D0227798

SPAWN'S BRAT

By

Patricia E. Walker

Copyright © Patricia E. Walker 2018
This book is sold subject to the condition that it shall not, by way of trade or
otherwise, be lent, resold, hired out, or otherwise circulated without the publisher's
prior consent in any form of binding or cover other than that in which it is
published and without a similar condition including this condition being imposed
on the subsequent publisher.
The moral right of Patricia E. Walker has been asserted.
ISBN: 9781718030046

With many thanks to my husband, Andrew, for his unfailing support. My thanks too to David Nunn, Museum Curator at London Hospital Medical College, for his kind assistance and invaluable help.

AUTHOR'S NOTE

The main problem in writing a historical novel is language. Every generation has had its own particular words and phrases which, over time, have mainly disappeared from daily use even though some of them can still be found in the dictionary. As an author, I have to bear in mind that the last thing the reader wants to do is to pause in order to clarify a word in the dictionary, at the same time however, I have to bear in mind that the story must be as realistic as can be told, which means using some period words or phrases, even in the vernacular, within the text.

CONTENTS

This is a work of fiction. Names, characters, businesses, organizations, places, events and incidents either are the product of the author's imagination or are used fictitiously. Any resemblance to actual persons, living or dead, events, or locales is entirely coincidental.

i

Chapter One

February, 1876

From outside, number forty-two was no different to any of the other houses which stood tall and erect on either side of Brook Street; its four storeys looking out upon what was usually a busy thoroughfare with calm respectability. But today the streets were virtually empty, due in part to the heavy fall of snow that had come down during the night. The already compacted ice on the pavements and the cobbled roadway, lying hidden under this fresh fall of snow, made it quite hazardous to venture out. Only the odd passer-by or carriage rumbling past on the cobbles evinced any sign of life outside the houses. But apart from these intrepid wayfarers who had dared to brave the elements on this raw, cold February day, Brook Street was practically deserted.

However, despite the inclement weather conditions, the inhabitants of number forty-two had had a busy morning. These few passers-by, eager to reach their destinations as quickly as possible, paid little heed to the fact that the several sets of footprints on the three shallow steps leading directly from the pavement up to the door, bore adequate testimony to the fact that something quite untoward was going forward. Nor did they stop and wonder why the servants, unlike those of their neighbours, had not cleared the snow away or that behind its respectable walls the inhabitants were gathering to await an event which was to change their lives forever. It was a well-preserved establishment, and even though the snow had not been cleared away from the steps or the iron railings on either side of them, they suffered from neither rust nor neglect, its neatness and propriety extending even to the basement steps behind the small iron gate.

Ordinarily, every particle of snow or unwanted piece of debris would be cleared away immediately. However, today was no ordinary day for the Harrington family; so much so that Harris, who far from being a martinet,

1

was nonetheless particular in all domestic matters, ensuring his subordinates carried out their tasks thoroughly, had been somewhat forgetful of his duty. Whatever his own opinions or feelings about the household he had served all these years, it was a day he thought he would never have lived to see, and he could not help wondering what the outcome would be.

No member of the household staff was under any illusion; the master would not live out the day. For nearly two weeks he had lain in that ornate four-poster clinging determinedly to a life which had spanned seventy-six years. No one, not even the overworked kitchen maid who, apart from never having set foot above stairs, had only laid eyes on the master once, could acquit him of denying them all the satisfaction of seeing him planted firmly underground.

But if they laboured under no illusions then neither did Matthew Carey Harrington. His days were numbered, he knew that well enough, and he was certainly not the man to repine now that settling day was almost upon him. He was about to cast up his accounts, but he would pay the reckoning never fear! Matthew Carey Harrington always paid his shot, and he would do so now. He would face his Maker the same as he had faced everything else in his life; boldly and unashamedly. He would not turn tail when confronted by the sum total of his life. No! Matthew Carey Harrington would look Him squarely in the face and take the consequences.

But there were some who would strenuously deny him the right to stand before his Maker at all. Matthew Carey Harrington, son of a Yorkshire brewer, had not exactly endeared himself to people let alone make friends, and even those who had been close to him were dubious of the honour that was about to fall upon him. No, he had no illusions about himself, and he certainly was under no misapprehension about what others thought of him. They feared him still. This sick old man, whose heart had almost given up on him, could still make them all dance to his tune and stand trembling before him. A twisted smile touched his thin, bloodless lips as he dwelled on the knowledge. Yes, by God! He was the master still.

Momentarily his eyes rested on the two people in the room, not that he wanted either of them here. He had always considered a deathbed depressing, and it was beyond his understanding why his wife and Doctor Rowley insisted on being with him. Observing the proprieties, no doubt! Such nonsense! He had ignored the proprieties all his life and he would be damned if he would start now.

Look at him! The old leech, hovering around like an expectant duck, waiting for the event yet dreading it too. The old bloodsucker! He could not wait for him to draw his last breath, no doubt thinking his long service to the family would be well rewarded. Well, he was in for a shock. He had been paid enough these past twenty years to see him comfortably through to his end. He would get no more out of Matthew Harrington.

Charlotte! His eyes softened for a moment. Yes, by God! He had loved her and married her in the teeth of her outraged family, too. Not good enough for the Lady Charlotte Beatrice Ambrose! Well, he had shown them. The brewer's boy may have lacked the breeding considered necessary for their daughter's future husband but he had not lacked the money which, in his opinion, got you more than any amount of breeding could. Something resembling a chuckle escaped his lips causing his two overseers to draw in their breath expectantly. But she had been a beauty; damn him to Hell if ever he had seen another like her! She had loved him too, but nevertheless she had had to be schooled; her outspoken ways curbed, but more particularly that tendency to independence restrained. There was only going to be one master in his household and that was himself. His will was law; his word final.

At sixty-three there were still traces of the beauty which had captivated him forty-six ago, but his gradual domination of her will had left its scars. The young and beautiful Charlotte Ambrose now looked every inch the dominated woman he had made her. She had eventually learned not to set up her will against his; to keep her opinions to herself and to accept without question his decision regarding the children, especially the boys. All in all though, he had been well pleased with her; not only had she been beautiful but also the ideal wife to adorn a man's home.

She had been fruitful too. Four sons and three daughters she had given him and not forced out of her either. He remembered so well how, in the early days of their marriage, she had welcomed his caresses, waited eagerly for the tap on her door after her maid had left her, but that had been before the brood he had spawned had taken over her life and love. He would strenuously have denied that he had killed her love, planting fear in her heart due to the obedience he demanded from her, until her only comfort and joy had been with her children. Overall though, he could not complain. He had been master in his own house and of his life, just as he had been over everyone else.

Those faded brown eyes glinted maliciously, still sharp and alive even though the end was near, as they once again focused on Doctor Rowley. Not long now, you old leech! Not long to wait for the end!

They were all here; the whole pack of them! Sitting downstairs waiting for the moment that would signal the end. Not one of them would be sorry to see the end of Matthew Carey Harrington. To the devil with the lot of them! He did not need their tears to see him through to the end. He could manage it on his own, the same as he had the rest of his life. By God though, he would give anything to see them now as they gathered in the drawing room with what patience they could muster. He could picture the scene as clearly as though he was down there with them. Sighing, waiting, watching for the door that would signal the end of the man they hated in varying degrees. Well, let them wait. He was not ready just yet. Soon, but not just yet. He would let them know when he was ready to say his farewells. The last thing he wanted was to be faced with the brood of a family he had spawned hovering over him. Not one of them would be sorry to see the last of him. It was enough to turn a man sick to his stomach. Dear God! Was there ever such a family as the one he had sired?

The expectant mourners sat with their own thoughts of the man who was holding desperately on to life in that mausoleum of a bedroom upstairs, two of whom at least had their own reasons for wanting the end to come quickly, and even though they seldom saw eye to eye they were as one in their desire to be free of having to dance to Matthew Carey Harrington's tune. Of course, they would do what was expected of them when the time came, but how like their father to drag the thing out. They supposed they should have known better than to believe he would have accommodated them by dying immediately after that heart attack nearly two weeks ago. No! Matthew Harrington had the constitution of an ox, fighting off the inevitable with the same determination that had characterised his whole life. Few of them could acquit him of staying alive out of spite! But he could not last much longer. Doctor Rowley had told them he was becoming weaker by the minute and had given him a few more hours, if that. Then what the devil was keeping him going? He would want them around his deathbed as little as they wanted to be there, but whatever the reason for his hold on life they wished he would get it over with.

No one observing the group gathered in the drawing room would ever have suspected these unloving thoughts, their demeanours just as they should be for such a solemn occasion, and anyone daring to suggest they were eager for the end would have been met without outraged denials.

Beneath the calm dignity which enveloped the house ran a fever of emotions, even the servants were conscious of it. It would certainly be the end of an era when Matthew Harrington died; in fact, no one could be in any doubt that life would never be the same again.

Harris, whose long service in the Harrington household had been an education, had accurately assessed their mood as they gathered in the drawing room. The air of gloom which pervaded the house was enough to give anyone a fit of the dismals, although he had to admit that until the arrival yesterday afternoon of Miss Emily and that scrawny bit she called her husband, informing him that they would be remaining here until matters were settled and that a room was to be prepared for them immediately, the atmosphere had at least been bearable. Her mamma, she informed him coldly, would no doubt welcome her presence and support at such a moment. Besides, she had added dismissively, it would create a very odd appearance if it became known that she had failed her afflicted parent in the hour of her need. Harris, maintaining a dignified silence as he received her coat and gloves accompanied by her rapid instructions, cast a knowledgeable eye in her husband's direction and read the expression on his face perfectly. If memory served him correctly, Miss Emily's husband had been no favourite with his father-in-law, and Edward, not quite able to forget the occasions when he had been subjected to that powerful personality's temper, questioned the wisdom of him being here. Nevertheless, experience had taught him that any kind of remonstrance with Emily would prove useless so, meekly doing as he was bidden, wisely kept his reflections to himself.

So too did her mamma when she learned of her decision to remain in Brook Street for the foreseeable future. It was not that she disliked the idea of her daughter and son-in-law coming to stay whilst matters were so unsettled, but it was so typical of Emily to expect everyone to fall in with her wishes without any prior notice or warning and to have her instructions carried out immediately. Like Harris, Charlotte knew the servants had more than enough to do right now with the house being in such an uproar, but as she was in no frame of mind to discuss this further with Emily, all she could do was distractedly request Harris to take care of them. Unlike her sisters, he had never taken to Miss Emily who, in his opinion, was too much like Mr. Charles for his liking, each of them taking it for granted that the servants should stop whatever they were doing to accommodate their wishes. It was therefore out of respect for his mistress that Harris instructed one of the maids to prepare a room, left to himself he would have willingly shown her and her husband the door.

It was also his opinion that Mrs. Charlotte had had a fair bit to put up with one way and another over the years, and since the arrival of Miss Emily and that rasher of wind she called a husband yesterday, it seemed that far from easing her mamma's situation she was doing the exact opposite. It was for Mrs. Charlotte's sake that Harris was prepared to do all he could to ensure things remained as near normal as possible, and it was for this reason that he instructed his spouse, who held full sway in the kitchen, to prepare the tea trolley. The roof could fall in on their heads but Mr. George would still expect to have his tea and refreshments! Having manoeuvred the trolley up the back stairs with the help of the boot boy instead of the footman William, who had been sent out on an errand, Harris eventually pushed this unwieldy piece of apparatus from the back of the large square hall to the drawing room. Knowing he could leave the task of pouring the tea to Mrs. Amelia or Mrs. Sophy, after ascertaining they required nothing else he quickly made his hasty exit, informing his wife upon returning to the kitchen that apart from Mr. Marcus and Mrs. Sophy he would sooner be caged up with a couple of hungry lions than his master's offspring.

Not until the door had closed behind him did George let out his pent-up breath. "I thought for a moment that…!"

"Please, George," begged his wife, "anyone would think you could not wait for the news."

"He can't," came a smooth voice.

George glared across the room at his brother, not for the first time feeling like a schoolboy in Charles's presence. "And you can, I suppose!" George felt a little better for saying that. Charles always made him feel inadequate, even where his wife was concerned. He could not prove it, of course, but George had always suspected that Amelia was not as impervious to Charles as she would have him believe.

Unlike the rest of them George was not a Harrington. Oh, yes, the man upstairs was his father right enough, but he had none of the hallmarks which distinguished him. He lacked the height as well as the physique of his father and brothers, indeed fate had played him a cruel trick when it endowed him with the Ambrose characteristics; the protruding pale blue eyes giving the impression he had just been startled, the unruly dark curly hair putting one in mind of an overexcited schoolboy, the heavy jowl and, worst of all, the tendency to corpulence. What was it his father had called him? Ah yes, the runt of the family! Well, the runt was about to become head of that family and then they would have to be careful. Every disdainful look, every cutting word and malicious taunt were about to be paid in full. He relished the moment. Taking the cup and saucer Amelia held out to him, their fine porcelain fragility smothered by his thick finger and thumb, a glow of pure satisfaction ran through him. Yes, they would all know that George was about to have his day; head of the family, head of the business. Let them see how they like that! He could barely stifle the smile which crossed his lips, the thought a delicious one to savour. More than the rest of them did he want the end to come.

"I thought that Reverend Handley had been sent for?" All eyes flew to Marcus.

"I am afraid your uncle refused to allow your aunt to send for him," Sophy told him.

A reluctant but appreciative smile touched Marcus's well-shaped lips. "I suppose I should have known."

"Your uncle told your aunt that if he so much as saw the Reverend's face he would have him thrown out," Sophy smiled shyly up at Marcus. "He could not be persuaded to change his mind."

"I can imagine." Marcus had no difficulty in imagining his uncle's reaction to the presence of a man of the cloth, and in spite of himself and his far from familial feelings towards his uncle, he could not suppress the gleam of pure amusement from entering his eyes. "He always was perverse," he remarked ruefully, his eyes softening instinctively as they held Sophy's.

Charles may be enjoying himself with Amelia behind his brother's back, content to ignore the many attractive qualities, even the very existence of his own wife, but Marcus had never given up hope of winning Sophy. He had no need to tell her how he felt, had done in fact ever since he had returned home following the accident which had left him with a slight limp, rendering it necessary for him to resign his commission. No words of love had been exchanged but both knew it lived and breathed between them, binding them irrevocably together.

Charles was unworthy of such a woman, but unlike her husband Sophy honoured the vows they had taken over two years ago. But Marcus did not want an affair with Sophy any more than he wanted to embark on a course which would involve stealing a few hours with her behind her husband's back; he wanted her as his wife, to love and cherish for the rest of his life.

It was what Sophy wanted too, although if she was honest no one could have been more surprised than she was herself upon realising that she had fallen in love. It was not simply because Marcus was good-looking, all the Harringtons were – well, except for poor George of course, and never more so than now. It seemed that the older they became the men of this family grew more handsome and, at thirty-seven, Marcus was very handsome.

"For once, I agree with you," Charles remarked idly.

Tearing his eyes away from Sophy, Marcus eyed his cousin, not for the first time wondering how the devil his uncle as well as Sophy's father could have sanctioned such a marriage.

"Since when have any of us known our progenitor do anything to please others?" Charles remarked. "I certainly can't recall such a sacrifice."

"Very true," Marcus conceded, "but did you really expect his death to be any different?"

"One can always hope," Charles drawled, "but my experience of my father has taught me always to expect the unexpected."

"I find this conversation in very bad taste!" Emily pointed out, her affronted gaze resting on her husband, who really had no idea what he was doing here anyway. From what he had seen of his father-in-law these past six months he could believe him capable of anything.

"Poor Edward," mocked Charles, "you really do find us most unnatural, don't you!"

Edward, who had never really known how to take his brother-in-law, stammered something about it certainly not being for him to say, but following an insistent nudge on his elbow from Emily, coughed and faltered, "Well, I... er... really... Of course, you know your father best."

"None better, Edward," affirmed Charles smoothly, enjoying his brother-in-law's embarrassment, "and had you been a member of this family for longer than six months you too would have been so privileged."

"Let me tell you, Charles," Emily nodded, her colour just a little high, "that Edward got along extremely well with my father, and had they become better acquainted I have no doubt he would have come to see that Edward is a valued member of this family as well as the business," her doting if concealed fondness for Edward almost blinding her to the weaknesses in his character.

"Indeed!" Charles mocked, his eyes contemptuously skimming over his brother-in-law, as aware as Harris of his father's opinion of Edward. "And since when, my dear sister," Charles demanded, "have you been outraged about any of us voicing our true feelings or exhibiting reticence yourself? I have yet to see that in you."

"You really are quite detestable, Charles!" Emily told him indignantly, her fingers agitatedly twisting the delicate lace-edged handkerchief which she used intermittently to dab at her eyes, her sense of propriety at such a moment outweighing her feelings of resentment over her father's lack of faith in Edward's abilities.

"I may be," Charles concurred infuriatingly, "but I am no hypocrite."

"Please, Charles," Sophy pleaded, "I think Emily is right. Now is not the time to say these things."

"Do you, my dear?" Charles asked dulcetly, his eyes cold as they skimmed dismissively over her.

"I agree," George said manfully, suddenly finding a new sense of worth in himself now the end was almost here. Charles, who had never really had anything but contempt for his older brother, let it show in the disdainful look he threw at him. Despite his valiant attempt, George inwardly winced, but trying to behave like the future head of the family said, with as much dignity as he could, "I know we have all had our differences with father over the years, but he *is* dying, after all."

"For God's sake, George!" Charles scorned. "Do try to be a little less boring than usual!" He watched in contented, almost malicious enjoyment as George struggled for something to say. A self-satisfied laugh sounded deep within Charles's throat as he watched his brother's mouth form words which refused to come out. "Very wise of you, for once," he mocked, his eyes alight with contemptuous amusement.

"Do you always have to be so insulting, Charles?" Amelia asked, not quite able to hide the answering smile in her dark blue eyes as they looked up at him.

"My dear Amelia," Charles replied smoothly, his glance appreciatively taking in every exquisite detail of her, vivid flashes of memory conjuring up her naked body as it had writhed wantonly in his arms last night, "it is irresistible when George makes it so easy."

"You have a damned unpleasant tongue, Charles," George managed, his temper exacerbated by being made to look ridiculous in front of his wife. He had not missed that look which had passed between them, which only served to reinforce his belief that they were in fact closer than he had ever suspected. Amelia may publicly accord him all the respect due to him as her husband but there were occasions, such as now, when she did tend to hold him up to ridicule, but he would make her pay for making him look a fool, they both would pay. See if they wouldn't!

To Sophy's relief, who had witnessed this interchange with despair, the sound of the bell clanging in the distance was a welcome diversion from the undercurrents hanging heavy in the over furnished drawing room. She knew only too well her husband's tendency for ridicule and mockery and that George would never be a match for him. Of all Matthew Harrington's sons Charles was the most like him. He did not lose control of his emotions like his father, but he was just as ruthlessly determined, and beneath that polished and self-assured exterior he was condescending and insufferably arrogant, both of which she found quite abhorrent. Coldly calculating and far more subtle than Matthew, Charles's smooth but venomous tongue could inflict acute pain. Charles was a product of his mother's aristocratic lineage and his father's money, and he exploited both to the full. She did not envy Amelia her liaison with her husband, on the contrary she was grateful. Sophy did not love Charles any more than he loved her, but she had tried to be the kind of wife her mother had raised her to be. It had been her duty to marry and since she had met no one for whom she had felt anything remotely resembling love, she had accepted his offer of marriage. But Charles was expensive. His father, who had been quite content to overlook certain indiscretions, had eventually reached the point where he had had enough of his son's financial excesses, categorically refusing to pay off any more of his debts or to raise his allowance again, considering the one he received more than adequate. It had therefore been far from complimentary, and certainly not what Sophy had expected, when she had discovered that Matthew had given Charles an ultimatum. "I'll pay your debts, whatever you owe, providing you marry Sophia Lessington." He had liked the connection even if Charles had not. But his arguments had fallen onto deaf ears. In Charles's opinion, it was degrading enough having to associate with those people at the brewery to please his father, but to marry a woman who held no appeal for him whatsoever to save himself from financial disgrace was unendurable. He had hated his father for it, and her too.

Sophy had not argued against the marriage, after all so many women of her acquaintance were locked into loveless marriages from one cause or another. She suffered all the slights of her own loveless marriage with dignity and resignation, never once allowing her feelings to show, not even when faced with Charles's contempt and bitter disappointment over her failure to give him a child. She endured rather than enjoyed his lovemaking, but since Charles wanted a son more than anything else, even if it meant with her, she had to endure it more often than she liked. She had come to believe that at the age of twenty-nine and tied to a marriage she could do nothing about, love was lost to her forever. Of course, falling in love was something only the lower classes indulged in, according to Mamma that was, but even though Sophy did not agree with this somewhat stern point of view, she had certainly not expected it to happen to her. It had therefore come as something of a shock to discover that she had fallen in love with Marcus, the only son of Matthew Harrington's youngest sister.

Marcus was a typical Harrington; tall, well over six foot but broader across the shoulders than Charles, his face leaner, more angular than the sculptured outline of his cousin, the deep tan a legacy from his days in India, emphasising the dark blond hair and the deep-set dark brown eyes which were the most expressive Sophy had ever seen. Like his uncle, Marcus knew precisely what he wanted, but that was where the similarity ended. He was the most gentle and caring man she had ever known, possessing an air of unassuming strength and reliability which made her feel very safe.

The interlude between George and Charles may not have surprised her, after all they had never really been what one could call friends, but that biting tongue of her husband, to which she herself was often subjected, never failed to upset her, even when directed at another. The brief touch of Marcus's hand on her shoulder was very reassuring and, as she waited for the drawing room door to open, she quickly stole a glance up at him.

Charles may have missed that fleeting intimacy, but Amelia had not. Of course, she knew of the state of affairs existing between Charles and his wife, and even though she was not its instigator she had taken full advantage of it, and if she played her cards well this little display could be turned to very good account.

"Are we expecting anyone else?" Emily asked of no one in particular, as the sound of voices could clearly be heard in the hall. "It can't be Jane, surely!"

"Since our dear sister is about to present Henry with his fifth *petit-pacquet*," Charles remarked disinterestedly, "I should think it most unlikely," adding, with a touch of wry humour, "unless, of course, Adam has decided to come home."

At the mention of their youngest brother's name, Emily cried indignantly, "I should not have thought he would dare show his face!"

"I agree it would be most inconvenient if he did," Charles acknowledged.

"Inconvenient!" Emily exclaimed, aghast. "It would be more than inconvenient!"

"After what that young fool did, I should have thought it would be far better for him to remain where he is," George pointed out, outraged. "Why, even now, it's all I can do to look old Marsden in the face!"

"A marvellous family, are we not?" mocked Charles, unconsciously echoing his father's thoughts. "A brother who forced a quarrel on a club member when in his cups one night and is fatally wounded in the duel they engage in next day; a sister who runs off with a stablehand and another brother who eloped to Gretna Green with the daughter of a knight of the realm and who is now languishing in some God-forsaken place because he dared not show his face in town!"

"Well, your mother certainly expects Adam to come home," Amelia reminded them, her eyes skipping past her husband to where Charles was standing beside the fireplace, his elegantly tailored person so very different to that of her husband who always presented the appearance of having scrambled into his clothes.

"I should have thought that rather than plead with him to come home Mamma would have been better advised to plead with him to remain where he is," George argued, his colour rising.

"I agree that Adam's presence could be a little embarrassing if it became known he was back in town so soon after what happened," Charles remarked smoothly, his eyes holding Amelia's for several appreciative moments.

"Is there no way he can be prevented from coming here?" Edward asked, not at all sure what the fuss was about.

"What do you suggest?" Marcus asked calmly. "We can hardly prevent him from returning home at such a moment, much less attending his father's funeral, no matter what absurdities he has committed. Far from being embarrassing it would be looked upon as most odd if he wasn't here to pay his respects. Not even Marsden would begrudge him that right."

"I agree that he had a right to be informed of Father's condition," George conceded reluctantly, "but had Mamma waited for my advice before she wrote to him, I should have strongly recommended her to refrain from requesting him to return to town." On which officious note he rested his case, firmly of the belief that his mother stood in constant need of his guidance.

"Marcus is, of course, right," Charles acknowledged unwillingly. "We may deplore Adam's impetuosity, but I fail to see how we can prevent him from coming home at such a time."

"*Impetuosity!*" George choked. "Is that what you call his scandalous behaviour? Impetuosity!"

"That's all…" Emily broke off as the door opened and Harris walked in.

Harris, who had been with the family ever since they could remember, had not once during that long if not entirely happy service ever allowed his feelings to show, but at the moment he looked visibly shaken. His eyes scanned the room as if seeking guidance, then, as if realising Mr. Marcus was the only one he could turn to, said faintly, "Sir… a… a young lady." He shook his head, nonplussed. "I really don't understand it, sir."

"What don't you understand, Harris?" Marcus asked quietly, never having seen him so shaken before.

"The young lady, sir, it's, well sir, it's… it's Miss Elizabeth's daughter, sir."

A stunned silence followed this announcement, each one, apart from Marcus, looking at Harris in stupefied astonishment. "Where is she now?" Marcus asked.

"I've asked her to wait in the library, sir," Harris informed him. "I didn't know what else to do with her," he apologised, "especially as the mistress is upstairs with your uncle, sir."

Marcus nodded. "Thank you, Harris. One of us will be along to see her directly."

"One moment, Harris," Charles forestalled him, before turning a haughty eye upon his cousin. "What do you mean precisely? One of us will see her!"

"What did you intend doing with her, Charles," Marcus asked coolly, "throw her out?"

"This is disgraceful!" George exclaimed, his colour rising alarmingly. "She has no right being here."

"I never thought I should ever agree with you, George," Charles informed him, "but you are right. Father threw her mother out twenty-odd years ago; we should do the same with the daughter."

"Her mother, in case you had forgotten," Marcus pointed out, the edge to his voice causing George to throw him a cautious glance, "was your sister. This girl is your niece."

"I must say she has a nerve!" Amelia said sharply, moved sufficiently to rise from her chair, her eyes accusing as they stared across at Marcus. "George is quite right. It is a disgrace her being here at a time like this!"

"Pardon, sir," Harris interrupted hesitantly, "but what do you want me to do with her?"

"Give us a few moments," Marcus told him, his eyes holding his cousin's, "then show her in."

Harris caught the anger on Charles's face and felt decidedly uncomfortable. Mr. Marcus, a real gentleman though he was, did not live here, having his own establishment, but Mr. Charles did, and Harris did not exactly relish the thought of going against him. It was therefore with considerable relief that he received a confirming nod from Mr. Charles, whereupon he quickly left the room.

"You seem to be taking an awful lot upon yourself, Cousin," Charles pointed out coldly. "Why should you interest yourself in a girl none of us have laid eyes on before?"

Marcus studied his cousin for several moments. "You don't have much compassion, do you, Charles?"

Compassion! Charles could barely hide his disdain, and his expression was eloquent testimony to his feelings.

George, on the other hand, never knew when to hold his tongue, his puffy cheeks suffused with angry colour as he again unburdened himself of his opinion.

"George is right," Emily declared, standing rigidly to her feet. "It's an outrage! How dare she come here in so brazen a fashion. I refuse to meet her." Beneath her tight-fitting bodice her breasts heaved in indignation and her naturally pale face was touched with colour as she sought support from her husband. "Are you going to sit there and do nothing?"

Edward looked his embarrassment, but before he could open his mouth Marcus forestalled him, his voice maddeningly calm. "Edward, my dear Cousin, is in no position to do anything."

Emily was forced to bite back the words on her lips as the door opened and Harris walked in. It was not for him to give an opinion but from the looks of it he had interrupted a pretty nasty scene. He had not been in the Harrington household for nearly thirty years without knowing the circumstances surrounding Miss Elizabeth or the fact that the master had never permitted her name to be mentioned, but if they were to ask him what he thought he would have to say that it had been a pretty rotten thing to do your own flesh and blood. This girl standing rigidly upright behind him was scared to death if he knew anything about it, yes, and determined not to show it either! He had a daughter of his own, about the same age too, and were it at all possible he would have liked to have been able to give Miss Elizabeth's daughter some words of encouragement, but unfortunately there was no time for that, so standing aside to allow her to walk past him into the room he silently hoped, though not very confidently, they would let her down easy. He had no need to worry about Mr. Marcus or Mrs. Sophy either, but it was that nasty piece of work Mr. Charles who would do the damage, yes, and that sharp-tongued sister of his given half the chance. In fact, if it came to that he would not put it past Mr. George's wife to have one or two things to say!

Chapter Two

Apart from Marcus and Sophy, the eyes directed on their uninvited guest standing nervously upright in front of them, were so blatantly hostile that Alexandra was momentarily taken aback. The hatred which emanated from them was so tangible she could almost taste it. Of course, she had herself built up an animosity towards them over the years, but her enmity had been the natural emotion of a young girl who had been forced to witness her mother's pain and grief; to watch in helpless despair the lengths to which she had gone to keep them clothed and fed, especially after her father's tragic accident. She had done nothing to them, yet they despised her! Her wide green eyes surveyed the room, her clear gaze taking in every one of her relatives, all but two of them finding her scrutiny as well as her presence intolerable.

Looking as she did, Matthew Harrington's granddaughter could easily have been mistaken for being no more than fourteen or fifteen years old, but the huge and slightly sunken eyes, the pale face pinched and drawn, completely belied the fact that she was just turned twenty. She realised only too well how she must look to these affluent relations; her thin boots, far from suitable for such weather, and the hem of her skirt, were soaked from her walk, not being able to afford the hackney fare to carry her all the way to Brook Street. From her hat to her flimsy coat, neither offering much protection against the icy conditions, everything she had on was old-fashioned and threadbare and had in fact been given her by a friend of her mother, as well as being considerably faded due to many washings, but despite her appearance Alexandra stood proud and unashamed as she faced her hostile audience.

The sight of this pathetic creature touched Sophy's heart and instinctively she rose to her feet, her hand outstretched in a gesture of welcome and friendship, but her husband's sharp disapproval made her pause, her heart pounding under that cold, warning stare. Dear God! What kind of a family had she tied herself up with?

Emily, who had always considered her sister to have been guilty of putting the rest of them to shame with her disgraceful behaviour, could barely bring herself to look upon the girl she adamantly refused to call a niece. The fact that she had been only six years old when the scandal broke did not seem to matter at all. In her opinion any woman who ran off with a stablehand, bringing disgrace and shame to her family, deserved the punishment she had received.

"Since everyone appears to have been struck dumb," Marcus said gently, his eyes smiling warmly as he took several halting steps towards her, "allow me to introduce myself. I'm Marcus, your mother's cousin, but you need not bother with the formalities if you would rather not. You must be Alexandra?"

"Yes." The voice which cut through the daunting silence was cultured and well educated.

"Won't you sit down, Alexandra?" Marcus offered, his hand clasping her cold one with a reassurance she found very comforting.

"Thank you, but no." She smiled gratefully up at him, recognising him instantly as the one her mother had always spoken of with affection. "I do not intend making a long stay."

"I don't know what it is that has brought you here or what you hope to gain," George told her unkindly, "but you are not welcome here, any more than your mother was." He had been eighteen when his sister had disgraced herself and never would he forget the scandal which followed. It had been bad enough having to endure the amused, not say ribald comments of his friends and acquaintances, but the snide whispers of the servants had been intolerable.

Alexandra's green eyes flashed, momentarily startling him. "You insult me."

"Oh, I hardly think so," Charles mocked, his eyes raking contemptuously over her thin and shabby appearance, bringing the colour flooding to her pale cheeks. "You really are wasting your time if you think you can inveigle yourself into my father's good graces." A none too pleasant smile twisted his well-shaped lips. "You see, he has none."

"You may as well take yourself off," Emily bit out. "There is no place here for the likes of you, indeed," she said nastily, "I cannot imagine what made you think you would be welcome here."

"I think," Marcus interrupted, the distinct edge to his voice causing

Emily to hold her tongue, "that it is time to cease this display of righteous wrath and ask Alexandra herself why she is here."

"I should have thought that was obvious," Amelia snapped, every immaculate inch of her disgusted by the sight of such a creature.

"Not to me," Marcus returned, his eyes softening as they rested on his favourite cousin's daughter. He had just turned eighteen when Elizabeth had presented her father with an ultimatum; she would marry the man she loved or she would marry no one. It was perhaps unfortunate that her lover was considered to be highly undesirable in all respects, but love was a rare commodity and Elizabeth was determined to hold on to it. Marcus had fond memories of his cousin and remembered his own feelings upon learning that she had not only been ejected from the parental home but disowned by every member of her family except her mother, but as everyone knew Charlotte Harrington had had no say whatsoever in the proceedings. His own intervention on his cousin's behalf had been met with outrage and abuse from his uncle, and the offer of asylum by his parents turned down by Elizabeth herself, to disappear without trace. He had never been able to forgive Matthew Harrington for the treatment he had meted out to his daughter and the pain he had inflicted on his wife because of it, and if it were not for the very deep and sincere affection Marcus had for his aunt, a very dear friend of his mother long before she became her sister-in-law, nothing would induce him to visit a house which possessed everything but love. However, since Sophy had taken up residence forty-two Brook Street had become a more welcoming venue, but even her warmth and capacity to love were being crushed by a cold determination which had been heartbreakingly witnessed only moments before. "You will have to forgive my relatives," he told her now, "but you have rather taken us unawares."

Alexandra responded to the encouragement in his eyes. "My presence here is not of my choosing, I assure you," she said earnestly.

"You expect us to believe that?" Amelia scorned, her outrage at the presence of a girl she would not have housed in the servants' quarters so blatantly obvious that she could only just bring herself to look at her. Amelia may despise her father-in-law, but she was proud and haughty, and although she had never met Elizabeth she had heard about her from her parents, and of course from George himself, and heartily approved her banishment.

"I think you could say that your visit is… well, let us say inopportune." Edward had not meant to say anything at all, but one look at his wife's face, a picture of horrified disgust, had been enough to tell him that she fully expected him to support her, and had therefore considered it prudent to show a little involvement. Being a naturally weak man who always bowed to a stronger will, he had silently acquiesced in his wife's decision to have him support her through this painful ordeal. For himself, he would much rather have been back at the brewery, albeit a menial clerking job Matthew Harrington had pushed him into.

"Inopportune!" exclaimed Amelia, unable to believe her ears. "Are you out of your senses, Edward? The girl's a baggage and should be thrown out on the instant!"

Before Edward could defend himself, Harris returned to say that the master was now ready to see the young lady if she would care to follow him to her grandfather's room. Apart from being too well trained in his duties Harris had long since grown accustomed to the ways of the Harrington family, and was therefore by no means surprised by their reaction to his announcement or to their reception of this unfortunate young girl, but keeping his views to himself he merely showed the assembled company his customary impassive face as he held the door open in readiness for her to pass through.

Alexandra, who was of the firm opinion that she owed none of them an explanation, was by no means pleased that they believed her to be making a last-ditch attempt to ingratiate herself into her grandfather's good graces, and it was therefore with a hauteur Harris had no hesitation in describing as typically Harrington, that she said, "I am here, not to inveigle myself with your father," looking directly at Charles, "nor to ask him for money, but at my grandfather's request."

Not unnaturally, this statement momentarily held her audience speechless, but without waiting to hear their reaction she turned on her heel and followed Harris into the hall and up the staircase to her grandfather's room.

*

Matthew Harrington had had his own reasons for paying the extortionate sum charged for finding his granddaughter, but if you wanted the best then you had to be prepared to pay for it and Ted Knowles was the best, if not the most honest, detective. If anyone could find her, he could, and no worries either about him blabbing your affairs to all and sundry. He could find anything or anyone – for a price! Well, the price had been well worth it. Ted Knowles had found the brat, but that had been over two months ago and the girl had not shown herself. As the search for his granddaughter had been arranged and conducted without his family's knowledge, his resultant anger over her defiance to show her face had confused them. How dare the brat defy him in this way! But he would bring her to heel, never fear. No one ever defied Matthew Harrington, and he would see himself damned before he would let himself be out-jockeyed by a spawn's brat!

Upon receipt of peremptory instructions to call again in Brook Street to verify his granddaughter's whereabouts, Ted Knowles had reaffirmed his findings, but when he had dared to suggest that his client either allow him to bring the girl to her grandfather or he visit her himself, he was met with such a violent outburst that he actually found himself pitying the girl. It was not only Matthew Harrington's physical strength which had carried him through his heart attack nearly two weeks ago, but his mental determination also. To the astonishment of his doctor and family, he had fought off death for one purpose only; he would not be outdone by a slip of a girl who should know better than to keep him waiting!

Like Charlotte, Harris had known about Miss Elizabeth's daughter almost from the day she was born, and under strict instructions from the master to say nothing about her to his offspring unless he knew what was good for him, he had kept his tongue, but he still believed that the family should have been told. He may not hold with the dismissive, not to say contemptuous behaviour they had displayed towards the girl, but in fairness to them, however, he could understand their shock upon coming face to face with a niece they never knew they had. As he had no idea that the master had employed a private investigator to find her, and he very much doubted Mrs. Charlotte had either, he had feared the worst, but since the master would have to be told, he had mentally braced himself to nervously inform him of her arrival. Matthew Harrington had a nasty temper and there was never any way of knowing which way he would go, but to Harris's astonishment and relief the old man had actually appeared pleased. It was almost as if he had expected it.

Charlotte had of course known of her granddaughter's existence ever since she was a few months old. She would never forget the day her maid had come to her as she sat in the drawing room to inform her that Miss Elizabeth had called and was at that very moment sitting in the kitchen, afraid to come into the main part of the house in case she met her father; her knowledge of him being such that he could, for some perverse reason, have elected to remain at home instead of attending the brewery as was his daily custom. How they had emerged from the safety of the kitchen into her own bedroom Charlotte would never know, but so overcome with joy and excitement was she at being reunited with her daughter and seeing her grandchild that every other consideration was forgotten.

The minutes had turned into hours and it was not until it became perceptibly darker that she became aware of the lateness of the hour and that Matthew could arrive home at any moment. In the hope of reaching the safety of the back premises before he came home she quickly hurried her daughter, holding the sleeping infant in her arms, down the stairs, but even before they had descended halfway the peal of the bell pull was heard. Harris, knowing full well that the mistress was upstairs with her daughter, prolonged opening the door for as long as he dared, quite as nervous as his mistress as he assisted in her heart rending efforts to shepherd her visitors to the sanctuary of the kitchen. But Matthew, impatient at the length of time it was taking Harris to open the door, had rushed matters to crisis point by inserting his own key into the lock, berating his harassed butler for dereliction of duty and demanding to know what the devil he was paid for.

It was not to be expected that the sight of his wife and daughter, standing almost rooted to the spot at the rear of the hall, would go unnoticed any more than he would refrain from comment. Charlotte's tearful entreaty for pity coupled with her appeal for him to look at his granddaughter fell on stony ground, and Elizabeth, earnestly pleading her father's forgiveness, fared no better. In one furiously delivered sentence Matthew ordered Harris to show the visitors out, informing him that under no circumstances was he to open the door to them again and should he or any member of his household dare to think they could flout his orders by admitting them clandestinely by way of the kitchen or any other means of entry, they were very much mistaken. He would not tolerate disobedience, and anyone found guilty of such or even breathing so much as a word about what had occurred let alone that his daughter had a child, they could expect instant dismissal without a reference, whereupon he shut himself up in the library.

Charlotte, heartbroken and distraught, knew that Matthew had meant every word he had said, but if she had thought for one moment that she would escape his lashing tongue she was mistaken. His reprimand had been scathing and to the point, informing her that when he said he would not tolerate disobedience this included his wife as well as the servants, and should today's occurrence be repeated then she could expect to suffer the same fate as her daughter. She may have endured this wounding interview in silence, but even though she did not expect to see her daughter again for some appreciable time, and certainly not in Brook Street, at no point did it occur to her that she would never see Elizabeth again, but as the years had passed it seemed that she was indeed destined never to do so. If only she could have written to Elizabeth it would have made their separation more bearable, but since she had no idea where her daughter could be contacted, Elizabeth having deemed it wiser, and infinitely safer for her mamma not to divulge this information, it was quite impossible for her to do so, and this knowledge together with being deprived of her granddaughter, rendered the pain around her heart even more heavy. But Matthew, impervious to his wife's wretchedness, continued to forbid all mention of Elizabeth as well as strictly warning her what he would do should she take it into her head to apprise their offspring to the fact that they had a niece.

It was an unbearable heartache for her to carry, but somehow Charlotte had managed to hide the pain which never left her, but just when she had begun to think that nothing else could possibly cause her so much agony as being parted from her daughter and grandchild she had read the offending sheet from a provincial newspaper which Harris had torn out and reluctantly taken up to her. How the newspaper had come into the hands of their vegetable purveyor who had used it to wrap the provisions which had been delivered in Brook Street earlier that morning he had no idea, and it was only because the name 'Elizabeth Dawes' listed in the obituary column caught his attention that prevented him from throwing it away, and so, after consulting with his wife, he realised he had no choice but to show it the mistress.

There was no doubting to whom the brief notice referred, but if Charlotte thought that the tragic death of Elizabeth, seemingly within a very short space of time after that of her husband, would bring about a change of heart in Matthew, she was mistaken. He acknowledged neither a connection with nor knowledge of the deceased much less the orphaned daughter she had left behind, so much so that he was easily able to ignore Charlotte's appeal for pity by angrily telling her that she was no grandchild of his before going on to warn her that he wanted to hear no more about it, and under no circumstances was she to speak of it to anyone. She had not done so, but her grief was such that Matthew could not fool himself into thinking that Charlotte's palpable shock and sorrow would not raise questions, and since he had no wish to acquaint his family with the news he had deemed it prudent to send her to stay with her sister in Hertfordshire until such time that she had overcome her emotions sufficiently.

That visit by Elizabeth all those years ago had been the last time she had seen her daughter as well as the only time she had seen her grandchild, and although it was extremely painful to know that she never would again she had, over time, come to reluctantly accept it. It was therefore in utter bemusement that Charlotte now heard Harris inform Matthew that Miss Elizabeth's daughter had called and was, at this very moment, downstairs.

The look on Matthew's face, far from exhibiting anger or disgust, was more than enough to tell Charlotte that not only was he by no means surprised but had clearly taken steps to find her, and waiting only until Harris had left did she exclaim, momentarily forgetting the presence of Doctor Rowley, "Matthew, why didn't you tell me what you were planning? That you had found her?" quite unable to believe what was happening; that at long last she was going to see her granddaughter.

"Because it was none of your business," Matthew snapped. "Now, get out of here, the pair of you. I want to see her alone."

"But she's my *granddaughter!*" Charlotte insisted, her faded blue eyes begging her husband. "You can't do this."

"She's your *nothing!*" Matthew bit out, his fingers agitatedly clutching the quilt. "And as for not doing what I choose in my own home," he told her forcefully, "you forget yourself."

"You really must not excite yourself," Doctor Rowley was unwise enough to advise. "You must remain calm."

Matthew was still a force to be reckoned with; venting his temper with an expletive which not only left the man who had been his physician for twenty years outraged, but made his wife gasp her shock. Ignoring both, he looked with loathing at the horrified doctor, no nearer to liking him now than he had been when he had first set eyes on him. "And as for *you*, you old bloodsucker, get out!" It was clear he was in no mood to listen to advice, especially from a man he found nauseating, but Doctor Rowley, either because he refused to believe that Matthew Harrington did not like him or whether his own conceit would not allow him to accept that a patient knew better, continued to chide him as though he were a child. "Are you deaf?" Matthew thundered. "I said out, both of you."

"I really must insist," persevered Doctor Rowley, ignoring the signs Charlotte knew so well.

Fearing the consequences, she quietly drew him to one side, suggesting that perhaps it would be better to do as Matthew asked. Doctor Rowley was not used to such treatment as this, and certainly the language his patient employed was so far removed from what he was accustomed to that he was genuinely shocked. Nevertheless, he took his calling very seriously and it was therefore with great reluctance that he left his patient, his thin lips pursing as he considered the possible outcome of too much excitement. The end was very near; a few hours, no more, and although he had no liking for the man he would like to think that Matthew Harrington would take the precious time left to him by making amends with his Maker, but as this seemed most unlikely, not only because he had already refused to see Reverend Handley but also because he had never taken the trouble to praise his Maker during his lifetime, Doctor Rowley supposed it was an empty hope. Unwillingly he followed Charlotte out of the room, leaving its sole occupant in a very dangerous mood. A mood that was still uncertainly balanced when the door opened a few minutes later to admit his granddaughter.

*

Despite her waif-like appearance Alexandra was made of sterner stuff than people realised. Although she had inherited those green eyes and dark red hair from her father there was no doubting that she owed her stubborn streak and sense of pride to the Harrington strain.

Those traits were evident now as she stood at the foot of that huge four-poster, looking dispassionately down at the man who was virtually only a step away from death as he lay back against a mound of snow-white pillows. He may well be, but those faded brown eyes had lost none of their keenness, and as he looked her over from head to foot, silently assessing her, he saw the determined thrust of her slender jaw and the uncompromising glint in her eyes, speaking volumes to the man who had deliberately fought off death for just this moment. The hatred which emanated from her did not surprise him, but the way she held herself, the unmistakable quality of her and the delicate bone structure, certainly did. He remembered her father, Joseph Dawes, a huge, uneducated bull of a man who was good enough to look after his stables but not his daughter, had mercifully passed on his colouring only.

Yes, by God! The girl hated him, but then she was not the first one to feel that way about him. "So! You've shown yourself at last!" Matthew stated belligerently. "What is it that keeps you over a month from getting here when I send for you?" His heavy jaws worked impatiently as Alexandra made no effort to answer him. "What's the matter?" he demanded. "Haven't you a tongue?" Still she did not answer, and Matthew, never one to be balked, ordered, "Come here girl, closer, where I can see you."

Despise him she may, but Alexandra was every inch a Harrington and hated taking orders like a servant. A thousand angry words rose to her lips, words she had stored up over the years, but as she slowly walked towards him, her feet sinking into the deep pile of the colourful Chinese carpet, she held her tongue; not because she had any love or sympathy for the man who was only a fraction from death nor because she found the circumstances precluded personal feelings, but simply because he was trying to goad her and she was certainly not going to give him the satisfaction of seeing her rise to his bait. Yes, she would open her mind to him before she left this room, but it would be conducted on her own terms and not his.

"Yes, you're my spawn's brat right enough!" Matthew told her with malicious satisfaction. "You have the look of her; defiant and impertinent." Her chin rose at this, causing a cackle of laughter to escape his bloodless lips. "Yes, I expect it pleases you to see me like this, doesn't it?"

"No." Her calm response made him stare harder. "As a matter of fact," she informed him with immense satisfaction, "it doesn't please me to see you at all."

"It doesn't, eh!" he purred dangerously, his talon-like fingers clutching the quilt.

"I see no reason why it should," Alexandra stated simply, her eyes holding his unflinchingly.

So, the brat wasn't afraid of him! "You don't, eh!" he said ominously, ignoring his doctor's advice to remain calm, his temper at this girl's lack of respect and stubborn defiance rising alarmingly.

Alexandra stared unrepentant at the remains of the man who lay before her. This giant of a man; her grandfather, who had ruled his family with a rod of iron, looked as though it would have given him tremendous satisfaction to strangle her.

As if by a superhuman effort Matthew controlled this overwhelming urge, saying provocatively, "But you are here, all the same."

"Yes," she nodded, "I am here, but not for the reason you think."

His eyes narrowed at this. "What other reason could there be other than doing as you are told?"

Without hesitation Alexandra replied, "Curiosity."

The sharp eyes narrowed even more. "Curiosity?" he repeated in disbelief. "What do you think I am, girl," he demanded thunderously, "a freak in a circus?"

"I wanted to see for myself what kind of man you are," she told him defiantly.

Damn her to hell! The girl needed bringing to bridle! "I did not ask you here to listen to your impertinence, girl!" Matthew shot at her.

"Ask me!" Alexandra scorned, her eyes flashing. "You delude yourself. I was not aware I had received an invitation. That man you employed to find me," she accused, "had the audacity to tell me that I must present myself to you without delay. I did not recognise an invitation in that demand." She waited to see the effect her words had on him, and she was not disappointed.

The claw-like fingers repeatedly clutched the quilt, the heavy jaws worked feverishly and the huge chest heaved as he struggled to raise himself. "I don't care what you recognised," he thundered. "You will do as you are told, girl!"

"The same as you expected my mother to do as she was told?" she scorned. "I think not."

"You think…" he began.

"You threw my mother out and then ignored her very existence," Alexandra accused. "You treated her worse than you would a servant instead of your daughter, and then," she continued inexorably, "when she did come here you issued instructions that she was never again to be allowed into the house." Her green eyes flashed, momentarily surprising the man who stared up at her as though he could not believe she was daring to say these things. "You made her wait for the rest of her life for a sign that she had been forgiven – it never came. So, I decided to make you wait too," she told him with immense satisfaction. "It's quite an insult, isn't it?"

"By God!" he fumed, when he had recovered from her accusations. "You *dare* to stand there, brazenly telling me that you intended to keep me waiting!"

His unrepentant granddaughter nodded. "I feel it also fair to tell you that had I not heard of your indisposition I should not be here now. Perhaps," she mused satisfyingly, "you could have been waiting even longer."

For the first time in Matthew Harrington's life he was utterly at a loss for words. This chit of a girl, who looked for all the world like an urchin, had the brass-faced nerve to say these things to him under his own roof. It was insupportable! "Who told you about me?" he demanded angrily, recovering his senses.

Alexandra shrugged. "Matthew Carey Harrington is a well-known pillar of society," she informed him sardonically, "his illness and the severity of it filtered through even to one of so lowly an order as myself."

For a fraction of a second it seemed as though her grandfather was about to draw his last breath, but the strength of will which had aided him so far came to his rescue again and in a very short while he had recovered himself sufficiently to say, "Yes, by heaven, you're Lizzie's girl right enough!" A fit of coughing brought Doctor Rowley hurrying in from his uneasy vantage point outside the door, but one look at his self-satisfied face was enough to cause his patient to send the water jug, thankfully empty, flying past him. "I don't want *you*," managed his tormentor, "get out." After watching him scurrying out of the room, Matthew brought his gaze back to rest on his granddaughter. "The old bloodsucker! Can't wait for me to draw my last breath." Exhausted by his efforts he slumped back against the pillows, life ebbing away with every breath he drew. His face was a ghastly hue but he managed to rouse himself once more, asking, "What did she tell you about me, your mother?"

It was several moments before Alexandra answered. "She told me all she considered I ought to know. I learned more about you, however, from the things she didn't say."

The old eyes seemed suddenly to light up with an amusement she could not understand. "And your father?" he prompted. "What did he tell you?"

Alexandra was tempted to lie, but mastering the impulse said contemptuously, "Do not waste your time in wondering about my father; all that need concern you is that he was a far better man than you and one, moreover, who deemed it unnecessary to even give you a moment's thought." The result of this scathing denunciation was all that she could have wished for. Matthew's face, turning purple at her dismissive contempt, mirrored his shocked disbelief. "You could have made things so much easier for her," she angrily threw at him, her eyes flashing. "Do you have the least idea of what she suffered because of you? The life she was subjected to? You forbid her to marry the man she loved because of your so-called pride! Well, she married him in spite of you, and was far happier than you have ever been. What kind of father are you?"

No one had ever dared say such things to him; oh, they probably thought them, but not one of them had the guts to openly accuse or question him, well, except for Marcus that was. Damn his impudence! He had always gone his own way. "The kind that will be obeyed," Matthew angrily shot at her. "Now, Miss," he bit out, "you listen to me." She stiffened at this, but another fit of coughing held her silent, and when he spoke again it was noticeable that most of the fight had deserted him. "I brought you here for a reason, and little though you may relish the idea I want you to know that I have changed my will to include you," he told her brusquely, "although God knows why when you show me little enough respect!"

"Respect has to be earned," she flashed.

"Hold your tongue!" he ordered. "Whether you like it or not I have made provision for you. No one, apart from my legal man Jenkins that is, knows of it," he informed her, his breathing more laboured. "Do you hear me, girl?"

"Yes, I hear you," she told him coldly, by no means pleased at the news. So, he thought he could buy her off, did he? Well, she did not need this belated display of family affection. "I did not come here for what I could get out of you," she bit out. "I couldn't care less about your money."

"Everyone cares about money," he ground out. "Even you."

"Yes, I care about it," she acknowledged, "but not yours."

"Ha!" he scoffed. "You expect me to believe that?"

"No." She shook her head. "I doubt whether you are capable of understanding or believing anything that does not come without a price tag. You changed your will to include me purely to ease your conscience," she rounded on him, her eyes darting green fire. "Well, if you think you can smooth your path to heaven through me, you are mistaken. I am not so accommodating!"

It was with a tremendous effort that Matthew Harrington controlled his anger. Alexandra could see the effort it was costing him but she was unrepentant. Her grandfather was dying right in front of her eyes, yet she could not relent towards him. What he was suffering now was nothing compared to what her mother had suffered because of him, and she knew she could never forgive him. She had come here today neither expecting nor wanting anything from him, but his announcement about his will had, instead of pleasing her, angered her. She wanted nothing from the man who had pushed her mother into a life of drudgery and poverty, her anger rising afresh as she recalled numerous occasions where her mother had strived beyond bearing to make their lives a little more tolerable. With the death of her father, her mother's will to go on living seemed to have deserted her; without the man she had never stopped or regretted loving life had taken on little meaning. Only she knew the full extent of his cold-hearted actions twenty years ago, and if Alexandra lived to be a hundred she would never cease to despise her grandfather!

Matthew Harrington had cared nothing for love or that her mother had found a man, albeit a stablehand, with whom she could be happy. All he had thought about was the shame his name would carry because of her behaviour.

"My conscience, girl," he growled, "is in no need of easing. The money is yours. Do with it as you will. Now leave me."

A twisted little smile touched her lips at this, but without uttering another word she turned on her heel and walked proudly towards the door. Just as she was about to turn the handle she heard him say, "You are a Harrington too, you know."

Alexandra regarded him steadily, and her voice, when she eventually spoke, was free of any gratitude as she replied, "A little late in the day to be remembering that, don't you think? Besides," she shrugged, "it is not something I am proud of, I assure you." Then, without a backward glance, she left the room, closing the door quietly behind her.

Chapter Three

"It's an absolute outrage!" declared Amelia as soon as the door had been firmly closed behind Alexandra. "She is lying, of course! Your father would never have asked her here."

"Apparently, he did," Marcus replied calmly.

"Well, I never knew what he was planning," protested George, his heavy jaws working, "and as the eldest I would surely have been told."

"Since when did father ever tell you anything?" mocked Charles, dismissing his brother contemptuously.

"Let me remind you, Charles," persisted George, "that I was deeply in Father's confidence."

"So it would appear," his brother scorned, removing a speck of dust from his sleeve. "Father, my dear brother, never confided in anyone, and if, for once in his life, he entrusted something of this nature to you, I should own myself astonished."

"Well, even if he didn't confide in me," George pointed out smugly, determined to put his brother in his place once and for all, "at least he never had to blackmail me into marriage because I was unable to pay my debts!"

A shocked gasp from Emily, a barely stifled titter from Edward and Sophy's flaming cheeks informed George of his error and the imprudence of being goaded into unguarded speech, but it was the ugly look on Charles's face which made him retreat a few steps; the sight of those clenched fists making him utter, "Charles, for God's sake!"

"You *miserable* little cur," Charles snarled menacingly. "You mealy-mouthed little…"

"I'm sorry," George swallowed, realising much too late the enormity of what he had said, "I don't…"

"I'll make you eat those words," Charles threatened, striding purposefully across the room towards him.

"If the two of you wish to discuss this further," Marcus intervened sharply, "then I suggest you remove yourselves."

George, who had inwardly quaked at the thought of being on the receiving end of his brother's meaningful fists, was more than grateful for his cousin's timely intervention. It was otherwise with Charles who bitterly resented the interference, and it was therefore several dangerous moments before he managed to get his temper sufficiently under control. "You are of course right, my dear Marcus," he drawled, resuming his poise. "What should we do without you to bring us to a sense of our surroundings?" The smile was now back on his face but the ugly look remained in those cold eyes, leaving Sophy in dread of the inevitable repercussions as they focused on her.

It was hardly surprising that she trembled for the consequences of George's unguarded words. Charles did not need reminding of the circumstances leading up to their marriage, quite the opposite. She herself was more than aware of his feelings towards her; his frequently expressed remarks never failing to remind her of the events which had prompted his reluctant proposal of marriage nearly three years ago. Of course, Charles never offered her physical violence, he didn't have to; that rapier-sharp tongue of his caused her far more pain than any blow could have. She had never pretended to love Charles, but she was a dutiful daughter and one who had never even considered going against her father's wishes, even though they differed widely to her own. She had therefore been prepared to accept Charles Harrington as her husband, but it was not until fifteen months ago when Marcus had returned home to England from India after being invalided out of his regiment, the result of receiving a bullet wound in his right leg which had failed to heal as it should, that she had come to know the meaning of love and all the emotions it evoked.

She had not fallen in love with him on sight. Not at all! It had been a gradual and wonderful awakening during Marcus's painful period of convalescence under his aunt's watchful eye. At first, Charles had resented his wife sharing a duty he considered to be both demeaning and unnecessary, but since he could not put forward any real objection he had unwillingly accepted the small tasks she performed to make his cousin more comfortable.

It had been those first few weeks which had done the damage to her heart. Through all the pain and discomfort Marcus had endured he had never once lost his temper; his warm smile and grateful thanks for even the smallest task so very different from her husband's demands and inflexible belief in what was his rightful due. Instead of impatience there had been understanding; instead of blighting criticism there had been acceptance and, for the first time in her life, Sophy had discovered that strength and determination could take a different form other than imperious demands. Where Charles ordered, Marcus requested; where Charles expected, Marcus awaited. Nor did he take for granted his aunt's unstinting care and devotion or the attendance of her daughter-in-law. His humane qualities and gentle nature in no way detracted from his masculinity, on the contrary they merely served to heighten it as well as her awareness of him. The time they had spent together had been the happiest she had ever known, and whilst neither of them had ever spoken of the love which was growing between them, they could not deny its existence.

Sophy may not love Charles but she was his wife, and no matter how much she loved Marcus she would not betray her husband, even though he had betrayed her with Amelia for the past twelve months. To allow herself to become the mistress of the man she did love would simply tarnish that love and reduce its value in her eyes. But Marcus had never even intimated at such an arrangement any more than he had made any attempt to kiss her, even though she knew it was what they both wanted more than anything else. But his eyes kissed her; every time they looked at her they caressed her soft lips, making her realise more and more how very vulnerable she was to him. He was looking at her now, but it was not a caress she could see but anger over her embarrassment at George's insensitive words.

"Really, George!" exclaimed Amelia, not without a touch of malicious amusement. "Can you *never* hold your tongue? You have quite embarrassed poor Sophy. It is too bad of you!"

Torn between his vexation for causing his sister-in-law any discomfiture, for he genuinely felt sorry for her, and his dislike of being placed in a disadvantageous position in front of Charles, George spluttered a disjointed apology, which only resulted in making him look even more ridiculous.

"Don't you think we are deviating from the point?" Edward pointed out, immediately coming under the glare of several pairs of eyes, of which one pair at least was filled with relief at his timely intervention. "Well, what I mean is," he swallowed, startled at his own temerity, "ought we not to discover what brings the girl here?"

A distorted smile twisted Charles's lips. "Have no fear, Edward, it shall be done."

"But how?" asked Emily, her faith in her husband strengthened by his support of her disgust at the presence of a girl she had no intention of acknowledging.

"By the simple expedient of asking her," Charles returned simply.

"I hope you do not intend to have her brought in here," Emily warned him.

"Do not be alarmed, dear sister," Charles mocked smoothly, "I shall, of course, meet her on her own ground."

"What on earth do you mean?" Amelia asked, bewildered. "Her own ground!"

"Why, what else should I mean?" he asked surprised, raising a supercilious eyebrow. "The gutter, of course!"

"Don't, Charles," begged Sophy. "That was uncalled-for." Too late to recall the words which had left her lips before she could stop them.

"Was it, my dear?" Charles asked, the menacing calm not lost on her, or the hard look which glinted in his eyes as they skimmed over her. "You know, my dear," he drawled, "between you and Marcus, I can see it is going to be extremely difficult to make an observation of any kind."

"Sophy's right," Marcus pointed out, deliberately drawing Charles's fire away from Sophy. "Whatever her circumstances it must surely be obvious that the girl has received a good standard of education and is also intelligent enough to realise that she would not be welcomed here without an invitation. As for your comment about the gutter, I can only say that, even for you, it was a damned offensive remark."

"You say an awful lot, Cousin," Charles told him icily, "considering you are merely a guest in this house."

Sophy's heart gave a sickening thud, dreading the outcome of this exchange. Marcus may have his own establishment, but should his visits to Brook Street ever cease, her life would indeed be intolerable.

It was not what Marcus had said precisely that Charles resented so much as the man himself. Regardless of the reluctant respect he had for his cousin, he hated the fact that unlike himself Marcus was not, and never had been, financially dependent upon his uncle.

Matthew Harrington's only surviving sister, the youngest of four daughters, had married exceptionally well, her husband's family having earned their reputation as well as their fortune in the woollen industry, and it had been on the death of his father that everything had passed to Marcus, placing him in the enviable position whereby he need not dance to his uncle's tune. Not that Marcus ever danced to any tune but that of his own playing, but at least it gave him the independence that Charles would have killed for. Not for the first time he found himself resenting the quirk of fate which had determined their parentage. It was damned unfair that Marcus had so much while he had only the allowance his father gave him. Not that it was not a generous allowance, after all his father was an extremely wealthy man, but he believed his sons should earn the money they received from him. Oh, nothing menial of course. Even so, it was degrading enough having to associate with those peasants at the brewery in order to live the life he considered should be his by right. Marcus, on the other hand, appeared to have no qualms or suffer any embarrassment about the source of his fortune or the fact that he was regularly required to journey north to associate with weavers or dyers or whatever they called themselves. Charles was every inch the aristocrat, hating his father's humbler side to such an extent that he had never really been able to acquit his mother of marrying beneath her. The thought had plagued him all his life. And if all that were not bad enough he had been blackmailed into marrying Sophy because his father had cut up pretty stiff about his debts. Left to himself he would have given her the go by after their very first meeting. His father, however, had had other ideas. Charles looked at her now, his eyes hardening as they dwelled on her, not quite certain whether it was his father, his wife or his cousin he resented the most.

Considering that Charles had spent a most agreeable interlude in the arms of Amelia last night, George having been conveniently delayed at the home of a business acquaintance, he had been in an uncertain temper ever since he had come downstairs. Sophy knew better than to ask the reason why, but she was rather surprised at the open animosity he was displaying towards Marcus. That Charles had a grudging respect for his cousin she knew, but unless she was very much mistaken, for reasons best known to himself, he seemed set on provoking a quarrel. But this last exchange very much alarmed her. Even though she could place the utmost reliance on Marcus's good sense, the outcome was hanging dangerously in the balance. For several awful moments the cousins eyed one another; the one steady and calm, the other cold and resentful. For the first time, Sophy found herself actually welcoming George's intervention.

"Never mind that," he dismissed. "What are we going to do about the girl? I mean, what if Father really did ask her to come here?"

"Are you out of your senses, George?" Amelia demanded irritably, wondering what next her husband would say.

"If he did ask her to come here," George mused, ignoring his wife's criticism as he turned it over in his mind, "then it looks as though he must have set someone on to find her."

"Oh, *well done*, George!" Charles mockingly applauded, the dangerous light in his eyes disappearing as they focused on other, if less worthy prey. "I am sure none of us would ever have thought of that!"

"Damn you, Charles!" George snapped. "You won't find it so very amusing if Father has made any provision for her. Which I'm bound to say, the more I think about it the more likely it seems."

"The only likelihood *I* can see," Charles said nastily, "is that you have clearly lost whatever sense you had." Before his brother could argue this point, Charles continued, "Do you honestly believe that having thrown her mother out and then refusing to have any mention made of her, my father would suddenly take it into his head to leave her daughter anything?"

"That's all very well," Emily put in, "but if he hasn't left her anything why employ someone to find her?"

As only to be expected, the news of their sister's death had gradually been imparted to them over time, either because Matthew had considered it necessary or Charlotte had let it slip in an unguarded moment, but at no time had any mention been made of a granddaughter, but whatever their feelings of loss over a sister they had not seen in over twenty years was far outweighed by finding themselves faced with a niece they never knew they had.

"More importantly," Charles said meditatively, suddenly struck by an idea, his eyes straying back to his cousin, "I for one had no idea that a grandchild existed until now," his eyes narrowing in thought. "My father clearly must have known about her for a long time, but how?" Since no one could enlighten him he took a step nearer to Marcus, his voice dulcetly smooth, reminding Sophy of a cat playing with a mouse. "If I recall correctly, Cousin, you were the only one amongst us who was not taken by surprise at the girl's existence, you even knew her name. It would appear, would it not, that you have the advantage of us," pausing before adding ominously, "would you care to share your knowledge with us?"

"I should be pleased to," Marcus told him, not at all intimidated by his cousin, "if I thought for one moment you were really interested in her."

"Oh, but we *are* interested, Cousin," Charles smiled thinly. "In fact, we should be only too delighted to learn at what point my father took you into his confidence."

"He didn't," Marcus returned shortly.

"Come, Cousin," Charles mockingly chided, "do you seriously expect us to believe that?"

"You may believe what you wish," Marcus shrugged dismissively.

"Why, Marcus!" Amelia smiled archly. "I do believe you have been holding out on us!"

"Yes, by God!" George exclaimed, taking a step nearer to his cousin.

"Explain yourself, Marcus."

"I owe none of you an explanation," he told them quietly, but there was no mistaking the inflexible note in his voice.

For the first time in his dealings with Marcus, George felt unsure of his ground. His cousin, always so calm and placid, had never spoken in quite that tone of voice before and it had taken him considerably by surprise. He was so used to parrying his brother's smooth-tongued barbs that it had become almost second nature, but that firm and authoritative voice had made him pause.

Amelia, however, had never been fooled by Marcus's quiet demeanour, firmly convinced that beneath the unruffled surface ran a will of iron and a resolution which she found very attractive. If it were not for the fact that there was no other man for her but Charles she was honest enough to admit to herself that she would have enjoyed prising Marcus away from Sophy.

"Really, Marcus!" Emily exclaimed, her thin bosom heaving. "I do feel we have a right to know from whom…!"

Marcus eyed her steadily for a moment, saying at length, "It was not from your father, but from your mother."

"Mamma!" George cried astounded. "But why, I mean… why _you?_"

"Because there was no one else to whom she could turn to unburden herself," Marcus told him, unperturbed. "Had any one of you shown the least tendency to understand your mother's feelings or let her know that she could confide in you," Marcus pointed out candidly, "she would doubtless have told you herself long since."

A shocked silence followed this quietly delivered accusation, only Sophy silently applauding it.

"My goodness!" Charles exclaimed in mock surprise, one slender forefinger rubbing his nose. "You really have put us in our place, have you not?"

Before Marcus could reply to this the door quietly opened and Harris walked in, but one look at his face was enough to inform them of his errand. "Sir," he said to Charles, "your mother has asked me to tell you that your presence is required upstairs. Your father…"

"Thank you, Harris," Charles cut him short. "We shall be up directly."

Harris may not be overly fond of the master, but he hoped he was human enough to feel some sadness at his parting. Even though he had always known of the state of affairs existing between Matthew Harrington and his offspring he nevertheless found this show of indifference not at all the thing.

Almost immediately Emily began to cry, refusing all Edward's clumsy efforts to console her. Charles watched this touching scene in sardonic amusement, not at all moved by the sight of his sister's distress over the imminent death of their father. "Very effecting," he drawled. "You would, however," he remarked callously, "be far more convincing had you shown this much affection before now."

"How dare you, Charles!" Emily cried, affronted at the very idea of being considered capable of anything but the most proper behaviour. "I have always loved Papa."

"When it suits you, certainly," her brother reminded her with maddening honesty.

"How can you say anything so abominable and untrue?" Emily demanded tearfully.

"Very easily," Charles shrugged, tired of this charade.

"I... I... h-hate you, Charles!" Emily hiccupped from the folds of her mangled handkerchief. "Have you n-no f-feelings?" she demanded.

"Most certainly," Charles nodded, casting a fleeting glance at Amelia, whose eyes glowed in response, "but unlike yours they are not misplaced."

George, who had missed that silent communication between his wife and brother, swallowed the unexpected lump which had appeared in his throat, saying, "I really think it is time we made our way upstairs. If you are ready, Amelia," he nodded. "Charles, are you coming?"

For once there was no trace of pomp or officiousness in either his tone or demeanour, but for some unaccountable reason this perfectly natural enquiry had the most adverse effect upon his brother, and this, coupled with what he considered to be his cousin's meddlesome involvement in dealing with the girl, rendered his hold on his temper even more fragile, a circumstance that made him say irritably, his hand outstretched imperatively towards his wife, "Come along, Sophy."

One by one they filed out of the drawing room, only Marcus remaining where he was.

"Coming, Coz?" Charles enquired sardonically, holding open the door.

"In a moment," Marcus nodded.

"As you wish," Charles bowed mockingly, adding, almost as if it were an afterthought, "by the way, Cousin, I shall look forward to hearing your explanation as to what you said a moment or two ago."

Marcus's eyes hardened slightly, their clear gaze looking directly at his cousin. "I don't have to explain myself to anyone, Charles."

This pointed rejoinder was not lost on his cousin, whose eyes glinted dangerously. "You know, Marcus," he returned silkily, "I have never been entirely certain whether to take you for a wise man or a fool. In either event, I find you extremely irritating."

A reluctant, if not unappreciative, smile, touched Marcus's lips. "Coming from you, Charles, that's quite a compliment."

"Make the most of it, Cousin," Charles warned ominously, "for you will not receive another."

As the door closed behind his cousin Marcus had the strong but not unamusing thought that had they lived fifty years ago they would in all probability end up firing pistols at dawn. It was not simply because his cousin was married to the woman he loved which had engendered his dislike of Charles, although his treatment of her did little to improve his feeling towards him. From childhood, Charles had displayed a proud arrogance which had gradually set him apart from his brothers and sisters; eventually creating an ever-widening rift between them, especially with George. Marcus, only three years older than Charles, had been aware from an early age that his cousin had, even then, resented the fact that he had not been the first born, and although the level of animosity between him and his eldest brother Richard had not run so deep, with his untimely death Charles had found it difficult to accept that George would be the one to step into their father's shoes. Not only did Charles hold his elder brother in the utmost contempt but looked upon him as being far inferior to himself. He had never been able to accept that George, by virtue of being older than himself, would precede him in all things. On his visits to Brook Street as a boy with his mother, Marcus had more than once witnessed the cruel taunts Charles had aimed at his elder brother, disliking the way he never lost an opportunity, even at that young age, to plague George into a frenzy of anger. If, at any time, the discord between them could remotely lay claim to having its roots in sibling rivalry, as time passed with no relenting of hostilities on either side and neither brother pretending to there being anything between them other than a heartfelt dislike, no evidence of this could be discerned.

Marcus had always enjoyed visiting his cousins, playing as boisterously as any of them, he and Richard always finding some new mischief to enter into. Being younger, Charles had naturally been excluded from these adventures; his banishment from these more grown-up games, far more exciting than the nursery where he was told he belonged, culminated in him venting his anger on any one of his brothers and sisters unlucky enough to be within his vicinity. This drastic though satisfying outlet had on more than one occasion resulted in the cousins coming to cuffs, especially when Jane unexpectedly found herself on the receiving end of a flying book, missing her by a fraction, from her furious elder brother.

Far from diminishing Charles's pride had grown with the years, his time at Eton and Oxford merely smoothing the rough edges of his personality, easing them into the cold and aloof man he had become. His friends and acquaintances from these establishments of learning had only increased his self-belief, filling him with an even greater desire to shed the stigma of his father's humble beginnings, dismissing as irrelevant the fact that it was his father's wealth, trade-earned though it was, which was enabling him to live the kind of life he enjoyed as well as frequently rescuing him from his more pressing obligations. As far as his mother was concerned, Charles accorded her all the respect due to her, his love for her tarnished as he secretly blamed her for making what he called a travesty of a marriage to his father. Adam and the rest of his family he tolerated with polite indifference, unless of course they committed some folly which he considered detrimental to himself, but George he still despised, although Marcus knew that nothing would ever really change that, and Charles's taunts, still cruel and calculated to hit home, were now far more sophisticated than the childish ones of the nursery and the schoolroom, guaranteed to make his brother more of a laughing-stock than ever.

As Marcus slowly climbed the stairs to join his family he found himself thinking, and not for the first time, that Charles would perhaps have been the better for a little army discipline, where a man was only as good as his courage allowed. For himself, Marcus had always hankered after a pair of colours, his only regret being that he had had to leave the life he loved before he was ready due to the accursed stupidity of a junior officer who had left an untrained man in charge of a loaded rifle.

Within the hour Matthew Harrington was dead. At last he had given up the fight to go on living. He had put his house in order and was well pleased with his efforts. In spite of the earnest entreaties of Jenkins, his long-suffering legal adviser, that a change to his will would only create ill feeling, he had gone ahead regardless. Let them fight! He would dispose of his assets as he saw fit, and if the brat did not touch a penny of the money he had left her, so be it. Even now, on his deathbed, he could give no explanation as to why he had changed his will to include her. Damn him if he could! She had given a good account of herself though; far from being intimidated by him she had treated him with contempt. The brat! Just like her mother. Stubborn and strong-willed – Elizabeth! Her name an indistinguishable whisper on his lips.

*

Having left her grandfather's room Alexandra released her pent-up breath, not entirely certain whether to be glad or sorry that she had seen him. She had by no means liked the idea that he had snapped his fingers and expected her to come running. She had intended to keep him waiting, but it had been pure chance she had come today. She had of course known that Matthew Harrington was ill, thanks to old Mr. Burrows who paid her a shilling a week to read to him, his eyesight almost gone, gleaning the information from his newspapers. She had had no intention of visiting Brook Street straightaway merely because she had been ordered to, but that she had come today, the day he was clearly dying, had been purely accidental and not from a sincere desire to see her grandfather before it was too late, but simply because it may as well be today as any other, besides which, she had no wish to receive another order to show herself in Brook Street. Not very commendable perhaps, but at least in her own small way she had paid him back a little of what she considered was owed him. For years her mother had waited for some sign that she had been forgiven, that she was welcomed once more into the family home, but none came. She had suffered hardships none of them could possibly imagine yet for all that the love her parents had shared, the love which had been scorned and condemned, had grown and strengthened – it had survived every setback. That love was something they were incapable of understanding.

"Alexandra!" From a small dressing room Charlotte emerged in a rustle of taffeta, her weary eyes glistening with unshed tears as she folded her granddaughter in a scented embrace. "My *dear* child!" she cried. "Let me look at you." Holding her at arm's length she eyed her from head to foot, her heart torn apart at the sight of her. So thin; so pale and drawn. "I can't believe you are here at last!" she told her between tears and laughter. "I had no idea what your grandfather was planning." Before Alexandra could say anything, Charlotte turned to Harris, who, all this time, had been hovering in the background as moved as his mistress. "Harris, take my granddaughter downstairs to my sitting room. Make her comfortable." Then, turning back to Alexandra smiled. "Harris will look after you. I cannot leave your grandfather just yet, you understand, but I will come to you just as soon as I can."

"I'm sorry," Alexandra told her in a hard voice, "but I really cannot stay."

"Cannot stay!" echoed her grandmother, surprised. "But you must, for a little while at least; just until I have had the opportunity to talk to you."

Alexandra eyed her grandmother without so much as a flicker of emotion, but managing to swallow her anger said curtly, "I do not think we have much to say to one another. Besides, there are things I have to do."

Charlotte blinked, momentarily taken aback at Alexandra's hostility and could only turn an anguished eye on Harris, who instantly came to the aid of his mistress. He had not been in the Harrington family for nearly thirty years without having to deal with some pretty awkward situations, and so to her undying gratitude Charlotte heard him say, "If I may suggest? If Miss Alexandra is pressed for time, you could talk in the dressing room here and I will wait outside in case the doctor needs you."

This suggestion found immediate favour with Charlotte, but before it could be carried out the sight of Doctor Rowley emerging from his patient's bedroom and the severity of his expression were enough to inform her that the end was very near. In her confusion, she had to leave her granddaughter in Harris's capable hands, never quite knowing how he managed to persuade Alexandra to go with him. Charlotte's love for Matthew may have died years ago but it would never so much have crossed her mind to leave his side, even though she knew he did not want her or his family at his bedside.

It had been her friendship with his sister which had brought them together, but whilst her parents had accepted Imogen Harrington as her dearest friend they clearly regarded her brother as being quite unsuitable as a husband for their daughter. From the social scale point of view they looked upon Matthew Harrington as being far beneath her, not even his money making him acceptable. There was no mistaking the vulgar tradesman behind the growing wealth and they were prepared to go to any lengths to prevent their daughter's association with such a man. Unfortunately, however, not even a prolonged trip to Italy to stay with an aged aunt who had long since found the climate beneficial for her frail health, had been successful. Immediately upon her return to London Charlotte had resumed her relationship with Matthew and, to the mortification of her parents, it had become increasingly clear that unless they wanted a breach with their daughter and the embarrassment of a public scandal, they had little choice but to accept, albeit with bitter reluctance, their betrothal announcement.

Those early years had certainly proved her parents wrong; she had been very happy with the man she had chosen for her husband. But Matthew had to be master in his own house. His mastery over her had been a gradual process, so much so that Charlotte had never been able to pinpoint the exact moment when she had ceased to love him. It had been little things at first; so trivial and insignificant and remarked upon so indulgently that she had accepted his scolds. Slowly though, his indulgence gave way to impatience and eventually to imperious demands until his stronger will crushed her. Where she had once looked forward to his company she had come to dread it, seeking solace with her children. Her solace had not lasted long. Two at least of her sons had inherited their father's temper and ruthless determination to have their own way, irrespective of the consequences. From being the most adorable children who had given her so much needed love they had grown into replicas of their father, the traits she had come to abhor in Matthew palpably manifesting themselves in Richard and Charles.

Richard, her beautiful first-born, by forcing a ridiculous quarrel with someone at his club, had been killed in the stupid and outdated duel which had resulted from it. He had allowed his temper to override his judgement, and even if he had not met his death he would now in all probability, like his opponent was being forced to do, spend the rest of his days abroad, not daring to show himself in England again.

Even Adam, the most even tempered of her sons, and certainly the most good-humoured and easygoing, had forced a situation which had come very close to creating a public scandal when he had eloped with Marsden's daughter. He had refused to accept that Marsden had someone else in mind for Isabel; he had loved her and was determined to have her. Their elopement had of course been hushed up, but Marsden had never forgiven the insult he believed Adam had brought to his name. Upon his return to town from honeymoon Matthew had instantly packed him off to Yorkshire with his new bride, believing that he would be far too busy with running the two breweries there to enter in to any more folly, besides which, it would give Marsden time to cool down.

From Adam's reply to her letter advising him of the seriousness of his father's condition, Charlotte had no clear idea when he would arrive home or if Isabel would come with him. Between Adam and his father there had never really been any animosity, only the expected differences of opinion which naturally existed between father and son, but as Charlotte looked at George and Charles, standing rigidly upright beside the huge four-poster, their expressions inscrutable, she could only guess at their feelings as they watched their father's life ebbing away. That he would not be greatly missed by them was certain. What was not certain was Matthew's reasons for having his granddaughter visit him. The fact that he had set plans in motion to find her and in the utmost secrecy, could only mean that his motives, whatever they were, would no doubt come to light at a later date. Matthew had never discussed his affairs with her let alone confide in her, but try as she did, Charlotte could not banish the thought that Alexandra's visit had been for a specific purpose. Matthew never embarked on something without a reason for doing so.

Elizabeth had not only been his eldest daughter but his favourite also, and Charlotte alone knew what a bitter blow it had been to him when she had disobeyed him over Joseph Dawes. When Matthew had made it clear that she either give him up or face the consequences it had not been an idle threat, but as Charlotte sat beside her husband's bedside with her family, all showing varying degrees of emotion, she had the distinct feeling that Matthew had still one more card to play.

His will had naturally been drawn up some years ago, and whilst she had not been privileged to know its contents she did not expect it to contain anything out of the ordinary. It had been by the merest chance that she had seen Jenkins enter the house that morning about two months ago, and although she had not paid too much attention to it at the time in view of Alexandra's visit today, Charlotte was left with only one conclusion. In her heart she prayed she was right and that Matthew had made some provision for her, but with Matthew one never could tell. For years Matthew and his sons, especially Charles, had argued over many things, not the least being money, and unless she was very much mistaken the question of money was about to raise its head again.

There seemed to be no end to the quarrels. If it was not one thing it was another, but worst of all was the ill-feeling between George and Charles, a situation Matthew had been well aware of, but unlike him Charlotte had neither the emotional nor physical strength to cope with it. Even though Matthew had made each of his sons responsible for a particular brewery there had never been any misunderstanding; their father had full and final authority and no decision could be made without his sanction. Now, George fully expected to take over where his father had left off. Charles may loathe the smell of the shop, but this would be an extremely difficult pill for him to swallow. Charles cared not at all that his father had taken old Joshua Harrington's small backstreet brewery in Halifax and turned it into a more profitable venture. Nor did he feel any admiration or pride in the knowledge that one brewery had soon become two, neighbouring Bradford, just seven miles away, a conveniently situated town for his father to spread his wings until finally bringing his business acumen to London where he soon had two more breweries bearing the name 'Harrington Ales', earning himself all the recognition he could have desired. Charles had never set foot in Yorkshire and as far as he was concerned he had no intention of ever doing so. For all he cared Adam was welcome to the God-forsaken place; a high price to pay in his opinion for running off with Marsden's daughter! But no matter how much Charles may despise the very lucrative business his father had built up from his grandfather's humble beginnings as well as the part he was expected to play in it, he would nevertheless be bitterly disappointed, even resentful, if he discovered that George had been automatically elected to take the leading role.

Charlotte may love her offspring, but she was painfully aware of

Charles's pride and arrogance as well as how he found the whole idea of associating with draymen and the like as too demeaning. But she also knew that his pride would take a far greater blow if Matthew had perversely decided to place the Islington brewery under Charles's authority under that of the one presided over by George at Deptford.

All his life Charles had fought the bitter anguish of not being able to live the life he considered his due by virtue of his mother's aristocratic lineage, but her marriage to his father had instantly rendered this very natural course out of the question. Nor did his time at Eton and Oxford help to lessen this belief, on the contrary it only served to intensify it. Being amongst the sons of lords and earls and visiting the homes of those with whom he had made friends, highlighted this thorn in his side as well as the bitterness he felt over the trick fate had played him by denying him what he considered was his by right due to his mother's aristocratic ancestry.

Charlotte knew that if Matthew had taken it into his head to make changes to his will at the last moment to provide for Alexandra, an action which would in itself mean that he had publicly acknowledged her, then Charles's humiliation would be twofold. Charlotte had not needed to witness firsthand her son's reception of her granddaughter this afternoon, she could well imagine his reaction and it would have been very far from avuncular, but what she did know for certain was that if Charles had to play second fiddle to George it would be an unbearable insult. Then of course there was Adam to consider. It was perhaps natural to assume that Matthew had made no changes where his youngest son was concerned, deciding that it would be far wiser to keep him in Yorkshire rather than have him show his face in town, but this could not be taken for granted. She knew Adam, the least contentious and certainly the most likeable of her sons, would have no objection to George stepping into Matthew's shoes, and although Adam was quite content to run his father's premises in Yorkshire she could not see him wanting to remain there forever.

Matthew could never be relied upon to do what one would expect, and it seemed to Charlotte that far from ending the family squabbles his passing would merely increase them.

Chapter Four

At three minutes past four o'clock on that cold and bleak February afternoon, Matthew Carey Harrington drew his last breath. He had lived barely an hour after seeing his granddaughter, the will-power which had kept him going for just that purpose finally deserting him. No one had been quite certain what it was that had passed his lips just before the end, the utterance hardly above a whisper, and Charlotte's attempt to get closer so she could hear was in vain.

Despite the fire burning fiercely in the grate, the atmosphere inside the impressive master bedroom was as cold and daunting as the weather outside. Perverse to the end, Matthew had adamantly refused to have the last of the daylight shut out, insisting that the heavy brocade curtains remain open even though the lamps had been lit some time before. With the discretion his late patient had despised, Doctor Rowley tiptoed reverently across to the window, shutting out the fading remnants of daylight. Apart from Emily, who, in spite of all she had ever said or thought about her father and his unreasonable attitude towards Edward, wept bitterly, unlike the rest of her family, who appeared to be quite unmoved by their father's death.

Being well versed in the ways of this unnatural family, Doctor Rowley had come to believe that there was nothing else they could say or do which could possibly shock him, but as he turned and looked at the group around the beside he found it almost impossible to believe that, apart from his daughter, no one shed a tear. Matthew Harrington had been a hard man and a refractory patient and had it not been for the handsome fees paid for his services nothing would have induced him to continually tend a man who had neither manners nor breeding to recommend him. He had shown neither courtesy nor respect to anyone, least of all to his wife, even so, Doctor Rowley had little doubt that nothing would be quite the same without him. Having satisfied himself that the deceased's family had looked long enough upon the remains of the man who had dominated the household for years, he respectfully pulled the sheet over the ashen face.

Charles, whose sharp eyes had not missed that tiny shard of broken china which had lodged itself into the pile of the carpet and had escaped detection when the pieces had been gathered up, knew precisely what had happened. Bending down to pick it up he glanced sardonically from the piece he held between his finger and thumb to the thin and harassed features of the man his father had frequently tormented and heartily despised, raising a mocking eyebrow. His agile brain accurately read the thoughts behind the insipid blue eyes as they looked back at him, and Charles, having no more liking for him than his father had, threw him a twisted smile which brought a tinge of colour to his face. Doctor Thadeus Rowley may have suffered all manner of verbal abuse from his late patient and, God forgive him, whilst he was not entirely heartbroken at his passing, it seemed a sad state of affairs when his own family regarded his death, if not as a happy event, then certainly as a welcome release from his controlling influence! It was not for him to either give an opinion or pass judgement, but to his way of thinking no one would ever suspect from their demeanours that they had just suffered the loss of a loved one!

Charles, who not only thought this touching scene quite nauseating, especially when he considered that not one of them would be entirely grief-stricken by the death of their patriarch, was of the firm opinion that he for one had played the role of grieving son for long enough. Apart from the medicines and phials on the bedside table there was no other evidence to suggest that a man had lain sick inside this room for the past two weeks. Everything was as it had always been, neat and tidy and spotlessly clean, but there was an indefinable odour attached to a sickroom which seemed to cling to one and which nothing could disguise and, as far as he was concerned, he was not prepared to remain in its grotesque atmosphere any longer.

Charlotte made no protest when Charles helped her to her feet, silently accepting his supporting arm as he led her out of the oppressive gloom and down the stairs followed by her family, her face as impassive as if it had been carved in stone. Having descended the last step, she removed his hand from her elbow, calmly announcing that she would join them in the drawing room in a little while, but first she must see her granddaughter who had been waiting for her in the sitting room.

Since none of them had the least idea that Elizabeth's daughter was still in the house, this calmly uttered statement considerably startled her offspring, believing her to have left long since. With a determination that was as firm as it was unexpected Charlotte adamantly refused the attempts of George and Charles to persuade her into leaving the matter in their hands, quietly reminding them that she had asked Alexandra to wait and no matter what their feelings were, she was her granddaughter and therefore she was going to see her.

Sophy caught the sparkle of admiration in Marcus's eyes at his aunt's resolution, watching her small upright figure as it retreated purposefully towards the rear sitting room, ignoring the protests of her family. Despite Alexandra's insensitive response to her greeting earlier, a reaction Charlotte had since put down to apprehension over meeting her relatives for the first time, it had not occurred to her that her granddaughter, having had time to collect herself, would not wish to see her. It was therefore something of a shock to find, upon entering the sitting room, that there was no sign of Alexandra especially having been told in a quiet aside by Harris that he had personally escorted her there. It was a painful blow to discover that at some point she had slipped away without anyone knowing or leaving a message of any kind. This discovery, following hard upon the heels of Matthew's death, took every last ounce of fight out of her, requiring all Charlotte's strength to return to the drawing room to reluctantly inform her family of Alexandra's unexpected departure, not at all surprised to learn that this intelligence only served to intensify their animosity towards their newly-found niece.

Such a sneaky departure, George informed her smugly, only went to prove that her manners were as reprehensible as her lack of breeding was to be deplored, and that any intention his mother may have of furthering the relationship ought to be discarded now. "Because I tell you, Mamma," he pointed out resolutely, "she will not be welcome here."

Her granddaughter's flight, following hard on the heels of realising that Matthew was dead, set the seal on Charlotte's despondency, but her son's insensitive words proved too much, and Sophy, recognising this, was moved to suggest that she may be better if she went to her room to rest. Like Charlotte, Sophy had cause to blush for her relatives, but she knew from bitter experience that any opinion she may put forward would either be ignored or, which was most likely, treated with disdain. Charles neither cared for nor desired her opinion, and George, who could never be brought to acknowledge that he could on occasion be wrong, merely humoured her.

Charlotte, kindly dismissing her maid who had come to tend her the moment she realised her mistress had entered her room, was extremely distressed as Sophy helped her to undress, her agitation so great that Sophy suggested asking Doctor Rowley to come and see her before he left the house. Charlotte, firmly vetoing this idea, said that she needed nothing to help her sleep. "She should not have gone!" she cried, wringing her hands distractedly. "Why did she not stay?"

Sophy could have given her several reasons, but said instead, "Do not distress yourself. We shall find her."

"We *must*, Sophy; we must!" she cried, sinking almost defeated onto the bed.

Charlotte's grip on Sophy's wrist was so urgent that she knelt in front of her, her warm hazel eyes smiling comfortingly up into the face which appeared to have suddenly grown so much older. "Of course we must," she nodded reassuringly, "but now, you must try to get some rest. There is nothing you can do about anything at the moment."

Charlotte nodded. "I know you are right, but I am so terribly worried about her."

"I know you are," Sophy soothed, wishing there was more she could do. "I promise you we *shall* find her."

"That poor child!" Charlotte cried. "You saw her, Sophy," she said tearfully. "So pale and drawn. What she must have suffered!"

"I know," Sophy said softly, her heart as wrung as Charlotte's over the sight of so pathetic a creature. "She has endured much in the name of pride."

Tenderly laying the palm of her cold hand on Sophy's smooth cheek, Charlotte said gently, "You always understand. It is such a comfort to me to know that I can talk to you without reserve." She sighed. "I know I should not be saying this, but I love you more than my other daughters-in-law."

This touching tribute brought a delicate flush of colour to Sophy's cheeks. "Thank you," she said huskily, adding, "but Amelia loves you too, you know."

Charlotte considered her daughter-in-law for several moments. "You have too much heart, Sophy. Do you really believe that Amelia would be so generous towards you?" Receiving no answer to this, she pointed out, "Amelia my dear, loves no one but herself."

"I think you wrong her," Sophy said truthfully. "Only consider how she idolises the boys."

"Very well," Charlotte conceded, "I grant you she loves her children, but that is all."

Sophy could have told her that there was one other whom she loved, but said instead, "And what of Isabel? You like her, don't you?"

"On the one and only occasion we met," Charlotte admitted, "I found her to be a very nice girl." Pausing only to tie the ribbons of her nightcap, she said, "Of course, had Adam done the thing right instead of running off with her I daresay I should have come to like her very well. As it is," she sighed, "I doubt I shall have the opportunity. Marsden will never forgive Adam for eloping with his daughter. I only hope the girl was worth it!"

"I am quite sure Adam has no regrets," Sophy smiled, considering Adam to be worth a dozen of his brothers.

"I hope not," Charlotte sighed wearily, allowing Sophy to help her into bed, "but despite his even temper and cheerful nature he can, once he has taken something into his head, prove quite determined."

"I am sure it will all come right in the end," Sophy told her, pulling the covers over her before drawing the heavy curtains part way round the bed. "From all I have ever seen of Marsden, which isn't much I grant you," she admitted, giving the fire a quick poke, "he will not keep his daughter out in the cold for very long, or Adam either."

"I hope you are right," Charlotte sighed again, "but Marsden is a very proud man."

"And *you*," Sophy smiled, sitting down on the edge of the bed, "are worrying unduly."

"A mother constantly worries," Charlotte smiled wanly.

"I know," Sophy nodded, realising her mother-in-law was in no hurry to let her go, and therefore she was quite prepared to remain with her for as long as she wanted her company. "I am sure though," she smiled encouragingly, "that they will be the first to tell you that they are adults and quite capable of taking charge of their own lives."

"Do you think so?" Charlotte enquired. "It seems they have not done very well so far." Sinking back against the pillows she eyed Sophy closely. "I have often wondered if I could have done more for my children."

"You did everything possible," Sophy assured her. "Besides," she added practically, realising it would do no good to encourage her mother-in-law to indulge in this fit of self-recrimination brought on naturally by all the events of the day, "you cannot hold yourself responsible for what they may choose to do, and if it is Adam you are worrying over," she pointed out, "I think you will find it not in the least necessary, and that in spite of the circumstances surrounding his marriage he is very happy and has no regrets whatsoever." Seeing that Charlotte still remained unconvinced Sophy said, with a lightness she was far from feeling, "You just wait and see. Adam will reconcile things with Marsden and before you know it he will be bringing Isabel on a prolonged visit. Now," she smiled, "it is time you tried to get some rest," reiterating her assurance that there was absolutely nothing for her to concern herself over as she kissed her cheek, before walking to the door.

"Sophy," Charlotte called, "I daresay you must be thinking how unnatural I am in shedding no tears for Matthew, but just now I find I cannot."

Sophy did not find it unnatural at all. Having been a member of this family for over two years she had witnessed her father-in-law's heavy-handed rule too often to feel either shock or surprise at her mother-in-law's feelings or that she was, for the moment at least, unable to shed any tears for Matthew. He may well have loved her in the early days of their marriage but, over time, his natural authoritarian disposition had taken its toll on a woman who had come to live in hourly dread of his temper outbursts and dictatorial rulings until it had become second nature to say or do nothing which could possibly go against her husband's wishes, gradually killing the love she had for him, and it was Sophy's opinion that from now on Charlotte would be a far happier woman.

Unlike Charlotte, Sophy had married to please her parents and not herself, and because no love had ever existed between her and Charles there was nothing he could say or do to kill or destroy it, even so, it had not escaped her notice that there were similarities between Charlotte's marriage and her own. Charles's control over her was far more subtle than Matthew's was over Charlotte. Charles's civility could cut like a knife, and his words, always politely delivered, had a razor-sharp edge to them which hurt far more than any physical injury he could inflict upon her. As she quietly closed the door to Charlotte's bedroom Sophy had to admit, however reluctant or ashamed she was to own it even to herself, that if their roles were reversed she too would find it difficult to shed tears for a man who missed no opportunity to exhibit either his contempt of her or his repugnance to a marriage neither of them had had any say in bringing about.

Upon reaching the first landing the sound of a familiar voice in the hall below was enough to inform her that Marcus was on the point of leaving. Sophy had long since come to accept that her feelings for her husband's cousin were very far removed from what they should be and that no possible good could come from them, especially when she considered that Charles, despite his resentment at being forced into a marriage he had had no mind for, would never sanction a divorce, but the truth was that the very thought of not seeing Marcus was more than she could bear. She had told herself that the only sensible course open to her was to try being in his company as little as possible but his regular visits to see his aunt rendered it rather difficult as more often than not she was at home when he called. Although she knew that being frequently in his company was only increasing her torment, even this seemed preferable to not seeing him at all.

It seemed her head and her heart were waging a never-ending battle one with the other and it was this which halted her descent, debating whether to remain where she was until Marcus had gone or to continue down the stairs, but Harris, whose well-trained eye had already caught sight of her, communicated her presence to Marcus leaving her with no alternative but to carry on walking down the stairs towards them.

Sophy's feelings for Matthew apart, it had never so much as occurred to her to either flout convention or hurt Charlotte by failing to mark his bereavement, and therefore she had taken a few minutes to change into mourning dress, but regardless of the fact that Sophy had a profound dislike of black there was no denying it became her admirably. Marcus clearly thought so, the admiration in his eyes as he watched her approach bringing a responsive touch of colour to her cheeks, and Harris, whose growing suspicions were now confirmed, decided he was most definitely an unwanted third party, and therefore discreetly removed himself to his own quarters, heartily wishing as he left them alone together that Mrs. Sophy had met Mr. Marcus well before the master had hitched her to Mr. Charles.

After responding to Marcus's enquiry about his aunt, Sophy, who wished he did not have to leave quite so soon, said sadly, "I had no idea you would be leaving quite yet."

"I wouldn't be," Marcus confessed, his attractive smile making her realise, and not for the first time, just how unstable were the defences she was trying to erect, "but since my patience can no longer tolerate their stupid prejudice and my opinion is condemned, I thought it perhaps advisable," adding truthfully, "my only regret is that I am leaving you to bear it alone."

"I am not really alone," Sophy told him lightly. "Should things become too unbearable I shall retreat to the safety of your aunt's sitting room." Her intention had been to dispel his look of concern but it only served to deepen it, causing her to say, more cheerfully than she felt, "Providing I put forward no opinions and keep my own counsel, I think I shall come out of it unscathed." She saw the frown crease his forehead and instinctively laid a hand on his arm. "I shall be quite all right, Marcus," she promised him, looking up into his eyes and taking comfort from what she saw in them. "The only thing I *do* mind," she told him shyly, "is that you were leaving without even saying goodbye."

"To say goodbye to you," Marcus told her in a deep voice, his eyes taking in every inch of her lovely face, his whole being aching to take her away from all she had to endure, "is becoming increasingly more difficult. Much better, don't you think, to have no such word pass between us?"

In their eyes was all the love they shared yet dared not express, longing to break free and, hovering just beneath the surface of the polite pleasantries they exchanged, ran a powerful force of emotions which could neither be ignored nor acted upon, but even though Sophy knew this as well as Marcus, there was nothing she could do to prevent that familiar and wonderful stirring in the pit of her stomach his nearness never failed to evoke. She felt the breath still in her lungs as she read the message in his eyes, making her realise how easy it would be to forget that just across the hall her husband and relatives were arguing earnestly about the events of the day and to cast herself into his eager arms, but somehow managing to clamp down on this overwhelming urge, she faltered, "I… we… shall see you again – soon?" In spite of her sound reasoning that it was far wiser to be in his company as little as possible, she nevertheless dreaded the thought that his visits to Brook Street may cease.

Removing her cold hand from his arm Marcus raised it to his lips, his eyes never leaving hers, making her feel as though her heart had momentarily stopped beating. "You must know you will," he told her warmly.

The brief touch, a warm intimacy which said far more than any words could, left her skin tingling long after he had gone. She had no need to see her reflection in the ornate hall mirror to know that her colour was very much heightened, and it took her several minutes to compose herself before she was able to enter the drawing room to rejoin her family, not at all surprised to discover that the conversation still centred around Alexandra, all of them instantly demanding to know if Charlotte had said anything to her and what her intentions were.

"I really have no idea," Sophy lied, not wishing to fuel their anger and resentment any more. "She was much too tired to discuss it."

"I shall of course speak to her later about it," George said officiously. "After all, we cannot possibly have the girl here."

After what had passed between her and Marcus before he left, it was hardly surprising that she had forgotten to mention Alexandra to him or to seek his aid in helping to find her. Sophy knew it would be futile asking George or Charles for assistance and equally futile to expect them to admit finding any details about her amongst their father's papers.

Unfortunately, dinner that evening set the pattern for the next few days and, as far as Sophy could see, the only topics of conversation which seemed of any interest to her in-laws and freely discussed across the dining table were Alexandra, Matthew's funeral and the reading of his will following the service. Both George and Charles had their own expectations from it, but even though they managed to contain their impatience to know its contents, there was no denying the importance they attached to it.

Having no desire to sit and listen to the same discussions night after night, especially as they always ended in acrimony, particularly between George and Charles, no matter how amicably begun, Sophy was more than content to sit with her mother-in-law in her sitting room who, it appeared, had neither the desire nor the inclination to join her family after dinner. Sophy's absence from these after-dinner talks was neither missed nor commented upon and certainly not by her husband, who considered her conversation at best to be little more than insipid statements which he regarded as being of no importance whatsoever.

Emily, who had taken the decision to remain in Brook Street until after the funeral despite Edward's tentative suggestion that they would be far better in their own home, had plenty of views to impart to her relatives, none of which her mother had any wish to hear having heard them time and again these past few days.

The fact that Jane had only yesterday been delivered of a third son, mattered not at all. This wonderful news, brought round in person by Henry, Charlotte's ecstatic son-in-law, early this morning, instead of brightening the gloom which hung over the household only seemed to deepen it.

Charles may have entered into matrimony as an unpalatable alternative to finding himself being faced with the daunting prospect of having to come up with sufficient funds to settle his unpaid debts, but since he had done so, however unwillingly, he could not help feeling aggrieved in knowing that after just over two years of marriage there was not even one child to show for his sacrifice. As he laid this deficiency unequivocally at Sophy's door, which clearly proved she was lacking in the necessary qualities a man required in a wife, it was yet another reason why he should not have married her in the first place. He did not love Sophy and knew he never would, which only went to feed his resentment over the way he had been forced into marrying her by his father, but this apart he had to admit she was exquisitely beautiful and, if nothing else, he supposed this made up for the rest, even so, it irked him to know that although she never repulsed his advances neither did she encourage them, and this knowledge, together with their childless marriage, all went to prove that Sophy was palpably failing in her duty to her husband. It was therefore with cold politeness that he received the news from Henry informing him that his sister Jane had made him an uncle for the fifth time, Charles's barely concealed frustration deflating Henry's joy over the addition to his family.

Sophy, conscious of her own disappointment in her failure to give her husband a child, was quick to recognise the annoyance on his face as Henry enthusiastically described the new arrival in minute detail, her pleasure at the news rapidly disappearing as she felt Charles's hard eyes silently accusing her.

George, who was perfectly aware of his brother's feelings, could not resist the temptation to drive it even further home by recounting his pride in his own two sons. To her credit, Amelia made strenuous attempts to send silent warning signals to her husband but determined to get the better of his brother in the only way he could, George pretended not to notice her efforts to catch his eye. Amelia had been aware of Charles's desire for a child, especially a son, for a long time, and whilst she was inordinately proud of her own two sons she had a profound sympathy for his own childless marriage. No one knew better than she did just how irritating George could be, but this latest attempt to get one over his brother pushed her patience to the limits. Her dark blue eyes flashed with anger as she heard him repeating again and again how he had felt when his own sons had been born, deliberately focusing his attention on Charles to see his reaction.

It was not long in coming. In a voice that cut through Sophy like a knife, Charles reiterated his congratulations to Henry on the birth of another son, adding coldly, "You are indeed most fortunate; which is more than can be said for some." Then, with a curt nod of his head, he left the room, leaving George the only happy one amongst them.

Deciding it was time he returned home, Henry wished his in-laws goodbye, Charlotte promising to pay Jane and her new grandson a visit immediately the funeral was over. If Charlotte thought that the arrival of a new baby would be enough to give her family's thoughts a new direction she was mistaken. Emily, for her part, could see nothing remarkable in her sister giving birth, especially when it was her fifth. Of course, she hoped to be able to advise her family of good tidings herself before very long; she and Edward having decided, for the time being at least, to wait a while until her suspicions were confirmed before making an announcement which could well prove to be false. She liked babies and could see no reason why she should not have a large family herself, after all her mother had had seven children so there was no reason to suppose she should not do likewise. Besides, it was a wife's duty to provide children for her husband, unlike Sophy, who, after almost three years of marriage, had still not given Charles a child. Mind you, this was hardly surprising! Emily had never really liked Sophy, considering her far too reserved and unwomanly to do her duty by her husband. Witness Charles's anger only this morning! It was really cruel of Sophy to deny her brother what he desired above all things. But all of this was beside the point! Nothing it seemed, not even her sister-in-law's iniquity, could take her mind off Alexandra, Emily's scathing comments pouring off her tongue.

"Emily," her mother said quietly, "I am of course delighted you have come to sit with me, it is not often you do, but I must insist you stop talking about my granddaughter in this way."

"Granddaughter!" Emily exclaimed, disgusted.

"Yes, *granddaughter*," Charlotte repeated, adding, "you seem to forget, my dear, that Alexandra is also your niece."

"That," Emily stated with determination, setting aside her embroidery frame with some force, "is something she will never be."

"You may not want to acknowledge it," her mother conceded, "but it is a fact nevertheless, and one you will have to face up to."

"I have no intention of facing up to it," Emily emphatically declared, bristling with indignation. "Surely, you cannot expect any one of us to accept a girl of her sort?"

"And what sort is that?" her mother asked, thoughtfully regarding her daughter.

"Really, Mamma!" Emily exclaimed irritably. "You saw for yourself what kind of a girl she is."

"What I saw," Charlotte informed her, eyeing her daughter disapprovingly, "was a young girl who has been denied her family."

"For which she has her mother to thank," Emily shot at her, her eyes sparkling with anger.

Charlotte eyed her daughter closely for several moments before saying, "I had never realised until now just how little feeling you have."

Emily coloured slightly, but unrepentant said proudly, "It is because I have feeling that I am trying to make you understand how impossible it is for us to accept her."

"That is not feeling," her mother pointed out, "that is pride. A very different thing altogether, but all of you had better try to accept her."

"You *are* serious!" Emily cried, aghast, unable to believe her ears.

"About what?" her mother asked, steadily regarding her daughter and not really liking what she saw.

"George said he had an idea you might try to do what you could to find her," Emily told her in a hard voice. "Well," she pointed out sharply, "you needn't think George will help you because he said won't lift a finger, and even if you do find her he will not allow the girl into the house. And Charles certainly won't help you to bring us to ruin by having the brat here." Emily encountered such a look of disgust from her mother that she shifted uncomfortably in her chair, her colour rather high.

Emily loved her mother of course, but she shared Charles's sense of misplaced pride, and therefore the mere thought of having her disgraced sister's daughter acknowledged as a member of the family was as repugnant to her as it was to her brother.

"I am sorry you feel that way, Emily," her mother said sadly, "but make no mistake, I am going to do my utmost to find her, and if George and Charles feel they cannot give me assistance, then I shall do very well without them."

"I suppose you will apply to Marcus for help," Emily remarked nastily, a malicious glint entering her eyes, "especially as it appears he not only enjoys your confidence but shares your sympathies."

"Marcus, my dear," Charlotte told her, rising to her feet, "has more compassion than any of you, but I should hesitate to admit, even to him, that I had no support from my children."

From childhood, Emily had never known her mother make a decision or express her feelings, on the contrary she had complied with everything that was put to her, but this unexpected show of independence and determination, neither of which Emily had ever before witnessed, threw her off balance, but not for long. She was not going to be deterred from her purpose in trying to make her mother realise that to publicly acknowledge the girl would make them all look rather ridiculous. "Edward and Amelia are of the same mind," she pointed out. "They quite agree that it would be unthinkable to have her here. What do you think, Sophy?"

Sophy, who had very early on recognised the similarities between Charles and Emily, had more than once witnessed her displays of prejudice; a mirror image of her brother, even though Emily herself would strongly deny this. Although they may disagree on many things that pride would always bind them together, and never more so than now. "I think your mother is perfectly capable of making decisions for herself," Sophy said quietly, "and that none of us have the right to deny her her granddaughter."

As this was not the response she had looked for, Emily twitched her sleeve with impatient fingers, saying coldly, "When I recall your behaviour the other day, I suppose I should have known better than to ask you."

"Perhaps," Sophy returned calmly, "but I certainly cannot find it in me to deny your mother the right to be with her granddaughter."

"I had no idea my brother had married a philanthropist," Emily grimaced, putting Sophy firmly in mind of Charles, into whose ear she had no doubt her sister-in-law would pour her part in the conversation.

Having heard enough of what her family thought, Charlotte walked across the elegantly furnished sitting room, so very different to the wholesome propriety of the rest of the house, reminding her daughter that as tomorrow was her father's funeral and it would most probably be an extremely exhausting day, she was now going to retire to bed.

"Of course, Mamma," Emily nodded, rising to her feet. "Would you like me to come with you?"

"No, thank you, Emily. I shall be perfectly all right on my own." Looking into her daughter's eyes she smiled, saying, not unkindly, "I realise that Alexandra has come as something of a shock to you all, but nevertheless I intend to find her."

"But Mamma…!" Emily began.

"No, my dear, no more," Charlotte broke in quietly. "You can tell George that although he would like to bar the house to a hundred people, since my father made a gift of it to me and your father and is now solely mine, that rather precludes him from doing so. As for Charles, you can inform him that any ruin brought to this family will not be through the acknowledgement of his niece!" On this parting shot she left the room, leaving her daughter speechless and her daughter-in-law extremely pleased.

*

All the ladies having retired, George, who had no wish to retire so early but equally disliked the idea of spending the remainder of the evening in the company of Charles and his brother-in-law, announced his intention of visiting his club. Since Charles had no more respect for convention than his father had, he put forward no arguments as to how it may be viewed in that on the eve of his father's funeral he whiled away the hours in the precincts of his club.

Never having quite understood what his sister had seen in Edward Machin to prompt her into marrying him, Charles found the prospect of his sole company so boring that no sooner had George left the house he offered his excuses, leaving Edward alone in the library with his whisky and cigar. Having leisurely climbed the stairs to the first landing Charles stopped momentarily, realising too late he had exchanged his brother-in-law's company for that of one equally as uninspiring. Glancing speculatively up at the next flight of stairs he thought a moment, then, as if thinking better of it, he turned to the right, walking unconcernedly past his father's room, his firm tread making no sound on the thick pile carpet as he approached the room he shared with Sophy.

No sound came from behind the mahogany door, but just as he reached out to take hold of the handle and turn it his hand stilled, thoughts of the sole occupant of the room above refusing to go away; his mind conjuring up the mental image of her while his body remembered with vivid clarity how good she felt in his arms. Quietly retracing his steps, he climbed the second flight of stairs, the house shrouded in silence and, for several moments, listened for any sound emanating from either his mother's room or the one currently being used by Emily and Edward. A quick glance up at the upper floor which housed the nursery and servants' quarters evincing no sign of life, he looked fleetingly down the well of the stairs before heading towards the room Amelia shared with George.

As he quietly turned the handle and slid open the door Charles experienced no qualms about his illicit visit. No twinge of conscience smote him as he dismissed the thought of his wife asleep in the room immediately below any more than he considered the fact that he was deceiving his brother. On the contrary both these thoughts added a certain piquancy to the whole affair. Amelia was not the first married woman with whom he had been on intimate terms, but she was certainly the most exciting and responsive.

From the very beginning, each of them had been aware of the attraction which had sprung to life between them, as compelling as it was instantaneous, but Amelia had been astute enough to realise that to embark on an affair with Charles, or any man for that matter, until she had presented her husband with offspring which would dispel any question of their paternity, was not only foolhardy but extremely dangerous. Her family, with its impressive connections, ensured that she could look as high as she chose for a husband, but she was honest enough to admit that had there been a surfeit of wealthy young men whose aristocratic background had made them an attractive proposition, poor George Harrington would never have been considered. Unfortunately, however, rich young aristocrats had been very thin on the ground, and even though George had neither looks nor personality to recommend him his mother's lineage and impressive connections were impeccable, whilst his father, irrespective of his background, was an extremely wealthy man, a consideration her father could not afford to overlook in view of his family's dwindling resources.

Well, there had certainly been no questioning the legitimacy of her sons! She had made certain of that! Within the first twelve months of her marriage she had presented her husband with James, and fifteen months later with Simon. After four years of marriage and two sons, the last of whom had rendered it impossible for her to bear any more children, Amelia had at last been free to concentrate her attentions on the man she longed for.

It was ridiculous to say that her attraction to Charles had nothing to do with the fact that he was the very antithesis of his brother or that he was remarkably good looking. It was impossible not to compare them, but it was also because he was the most exciting man she had ever met, his masculinity enhanced by that dangerous element of uncertainty which she found exhilarating. She had never once ceased to regret the fact that at the time she met George his brother had been enjoying an extended holiday on the Continent with some friends, not returning until their betrothal announcement had been made, by which time it had been far too late; besides which, her father would not have considered for so much as a second setting aside her betrothed for a younger son. The timing could not have been worse. Fate had certainly played them a cruel trick! It had made no difference to their feelings, however. From the very first moment they met she had recognised the strong physical attraction which had sparked to life between them, but it was not until that weekend at Langley House just over twelve months ago that they were at last free to embark on the relationship which had continued as fervently as it had begun. Amelia's strict upbringing and the knowledge of what she owed to her family had ensured that there had been no lovers prior to her marriage, only mild flirtations which had been quite acceptable providing of course they did not go beyond the line of what was considered proper. But now her duty to George had been discharged, she could, if she wished, and providing she was discreet, embark on an extramarital liaison.

That shooting party at Langley House had provided all the seclusion two lovers could have wished for, with their respective rooms located in the same wing of the house and the added bonus of the absence of George and Sophy, it had been the ideal opportunity for two people to spend time alone. It had not been deliberately planned, not at all, but as Sophy had found it necessary to make her excuses at the last moment due to her mother's sudden indisposition and George had declined the invitation on the grounds that he did not like his hosts, it had presented them with the perfect opportunity. The passion and intensity of their lovemaking had not waned during the twelve months they had been secretly seeing one another, and even though Amelia was fully aware of the flaws in Charles's character she loved him in spite of them, and after twelve months of unrestrained passion she still craved for him, yearning for the moment when they could be together again.

Charles had never told any woman that he loved her, not even Amelia, nevertheless he knew perfectly well that he could not live without her, and far from diminishing his desire had grown. He still needed and wanted her to such an extent that he was even prepared to risk discovery by coming here tonight.

Seated at the intricately carved dressing table, littered with perfume bottles, innumerable jars and her discarded jewellery, was Amelia. Having startled her maid by refusing her services, stating sharply that she wished to be alone and could manage very well without her, she had prepared herself for bed, the evidence of which was all too visible. Over the back of a blue brocade *chaise longue* lay her bodice and skirt, while her petticoat and other undergarments, which had been flung unceremoniously onto the cushioned seat and was now looking in imminent danger of falling off and, next to her shoes on the floor, lay her bustle cage. Comfortably established in front of her mirror, wearing only her elegant stiffened black lace corset, her deft fingers removed the pins from her hair, but at the sound of the door sliding open her hands stilled, a slight frown creasing her forehead. She had not expected to see George for quite some time, convinced that he would be enjoying the contents of the decanters in the library with Edward to be in any hurry to come upstairs, but upon raising her head to find Charles standing in the doorway, her face immediately relaxed, her eyes softening perceptibly.

For several moments their eyes met and held in the mirror, her full sensual lips parting in a silent invitation which her visitor found irresistible. Even from this distance Amelia could see the glint in his eyes as he silently regarded her, her body instinctively reacting to him. Charles may have no qualms about his affair, but as he stood looking at Amelia he could not prevent himself from comparing her with Sophy. No two women could be more dissimilar. Amelia may not be as tall as Sophy but she was far more curvaceous, her voluptuous body far more alluring than Sophy's slimmer and, for the most part, unwelcoming one, not that she ever denied him his rights! Not Sophy; she was far too dutiful! The cold rigidity of Sophy may have to be endured if he wanted a son by her, but it was Amelia's warm and responsive one that gave him pleasure and satisfaction. Looking at her now no one would ever suspect that she had given birth to two children, her body still firm and desirable, making it impossible for him to give her up.

"Charles!" Amelia cried. "What are *you* doing here? Are you mad?" her heart racing at the sight of him.

"Only for you," he confessed warmly, his lips parting in a rare but not unattractive smile as he walked towards her.

"But what if George…?" she began, her eyes still holding his through the central mirror.

"At this very moment," Charles informed her smoothly, his hands coming to rest on her bare shoulders, "he is on his way to his club. He will be gone, I imagine, for some considerable time."

"His club!" Amelia echoed. "Has he no sense? Tonight of all nights!" her voice rapidly losing its sharpness as Charles's lips tantalisingly brushed the back of her neck. "I suppose you made no attempt to stop him?" she accused weakly.

"Had I suspected for one moment that is what you wanted," he told her, his breath warm on her soft skin, "I should certainly have done so."

"You are all consideration, Charles," she mocked huskily, enjoying his caresses too much to regret her husband's folly.

"You're wasted on George," he told her, raising his head so he could see her reaction to his kisses through the mirror, "do you know that?" Without waiting for a response, he straightened up, his eyes glinting as they searched her face, provocatively entwining his fingers through her blonde curls, exposing more of her neck to his lips.

"I always knew I had married the wrong brother," she admitted a little breathlessly, her skin tingling in response to the seduction of his lips.

"He doesn't deserve you," Charles told her unsteadily, his lips tracing an erotic path to her shoulder while his hands slowly and sensually slid up and down her arms. "I resent every minute you spend with him," he confessed hoarsely.

"Do you think I enjoy it?" she asked on a sharp intake of breath as his hands gently cupped her breasts, heaving beneath the tightly fitting corset.

"Does he make you feel like this?" Charles demanded thickly, satisfyingly watching her reaction in the mirror as his fingers stroked their eager fullness with a slow deliberation that drew a deep throated groan from her. "Does he?" he repeated urgently.

"You know he doesn't," Amelia confirmed weakly, her body burning with increasing desire as his hands slid down to her stomach, his fingers gently caressing its softly rounded surface before travelling provocatively to her thighs.

"I can't bear to think of you being pawed by him," he admitted, the vehemence muted by desire.

"Then don't think of him," Amelia advised, the throbbing of her voice inciting him, her thighs warm and trembling beneath the feather light touch of his fingers.

"I nearly didn't come here tonight," he told her, his desire growing with every unashamed and excited response which emanated from her, his lips erotically teasing and caressing the soft creamy skin of her neck and shoulders.

"Then why did you?" she gasped, the exquisite pleasure he was arousing inside her breaking down her will to think.

"Because I can't resist you," he told her thickly, his teeth gently tugging her susceptible ear, "and because I want you." Turning her head to look up at him, her eyes as darkened with desire as his, her parted lips eagerly met his in a searing kiss. "You're mine," he ground out fiercely when he eventually released her lips, *"all mine!"* he groaned, pulling her out of her chair with such force that she reeled against his hard body, his breathing laboured as he gathered her in his arms, his control snapping as he kissed her with a need that weakened her into joyous submission. "This is very becoming," he told her hoarsely when he eventually recovered his breath, appreciatively indicating her corset, "and far be it from me to dissuade you from wearing such a garment, it *is* rather in the way," his unsteady but deft fingers making easy work of the laces, the stiff creation falling silently to the floor.

Amelia was not in the least embarrassed as she stood naked before him, on the contrary she was proud of her body, still firm and desirable, but more than this she was thrilled that she had the power to render a man like Charles weak with desire. Those eyes, usually so cold and mocking, were now burning with a need which not only sent the blood rushing through her veins but totally belied the fact that it had only been a few nights ago when they had last been together, but if Charles wanted her, she most certainly wanted him.

Gripped with an urgency which demanded immediate satisfaction her impatient attempts to rid him of his clothes were severely hampered by the provocative wandering of his hands and lips on her body, subjecting her to the most exquisite pleasure, but one by one she at last managed to divest him of his clothing, carelessly strewing them onto the floor without a thought for the usual care he bestowed on them. All considerations except one were lost sight of, even the possibility of her husband returning home earlier than expected, and when Charles effortlessly picked her up in his arms and carried her over to the bed, Amelia's only conscious thought was the burning need to make love to the man who was filled with the same urgency as herself, waiting impatiently for him to fling back the bedclothes, his mouth covering hers almost before he had lain down beside her.

Their lovemaking was as demanding as ever, leaving their damp and glistening bodies satisfyingly exhausted as they slumped back against the pillows, but both knew their repletion was only temporary, it always was. Their need of each other was such that it never seemed to be fully satisfied, the only regret being that Charles would soon have to leave her. There were times when Amelia almost wished that George would find them together, at least then she would not have to endure his clumsy lovemaking. He not only lacked the finesse of his brother but also that exquisite delicacy which was calculated to please. Even to think of her husband's thick fumbling fingers on her body and his wet lips on hers repulsed her, so much so that Amelia could only just manage to stop herself from flinching when he touched her. Charles though, knew exactly how to please and arouse her; she did not have to feign pleasure or create excuses to prevent him from making love to her, on the contrary she yearned for the moment when they could be together again. She ached for him with such intensity that it frightened her, dreading the thought that one day it may end. She wanted and loved Charles more than she thought it was possible for any woman to do, and bitterly resented the fact that it was Sophy who was his wife and not her.

Although Charles seldom discussed his marriage with her, she knew enough to realise that she gave him what Sophy could not. The ironic thing was Amelia rather liked her sister-in-law. Of course, Sophy was totally the wrong type of woman for Charles, but she was by no means the cold and unresponsive woman he believed her to be any more than she was averse to a man's attentions; especially if he were the right man! Amelia had seen the fleeting intimacies and unspoken messages which had passed between Marcus and Sophy and how she suddenly seemed to come to life when he was around, but although Charles may dismiss his wife as cold and unwelcoming, Amelia doubted Marcus did. Behind Sophy's quiet reserve ran a passion as deep and intense as her own, but unlike herself Sophy would shrink from an affair. Amelia had a shrewd notion that despite the fact they were very much in love, Marcus was too much the gentleman to coerce Sophy into betraying her husband, even though they longed to be together. Of course, the most surprising aspect of all this was that Charles, usually so astute, had not yet seen what she had known for some time. Amelia really did find her lover's lack of perception rather amusing, but perhaps it might be as well to keep such provocative news to herself for a while longer; it could prove very useful at some point in the future. In the meantime though, Charles was sharing her bed and there was still a little time yet before George would return.

*

Amelia however, was not the only one thinking of Sophy. Marcus, who had elected to spend this evening by his own fireside, was thinking of her too. Like his cousin, he had had his share of amorous liaisons and thoroughly enjoyed them while they had lasted, but he had never been in love with any one of the ladies with whom he had shared some very pleasurable moments. He had been a good officer, liked and well respected by all who had served with him, and whilst he had known the day would come when he would have to consider his business interests and his Uncle Lionel, his father's youngest and only surviving brother, who had been capably holding the reins on his behalf, his life as an unattached officer had suited him very well. The accident however, had rushed things along and hastened his return to England where, after a long and painful convalescence, he was at last able to turn his mind to the business he had inherited from his father.

Marcus had learned of Charles's marriage and the reason for it from his aunt's letters, but the only member of the Lessington family he knew was Timothy, Sophy's older brother, and although they had been good friends at Oxford, apart from briefly running across one another now and then when Timothy had occasion to come to town, they had not really had the opportunity to spend time together and exchange news since before Marcus had left with his regiment for India. He seemed to recall Timothy telling him he had two sisters, both younger than himself and that Sophy was the youngest of the two, but even though Marcus had never set eyes on either of them and had no idea what they looked like, he could not help having some sympathy for Sophy Lessington as Charles, not the easiest of men to get along with, would be far from happy in being tied to a woman he had been forced into marrying.

The news that Major Ingleby had been shot by a wayward bullet from a rifle in the hands of a young and inexperienced Sepoy had spread through the barracks like wildfire. Despite the sterling efforts of the army surgeon, who had himself only been in army service a short time and had therefore limited experience of bullet wounds, Marcus had lost a tremendous amount of blood, and coupled with the fact that the bullet had lodged deep in his leg and shattered the bone, its removal had not been a clean operation, leaving him extremely weak.

Marcus had never intended to saddle himself on his aunt, having the intention of resuming residence in the Knightsbridge house which, apart from regular visits to his father's family home in Yorkshire, had been his home from childhood, but no sooner had she discovered the exact date and time of his arrival than she had met him in her own carriage and whisked him off to Brook Street. How she had managed to reconcile Matthew to the scheme Marcus never knew, but apart from the occasional, and thankfully very brief meetings they had had, they hardly laid eyes on one another. His aunt, having taken the decision upon herself to call in his own doctor to examine his leg, telling him worriedly that she was not entirely satisfied with the handiwork of the army surgeon, a further operation had been deemed necessary. Unfortunately, it had been no more successful than the first, the result being weeks of agonising pain.

He had, in the beginning, been in too much pain and discomfort to take any notice of his aunt's daughter-in-law, nevertheless, he had been aware of a gentle pair of hands and a quiet, soothing presence. Through a haze of pain, he had registered a tall young woman with a cloud of silken auburn hair and a pair of large hazel eyes, whose full and generous mouth would smile encouragingly at him and a soft and persuasive voice that could coax him into doing anything. Every movement of that leg had been excruciatingly painful, but, somehow, he had never seemed to mind it when she was there, making his convalescence far more endurable than it would otherwise have been, especially so when he had been told that he would be left with a slight limp.

Being in her company almost every day Marcus had gradually come to know the woman who had married his cousin and who was devoting so much of her time to a man she had never met before. From exchanging polite pleasantries and catching up on news of Timothy to discovering the things that interested her and what made her laugh, taking great pleasure from listening to her amusing anecdotes of what she had seen at the theatre the previous evening or on a shopping trip with his aunt, had been a relatively short step. Marcus had soon found himself waiting expectantly for Sophy to come to the sitting room which his aunt had temporarily turned over to him, strangely disappointed if she could not stay long or, worse, did not come. He had liked being with her and talking to her, but, also, he had been perfectly content to just lie back and watch her as she moved serenely around the room, discovering a pleasure he had never known before. He had no precise idea of the exact moment he had fallen in love with her; it seemed to have crept upon him gradually before exploding in a crescendo, taking him completely by surprise. So very different to what he had felt for those women who had previously shared a brief moment or two of his life.

Charles may have been forced into marrying Sophy but his treatment of her had merely made their relationship worse. From the outset, he had never failed to remind her of the reason for their marriage, taking every opportunity to subject her to his insufferable indifference and cold disdain, rendering it impossible for him to see how vitally alive his wife really was. Her natural shyness had therefore become a protective shell, but in the secluded haven of his aunt's sitting room Marcus had seen the real Sophy gradually emerge from the safety of the cocoon in which she had hidden herself, and that was the woman he not only yearned to know but could not live without. There had been times when he had awoken from a medicinally induced sleep to catch her unawares, her book or embroidery lying forgotten on her lap as she sat looking at him, but even though the colour had flooded her cheeks as she saw him suddenly open his eyes to see her looking at him, she had not turned away.

No protestations of love had ever passed between them, but their eyes often met and held saying far more than words ever could, but never before had he found it necessary to exert so much self-restraint to prevent himself from taking her in his arms and kissing her and, as time passed, it had become increasingly difficult. He wanted nothing more than to show her how much he loved and needed her, not that it was in the least necessary; Sophy had seen it for herself whenever he looked at her, heard it in his voice whenever he spoke, felt it every time she had touched him, and although neither of them had ever spoken of, it lived and breathed between them. Even to feel the touch of her fingers against his lips when he kissed her hand was enough for him to want to throw caution to the wind and take her in his arms and to the devil with the consequences! He had not done so, but he was honest enough to admit that having to continually hold his emotions in check was becoming ever more difficult.

Whether Charles loved Sophy or not was immaterial, there was not the slightest possibility of him ever sanctioning a divorce. Apart from the fact that his pride would never tolerate the stigma and scandal that such an action would give rise to, divorces were seldom granted and certainly not for a husband's treatment of his wife, much less his infidelity. The unspoken code governing society meant that a woman virtually became her husband's property upon marriage as well as giving him the right to treat her in any way he saw fit, but it also meant that she was supposed to accept it as well as ignore his little affairs, indeed, she was supposed to know nothing about them!

Sophy may not love Charles but at no time had she given him cause to treat her with such dismissive contempt, but even if he did not subject her to such despicable treatment Sophy would never consider a divorce in order to marry the man she loved. Marcus knew perfectly well that he held Sophy's heart, and even though she strenuously resisted the temptation to surrender herself to the man she loved he knew too that she could not lightly turn her back on the vows she had made.

It would of course be far easier for him to make her his mistress rather than to strive for something which, at the moment at least, was well out of reach. It was of course perfectly acceptable to visit a married lady in the afternoon and to spend some time with her, to be received by her in the drawing room wearing a very fashionable and most convenient tea gown; to while away a few hours to whatever degree your passions demanded; but be that as it may, Marcus shrank from the thought. It was not simply because Sophy did not fall into that category of women who sought a man's patronage and protection or because she did not love her husband, but because he loved and respected her too much to force her into something he himself found quite repugnant and totally unacceptable.

It seemed the more he considered the matter the worse it became, seeing no way out of a situation which was putting an intolerable strain on them both. It had struck Marcus some time ago that Charles's affair with Amelia was far more serious than he had at first thought, but the for the life of him

Marcus failed to understand why Charles, who obviously had more feeling for his sister-in-law than he did for his wife, preferred the situation as it now stood rather than trying to untangle a knot which was becoming tighter every day. It could of course be that Charles liked the deception he was playing on his brother; an ace in the hole he was keeping in reserve until it suited him. Whether George knew of the affair or not Marcus was not certain. So far at least George had given no sign of it, but Marcus doubted it. Given the mutual dislike which existed between the brothers Marcus felt reasonably certain that his cousin had no idea of the affair because if he did Marcus could not see George letting something like this pass.

As far as Sophy was concerned Marcus was unable to say for certain whether she knew of the affair between her husband and sister-in-law or not, but if she did she would never discuss it, but he had a shrewd notion that she could not fail to be aware of it. Even to think of Sophy being subjected to his cousin's cold indifference as well as any sexual demands he may impose upon her not only served to increase his vexation but to hasten his desire to put an end to a situation which was unbearable. Ideas followed one another in quick succession only to be discarded, and by the time Marcus finally retired to bed he was no nearer to finding a solution than he ever was.

*

Having ascertained that the ladies and Mr. Charles had all retired and Mr. George had gone to his club, Harris could finally look forward to a brief period of quiet in his own domain below stairs for a read of the newspaper. It was not often he was able to steal a few moments to himself, one or the other of them keeping him pretty well occupied for most of the time. Having comfortably settled himself in an armchair which had long since found its way into the downstairs quarters, and with a nip of something just to keep the cold out, he opened the newspaper, considerably startled a few minutes later by the urgent tugging of the front door bell.

Edward, having been deserted by his brothers-in-law, was enjoying his whisky and cigar in a rare moment of peace and quiet when the sudden and insistent clanging of the bell startled him into jumping out of his seat, a heavy fall of cigar ash dropping onto his trousers.

Considerably out of breath from his hasty climb up the back stairs, Harris barely had time to recover his poise before Edward emerged from the library, his enquiring gaze being met with only a brief nod of acknowledgement. Whoever it was seeking admittance was certainly impatient, the violent tugging of the bell ceasing only when Harris opened the door, his eyes staring in disbelief as Adam brushed past him with a careless, "Hello, Harris. How's things?"

"Very well, sir, thank you," Harris replied faintly. Apart from the fact that he had given up hope of Mr. Adam coming home, Harris noted with disapproval that six months of married life had done nothing to change his haphazard ways. Edward, who secretly envied the exploits of his in-laws, looked at Adam with frank appraisal, wishing that his black frock coat sat on his own narrow shoulders as well as Adam's impeccably tailored one did on his far broader ones.

After a brief word with his brother-in-law, Adam asked casually, "Where is everyone?"

Relieving him of his heavy top coat as well as his hat and gloves, Harris informed him that the ladies had all retired and that Mr. George had left a short time ago for his club. Adam looked a little taken aback at this, which immediately raised him in Harris's esteem, but upon being told that Mr. Charles had also retired, Adam exclaimed, "Good God! At this hour! Not ill, is he?"

"Not as far as I am aware, sir, no," Harris replied, ignoring the titter from Edward, his voice noncommittal as he kept his reflections to himself. Clearing his throat, he said, "Your room is quite ready for you, sir, your mother having expected you several days ago."

"I daresay she was," Adam conceded absently, his concentration solely on straightening his necktie in the mirror, "but I couldn't get away any sooner. Besides, once I received her last letter a couple of days ago telling me that m'father had died and the funeral was tomorrow, it seemed pointless me breaking my neck to get here any sooner."

"I take it, sir," Harris coughed, ignoring the latter part of Adam's speech, "that Mrs. Harrington is not with you." Upon receiving a careless no, Harris said resignedly, "If you will excuse me, sir, I will get the maid to air your bed and put a light to the fire."

"And while you're about it," Adam forestalled him, "you might see about some supper. I've eaten nothing since early this morning."

"Very good, sir," Harris nodded. "Would you like me to inform your mother of your arrival, sir?"

"No," Adam shook his head, "I won't disturb her. I'll see her in the morning. By the way," he asked with an insouciance Harris deprecated, "what time does it start tomorrow?"

"*If*, sir," Harris said disapprovingly, "you mean what time your father's funeral is to commence...?"

"I do," Adam cut in unblushingly.

"The cortège will leave here at eleven o'clock, the service being at half past."

Adam nodded, then, indicating the bulging portmanteau with a nod of his head, asked, "Can you get someone to press my gear?"

"Of course, sir." Harris hesitated before saying tentatively, "If you will permit me, sir, the master is…"

"If you're trying to tell me that m'father's on view upstairs for all to see," Adam cut in unceremoniously, "then don't!"

"Very good, sir," Harris sighed, retreating to his downstairs domain, wondering what on earth he had done to deserve being in such a household.

Chapter Five

The following morning was raw cold with the threat of more snow looming ominously as Matthew Carey Harrington was finally laid to rest, his huge oak coffin taking the efforts of four strong men to ease it into the rock-hard ground. Having performed the service with a dignity Matthew Harrington had never shown to anyone during his lifetime, Reverend Handley was determined to accord the deceased every respect, even though he was still smarting from being denied the house in order to prepare one of his flock for his demise.

Unlike his wife, Matthew Harrington's visits to church had been few and far between, as had those of his sons, in fact, their attendances still were, and Reverend Handley could not help but bemoan the fact that it had taken a burial to get the whole family here. Taking his calling very seriously, Reverend Handley's sermon was lengthy as well as sincere, leaving Adam to wonder how long it had taken him to prepare it, his father having been a man who had had little or no virtues to expound. On and on went the sermon, the zealous cleric quite impervious to the weather, his small rotund figure standing firm as a rock against the wind, his every word slicing through the icy cold air as clear as the ringing of a bell. Up above, a watery sun filtered down from a leaden sky, the thick covering of compacted ice glistening in its weakening rays. Inside their muffs the ladies' gloved hands were numb from the cold, their tingling faces finding no protection beneath their black veils from the clawing icy fingers which stabbed painfully at their delicate skins, Emily's tears burning her face as they ran down her smarting cheeks.

At long last Reverend Handley's resonant voice stopped, the mourners filled with heartfelt relief as he finally brought the surprisingly lengthy sermon to a close. Charles, whose face had remained impassive throughout, now visibly relaxed, his eyes travelling across the dug-out oblong to his brother standing with his head reverentially bowed between his wife and mother. Charles had no way of knowing whether George's reddened cheeks stemmed from emotion or the biting cold, but whichever it was he certainly appeared to good effect in the eyes of the middle-aged clergyman.

To the sound of soil being hurriedly shovelled onto the coffin, the mourners made their way back along the path through the churchyard to the waiting carriages, the gleaming black horses with their tall black plumes snorting impatiently, being quickly uncovered ready for the slow journey back to Brook Street.

In the first carriage Charlotte sat in silence with her three sons, followed by her daughter and daughters-in-law in the second. Marcus and her two sons-in-law, Edward and Henry, who had allowed himself to be persuaded by his wife at the last moment to attend the funeral, were in the third. The hot bricks which had been thoughtfully provided by Harris had long since gone cold, rendering the atmosphere inside the carriages even more dismal as they made their dignified way home.

Having politely declined Charlotte's invitation to return to Brook Street for a glass of sherry, Reverend Handley watched the departing mourners, his heart saddened at the death of a man whose family, with the obvious exception of Mrs. Matthew Harrington and her daughter, appeared to be by no means grief-stricken over his passing. He would not go so far as to say that the attitude of the rest of them was indifferent, but it could not be argued that they had certainly been somewhat undemonstrative when it came to exhibiting sorrow, and in view of this he much preferred a glass of sherry in the peace of his own home, at least there he would not be obliged to offer sentiments they clearly did not wish to receive.

He was not the only one to shake his head over the Harrington family. Fortified with a glass of Matthew Harrington's excellent Madeira, Silas Jenkins awaited the return of his late client's family with a mixture of apprehension and resignation. It was only to be expected that during the course of his many years of legal counselling to Matthew Harrington he had learned of his eldest daughter's fall from grace. It was not, however, until he had been summoned by his late client just over two months ago that Jenkins had discovered the existence of a granddaughter. Familiarity with Matthew's volatile temperament had made him hold his tongue, listening to the angry admission with a mixture of sympathy and shock. Whatever his own thoughts were upon hearing such a confession, Jenkins had kept them admirably in check, but upon being informed that a codicil was to be inserted into the will to include his granddaughter he had been shaken out of his stupor. It had taken him several minutes to recover his senses sufficiently before strongly advising Matthew against such a decision, pointing out that without knowing the first thing about the girl, let alone never having set eyes on her, he could not be certain of her credentials. Matthew's face had become suffused with angry colour, barking out, "Do you think I don't know my own business?" Hastening to assure him that he meant no offence, Jenkins knew he would be failing in his duty if he did not try to make Matthew see the imprudence of such a decision. His arguments were as sincere as they were just, emphasising as earnestly as he could the ill-feeling it would create within the family. The angry tirade that followed had stemmed any more arguments Jenkins may have put forward, finally agreeing, much against his better judgement, to carry out the necessary amendments, his reluctant acceptance bringing a satisfied smile to his late client's lips.

That George would not like it Jenkins knew only too well, but he knew too that once his initial blustering had worn itself out he would accept it well enough. Charles, however, was a different matter altogether. Jenkins knew perfectly well that his temper, uncertain at the best of times, could turn pretty ugly on the least provocation. Well, the amendments in that will held sufficient provocation for Charles to turn very ugly indeed. Silas Jenkins was not unfeeling, and of course it was only natural that a man should want to provide for his granddaughter, but he would have felt much more comfortable about the whole business if he himself had undertaken the search for her rather than leave it to a man about whom, despite Matthew's assurance, very little was known. In view of the amendments he intended making in his will, Jenkins could well understand why his late client had employed the services of a stranger, even so, any shady character could set himself up as a private detective! A circumstance that did very little if anything to assuage his concerns.

Naturally, Jenkins had been rather shocked himself upon discovering the existence of a granddaughter and could well imagine how the family had felt when a niece they never knew they had unexpectedly descended on them, but what had shocked him even more was Matthew's magnanimity, especially in one who was not known, for the most part at least, for his generosity. That the contents of the will were inflammatory Jenkins knew, he only wished he were out of it!

Suddenly the silence in the library seemed oppressive, the ormolu clock on the mantelpiece remorselessly ticking away, every second increasing his apprehension, making him wish that Matthew had taken his family into his confidence. If all Harris had told him about the family's reaction to Alexandra when she had come to see her grandfather, inflamed even more upon discovering her flight from the house, was true, then he could expect a pretty uncomfortable time this afternoon. Never had Jenkins faced a task with more reluctance. The reading of a will, normally a simple and straightforward matter, suddenly took on immense difficulties, so much so that he found himself almost dreading the family's return home from church. Unlike the previous occasions when he had been privileged to enter this room he found himself quite unable to appreciate the warm intimacy of his surroundings. The rare volumes and first editions lining the walls were a joy to behold and the well-worn leather club chairs ensured one could read a favourite author in total comfort. In the flickering flames of the fire, the highly polished table and neatly arranged chairs gleamed with pride. The heavy velvet curtains draped across the window enhanced the richness of this lofty room, their deep red collaborating perfectly with the colourful carpet. Unfortunately, however, none of these things had the power to take Jenkins's mind off what was to come, his straining ears listening for the sound that would signal the family's return.

Eventually, the moment he had looked upon with foreboding had arrived. The sound of carriage wheels pulling up on the cobbles outside told him that the family had returned home, and Harris, who had obviously been on the watch for them, had the front door open in readiness. The sound of voices in the hall gradually wafted through to Jenkins and instinctively his eyes darted warily to the door of the library as it quietly opened to admit Harris, swallowing uncomfortably as he was calmly informed that the family would be with him directly.

Marcus, who had neither the desire to sit in at the reading of his uncle's will nor any expectations from it, had elected to while away the time with a glass of something warm and invigorating in the peace and quiet of the drawing room. He was considerably surprised therefore, when George unexpectedly put his head round the door and requested him to join the gathering in the library, adding gravely, "I think Mamma would like it." Against his better judgement Marcus allowed himself to be persuaded, reluctantly following his cousin across the hall and into the library, still redolent from Edward's cigar smoke the night before.

Apart from a raised eyebrow Charles made no comment at the sight of his cousin, who, making himself as unobtrusive as possible, sat down in a chair immediately behind the door, crossing one long leg over the other, questioning the wisdom of his being here as he did so. From his vantage point Marcus had a clear view of every member of his family and could only guess at their thoughts as they waited for Jenkins to begin the reading of his uncle's will. George, whose colour was still considerably heightened, sat at Jenkins's right elbow, his protruding eyes staring expectantly at the parchment only inches away from him, barely able to hide his impatience to know its contents and to have his new-found status confirmed. Immediately opposite sat his aunt, whose small upright figure looked lost in her chair. From the top of her neatly coiffured silver-grey hair to the soles of her black leather boots she exuded a quiet dignity which totally belied her inner tensions, her thoughts hidden as she looked down at her hands folded limply on her lap. With one ankle crossed negligently over the other, Charles lounged at his ease beside her, only his eyes giving any indication as to his eagerness to hear the contents of his father's will. Nearest to Marcus sat Adam, whose careless disregard for appearances had prompted him to help himself to a sustaining drink before taking his seat at the end of the table, his concentration more on savouring his late father's malt than the contents of his will. Edward, who had been firmly pushed as near to the top of the table as was possible by Emily, unwillingly took his seat next to George, his thin, rather sallow face flushing as he caught Charles's mocking glance. Useless to tell his brother-in-law that Emily was determined he was not going to take a back seat; that he was as much a part of this family as the rest of them. Seated next to her husband, Emily awaited the reading of her father's will with the same impatience as her two older brothers, unlike Amelia, sitting as one thoroughly bored with the whole affair, beside Charles. It was hardly surprising! George had talked of little else since his father's death. Seated next to Emily at the end of the long table and directly facing Adam, was Sophy who, having received a very handsome settlement upon the death of her father, looked for no mention in her father-in-law's will, but she was perfectly aware of her husband's expectations from it. That careless pose did not fool her. Like Charlotte, she knew that should George be granted sole authority Charles would take it very badly; the insult, for he would see it as nothing less, would be intolerable!

Satisfied that they had all settled themselves, Silas Jenkins placed his spectacles on his nose, looking anxiously from one to the other before removing the tape securing that all-important document, the parchment crackling abnormally loud in the overcharged silence. Having successfully read out the preliminaries, in which there had been nothing to instigate either discussion or debate, he took a moment to eye his late client's family over the rim of his spectacles, most of whom were looking at him with a mixture of eagerness and expectation. It could not be said that he was looking forward with any degree of enthusiasm to reading the following clauses, in truth, he was honest enough to admit to himself that he wished he were anywhere but here. Unfortunately for him, however, he was here and it was his duty to carry out his late client's wishes irrespective of the furore which he knew full well would follow, but since he could not delay the inevitable he cleared his throat and resumed the reading.

To Charlotte's profound relief, Matthew, in a rare show of wisdom, had decreed that his lawyer set up a board of directors with George, Charles and Adam holding equal shares of the business, but although they had full authority over their own particular brewery regarding its today to day running, they would require the approval and sanction of their fellow directors in order for any major changes to take place or the selling of their shares and all pertinent matters. As far as their quarterly allowance was concerned, this would cease with immediate effect to be replaced by them drawing a salary every lunar month commensurate to their new status as directors. The annual profits were to be halved; one part to be put back into the business and the other to be shared equally between the brothers. Charlotte was not the only one to receive this news with heartfelt relief. Having sent up a silent and sincere thank you to her father-in-law, Sophy glanced across at Charles, noting the satisfied smile which touched his lips who, in turn, threw his brother a look of pure triumph, thoroughly enjoying the moment. This was certainly preferable to being under George's sole authority, the mere thought too unbearable to be contemplated.

George, who had fully expected to take control as his father had done, spluttered his anger and disbelief, challenging the harassed lawyer as to the veracity of such a surprising announcement. Jenkins did his best to assure him that he had carried out his father's wishes to the letter, but George was determined to argue the point. His face was dangerously suffused with angry colour, putting his mother firmly in mind of Matthew. Charles, to whom the news could not have been better, advised his brother in a few short words to stop being a bore and let the man continue. With a brief nod of thanks Jenkins resumed the reading, only to be interrupted by George's belligerent muttering. "This is *your* doing!" he threw at Charles, pointing an accusing finger. "I don't know how you managed it, but m'father would never have done this on his own."

The ugly look which crossed Charles's face was not lost on Jenkins and deeming it wise to intervene before a pretty nasty scene could be enacted, said hastily, "I can assure you that your father's wishes were entirely his own."

"Of course they were," Charles said coldly, "but you will never get George to believe it."

"Why should I?" George demanded, determined to have this thrashed out. "How am I to know that the three of you didn't plan this to do me out of what is rightfully mine?"

"I *hope*, sir," Jenkins cried, aghast, "that you are not accusing me of being a party to or condoning coercion!"

Realising he had allowed his tongue to run away with him, George quickly apologised, stating that he had meant no offence.

"If you have quite finished honouring us with your opinion," Charles bit out, "perhaps you would allow Jenkins to continue."

George glared across at his brother but thinking better of the angry retort that rose to his lips, relapsed into smouldering silence. Adam, who was totally unconcerned by the revelation, in fact he could not think what all the bother was about, merely shrugged a careless shoulder in response to the accusing look he received from George, but he knew from experience that his eldest brother would not let this pass. He knew too that George had fully expected to take over where his father had left off, but this setting up of a board of directors had killed any such hope at a stroke.

Silas Jenkins had wholeheartedly agreed with Matthew Harrington when he had decided upon this course of action. His late client had been no fool and although he may have deprecated Adam's occasional impetuous and headstrong behaviour, he had nevertheless been fully alive to the fact that his youngest son bore no animosity towards either of his brothers or they to him. The same could not be said of George and Charles, however. Matthew had been perfectly aware of the ill-feeling which existed between them and that one would never be brought to take orders from the other, and unless he wanted his business to fall into ruin after his death because of this, it seemed the only way of protecting and ensuring its successful continuance was to ensure such authority did not rest in one pair of hands. To Jenkins's relief Charles had accepted this remarkably well, indeed from his point of view it could not have been better, especially as it pulled the carpet right from beneath George's feet, but the atmosphere in the library was still very tense, to which George's constant mutterings under his breath and the fulminating looks he cast in Charles's direction were not helping. Taking advantage of the uneasy silence which had descended, Jenkins resumed the reading, trying not to think of their reaction to the clause he was fast approaching.

As expected, Matthew had made ample provision for his wife, ensuring her financial comfort for the remainder of her lifetime. To his daughters he left equal amounts as well as smaller, but by no means ungenerous amounts to his daughters-in-law for their sole use. To his sons-in-law, he left minor sums only, merely a gesture of recognition, a circumstance which by no means pleased Emily who had fully expected Edward to have been more adequately recompensed by her father.

For the second time Jenkins was obliged to stop the reading as Emily stated that it was grossly unfair, especially as Edward's contribution to the family as well as the business had been considerable and that Amelia and Sophy had received far more for doing absolutely nothing, and as for Isabel, it was a disgrace, particularly when she considered the circumstances surrounding her hasty marriage to Adam. She eyed her youngest brother accusingly as if he were personally responsible, but the only response she received in answer to her angry indictment about his marriage and the inclusion of his wife in her father's will was the raising of his glass in salute, to which she took a great exception.

Henry, who had not stayed to hear the reading of the will, not only because he had no desire to benefit personally from it, his lucrative medical practice providing all he needed but also because apart from three of its members he could not bear being in his wife's family's company for any longer than he could help. As far as Edward was concerned he had received far more than he had ever expected, secretly of the opinion that his father-in-law had not liked him over much, but from the look on his wife's face it was obvious that she not only regarded such a paltry sum as an insult but was determined not to let it pass unanswered. For several moments Emily argued hotly against the bequest to her husband, shrugging off Edward's restraining hand. "No, Edward," she cried, "I will *not* hush! You have worked so hard for this family only to be rewarded with what amounts to nothing more than a pittance." Swallowing the lump in her throat, she scorned, "A measly one thousand pounds! Why, I had much rather he left you nothing than such a paltry sum!"

"We can discuss it later," Edward soothed, embarrassingly conscious of Charles's growing impatience.

"We will discuss it now," she said determinedly.

"You have discussed it enough," Charles told her sharply. "Either be quiet or leave the room until you can conduct yourself in a reasonable manner."

Edward may not have liked his brother-in-law's tone but being a man who had neither the desire nor the courage to take him to task, remained silent. After throwing her brother a resentful stare, Emily sniffed into her handkerchief, astute enough to know that he was more than capable of forcibly ejecting her from the library.

"Thank you," Charles mocked. "Go on, Jenkins," he waved irritably, "let's get this over with."

If two such bequests could create this kind of scene Jenkins dreaded to think what the outcome would be to the next one, and it was therefore with a sickening feeling in the pit of his stomach and an extremely dry mouth that he cleared his throat. "To my grandsons, James Matthew Harrington and Simon George Harrington, I leave the sum of thirty thousand pounds for their sole use upon reaching their majority. Their education and welfare to be maintained by the trust which was set up at their birth." After a brief pause, during which Jenkins scanned his audience over the rim of his spectacles, he continued, "To my granddaughter, Alexandra Beatrice Dawes, only child of my eldest daughter Elizabeth Georgiana Dawes, I leave the sum of thirty thousand pounds for her immediate and sole use together with all her mother's jewellery of which I die possessed."

To Charlotte's profound relief her prayers had been answered! What Matthew's reasons were for this she would never know, but at the very end he had relented, finally acknowledging his granddaughter. At last she could take her rightful place in the family where she belonged! So overwhelmed was she at Matthew's unaccountable generosity that she could actually find it in her to forgive him everything. Sophy saw her eyes fill with tears and for the first time acknowledged that this was perhaps the only good thing her father-in-law had ever done. They were the only ones who shared this view, however.

The outcome of Alexandra's inclusion in Matthew's will was exactly as Jenkins predicted it would be. He had always served his late client with diligence and loyalty, but he had to admit that Matthew Harrington had not played fair with his family. He was of the same opinion now as he had been two months ago; Matthew should have confided in them or, at least, forewarned them of his intention, instead of which he had dropped onto them nothing short of a bombshell!

The scene which followed was most unpleasant. Disbelief quickly turned into anger as the full realisation of what they had just heard hit them, questions and accusations being hurled at him one after the other. "I take it that thing *is* legal?" George wanted to know, nodding at the document Jenkins was holding, his heavy jaws working feverishly as he glared at him.

"It *is*, sir," Jenkins replied firmly, "and I hope you are not suggesting that I would be a party to something that was *not* legal?" his affronted gaze making George hastily assure him that no such thought had entered his head.

"Of course he ain't!" Adam dismissed, to whom the warming effects of his father's malt had had a most beneficial influence. "But you must admit," he pointed out reasonably, "that it does seem most odd, especially when you consider m'father's behaviour over the whole affair!" Adam, who had had no more knowledge of Alexandra than the rest of them until told of it that morning by his mother, had fond memories of his sister and, like his mother, had had no dealings in her banishment, always believing that she had been harshly dealt with. For himself, he considered that her daughter deserved something at least, but at the same time he found it incredibly hard to understand his father's change of heart at the very last minute.

"I am afraid your father did not seek or take heed of my advice," Jenkins told them truthfully, his thin lips pursing. "I merely carried out his instructions."

"I take it my father *was* of sound mind?" George questioned, the only glimmer of hope on his horizon, still furiously angry that he had had the reins taken out of his hands at the very last moment.

"You *can*, sir," Jenkins confirmed, "very much so."

"There is, then," Charles put in coldly, very white about the mouth, "no possibility of this bequest being overturned?"

"None, sir," Jenkins shook his head, adding firmly, "there is no reason of which I am aware to necessitate such an action. There is nothing whatsoever to prevent your niece from receiving her inheritance."

He saw Charles stiffen, and for the first time since becoming aware of the girl's existence Jenkins actually found himself feeling sorry her. It was going to be no easy task for her to be accepted by such resentful relations and, from what he could see, apart from her grandmother and Mrs. Charles Harrington, who seemed to have more feeling than the rest of them put together, no one else would welcome her into the fold, in fact, he considered it to be a pretty foregone conclusion that she was going to be in for a pretty rough time. As far as he could ascertain he did not envisage Marcus putting forward any objections, but then his uncle's will was of no particular concern to him, even so, Jenkins could not help regretting the fact that Marcus was only a nephew and not a son – pity, because from the little he had seen of him since his return from India his apparent calm good sense was sadly lacking in the others. He could not speak for Adam, but Jenkins would hazard a pretty good guess that the girl, should she ever step foot across the threshold, would meet with no antagonism from him.

Charles, to whom the news of the girl's inclusion in his father's will had come as a profound shock, had challenged his mother at the earliest opportunity about the girl's existence as well as demanding to know why neither she nor his father had ever mentioned her, besides taxing her as to why she had seen fit to confide the truth to Marcus and not to her children, to which her tearful and distressed response had done nothing to either lighten his mood or endear him to Alexandra or his cousin. It was therefore in an icily cold voice that he asked Jenkins when it was his father had decided to include the girl in his will.

"A little over two months ago," Jenkins informed him, not liking the look in Charles's eyes or the way his face had become grimly taut, his lips compressed into a thin forbidding line.

"Why did you not say anything?" Charles demanded curtly, his eyes accusing as he looked at Jenkins. "Did you not at least try to dissuade my father?"

Jenkins swallowed, acutely aware of the justification of these accusations, but said, with perfect truth, "I understand your feelings, they are of course perfectly natural, but my client's instructions had to be treated in confidence as I am sure you will appreciate, and as for trying to dissuade your father, did you ever succeed in such a venture?"

"That is quite beside the point," Charles dismissed curtly, still reeling from the shock.

"The *point*, sir," Jenkins sighed, "is that as your father's legal adviser I was duty bound to carry out his wishes and in the strictest confidence."

Charles looked far from satisfied with this reply, indeed he looked most forbidding, and Sophy, standing with her hands resting nervously on the back of her chair, looked anxiously at her husband's formidable expression, inwardly trembling at the repercussions. Whatever her own feelings about Alexandra's inclusion in her father-in-law's will it was clear that Charles did not share them, on the contrary he had taken it very badly, in fact she would go so far as to say that the news had acted upon him like a body blow, but why this should be she had no idea. Even taking into account his reaction to Alexandra upon the occasion of her recent visit, it did not fully explain away his attitude now.

"Are you seriously suggesting that we calmly hand over thirty thousand pounds to a girl whose mother brought disgrace to the family?" Emily demanded, her face flushed with anger. "It's unthinkable!"

"If I may be permitted to point out," Jenkins told her reasonably, "it is not your money that has been bequeathed to her but your late father's. There is nothing anyone can do to overturn the will. The only thing you can do is to find the girl as quickly as possible."

"We shall do no such thing!" George exclaimed angrily.

"I am afraid you have no choice, sir," Jenkins told him firmly. "You cannot legally withhold the money or the jewellery from her." Then, with equal firmness, said, "I can, if you wish, locate the girl on your behalf or, if you prefer, you can undertake the search yourselves. However," he pointed out, "I must tell you that I was not the one who found her in the first place, your father having employed a private detective without my knowledge. Since I have no idea who this man is, your father declining to furnish me with his name and direction, and there are no details amongst your father's papers concerning him, it will of course take a little time to find her."

Charlotte, seeing that Charles was about to turn this suggestion down, quietly but firmly accepted Jenkins's services, to which he nodded agreement, relieved that at least one member of the family was not going to raise any more arguments or objections. "Thank you," she smiled, then, looking from one to the other of her family, suggested they all go into luncheon.

Silas Jenkins, declining her very kind invitation to join them for luncheon, deciding he would much rather make good his escape, confirmed he would set plans in motion immediately to find Alexandra, ignoring George's blustering arguments to the contrary.

"One moment, Jenkins," Charles forestalled him quietly when the others had left the library. "Are you seriously suggesting that you are indeed intending to look for the girl?"

"Yes, sir," Jenkins nodded, not liking the look on Charles's face. "Indeed, there is nothing else to be done. Once I have discovered her whereabouts and her credentials are found to be satisfactory, she will be at liberty to draw on the account your father arranged for her at Mercers and, of course," he added, "be allowed to take possession of her mother's jewellery. I do believe," he nodded, not really expecting Charles to agree with him, "that she would be well advised to leave the jewellery where it is until matters have been arranged to suit herself."

"To suit herself!" Charles scorned. "You are not seriously suggesting that we calmly hand over thirty thousand pounds plus a collection of jewellery worth a small fortune to a brat we have only laid eyes on once," Charles snapped, "and never even knew existed until a few short days ago?"

Jenkins sighed, then, shaking his head, said as firmly as he could, "Mr. Charles, there is nothing any one of you can do to prevent her from having either the money or the jewellery."

"Is there not?" Charles smiled menacingly.

"No, Mr. Charles, there is not," Jenkins confirmed.

"We shall see," Charles nodded.

Jenkins pursed his lips but deeming it prudent not to get into any further discussion on this very sore point, bid him good day.

"We have heard nothing from you yet, Coz," Charles commented smoothly as he came upon his cousin in the hall. "I felt sure that you at least would have had a comment or two to make."

"I can't imagine why," Marcus dismissed.

"You are too modest, Cousin," Charles smiled superficially, his eyes hard and cold.

"Not at all," Marcus smiled. "Apart from the fact that I fail to see the need for comment in the first place I had no idea my opinion mattered so much to you."

"It doesn't," Charles replied candidly, "but I am so used to you offering it that your silence *has* rather surprised me."

"I'm sorry to have disappointed you," Marcus apologised, fully aware of his cousin's annoyance.

"I seriously doubt that," Charles returned coolly.

"You're too proud by half, Charles," Marcus told him truthfully, eyeing his cousin steadily.

"It is a good thing that I am," Charles returned firmly. "Left to you and my mother any ragtag could take what does not belong to them."

"I would hardly call Alexandra a ragtag," Marcus pointed out tersely, wondering when this insane prejudice would end.

"You have proved my point admirably!" Charles bowed mockingly. "You are not obtuse, Marcus," he remarked, "you must surely realise that by leaving her thirty thousand pounds as well as her mother's jewellery my father actually acknowledged her."

"I realise that," Marcus nodded, "but you seem to be forgetting, they are hers by right and long overdue."

"I suppose I should have expected you to say something like that," Charles remarked contemptuously, "after all, you never did have to wait upon my father's whims, did you?"

"Perhaps I didn't," Marcus acknowledged, "but your father's bequest to his granddaughter takes nothing away from the rest of you."

"Granddaughter!" Charles exclaimed derisively.

"Accept it, Charles," Marcus advised, not unkindly. Blessed with a more generous nature than his cousin he could not understand such deep-rooted prejudice, but he was not unmindful of what a shock it must have been. But Charles, far from receiving his advice in the spirit it was given, gave his cousin to understand in no uncertain terms that under no circumstances would he sit back and allow a brat to take what did not belong to her. Realising that it was useless to argue the point Marcus joined the others in the dining room, leaving his cousin to his own reflections as he followed unhurriedly behind.

Not surprisingly, the luncheon table proved an ideal battleground for those who felt aggrieved over Matthew's will, giving voice to their views and opinions as soon as Harris had closed the door to the dining room behind him. Amelia, smiling archly at no one in particular, said that for herself she was at a loss to understand what could possibly have got into Matthew to cause him to do such a thing as leave the girl not only a fortune in jewellery but also the staggering sum of thirty thousand pounds. Emily, two spots of angry colour on her pale cheeks, immediately picked up on this by declaring vehemently that it was an absolute disgrace to think that Edward had been treated so shabbily while a brat from the gutter stood to walk away with so much. George, whose shock and anger were equally divided between having had the ground kicked from under him without any prior warning followed by the girl's inclusion in his father's will, was not at all sure which insult to comment upon first. He wanted nothing more than to take Charles to task over what he believed to be his conniving influence, but not only because it was obvious to the meanest intelligence that Charles was in no mood for conversation any more than he was for his brother's pompous moralising and would have no compunction, irrespective of who happened to be present, in responding to his accusations in a way which would be guaranteed to make him look ridiculous, but this question of the girl's inheritance could not be ignored, and therefore George decided to err on the side of caution. Although he vented some of his spleen by disparaging the girl and condemning her for worming her way into her grandfather's affections at the eleventh hour by means unspecified, his vexation was by no means assuaged and could not resist the temptation to throw Charles a smouldering and accusing look across the table. Charles, who knew perfectly well that his brother's nose had been put well and truly out of joint by his father's unexpected decision regarding a board of directors and that George believed he was responsible for it as well as knowing the reason for him refraining from commenting upon it, replied with a contemptuous curling of his lips, blatantly inviting him to retort.

Charlotte, who, like Sophy, not only found all this hostility distressing, which would achieve nothing to the purpose, but quite unable to account for such animosity, believed that it was time to call a halt to a conversation which bore all the hallmarks of turning into a full-scale argument between George and Charles. Marcus may have been engaged in conversation with Adam throughout most of luncheon at the far end of the table, but Charlotte had seen the look of vexation which had crossed his face at the prejudiced and vituperative comments which had been voiced and knew that he would not hesitate to bring them to a speedy conclusion should they continue. However, she knew too that since both George and Charles were more than likely to take exception to such a rebuke and equally likely to act upon it, perhaps even going so far as to suggest that Marcus's visits to Brook Street cease, she chose this moment to intervene. Her calm words bore fruit, bringing forth apologies or lowered eyes from her offspring, all except Charles, who merely shrugged his shoulders, and Sophy, briefly glancing across at Marcus where he sat opposite her, smiled in response as he turned brimming eyes in her direction.

Remaining only long enough to speak to his aunt and Adam followed by a brief word with Sophy, Marcus left not long after luncheon had finished. It was just as he was shrugging himself into his overcoat when he saw Charles emerge from the dining room into the hall, strolling leisurely towards him with an amusing look on his face, nodding dismissal to Harris. "Going so soon, Coz?" he enquired, raising a questioning eyebrow. "Do not tell me," he exclaimed in mock horror, "it is because we have given you a disgust of us!"

"Not at all." Marcus shook his head, too used to his cousin's humour. "It is time I was taking my leave."

"It could not be," Charles smiled provocatively, "that you are perhaps beating a somewhat strategic retreat in the face of overwhelming opposition to your opinions."

Marcus paused in the act of pulling on his gloves and after eyeing his cousin, considering for a moment or two, said quietly, "Is that what you think I am doing, Charles?"

Charles shrugged. "Let us just say that the thought *has* occurred to me."

"And has it also occurred to you, Charles," Marcus said significantly, "that a strategic retreat does not necessarily mean the battle is lost; merely regrouping one's forces?"

Charles mockingly inclined his head, his eyes narrowing. "I understand the simile perfectly, Marcus," he said softly, "but it does not alter either my sentiments or my intentions."

Marcus looked thoughtfully at his cousin, saying at length, "Your sentiments I know; your intentions, however," he nodded, "are a little less clear."

Charles raised a surprised eyebrow, his lips parting into a thin cold smile. "Why, Marcus!" he cried in mock astonishment, "I should have thought that a man of your acuity would have known; to thwart the girl, of course!"

"To thwart the girl?" Marcus repeated slowly, looking intently at his cousin. "What am I to understand from that?"

"Anything you please," Charles shrugged.

Marcus sighed, then, looking straight at his cousin, said, "Take my advice, Charles; accept it, if not with enthusiasm then at least with resignation." Upon which he donned his hat and left.

It was some time after Marcus had left that Adam, enjoying a glass of his father's excellent malt in the solitude of the library, Harris having since concertinaed the table to its customary length, considered his father's bequest to Alexandra in more depth. He had played no part in the discussion which had taken place at luncheon, but the truth was he could not explain his father's last-minute decision to include her in his will any more than he could his reasons for making provision for Isabel. It was not difficult to understand why Sophy and Amelia had been mentioned, but then, his father could, despite his shrewdness and business acumen, on occasion, do something totally out of character which could not be understood or explained.

For himself, Adam had no problem where Alexandra was concerned, but there was no denying that Charles had taken it very ill. It was of course early days and such a clause would take a lot of getting used to, even so, it would be interesting to see if he would make any attempt to overturn that bequest or whether he would gradually come to accept it as well as the girl, although if Adam was honest he had to admit that it seemed most unlikely.

He was naturally pleased that his mother was happy about the contents of his father's will, after all she had had very little joy over late years, nevertheless, it was going to take all her resolution to fight the combined efforts of Charles and George in having the girl with her. His mother was the kindest and most gentle of creatures who deserved some good fortune, but it was extremely doubtful whether his brothers would see it in the same way. They may dislike one another intensely, and of course Adam knew that his father's decision about setting up a board of directors had not exactly helped to endear Charles to his brother, but they were for once as one on this issue of the girl. Whether George would finally come to terms with Alexandra's inheritance as well as his mother's wish to have her residing here remained to be seen, but if he ran true to form there was every chance he would, especially as he had the tendency to vehemently argue a point to death until gradually climbing down, but from what Adam could see of it he doubted very much that Charles would. The look in his brother's eyes had been implacable, and Adam knew him well enough to say that nothing would move him from the stance he had taken.

The quiet entrance of Sophy curtailed his thoughts and, rising to his feet, he smiled, heaving a sigh of relief. "Sophy! Thank God it's you! I came in here for a bit of peace and quiet because if I have to listen to any more nonsense today I shan't be answerable for the consequences!"

Sophy laughed. "I know, and I am sorry to disturb you," eyeing the glass in his hand indulgently, "but your mother would like to see you; *after* you have finished your drink, of course!" she smiled. "She is in her sitting room."

Adam nodded, then, after looking from the glass he was holding to her smiling face, grinned, "You're a real brick, Sophy!"

"Why," she laughed, unable to resist his smile, "because I don't tell tale on you?"

"Precisely," he grinned again.

"As if I would *do* such a thing!" Sophy exclaimed in mock horror, bringing a huge grin to his handsome face.

As if a thought had suddenly occurred to him he looked at her, considering for a moment or two before saying tentatively, "Sophy, you had no objection to Isabel being included in m'father's will, did you?"

"Of course not." Sophy shook her head, taking several steps towards him. "Why should I?"

"Oh, no reason," Adam shrugged, "but I thought that if Emily…"

"You must not take any notice of that," Sophy said softly, "your sister is naturally very upset over her father's death."

Adam nodded. "Tell me, what do you think of Alexandra…? I mean," he corrected himself, "about her inheritance?"

Sophy swallowed, saying hesitantly, "Well, Adam… you see, it is really not for me to say."

"Yes, it is," he told her firmly, "you are a member of this family too."

"Yes, I know, but… well, you see, Adam," she faltered, mindful of Charles's dislike of her offering any views, but knowing she could trust Adam offered tentatively, "the truth is I had not looked for such generosity from your father; he could be a most unforgiving man, but I must confess to being very pleased with that bequest."

Adam nodded. "Yes, so am I, but you heard them yourself at luncheon," he reminded her. "I can see it's going to cause the devil of a lot of trouble."

"What is?" came a cold voice from the door.

"Charles!" Sophy cried, startled, raising a hand to her throat, not having heard him enter. "I came in search of Adam," she explained nervously. "Your mother would like to speak to him in her sitting room."

Charles eyed her coldly before glancing across at his brother, hurriedly tossing off the remainder of his whisky. "Do not choke yourself on my account," he advised smoothly. "But do, please, go on with what you were saying."

Sophy trembled, but Adam, by no means overawed by his brother, said, "If you must know, we were discussing m'father's will."

Charles raised a questioning eyebrow, but said smoothly, "Indeed, and what have you concluded about it?"

Adam shrugged. "Oh, apart from the fact that I did not anticipate anything like a board of directors being set up, not that I have any qualms with it, nothing much. Of course," he shook his head, "I did not expect Alexandra to be mentioned at all, but aside from that," he shrugged again, "it's very much as I thought it would be."

Charles, dismissing Adam's opinion, was more interested in what his wife had to say about it, asking politely, "And what did *you* conclude, my dear?"

Despite Marcus's encouraging words to her before he left, Sophy swallowed, knowing that disapproving look on Charles's face only too well, but even though he clearly expected an answer from her she felt quite unable to give him one. She glanced helplessly from her husband to Adam, not realising how vulnerable she looked to her brother-in-law, who, disliking his brother's treatment of her, felt it incumbent upon him to say in her stead, "It makes no difference what any of us thinks about it, the fact remains it can't be changed."

"You seem very sure of that," Charles said smoothly.

"There's nothing we *can* do," Adam told him, moving towards the door, "and to be honest with you," he pointed out, "I have no desire to make the attempt."

"So, you would much prefer to see some little guttersnipe walk away with a fortune," Charles said coldly.

"She's hardly a guttersnipe!" Adam returned sharply.

Charles eyed his brother disdainfully, saying coolly, "You are beginning to sound like Marcus; they are precisely his sentiments."

"Has it ever occurred to you," Adam pointed out, "that he could well be right?"

Charles appeared to give this due consideration before saying at his most urbane, "I am perfectly aware that our estimable cousin has many excellent qualities and equally as many noble ideas, but I have no intention, either now or in the future, of allowing any of them to weigh with me. Whatever you and Marcus may think," he emphasised, "I am not going to stand idly by while a brat like that takes possession of something which does not belong to her, and to which she certainly has no right."

"But Charles…" Sophy began.

The look Charles gave her made her draw in her breath and his voice was cuttingly polite as he said, "I am already well acquainted with what you think, but as your opinion is neither sought nor required I should be obliged if you would refrain from offering it."

"I'm sorry," she said huskily, lowering her eyes so he would not see her fear and hurt.

It had not taken this exchange to tell Adam that his sister-in-law was by no means happy in her marriage or that she was frightened of her husband, but since it was not his place to take his brother to task for the way he treated his wife, he bit down the angry retort on his lips and left the library, wishing there was something he could do to ease Sophy's situation.

*

Having awoken to the news that his brother had arrived home the previous evening, Charles had been in no very good humour ever since. It was not that he begrudged Adam the right to attend his father's funeral, but his presence in town would undoubtedly be frowned upon in a certain quarter. Even now, six months on, there were still those who dared to question him about the circumstances surrounding his brother's sudden departure to Yorkshire and his hasty marriage to Isabel Marsden, and since Charles disliked his family's affairs being broadcast to all and sundry, apart from which he was not his brother's keeper, he was sick and tired of parrying these pointed questions.

Marsden, as George had rightly remarked, was still smarting from the episode, and only his paternal feelings coupled with his horror of scandal prevented him from blurting the truth to all his acquaintance. Like Harris, Charles had noticed that Adam's enforced absence from town and the shackles of matrimony had done nothing to moderate his careless attitude, and upon mentioning to him at breakfast that he would be well advised to leave for Yorkshire as soon after the funeral as possible, he had been met with, "Not until I have seen Marsden."

Not unnaturally, this calmly uttered announcement had startled Charles out of his usual indifference, momentarily rendering him speechless as he stared across the breakfast table at his brother, who seemed more intent on his breakfast than any worldly considerations. It seemed that Adam was as unperturbed over meeting his father-in-law as he was about the existence of Alexandra or the fact that his father may have included her in his will at the last moment. His blasé acceptance of such important issues was sufficient for Charles to deliver a sharply worded rebuke, which may as well have been left unsaid for all the notice his brother took of it.

"The thing is," Adam pointed out reasonably, his mouth full of kidney, "there's nothing any of us can do about Lizzie's girl or any changes Father may have made in his will, so we may as well accept them, and as for Marsden," he commented calmly, helping himself to another kidney, "I aim to get things settled between us once and for all because although I've nothing against Yorkshire he's not going to keep me away from town.

Besides," he added fairly, quite unperturbed by the look on his brother's face, "Isabel worries over the rift between us, and I don't want that." Realising that it was useless to try to bring Adam to a sense of what was due to the family, Charles left his brother to finish his breakfast alone, angrily walking out of the dining room just as George entered it.

George, having been informed of Adam's arrival by his mother, who had enjoyed a long talk with her youngest son less than an hour earlier, frowned down at his sibling who was calmly tucking into a substantial breakfast. George knew from painful experience that Charles was not the easiest of people to get along with at the best of times, but first thing in the morning he was positively lethal. George did not need to be told what had put that look on Charles's face, he could hazard a pretty good guess. Adam, on the other hand, was totally unconcerned by Charles's display of annoyance, his cheerful good morning irritating George to such an extent that he was moved to remonstrate with his youngest brother over the imprudence of upsetting Charles.

"He'll get over it," Adam shrugged.

"Much you know!" George snapped, helping himself from a selection of dishes. "He'll be in the devil of a temper for the rest of the day."

"And why should that bother you?" Adam wanted to know, refilling his tea cup.

"Why?" George repeated bitterly. "You'd know why if you lived here," adding unnecessarily, "Charles has a damned unpleasant tongue."

"So, what's new?" his brother shrugged.

"Is that all you can say?" George thundered.

"What else do you want me to say?" Adam asked.

"I don't want you to say anything," George told him forthrightly, pointing his knife at him, "that's the point. The least said to Charles the better."

"Still pandering to him, are you?" Adam remarked, his attractive smile having a most adverse effect on his brother. "That's his trouble," he pointed out calmly.

"Let me tell you," George spluttered furiously, "that I don't pander to anyone!"

"Well, if that's the case," Adam argued reasonably, "why should you care what mood he is in?"

George threw him a smouldering look and, after swallowing a mouthful of ham, spoke at length on their brother's uncertain temper and the folly of crossing him, ending this angry sermon with a demand to know what the devil he had said to Charles.

An impish gleam entered Adam's eyes as he imparted what had passed between them, his insouciance causing his brother as much annoyance as the disclosure.

George's pale blue eyes protruded even more as he stared incredulously across the heavily laden table at his brother, his heavy jaws working feverishly as he struggled to find words suitable to convey his feelings. No wonder Charles had looked thunderous! Was Adam totally mad? "Good God!" he exclaimed. "Are you out of your senses?"

"No." Adam shook his head. "What makes you think I might be?"

"You calmly sat there," George said, aghast, "and told Charles all this?"

"Yes, why not?" Adam shrugged, his concentration more on deliberating between another kidney or a slice of ham.

"Why not!" George cried. "No wonder he's furious! Well," he told him firmly, "I'm with this Charles in this. There is no way if I can prevent it that the girl will ever enter this house again, and if my father did change his will to include her I can promise you there is no way one penny will be released to her!" Pausing only to wipe his mouth with a napkin, he pointed out, "And as for you calmly announcing that you're going to see Marsden, I warn you here and now that he will most probably bar you the house!"

Chapter Six

Marsden may not have gone as far as barring the house to him, but upon Adam's arrival on his doorstep three days later, his father-in-law having only yesterday returned to town, he was certainly coldly received. Sir Thomas Marsden's appearance was as impressive as his lineage. Having inherited his title from a long line of venerated ancestors he had good cause to be proud of the name he bore. The first of his illustrious forebears had received the hereditary title and lands from a grateful Henry VIII, and his descendants had continued to distinguish themselves in the service of their sovereign and country ever since.

Adam did not need reminding of the family's proud history; like everyone else he knew there had been a Marsden in nearly every campaign recorded in the annals of British military history; from Sir Neville raising the royal standard at Bristol to Sir Aubrey's heroic efforts in the Crimea. Every inch of the man who glared ferociously at Adam from out of a pair of piercing blue eyes was the embodiment of pride and self-worth, and he had no intention of relinquishing either.

Harris may deprecate Adam's blasé attitude but he was not so blind that he did not recognise, like everyone else who came into contact with him, the integrity and strength of purpose concealed behind that careless demeanour, both of which enabled him now to withstand that penetrating stare without a blink, even though he by no means liked the way his father-in-law was trying to reduce him to schoolboy status. "Thank you for seeing me, sir," Adam managed, determined to keep this meeting as friendly as possible. "I very much appreciate it."

The scowl on that craggy face did not lift as Marsden listened to this polite introduction, on the contrary it deepened, but his voice was perfectly controlled as he said, "I did not invite you here, Harrington; so make it brief. What do you want?"

Adam did not exactly relish the idea of being addressed in such dismissive terms and were it not for Isabel's distress over the rift between him and her father, both of whom she dearly loved, and the promise he had made her to speak to her father in an attempt to reconcile their differences, he would not be here now, nor would he be struggling to bite down the angry retort which rose to his lips. "Actually, sir," he said civilly, "I am here to offer you a very belated apology for the way in which I married your daughter, and also to see if we could perhaps overcome our differences."

"Indeed!" Marsden replied, not very encouragingly, his massive frame rigidly upright as he stood with his back to the roaring fire.

"Yes, sir," Adam nodded, his clear gaze unflinching as he held his father-in-law's hard stare.

"You run off with my daughter," Marsden accused, "and then you expect me to calmly forgive you?"

"Not calmly, no," Adam smiled, "but I would very much welcome it."

"I've no doubt," Marsden scorned, adding implacably, "but I have no intention of doing so. Not now; not ever."

For himself, Adam cared nothing for his father-in-law's forgiveness much less his approval, but it pained him to see the effect it had on Isabel. She may have eloped with an eagerness which would have condemned her in the eyes of society had it ever become public knowledge, but she loved her father too much not to want the opportunity to apologise for hurting him and to repair the damage to their relationship. Isabel did indeed love Adam and she certainly had no regrets in her choice of husband, but her sole desire now was to appease her father and to bring about a reconciliation between him and Adam. Immediately prior to his departure Adam had read the silent plea in her eyes and found himself incapable of resisting it, and therefore he had reiterated his promise that he would speak to her father. He had not exaggerated when he had told his brothers the other morning that he was not going to allow Marsden to keep him away from town, but it had been Isabel's pain and distress which had brought forth his apology. To have it brusquely turned aside made Adam stiffen, his long slim fingers gripping the ebony cane as he fought to control his rising temper. Marsden watched his efforts unmoved, dismissing him with a half turn of his head. Adam's lips thinned and his face turned slightly pale, and it was therefore with a considerable effort that he managed to say, "Is that your last word?"

"It is," Marsden bit out with finality, digging his hands into the pockets of his trousers.

"And what of Isabel?" Adam wanted to know. "Have you no desire to pardon her?"

"I have no wish to discuss my daughter with you," Marsden informed him icily.

"Why not?" Adam demanded, "she is my wife, after all."

"Your *wife!*" Marsden exclaimed disparagingly. "Do you call such a ceremony a marriage?"

"Our wedding was perfectly legal," Adam told him firmly. "Unorthodox perhaps, but legal nonetheless."

"Ha!" Marsden scorned. "You may bamboozle my daughter into believing that, but you and I know better!"

A tide of hot anger had Adam in its grip, but even though his eyes were blazing his voice was perfectly controlled, every word icily delivered. "If you are suggesting that I have taken advantage of Isabel, then you are a damned liar!"

"Understand me, Harrington," Marsden bit out, "I don't like you any more than I liked your father, or the rest of your family for that matter. I should never have sanctioned the connection no matter what! Why, the mere thought of my name being tied up with yours turns me sick to the stomach!" Before Adam could reply to this, Marsden continued, "Your mother may have an acceptable lineage but your father was nothing but an upstart, and I tell you to your face that his background was as vulgar as his manners!"

Adam may have had his differences with his father from time to time but to hear him insulted in this way was going beyond what he could accept or tolerate. It was seldom Matthew Harrington's youngest son lost his temper, his natural friendly disposition and casual unconcern making him the most popular member of his family, but this was too much. "You accuse my father of being vulgar! Yet you, sir," Adam nodded, "what are *you?* You may have been born a gentleman, Marsden, but *your* manners are far removed from those of any gentleman *I* know. But I did not come here to discuss my family or to listen to your offensive remarks, but about my marriage to your daughter. I think you owe me an apology, Marsden!"

"You damned little upstart!" Marsden fumed, his colour darkening. "You'll wait forever! I never apologise for speaking the truth."

"You cannot fail to be aware that I buried my father only three days ago," Adam stated coldly, "yet you have shown not the slightest respect for that. However," he nodded, "if that is your last word, then you leave me with little choice."

"What the devil do you mean?" Marsden demanded, a sudden wariness entering his eyes.

Adam looked straight at him, a strange glint entering his eyes. "It would be a pity, don't you think, if you were never to see your daughter again." Despite his anger, his words were spoken quite calmly and he could see they had hit home. "I flatter myself that I have considerable influence over Isabel. I only have to…"

"You wouldn't *dare*!" Marsden thundered, taking several menacing steps towards his son-in-law.

"You underrate me," Adam returned ominously,

"You miserable little…!" Marsden began, but the determined look in Adam's eyes made him pause, thinking better of what he had been about to say.

"Enough of this!" Adam dismissed. "You have spoken your mind to me very plainly, and now I will do likewise. You know as well as I do that as Isabel's husband I have certain rights, and I *will* exert them if you continue in this vein, but I should prefer not to." He paused only long enough to allow this to sink in. "Speaking for myself, I don't care whether you give me the cut direct or not. I care nothing for you or your opinion of me but Isabel does. I am here purely for her sake, not mine. I wouldn't lose any sleep over you or your opinion, but it upsets Isabel and I don't like that. Whatever you think of me is neither here nor there, but I love your daughter and I don't like seeing her unhappy. She loves you very much and it hurts her to know how things are between us. For that reason, and that reason alone, I am here to see if we can mend our differences. If not… well," he shrugged, "as I have already said…"

"Damn you, Harrington!" Marsden ground out. "I heard you the first time." For several minutes he struggled with himself, his jaws working feverishly as he considered all Adam had said, eventually barking out, "I don't like being blackmailed."

"That's a very ugly word, Marsden," Adam returned coldly, "and not one I'm fond of."

"What else do you call it when you threaten to withhold my daughter from me?" he demanded angrily.

"Certainly not blackmail," Adam stated firmly, "but you know Isabel as well as I do; her loyalty is very strong, especially to those whom she loves. It would not be right or proper to expect her to choose between us, which is what it will come down to if you persist in taking this line."

Adam watched his father-in-law's inner battle unsympathetically. In his view, Marsden had only himself to blame for forcing him and his daughter into a course of action which could easily have been avoided. Marsden had known from the beginning that Isabel disliked Ronald Erskine and that she had made it clear she would never marry him, not even to please her father, but had in fact met and fallen in love with someone else, and that she could not do as he wished. Adam's visits to Marsden, pleading with him to allow the two of them to be married with his blessing had been coldly and implacably dismissed, ignoring the warning as to what could result from his refusal.

Marsden had known perfectly well that his only daughter loved Adam Harrington, but his long-standing friendship with Ronald Erskine's father had swayed his decision. To have that decision taken out of his hands by the son of a man he had never been able to tolerate had been too much. But as Marsden looked at his son-in-law he realised, albeit reluctantly, that he either had to accept the situation or remain estranged from his daughter until such time that he relented. His begrudging acceptance of Adam's terms was immediately followed up with the angry warning, "But understand me, Harrington, whilst I agree to accept you in the presence of my daughter outside her company I shall consider myself justified in ignoring the connection between us!"

Adam accepted this ultimatum without reservation. He had got what he came for and that was all that mattered, not at all put out when his outstretched hand was refused. Marsden was certainly not the easiest of people to deal with, in fact he had been blunt to the point of rudeness, and had he been anyone other than his father-in-law or even a younger man, Adam would have known how to act, but for Isabel's sake he had curbed his temper. He had not relished the thought of being treated so dismissively, even so he could live with the uneasy truce which had been made between them, and as he descended the steps and hailed an approaching hackney he was able to congratulate himself on a reasonably successful interview.

Eventually arriving at his destination, Adam stepped lightly out of the vehicle, whereupon he threw a coin up at the muffled coachman on the box before ascending the steps of the house in the secluded Knightsbridge square, which, on a raw day such as this, was quite deserted. It was not until he was standing on the top of the three shallow steps waiting for a response to his vigorous tug on the bell pull that he wondered whether his cousin would be at home, having given him no warning of his visit, but upon being informed by Webster, Marcus's very correct butler, that his master was at home, Adam quickly stepped inside out of the cold.

*

Having been occupied for most of the morning with the accounts he had received from his Uncle Lionel, Marcus was more than willing to set them aside for a while to speak to his cousin. Like Sophy, he had always had a soft spot for his careless younger cousin, greeting him with the smile that had won Marcus many friends. "This should help thaw you out," offering him a glass of very excellent Madeira.

"You're a gentleman and a scholar!" Adam grinned, raising his glass in mock salute. "Not interrupting anything, am I?" he asked, nodding towards the papers on the desk.

"They'll keep," Marcus assured him, easing himself into a wing chair on the opposite side of the fireplace facing his cousin, then, after accepting his compliments on the quality of his cellar with an inclination of the head, he sat contentedly back to spend the next ten minutes or more listening to his cousin pass observations on nothing in particular before deeming it time to inform his insouciant young relative that he was not such a fool as to believe he had paid him this visit merely to discuss pleasantries. "This is all very interesting," he pointed out, amused, "but I don't think you came here simply to pass the time. What is it?"

Adam's decision to seek his cousin's advice on a matter which was extremely delicate to say the least was one thing, but when actually faced with the task he discovered, to his discomfiture, that it was not so easily accomplished. As he sipped his wine and eyed his cousin over the rim of his glass he began to wonder whether he had totally misread the situation, and so instead of broaching the subject he had come to discuss took refuge in prevarication by giving Marcus a rather indignant account of his misfortune in being blessed with a family who knew no better than to give one a lecture at the breakfast table.

Marcus laughed. "That was certainly inconsiderate of them, but what cause had they to give you a lecture so early in the morning?"

"I told them I was going to see Marsden," Adam told him, adding, "as a matter of fact, I've just left him."

Marcus eyed his cousin with a nice mix of admiration and surprise. "I see," he said slowly. "And how did it go?"

Adam recounted the meeting in a better frame of mind than he had been in at the time, only his eyes kindling at the memory.

"I'm not very well acquainted with Marsden," Marcus shook his head, "but I hear he is quite stiff rumped."

"Stiff rumped!" Adam echoed. "I should rather think he is!"

Marcus eyed his cousin closely, shrewdly suspecting that there was more to this visit besides informing him of his meeting with his father-in-law.

Stretching out his right leg, which had been giving him some discomfort all morning, he eased himself into a more comfortable position before saying, not unkindly, "You know, Adam, as much as it gratifies me to receive this visit from you, I find it hard to believe that you have come here solely to advise me of your meeting with Marsden." Adam met his cousin's steady gaze a little sheepishly, realising, and not for the first time, that Marcus saw far more than was comfortable. "Why do I get the feeling that you are going the long way round to tell me something?" The smile on those finely chiselled lips never wavered, but that steady and searching gaze made Adam move uneasily in his chair. "What is it?" Marcus encouraged. "Money?"

"What! Oh Lord, no," Adam said vehemently. "It's nothing like that!"

"I am relieved to hear it. Then what is it like?" Marcus urged encouragingly, swallowing the remainder of his wine.

After eyeing his cousin considering for a few moments, Adam decided he may as well say what he had come for, but it was not without a little hesitancy that he asked, "What do you make of this business about Alexandra?"

It was several moments before Marcus answered, his attention seemingly taken up with adding another log to the fire. "Why should I make anything of it?"

"Well, I understand from m'mother that you've known about her for some time," Adam stated simply.

Marcus looked steadily at his cousin, saying, unperturbed, "Your mother did tell me about her, yes, but since it was said in confidence it would have been quite wrong of me to relate it to the rest of you."

"Damn it, Marcus!" Adam exclaimed, horrified. "I'm not blaming you for anything, but what beats me is how the devil she kept it a secret all these years!"

Marcus hesitated before saying calmly, "It is not so difficult to understand when you remember that your father, having discovered his banished daughter had a child, strictly forbid your mother to mention it. She knew better than to go against him."

Adam swallowed, his voice a little taut, "Yes, I can imagine him warning her to keep silent," taking a generous mouthful of his wine. "He could be very intimidating, and m'mother would know better than to disobey him." Marcus nodded his acknowledgement of this, and Adam, after giving the matter a little more thought, let out a long low whistle, exclaiming, "Lord, he must have been furious to discover his daughter and grandchild making their escape from the house! Of course," he nodded, "knowing m'father he wouldn't have spoken of it to any of us, in fact," he pointed out, "I'm surprised he told us about Lizzie's death!" Taking a revivifying drink of his wine, he exclaimed, "What has me in a puzzle though, is why he took it into his head to make provision for her! Not but what I think she deserves something but knowing m'father's attitude about the whole affair I can't for the life of me understand him doing such a thing!"

"I can't answer that," Marcus told him, "but you know as well as I do that he never confided in anyone, much less accounted for what he did."

"Lord, yes!" Adam acknowledged. "Mind you," he confessed, "I was only a boy at the time, but I have always thought that Lizzie was treated pretty badly. But you know, Marcus," he pointed his glass at him, "this bequest to Alexandra is going to cause the devil of a stir! George is far from happy about it, and Charles — well, you know how he feels about it. If Jenkins does find her she'll be in for the devil of a time!"

"I've no doubt," Marcus agreed, "but if George and Charles have any sense they will accept it with as good a grace as possible."

"George may come round in time," Adam mused, giving it a little thought, "but Charles won't. Believe me, Marcus, he is absolutely determined to do all he can to prevent the girl from having a penny of the money m'father left her, and as for Lizzie's jewellery, he was saying only last night that he would rather sell the lot than let her have so much as a piece of it."

"I can imagine," Marcus nodded, "but Jenkins was quite right when he said that the codicil is perfectly legal and cannot be overturned. If Charles is thinking along those lines he is wasting his time."

"What *I* don't understand, though," Adam shook his head, "is who is this private detective m'father hired? Why not employ Jenkins to find her?"

"Again," Marcus shook his head, "I can't speak for anything your father did, but I agree it would have been far better to have left it to Jenkins than to employ a stranger."

"I know Jenkins said that it would take a little time to find her in view of there being nothing amongst m'father's papers to indicate who this man is so he could point him in her direction, but unless I miss my guess," Adam pointed out, "Charles for one won't mind how long it takes; as far as he's concerned he hopes she's gone to ground for good."

"I realise, of course," Marcus conceded, "that Charles is finding it difficult to accept the girl, indeed, I have seen and heard enough myself to be in no doubt of that, but the sooner he *does* accept her as well as her inheritance the better it will be."

"Well," Adam shook his head, "I fail to see what he *can* do to prevent her from taking up her inheritance. You were there, Marcus," he nodded, "you heard Jenkins assure us that the will was legal and that m'father knew precisely what he was doing."

"We must hope that Charles will come to recognise that. I am sure he will," Marcus nodded, though not very hopefully, "but in any event, once Jenkins finds her there is absolutely nothing whatever to prevent her from taking up her inheritance."

"I know," Adam agreed, "but I have a feeling there is going to be no happy ending to this." In response to Marcus's look of enquiry, he then went on to recount the exchange between his brother and Sophy in the library the afternoon of his father's funeral as well as other instances over the last couple of days when Charles had expressed his feelings on this very point and how, if he could help it, the girl would never take up her inheritance.

Having witnessed Charles's callous usage of Sophy more than once, Marcus did not need reminding of his behaviour towards her, but hearing of this latest verbal attack only served to intensify his impotence and frustration in being unable to do anything to either offer her protection or assistance. Not by a word or gesture did he betray these feelings to Adam, merely reiterating his opinion that once the initial shock had worn off not only George but Charles too, would be brought to accept the inevitable.

"You may be right about George," Adam conceded cautiously, "but you didn't hear Charles last night or see the expression on his face, and I tell you, Marcus, I can't help feeling that this goes deeper than his pride."

"What makes you say that?" Marcus asked thoughtfully, looking at his young cousin with interest, knowing him to be a man who was neither prone to exaggeration nor deliberately making mischief.

Adam paused a moment before saying, "It's probably nothing, you understand, and I could be completely wrong." Marcus waited in patient silence while Adam poured himself another drink. "The thing is," Adam continued slowly, "it was something Sophy said last night over dinner; something about Lizzie's jewellery. I can't recall her words precisely, but it was something about never having seen them and that perhaps it would be a good thing if they were cleaned before Alexandra sees them. I probably wouldn't have paid much attention to it had it not have been for the way Charles suddenly seemed to turn quite pale, in fact," he added, shuddering at the recollection, "he was damned unpleasant, telling Sophy, in front of all of us," he scorned, "that he had already advised her about keeping her thoughts to herself, and in future he would thank her to remember it." After swallowing a generous mouthful of his Madeira, he resumed, "Anyway, just when I thought he had finished raking her down, he told her, you know that voice he uses when he wants to be particularly cutting, that he would thank her if she would refrain from meddling in affairs which were no concern of hers."

Marcus was not entirely certain whether the danger he sensed was a legacy from his army days or simply the natural protective instincts for the woman he loved; but in either event the feeling was so strong that he could not prevent himself from wondering if his young cousin had inadvertently stumbled upon something Charles wanted no one to know about or if it was nothing more sinister than his excessive pride.

"Well," Adam continued, "naturally I thought no more about it, but after dinner I sat with m'mother in her sitting room, you know how it is; she wanted to talk about Isabel and everything, well, after I left her and was passing the library I heard voices coming from inside. It was Charles and Sophy, one or the other of them had failed to close the door properly. Well, I wouldn't have stayed and listened to a private conversation as I hope you know, but just as I was level with the door I could distinctly hear Charles's voice; he was giving Sophy a thorough dressing down, informing her that if she thought for one moment he was prepared to sit by and allow the girl to enjoy one penny of her inheritance she was very much mistaken, and that as far as the jewellery was concerned he personally would ensure that not one piece would be released to her. He then followed this up by saying he would be grateful to her if she would keep her thoughts and views to herself, and that when he wanted her opinion or suggestions he would ask for them, until then he would thank her to keep her tongue still and hoped that this would be the last time she would give him cause to speak to her on this matter. In the meantime, he would be extremely obliged if she would mind him better in the future!"

Marcus was too much in control of himself to allow his emotions to show, and Adam, looking at the ruggedly handsome face opposite him without the slightest change of expression on it, was beginning to think that his mother had totally misread the situation between his cousin and Sophy. He was convinced that his mother had not meant to say anything at all about her nephew and daughter-in-law, not that she had actually said anything to the purpose, a mere passing remark which could in fact have meant something quite different, but he too had seen the subtle change which came over Sophy whenever Marcus was around and although Adam had never taken any heed of it before, in view of his mother's unconscious remark he had begun to wonder. He would lay a considerable sum on the chance that she had no idea what she had allowed to slip out, and certainly she would never maliciously say or do anything to hurt anyone, all the same it had set him thinking which had rendered him a little uncomfortable in confiding his thoughts to Marcus, especially about what he had witnessed between his brother and Sophy. Upon reflection, however, it was hardly surprising that Sophy and Marcus got along extremely well. Not only was his cousin an easy man to get along with but Adam knew that Marcus and Sophy's brother Timothy were acquainted, and since Sophy and her brother were very close it was perhaps natural that she should lean towards Marcus more than the rest of them.

But whatever his mother may have accidentally let fall last night there were certainly no signs as far as Adam could see to confirm that Marcus's feelings for Sophy were anything other than what they should be for his cousin's wife. Indeed, his face was as impassive as if it had been carved in stone. Of course, it was nothing to do with him what the rest of his family did, and although it was true that he liked Marcus, Adam doubted whether Charles would welcome his interest in his wife, if such an interest existed, which Adam was now beginning to doubt. Charles may be his brother but he had often thought Sophy deserved better than him for a husband, and if she and Marcus were in love, apart from the fact that it had nothing whatsoever to do with him, Adam would certainly raise no objections. Even though his brother never spoke of it, he knew perfectly well that his father had forced Charles into a marriage he had by no means wanted, but when faced with the alternative his brother had, however reluctantly, accepted Sophia Lessington as his wife. Like his mother, Charles was not the kind of man Adam would have given Sophy to in marriage, but from the very beginning she had tried to make Charles a good wife; certainly, she gave him no cause to either doubt her fidelity or her loyalty, and that she was dutiful was beyond question. Charles may have railed against the marriage, still did in fact, but it was not as though she did not do him justice, on the contrary her behaviour and manners were impeccable, never saying or doing anything to deserve the treatment he handed out to her, and that she was as beautiful as she was kind and generous could not be argued. If anyone were to ask him for his opinion, Adam would have to say that from what he had been privileged to see of Charles's marriage it was not at all as it should be, for which he put whatever the problem was down to his brother's autocratic temperament.

There may not have been any outward display of emotion from Marcus, but inwardly he was straining every nerve and sinew in an effort to hide the anxiety and anger running through him when he considered all Sophy had to endure at his cousin's hands. He did Charles the justice of owning that he never offered her physical violence, but then he did not have to, that tongue of his inflicting more pain than any blow possibly could. No one knew his world better than he did; censorious and disapproving, and whilst Marcus cared nothing for what people may say of himself, for him to openly declare his love for Sophy the consequences for her would be catastrophic. Like Adam, Marcus knew only too well that it was not his place to take Charles to task for his treatment of her. As her husband he had the right to deal with her in any way he chose, but for Marcus, who loved her more than life itself, it was becoming increasingly more difficult to fight the overwhelming desire to tell his cousin the truth, longing for the day when he could not only offer Sophy the protection of his love but his name as well. Since Adam had only been back in town a few days it was impossible to tell whether he had guessed the truth or not; from the looks of it though it certainly seemed that he had not, but this assumption could not be taken for granted. Marcus knew he could trust Adam, even so, the thought of disclosing a confidence to which he did not hold the sole rights was quite repugnant to him, little realising that his aunt, whom he knew to be far more alert than her family gave her credit for, had innocently set Adam thinking.

In view of Marcus's apparent unconcern, Adam's thinking was beginning to undergo a change. In his opinion, no man could look so calm and unmoved when told that the lady he loved was in distress, so dismissing the thought as mere fancy, said, "I couldn't quite make out Sophy's reply but she was certainly upset, and unless I mistook the case, which I doubt," innocently adding to Marcus's fears for Sophy's well-being, "by the time she returned to the drawing room several minutes after Charles, I could have sworn she had been crying. Anyway, Charles said, and I heard him distinctly," he nodded at his cousin, "'Make no mistake about it, the girl will never enjoy a penny of her inheritance, and as for the jewellery, believe me, that is *quite* out of the question.'" Adam shrugged. "As I said, I could be quite wrong about the whole thing, but I can't rid my mind of the way Charles looked and spoke. I've never known him be so determined about anything before as he is about this. No wonder Sophy did not come down to breakfast this morning!"

No sign of the anger surging through Marcus on hearing this was visible on his face, and when he eventually spoke his voice was perfectly calm as he asked, "I take it Elizabeth's jewellery is at Mercers still?"

"As far as I know," Adam shrugged. "Why do you ask?"

"No reason," Marcus shook his head, "except that I saw them once, not long before Elizabeth left."

"Well, I've never laid eyes on 'em!" Adam exclaimed, "so I couldn't tell you what's there or not."

"It's quite an impressive collection as I recall," Marcus told him. "As you know, before she died your maternal grandmother willed her jewellery between the three girls; so most of the pieces that belonged to Elizabeth are what she left her, the rest I believe were gifts from your father."

"How much is the lot worth in your opinion?" Adam asked interestedly, his eyes narrowing fractionally.

"I really have no idea," Marcus admitted, "but I should think their value is quite considerable."

Adam nodded absent agreement to this, his mind suddenly taken up with an idea which, however absurd or distasteful, refused to go away and, after eying his cousin thoughtfully for a moment or two said, "You don't think that Charles has…? No," he shook his head, "he wouldn't be so stupid, surely!"

Marcus did not pretend to misunderstand him, but not wanting to encourage this line of thought which, however disagreeable, had already occurred to him, said, "Charles is not fool enough for that."

"I should like to think not," Adam nodded, a frown creasing his forehead. "What do you think he meant though? I mean," he shrugged, "what he said to Sophy."

Until Marcus had had time to think it calmly through and to make his own discreet enquiries he was not prepared to commit himself, saying instead, "Oh, I should think it was nothing more than an excessive attack of pride. You know how he is."

Adam did know; but the seed having been sown would not go away, but by the time he took his leave of Marcus, thanking him for the excellent Madeira and to invite him to visit them when next in Yorkshire, his cousin's calm good sense had gone a long way to easing his mind.

Not until he had closed the door behind his cousin did Marcus release the iron grip with which he had held his emotions in check, his mind filled with thoughts of the woman he loved more than life itself, and the frustration of knowing that as things stood right now he was virtually powerless to help her. As far as Charles was concerned, for the time being at least, everything was conjecture and hearsay, but that he was more than capable of denying Alexandra her inheritance Marcus had no doubt at all. The only doubt he did have was how Charles would accomplish it. Of course, he had no legal right to involve himself in Matthew's affairs, and Marcus realised only too well how his interference, for Charles especially would see it as precisely that, would be looked upon; all the same, Marcus knew he could not stand by and see Alexandra deprived of what was rightfully hers. Even before Adam had voiced his concerns, Marcus had considered Charles's attitude to be rather disproportionate, but at the same time he could hardly accuse him of having designs on her inheritance!

Completely ignoring the work which had been interrupted by Adam's visit, Marcus walked straight past his desk to stand staring out of the window which overlooked the square's well-kept garden, his mind conjuring up the image of Sophy, his whole being aching with the need to take her away from a situation she neither asked for nor enjoyed, to make her his own in the eyes of the world. The very thought of Charles treating her in the way he did made Marcus clench his fists in anger and frustration. As her husband Charles had the right to behave towards her in any way he saw fit, while he, who would willingly give his life for her, could only look on in anguish, powerless to do anything to help her. Charles may be finding it difficult to come to terms with that bequest, but that he should dare to rake Sophy down because of a comment she had made as well as his regularly displayed contempt and indifference, made Marcus hasten his desire to find a solution to the unbearable situation she was in. In the meantime though, it would not be a bad idea if he renewed his acquaintance with Oswald Mercer!

Chapter Seven

Marcus was not the only one who recognised Charlotte's alertness; Sophy too had realised long ago that her mother-in-law was far more astute than her family gave her credit for. Nevertheless, she would have been astonished to learn that Charlotte was by no means in ignorance of what she had been striving to hide all this time. Not by a word or gesture had Sophy conveyed her feelings for Marcus to Charlotte, even though she knew her confidences would be strictly kept. Sophy's relationship with her mother-in-law was a close one, in truth, her life in Brook Street would be insupportable if it were not for her, but for all that she was extremely loath to confide anything so personal to her, or indeed to anyone, and certainly not to Amelia or Emily. Sophy would have been acutely embarrassed had she known that Adam had been unwittingly made aware of her feelings for Marcus, but the mere thought of either of her sisters-in-law suspecting her secret caused her grave concern as both of them were more than capable of informing against her to Charles.

The sad thing was Sophy did not dislike Amelia, but for reasons of her own she may consider that it could serve her well at some point suitable to herself to advise Charles of his wife's guilty secret, conveniently overlooking the betrayal of her own husband with his brother. Emily she could neither like nor trust. It had struck Sophy at the outset that her sister-in-law possessed a spiteful streak, which had been all too evidently demonstrated on the day Matthew had died. She knew Emily well enough to say that she would not only consider it to be her duty to tell her brother that his wife was in love with their cousin but that she would be more than capable of adding to it until her tale bore no resemblance to the truth. Her sharp-eyed sister-in-law missed very little especially where Sophy was concerned, of whom she was extremely jealous. In her heart Emily envied Sophy her beauty and graceful elegance, so very different to her own lack of inches and thin, shapeless figure which no amount of embellishment could improve. Sophy had no need to fear Jane, a sweet and gentle creature who interested herself in no one's affairs but her own, her growing family and loving husband her only concerns. Sophy had more than once envied them their idyllic life and always looked forward with real pleasure to her visits to her sister-in-law, their happy and loving home far more to her taste than the undercurrents prevalent in Brook Street, her only respite from the unbearable tension being when Marcus called.

There was no need for words between her and Marcus to express the love they shared; it was there in their eyes whenever they looked at one another, mutely confirmed in every gesture or polite enquiry from one to the other and excitingly conveyed with every warm touch of his lips as they brushed her fingers. No doubts or uncertainties had ever plagued her about the love she had for him and which continually threatened to overwhelm her, especially when in his company. Sophy had never known such all-consuming emotions existed, much less to knowing that she could feel them, and although she was neither afraid nor shocked at the depth of her love her fear was inadvertently betraying herself, for however much Charles may pay no attention to her he was no fool and it would only take a momentary lapse on her part for him to guess the truth.

Charlotte, however, had always known that her son's marriage was not a love match, and although she had had no dealings in its arrangement she had hoped, rather optimistically perhaps, that in time it may prove to be successful, after all most marriages of this kind usually worked out very well, but unfortunately it had not been so. Charles was not the man to whom she would have given Sophy in marriage and, over time, she had been right. Sophy was never at her best in Charles's presence and although she was a dutiful and loyal wife she was not in love with her husband, or he with her.

When Charlotte had taken it upon herself to nurse her nephew upon his return to England it had never so much as crossed her mind that Marcus and her daughter-in-law, both of whom she loved very much, would come to love one another. Upon reflection, however, she supposed she should have been prepared for such an eventuality, but it was not until Marcus had been in her care for some little time that she had noticed a distinct uneasiness in him, as concerning for her as it was out of character for him. At first, she had thought it was because he was missing his military life and the friends he had left behind, but it was not long before she realised that his uneasiness stemmed from the frustration of having fallen in love with a woman who was already the wife of another man, and the knowledge that the other man was his own cousin only served to increase his disquiet. In her unobtrusive way Charlotte had observed the love which had blossomed between them throughout his convalescence, and whilst Marcus's behaviour towards Sophy had been exemplary and precisely what Charlotte would have expected from him, she had nevertheless seen Sophy's reserve disappear in his company. Marcus's gentle coaxing and easy manner had gradually exposed the woman she kept hidden, all the traits of her personality coming to the fore, her face glowing with a radiance which would have fooled no one privileged to have seen her.

But it would not do! Charles was neither stupid nor blind, and sooner or later he would see the truth. But neither Marcus nor Sophy had betrayed themselves or each other; Sophy because it was unthinkable to go against her upbringing or neglect her commitment to her marriage, and Marcus because he loved her too much to expose her to the criticism which would inevitably follow.

No one looking at Marcus would ever guess he was deeply in love or how increasingly difficult he was finding it to feign an indifference he was very far from feeling. Not only that but it had become noticeable of late that Sophy too was clearly feeling the strain, and the episode over dinner last night, only one of many instances of Charles's treatment of her, was more than enough for Charlotte to acknowledge to herself that she could not blame Sophy for finding Marcus's company far more agreeable than that of her husband. Charles may not love Sophy but at no time had she ever given him cause to be ashamed of her, much less treat her in a manner which, however painful it was for Charlotte to acknowledge, made her feel quite ashamed that a son of hers could treat his wife so contemptuously. Last night's episode was only one of many occasions when he had spoken to Sophy so harshly, and if he behaved towards her in such a way in front of his family, then it left Charlotte wondering how he dealt with her in private, and she would not have been at all surprised to discover that his anger had not abated when dinner had come to an end.

Sophy's absence from the breakfast table had occasioned comment from no one except Adam, who, in George's considered opinion, was unwise enough to ask, "Not ill, is she?"

Having cooled his temper by visiting his club after dinner, Charles had enjoyed a convivial few hours with some of his friends over several glasses of excellent cognac, which had considerably mellowed him, and by the time he returned home he was certainly feeling a little more generous towards his wife. He would never be in love with her nor would he ever find himself irresistibly drawn to her as he was to Amelia, with whom he could not wait to make love, but, right now, in the fading glow of the bedroom fire, Sophy was by no means undesirable. Her simple but very expensive nightgown having slipped a little way down over her shoulder, exposing the soft silken sheen of her creamy skin, and with her long hair spread invitingly on the pillow, Charles was certainly in the right frame of mind to make love to his wife. The movement of him sliding into bed beside her had the effect of rousing Sophy from the only time she had fallen asleep, and as he watched her eyes drowsily open he actually found himself wanting her more than he could ever remember. She did not resist him, but for some unaccountable reason Sophy's customary submissive response on this occasion rankled more than ever, and when, this morning, he found his kisses being met with her cheek instead of her lips with the news that she had a severe headache, did nothing to improve his mood. So when Adam had asked him about Sophy, which George clearly regarded as disastrous, it had immediately caught Charles on the wrong side, but although his eyes glinted narrowly he said quite smoothly, "Merely a headache, I assure you."

Charlotte, upon discovering that Sophy was still in her room, wisely kept her thoughts to herself, visiting her daughter-in-law immediately after breakfast, carefully refraining from commenting about Charles's annoyance at dinner the previous evening, which she shrewdly suspected had not ended there, or the dark circles under Sophy's eyes, knowing that they had obviously resulted from a sleepless night.

Unable to account for her unguarded words, Sophy had indeed lain awake for some considerable time, her mind going over those careless words and wondering how on earth she could have been stupid enough to say something she should have known would have been better left unsaid, and what her husband had clearly regarded as provocative. She really should have known better! Of course, she acknowledged now that they were provocative no matter how innocently said, but it had made her realise, perhaps for the first time, just how determined Charles actually was in preventing Alexandra from taking possession of her inheritance.

Sophy had not heard him enter their room, but as soon as the bed had depressed under his weight it had instantly roused her from the light sleep she had eventually managed to fall into after being unable to close her eyes for so long, but after what had passed between them earlier in the evening the last thing she had wanted or, indeed, expected, was to find herself being faced with an amorous husband. It had been impossible for her to feign sleep after that, his intention perfectly clear from the moment he had lain down beside her to feel his hand slowly sliding up and down her arm and his lips caressing her exposed shoulder. His lovemaking had certainly been passionate, more so than she could ever recall, and although it was not what she wanted she had allowed him to make love to her, not only because she was fully conscious of her husband's rights but to refuse could so easily have resulted in him losing his temper again and having not long before been on the receiving end of his rapier-sharp tongue she was in no hurry to have a repeat performance. Never had she known him be so aroused and even though she had not resisted him she had seen the annoyance on his face when she had awoken this morning to see his lips seeking hers only to find her cheek instead, his voice dulcetly smooth as he had sardonically apologised for forcing his unwanted attentions upon her yet again, especially as she was not feeling well. Her headache was no excuse, indeed her head throbbed painfully. It was not only because every inch of her body felt bruised but that such passion had come hard on the heels of his loss of temper only hours before had shaken her, and she knew she could not have faced even a mouthful of food let alone take her seat opposite Charles at the table while his mood was still uncertainly balanced.

Sophy had welcomed Charlotte's visit this morning as well as her tactful avoidance of the previous evening's incident. She knew Charlotte would naturally assume that the reason for her not joining the others downstairs for breakfast was because she thought Charles would still be angry with her, and although this was partly true Sophy much preferred this than telling her that her husband's unlooked-for passion last night had totally shaken her. Yesterday evening, during that never to be forgotten episode in the library, she had not only been subjected to the most severest interview yet with Charles but she had seen the ruthless determination on his face, his voice cuttingly sharp as he had made his feelings clear. She knew then that he meant what he said in that he would do everything in his power to prevent Alexandra from receiving a penny of the money Matthew had left her and, as for the jewellery, not one piece of it would ever be hers if he could help it. Sophy had no precise idea how he would set about it, but she was convinced that he would stop at nothing to achieve his aims. Unconsciously echoing Adam's thoughts, it had struck her most forcibly that for some inexplicable reason Charles seemed more concerned over the jewellery than the thirty thousand pounds. Although she had seen some of the jewellery belonging to Jane and Emily, Sophy had never seen Elizabeth's, but from what Charlotte had confided to her, her mother had bequeathed all her jewellery to her three granddaughters; Elizabeth, being the eldest, received the greater part of it, and even though the other pieces were gifts from her father, the whole collection, apart from being quite impressive, was worth a small fortune.

Unfortunately, Elizabeth had not enjoyed their beauty for very long. Matthew, upon discovering his daughter's illicit and disgraceful affair with his stablehand, followed by her ultimatum that she would marry him or no one, had not only disowned her but had, in a fit of uncontrollable rage, made certain that she vacated the house with nothing except the clothes she had stood up in, every exquisite piece of jewellery being denied her. From that moment on they had been locked away in Mercers' vaults; never to see the light of day again – until now!

*

Charles though, knew every item in his sister's collection by heart and exactly how much each piece was worth, and collectively their value was enormous! Until his father had made that disastrous inclusion in his will Elizabeth's jewellery had become a forgotten asset, never spoken of or thought about, not even by his father. It had therefore come as a terrible blow to discover that far from being forgotten they had formed part of that catastrophic bequest, the very last thing he had expected. Whilst it may have crossed his mind that his father might make some provision for her it had never really been anything more than a fleeting thought, unlike George, who was convinced that his father, having taken the trouble to find the girl, would leave her something, but that he should have left her with what was, to all intents and purposes, a forgotten hoard, had been a severe shock. Charles thought he had known his father so well, or at least well enough to say that he would never have left the girl anything, but to learn that this was precisely what he had done as well as knowing of her existence all these years, then deliberately setting plans in motion to find her and without his family's knowledge, had shaken him out of his calm assurance. It was unthinkable that the brat should have anything at all! By making provision for her, his father had not only accepted and acknowledged her but had placed him in an impossible situation; a situation he was presently in no position to do anything about, any more than he had been four years ago when first faced with the problem which, regrettably, had come back to haunt him.

It was unfortunate that a certain married lady who had once enjoyed his interest had not played the game according to the rules, vulgarly demanding an extortionate sum in exchange for some rather revealing letters he had been fool enough to write to her. It really had been a crass mistake to make, especially for one of his amatory experience, and not one he had repeated, but since the lady, or so she had said, was in urgent need of funds for which she could not apply to her husband, those fatal letters, apparently, were her only means of financial salvation – they had been his financial ruin! Unquestionably beautiful and utterly desirable, Charles had indeed spent more than one pleasurable hour in her company and when the affair had ended they had parted on the most amicable of terms, but the lady had undoubtedly known her worth! Five thousand pounds! An extremely high price to pay for having enjoyed her many charms. It had been a devastating blow to find himself faced with such a demand, even though it came wrapped up in the most feminine of packages.

His finances had not been any too healthy at the time and certainly could not have supported such a sum. He had rather hoped that a successful couple of days at the races or, perhaps, a run of luck at the tables would do the trick, but since neither of these precarious sources of income had proved rewarding Charles had been obliged to set his sights in other directions. Unhappily, however, there were no other avenues of escape available to him, and he would rather have died than approach George, who never seemed to be faced with monetary problems, and since applying to his father was equally out of the question, especially as he had not long previously come to his aid, there seemed to be no other option but to visit a money lender. Distasteful though the thought was Charles had swallowed his pride and made the acquaintance of the one and only usurer he had ever met, but apart from taking an instant dislike to the glibly tongued individual on sight the interest he would have been required to pay was extortionate, and consequently he had bid the man a curt good morning, having to rethink another course of action.

Although this was not the first financial crisis he had encountered it was certainly the heaviest, but since he had every hope of solving the problem he did not allow himself to become too despondent, that was until the lady began to press him hard. At first there had been nothing in her scented notes other than the hope he would not fail her, but over the ensuing days each subsequent communication, whilst conveying the embodiment of feminine distress, was noticeably more pressing than the one before until those scented reminders began to delicately stress how urgent her need had become. Charles had read the faintly hinted warning that unless she received the sum agreed upon within the following week she would, regrettably, have no alternative but to put the whole matter before her husband, a circumstance which, she felt sure, he would find as repugnant and embarrassing as she would herself. Too late to regret the insane impulse which had prompted him to write those few letters. It was imperative therefore, that he retrieve them and then destroy them; the cost – a mere five thousand pounds!

All options having been considered, tried or discarded, it had seemed to Charles nothing short of divine intervention when he was suddenly struck with the thought of his sister's jewellery, doing absolutely nothing except gathering dust in Mercers' vaults. The idea, so blindingly audacious, had to be worth a try especially in view of the heavily scented reminder he had received that morning. It had been a relatively easy matter to gain access to Mercers' vaults, after all his father was a highly respected businessman and what could be more natural than one of his sons transacting affairs there? There had been no difficulty in finding a jeweller not only expert enough to copy the pieces he had discreetly removed from his sister's collection but also disreputable enough to carry out the work with no questions asked. For a price Linas Webb could be discretion itself and, for a little extra, he could not only guarantee the finest quality workmanship within a few days but promised to be deaf, dumb and blind into the bargain.

Charles knew perfectly well that the two pieces he had extracted from the vaults of that most renowned bank, a sapphire and diamond bracelet and a ruby and pearl necklace, could not be sold, but copies could be made and replaced without anyone being the wiser. Linas Webb, a great exponent of his art if not the most honest, had had the privilege of providing trinkets for the ladies of his client's acquaintance in the past, and therefore he experienced no qualms in coming to his assistance on this occasion. His lucrative, if somewhat dubious sideline, had earned him a small fortune over the years and although he may look as though he could not rub two pennies together he was in fact a very rich man, thanks in part to more than one client like Charles Harrington who found themselves temporarily in straightened circumstances. The matter was simple! He would copy the pieces, which he would give to Charles plus the five thousand pounds and hold on to the originals until such time that his client found himself in a more affluent position to redeem them. The transaction, conducted along the most gentlemanly lines, suited both parties very well, and Linas Webb, equally as astute as his client's father, knew that if he held those pieces for ten years the interest would more than compensate for the lack of any ethical considerations.

If Charles had held any doubts as to the lady's integrity he soon discovered that he had wronged her. Upon receipt of the money she had immediately handed him the bundle of letters for which he was paying such a high price, their acquaintance permanently severed as soon as those incriminating sheets had been consigned to the flames. It had been as easy to substitute the fake jewellery as it had to remove the originals from their forgotten hideaway, and even though he had every intention of redeeming the bracelet and necklace from Linas Webb, over time they had ceased to become of paramount importance, so much so that they had almost faded from his memory. His father's will, however, had brought them to the forefront of his mind with horrendous clarity! Now, Charles could think of little else.

He knew that Jenkins would have no difficulty in finding the girl; for a man of his ability it would not be too strenuous a task. Charles's own difficulty was preventing his deception of four years ago from being discovered. He was not afraid of being dunned by Linas Webb, that astute individual knowing there was no need to call in the debt as long as he held those pieces of jewellery. Whilst the girl had been non-existent in their lives and the jewellery hidden away, Charles had been perfectly safe, but now he was hovering on the brink of an embarrassing disclosure which he could find no way of averting. With hindsight, it was safe to assume that his father had told the girl of his intention of making provision for her, but he could not be certain just how much he had confided to her. He had seriously toyed with the idea of running the girl to earth himself before Jenkins did but that would mean telling her things he would much rather not, and if he did attempt to buy her off she would almost certainly want to know why, and it was equally certain that she would want far more than he was offering. In either event it would unquestionably lead her to suspecting that he had something to hide and, once she discovered the truth and just how damaging it would be to his reputation, she could so easily bleed him dry! After all, a girl of her sort would hardly think twice about resorting to blackmail!

Whatever his decision it had to be made – and quickly. He could not afford delay. Once Jenkins found the girl and she was put in possession of her inheritance, it would not be long before the bracelet and the necklace were seen to be nothing more than copies. Charles knew perfectly well that whilst they would pass a cursory inspection they would not escape close scrutiny by someone who knew their business, and at the moment he was certainly in no position to redeem them. Useless to expect Linas Webb to hand them over on trust; disreputable he may be but a fool he was not! To make things worse his mother, who had made it quite clear that once the girl was found it was her express intention to keep her with her despite all his efforts to persuade her to the contrary, was not only showing a determination which was as surprising as it was inflexible, but it was rendering his position even more untenable. The last thing Charles wanted was Alexandra residing in Brook Street, not only because she would no doubt take satisfaction from exposing his deception when she discovered that two of the pieces which comprised her mother's jewellery were fakes or, which was more than likely, attempt to blackmail him in return for her silence, but the mere thought of housing a brat from the gutter was too objectionable to contemplate.

The fates were certainly against him at the moment! Something had to be done to stave off disaster; for the life of him though he could not think what. Given time he would doubtless arrive at a solution, but time was not on his side and this knowledge did little to ease his growing frustration and brittle temper. Over the next few days no one, apart from Amelia, escaped his sharp tongue or biting criticism. It seemed that she alone had the power to take the hard look out of his eyes and the severity from around his mouth, easing his irritation into more pleasurable channels.

*

Following his visit to Marcus, Adam, after giving more thought to his brother's inexplicable attitude, had decided against returning home to Yorkshire as planned and wrote a hastily but carefully worded letter to Isabel, deliberately omitting telling her what was in his mind. What this was exactly he could not say. All he knew for certain was that his brother was taking this affair of Alexandra far worse than he had at first suspected, and from what he had seen over the last few days he could not rid himself of the feeling that it went deeper than his pride and also that something more than the contents of his father's will was at the root of Charles's present mood. Adam knew that he would be the last person his brother would confide in, not that he could see him confiding in anyone, but he knew Charles well enough to say that he was more than usually grim. Beneath that smooth veneer Charles had an extremely nasty temper, but whatever the underlying cause responsible for his present mood as well as that dark forbidding look which had descended onto his face, Adam was quite certain that Sophy was carrying the brunt of it. His prolonged visit may be most agreeable to his mother and Sophy, who not only found his company like a breath of fresh air but also extremely enjoyable, but as far as George was concerned the sooner he returned to Yorkshire the better. Charles, who now had far more important things on his mind other than his youngest brother, did not care whether he stayed or went, it had become a matter of complete indifference to him.

It was otherwise with George, who still believed that Adam was a constant source of embarrassment. "I'm damned if I know what keeps you here!" he said peevishly. "I should have thought you would be better employed in looking after things at the brewery, unless of course you are in no hurry to return to Isabel!" He encountered such a look from his brother that it momentarily startled him, especially as Adam was usually so easygoing, stammering, "I'm sorry. I don't... I mean, well... what I meant..."

"I know damn well what you meant!" Adam snapped angrily, taking several hasty steps towards his brother. "But I would strongly advise you to keep your mouth shut in future."

"Yes, of course! I just..." George apologised quickly, not liking the look in his brother's eyes. "I simply thought..."

"Then don't," Adam said curtly, adding, "I shall stay here for as long as it suits me, and if you so much as hint at anything about Isabel I'll make you sorry you ever opened your mouth."

"You're very quick to take one up!" George exclaimed, looking extremely hot. "I merely wondered if you were considering seeing..."

"Let me remind you," Adam said firmly, knowing precisely what was in George's mind, "that my affair with Lily Southam ended the moment I met Isabel. I have no intention of resuming it, and my decision to remain in town for a few more days has nothing whatsoever to do with her – or with you for that matter."

George, who was still finding it difficult to believe that Marsden had not only received Adam but had actually agreed to such a fait accompli, remembered Lily Southam very well; a dark-eyed brunette who had captivated his brother from the moment he first saw her on stage at the Theatre Royal, and found it incredible that such a warm-hearted creature could have been so quickly supplanted in his brother's affections by Isabel Marsden. Isabel was pretty enough, but nothing remarkable when compared with Lily. He had been impressed with her himself, such an exciting armful and one no right-minded man would surely even consider turning away, especially for someone, in George's opinion at least, as unexciting as Isabel Marsden. Of course, Lily and her kind were not the sort of women one would introduce to the family, even so, she could certainly help pass the time, but to exchange her welcoming arms for those of one whom he would have thought would hold no appeal for his adventurous youngest brother was something he did not understand.

Something of this nature was on the tip of his tongue, but his brother, who shrewdly guessed what he was about to say, forestalled him. "Marsden may be an irascible old cuss but there's nothing wrong with his daughter or her pedigree. Of course I enjoyed Lily's company," Adam pointed out irritably, "what man wouldn't? But you know as well as I do that the Lily Southams of this world are ten a penny and not the kind a man marries, and I tell you now that the only regret I have is that I did not meet Isabel sooner!"

This speech not unnaturally silenced George, and Adam, who had previously regarded Charles's contempt of him as being rather harsh, unexpectedly found himself more in sympathy with him that he would ever have thought possible. George's tendency for pompous sermonising was something Adam had never really taken much notice of before, but since he had been back home, albeit for only a few days, it had struck him most forcibly, and although he would never deliberately hurt or offend anyone, it was fast becoming clear to Adam that nothing short of an insult would stop his brother.

Amelia's unexpected entrance at such a moment was looked upon as extremely timely by her husband who had realised too late that he had not only spoken out of turn but had virtually charged his brother with something which was not only untrue but had nothing whatsoever to do with him. After all, Adam was not a child! Amelia of course, knew immediately what she had interrupted, but not by a word or look did she betray this or her irritation, merely bestowing her glowing smile upon them. "I hope I am not intruding?"

"Not at all," Adam returned stiffly before George could speak. "I was just on the point of leaving anyway."

Amelia had had only one purpose in mind when she had gone in search of her husband, which was to discover when he intended bringing the boys back from their uncle's home in Norfolk where they had been staying during Matthew's illness, their visit being hastily extended until after the funeral. Amelia's brother had kindly suggested the boys go to him, considering it would be far better than being in Brook Street while things were so unsettled. She had found nothing to object to in this but had genuinely been sorry to see them go; for all her faults, she truly loved her two sons, but now it was all over she wanted them with her again and as George had remarked the other night it was time they were back in their own home, and unless anything arose to prevent it he aimed to see his brother-in-law this weekend and return with the children. She knew very well that George would be away for the better part of the week as he not only got along extremely well with Giles but very much appreciated his well-stocked cellar; besides, it would give her and Charles a little time together.

Amelia, who was always exquisitely coiffured and immaculately dressed, unlike Sophy, had no objection whatsoever to wearing black; it became her beautifully, and the expensive creation she was now wearing, and which she had chosen with great care, was certainly worth every penny she fully expected George to pay. As she wanted him out of the way as soon as possible she knew she would have to exercise great tact if she wanted to urge him to go this weekend as he had suggested without arousing his suspicions that she was eager to be rid of him and was, therefore, determined to show him her most mellow mood. "What did you say to him?" she asked gently as soon as the drawing room door had closed behind Adam, briefly adjusting the broach at her throat in the mirror.

"Why should I have said anything?" George demanded irritably, his colour a little high at her accusation.

"Because you usually do," Amelia chided gently, casting him a sidelong glance, admirably concealing her contempt.

"I suppose you would prefer it if I said nothing at all!" George said tetchily.

"No," Amelia shook her head, her blonde curls catching the light, "but I do think that you may pause and consider a little before you speak," adding smoothly, "you do have a tendency to say things which would perhaps be better left unsaid."

"I said nothing amiss," George defended himself uncomfortably.

"Then why did Adam's face look like thunder just now?" Amelia enquired.

"How the devil should I know?" George exclaimed impatiently. "It seems to me that no one in this house can bear to have anything said to them."

"So, you *did* say something to him," Amelia smiled knowingly, throwing him an arch look.

"All I did," George told her irritably, "was to ask him why he was in no hurry to return to Yorkshire, and if the reason for him extending his stay here was because he was hoping to renew his acquaintance with a certain young woman who took his fancy before he..." George stopped, his colour rising as he realised what he had been about to say.

Amelia knew all about her brother-in-law's little fling with that dancing girl, and although it did not take much imagination to know the kind of woman she was, Amelia knew that no man liked to have his past affairs thrown at him, but that her husband should have been tactless enough to mention her, surprised even her. *"Now* I understand," she nodded, turning round to face him. "No wonder Adam was furious!"

"What do you understand?" George asked sharply, watching her closely.

"You know, George," Amelia mused, determined to keep her temper, her fingers smoothing down the lapels of his coat, "I am surprised that even *you* could have been insensitive enough as to touch upon a subject which is not only past history but one Adam plainly wishes forgotten."

As his wife seldom spoke to him in so soft a voice or troubled herself over his appearance George was considerably surprised by this unexpected show of solicitude, which had the immediate effect of smoothing his ruffled feathers at her accusation. "And what do you know about it?" he asked in a more mollified tone than he otherwise would have, his bemused brain just a little confused as he looked down into his wife's wide blue eyes which for once held no contempt, her full sensuous lips parted in a rather provocative smile which he had not seen for some time and which was having the most mellowing effect upon him.

"The exploits of this family," Amelia told him smoothly, "are hardly conducted with discretion."

"You don't have to tell *me* that," George told her regrettably. "It seems to me that no member of this family can do anything without advertising it to the whole world!"

"I know," Amelia soothed, her fingers beginning to work on his cravat, "but you have nothing to reproach yourself for, any more than you can hold yourself responsible for what they may choose to do, which is why," she said cleverly, "you deserve this visit to see my brother, and the boys will be delighted. You know they will, and I so want them home again."

George, confronted by this unexpected change in his wife's attitude, blinked in surprise, which was hardly surprising; it had been a very long time since she had behaved towards him in this way. In fact, if memory served him correctly he could not bring to mind, even in the early days of their marriage, an occasion when she had ever deliberately enticed him as she was now doing and, for a brief moment, he wondered if she was playing some kind of game. But the look in her eyes did not suggest this, and unless he was very much mistaken he could almost believe she was actually enjoying his company.

"Please, George," Amelia begged, "won't you bring my boys home? I miss them terribly."

As George had not been prepared for this feminine attack on his defences, the gentle touch of her fingers on his cheek had an immediate weakening effect on him, so much so that he was moved to clasp her hand, feverishly kissing its soft palm. "Come with me then," he suggested, his eyes suddenly burning.

Amelia had known what to expect and was therefore fully prepared for it, saying easily, "You know I cannot. I want to have everything ready for them when they come home. Besides, I think I ought to spend a little time with your mother; I have sadly left too much on Sophy's shoulders. Anyway," she smiled archly, "you wouldn't even know I was there once you and Giles started talking and sampling his cellar; I should be consigned to the devil!"

At any other time George would have stared at this, never having known his wife consider anyone but herself, but, right now, his thoughts were solely concentrated on the beautiful face smiling up at him, his reaction to her initial allegation completely forgotten. *"Never!"* he exclaimed, his heart beginning to race, unable to believe his good fortune. Amelia was certainly at her most charming, and unless he had misread the signs she was definitely in a receptive mood.

"You say that," Amelia shook her head playfully, "but you know it is true."

To her relief George released the tight grip on the hand he had been holding but unfortunately it was only short-lived, her husband considerably startling her when he suddenly grabbed her in his arms and pulled her roughly against him. This unwanted display of desire had not formed part of her calculations, but even though she could not bear him to touch her she was far too clever a woman to repulse him outright. Amelia may love Charles with every fibre of her being but she was astute enough to know that a husband was a far more valuable asset than a lover, no matter how much pleasure and excitement he gave one. Besides, if she wanted to spend time with Charles over the coming weekend she had to get George out of the way, and if this meant humouring him for a few minutes she was quite prepared to do so.

Suddenly, all George's suspicions about his wife and brother seemed absurd. No woman, surely, could look at her husband as Amelia was now doing if she was in love with another man? It had been a long time since he had made love to his wife, not that he had not wanted to, but she had been rather elusive recently; if it was not a headache or the boys demanding her attention it was something equally as preventive, but right now he wanted nothing more than to take her to bed and make love to her. He had not experienced this urgent need for some time, although she had hardly been in the mood to receive his advances!

Amelia knew in which direction George's thoughts were going and tried her best to humour him out of his increasingly growing desire, even by laughingly remarking that it was only five o'clock in the afternoon, but his escalating arousal accompanied by an enforced abstinence fused into a powerful combination which was acting upon him like a flame to gunpowder, and as he held her in his arms such a minor consideration as the time of day never entered his head.

"Please, George!" Amelia begged, ineffectually trying to struggle out of his arms. "Someone may come in."

"There's no fear of that," George told her thickly between kisses. "Mamma and Sophy have gone to visit Jane, Charles is at the brewery and Adam has now left to keep an engagement with Stillington," adding in a deep voice, "so, you see, my dear, we are quite alone."

It was a pity Emily and Edward had returned to their own home only this morning as Amelia actually found herself wishing they were still here because with every kiss George's desire was growing and she began to wonder whether even her powers of persuasion would be enough to stop his amorous onslaught. Instead of cooling his passion her efforts to break free only seemed to arouse him more, but when his hands began roaming her body, having released her from his suffocating embrace, she made a further attempt to escape him which, unfortunately, only served to heighten his excitement.

"George, please!" she begged, disliking the way he was pawing her. "You know we cannot."

"Why?" he demanded thickly. "I want you; it has been an age since we have been together like this, and you are my wife. What could be more natural than wanting to make love to you?"

It was obvious he was not going to be put off so easily, chiding herself for allowing things to get this far, but unless she wanted to arouse his suspicions she had to tread very carefully, saying, with as much briskness as she could, "Really, George! We are surely past the age of stealing kisses!"

"I don't just want your kisses," George told her hoarsely, "I want all of you, and it won't be stealing."

Before Amelia realised what George intended he took hold of her hand, giving her no opportunity to slip away, guiding her out of the drawing room towards the stairs, leaving her with little choice but to follow him, her mind frantically searching for a way of escape, realising too late that it was her own actions which had incited this desire in her husband. She had no one to blame but herself for this unexpected turn of events, never dreaming George would have reacted in a way she neither wanted nor was in the least kind of mood for.

Despite his moralising, George was a very passionate man whose ardour, unfortunately, was far greater than his expertise, but like Sophy, Amelia was fully aware that to deny a husband certain rights could be a very dangerous thing indeed. She knew without any doubt that her husband had no feminine interest tucked discreetly away and this being so, his emotions at the moment were extremely highly charged. His desire was such that it would take nothing short of a miracle to prevent him from making love to her. Distasteful though the thought was, she was practical enough to realise that if this was the price she had to pay for spending time with Charles, then it would be well worth it! George had never aroused her, but unlike her sister-in-law Amelia was an excellent actress and knew precisely how to make her husband believe that she was enjoying the experience as much as he was. She had become accustomed to George's fumbling attempts at lovemaking and even though her flesh crawled at his touch she was adept enough to hide her feelings, such as now when his eyes and lips were hungrily devouring her, his thick clumsy fingers tearing off her clothes in his impatience, her mind and body silently crying out for the man she loved as her husband's slack lips spluttered wet kisses on her soft skin, his heavy body hot and repellent as he pressed it against her.

How very different it was with Charles, who instinctively knew every vulnerable spot as well as knowing precisely how to arouse her ardent and eager responses to his lovemaking! George had no such knowledge. He did not aim to please her so much as himself, concerned only with his own gratification and repletion, and when he eventually moved away from her to his own side of the bed, satisfied and fulfilled, she had to fight down the tears welling up at the back of her eyes. For the first time Amelia actually found herself sparing a thought for Sophy; after all, it was no pleasant thing to have to make love to a man you had no feelings for, even though he was your husband! If Sophy's love for Marcus was anything like her own for Charles, then Amelia could well understand why her sister-in-law was not happy in her marriage, but as she turned her head to glance at her husband she knew, had known in fact from the very first moment she had met Charles, that were it at all possible she would willingly exchange George for his brother!

Amelia was neither fulfilled by George's lovemaking nor fired with the desire to repeat it, and when, sometime later, she entered the drawing room on her husband's arm no one looking at her would ever have guessed that she had spent the better part of the last two hours in his arms. It had not been enough for him to subject her to his passion once only, she had unfortunately to endure it a second time. George, on the other hand, was in an extremely buoyant mood, so much so that not even Charles's sharp tongue had the power to deflate his near state of euphoria.

*

Having spent most of the day at the brewery followed by a fruitless hour-long interview with Linas Webb, Charles was in no mood for his brother, or anyone else for that matter. Linas Webb had been politeness itself, in fact he had fully sympathised with his client's dilemma, but after all he was only a poor businessman, and therefore without the full redeeming sum plus the interest being handed over to him he could not allow those precious gems out of his possession. Charles's strenuous arguments had been received with complete understanding, indeed, Linas Webb had genuinely felt for him in his predicament, but he could only repeat that under the circumstances his hands were tied. Over his long career he had naturally dealt with more than one client in straitened circumstances, but never had any one of them looked at him as though it would have given them the greatest satisfaction to take him by the throat and throttle him. It had been with considerable difficulty that Charles had managed to master this overwhelming impulse, in fact, it was close on a full minute before he could control himself sufficiently to bid his last hope a terse good evening.

Where he went from here he was not quite certain, but it did not lighten his mood when, upon the following morning, he entered the dining room just as his mother was reading out to Sophy the contents of a letter which she had received only minutes before from Silas Jenkins. Charles's eyebrows snapped together and his lips compressed into a thin forbidding line, but even though his mother immediately folded the letter and put it into the pocket of her skirt upon catching sight of him, he had heard enough to know that every effort was being made to find the girl, and that Jenkins hoped to be in the position to relate good news within the next few days. Even though Charlotte knew Charles's feelings on the matter very well it did not entirely explain the dark, almost brooding look in his eyes or the severity of his expression and decided that now was not the right moment to either comment upon the letter or ask him any questions. He may not have remarked upon it but Sophy knew from the look on his face that he was far from pleased, the glance he cast at her doing very little if anything to improve her appetite. She watched him turn away from her to make his selection from the numerous serving dishes on the sideboard in ominous silence, an uncomfortable lump suddenly forming in her throat, but upon his return to the table followed by a dulcetly smooth, "Sophy, my dear, I wonder if you would spare me a moment after breakfast," her stomach lurched in apprehension, bracing herself for the inevitable.

Sophy had certainly expected a none too pleasant interview with Charles, but she had certainly not expected him to angrily demand an explanation as to why, having made his views clear on more than one occasion, she continually disregarded him by encouraging his mother in a course of action which she knew he thoroughly disapproved of! Taken a little aback by this scathing attack, her somewhat apprehensive response, being all Sophy could manage, in that such had not been her intention, was acerbically dismissed with the warning that, unless his memory erred, he felt sure he had cautioned her before about interfering in what did not concern her and, he trusted, this would be the last occasion he would have cause to remind her. Not until she heard the front door close behind Charles, signalling he had left the house to go to the brewery, did she make any attempt to leave the library, but instead of joining her mother-in-law in the sitting room Sophy made her way upstairs until she had recovered her composure sufficiently to avoid questions being asked if something was amiss.

As Adam had correctly guessed, Sophy was certainly taking the brunt of Charles's temper; never had she known him be so severe in his dealings with her, and whilst she knew better than to ask him questions she suspected that something other than his mother's desire to have her granddaughter stay with her and the startling contents of his father's will, was at the root of his dark mood. Never had she longed for Marcus so much as she did now, just knowing he was here, even for only a short while, made her feel not quite so alone and isolated. To see his tall, broad-shouldered figure and to feel his quiet strength filled her with a reassurance she badly needed, and although he had called twice since the day of Matthew's funeral she had unfortunately missed him on both occasions, and therefore she had not seen him since then when, regrettably, apart from a few parting words, there had been no real opportunity to speak to him.

There may be no future for her and Marcus but that did not prevent her from imagining how good it would be to spend the rest of her life with him any more than it put an end to those wonderfully warm stirrings in the pit of her stomach whenever she thought of him. Sophy had never believed herself capable of feeling such intense emotions, but she only had to bring to mind the times when Marcus had kissed her hand to feel again the delicious tingling which coursed through her at the soft touch of his lips on her skin, or the way her heart somersaulted at the warmth in his eyes whenever he looked at her, to know that she was indeed capable of such responsiveness, as well as aching with the need to explore such alien but wonderful sensations further. Try as she did she could not still the breathtaking upheaval he had awakened inside her, the force of it shocking and exciting her at the same time, and it therefore took every ounce of will-power she possessed to hold back the despairing tears when she considered that these brief intimacies were all she would ever have to carry her through the rest of her life.

Marcus, who was as moved by Sophy as she was by him, was himself beginning to believe that these fleeting demonstrations which passed between them were all they would ever share. He wanted nothing more than to be allowed to love her, to show her that what she was feeling was nothing to what he could make her feel, but he was realistic enough to know that unless a miracle occurred it would never be. Her marriage may be far from happy, but however harshly Charles treated her he was her husband, which gave him rights he himself did not possess, and although it tore Marcus apart to know that the woman he loved was subjected to such treatment, as matters stood he was powerless to do anything about a situation to which he could find no solution. Whilst Sophy was married to his cousin his hands were tied, and frustrating though it was to have to stand on the sidelines, intensifying his feelings of impotence in being unable to shield her from Charles's callous treatment, unless his cousin consented to a divorce, which Marcus knew full well he would never do, he could see no end in sight to the emotional torment they were both suffering. If his visits to Brook Street to see his aunt only ensured him a short time in the company of one who had for long been an indispensable part of his life and without whom he could not envisage his future, then he would rather that than not see Sophy at all, the very thought of which being more than he could bear.

Even though Marcus realised it would not do to let it be seen she meant more to him than life itself or that he was haunting the house just to be with her for a little while, he had nonetheless fully intended to pay his aunt a visit within a day or two of Matthew's funeral, but due to the accounts he had received from his Uncle Lionel taking longer to deal with than he had thought, it had not been possible. However, as a result of Adam's visit and what he had confided, Marcus had readily set these aside and visited Brook

Street the next day, but although he was relieved to be informed by his aunt, in response to his broad enquiry, that whilst Alexandra was still the main topic of her family's conversation nothing untoward had occurred, he was nevertheless only just able to conceal his disappointment when told that Sophy had taken the opportunity to visit her widowed mother who shared her luxurious seclusion in the expensive Mayfair home with her unmarried daughter. However, he was pleased to learn from his aunt that according to the letter she had received from Silas Jenkins he was putting forward every effort into finding Alexandra. Marcus had not known whether to be glad or sorry to learn that Sophy was again not at home when he called the following day, having accompanied her sister on an errand for their mamma.

He was disappointed not to have seen Sophy, but before he called in Brook Street again there was his luncheon engagement with Oswald Mercer. They may not have seen one another for some years, but it had been an easy matter to invite his old friend to luncheon at his club on the pretext of seeking financial advice and talking over old times. Oswald Mercer was as cheerful as he was generous and greeted his old friend with genuine pleasure. The last time they had met had been before Marcus had left with his regiment for India nearly six years ago, but he noted that during his absence from England his friend had altered hardly at all.

Oswald Mercer was the same height as Marcus, but rather lanky, giving the impression that he was taller than he actually was. He had a slightly sallow complexion and light brown hair, now beginning to thin on top, brushed back from a high forehead, emphasising his rather prominent nose and bony chin, making him look older than he really was. He had narrow, slightly stooping shoulders which did little justice to the black frock coat he wore, giving the impression that it was by far too large for him, as was his shirt, the butterfly collar swamping his neck, but he seemed as unconcerned over these irrelevancies as he was in knowing that his unprepossessing features could never be regarded as handsome. Only his pale grey eyes caught the attention, smiling humorously upon the world with an innocence Marcus knew perfectly well hid an astuteness no one would ever have realised he possessed.

Marcus, who had long been a member of the exclusive Military Club situated in Shepherd Market in Piccadilly, only seldom took advantage of its amenities. Within its elegant portals members could not only be assured of a quiet haven from the humdrum of everyday life but also an excellent luncheon. It was over one of these gastronomic feasts that the two friends sat and talked, regaling one another with what they had been doing since they had last met, but it was not long before they were indulging themselves in reminiscences over their carefree days at Oxford and the friends they had known, laughing over incidents which had been long forgotten. Not until they had settled themselves into two comfortable armchairs by a roaring fire with their glasses of brandy in the smoking room, did Oswald refer to the reason for their get-together.

"Filthy habit!" Oswald grinned, watching the smoke from his cigar curl up into a thick cloud. "You were right not to adopt the habit when I tried to coax you into it at Oxford," he nodded wisely. "So," he mused, looking searchingly at the calm face opposite, "to what do I really owe this luncheon? Not that I'm not pleased to see you, of course," he said affably, "but whilst I admit that talking over old times has been most enjoyable, I find it hard to believe that you of all people stand in need of advice!"

Trust Oswald! He always had been far brighter than he looked! If at first Oswald was a little surprised to find himself being asked to offer advice to a man who, like his father, had always banked with Boultons, the fabricated tale which fell off Marcus's tongue was sufficient to fool his friend, but whilst Marcus may deprecate the deception he was playing on him it was nevertheless very necessary. He knew that whatever suspicions he held about Charles it would be quite wrong of him to voice them, even to Oswald. Nothing could be more fatal than to let it be seen that he was questioning his cousin's integrity, and should his doubts be proved wrong it would certainly open him up to the well-deserved criticism he would receive.

Trying to forge the right kind of opening about Elizabeth's jewellery had teased Marcus's mind throughout luncheon, after all he could not just come out and tell Oswald that this reunion was purely to ask him if he thought it was possible for Charles to simply walk into Mercers and take them or merely remove one or two pieces without anyone being the wiser, so it was therefore with a sigh of relief when Oswald provided it for him.

"Naturally," Oswald smiled, "I will assist in any way I can, after all m'father's always pleased to welcome new business, and since your uncle was a most valued client I have no doubt at all he will welcome you with open arms. The only snag of course," he pointed out fairly, "is that Boultons will be far from pleased to lose you to us."

"I've no doubt," Marcus nodded, taking a sip of brandy, "but as I said, I'm just turning things over in my mind at present."

"Of course," Oswald acknowledged, "but think it over anyway and let me know what you decide. We'll be pleased to help. By the way," he offered, "I was sorry to hear about Matthew. I know I should have mentioned it sooner," he grimaced, "but with one thing and another it slipped my mind."

Marcus dismissed the oversight and Oswald, grateful to his friend for overlooking this social solecism, said tentatively, "I… er… I take it you know of your uncle's bequest to his granddaughter?"

No one looking at Marcus would ever have guessed the relief he felt at hearing these words, his calm expression raising no suspicions in Oswald's mind. "I was aware of it," he nodded.

"Well, as you know," Oswald explained, "your uncle appointed us as his executors, but when we saw the changes he had planned I don't mind telling you that the girl came as quite a shock. Of course," he shrugged, "I knew something had happened way back in the dim and distant past concerning his daughter," inhaling on his cigar, "but according to m'father the whole thing was hushed up pretty quick, but I never knew anything about the girl any more than he did."

Marcus refrained from telling him about his own prior knowledge of her, merely giving him a brief outline of what had occurred on the day she visited Brook Street. "My uncle never talked about Elizabeth and strictly forbid his family to even mention her name," he pointed out, "so it was hardly surprising he kept his granddaughter a secret."

"God!" Oswald suddenly exclaimed, an irrepressible twinkle lighting his eyes. "Can you imagine the shock when they heard that Matthew had included her in his will? I'd have given a monkey to have seen them!"

"You wouldn't have been disappointed," Marcus told him.

"Don't tell me you were there!" Oswald exclaimed, unable to hide his surprise, signalling the waiter hovering discreetly in the background.

"Yes," Marcus nodded. "As I had no expectations from it and neither wanted a mention nor looked for one, I had no intention of sitting in at the reading, but unfortunately George considered my presence indispensable."

"What the devil for?" Oswald demanded.

"Your guess is as good as mine," Marcus shrugged, declining the offer of another brandy. "He told me that he thought my aunt would like it."

"And how did he take it?" Oswald enquired.

"As you would expect," Marcus nodded.

"Tell me something," Oswald asked confidentially, leaning forward a little, "does George always prose on about things?"

"Always," Marcus confirmed, unable to suppress a smile.

"I thought so," Oswald sighed. "He's the same whenever he comes into the bank. A most irritating man! He can set your back up quicker than anyone I know!"

"Yes, he can," Marcus agreed, pausing only to raise an acknowledging hand to a passing acquaintance. "I really don't think he can help it."

"I daresay. Mind you," Oswald pointed out fairly, "irritating or not, I'd rather deal with him than Charles. I know he's your cousin," he acknowledged, "and I've no wish to upset you, but he's a damned nasty piece of work if ever I saw one, I can tell you," he told him with feeling, "and I don't mind admitting, I'd hate to cross him; that's certain!"

"He can be a little off-putting," Marcus said circumspectly.

"Off-putting!" Oswald echoed. "You know, Marcus," he remarked candidly, pointing his glass at him, "you're either a master of understatement or you know nothing about it!" Pausing only to inhale on his cigar, he continued, "Well, whatever he is, I can tell you this; from what I've ever seen of your precious cousin Charles, he's not likely to want to relinquish anything to the girl, and certainly not the jewellery!"

Taking the opportunity offered, Marcus remarked casually, "It's quite a collection, and I believe worth a small fortune."

"It's a magnificent collection!" Oswald told him seriously. "And you are right in saying it's worth a small fortune; why, the one bracelet alone is worth at least three thousand! Someone in your aunt's family certainly knew about precious stones," he nodded, "because I've never laid eyes on anything quite like them."

Calmly swirling the remains of the amber liquid in his glass Marcus's mind was racing ahead, but the unperturbed look in his dark brown eyes gave nothing away. "I saw them once, you know."

"Really!" Oswald sounded surprised.

"Mm," Marcus nodded.

"You don't mean you actually saw them at the bank?" Oswald asked, surprised.

Marcus shook his head. "No, it was before they were handed over to you; Elizabeth showed them to me one day."

"They should of course be adorning some beautiful woman," Oswald commented, "not languishing in our vaults!" Marcus nodded and Oswald asked, "This granddaughter of Matthew's, is she beautiful?"

"I think I can safely say that given the opportunity Alexandra could be very beautiful," Marcus told him truthfully.

Oswald did not pretend to misunderstand him. "Had it pretty rough, has she?"

"Unnecessarily so!" Marcus confirmed firmly.

"Well," Oswald was pleased to tell him, "when Jenkins finds her and we are satisfied with her credentials, we shall be pleased to do all we can for her. Of course," he remarked, "she would be well advised to leave the jewellery with us for safe keeping. My father I know," he nodded, "will recommend she does."

"I know I can rely on you to deal sensitively with her," Marcus stated simply. "She may have had to endure deprivation, but she is extremely proud."

"As one would expect of Matthew's granddaughter!" Oswald commented. "Don't worry, Marcus," he assured him, "we will take great care of her."

"Thank you. I knew I could rely on you," Marcus nodded, ordering another brandy for his friend.

"You know, Marcus," Oswald mused, "what beats me is what made your uncle decide to leave her anything! I'd nothing against him, mind," he shrugged, "but knowing him as I did I can't for the life of me fathom it out."

"I am afraid my uncle's reasons for doing anything were very much his own," Marcus assured him. "The important thing," he nodded, "is that he did, whatever the reason."

Waiting only until the waiter had deposited his brandy onto the table beside him followed by taking a moment to swallow some of the amber liquid, Oswald, who had suddenly been struck with an idea, exclaimed, "I've been thinking, would you care to see your cousin's jewellery?"

Marcus's expression was one of complete surprise. "Well, yes," he nodded, his faith in Oswald's taste for brandy not misplaced. "Would that be possible, do you think?"

"Nothing easier," Oswald shrugged.

Marcus may have considered Charles's attitude towards Alexandra and her inheritance as being rather extreme, but it was not until Adam had put forward his doubts that his own increased. From his aunt, Marcus had learned of Matthew's growing impatience over Charles's expensive lifestyle and, repugnant though the thought was, he had, over the last few days, wondered if his cousin had been stupid enough to sell some of the jewellery as Adam had almost suggested. Marcus could of course be doing Charles a great disservice but try as he did he could think of nothing else which explained his cousin's hard line. He knew it would be a fairly easy matter for Charles to gain access to them, after all Matthew was his father and no suspicions would be aroused.

It had been a long time since Marcus had seen Elizabeth's jewellery and therefore he would not be able to say for certain if any of the pieces had been removed and replaced with copies, but whilst he disliked treating Oswald so shabbily, it was nevertheless very necessary, and accepted his friend's invitation without showing too much eagerness.

"Very well," Oswald nodded, surprising Marcus by saying, "if it's alright with you, how does right now suit? That is," he cocked his head, "if you have no further engagements this afternoon. I know m'father will have no objection to you seeing them."

It suited Marcus very well and, after assuring his friend that he had no further engagements, Oswald tossed off the remainder of his brandy, whereupon they strolled out of the club to hail a hackney to take them to Cornhill.

Chapter Eight

When Silas Jenkins had offered his services, he had known that his self-appointed task was not going to be easy. Nevertheless, he had every confidence in the ability and discretion of his clerks to carry out the search for his late client's granddaughter successfully. This genuine belief had prompted him to write that letter to Charlotte, never for one moment thinking that after almost two weeks of intense effort they had found no trace of her.

Whatever sympathy he may have towards Matthew's family, his duty was clear! Alexandra must be found and informed of her inheritance, and if it took him a whole lifetime he was determined to seek her out. He could not believe it to be possible that one young girl could, to all and intents purposes, completely disappear, even in such a large city as London, and pride as well as professional integrity spurred him on. However, over the ensuing days frustration soon began to border on despair when no news came of her; but he had by no means given up hope. Despite a thorough search of Matthew's papers there had been nothing amongst them to give any indication as to Alexandra's whereabouts or anything relating to the private detective he had hired, which was a pity because if only Jenkins could locate this man then the search would be over.

In view of George's angry and suspicious accusations and Charles's antagonism, whatever hopes Silas Jenkins may originally have had about either of them passing any information onto him should they come across anything, soon died a death. Nevertheless, he was not a man to give up easily and certainly not until every avenue had been explored, but as the days relentlessly dragged by without any news of Alexandra it was becoming increasingly obvious that if she was to be informed of her grandfather's bequest his only option, however distasteful, seemed to be inserting an advertisement of some kind in the newspapers. He had initially toyed with the idea of appealing directly to the girl herself but no sooner had he considered this than it was immediately discarded. In view of what he had learned about her precipitate flight from Brook Street it was enough to convince him that there would be very little likelihood of her responding to his plea. The only way forward as far as he could see was to appeal instead to the man who had originally located her.

Although this seemed at first to be the answer to his difficulties it soon raised the question as to which newspaper this unknown individual would be likely to read, but as no more time could be wasted on this matter he elected to place his advertisement in a number of popular editions, concluding that this man, whoever he was, must take one of them at least. Naturally, it would have to be very carefully worded; his late client's family, who would be far better off not knowing anything about it, could certainly be relied upon to take an exception to having their affairs made public knowledge. Even so, he could find no other alternative and immediately set about preparing a notice which would be suitable to all parties concerned, little realising that it would take considerably longer to compose an appropriate message than he had thought, but when he eventually read the final draft, neatly written on a sheet of white vellum, he was more than pleased with his efforts.

*

Ted Knowles, reading the advertisement the day after it had been published, had no difficulty in interpreting its meaning; the very words, *'Will the gentleman who recently had occasion to speak with a lady bearing the initials AD on behalf of a mutual client bearing the initials MH, please apply to the editor for contact details and respond to the writer as soon as possible'* were more than enough to inform him that it related to himself and Matthew Harrington's granddaughter.

Ted Knowles had of course learned of his late client's demise, after all the death of such a wealthy and successful man like Matthew Carey Harrington could not be expected to escape the notice of the newspapers. Although Ted Knowles had been amply rewarded for his services he was not the man to let opportunity slip through his fingers, and unless he was very much mistaken, which he doubted, he smelled further financial gain in the offing. Matthew Harrington had not taken him into his confidence as to why he was seeking his granddaughter, but Ted Knowles was astute enough to realise that for a man of Matthew Harrington's volatile temperament and rigid standards of behaviour it must have been for a pretty important reason, and the only possible reason as far as Ted Knowles could see was that he had most probably made provision for her in his will. The advertisement proved that surely!

This of course could take many forms, but the seed which had taken root in his fertile brain suggested that this was the most logical explanation. If this was indeed the case, which seemed likely, then it would go a long way to explaining the situation. Servants, no matter how highly one regarded them, talked. Temptation came in all shapes and sizes and few of them would turn down a handsome largesse for passing on a juicy piece of gossip for certain interested parties or miss the opportunity to impress their cronies over a pint. Small snippets of gossip spread and grew, and as these seemingly harmless utterances formed part of Ted Knowles's stock-in-trade his ear always remained very close to the ground and his mouth firmly shut.

Naturally, he had heard about Elizabeth Harrington from a most reliable source, but even though he had discounted half of it the fact remained there was never any smoke without fire, and in his own inimitable way he had questioned and ferreted around, slowly putting little pieces together until the picture became clear, storing it away until such time when it could prove useful. Such as now! He had seen enough of Alexandra to know that she was more than a chip off the old block, and her resentment at being summarily ordered to visit her grandfather still made him blink in surprise. Her condemnation had been brief and scathingly to the point, making him believe that he could have actually been talking to her grandfather himself. Whatever his own thoughts may have been about her obviously straitened circumstances when compared to the luxurious comfort he had seen in Brook Street he had kept to himself, but there had been no mistaking that streak of pride or the cold disdain he had seen in her eyes. In fact, far from receiving his news with open arms she had been furiously angry, as though he personally were responsible and not her grandfather.

Ted Knowles had no way of knowing for certain if she had ever complied with her grandfather's request, but human nature being what it was he shrewdly suspected that she had, from curiosity if nothing else, and if, as he again suspected, the old codger had left her something, then his services could still come in very useful. Why else would that advertisement have been inserted in the newspaper? He had seen enough of Matthew Harrington to be quite certain that finding his granddaughter had been out of necessity rather than love, which would explain why the transaction had been conducted in the utmost secrecy, his late client forcefully stressing that no one must know of his visit to Brook Street or the commission he had been given. It was therefore safe to assume that the family had been, and perhaps still were, in complete ignorance of her existence, in which case they would be far from eager to welcome her into the fold never mind letting her take possession of whatever it was Matthew Harrington had most probably left her. If Ted Knowles's calculations were correct, then from what he had seen of the girl he would not put it past her to sling her grandfather's generosity back in his face; and no doubt enjoy doing it too. If this was in fact what happened, then he could well imagine the outcome of such a meeting, and from his experience of both parties concerned he did not think that it would have been a very amicable one.

Of course, all of this was mere conjecture. He could be barking up the wrong tree entirely, but somehow he did not think so. If Matthew Harrington's solicitor had found it necessary to get in touch with him, albeit via the agency of the press, it not only meant that they had no knowledge of the girl's whereabouts but that it was imperative she was found. Ted Knowles had worked for well-breeched swells too often to be under any illusion as to the way their minds worked, and Matthew Harrington, despite his working-class roots, had been very much in the mould. Oh yes! Ted Knowles knew the type well enough! Proud, haughty and totally unforgiving! Why else would a man undertake a surreptitious search for his granddaughter and without his solicitor's knowledge or that of his family if circumstances had been different? Unless he missed his mark, and he was certain he hadn't, then the author of that advertisement would be more than willing to pay for the information he was only too willing to sell.

When Silas Jenkins had inserted that advertisement, he had no way of knowing how long he would have to wait for the private detective Matthew Harrington had hired to get in touch with him, but he had certainly not expected to receive a visit from him within two days of its insertion. As he looked at the card handed him by his clerk with its florid legend he was conscious of a feeling of caution tinged with relief. Caution because Matthew Harrington had never told him the name of the man who had acted on his behalf, and despite Matthew's assurances of his competence and credentials Silas Jenkins remained very sceptical. Of course, if this Ted Knowles turned out to be genuine it would be an enormous relief to get the matter settled once and for all because there was no denying that the longer it took to find the girl the more time George, and Charles in particular, would have to argue against her coming into her inheritance. Even so, Jenkins was certainly not going to be hurried into making any rash decisions until he was perfectly satisfied with the credentials of a man who, in his considered opinion, was not the type he would wish to do business with, and when the full force of Ted Knowles's flamboyance eventually burst into his office he was sure of it.

Ted Knowles was so far removed from what Jenkins knew of the detective fraternity that initially he could only stare in surprise, horrifyingly conscious of the thought that Ted Knowles looked to be very much the type of man who was far more than a private detective. In fact, Jenkins would not put it beyond him to undertake work which had very little to do with the profession he claimed to be a member of, and well outside the boundaries of the law.

Having chosen his attire with more particular care than usual, Ted Knowles interpreted Silas Jenkins's incredulous stare as one of approval, never for one moment thinking that to one of his fastidiousness and dislike of anything showy, the sight of the woollen tan suit with the bold red check was not only vulgar but made one question his ability to carry out any kind of investigation with the discretion one would have liked. In fact, his whole appearance hardly inspired confidence, and Jenkins could not help but think that should any kind of physical activity be required during the course of one of his investigations he could find himself considerably hampered as his bulky proportions looked far from agile.

Removing his brown bowler and holding it firmly by the rim in front of him, Ted Knowles nodded, wishing Silas Jenkins a cheerful good morning in a deep and hearty voice.

"Good morning," Jenkins returned faintly, struggling to hide his surprise, offering his hand to find it swamped in a huge paw. "Please, won't you sit down?"

"Thankin' yer kindly," Ted Knowles beamed. "Don't mind h'if H'I do."

Glancing from his visitor to the card, then back at his visitor, Silas Jenkins cleared his throat. "I take it you must be Ted Knowles?" he managed.

"That's me," Ted Knowles nodded. "Glad ter make yer h'acquaintance." His pale blue eyes twinkled merrily across at the thin, wary features of the man who was having considerable difficulty in believing that his late client, who had always been so discerning, had not only engaged this man on such a delicate commission but had clearly trusted him into the bargain.

A hesitant smile touched Jenkins's lips as he flicked the calling card with his forefinger. "I take it then, that I can assume you know the reason why I placed that advertisement?"

"Oh, ah!" Ted Knowles nodded. "As soon as H'I clapped eyes on it H'I says to meself, 'Ted' H'I says, 'this be you them afta.'"

"It is good of you to reply so promptly," Jenkins acknowledged, "but you will, I am sure, understand that I need something a little more convincing than a calling card to prove who you are."

A rich chuckle escaped Ted Knowles's lips at this, his face turning a deeper shade of red as he appeared to be enjoying a private joke. "Lord luv yer!" he gasped. "You'm as cagey a one as H'I've eva clapped eyes on!"

Ignoring this with the contempt it deserved, Jenkins said firmly, "I feel sure if our positions were reversed you would be asking me for proof of my identity."

"Now, look'ee 'ere," Ted Knowles said conspiratorially, leaning forward on his elbows, "we both knows what we know. No use pretendin' we don't, an' that is a certun gen'leman asked me ter 'elp 'im. A gen'leman we both knows; so wot do yer say we gets down to brass tacks?"

"Very well," Jenkins reluctantly conceded, deploring his brash manner. "I will come straight to the point."

That's more like it!" Ted Knowles nodded approvingly. "I al'as said there's no sense in beatin' about the bush."

"Quite!" Jenkins dismissed. "I am aware that my late client, Matthew Harrington, prior to his death, asked you to undertake a commission for him," pausing before saying cautiously, "that is to say, to prosecute a search for his granddaughter."

"I knowed I wos right!" Ted Knowles exclaimed, slapping his thigh. "H'I says ter meself, 'Ted,' H'I says, 'them gonna need yer ter give 'em 'and,' an' yer see," he beamed, "I wos right!"

"Yes, well," Jenkins coughed, "what I need now is for you to furnish me with her direction."

"Thawt yer wud," Ted Knowles smiled. "That's wot I'm doin' 'ere."

Under normal circumstances Silas Jenkins would have known no hesitation in showing this coarse and vulgar individual the door, but as this was totally out of the question, primarily because he needed his help too much for that but also because he had seen enough of Ted Knowles to know that he was not the kind of man to go quietly, so hiding his dislike as best he could, enquired, "You can then, tell me where I can find the girl?"

"That's it," he nodded. "H'I 'as 'er address 'ere in me very pockit."

"May I have it?" Jenkins asked, holding out his hand. When Ted Knowles made no immediate effort to hand it over, Jenkins pointed out firmly, "It really is extremely important that I find her. I am sure my late client stressed the urgency of this matter to you at the time you undertook the commission, and that it was imperative the girl was found?"

"Ah!" Ted Knowles mused, "fer bustin' wi' it, 'e wos. I thawt it mus' be. 'Ted,' I says ter meself, 'it mus' be sumthin' mighty important; the old guvna chasin' all ova fer 'er.'"

Silas Jenkins, having waited in growing impatience for his visitor to finish his monologue, said briskly, "So, surely you must realise the urgency of this matter and how vitally important it is that I find her as soon as possible?"

"Ah!" Ted Knowles nodded informatively, "slippery as an eel, that one!"

"I daresay," Jenkins dismissed. "However, you clearly managed to carry out the task excellently. Now though, I am most anxious to be put in possession of her direction."

"Bound ter be. 'Cus," Ted Knowles added, reflectively rubbing his nose, "it was no easy thing findin' the gerl."

"I can imagine," Jenkins replied, having a very shrewd idea what was going through his mind.

"No," Ted Knowles confirmed. "Traipsin' 'ere an' there like a dunno wot till I wos fer flummoxed!"

"Quite!" Jenkins nodded. "However," he remarked astutely, "I have no doubt that you were more than adequately recompensed for your efforts."

As this was not quite the response Ted Knowles had expected, a sharp look entered his eyes. "Wot's that yer say?" he queried at length, his voice questioningly suspicious.

"Well," Jenkins pointed out innocently, "I assume that Matthew Harrington *did* pay you for your services."

It would have been so easy for Ted Knowles to have denied receiving any payment, but he was shrewd enough to know that a man in Silas Jenkins's position could quite easily find out whether or not he had been paid, and although he was never one to turn down money it would not do to let it be known that Ted Knowles was a swindler. What he did behind the scenes was one thing but up front for all to see was quite another, even so, he saw no reason why he should be cheated out of what he judged to be his due, especially when he considered that the Harrington family were as wealthy as they were proud and would not miss a bob or two out of the funds. If he played his cards right, then he saw no reason why he should leave here out of pocket, so temporising said slowly, "Well, 'e did gimme a little sumthin' fer me trubble, yes."

"I suspect he gave you more than a 'little something'," Jenkins nodded knowingly.

"Ah!" Ted Knowles nodded. "I knowed yer fer a knowin'un the minit I clapped eyes on yer. Now, lookee 'ere," he invited confidentially, leaning forward on his elbows, "are yer by any chance tellin' me that this 'ere address I 'ave in me pockit ain't werth sumthin'? Without giving Silas Jenkins time to respond to this, he inclined his head as if inviting him to come closer, then, lowering his voice, said, "I 'ea the wench is gonna walk away wi' a pritty penny, not ter menshun a set o' sparklers that'd mek yet blink! Now," he rallied, "are yer tellin' me that the 'Arringtons 'ud argue the toss ova a few quid in orda that yer can let the wench 'ave wot's cumin' to 'er?"

Silas Jenkins, revolted by such brash tactics, was seriously alarmed at the extent of Ted Knowles's knowledge concerning the contents of his late client's will, and felt he would be failing in his duty if he did not try to ascertain from whom this offensive and crude individual had obtained such information.

Ted Knowles, having made it his business to discover certain facts before coming here this morning, had no intention of revealing his source, for one thing it would do his reputation immeasurable harm if it became known that he was a gabster and, for another, he had no intention of stemming a source of supply that could still produce substantial reward. "Ah!" he nodded, patting the side of his nose with a thick forefinger.

"Mr. Knowles…" Jenkins began coldly.

"Now there's no need ter fret yerself," Ted Knowles broke in soothingly, raising a pacifying hand. "I ain't no gabster, so there's no need to think I'm gonna blab, 'cus I ain't. It don't mek an 'apporth o' diffrence ter me wot 'ers got cumin' to 'er, it's jus' that, in the way o' bisniss so ter speak," he shrugged, "I thawt yer might pay well fer the wench's address."

Swallowing his frustration as well as his disgust, Silas Jenkins looked searchingly at the man he devoutly trusted it would never again be his misfortune to encounter, sighing, "I am, of course, prepared to remunerate you, but I think you possibly expect far more than I am prepared to pay."

For several moments it looked as if Ted Knowles was going to argue the point, but as if he thought better of it he suddenly chuckled, shaking his head and running his thick fingers through his sandy hair, considerably relieving Silas Jenkins who, apart from the fact that he had so far regarded the meeting as not one he would like to repeat, had gained the very strong impression that lurking beneath Ted Knowles's bluff joviality was a rather unpleasant temper.

"Dang me!" Ted Knowles exclaimed. "I wos right; you'm as cagey a body as H'I've eva met. Now, look'ee 'ere," he said a little resentfully, "yer wudn't by any chance be tryin' ter do me out o' wot is me due, wud yer?"

"Not at all," Jenkins shook his head, leaning back in his chair, "but neither am I prepared to pay for something that has already been paid for. However," he added in an attempt to placate him, "I *am* prepared to pay you a token sum for the information."

"Ow much 'ad yer in mind?" Ted Knowles asked warily, his eyes narrowing sharply.

"Shall we say, five pounds?" Jenkins offered.

"Five!" Ted Knowles repeated incredulously, believing the information

to be worth far more.

"I think that is more than adequate to cover any extra costs you may have incurred," Jenkins told him firmly.

"Well, I dunno," Ted Knowles mused, rubbing his chin meditatively. "Mek it ten an' yer might 'ave a deal." But when he could see that Silas Jenkins was not prepared to go any higher he grudgingly accepted the five pound note he was handed, carefully checking it before digging his hand into his coat pocket to retrieve a screwed up piece of paper which he tossed onto the desk.

"Thank you," Jenkins nodded, quickly picking it up in case Ted Knowles changed his mind, hurriedly reading it before thrusting it into his own pocket.

"Well," Knowles grinned, holding out a huge paw, gripping the hand reluctantly held out to him and vigorously shaking it, "it's bin nice doin' bisniss wi yer," rising to his feet and making his way to the door.

"By the way," Jenkins forestalled him just as he was about to reach out for the handle, "I take it there is no need for me to stress the importance of keeping this transaction to yourself," he nodded, "in fact, everything you have gleaned about my late client and his family? It would be most inadvisable to discuss it with anyone."

"Lord luv yer!" Ted Knowles exclaimed, his shocked expression not impressing Jenkins. "That's cut me ter the very quick that 'as 'an no mistake. I knows wen ter keep me tung between me teeth."

"I am very glad to hear it," Jenkins told him quietly. "It would not do for you to break your word."

Ted Knowles eyed him cautiously; so, the old snipe had friends eh! Well, so did he! "Ah! Yer've no need to fret yerself," he nodded. "You play fer wi me, an' I'll play fer wi you." Then, as if a thought had suddenly occurred to him, he grinned, "H'if you'm eva in need o' me servicis agen…"

"Yes," Jenkins nodded hastily, eager to be rid of him, "I will keep you mind," dismissing the thought immediately the door had clicked shut behind him.

Neither party could claim to being entirely happy with the outcome of the meeting; Silas Jenkins because he doubted Ted Knowles's ability to keep his mouth shut about the affairs of the Harrington family and Matthew's will in particular, and Ted Knowles because he had expected far more remuneration than a measly five pounds. Nevertheless, all was not entirely lost, and even before he had descended the narrow stairs that led to the street his fertile brain was rapidly turning over ideas as to how he could recoup his losses.

Silas Jenkins, seriously concerned as to the extent of Ted Knowles's knowledge, found it hard to believe that a man of Matthew Harrington's character would confide too much if anything to a man of Knowles's obvious calibre, and Jenkins could not help but wonder from whom he had acquired so much information; a circumstance which could lead to unpleasantness if he questioned the family and gossip if left unchecked. The only saving grace being that since no tittle-tattle had yet come to his ears about the Harrington family and they themselves had mentioned nothing about hearing anything to their detriment, it was perhaps safe to assume that whoever was feeding Knowles information was being paid handsomely to keep his mouth shut. If Jenkins had read Knowles's character correctly, and he believed he had, then it seemed likely he would not be any too inclined to share whatever information he had gleaned with a third party as this would doubtless mean handing over a part of any profits he may gain from putting it to further use, and for a man of his apparent avarice Jenkins could not see him taking kindly to handing over a percentage of any proceeds. He may find the whole thing distasteful but the more he thought about it the more disposed he was to think that in view of the kind of man Knowles was he would keep silent as promised, leaving Jenkins to believe that there could well be honour among thieves after all, and if Knowles was anything to go by, then from this standpoint alone Jenkins considered that the name of Harrington would not be the subject of talk.

Jenkins may condemn his late client for using the services of such a man but he had never known Matthew Harrington make a wrong decision in business, and although he personally deprecated a man of Knowles's type being involved in the affairs of one of his clients, he was able to take some consolation from knowing that whatever Matthew Harrington may or may not have been he had certainly been no fool and more than capable of seeing through Ted Knowles and his ilk. But for all Matthew's shrewdness and business acumen he had been sadly lacking in foresight as well as common sense when dealing with this matter of his granddaughter. Whilst admitting to feeling some sympathy for a man whose daughter had behaved in a way which was not only calculated to bring shame on her family but condemn her in the eyes of the world, Silas Jenkins could see no possible good resulting from hanging the same mantle around his granddaughter's neck and ignoring her very existence into the bargain.

During the months preceding Matthew's death, Silas Jenkins had not been taken fully into his client's confidence and certainly not to the extent that he had a granddaughter or that he had set someone on to find her, this information only forthcoming at the very last moment when he had been instructed to insert that codicil in his will. He supposed he should have known his client better, but for all that this had not only hurt his pride but his professional integrity as well, all the same Jenkins was more than prepared to go to any lengths to fulfil his late client's instructions and if this meant associating with the likes of Ted Knowles then so be it. 'Slippery as an eel' was how he had described Alexandra, well, in view of her hasty escape from Brook Street on the day of Matthew's death Jenkins could well believe it, and he certainly had no wish to cause her to embark on another such flight. For this reason then, he decided that his best course of action, indeed his only course of action if he wished to avoid the same thing happening again, was to give her no prior warning of his visit thereby granting her no opportunity to do so.

Had the object of his thoughts and investigations the least idea of what was going forward she would most certainly have done just that, but as Alexandra had not seen the advertisement she remained in happy ignorance of what was to come. Still furiously angry over the treatment she had received at her family's hands as well as her grandfather's disclosure, Alexandra was in no hurry, and certainly in no frame of mind, to receive yet another representative of the Harrington family.

Ted Knowles had offered no reason to account for the peremptory summons issued by her grandfather demanding her immediate attendance in Brook Street, but when, in due course, she heard him announce that he had made provision for her in his will, far from being elated she had felt nothing short of insulted. She did not regret one word she had said to him, it was all true; she wanted nothing from him – nothing! She only had to think of her mother's pain and suffering and her secret hope that one day she would be forgiven and Alexandra's anger rose afresh. Her grandfather had dismissed her mother from his mind as easily as he had dismissed her from the house, then mistakenly believed that by offering recompense at the very last moment he was making amends for what had gone before – how misguided he had been! Alexandra had had no intention of making it easy for him; she had wanted to hurt him, to repay him as best she could for all the years he had hurt her mother, but if she had thought she could make her grandfather beg and plead for forgiveness as well as her acceptance of his financial offering, she could not have been more wrong. The brief period of time she had spent with her grandfather had been more than enough to tell her he was not the type of man to beg or plead for anything, and certainly not from a young woman who, apart from having denied all knowledge of her, cared nothing for her opinion of him. She had accused him of trying to ease his conscience through her. She still thought it. He had neither known nor cared about the life he had pushed his daughter into, nor had he shown the slightest interest in what had happened to her once he had ejected her from his life, and Alexandra had instinctively known it would have been a waste of time in telling him.

She could well imagine what his reaction would have been had she told him that his daughter had been forced into taking refuge with her future mother-in-law; a widow who had been allowed to continue living in the cottage which had formed part of her late husband's work as a farm labourer, not out of the goodness of the landowner's heart but simply because she was still able to carry out light work in the main house. The cottage, which should have been demolished years before, had not only stood in urgent need of essential repairs but was hardly conducive to comfortably accommodating three people. Her grandfather would doubtless have looked upon it as fitting punishment for a girl who had disgraced him, as indeed he would the unattended wedding which had been performed by the pompously outraged vicar of the parish, who had deemed his front parlour more suitable for the ceremony than the sanctity of his church; more than good enough for a woman so far gone in sin to merit anything better. Although her mother had been extremely careful in what she confided to her, Alexandra had learned enough to make her hate the very name of Harrington. Too often she had caught sight of the tears which her mother had hurriedly blinked away as soon as she had become aware she was being watched, her beautiful smile lighting up her face, quickly hiding the pain.

Alexandra knew her grandfather would have been totally unmoved by such a story as indeed he would have been had she told him how her father had struggled to find work after he had dismissed him without a reference; to go from place to place looking for whatever work he could find, finally ending up as a farm labourer on the Maybury estate like his father before him. The border of Surrey and Sussex, an area of outstanding pastoral beauty, was certainly an ideal place in which to bring up a child, but the conditions endured by the workers on Sir Donald Maybury's estate were appalling and the farm workers' cottages, which had been crying out for repairs with not one of them being carried out, were so very different to the luxurious splendour of Maybury Hall, where her mother had been fortunate enough to gain work as a scullery maid, joining the army of domestic servants employed by Lady Maybury.

Not only was a scullery maid considered to be the lowest form of domestic life and never allowed to set foot above stairs but also regarded as being far too unworthy to even merit an interview with the lady of the house, her employment commenced and terminated by the undisputed powers of the cook, whose authority over her domain was absolute. Whatever Mrs. Singleton, who had been the cook at Maybury Hall for a good many years, thought about her newest recruit, who was clearly not the type who usually undertook such lowly work, she kept to herself, but not by a word or gesture had her mother betrayed herself to her employers, none of them having the least guess that the latest addition to the kitchen staff was in fact the disgraced daughter of Lady Charlotte Beatrice Ambrose, a once beautiful socialite who had married the wealthy businessman Matthew Carey Harrington.

Alexandra could only guess at her mother's thoughts as she did endless loads of washing up and scrubbed the stone-grey floors of the huge kitchen, her once beautiful hands roughened and chapped from being constantly immersed in scalding hot soda water. No, her grandfather would not have been moved by his daughter's terrible ordeal, any more than he would have been to know that she had more than once gratefully accepted untouched leftovers given her by Mrs. Singleton, who not only ruled her downstairs domain with a rod of iron as well as demanded the highest standards of work as well as behaviour from her kitchen staff, but had, for some inexplicable reason, taken a liking to her young scullery maid.

These tasty morsels may have helped to stretch out their meagre income, but more than once Alexandra had wanted to shout aloud who her mother was, that she was far above taking handouts, however kindly meant. But her mother, reading the thoughts behind her stormy face, had merely smiled and shook her head, her soft voice reminding her that it was of no consequence; that the man she loved and for whom she had forsaken everything together with her daughter, were far more important than claiming her identity. However much Alexandra had railed against this, her childhood had not been as unhappy as some might suppose; at least she had had the love of her parents who in turn loved one another, providing an emotional security and comfort denied to many. Apart from attending the village school where she had been taught to read and write and do her sums, her mother had, incredibly, found the time to instruct her in all the things a young girl in her position would never need to know. She had taught her to speak grammatically correct, which meant that her cultured voice rendered her open prey to the other children, her mother also insisting she learn to speak French as well as how to behave in every conceivable social situation. Alexandra had been tutored in everything a young woman from her mother's background would have been taught from childhood, her mother believing that one day her daughter would take her rightful place in the world where she really belonged and should be prepared for it, but which Alexandra herself could never visualise. Even so, she had learned quickly, her lively mind and keen intelligence making her a very apt pupil.

As a child, one of her greatest pleasures had been to sit in front of the black leaded grate while her mother had prepared vegetables or darned a torn garment, listening to her describe some of the parties she had attended and the dresses she had worn, but these reminiscences had been rare and never when her father was present, her mother always careful to save him as much pain as possible. Her father, who had always kept his feelings towards his father-in-law to himself, had, on occasion, inadvertently let something slip which had made Alexandra realise that although he could not imagine his life without her mother, he was nonetheless fully conscious of what his love had brought her to. He had certainly not expected to be rewarded for his impudence in daring to fall in love with his employer's daughter, in fact he had known only too well that he was treading on very dangerous ground, but once having set eyes on the beautiful Elizabeth Harrington he could not have stopped himself from falling in love with her, unable to believe his good fortune when she had made it abundantly clear his feelings were fully reciprocated.

It would have been useless for Alexandra to have told her grandfather that his accusations had been wrong and that far from taking advantage of his daughter's youth and vulnerability, in some obscure hope that he would be compelled to make some kind of financial offering to induce him to end the affair, no such thought had ever entered her father's head. She had no need to hear her grandfather toss her denial aside as nonsense, she could well imagine every scornful word he would have uttered. As she grew older, Alexandra had discovered that it was she who bore the resentment for their way of life rather than her mother, never being quite able to understand why she so calmly accepted her lot with such serenity while she herself had built up such an animosity towards her mother's family and their treatment of her that she was ashamed to have their blood in her veins. She seemed to lack the contentment which had filled her mother, who saw her life as somehow inevitable rather than something to be deplored or pitied. Alexandra envied not only the warmth her mother had radiated and which had endeared her to everyone who knew her but her love of life, which seemed to stem from some kind of inner peaceful source she herself did not possess. It was not until her father's tragic accident that her mother's resolve and buoyant spirit began to wane. Alexandra knew her mother had loved her, devoted her life to her, but it was her father who had been the mainstay of her existence, the foundation upon which she had rebuilt her life. Her grandfather had denounced the love her parents had shared and which he had tried so hard to end, yet in spite of his condemnation and angry outbursts, even the expulsion of his daughter, it had survived it all, binding them even closer together.

Except for her grandmother, her family had made their feelings perfectly clear; they wanted no association with her whatsoever – well, Alexandra had no wish to further her acquaintance with them either, but for all that she was conscious of a desire to see her grandmother again as well as a deep sense of remorse over the way she had so abruptly dealt with her. Her only excuse was that she had been too angry to assess her own feelings on the day she had visited her grandfather, but upon reflection Alexandra had to admit that from what she had seen of her grandmother it had not been necessary to have her mother's words reinforced in that she had had no hand in her eviction and was certainly no match for Matthew, her wishes and desires being easily overborne by his stronger will. Alexandra may possess more than her fair share of the Harrington strain, but she was too much her mother's daughter to be unfair or prejudiced in her dealings with people or to be less than honest with herself and knew she had treated her grandmother unjustly. This did not mean she acquitted or forgave the rest of them. Not for a moment! Their attitude towards her had been both insulting and insufferable, and for as long as she lived she would never forget the things they had said to her.

No amount of money could possibly compensate for what her grandfather had done in banishing her mother from her home and family. By denying her the right to live her life in love and happiness with the man she had chosen for her husband he had pushed her into a life of penury and virtual slavery, leaving her nothing short of an outcast; to make her way in a world for which she was totally ill-equipped, and for that reason alone Alexandra had slung her grandfather's generosity back in his face; just as Ted Knowles had rightly guessed she would.

Similar thoughts had been going through Silas Jenkins's mind also, and if everything Harris had told him was true, then he was going to find his forthcoming meeting with his late client's granddaughter far from easy. If she was anything like her grandfather, and Jenkins had every reason to suppose she was, then convincing her that the bequest he had made in her favour was hers by right was beginning to bear all the hallmarks of being anything but the straightforward matter it should be. If she could calmly walk out on her grandmother without so much as a by your leave, then he could expect a very cold reception, in fact he would not put it beyond her to slam the door in his face. It was perhaps unfortunate that he had a rather limited experience in dealing with young ladies, and what eloquence and ability he did possess he doubted very much if they would be sufficient to carry him through what he suspected was going to be a rather difficult interview. Ideally, what he needed was someone to accompany him who could not possibly be accused of dissimulation and whose integrity was beyond question, and preferably one who was already known to the girl. If Harris was right when he had said that except for Mr. Marcus, Mrs. Charles Harrington had more heart than the rest of them put together, then perhaps she would be the very person to give him assistance. Of course, Jenkins realised that he could not rely upon her agreeing to accompany him, especially when he considered her husband's opinion about the whole affair, after all she may not be any too eager or comfortable in doing something which would run counter to his views. He was not unmindful of the awkward position such a request would place her in, but Alexandra had to be informed of her inheritance and it was his duty to do so regardless of personal feelings. There had been far too much time wasted already and he could no longer afford any delay in discharging the obligation he was honour bound to execute, and therefore decided that his best course of action would be to call in Brook Street the following morning on his way to see Alexandra.

Irrevocably determined on this course, Jenkins arrived in Brook Street to the pleasing intelligence that Mrs. Charles Harrington was at home, but upon Harris entering the drawing room to inform Sophy that Silas Jenkins had arrived and was most desirous of a moment of her time, she was considerably surprised. She was both gratified and alarmed by Jenkins's request and although she was firmly of the belief that Alexandra had every right to take possession of her inheritance and as quickly as possible, she was also extremely wary to do anything which would run counter to Charles's wishes. Sophy knew perfectly well what his reaction would be if he ever discovered she had visited Alexandra in order to assist Jenkins conduct a transaction of which he was most definitely not in favour and trembled at the thought, having no desire to experience another interview like those she had already had with Charles in the library. Even if Matthew had not made provision for Alexandra, Charles's feelings towards her were very far from avuncular, in fact they were totally antipathetic, but the very fact that Matthew had included her in his will just went to strengthen them.

Sophy's hazel eyes revealed more than she realised to the man silently watching her, who had his own views about her husband, but although Jenkins would be grateful to receive her help at the same time he had no wish to place her in a position which would expose her to his anger, and therefore immediately apologised for the intrusion.

He was just about to take his leave when Sophy cried, "No! I will go with you. Just give me a moment," deciding to leave the question of the possible consequences until later. She had no idea what help she could possibly offer, even assuming Alexandra would listen to her, after all there was no reason for her to do so, but in her heart Sophy knew she was doing the right thing. She may incur her husband's displeasure, but what was that compared with doing what she knew to be right? Nevertheless, she could not help feeling somewhat relieved to know that Amelia had left the house half an hour before, knowing how difficult it would have been to explain away her sudden departure with Matthew's solicitor.

It was not until the hackney driver had whipped up his horse that Sophy realised she had no idea where Jenkins was taking her, but upon his calm response to her enquiry, she exclaimed, "Hoxton!"

"That is the address I have for her," Jenkins replied uncomfortably, embarrassingly conscious that it was hardly the place a lady of Sophy's quality would visit much less where a client's granddaughter would live.

"Good heavens!" Sophy cried, considerably startled, as familiar with the type of locality as her companion, staring at him in disbelief. "Then we must get her away from there as quickly as possible."

"I am afraid that may not be so easy as either of us would like," Jenkins pointed out.

Sophy was very much perturbed at this, saying firmly, "Well, I think we ought to do everything possible to make sure that we do."

"Until we have spoken to the girl," Jenkins offered practically, "and informed her of her grandfather's bequest, which," he nodded, "she may refuse, indeed she may even decline to see us, everything else is meaningless."

Sophy reluctantly agreed to this, but when the hackney carriage eventually drew up outside a dilapidated red-bricked house set in the middle of a run-down terrace, her heart sank. However, a closer inspection revealed that despite the fact that the small front garden was overgrown and the weeds grew freely between the paving stones of the path which led from the broken gate to the door, at least the curtains at the window, although torn, looked reasonably clean, making her feel more hopeful about the conditions inside.

After handing her down onto the pavement and paying off the man sitting patiently on the box, Silas Jenkins trod purposefully up the path, banging the tarnished knocker against the door, causing some of the old and flaking paint to fall away. At first it seemed as though no one was at home, but within seconds of banging the knocker a second time the door was finally opened to reveal a stout middle-aged woman whose asthmatic enquiry was anything but welcoming, and her stale breath, tinged with drink, was far from pleasant. Silas Jenkins, upon asking her to whom he was addressing, received a suspicious look before being grudgingly told, "Mrs. Drew. Tho' wot that's got ter do wi' you I don't know. Now," she nodded, "wot is it yer want?" Upon being told that he would like to speak to Miss Dawes whom he had reason to believe resided at this address, she asked gruffly, "'Oo wonts 'er?" pulling the faded woollen shawl closer around her. "Yer ain't the law, are yer?"

"Good God, no!" Jenkins quickly assured her, appalled. "Certainly not," hurriedly handing her his card in the hope that she would believe with her own eyes what his profession was, but which Sophy shrewdly suspected she could not read.

"Wait 'ere. I'll see if 'ers in," adding suspiciously, "not in any truble, is 'er? This is a respectable 'ouse this is, an' I'll 'ave no truble 'ere!"

"No, none at all," Silas Jenkins hastily confirmed. "It is merely a private matter."

She looked doubtfully at the card then back at her uninvited callers before shuffling away into the back of the house, emerging a few minutes later with Alexandra following closely behind looking anything but pleased at the sight of her visitors, causing Sophy to question which concerned her more, Mrs. Drew's gin-ravaged features or Alexandra's angry ones, both of which were rather daunting.

After assuring her landlady that she was very well able to deal with the matter herself without resorting to the strong-arm tactics of Ned to do it for her, a circumstance which made Silas Jenkins swallow nervously, devoutly trusting that whoever Ned may be he would not be called upon to do his duty, Mrs. Drew once again shuffled away, muttering to herself about the nerve of some people, poking their noses into what was no concern of theirs as she went.

At first it seemed as though Alexandra's only inclination was to close the door on them, her stormy face and sparkling eyes warning them that their visit was as unwelcome as it was unwanted, listening to Silas Jenkins introduce himself for the second time with barely concealed annoyance.

"Of course," he was unwise enough to add, "you have already met your Aunt Sophy."

Since Alexandra was in no mood to meet another member of her family the acknowledged relationship was not only inappropriate but inopportune, inciting her to purposefully disregard Sophy's outstretched hand. Alexandra had not forgotten the last occasion when Sophy's gesture of friendship had been coldly dealt with, but deliberately thrusting this recollection to the back of her mind she determinedly ignored the hurt expression she could see in those hazel eyes as well as her mother's strictures in that there was no excuse for bad manners, taking immediate refuge in anger, momentarily making Sophy almost believe that she could be looking at Matthew himself; as had Ted Knowles before her.

Handing Jenkins back his card, Alexandra said coldly, "I can guess what brings you here, but you would have been better advised not to have come."

"Don't you think it would be better to reserve judgement until after you have heard what we have come to discuss? Preferably indoors." Silas Jenkins, who, apart from the fact that he had been eyeing the weather unfavourably for some little time, had, for the past few minutes, become uncomfortably aware of the unsavoury group of individuals who had congregated on the pavement watching with interest at the goings-on at number eighteen, disliking the idea of conducting business on the doorstep.

"Discuss!" Alexandra exclaimed scornfully. "I don't think we have anything to discuss."

"I am sure you will agree," Jenkins pointed out, "that neither of us would be here if that were the case."

As Sophy had also noticed the interested parties staring curiously at them and was equally as reluctant as Jenkins to discuss anything so private on the doorstep, she said gently, "Indeed, I think it would perhaps be better for all concerned if you allowed us to step inside. I am sure you have no wish for your private affairs to be broadcast for everyone to hear," adding, with her lovely smile, "and far warmer, don't you agree?"

Apparently she did, because after debating the sense of these words Alexandra eventually stepped aside to allow them to walk past her into the dingy narrow passageway, the dark and faded wallpaper, which, due to the damp, was peeling off the walls in places, as unwelcoming as it was oppressive. "In here," she said brusquely, brushing past them to open a door just a little way down the passage on the left-hand side.

As the occupants of number eighteen Mansion Gardens were seldom visited by two people whom they had no difficulty in recognising, the one whose whole demeanour unmistakably advertised his calling and the other whom they saw at a glance as being a well-heeled piece, their arrival had the effect of bringing two women from the back premises into the passageway to stand staring in open-mouthed surprise. Silas Jenkins, by no means liking the look of them, may not have been able to determine how old they were from their rather unkempt and dishevelled appearance, but there was no mistaking the avarice mixed with curiosity in their eyes as they saw the opportunity for largesse. The more bold of the two, having taken one look at Sophy, began to slowly draw near with her hand suggestively outstretched, but even before the whining plea for money left her lips Silas Jenkins hurriedly steered Sophy into the privacy of Alexandra's room.

It was far larger than Sophy had expected but it benefited hardly at all from the small fire which burned in the grate, the flames desultory and ineffectual, giving off very little heat, leaving the air cold and chill and not encouraging her to remove her gloves. Apart from a rather uncomfortable-looking bed in the corner, a scrubbed topped table in the middle of the room on top of which were several items of clothing and reels of cotton and pins, along with three upright chairs which looked decidedly the worse for wear and a battered item of furniture which acted as a wardrobe, the room was sparsely furnished, but even though there was not so much as a rug on the floorboards it was spotlessly clean, relieving Sophy of one of her concerns at least. What did concern her, however, was knowing that Alexandra was forced to share her lodgings with other tenants whose apparent understanding of communication was screaming and shouting, and Sophy could only marvel at Alexandra's seeming imperviousness to the pandemonium going on around her. Emanating from the room immediately above a loud and vociferous altercation could be heard taking place, and Silas Jenkins, to whom the vocabulary was more intelligible than it was to Sophy, raised his eyes to the ceiling then back to Alexandra, who returned his dismayed look quite unmoved.

The searing cries of a child intermingling with raised voices and the sound of breaking glass coming from upstairs, made Sophy's heart cry out in agonised silence at the conditions in which Alexandra lived. She was very much saddened by what she saw, despising the attitude which had brought about this unnecessary state of affairs, and knew that the sooner Alexandra removed herself from this place the better. Unfortunately, however, Sophy needed no reminding that her own hands were very much tied and therefore she was hardly in a position to hasten Alexandra's removal from this dreadful place, nor could she argue against the sense of what Silas Jenkins had said in that until Alexandra had come to certain decisions herself everything else was meaningless.

"I suppose it was that private detective who told you where to find me?" Alexandra said scornfully, closing the door with a snap behind her. Upon receiving an assenting nod from Jenkins, she shrugged. "Well, it makes no difference; your journey has been for nothing!"

"Miss Dawes…" Jenkins began.

"As you are not here by my invitation," Alexandra broke in, "please say what you have to and then leave. As you can see," she added, indicating the pile of sewing on the table which she had been working on, "I am *quite* busy."

"I… er… I take it," Silas Jenkins said tentatively, glancing across at the table, "this is how you earn your living?"

Alexandra eyed him shrewdly, her eyes sparkling dangerously in her pale face. "Of course. How else did you think I earned it?"

Considerably embarrassed by this pointed question, Jenkins looked rather discomfited, helplessly shrugging his narrow shoulders as he told her lamely that he had meant no offence. "I also read the newspapers to an elderly man several streets away," she further informed them. "He is almost blind, but he enjoys the hour I spend with him. The money he pays me is not much but it comes in very useful."

"I can imagine," Jenkins nodded, eyeing his surroundings with barely concealed horror, taking the opportunity offered to explain the reason for their visit. "But since you raise the question of money, you must know that is why we are here," pulling out two chairs, one for himself and the other for Sophy.

"I thought so," Alexandra nodded, resuming her seat. "It's about my grandfather's will, isn't it?"

"Yes," Jenkins confirmed, clearing his throat. "I take it then, that he did mention it to you the day you went to see him?"

The martial light was back in her eyes but she replied with perfect calm, "He did touch upon it, yes," adding defiantly, "but I told him I neither wanted nor needed anything from him. I still don't."

Realising that his task was going to be even more difficult than he had envisaged, Silas Jenkins looked anxiously across at Sophy who had also come to the conclusion that it was going to be far from easy to overcome Alexandra's pride as well as her prejudice by trying to convince her that her grandfather's bequest, made with whatever reason in mind, was hers by right.

"You really have wasted your time," Alexandra told them, glancing from one to the other. "Nothing could prevail upon me to take anything from him."

"I should hardly describe it in those terms," Jenkins remarked, moving uncomfortably on his chair. "It is not a case of taking anything; quite the reverse in fact. You would merely be receiving something he wanted you to have."

"That was very well put," Alexandra smiled sardonically, "but it means the same thing. All you have done," she told him forthrightly, "is wrap up something dirty in clean linen."

"Well," Jenkins persevered, wondering what on earth he had done to be saddled with such a stubborn family, "why not reserve judgement until you have heard the full nature of the bequest?" he suggested, convinced that once she learned the full sum of her inheritance she would feel differently.

"The nature of the bequest is immaterial." Alexandra shook her head, adding firmly, "Besides, it really is rather late in the day for my grandfather to be making amends."

"Is that how you look upon it," Jenkins questioned, "as making amends?"

"Wasn't that his intention?" Alexandra asked, raising a supercilious eyebrow.

"I don't know *what* his intention was," Jenkins told her truthfully. "I doubt if anyone does."

"Do you honestly expect me to believe that my grandfather never confided in you?" she demanded incredulously. "His own solicitor!"

"Your grandfather never confided in anyone," Jenkins informed her firmly, "much less seek advice."

"I find that extremely hard to believe," Alexandra told him sceptically.

"It is quite true, however," Sophy assured her quietly, coming to Jenkins's rescue. "Your grandfather's reasons for doing anything were very much his own, and if at any time he did seek advice it more often than not went unheeded."

"Well," Alexandra said at length, "whatever his reasons may have been he certainly miscalculated on this occasion. I don't want his money!"

It was obvious to Silas Jenkins that although Alexandra may despise her grandfather she was every inch his granddaughter, exhibiting the same temperament and stubborn pride he remembered so well. Daunted but by no means despairing of bringing her round to accepting her inheritance, he explained in detail the precise nature of the bequest.

Never having heard her mother mention anything about jewellery, this disclosure was just as much of a shock to Alexandra as discovering that her grandfather had left her thirty thousand pounds, her incredulous stare confirming Silas Jenkins's belief that once having heard the full sum of the bequest she would feel differently and accept it well enough.

It was several minutes before Alexandra could trust her voice sufficiently to say, and then faintly, "There must be some mistake!"

"There is no mistake," Jenkins told her unequivocally. "Your mother's jewellery and the money are yours. The jewellery is where it has been ever since your grandfather disowned your mother; in the vaults at Mercers' bank, where, incidentally, an account has been opened in your name. All I require from you is your signature on this document," removing the appropriate sheet from his case. "Once I have that I can then give you the necessary letter of introduction authorising the bank to release whatever monies you require."

Like Marcus, Silas Jenkins had noted her quick intelligence as well as her cultured voice, clearly the results of the high standard of education she had doubtless received from her mother. In view of this then, he had every expectation that she would, after only a very little thought, sign the document he was holding out to her. Alexandra was certainly no fool and surely must realise that what was being offered her was something no one in their right mind would turn down.

The anger and pride which had aided her over the years and carried her through all the dark times gradually began to ebb away, rendering her speechless as she stared helplessly from one to the other, seeking the enlightenment which neither of them could give her. Silas Jenkins was too much the professional to allow his feelings to show, but it was otherwise with Sophy, her eyes filling with tears at the pathetic sight in front of her, but she knew better than to follow her instincts which were to wrap the small and insecure bundle of shocked vulnerability in her arms. Instead, she said gently, "I know this has come as something of a shock, but indeed it is true."

Alexandra stared almost blindly at her, her hands slightly agitated as they rested on her lap. "I don't understand!" she cried at last. "After all these years! Why now? Why could he not have allowed my mother the enjoyment of them?"

"I wish I knew," Sophy said sincerely, aware of how inadequate she was to deal with a situation she could not explain even to herself.

"All those years!" Alexandra exclaimed, raising a distracted hand to her forehead, as if by doing so it would clear her mind and everything would be explained. "For years my mother waited and hoped for a sign she had been forgiven; that my grandfather actually felt remorse at what he had done; that he still loved her, but nothing came." She swallowed her angry tears, giving Sophy a watery smile. "She could not be brought to write to him, especially after that visit not long after I was born, and strictly forbid me to do so for her."

"And your father?" Sophy prompted gently.

"My father never spoke about it; at least not to me." Alexandra shook her head. "Whatever his feelings were, he kept them from me." Fighting to control another surge of tears she eventually managed, "My father could not have written to my grandfather even had he wanted to; you see he... he could not read or write."

Jenkins, less vulnerable to sad stories than Sophy, said briskly, "Yes, well, that is over and done with now, and there is nothing you can do about it, but you can do something about your future."

This rather tactless speech not only made Sophy inwardly wince but necessitated her stepping quickly into the breach as Alexandra clearly bristled with renewed anger at his words. Without pausing to think what she was doing Sophy leaned forward so she could clasp one small cold hand in her own, its violent trembling betraying just how upset she actually was, saying softly, "No one can turn back the clock and undo what has gone before, no matter how painful it may have been; all any of us can to is to learn from it; to try to ensure that it does not happen again." Waiting only until Alexandra had dried her tears with the delicately laced handkerchief Sophy offered her, did she continue, her voice quietly soothing, "Listen to me, Alexandra," she pleaded, "no matter how much you may dislike it you have been given the opportunity to not only remove yourself from this dreadful place but to dictate your own future; to live your life as your mother would have wanted you to."

"What do you know…?"

"About your mother?" Sophy broke quietly into the heated accusation, smiling warmly. "Nothing, but from everything I have ever heard your grandmother say of her I feel I do know her; and it is because of this that I strongly urge you to reconsider and accept your grandfather's bequest." Seeing that Alexandra was about to argue the point, Sophy continued, "Your mother's jewellery and the thirty thousand pounds are yours, not just legally but morally. Your mother would have wanted you to have them."

"I don't want them," Alexandra shot at her, her eyes blazing. "There is nothing to reconsider. Why should I ease his conscience by accepting them?" snatching her hand out of Sophy's as she rose jerkily to her feet to begin pacing up and down, wringing her hands in anguish. "He neither knew nor cared about our life," she raged. "We could have starved in the gutter for all he cared! Not once did he ever take the trouble to find us. What kind of man treats his daughter in the way he did?" As Sophy had often asked herself this question without any satisfactory answer, she was unable to make any suitable reply. "He not only disowned her but made it impossible for my father to obtain work. He never knew, never wanted to know, the life he had subjected them to," Alexandra panted, tears running down her face.

Sophy, deeply concerned that Alexandra was working herself up into a state of hysteria with her impassioned outburst, rose to her feet, trying to stem the flood of her outpourings by calmly advising her not to distress herself, that she would only make herself ill, but Alexandra refused to be still, until finally, emotionally exhausted, she came to an abrupt halt, her eyes sparkling and the tears running freely down her face. Instinctively, Sophy held out her hand in a mute invitation for Alexandra to come to her, her smile warm and welcoming. At first it seemed as though she was going to be rebuffed, but after a few moments of struggling with her cauldron of emotions Alexandra stumbled into Sophy's arms, crying helplessly into her shoulder. Sophy welcomed her eagerly, happy and contented to cradle the child, for she was nothing more, her voice calm and comforting as she encouraged Alexandra to unburden herself, deliberately closing her eyes in an effort to shut out the mental image of her husband's face; contemptuous and scornful. Like his father, Charles neither knew nor cared about anything or anyone other than himself, Sophy knowing exactly what his reaction would be if he could see her now.

Alexandra had no idea why she should feel such empathy towards this woman who was really nothing more than a stranger, but in some obscure way she reminded her of her mother, so much so that she forgot everything and allowed herself to be comforted.

After staring dumbfounded at the scene being enacted in front of him for several stunned moments, Silas Jenkins considered it rather prudent to leave them alone for a while as it appeared that Mrs. Charles Harrington would do very much better without him. When he had enlisted her support, he had had no very clear idea as to what she could realistically do to help; all he knew was that the presence of a woman already known to Alexandra may just serve to set her mind at rest as well as convincing her as to the integrity of his visit, but in view of the way things were turning out he could not help priding himself in that his idea had not only been inspirational but nothing short of a masterstroke.

It was some little time before Alexandra's tempestuous fit of crying burned itself out, leaving her limp and drained as Sophy helped her onto a chair, drawing her own nearer. Removing her gloves, she gently pushed back a strand of stray hair from Alexandra's flushed face, her hazel eyes smiling warmly into those wide green ones, which had, thankfully, lost a lot of their fire. "That's better," Sophy soothed. "Can I get you something? A drink of water, perhaps?"

Alexandra shook her head. "No, nothing, thank you." A deep shudder racked her thin body. "I'm sorry," she apologised, "I don't know why I did that. I have not cried in a long time."

"Then it was long overdue," Sophy smiled, "and nothing you have to apologise for."

Alexandra eyed Sophy closely, her frank gaze taking in the tenderness as well as the humanity behind the beautiful face, her heart and mind no longer in conflict. Alexandra had wanted to hate this woman who represented the family she heartily despised, but she knew it was impossible. Not only because Sophy was not a Harrington by birth but because she genuinely liked her; had done so in fact the day she had first seen her when she went to visit her grandfather. Sophy was not tainted with the

Harrington strain, full of pride and prejudice, on the contrary she was warm and kind with a generosity of spirit which reminded her very much of her mother. "I'm sorry I was rude to you earlier," Alexandra said ashamedly.

"You don't have to be," Sophy assured her. "We did take you rather by surprise, after all."

"Yes, but that is no excuse," Alexandra shook her head. "My mother," she told her, "always believed in good manners, in fact," she confessed, "she severely reprimanded me on more than one occasion for not observing them."

Sophy smiled, content to let her talk and unburden herself, honoured that she was the one Alexandra had chosen to be her confidante. It was evident she had loved her parents, her mother especially, who deserved the highest praise for the way she had raised and educated her daughter under what must have been extremely difficult circumstances. As Sophy sat and listened to the jumbled mass of reminiscences and explanations she found herself unable to prevent the renewed surge of condemnation which rose inside her over the way Matthew had treated his daughter. So strong was this denunciation that she was rather surprised to discover that running parallel to it was a feeling of pity for the man who had missed so much because of his stubborn pride.

"You know," Alexandra told her when she had come to the end of her disjointed utterances, "I really believe my mother actually forgave him."

"I think so too," Sophy confirmed quietly. "In which case," she said tentatively, "do you not perhaps think you too could forgive him?"

Immediately Sophy felt the thin body stiffen. *"Never!"* Alexandra cried vehemently.

"But what about your grandmother?" Sophy pressed gently. "Can't you forgive her either? After all, she had no hand in it." When Alexandra made no attempt to speak, Sophy said gently, "You saw your grandmother for yourself; surely you must have realised that her wishes never counted for anything. Indeed, you must not hate her, Alexandra. Whatever you may have accused her of she is totally innocent. She loved your mother very much and it hurt her more than she ever owned when your grandfather behaved the way he did, but I promise you she had no dealings in it. You must know it is true," squeezing the cold hand cradled in her own. "Can't you forgive her? She loves you very much indeed, and she was very upset when you left without saying goodbye. She longs only for the day when the two of you can be together." She felt the small hand move within her own, betraying just how emotionally vulnerable Alexandra really was.

"Oh," Alexandra shrugged wearily, "I know I should not have left without saying goodbye, and as for my grandmother being a party to what happened," she shook her head, "I never believed it. My mother told me enough to convince me of that."

"I can't tell you how happy that makes me," Sophy sighed, relieved. "You see, I am extremely fond of your grandmother and I would hate to see her hurt any more than she has been already."

"But the others," Alexandra said determinedly, *"never!* I shall never forgive the things they said to me." Sophy had no idea how to respond to this, still painfully aware of that distressing scene in the drawing room and the part her own husband had played in it. "I am not blaming you," Alexandra assured her as Sophy hung her head. "It was not your fault."

"Perhaps not," Sophy acknowledged, "even so, it makes me feel quite ashamed."

"There is no need," Alexandra dismissed, "you cannot be held responsible for their behaviour, but I admit that Marcus certainly made up for their rudeness. I was indeed most grateful to him; his conduct was such that I knew instantly what my mother meant." In answer to Sophy's look of enquiry, she explained, "You see, she often spoke of him, and always with affection. She was extremely fond of him," she nodded, "and I can see why," she smiled. "He was most kind to me that day."

"Yes," Sophy agreed faintly, unable to prevent the tinge of colour from creeping into her cheeks at the mention of his name, "Marcus is most *truly* kind."

"But even if I were in agreement about staying with my grandmother," Alexandra conceded, accurately reading the affection Sophy had for her mother's cousin in her heightened colour, "surely you must see how impossible it would be for me to do so. They would never tolerate it. They would very soon prevail upon her to let me go."

"No, no they would not," Sophy told her firmly. "She is determined to have her own way in this. They know that." Alexandra shook her head, but Sophy persevered. "Listen to me, Alexandra. It is true that your grandmother has been overborne in many things, indeed she is the most gentlest of people and will do almost anything to avoid unpleasantness, but she is adamant that for once in her life she is going to do as she wishes."

"I want to believe it, Sophy," Alexandra said fervently, "but I saw enough that day to convince me that I should be as unwelcome as if I were the plague!"

"I can't promise you a warm welcome from any one of them," Sophy told her truthfully, "but I *can* from your grandmother, but if nothing else at least promise me you will think about it," she pleaded, her hazel eyes imploring as they searched the pale face only inches from her own. "It would make your grandmother so very happy."

"Yes," Alexandra nodded, "I believe it would."

"I too would like it," Sophy admitted sincerely. "In fact, I think you and I are going to become very good friends," she prophesied, adding, "indeed I know we are. You have already called me Sophy."

Alexandra smiled. "I can see you are a very persuasive advocate."

"Then you will think about it?" Sophy pressed.

"Yes, I will think about it," Alexandra nodded.

"And your grandfather's bequest?" Sophy urged. "You will think about that too?"

The green eyes sparkled, but Alexandra said quite calmly, "You told me just now that my mother would have wanted me to accept the money and her jewellery."

"Yes, I did," Sophy confirmed, "because I am sure it is what she would have wanted for you." Without allowing her time to say anything Sophy pressed home her advantage. "I am not going to try to defend your grandfather; his treatment of your mother was both despicable and cruel, but I believe that he *was* trying to make amends at the end. Perhaps he was trying to ease his conscience as you seem to think, but none of us will ever know the real reason, but whatever it was, the money and your mother's jewellery are yours. You not only owe it to your parents to accept them, but to yourself."

"Could you forgive, Sophy?" Alexandra asked, a frown creasing her forehead.

"I don't know," Sophy replied frankly, her eyes clouding as she considered her own humiliation at Charles's hands. "I would certainly like to think I could."

"It's not easy, is it?" Alexandra pointed out tiredly. "I mean, if someone has hurt you, very badly, destroyed your life almost, how can one begin to forgive them?"

"I'm not sure," Sophy sighed, rising to her feet. "All I do know is that you must not allow yourself to be blinded by hatred and dictated to by revenge until you are eaten up by them. If you do, they will destroy you, until you are no better than the person who instilled them in you."

"The day I visited my grandfather," Alexandra confessed, "I *was* full of hatred, so much so that I wanted to hurt him. I thought I had too," she added on a twisted little smile. "Now," she sighed resignedly, "I don't think

I even scraped the surface."

"Well," Sophy shook her head, "if it is of any consolation, I doubt if anyone had the power to do that. Your grandmother least of all."

"Will you tell me something, Sophy?" Alexandra asked curiously, rising to her feet.

Sophy half smiled, her fingers stilling in the act of buttoning her black leather glove. "If I can."

"Does your husband know that you have come here today?" Whatever Sophy's feelings towards her husband it would be quite wrong of her to voice them, but the tinge of colour which crept into her cheeks gave Alexandra her answer. "I thought not," she smiled knowingly. "From what I saw of him," she stated candidly, "he would be far from pleased. You have taken a great risk on my behalf, haven't you?"

Again, Sophy did not answer this, but she knew it was true. She may have no regrets about her actions this morning, in fact she was glad she had come, even so, she trembled to think of Charles's reaction should it ever come to his ears.

"I do thank you for that," Alexandra said earnestly.

There was no doubting the sincerity of Alexandra's words, but even though Sophy shook her head in silent denial she realised that this young girl saw and understood far more than anyone would have thought.

"I *will* think about all you have said," Alexandra promised.

Raising her gloved hand to the soft cheek, Sophy smiled, her eyes warm and misty as she acknowledged her own unhappiness and her new friend's recognition of it. In some strange way she felt they were kindred spirits, both of them in varying degrees suffering at the hands of the Harrington family. "That's all I ask," Sophy nodded, turning on her heel before her emotions got the better of her.

Chapter Nine

The morning's post had brought Marcus yet another letter from his uncle, but this time his request that his nephew come to Yorkshire on affairs of business was more urgently expressed than the others he had received to date. Marcus knew the journey could not be delayed for much longer and that it was not only unfair of him to shelve a duty he took very seriously but which was totally uncharacteristic of him. Even so, it would have to be postponed for a week or so at least, or until he was convinced in his own mind that what he suspected was in fact nothing more than mere fancy.

It had been his suspicions which had brought about that luncheon engagement with Oswald Mercer and the subsequent visit to his family's bank to try to make sense of Charles's irrational attitude towards Alexandra and the stance he seemed to be adopting regarding her inheritance, but if Marcus had thought that his private viewing of Elizabeth's jewellery would put everything into perspective, then he had been doomed to disappointment. All it had achieved was to make him question his own uncertainties even more, and by the time he had said goodbye to Oswald he had been no nearer to distinguishing the fact from the fiction than before.

At one point, Marcus had begun to wonder whether it was his own judgement which was at fault, or merely that he had allowed his distrust of Charles to persuade him that he was involved in something sinister when in fact nothing could be further from the truth. The only positive thing to result from his visit to Mercers' vaults was that his cousin's jewellery was even more magnificent than he remembered. Every exquisite piece was a work of art, created by the most gifted of artists with such care and expertise that the whole collection could, without any doubt, be rightly assessed as being worth a fortune, corroborating Oswald's observation in that someone in his aunt's family had certainly known about precious stones. Marcus had only been able to stand and stare in awe and admiration at the array of diamonds, rubies, emeralds and pearls glittering up at him from their beds of blue velvet, unable to find words adequate enough to express their beauty, but he had also been quite unable to say whether all or some of the pieces were fakes. He was certainly no expert and to his untrained eye every piece appeared real enough, but although he could see nothing amiss with the collection or offer any concrete reason the nagging doubts at the back of his mind persisted.

Other than Adam's confidences and his own knowledge of his cousin, there was absolutely nothing on which Marcus could accuse Charles, but that did not prevent him from thinking something was very wrong and that for some obscure reason it all centred around Elizabeth's jewellery. Marcus could not prove anything, assuming of course there was something to prove in the first place, but Charles's excessive pride and extreme prejudice did not entirely explain away his reaction to his father's bequest to Alexandra. His contemptuous treatment of her did not surprise Marcus, but he failed to understand Charles's rigid stance regarding her inheritance or his anger with Sophy simply because she happened to mention his sister's jewellery. Marcus could not even put forward the argument that such a bequest deprived his cousin of his share of his father's estate, on the contrary all three sons had done extremely well out of it. If only he could be certain that his conjectures and suppositions were exactly that and not grounded in fact he would feel far happier, but Marcus knew perfectly well that he could not openly charge his cousin with something that even he was not sure of, and this knowledge, instead of assuaging his concern, merely served to increase it as well as his growing frustration.

He could not possibly approach Sophy with his suspicions, not only because she would be the last person Charles would take into his confidence but Marcus wanted to do everything in his power to shield her from a situation which she would find deeply distressing but, more than this, should it ever come to Charles's ears that he had been discussing his affairs with his wife, it could make things extremely difficult for her. Sophy's situation was intolerable enough without him adding to it, and therefore it seemed to Marcus that for the time being at least all he could do was keep a close eye on his cousin.

Having received an invitation from his aunt to dine in Brook Street this evening it would, if nothing else, give him the opportunity to see if Charles had had second thoughts about his intentions to thwart the girl, especially now he had had a little time to adjust to the contents of his father's will, but Marcus had to tread carefully; nothing could be more fatal than for Charles to suspect he had come under suspicion. Marcus may not like his cousin over much, but he was honest enough to admit that he was far from proud of the thoughts he was harbouring and had to acknowledge that if they were the product of someone other than himself he would laugh at their absurdities. But he knew Charles as well as he knew himself and what he was capable of, and unless Marcus was very much mistaken he was as convinced as he could be that Charles had got himself into something which was about to come to a head, particularly now that Jenkins was putting a thorough search into operation to find Alexandra and, for this reason alone, Marcus could not be brought to leave London even for a few days. However regrettable, it was nevertheless very necessary, and therefore his letter to his uncle was at once brief and apologetic, knowing that when he did eventually arrive in Yorkshire he would be in for a rare dressing down, the thought bringing with it happy memories of his childhood and a fond smile to his lips.

Charles, on the other hand, had very little to smile about. He was no nearer finding a solution to his difficulties than he ever was and the frustration of knowing that he was floored on all points did nothing to improve his temper. He disliked being out of control and dependent upon others, but he was forced to admit that at the moment he would accept help from Lucifer himself if he could provide the answer to his problem or, more to the point, sufficient funds to redeem those two pieces of jewellery.

He did not know whether to feel relief or anxiety when no further communication came from Jenkins, but Charles felt it reasonably safe to assume that had he located the girl he would have notified them of it; his mother certainly would not have withheld such news from him. Although it was some comfort to know that the longer it took Jenkins to find her the better it was for him, it did mean that he could only speculate as to how much time he had available in which to try to raise the money to buy back the necklace and bracelet from Linas Webb before she was found. At one point he had even toyed with the idea of breaking into his place of business, but it had only taken Charles a matter of moments to realise that he would be the first one to come under suspicion. Once Linas Webb discovered the loss of those two precious items of jewellery he would know instantly who the culprit was, and whilst he may not be in a position to report the theft to the authorities, his affairs being such that they would not take too much scrutiny, he no doubt knew all manner of unsavoury individuals to whom he could turn to help him recoup his losses. Should he be proved wrong in this assumption and Linas Webb did report the theft to Bow Street after all, then it would not be long before the whole sorry story became known and at all costs Charles had to avoid a scandal and subsequent denunciation, the very thought not only being too horrendous to contemplate but firing his determination to settle the affair as soon as possible.

With so much to occupy his mind the last thing he had needed was to be informed by his mother that not only had she invited Marcus to dine with them this evening but also the Reverend Handley, neither of whom Charles had the least desire to share his company with. Making small talk, especially to a man of the cloth, not to mention his cousin, had never been one of his favourite pastimes and never less so than now when he had far more important things to think about.

George's pompous officiousness may incite his employees at Deptford to laugh at him behind his back, but they did not hate or stand in fear of him as did their fellow workers at Islington with Charles, all of whom were more than familiar with his arrogance and rapier-sharp tongue. They had witnessed more than one dismissal for a slight misdemeanour and unless absolutely compelled to do so they did not approach him, keeping their distance as much as possible, his uncertain temper making them extremely wary of him. Unfortunately for Samuel Perry however, his long-suffering clerk, there was no such luxury as not only was his office situated immediately next door but his very position demanded he attend him.

He had known Mr. Charles for a good many years, in fact ever since he had been a boy when he had occasionally come to the brewery with his father, but even at that early age he had exhibited an aloof detachment which, over the years, had grown into an arrogance which rendered any contact with him a rather daunting experience. Like his father, Mr. Charles ran the brewery not only efficiently but at a profit, but unlike Matthew, who, despite his exacting ways and volatile temperament, had always been fair and just in his dealings with the men, who, in return, gave him their loyalty and respect, both of which they denied to Charles Harrington, as he did himself, especially having been on the receiving end of his haughtiness and temper more than once as well as witnessing his abruptness with the men. Nevertheless, Samuel Perry had never before known Mr. Charles be in the devil's own humour as he had been of late and, with the exception of himself, who really had no choice, only the bravest, or the most foolhardy, would dare approach him. All the same, he would give a week's wages to know who or what had brought that look of thunder to his face, but familiarity with his employer made him refrain from politely enquiring if anything was amiss, knowing full well that he would be given a sharp reminder of his position for his pains.

Charles, having spent another fruitless morning considering what options were available to him and concluding that there were absolutely none at all, was far from pleased to hear the tentative tap on his door followed by Perry putting his head round it. "I thought I had made myself quite clear, Perry," he reminded him coldly, causing his underling to swallow nervously. "I said I did not want to be disturbed."

"I'm sorry, Mr. Charles," Perry apologised hastily, "I would not have done so now, but there is a gentleman…"

"Get rid of him," Charles told him brusquely, his eyebrows snapping together and his lips thinning into an angry line.

"That may be a little difficult, sir," Perry said fearfully, torn between his employer's anger and his visitor's refusal to leave. "He is most insistent, and refuses to leave the premises until he has seen you. In fact," he ventured nervously, "he particularly desired me to bring you in his card."

"Perry," Charles warned, his eyes narrowing, "unless you want to find yourself in the unenviable position of seeking other employment I strongly advise you to remove yourself, and while you are about it you can take that fellow with you!"

Perry swallowed uncomfortably; he knew that look and ominously calm voice from painful experience and realised only too well that Mr. Charles meant what he said. He would have no compunction in dismissing him and he was far too old to be seeking further employment, but the man waiting in his office, coarse and vulgar though he was, was not going to be dismissed so easily. Swallowing again, Perry said weakly, "I will try to get rid of him, sir, but he said it would be of considerable advantage to yourself if you could spare him a few minutes of your time."

The brown eyes glinted dangerously and the handsome face took on an ugly look which made Perry tremble as he bravely placed the calling card on the desk in front of him, his spare frame shaking alarmingly as he feared for the consequences.

"You are either deaf," Charles remarked nastily, glancing dismissively at Perry before briefly eyeing the card, "or you are incapable of understanding plain English. Which is it?"

"N-neither, sir," Perry stammered, his eyes watchful as Charles's long fingers flicked over the card.

"I will not tolerate insubordination in my staff, Perry," he told him absently, his attention momentarily diverted. "Do you understand?"

"Yes, sir," Perry nodded, edging his way cautiously towards the door.

"This man," Charles forestalled him, "where is he now?"

"In my office, Mr. Charles," Perry replied, thankful for the stay of execution.

"Did he say what he wanted?" Charles demanded, leaning back in his chair, eyeing his underling closely.

"No, sir," Perry shook his head, "only that I was to inform you that you would not be wasting your time if you spared him a few moments."

Charles eyed the card again. He had never heard of anyone by the name of Ted Knowles and could see no reason why he should choose to honour him with a visit, but curiosity tinged with something he could not quite define made him pause. "Very well," he nodded at length, having deliberated the matter, "I will see him."

"Very good, sir," Perry nodded.

"And Perry," Charles warned him ominously, "the next time you disobey me will be your last. Remember that."

"Yes, sir. Thank you, sir," Perry nodded again, relieved to be leaving with a whole skin.

Having been most unsatisfactorily treated by Silas Jenkins, Ted Knowles was determined to take further advantage of the situation as much as he possibly could. In his considered opinion five pounds had been nothing short of miserly, even an insult, and he was not the type of man to suffer such treatment tamely. The Harrington family were as wealthy as they were proud and unless he was very much mistaken, and he was sure he wasn't, then they would be none too pleased to find themselves faced with a young slip of a girl who was not only about to take possession of a sizeable fortune but a collection of sparklers reputedly worth a King's ransom, and one who would be nothing short of an embarrassment to them.

For a man of Ted Knowles's ingenuity and considerable enterprise, it had been a relatively easy matter to put himself in possession of certain facts about the family, and his reliable source of information, who had never yet steered him wrong, had shown him that his safest bet was to approach Mr. Charles Harrington. Not being a man who worried himself unduly over ethics, Ted Knowles thought no more about receiving inside information from a trusted servant any more than he did from anyone else, on the contrary it merely reinforced his belief that servants, like most people, could be bought. The trouble of course was that some employers considered their servants to be deaf, dumb and blind, speaking as freely in front of them as they would to a valued friend. Not that it mattered one bit! Of course, it was a pity that the information came via a third party who, no matter how reliable a go-between he was, required payment up front, but then he consoled himself with the knowledge that he could more than adequately recover his losses with the money he would receive from Mr. Charles Harrington. In view of the ingratitude shown him by Silas Jenkins in offering him no more than five pounds for his trouble, Ted Knowles saw nothing to prevent him from seeing Charles Harrington as soon as possible. If he was as dead set against the girl as Ted Knowles had been led to believe, then he would no doubt be very interested in her whereabouts and pay very handsomely for the information. If all he had been told were only half true, then Charles Harrington had no intention of ever allowing the girl to lay a finger on her inheritance, never mind accepting her into the family. Being a man of few scruples, it never even occurred to Ted Knowles that his devious methods of working were far from honourable and he could see no possible reason why he should come out of this whole affair a loser and bearing in mind what he had been told about Charles Harrington he envisaged a very rewarding meeting. In his experience, well-breeched swells like him were always in need of the services of a man of his particular talents and, this being so, there was absolutely no reason why he should not expect a very rosy future resulting from their collaboration.

Having been kept kicking his heels in Samuel Perry's office for far longer than he had expected, by the time Ted Knowles was eventually shown into Charles Harrington's room he was rather frayed around the edges and his temper well and truly on the rise. He had not anticipated being kept hanging around like a schoolboy, especially when he had come here specifically to do him a considerable favour, but no sooner did Ted Knowles set eyes on Charles Harrington than the belligerent retort hanging on his lips died at birth. It took him only a matter of seconds to recognise that he was a very different kettle of fish altogether to Silas Jenkins, and certainly not the type of man one took liberties with, and if Ted Knowles was any judge a man would have to be pretty desperate to cross swords with him.

Like Silas Jenkins before him, Charles looked at the man standing respectfully in front of him with barely concealed horror, his face clearly reflecting his revulsion at the sight of the tan suit. To one of his impeccable taste, Ted Knowles was not only vulgar but offensive and Charles seriously questioned the possibility of him being able to do anything remotely advantageous for anyone.

Impervious to snubs, verbal or otherwise, Ted Knowles removed his bowler, his face breaking into a smile which yielded no response from the man looking disdainfully up at him. Undeterred, he said cheerfully, "Mornin' yer 'oner."

Upon receiving no reply to his greeting, Ted Knowles merely ambled over to the large mahogany desk, behind which Charles lounged at his ease in a comfortable leather chair, his elbows resting on the wide arms and his long slim fingers propping up his chin. Several minutes went by before he spoke, during which he calculatingly eyed his visitor; accurately assessing the character of the man. Again, like Silas Jenkins, Charles saw beneath the hearty surface, instantly recognising him for what he actually was. Ted Knowles may advertise himself as being a private investigator, but Charles saw the grasping avarice behind the course joviality and knew that he would be none too particular in lending his hand to any task if it proved to be gainful. If his calculations were correct, and he was certain they were, then this common and vulgar individual, distasteful though the thought was, may be of some use to him after all. But however critical his predicament, Charles was by far too intelligent and shrewd to jump in with both feet before he had tested the water. "I understand you wish to see me," he stated, not very encouragingly, "although I cannot possibly conceive why."

"Ah!" Ted Knowles nodded, presumptuously taking a seat.

"Please, do make yourself comfortable," Charles invited sarcastically, his lips parting in a none too pleasant smile.

"Thankin' yer kindly," Ted Knowles beamed.

"Well," Charles said abruptly, "what is it you want? I am extremely busy and have neither the time nor the inclination to indulge in polite conversation." For some obscure reason this seemed to amuse his visitor, considerably surprising Charles when he broke into a deep-throated chuckle which made his face turn an even deeper shade of red. "I fail to see the humour," Charles told him coolly when Ted Knowles's paroxysm had abated. "Either state your business or leave."

"I'm cumin' to it," Ted Knowles gasped. "Jus' gimme a minit." After wiping his streaming eyes with the large handkerchief he pulled from out of his coat pocket, he said, "Well now, I dessay you'm wundrin' wot I'm doin' 'ere."

"I thought I had made that abundantly plain," Charles drawled sarcastically, eyeing him with fervent dislike.

"Well, it's like this," Ted Knowles explained. "I 'ave 'ere in me very pockit sumthin' I thinks yer'll find interestin'."

"Indeed!" Charles replied haughtily, his eyes wary as he crossed one long and impeccably tailored leg over the other. "And what might that be?"

Digging deep into his inside pocket, Ted Knowles retrieved what looked to be a folded sheet torn out of a newspaper which he subsequently handed over, saying, "This."

Charles may not subscribe to this particular newspaper but he recognised the personal section when he saw it and it was his experience one only interested oneself in an advertisement page to either consult or insert one. He did not need to have the message explained or the initials translated, he knew immediately what they signified and that Silas Jenkins was its author. Charles's expression may have been inscrutable but he felt as though the ground had opened up beneath him. It did not take much ingenuity to conclude that Ted Knowles was clearly the man his father had employed to find the girl and that Silas Jenkins, as a last resort in his efforts to locate her, had inserted that advertisement.

If ever Charles had needed proof that the fates were against him, surely this was it! Now Jenkins was in possession of the girl's direction it was only a matter of time, perhaps days, before his deception was made known. There was no possibility of recovering the situation in so short a time! Admirably concealing his feelings, Charles tossed the sheet onto the desk with hands that were far steadier than he would have thought possible. "I fail to see how this is of any interest to me," he shrugged nonchalantly.

"Well, now," Ted Knowles said thoughtfully, picking up the sheet and slowly folding it before returning it to his inside pocket, "seems as if I've picked up the sow by the 'rung 'ea!"

"It would appear so," Charles remarked disinterestedly, his brain racing ahead. If only he could ascertain whether or not this obnoxious individual had already responded to the advertisement or if he had decided to delay contacting Jenkins in order to play his own game first, then he could probably still salvage the situation. If he had not contacted Jenkins yet, and from the date of the newspaper it seemed unlikely, then all was not lost. Gradually he was beginning to feel his way and eyeing Ted Knowles meditatively said, with perfect sang-froid, "I must be extraordinarily obtuse today because try as I do I cannot understand why you have come to me with this rather than to the author of the advertisement."

Ted Knowles looked searchingly at him, but he could read nothing in the impassive face calmly regarding him to suggest he was on the right track. If Charles Harrington did have a particular interest in the girl as his informant had led him to believe, then he was giving no sign of it, but being a man who did not give up on something so easily, and certainly not when it came to the prospect of earning money, then for that reason alone Ted Knowles was prepared to press ahead. "Am yer tellin' me that yer dunno the gerl?" he asked, his eyes watchful.

"Of course I know her," Charles replied with more composure than he felt, "but that does not explain why you have come to me with this. I should be glad of enlightenment."

"Ah," Ted Knowles nodded, "I knows I was not mistook."

Charles eyed him with distaste. "In what?"

Resting his elbows on the desk Ted Knowles leaned forward, saying confidentially, "Now, lookee 'ere. I knows wot I knows, an' that is that a fine gen'leman like yerself wud be int'restid in findin' the gerl."

"For what purpose?" Charles enquired, raising a supercilious eyebrow.

Tapping his nose with a thick forefinger, Ted Knowles nodded conspiratorially, "Well, from wot I 'ears 'ers gonna walk away wi' a fer bit; not ter menshun the sparklers!"

Charles looked searchingly at him for several moments, his steady gaze by no means disconcerting his thick-skinned visitor. So, Ted Knowles knew that much, did he? "How do you know this?" he asked sharply, not at all pleased to learn that his family's affairs were known to this man.

Ted Knowles shrugged as he straightened up. "Like I says, I knows wot I knows."

"You are not by any chance going to tell me that Silas Jenkins told you, are you?" Charles asked with credible surprise, cunningly seeking the answer to his burning question. "Because if you are, I tell you now I do not believe it."

"Wot 'im!" Ted Knowles scoffed. "Close as a clam that one," he told him disgustedly. "Scared ter let 'is one 'and know wot 't'others doin'."

This was not what Charles wanted to hear but he hid his vexation, saying, quite unperturbed, "So, he knows the girl's direction. When did you see him?"

"Yesterdee mornin'," Ted Knowles confirmed.

Yesterday! A whole twenty-four hours wasted! But it could have been worse. In his estimation Silas Jenkins would surely be far too busy to visit the girl at a moment's notice, nevertheless he would be a fool to take this assumption for granted. Charles knew enough about Jenkins to realise that a man of his professional integrity would carry out his father's instructions to the letter, and as soon as possible. He had to suppose that Jenkins had already seen the girl, either yesterday afternoon or this morning, in which case it may already be too late for him to salvage the situation, even so it did not necessarily follow that he had met with success, it could well be that the girl was not at home when he called or, and Charles would not put it past her, she could have slung Jenkins and his client's bequest through the door!

He was still deliberating this when Ted Knowles helpfully offered his opinion of the girl. "A propa little firebrand that one! Wy, it wos like I wos talkin' to the old guvna hisself. Wen I tells 'er that 'er gran'pa wonted to see 'er wy, I wos givun a rare talkin' to."

Charles nodded absently, his brain thinking several steps ahead, but eventually he said, "You still have not answered either of my questions. How did you know about the girl's expectations? And why come to me when you have already furnished my father's solicitor with her direction?"

Ted Knowles may be unscrupulous and quite prepared to use anyone who could serve his own devious ends, but he was no fool and he certainly did not underestimate Charles Harringon. He recognised the ruthless determination lying beneath the polished exterior and instinctively knew that his retribution would be as swift as it would merciless and once he was in possession of certain facts, his source of information for one, he would very soon put an end to any more gossip emanating from Brook Street. Shrugging, Ted Knowles prevaricated, "Stands ter reason the old guvna left 'er sumthin', othawise wy wud 'e 'ave 'ad me chasin' all ova fer the gerl?" Allowing a few seconds for Charles to digest this, he went on, "Now, I asks yer, if yoo were me, wot wud yer think? Stands ter reasun yer ain't gonna be any too pleased. I wudn't meself. A yung slip of a wench out o' now'ere cumin' along ter tek a nice little earna!"

Charles eyed him coldly, saying unpleasantly, "You seem to have done a great deal of thinking, but you could not possibly have known about the jewellery, and if, as you say," he inclined his head, "Jenkins did not inform you of her inheritance and what it consists of, you must have had the information from someone." His eyes narrowed suddenly and his voice dropped to an ominous calm. "Someone has been talking, Knowles."

"Now there's no need ter fret yerself ova that," Ted Knowles assured him. "It's jus' that a man in my posishun gets ter 'ear things, an'… well," he shrugged, "puttin' two and two togetha…"

"I am not interested in your arithmetical abilities," Charles purred dangerously, "but I *am* interested to learn from whom you 'heard' these things."

Too late to realise that he had perhaps been a little too clever by telling Charles Harrington precisely what he knew about the girl's expectations and equally late in realising that he would not allow it to pass. Ted Knowles had seen at the outset that Charles Harrington was no dupe and that he would not be easily pacified, but it would do his reputation no good at all if it became known that he snitched on his accomplices, although if it came to that it would not do him any good to cross this man either, so deciding that his only chance was to try to bluff his way through it, Ted Knowles shrugged, "Well now," he rubbed his chin thoughtfully, "can't say as I rightly rememba."

"You had better remember, Knowles," Charles warned, "because if the affairs of my family become public knowledge I shan't take it kindly."

"They *won't,*" Ted Knowles said emphatically. "Nobudy's gonna say nuthin'," he nodded, "so there's no need ter fret yerself," he reiterated. "It's jus' that I gets ter 'ear lots o' things from lots o' peeple, but they ain't no gabsters," he shot at him, emphasising, "an' nor am *I!* Wudn't do me a mite o' gud if I startid blabbin'."

"You clearly hear a great deal," Charles bit out, far from pleased, "and no doubt you have concluded I would be willing to pay you handsomely for the girl's direction."

"Ah!" Ted Knowles nodded approvingly, his habitual buoyancy resurfacing. "I says to meself, 'Ted,' I says, "ere's as knowin' a body as I've eva clapped eyes on!'"

Revolted by his visitor's lack of address as well as his manners, Charles commented scathingly, "It appears you do a deal too much thinking!"

Unperturbed by this rebuke, Ted Knowles grinned, "Ain't no sense in goin' in 'arf cocked. Al'as mek shua o' yer ground before yer meks a move."

Despite his revulsion, Charles had to acknowledge that here was a man after his own heart and one, moreover, who would have no compunction in doing whatever he considered necessary to further his ends, and certainly not one who would shrink from a task no matter how distasteful. "You seem to me," he commented, "to be a man entirely without scruples."

Ted Knowles accepted this as quite a compliment, confirming unashamedly, "Can' afford 'em. 'Sides," he added truthfully, "they don't do nobudy no gud. Betta orf without 'em."

After considering the burly faced individual opposite for several moments, Charles mused, "You know, considering you have apparently gone to such great lengths to gather so much information about my family, by what devious methods I can only hazard a guess, I am surprised you have approached me and not another member of my family!"

Having expected something like this Ted Knowles had his answer ready. "Ah," he offered glibly, "but none of 'em wud appreshiate me paticler talents like yerself," nodding in response to the appreciative twitch of Charles's lips that he was not quite able to suppress.

Providence may have unexpectedly come to his aid in the guise of this crude and vulgar individual to help save him from a most embarrassing disclosure, but Charles was certainly not about to take him into his confidence. It was unfortunate that time was not working in his favour which meant that he could not afford to be too nice in dealing with a matter which was rapidly approaching crisis point; indeed, for all he knew it may already be too late to prevent that substitution from being discovered. The very thought of having to use the questionable talents of the man sitting comfortably opposite him may be too horrendous to contemplate, but whether he liked it or not he was forced to admit that his only hope of emerging from his dilemma seemed to lie in this coarse and vulgar individual. Charles may still be finding it difficult to believe that his father, as astute a man as one would find anywhere, had resorted to using the services of someone like Ted Knowles, but however much it pained Charles to own it, it was patently obvious that he was far more capable than one would suppose. If he could find one solitary girl in the midst of a sprawling city like London, then, surely, he could fulfil whatever task was given him with equal competence, and without any qualms as to how he accomplished it. "You came here this morning for a reason," he shot at him, his eyes narrowing. "What is it you want?"

Totally unabashed by this forthright question, Ted Knowles rubbed his fingers and thumb together.

"How much?" Charles demanded.

"Well now," Ted Knowles said thoughtfully, "that's dependin'."

Charles did not pretend to misunderstand him, but he considered long and hard before saying, "These particular talents of yours, I take it they are to be relied upon?"

"I ain't 'ad no complaints so far," Ted Knowles pointed out, affronted, unused to having his methods of working called into question.

"My apologies." Charles mockingly inclined his head. "However," he said smoothly, "since you have taken it upon yourself to discover so much about my affairs, you must therefore have concluded that the girl as well as her prospects are most unacceptable to me, and could, at some point in the future, create something of a problem?"

"Bound to," Ted Knowles nodded. "O'cus," he said suggestively, "problems can be ovacum."

"I daresay," Charles acknowledged, "but this particular problem could prove a little difficult to overcome."

Ted Knowles may be in the dark as to the truth surrounding the significance of the jewellery which formed part of that bequest and Charles Harrington's desperation to prevent that substitution of four years ago from coming to light, but he was perfectly well acquainted with human nature and found nothing to marvel at in his newly acquired client's dislike of having to hand over such a hoard to a slip of a girl out of nowhere, and fully appreciated how he must resent her having anything at all. Being an avaricious man himself, Ted Knowles had every sympathy for his client's reluctance to accommodate the girl in any way whatsoever, and therefore felt no twinge of conscience in offering his services to rid him of his predicament by any means available. "O'cus," he shrugged, leaning forward on his elbows, "h'if the problum wos removed now…"

Charles knew precisely what he was suggesting, but although this idea had already crossed his mind it had been more wishful thinking than serious contemplation, let alone actually planning it. Even without his urgent need to recover those items of jewellery from Linas Webb, the very thought of the brat having anything at all was unthinkable, and as for having her residing in Brook Street the prospect was too horrendous to contemplate! Of course, the idea was not entirely without its merits and one which would certainly solve his immediate problem, but he was astute enough to realise that removing the girl would be no easy matter, not to mention the scandal it would generate should it ever become known that he had engineered his niece's demise. Given time he would doubtless arrive at a solution, but this precious commodity was not on his side, even less so now that Jenkins was in possession of her direction. Charles may not be a man given over to panic but he could not help feeling some uneasiness when he considered that public disgrace was getting ever nearer and, at all costs, he could not allow his actions of four years ago to come to light. This common and vulgar individual may have been put in the way of certain information, but he could not possibly know anything about those two pieces of jewellery which he had used to borrow on and which he was now trying to redeem without anyone being the wiser. The less this man knew the better, even so, his services could prove very useful particularly as time as well as desperation were forcing his hand.

Ted Knowles had not disappointed him; he was everything he had calculated him to be, and far more. Not only was he unscrupulous and totally devoid of principles but he clearly had no reservations about doing anything which may be considered outside the law. He was not only a stranger to the codes of honour governing society but to finesse as well, but he was the very person Charles had been looking for, and instinctively knew that he need have no fear of him blabbing to all and sundry. Apart from the fact that he would not risk jeopardising his disreputable career and bringing his own particular brand of integrity into question, there was no doubting that the law would be very interested in Ted Knowles. Charles eyed him narrowly. "Removed," he repeated slowly. "It certainly covers a multitude of possibilities."

"I knowed yer'd like it!" Ted Knowles smiled, his eyes lighting up.

"I may do," Charles conceded, disappointing him almost at once by saying, "but I am certainly not prepared to engage on such a venture unless it becomes absolutely necessary." He saw the effect this had on Knowles. "I realise of course," he mockingly apologised "that this will deprive you of the opportunity to exhibit your many talents, but regrettable though you may find it before I embark on such a drastic course I would much prefer to adopt other measures."

Rubbing his chin reflectively, Ted Knowles eyed his client with a mixture of disappointment and resignation. He knew without even trying that it would be a waste of time in pushing Charles Harrington into something he had no mind for. Perhaps later, when he discovered that his other options had failed, as they undoubtedly would, because even he had seen that the girl was no fool. Nevertheless, his client's reluctance to permanently rid himself of the hurdle which held out every likelihood of being the source of future difficulties, came as something of a surprise, but telling himself that it was no bread and butter of his and as long as he was paid for his services it was all one to him. "Er…" he began tentatively, "jus' wot *did* yer 'ave in mind?"

"Like you, Knowles," Charles smiled, "I too always make sure of my ground." Eyeing his visitor closely, he said circumspectly, "My needs as well as my aims are really quite simple; and my main aim at this moment is to ascertain precisely what the girl has in mind," adding smoothly, "which is where *you*, my dear Knowles, come in."

Ted Knowles listened to his client acquainting him with what he had in mind with barely concealed surprise, at the end of which he said with polite sarcasm, "That's jus' dandy, that is! An' jus' 'ow do yer suggest I do that? The wench ain't likely ter welcum me wi' open arms yer knows!"

The brown eyes mocked him but the voice was perfectly affable. "Why, I shall leave that to your ingenuity and infinite resource."

"That's all very well," Ted Knowles snorted, "but even if 'er does speaks ter me, wot meks yer think 'er'll tells me wot I wonts ter know?"

"You must ensure that she does," Charles replied. "Besides," he pointed out, "I have great faith in your extraordinary capabilities!" This quietly delivered speech left Ted Knowles in no doubt as to the kind of man he was dealing with and that it would go ill with him if he failed, confirming his initial estimation that Charles Harrington was not a man he would willingly cross. "I shall expect your report this afternoon," Charles told him.

"This *aftanoon!*" Ted Knowles repeated, aghast. "That don't leave me much time," he pointed out. "'Sides, the gerl may not be in."

"Unfortunately, I can offer you no more time. As for the girl," Charles mocked nastily, "I doubt very much whether she is inundated with social engagements!"

"Mebbe 'er ain't," Ted Knowles acknowledged, "but even so it's pushin' it a bit."

"Half past four this afternoon," Charles said with finality. "I shall meet you at the Piccadilly entrance to Green Park."

Ted Knowles sighed, knowing it was pointless arguing. Unless of course he wanted to be on the receiving end of Charles Harrington's tongue and perhaps even lose this golden opportunity to make some extra money, he had no choice but to follow his instructions. But there was not much time to play with, it was getting on for twelve o'clock now!

"Of course," Charles shrugged, "if you think the task is too much…"

"It ain't," Ted Knowles broke in, "but a bit more time wud'nt cum amiss."

"I do sympathise," Charles mockingly soothed, "but I am afraid you will have to make the best of it. Now," he reminded him, holding out his hand, "I think you were going to give me the girl's direction."

Ted Knowles had a good mind not to give it to him, but it did not take him many moments to realise the futility of such a refusal, so biting down on this inclination he did as he was asked, then, after watching Charles slip the piece of paper into his inside pocket said that if that was all he had best be on his way.

"Not quite," the smile not wavering on Charles's lips, to which Ted Knowles cocked his head. "Before you leave here there are one or two points I wish to make clear."

"Such as?" Ted Knowles asked warily, shifting uncomfortably in his chair.

"Such as, Knowles," Charles said with slow deliberation, "that it would be most unwise of you to divulge my commission to you to anyone."

Even though there was no need for Ted Knowles to have his meaning spelled out the subtle warning about keeping his tongue between his teeth nevertheless rankled. "There's no need to fret yerself," he said tetchily, "I'm no gabster!"

"I sincerely hope not," Charles warned.

"I knows when ter keep me mouth shut," he nodded firmly, rising to his feet.

"I am so glad we understand one another," Charles smiled thinly, "and that there is no need for me to further impress upon you the imprudence of crossing me." He paused momentarily, his smile disappearing as he said menacingly, "I make a dangerous adversary, Knowles. Remember that!"

"I'll remember," Ted Knowles nodded. "If that's all then, Guvna, I'll be on me way."

"Just one more thing," Charles forestalled him. "Do not make the mistake of failing to take me seriously or, worse, underestimate me in any way. If any of what has been discussed here today, or whatever passes between us in the future, becomes public knowledge, I shall personally ensure that you will come to regret the day you ever came in my way."

Having already given his word on these points Ted Knowles looked rather affronted, but, unfortunately, he was given no opportunity to put forward any protest as to the slur on his integrity as he found himself dexterously manoeuvred out of the room, his dark mutterings going unheeded. Thick skinned he may be but he was astute enough to realise that Charles Harrington would have no hesitation in carrying out his unspoken threats or, to be more accurate, his promises, should he go against him. Ted Knowles was not afraid of a fight, in fact he could hold his own very well, and although Charles Harrington looked to be pretty handy with his fives he felt reasonably certain that his retribution would go further than using his fists.

It never so much as crossed Charles's mind that Knowles may fail him, in fact he had every confidence in the questionable tactics of his new-found acquaintance to doubt his eventual success, and therefore spent the few hours remaining before their assignation in Green Park in happy contemplation of a speedy end to his difficulties.

Unfortunately, however, Ted Knowles did not share his optimism. He had no cause to question his own abilities, in which he had great faith, but as he slowly made his way from Islington to Hoxton he saw all too clearly the many pitfalls which could arise to prevent him from being in Green Park at half past four. It was all very well for Charles Harrington to scoff about the girl having no social engagements, but there were other reasons why she may not be in when he called which would mean he either hang around for goodness only knew how long waiting for her to return or, which was infinitely worse, going in search of her which would necessarily mean making enquiries with her landlady, a prospect he did not look forward to with any pleasure, especially when he remembered her previous reception of him. Even if he did find the girl at home there was no guarantee she would talk to him, and although he had no qualms about using his various methods of persuasion on her he would much prefer not to at this stage of the game. In his unchallenged opinion he could see no sense in showing off your wares if you were not ready to sell them! Besides, it would create a great deal of talk, something Charles Harrington particularly wished to avoid. For himself though, Ted Knowles was still of the view that his client would be far better off by disposing of the problem at the outset, getting it over and done with, nice and quiet like, eliminating the possibility of being seen as well as cutting down the risk of wagging tongues! Being of an avaricious nature himself he regarded Charles Harrington's desire to remove the girl from his life as perfectly understandable, especially when Ted Knowles considered how she stood to gain at his expense. It never even occurred to him to delve any deeper into his client's motives in case he had a far more devious reason entirely for wanting her out of the way, and even if he had questioned him it was doubtful he would have told him, not that it was any of his business anyway, providing he was paid it was all one to him irrespective of Charles Harrington's real motives.

But good fortune was apparently smiling upon Ted Knowles. During the slow and extremely uncomfortable journey to Hoxton he had set his mind to the task of how best to approach his quarry, vivid recollections of their previous encounter not exactly filling him with hope of a successful interview. He had little reason to suppose she would welcome him with open arms much less confide in him, but as the hackney carriage neared its destination the foundations of a plan were beginning to formulate in his brain. The hackney driver, either because he had misheard the number of the house given him or because he had taken Ted Knowles in dislike from the moment he had unceremoniously deprived him of his original fare which would have given him a bigger largesse, dropped him almost five doors away, necessitating him walking the short distance to the one he wanted. Angrily tossing a coin up at the driver with the dark warning as to what may befall him if he continued to treat his fares in this way, Ted Knowles strode along the pavement towards number eighteen, his mood lightening at once when, within stepping distance of the gate, the door opened and a lady emerged from the house immediately followed by Silas Jenkins. For a man of his bulk Ted Knowles moved with surprising swiftness into the side entry which conveniently separated number eighteen from the house next door. He had no idea who the woman was but her clothes and the way she held herself told him that she was unquestionably a lady. Pinning himself flat against the entry wall he strained his ears in an effort to listen to what they were saying above the noise in the street and was just able to make out a part at least of their conversation.

"You say she has promised to think about it?" Silas Jenkins said as he handed Sophy down the step onto the path.

"Yes," she nodded, her soft voice just audible. "Of course, it has all been rather a shock to her, but I believe that after she has given it some thought and had time to become adjusted to it all she will accept her grandfather's bequest."

"I don't suppose she gave any indication as to how long it will be before she arrives at a decision?" Jenkins enquired of his companion.

"No, but although I cannot bear the thought of her remaining in this dreadful place any longer than is necessary, under no circumstances must we coerce her into making a decision until she is ready."

"No, of course not," Jenkins agreed. "Do you think we should tell Mrs. Matthew Harrington? I mean," he shook his head, "if Alexandra does not want anything to do with her grandmother…"

"I don't like deceiving her," Ted Knowles heard Sophy say, "but should that be the case it would hurt her dreadfully! I think it may be best to leave it for a little while."

"Yes," Jenkings nodded, "I agree," opening the gate for her to pass through. "However, I must own to some relief," he remarked with feeling, making a not very successful attempt to close the broken gate behind them, "that you agreed to accompany me today; I doubt I should have coped half so well with her."

"She is understandably very upset," Sophy pointed out. "Perfectly natural of course considering what she has had to endure all these years."

"Very well," Ted Knowles heard Jenkins say, "I will not approach her just yet."

"No, I do not think that would be very wise. Far better to allow her a little time. After all…" Sophy's voice had now become quite inaudible as they walked out of earshot.

Ted Knowles, inching his way out of the entry, saw them walk to the end of the street where, just on the corner, Silas Jenkins hailed an oncoming hackney, but not until they had climbed into the vehicle and it disappeared from his view did Ted Knowles emerge onto the pavement, still unable to believe his luck.

A miracle, that's what it was! Nothing short of a miracle. Who would have thought it? Shaking his head in disbelief at his good fortune he could not get over the fact that he had done a job successfully with absolutely no effort required on his part to do it. To think that he had been wondering how to find out what he wanted to know without arousing suspicion in the girl and here he was on the very day that Jenkins had come to see her! It was an omen; that's what it was – an omen! Rubbing his hands together with immense satisfaction at having acquired the information he had been sent to obtain without any exertion whatsoever on his part, he decided that he had more than earned a drop of something warm and invigorating at his favourite watering hole, besides which, it would help keep the cold out. If Charles smelled alcohol on his co-conspirator he certainly could not accuse him of being drunk; Ted Knowles had an extremely hard head and it would take more than several glasses of the landlord's best brandy to put him under the table.

Having strolled across Piccadilly to the entrance of Green Park, which, at half past four on a dark and bitterly cold February afternoon, was deserted, Charles spied his associate looking extremely cold and uncomfortable as he stood beneath one of the trees in an attempt to keep out of view of any late wayfarer.

Upon seeing Charles walk towards him Ted Knowles emerged from his shelter, doffing his hat. "Aftanoon yer 'oner."

"Well," Charles bit out, forgoing any greeting, "what have you been able to discover?"

"Ah," Ted Knowles nodded, "d'ain't I tells yer ter trus' me?"

"Knowles," Charles drawled dangerously, absently eyeing the silver tip of his ebony cane, "I have neither the time nor the patience to stand here passing pleasantries with you. Get on with it," he snapped.

Doing as he was bidden, Ted Knowles related the events of the past few hours, pleased to be able to give his client good news, eagerly looking forward to the largesse he would soon have in his pocket.

"So," Charles mused, almost to himself, "Jenkins has been quick off the mark, has he?"

"Ay," Ted Knowles confirmed, "'e ain't wasted no time."

"This woman," Charles said slowly, eyeing his companion closely, "did you manage to discover her name?"

"No," Ted Knowles shook his head, adding defensively, "'ow cud I wi'out showin' meself?"

"Quite!" Charles drawled. "So, you have no idea who she is?"

"No," Ted Knowles said firmly, "but wot I *can* tells yer, is that 'er's unqueshionably a lady."

"Unquestionably a lady," Charles repeated, drawing in his breath. "What did she look like?" he demanded, not quite able to keep the urgency out of his voice. "Can you describe her?"

"Well now," Ted Knowles considered, rubbing his chin, "I only got a glimpse of 'er mind, but from wot I cud see 'er wos pritty tall."

"Pretty tall," Charles repeated slowly, feeling as though the ground was being kicked from under him, the ugly look crossing his face not lost on Ted Knowles.

"Ay," Knowles nodded, "an' o'cus 'er 'ad 'er 'at on, but I'd say 'er wos red 'aired, awbun like."

"Tell me," Charles asked, an odd inflexion creeping into his voice, "this lady, she is of slim build?"

"That's it!" Knowles nodded. "An' I'd say 'er's a fer dazzla." When Charles made no response to this extra information, he asked warily, "Yer knows 'er?"

"Yes, I know her," Charles confirmed quietly. "Unless I am very much mistaken, which I doubt," he told him tautly, a strange glint entering his eyes, "that lady happens to be my wife."

Apart from pursing his lips Ted Knowles gave no other indication as to his surprise, but as far as he was concerned the only thing that mattered was that he had done what he had been asked to do and now he wanted paying, but one glance at Charles Harrington's face was enough to tell him that now was not the time to ask him for what he considered to be his due.

Charles's expression was certainly forbidding, and it was several minutes before he was able to bring his temper sufficiently under control to enable him to ask, "You are certain they did not see you?"

"O'cus I'm certain," Ted Knowles said indignantly.

Charles nodded, but it was obvious he was paying no heed to Ted Knowles's resentment over the aspersions cast upon his prowess. The intelligence Charles had received, apart from acting upon him like a body blow, put quite a different complexion on the matter altogether.

If Sophy was taking a hand in the affair then he would lay his life that she would do everything possible to persuade the girl to accept her grandfather's bequest without any further loss of time in spite of the fact that she had urged Jenkins not to press her. Like everyone else, Charles was aware of the run-down conditions which existed in that part of London, and he knew his wife too well to be misguided into thinking that she would have remained unmoved by the far from salubrious locality in which the girl lived and the conditions which clearly made up her domicile. Her innate compassion would doubtless have been stirred by what she saw, and this, added to what he knew were her true feelings regarding the girl even though she may not voice them, he could well imagine her doing all she could to try to bring about a speedy conclusion.

He could not help thinking that without his wife's persuasions the girl would no doubt take her time in claiming her inheritance, if for no other reason than defiance, in some ill-bred attempt, in a manner the lower classes always had towards their betters, to repay her relatives for their unconcealed contempt of her as well as increasing their dread at the prospect of having someone like her residing in Brook Street, but he was in no doubt that she would ultimately accept what was being offered her. The longer she delayed declaring her intentions the more time he had to try to arrive at a means of redeeming those two pieces of jewellery from Linas

Webb, but as Charles was perfectly well aware of Sophy's sentiments in this he could not fool himself into believing that she would refrain from urging the girl to come to an early decision.

The girl was by no means stupid, on the contrary she was typical of her kind, cunning and wily, and would know that what she was being offered was too tempting to turn down, and Charles could not delude himself into thinking that she would turn her back on thirty thousand pounds. Having once decided to accept her grandmother's protection as well as her inheritance, then if for no other reason than curiosity she would want to see her mother's jewellery. Once that collection was removed from its protective confines, then it would only be a matter of time, perhaps even hours, before someone identified the necklace and bracelet as being copies, and quite useless to suppose that the girl would want to hush up the deception; on the contrary she was just low and vulgar enough to take satisfaction from exposing and humiliating him, and at all costs this contingency had to be avoided.

As it was only a matter of time before the truth about the substitution emerged, he knew he could no longer afford to waste any more time or thought in indulging the hope, never very strong at the best of times, of coming to some kind of arrangement with the girl; and equally a waste of time to go on deceiving himself into thinking that he could raise the money to redeem those two pieces of jewellery within the foreseeable future. Added to this was his mother's expressed wish to have the girl reside with them in Brook Street, the very thought of which was not only quite repugnant to him but something he could not contemplate without revulsion, and consequently concluded that no option remained open to him other than that recommended earlier by his confederate. Dire it may be, but rather that than having to suffer the presence of one who was nothing more than a low-bred upstart, aping her betters instead of knowing her place, besides having to most likely witness her smug satisfaction over the public scandal which would ensue when it became known of the deception he had perpetrated.

Charles was conscious of none of the finer feelings attached to making such a drastic decision, only an overwhelming sense of relief to know that very soon this thorn in his flesh would no longer be around to create difficulties. As if suddenly aware of Ted Knowles's presence, Charles absently dug a hand into his overcoat pocket, drawing out a roll of notes which he handed to him. "I shall be needing you again. Meet me here tomorrow, the same time."

"Very well, Guvna; termorra it is," Ted Knowles nodded, asking no questions as he put the roll of notes into his pocket. By now the temperature had dropped considerably, and since he was no believer in too much fresh air, especially when it was as raw cold as this, he bid Charles a hasty good evening before hurriedly making his way to the gate, whereupon he turned round to see his newly acquired client still standing where he had left him, clearly in no hurry to leave.

There was no doubting that the lady Ted Knowles had described was Sophy, and the knowledge that she had deliberately gone against his wishes filled Charles with a white-hot anger that held him almost paralysed. His slim fingers tightened on his cane as he considered her duplicity, the soft leather of his glove stretched taut as he gripped it. As he had made his views perfectly clear her interference was all the more inexplicable. He could only guess at her motives but for him to allow such behaviour to remain unchecked was not only foolhardy but extremely dangerous, besides which, he would not tolerate disobedience nor permit it to continue, especially from his wife. He could not deny that the decision she had taken in conjunction with Jenkins not to tell his mother, whilst going a long way to working in his favour, by no means assuaged his temper. Sophy would very soon discover what he not only expected from her but demanded as a husband's right.

By the time he had crossed over Piccadilly into Half Moon Street his anger had subsided sufficiently for him to consider how best to deal with his wife's sudden and unaccountable waywardness. His initial intention had been to confront her outright, but it only took him a moment or two to see that this would not serve his purpose, apart from which it could very well set her thinking, and as she had already demonstrated how prepared she was to go against him he decided not to raise this with her just yet. Sophy may be free of guile but she had never once confided in him and, quite frankly, he could not see her doing so now, especially about something she knew full well he would strongly disapprove of, but there was always the possibility that she could, in an unguarded moment, let something slip, and there was more chance of this happening if he feigned ignorance of her morning's activities. Of course, he could be quite wrong, she may well inform him of her visit to the brat, but, somehow, he knew she would not.

Jenkins, a man whom Charles knew to be not only diligent but really quite tenacious, must have enlisted her aid at some point over the last twenty-four hours irrespective of the fact that he was well aware of his own firmly held views. Jenkins would know that Sophy was perhaps the only one the girl would listen to, and by all accounts she had done just that! Momentarily Charles's anger flared up again. It may be only a matter of days, even hours, before the girl claimed her inheritance, after all she was no fool and would very soon see that living in comfort was a far better prospect that continuing to live in poverty. With the help of his wife public denunciation was staring him in the face, and where before today he had at least some hope of coming out of his difficulties unscathed she had, by her meddlesome interference, considerably shortened the odds.

Whichever way he looked at it, ridding himself of the girl was essential if he wanted to keep his reputation unsullied. How to achieve it without revealing his own part in it had him in something of a quandary, but by the time he arrived at Berkeley Square an idea, so blatantly obvious and ridiculously simple, came to him. It would of course have to be carefully thought out but he felt sure that Ted Knowles's particular talents would not be stretched too far by the task, indeed Charles felt it reasonably safe to say that he would give it no more thought than he had to the task he had undertaken this afternoon.

No feelings of regret or remorse invaded Charles's conscience as he turned over in his mind this drastic solution to his difficulties, on the contrary he was conscious only of immense relief at the prospect of finally scaling what had become an insuperable hurdle without any finger of suspicion being pointed in his direction. Even if that precious collection was not an issue and his father had left the girl a token sum only, it would have made no difference to his feelings; the very thought of acknowledging a connection with someone he regarded as totally unworthy of his notice was as repugnant as it was offensive, considering himself as being far above a brat from the gutter. And Sophy? Ah yes, Sophy! Well, one step at a time, he would deal with her in due course, and in a way she would not forget; he would teach her to mind him better in future!

Having walked down Davies Street to the corner of Brook Street, his idea having by now become a fixed resolve, Charles's mood had lightened considerably, so much so that when the door was opened to him he was actually smiling, a circumstance which Harris found rather disconcerting; Mr. Charles seldom smiled! Having handed his cane, hat and gloves into Harris's keeping followed by his overcoat, Charles briefly enquired after his wife and upon being informed that she had gone upstairs not ten minutes before, he nodded his head and leisurely climbed the stairs.

*

Since the courage which had temporarily invaded her this morning and had been responsible for her accompanying Silas Jenkins had long since worn off, Sophy had had the rest of the day to ponder her actions, growing more nervous with every tick of the clock. She certainly had no regrets about her morning's work, indeed she was proud and honoured that not only had Silas Jenkins valued her opinion enough to enlist her help but that Alexandra had trusted her sufficiently to listen to what she had to say. Whether she would take that trust further and accept her grandmother's invitation as well as her grandfather's bequest remained to be seen, Sophy certainly hoped so, but since she could see no good resulting from pressing Alexandra for a decision, especially in her confused state of mind, Sophy failed to see what else could be done for the time being. Deep in her heart she knew she had done the right thing; to have done otherwise would have been to condone Matthew's unforgivable actions all those years ago whereby he had not only propelled his daughter into a life for which she had been totally ill-equipped and forcing her into forfeiting what was hers by right but also by depriving his granddaughter of the same. Alexandra had a right to the money and her mother's jewellery as well as taking up her rightful place in the world where she belonged, and it would be almost criminal to deny her any of it. Although Sophy told herself that Silas Jenkins would not betray her participation in today's events any more than Alexandra would, Sophy nevertheless dreaded it coming to Charles's ears, and had spent all afternoon in trying to think of any way he could possibly find out.

Not having expected Charles to arrive home quite so early, Sophy's already overstretched nerves suffered a severe jolt when the door unexpectedly opened and he walked in, startling her so much that she instantly dropped her brooch, staring somewhat blankly at him through the mirror of her dressing table, exclaiming in a choked voice, "Charles!"

"Was is it, my dear?" he asked, surprised, closing the door behind him without a backward glance. "You have gone quite pale."

"You took me by surprise, that's all," she smiled tremulously, jerkily turning round in her chair. "I wondered who it could be."

Biting down his renewed surge of anger when he thought of her duplicity, Charles raised a questioning eyebrow, his voice silky smooth, "Why, who else but your husband would come here?"

"Yes, of course," Sophy swallowed nervously. "It was stupid of me."

"You do not object to my being here, I trust?" Charles queried ominously. "I *am* your husband, after all; and husbands you know, *do* have certain rights."

This was certainly not a promising start to the evening ahead but conjuring up her lovely smile Sophy said as lightly as her overstretched nerves would allow, "Of course I have no objection. What can you be thinking of?"

"Why, you are trembling," Charles commented as he came up to her.

"It is nothing," Sophy shook her head, "merely a headache."

Picking up the brooch from where it lay on the floor at her feet, Charles said smoothly, "Allow me, my dear."

Sophy felt the warm touch of his fingers against her throat as he attached the brooch to the collar of her dress, but instead of straightening up when he had finished she saw him lower his head slightly to enable him to kiss her, the breath constricting in her lungs when he lightly brushed her lips with his own, his long slim fingers entwining themselves in her hair as his kiss gradually deepened until she felt almost suffocated by it. That something had annoyed him had been patently obvious from the moment he had walked in; in fact, he had been in a most uncertain mood for the past few weeks, but there was no suggestion of anger in his kiss. Amelia would have known precisely how to respond to this amorous attack, but Sophy, whose nerves had undergone a great deal during the day and who had neither wanted nor expected this display of desire from Charles, unhappily allowed him to kiss her. She did not repulse him for fear of fuelling his anger, but her whole being cried out in silent protest, her mind blotting out the harsh reality by conjuring up the face of the man she would never want to repulse.

After what seemed an eternity Charles finally freed her lips from his, raising his head to look down at her, his eyes intently searching her flushed face. "You know, my dear," he drawled, "I really must make a point of assisting you with your toilette more often." No one chancing to look at him would ever have guessed that he had just been passionately kissing his wife; no traces of desire or satisfaction could be seen on his face or in his eyes or any of the telltale signs which were clearly evident when he had kissed Amelia. Without giving Sophy time to respond to this, he asked, "So, tell me, how have you spent your day?"

So many emotions were rioting inside her as a result of his kisses but this mundane question, coming immediately after what had just happened, made Sophy feel sick. Since Charles never asked or cared about how she spent her time this unexpected enquiry threw her into confusion, the colour deepening in her cheeks. As she had told no one about her visit to Hoxton, not even Charlotte, Sophy had no choice but to tell him the same story as she had everyone else, but somehow the words stuck in her throat. "Oh, nothing very exciting." She shook her head, standing up and straightening her skirts. "I merely called in Bond Street to make a few purchases."

"You know," Charles drawled, removing his coat, "I never thought I should hear any woman say she found shopping unexciting." After eyeing her closely for a moment or two, he said, "You are obviously an exception, my dear. So," he asked without warning, "what did you purchase? Am I quite bankrupt?"

Not having anticipated this question, it took Sophy several agonising moments to think of an answer which would satisfy him. "Well, actually," she confessed, hoping her smile would dispel that rather penetrating look in his eyes, "I only purchased a few tablets of my favourite soap," devoutly praying he would not ask to see them. "I had hoped," she offered as lightly as she could, "that Wilton would have had my new pair of gloves ready, but unfortunately he did not."

"That certainly was a pity," he said dryly, his eyes narrowing as he looked at her. "I trust he will soon do so, however."

Sophy's earlier claim of a headache suddenly became a reality as her head began to throb. Despite her plausible lies she felt he knew that this was precisely what they were, but then with Charles one never quite knew what he was thinking. As he had by this time shrugged himself into his brocade dressing gown and rung the bell for Farley, she took the opportunity of hastily excusing herself on the pretext of offering his mother some assistance, wishing to avoid any more probing questions about how she had occupied her day. Unlike George, Charles considered the services of a valet not only indispensable to his comfort but to his dignity as well, but it was several moments after Sophy had left him before he entered the adjoining dressing room to join him, a dark forbidding look descending onto his face.

The only thing which had sustained her throughout the day was knowing that Marcus would be joining them for dinner, and although she knew there would be very little opportunity for any private conversation between them, just having him near made her feel so much better, especially now after what had been a most eventful day culminating in those unnerving moments with her husband. Sophy did not think her startled response to Charles's unexpected entrance had been the cause of his annoyance, but there was no disputing the fact that it had certainly exacerbated it, and therefore his display of passion had been quite unlooked-for. Her nerves, which had see-sawed alarmingly during the day, had certainly plummeted upon seeing her husband well before she expected to, causing her suddenly nerveless fingers to drop her brooch, bringing about that kiss which, like their marriage, had had no roots in love or affection.

She had accepted Charles as her husband not out of love but because her parents had desired it, and since her father had been a business acquaintance of Matthew, that, as far as he was concerned, clinched the matter. Charles, for whom the marriage had been a means of financial expediency instead of the dictates of his heart had, at no point, even tried to accept their marriage or made the least effort to deal comfortably with her, on the contrary he had made his feelings perfectly clear from the outset that he resented being forced into matrimony with a woman who held no appeal for him whatsoever. Nevertheless, he certainly expected her to conform to his wishes as well as any physical demands he made of her, fully expecting to claim his rights as a husband. Sophy may not reject Charles but her response to his lovemaking was dutiful rather than pleasurable, leaving her unhappy and disconsolate, and since the advent of Marcus in her life, who had awakened her to emotions she never knew existed, even more so, but never before had she mentally substituted him for Charles as she had tonight when he kissed her. It shocked her to discover that she was actually capable of betraying her husband, if not physically then mentally, and the feeling of wretchedness which swept over her, exacerbated all the more in knowing that she wanted Marcus to make love to her, was so overpowering that she had no idea how she was to face him when he arrived this evening. Her feelings for Charles may not encompass love and desire, she knew they never would, but she could at least offer him the fidelity and loyalty he constantly denied her.

*

Reverend Handley, who had accepted Charlotte's invitation to dinner more out of respect for his hostess than any desire to spend the evening with her family, looked decidedly uncomfortable as he took his seat at the table. It was perhaps unfortunate that he had been placed opposite Charles, who made not the slightest effort to welcome the middle-aged cleric. Never having quite understood Charles's witticisms much less his smooth-tongued utterances, Reverend Handley had, on more than one occasion during the course of the evening, to severely remind himself of his calling and the duty of every Christian to love his fellow men.

George, who had not only suffered verbal mutilation at his brother's hands over the last few weeks and was still bristling with indignation, not to mention his festering belief that Charles had somehow managed to cheat him out of what he believed was his by right, was also still suffering acute embarrassment over Adam's continued presence in the house. Following an accidental meeting with Marsden only yesterday, whose acknowledgement had been icily polite, George had made the error of approaching Adam about the length of his stay in town, to which he merely received a mischievous grin and a careless shrug of the shoulders. Had George sought advice, he would have been strenuously cautioned against mentioning the subject again this evening, but since he was strongly of the opinion that he was totally disregarded in his role as head of the family, especially now that he had had the reins of power snatched from him, he was determined to impose his authority and, unwisely, chose this evening to assert himself.

Considering himself as being well past the age of having to render himself accountable to his brothers, Adam took instant exception to George's demand to know when he intended returning to Yorkshire. "Not at that again, are you?" Adam asked irritably. "I'll return home when I'm good and ready and not before." He eyed his brother closely across the dinner table. "You seem mighty eager to see the back of me. Why?"

"Not at all," George blustered, discomfited by this pointed question. "It just seems a little odd, that's all."

"What's odd about it?" Adam demanded. "Can't a man visit his family without undergoing an inquisition?"

"Fear not, Brother," Charles drawled, his eyes glinting wickedly across at George, "it is merely that he had the misfortune yesterday to run cross Marsden."

"Damn you, Charles!" George spluttered. "I can speak for myself."

"All too often it seems," Charles mocked.

George's pale blue eyes glared furiously at him. "What the devil do you mean by that?"

Charles's smile was insultingly contemptuous. "You know, George," he drawled nastily, "you are the only person I know who can make a speech without managing to say anything at all."

George's face turned an alarming shade of purple and his jaws worked feverishly as he struggled to find words cutting enough to put Charles in his place, but as nothing suitable came to mind he merely spluttered something to the effect that one of these days he would meet someone who would knock his cutting remarks down his throat.

"But not by you, Brother," Charles warned menacingly. "Not by you."

As this naturally killed any desire for conversation it was left to the embarrassed cleric to step quickly into the breach. "Please accept my felicitations, Mrs. Harrington," he said hastily, "on an excellent dinner."

Saddened and distressed by the behaviour of her offspring as well as being quite powerless to stop it, Charlotte smiled gratefully at him. "Thank you, Reverend. Although," she added, "I must confess to a little cheating. You see," she offered, "I recall you saying once how very partial you are to goose."

"I am indeed," he smiled warmly, "especially when it is cooked and dressed as excellently as this."

Acutely aware of the silent battle that was taking place between George and Charles, Charlotte went on hurriedly, "Of course, the dessert I have chosen is Mrs. Harris's speciality. I advise you to reserve judgement until afterwards. I promise you," she smiled uneasily, "you will not be disappointed."

Reverend Handley laughed politely at this, but he was profoundly shocked by the open animosity which existed between the two brothers, and it was only his deep regard for his hostess and his punctiliousness to social conduct which prevented him from making his excuses and leaving before the promised dessert.

Marcus was too used to George and Charles trading verbal attacks one with the other to feel surprise at this latest exchange, but it annoyed him to know that it deeply distressed his aunt, a circumstance which seemed to escape them in their desire to score points off one another.

Charles had been in a dangerous mood all evening, his temper balancing on a very fine line, in fact upon his arrival Marcus had realised straightaway that he had interrupted a cuttingly polite though bitter verbal encounter between them, which, unfortunately, had resulted in Sophy being caught in the backlash when she had dared to remind them that their guests would soon be arriving. For the remainder of the evening she had said no more than was required of her, and even though Marcus was sitting directly opposite her at the dinner table she had deliberately refused to look at him unless she was obliged to do so.

Whatever the reason was to account for Charles being in the devil's own temper George's inflammatory words had only served to darken his mood even more, as anyone but a fool would have known. But George never did know when to keep his own counsel, and Charles was not the type of man to listen to his pompous remonstrating at the best of times.

Amelia had long ago given up hope of George cultivating a little wisdom and witnessing his display this evening she knew he never would any more than he would ever learn his lesson or accept the fact that he would never come out on top over Charles. Charles not only outthought him but outshone him in every way and never let an opportunity slip in order to make his brother feel his inadequacies. Whatever she may feel or say to her husband in private, she was publicly dutiful and had sat in silent irritation while George had attempted yet again to impose his authority. George would never be the equal of his brother, and Amelia's only regret was that Charles was her brother-in-law and not her husband. Unfortunately, George's journey into Norfolk to bring her sons home had been unexpectedly curtailed due to her sister-in-law succumbing to the influenza, but the time she and Charles had spent together during the night-time hours when the whole household had been asleep, had proved to her beyond any doubt that not only would she go to her grave loving him, but that if it were at all possible she would willingly exchange her husband for his brother. Amelia wondered what this homely parson would say if he knew of her clandestine affair with her brother-in-law; most probably he would refuse to sit at the same table with her.

It came as no surprise to Sophy when Charles announced his intention of visiting his club after dinner, having no desire to spend the remainder of the evening either with his wife or family. She had no idea what had brought this black mood on her husband, but George's ill-timed words had certainly inflamed it.

"You're a fool, George," Adam told him as soon as Charles had left. "Why can't you keep that tongue of yours still?"

"It's about time Charles realised that he cannot ride roughshod over everyone," George said officiously.

"Well, you're not the man to make him realise it!" Adam told him forthrightly.

"Come along, George," Amelia said quietly, tucking her hand under his elbow, admirably concealing her annoyance. "You know you promised to say goodnight to the boys."

George hesitated while he debated whether or not to challenge Adam's comment, his colour rather high at the suggestion that he was not capable of handling Charles, but one look at Amelia's face decided the issue and he reluctantly allowed her to guide him out of the room.

Adam grinned. "It'll take more than George to teach Charles a lesson!" Then, looking at Marcus, he asked, "Coming, Marcus? There's a damned good port I want you to try! You will excuse us, won't you Sophy?" Adam coaxed irresistibly as he assisted her out of her chair.

"Yes, of course," she smiled indulgently, deliberately avoiding looking at Marcus, still acutely conscious of how she had mentally supplanted her husband earlier with the man whose eyes had hardly left her all evening.

"Ready?" Adam raised an eyebrow at his cousin as he opened the dining room door.

"In a moment," Marcus nodded. Waiting only until Adam had gone Marcus turned his attention back to Sophy, whose pale face had caused him concern all evening, and after studying her closely for several moments, asked considerately, "What's wrong, Sophy?" When she merely shook her head in silent denial, he remarked gently, "You have kept me at a very discreet distance all evening." Her eyes flew to his. "I have been endeavouring to discover what I could possibly have done to offend you."

These softly spoken words brought a flood of colour to her cheeks and her eyes glistened as she quickly turned away from him. "I have no recollection of you offending me," she prevaricated, attempting to walk past him towards the door but was prevented from doing so by a gently restraining hand on her arm.

"But you are out of sorts with me!" he confirmed a little ruefully.

"Of course I am not," she shook her head. "It is merely a headache that refuses to go away." The love and tenderness she saw in his eyes made her draw in her breath, neither of which did anything to stem the tide of emotions coursing through her.

"What is it, Sophy? What's wrong?" Marcus urged. "Please, do not say nothing," he smiled disarmingly, "because I shan't believe you." When she made no reply, he asked, "Don't you trust me enough to confide in me?"

"Oh, Marcus!" Sophy cried involuntarily, her eyes flying to his. "Of course I trust you," she told him earnestly. "You are the only one I *could* confide in."

"Then do so now," he pressed, his hand still resting on her arm. "You will feel so much better when you have told me what it is that is worrying you."

The reassuring touch of his hand may not have done anything to contain the wonderful sensations it evoked, but it certainly filled her with a warm sense of well-being that she badly needed. Her trust in him was so implicit that without any more urging she found herself telling him how she had spent the morning, relieved to be able to unburden herself, to put into some kind of perspective what had become, during the course of the day, nothing short of a crime, at least that is how Charles would see it should he ever discover it.

Marcus listened to her without interruption, biting down his anger when he thought of all she was subjected to at her husband's hands and her fear of him finding out about her visit to Alexandra. Whilst he acknowledged that it was characteristic of Sophy's generous nature and what he would have expected of her, he knew perfectly well that the implications resulting from it could have far-reaching results. "Have you told my aunt about this?" he asked.

"No," Sophy shook her head, "I thought it wiser not to. It would only do more harm than good if she built up her hopes only to discover that Alexandra does not wish to come here."

"We cannot discount that possibility, of course," Marcus acknowledged, "but my aunt will have to be told something at some point."

"Yes, I know," Sophy sighed, "but even though I want nothing more than to remove Alexandra from such a dreadful place, I think Jenkins could well be right in that until she has come to a decision nothing can be done. After all," she conceded reluctantly, "we cannot force her into doing something against her wishes. I think too," she told him sadly, "that we should not press her, at least for a few days."

"Very well," Marcus nodded, a slight frown creasing his forehead, his eyes full of concern as he looked down at her.

"You think I should not have gone, don't you?" she asked quietly.

It was several moments before Marcus spoke. "Not that precisely."

"What then?" Sophy asked quickly.

Again, Marcus hesitated. "I quite agree that Matthew's treatment of Elizabeth was nothing short of brutal and that her daughter does not deserve to suffer because of it, but I do feel that Jenkins was wrong to have asked such a thing of you." She saw the frown deepen and heard the grimness in his voice. "You know as well as I do that if Charles ever finds out you went to see her, he will take it very badly."

Sophy inwardly shuddered at the thought, her smile merely a camouflage to hide her fear, but managed to say optimistically, "You are worrying unduly, Marcus."

"You know I am not," he said quietly. "Charles will not like to think that his wife has not accorded him the loyalty and respect he considers his due."

Despite her attempt to lessen the consequences of her actions, Sophy knew Marcus was right. Charles would be furiously angry!

Unlike some, Marcus had never fallen into the trap of underestimating his cousin. No one knew better than he did the lengths to which Charles would go to achieve his own ends, and his retribution would be swift as well as severe. Marcus trembled for Sophy. She had put her head into the lion's den and was now left dependent upon the discretion of two people for her salvation, neither of whom he knew well enough to put his complete trust in. Not for the first time he found himself railing against the ties which bound him. Legally he had no rights whatsoever where Sophy was concerned, and certainly none when it came to offering his protection to another man's wife. As her husband Charles was at liberty to treat her in any way he chose, while he, who would willingly give his life for her, was powerless to shield her from a husband who neither loved nor wanted her. For himself, Marcus would readily face any criticism or social condemnation in the defence and protection of the woman he loved, but for Sophy the results would be disastrous. At all costs he had to save her from narrow-minded prejudice and social disgrace whilst at the same time doing everything he could to shield her from her husband's wrath. "Charles is no fool," he warned her softly, his fingers comfortingly squeezing her hand. "He would certainly not condone or pardon what he would consider to be nothing short of betrayal."

He was right, of course. Charles was coldly unforgiving! Sophy looked up into Marcus's eyes, her own deeply troubled. "He would never forgive me," she acknowledged, her voice hardly above a whisper. "But I could do no other than go with Jenkins," she told him, shaking her head. "I could not refuse him!"

Marcus doubted his cousin would see it that way, especially now when he was in the devil's own humour, and his eyes clouded, reflecting his concern for Sophy. "Do you have any idea what has brought this black mood down on him?"

Sophy shook her head, saying truthfully, "No, but I do know that ever since Jenkins read out Matthew's will Charles has been most forbidding and more unapproachable than ever." Then, as if all restraint left her, she cried urgently, "Oh Marcus, I am so afraid! I know I am most probably allowing my imagination to get the better of me, but I cannot rid my mind of the thought that something dreadful is going to happen!"

He thought so too but decided to say nothing to Sophy, seeing no point in escalating her fears by alerting her to his own thoughts as to the reason for Charles's ill humour and his confession about thwarting the girl. "There is no need to be afraid," Marcus told her in a deep voice, "I promise you."

"I am never afraid when I am with you," the words leaving her lips before Sophy had time to consider what she was saying, and her face flamed when she thought what her admission signified.

There was so much Marcus wanted to say to her, not the least being how much he loved her, but now was neither the time nor the place. At any moment they could be interrupted and he had no desire to make Sophy the object of gossip or speculation. If things were different he would have no hesitation in openly declaring what they both already knew any more than he would resist the temptation to take her in his arms and kiss her. Yet even though he knew it was impossible, his whole body cried out with the need to hold her, to show her how much he loved and needed her, but the look in her eyes and the quivering response of her hand as he held it in his, telling him more than any words possibly could that she felt the same, did nothing to help him maintain the frail hold he was keeping on his self-control.

No words were necessary between them, each knowing precisely what the other was thinking and feeling, and Sophy, who wanted nothing more than to be held close against him, dug into her mental and emotional reserves to fight the need to cast herself into his arms, arms she knew would welcome her eagerly. "I really must go, Marcus," she managed unsteadily, removing her hand from his. "Your aunt will be wondering where I am. I cannot leave her to entertain Reverend Handley alone."

Marcus made no attempt to detain her, merely saying, "Sophy, if ever you should need me."

Sophy nodded. "Yes, I know," she smiled. "Thank you, Marcus."

She was gone on the words, leaving Marcus prey to so many thoughts and emotions that it was almost a full five minutes before he left the dining room to join Adam in the library.

Chapter Ten

Adam was well aware of the connotations George put upon his protracted stay. Even so, he had no intention of confiding his thoughts to him. Nothing could be more fatal than imparting his suspicions to his eldest brother in that Charles could well be trying to deprive Alexandra of her inheritance. George may despise Charles with every fibre of his being, even more so now that he had had the reins of power taken out of his hands, for which he held Charles solely responsible, and although nothing would give George greater satisfaction than to be able to throw something as damaging as this at his brother in an attempt to topple his arrogance once and for all, of which he stood in considerable awe, he was such a gabster that when he was in a temper he could not be relied upon to keep his tongue between his teeth!

Like everyone else, Adam could see that Charles was in no very good humour, in fact he had not been in the best of moods ever since the reading of their father's will, the contents of which had been explosive enough to inflame someone with a more even temper than Charles. The doubts which plagued Adam about his own brother gave him no pleasure or satisfaction even though he knew Charles could be insufferably arrogant when he chose, but for all that Adam would not like to think him capable of doing something which was not only against the law but would be guaranteed to bring scandal down on their heads. Nevertheless, the more he saw of Charles's forbidding humour the more convinced Adam became that something was very wrong.

Unfortunately, George's pompous and constant attacks as to his brother's complicity in the compilation of their father's will did not help matters, on the contrary they only served to set Charles's back up all the more and from what Adam had been privileged to see the only one who seemed to be suffering the consequences was Sophy. Not that she ever discussed her situation, but anyone with only half a mind could see that Charles failed to treat her as she deserved at the best of times, let alone now when his temper was even more stretched than usual.

Adam had not been overly surprised when Marcus had made light of his concerns, in fact he had simply run true to form. Despite the six years that separated them and the time Marcus had been away serving with his regiment, Adam was perhaps the only member of his family, with the exception of his mother, who could say he knew his cousin better than most, and this being so he knew Marcus never made any kind of move until he was in possession of all the facts, and then only when he had assembled and assessed them did he act. Nevertheless, Adam was as convinced as a man could be that his brother was up to something and if it took him all night he was determined to speak to his cousin about it. But when Marcus eventually joined him in the library and he put his concerns to him, Adam was unable to offer him any concrete evidence apart from his own suspicions.

"I am afraid suspicions are not enough to accuse him of anything," Marcus pointed out reasonably.

"Damn it, Marcus!" Adam exclaimed. "Charles has been in the devil's own humour now for weeks; ever since m'father's will was read out in fact!"

"He may well," Marcus acknowledged, swirling the brandy around in his glass, which he much preferred to port, "but it proves absolutely nothing."

Adam eyed his cousin, of whom he was extremely fond, aghast. "Y'know, Marcus," he exclaimed exasperatedly, "you can be the most infuriating man when you've a mind!"

"No, really?" Marcus enquired, raising a surprised eyebrow.

Adam, finding it difficult to resist that disarming smile, demanded as firmly as he could, "What will it take to make you see?"

"A lot more than mere conjecture," Marcus replied calmly.

"Conjecture!" Adam cried disgustedly. "I suppose you call Charles's present mood normal! I wonder if you'll take it so calmly when he lands us all in Newgate?"

"Oh, I hardly think it will come to that." Again, his irresistible smile dawned, exasperating his young cousin who snorted his disgust at Marcus's seeming unconcern over something which could have far-reaching consequences.

Marcus had not intended taking Adam into his confidence, at least not at this stage, but in view of his cousin's vigorous insistence and growing doubts it only took Marcus a matter of a few minutes to see that his mad-cap young relative was more than capable of taking matters into his own hands, and that by going off half-cocked he was more than likely to make bad worse. More than once during his military career he had come up against half-fledged young officers of his cousin's stamp, full of pluck and backbone, possessing too much enthusiasm and not enough experience and ultimately finding themselves in an entirely helpless position which they could not possibly hope to defend.

"You know something, don't you?" Adam said suspiciously, regarding his cousin closely.

"No more than you," Marcus dismissed.

"Come on Marcus, out with it!" Adam demanded frustrated. "He's up to something, isn't he?"

Infuriating his young relative by taking time to savour his brandy, Marcus smiled across at him, saying, quite calmly, "Very well, if you insist."

"I *do*," Adam confirmed, refilling his glass. "And don't try to fob me off by humouring me, because I know *you.*"

Marcus laughed. "And when have I ever tried to fob you off?"

Adam grinned. "Well," he admitted sheepishly, "I daresay I shall bring an occasion to mind eventually, not that it matters," he pointed out, "the fact is I have a right to know what my own brother's up to, especially if he's on the point of bringing us to ruin, and whilst I'm not proud of my suspicions there's m'mother to consider. Apart from the fact that she's had enough to cope with, I doubt she'd recover from the shock. I don't want her to go through that."

"I agree," Marcus nodded, applauding Adam's sentiments.

"Well," Adam urged, "have you discovered anything?"

"No," Marcus shook his head. "If Charles is indeed planning to disinherit Alexandra he is far too clever to overlook anything which could be regarded as incriminating." Stretching out his right leg he sighed his indecision, still debating whether or not to open his mind to his cousin, but when faced with his persistence and barrage of questions Marcus finally gave in to his better judgement. "You realise, of course," he told him resignedly, "that my suspicions as well as my motives could easily be misconstrued?"

"Damn it, Marcus!" Adam exclaimed irritably, perfectly aware that Charles was no favourite of his cousin. "I know you wouldn't fabricate something out of spite!"

"Not out of spite, no," Marcus replied, an odd inflexion in his voice, "but there are other reasons equally as influential." Not being the type of man to readily discuss his innermost feelings, Marcus held his cousin's comprehending look, neither confirming nor denying what had been left unsaid.

But there was no need for Adam to have his cousin's meaning explained, the intimation was plain enough. Marcus may not have mentioned Sophy by name much less admitted to being in love with her, but Adam knew his cousin well enough to know that he would not have mentioned it at all were it otherwise. His cousin may have his emotions sufficiently under control so as not to alert anyone to the fact that he was very much in love with Sophy, but there had been a number of times over dinner this evening when Adam had caught the look which had entered Marcus's eyes whenever they had rested on her, and although Adam had discounted his mother's harmless remark on the day he had called to see him, after what he had witnessed this evening he was left in no doubt. He was also left in no doubt that Sophy fully reciprocated Marcus's feelings even though she would never dream of betraying her husband, but where the two of them went from here Adam had no idea, especially when he considered the type of man his brother was. As he was not one to interfere in the affairs of his relatives, unless of course it was something serious enough to involve each and every one of them, such as the possibility of Charles plunging them all into scandal, whatever the two of them felt for one another was nothing to do with him. Adam was certain his cousin had not meant to say as much as he had and that it was his own insistence which had brought about that unspoken confession. He had no wish to interfere in Marcus's private affairs, but this matter of the girl's inheritance and his brother's probable intentions could not be ignored. "You mean Sophy?" he said at length, raising his eyes from the glass in his hand.

"Yes," Marcus nodded, "I mean Sophy."

"I see. I'm sorry, Marcus," Adam quickly apologised, "I didn't mean to pry."

"You're not," Marcus shook his head, "but since you pressed me for my opinion I thought you should perhaps know how my behaviour in this could be looked upon."

"Not by me," Adam assured him.

"No, not by you," Marcus smiled, "but by others less well-informed."

Adam smiled his thanks. "I don't mean to intrude into your private affairs, Marcus," he told him, "but whilst I appreciate the awkward position this may place you in, I do think that if you have something on your mind you should tell me."

"You are right, of course," Marcus inclined his head, acknowledging the justification of this, "but if what we conjecture is found to be fact, whatever the outcome it could place Sophy in a most unpleasant situation. Do you still wish to go on with this conversation?"

"Of course!" Adam exclaimed. "Look, Marcus," he said earnestly, "I have no wish to embarrass anyone, least of all you and Sophy, besides which," he added irrepressibly, "next to m'mother the two of you are the only members of this family I can tolerate. I do know that you would not do anything underhand simply because of any personal considerations."

"Well," Marcus nodded, "since you know that you must also know that, like you, I am not proud of harbouring these suspicions, but since you have pressed me to tell you what conclusions I have come to, then I have to say yes, I too have come to believe that Charles is planning how best to deprive Alexandra of her inheritance."

Adam, not at all sure whether to be glad or sorry to have his suspicions confirmed, asked, "Did you suspect any of this before I raised it with you?"

Marcus thought a moment, choosing his words carefully before saying, "I never intended sitting in at the reading of your father's will, but George, for reasons best known to himself, thought it would be a good idea. Discounting Sophy and myself, apart from you and my aunt," Marcus inclined his head, "the bequest to Alexandra was hardly well received, and whilst George argued the point vociferously with Jenkins, we both know how his tongue runs away with him until eventually he comes to accept whatever it is he has been arguing against. Charles though," he nodded, "is a different matter entirely. He may not have reacted as passionately as George, but his disapproval was no less real for all that, and you know as well as I do that he did not exactly hide his feelings or his resentment, in fact," he reminded Adam, "not even when Jenkins made it quite clear that there were no legal reasons whatsoever to warrant invalidating the will or overturning that codicil, Charles made his feelings as well as his intentions quite clear and has," he pointed out, "continued to do so, indeed he told me himself following the reading that his intention was to thwart the girl.

"As you know," he nodded, "unlike George, Charles never gives up on something, which is why I cannot rid my mind of the feeling that he will not just sit back and allow Alexandra to take what he firmly believes does not belong to her. At first," he shrugged, "I thought it was nothing more than an initial reaction, simply the shock of realising that Alexandra was firmly in his life whether he liked it or not, but Charles's continued anger and resentment over her inclusion in the will seemed to me to go far deeper than just his pride. However," he admitted, "I did not realise how badly he had taken it until you came to see me that day when you related what had passed between you on the afternoon of your father's funeral as well as how Charles had raked Sophy down over dinner the evening prior to you coming to see me. Since then, I have had only the odd conversation with Charles, but they have been sufficient to make me realise just how determined he is to do everything in his power to prevent the girl from having anything." He saw the frown crease Adam's forehead. "Unless I am mistaken," Marcus pointed out, not unmindful of his cousin's feelings, "I gain the impression that his resistance to her inclusion in your father's will goes far beyond the money."

"You mean the jewellery?" Adam supplied, the frown on his forehead deepening.

"I am afraid I do," Marcus confirmed at length. "For reasons I cannot explain, much less prove," he inclined his head, "I have the growing suspicion that Charles is most anxious to ensure that Elizabeth's jewellery continues to remain hidden in Mercers' vaults; never to see the light of day."

"But why?" Adam asked, bewildered. "I should have thought Lizzie's jewellery would be of far less importance to him than the money; after all, he's never a feather to fly with six times out of ten!"

"That's as may be," Marcus acknowledged, "but from what you yourself have told me about the conversations you have had with Charles as well as him taking Sophy to task on more than one occasion on this very point, I am convinced of it." He saw the look of horror on Adam's face, and said calmly, "Try as I do, I can find no other explanation to account for his temper being so uncertain or the rigid stance he is taking over the girl which, you must agree," he nodded, "goes far beyond his pride, and certainly not for him lashing out at Sophy simply because she happened to mention she had never seen your sister's jewellery and that they ought perhaps to be cleaned before Alexandra takes possession of them."

At no time had Adam suspected his cousin of maliciously trying to implicate Charles in something he could well be innocent of, after all he was of the same opinion himself, but it seemed the deeper they dug the more certain it became. In a desperate attempt to try to make sense of it all he rose jerkily to his feet to begin pacing up and down as if by doing something energetic it would help clear his mind, eventually coming to an abrupt halt in front of Marcus. "I know I thought he may have done something stupid with the jewellery," he exclaimed, "sold one or two pieces perhaps, but to be honest with you I don't think I ever really believed it, after all," he said truthfully, "it's not something one likes to think their own brother capable of." A deep frown creased his forehead. "If it is the case, then for the life of me I can't imagine what could possibly have arisen to make him do anything so rash!"

"I confess," Marcus admitted, "that that unpalatable thought has occurred to me," going on to relate his luncheon engagement with Oswald Mercer and his subsequent private viewing of the jewellery.

Adam stared incredulously. "Good God! You don't mean that he really *has* gone and sold some of the pieces?"

"I couldn't honestly say." Marcus shook his head. "From what I was privileged to see of Elizabeth's jewellery it appears every piece is accounted for."

Adam's eyes clouded as he considered this, saying thoughtfully, "Well, if Charles did find himself at the point of no return, using Lizzie's jewellery as the last resort, I suppose he could easily have borrowed them to have them copied and then returned the copies without anyone knowing."

"I wondered that," Marcus sighed, "but if Charles *has* substituted any of the originals with copies in order to hide the fact that he has removed some of the pieces, not to sell but to borrow on because to sell them would be bound to raise questions, and I say *if*," he stressed, "because at the moment we are working on nothing other than pure conjecture, then, like you, I fail to see what exigency could have arisen to prompt Charles into taking such drastic measures, but as I am no expert on diamonds and precious stones from what I saw I could not, in all honesty, swear that all or any of the pieces were copies."

"If he *did* have some copied," Adam mused, feeling sick at the thought, "what beats me is how no one knew about it or saw him take them! And when?"

"Well," Marcus sighed, "assuming he has removed one or two pieces, I have no more idea than you as to when; it could have been any time. As to gaining access," he pointed out reasonably, "who would question one of Matthew's sons? Any one of you could gain access to the vaults without enquiries being made as to the reason, after all there is more than your sister's jewellery housed there."

"Yes, I know," Adam acknowledged, "but if Charles did take any of them," he remarked thoughtfully, "then who on earth would he employ to copy them for him? I mean," he shrugged, "no reputable jeweller, surely, would touch such a job!"

"No," Marcus agreed, "but you must admit there are any number of Cranbourn Alley merchants who would be only too willing to do it, providing of course the price was right! My guess though," he nodded, "is that Charles would not have risked taking them to someone he did not know."

Adam shuddered at the thought. "Assuming Charles *has* taken such a drastic step, he had the devil of a nerve! Puzzles me how he managed it!"

He saw the smile dawn on his cousin's lips. "What puzzles *me*," Marcus told him, "is what the devil you think you can do by remaining here."

Adam grinned, reminding Marcus of a mischievous schoolboy. "I've been keeping my eyes on him."

In spite of the seriousness of the situation facing them Marcus laughed, a deep-throated sound which immediately infected his cousin with the same affliction. "And what have your observations determined?" he asked.

"That's just it," Adam informed him dejectedly, a reluctant smile touching his lips, "nothing."

"I thought not," Marcus acknowledged, rising to his feet. "If you take my advice, you will return to Yorkshire. Apart from the fact that Isabel will be wondering what has happened to you, you are only making George uncomfortable, and when he is uncomfortable it leads him to saying things which are guaranteed to set all your backs up, especially Charles." After emptying his glass, he warned, "Listen Adam, Charles is no fool; in fact, I would go so far as to say that should he find himself in a corner he could be a very dangerous man, and if he discovers he has come under suspicion, as he will if you continue in your present endeavours, your relationship will mean nothing to him. Once he senses his back is against the wall he will do everything to save himself, even at the expense of a brother."

Adam knew this was true; Charles had always liked things his own way and disliked being thwarted, long forgotten incidents involuntarily springing to mind. "You needn't worry," he consoled him, "I've written to Isabel so she won't be fretting, and as for George, I can handle him."

"That's as may be," Marcus acknowledged, "but do not forget there are others who will suffer from Charles's irritation resulting from George's persistent sermonising."

Adam instinctively knew he was referring to Sophy who was already bearing the brunt of his brother's temper, but although he had no wish to be the one responsible for causing her any further distress, he nevertheless firmly defended himself and his actions. "But I'm not leaving here until I've got to the bottom of things!" he added determinedly.

Realising that his well-meaning but headstrong young cousin could not be moved, Marcus reluctantly accepted the inevitable, but not without warning him to be careful. "Very well, watch Charles if you must, but whatever you do, do not let him know it." Gripping Adam's shoulder, he urged, "Do not try to be a hero, Adam. If anything happens come to me, do not attempt to deal with it alone."

After giving his word, Adam asked, "But what happens now?"

"We wait," Marcus told him, rather amused at the disappointment on his cousin's face.

"Yes but…" Adam began.

"No 'buts'," Marcus shook his head. "Besides, there is nothing we *can* do at the moment, and under no circumstances are you to approach Charles on this, and I forbid you to force any kind of an issue. Remember," he warned, "not only do we have no proof on which to accuse him, but as things stand at the moment we can't say for certain that Charles is planning *anything*, but once he suspects the way our thoughts are going he could be extremely unpleasant."

Familiarity with his brother forced Adam to concede the painful truth of this and assure his cousin that he would do nothing to alert Charles to their suspicions, but it also told him that should his brother ever discover the truth about Marcus's feelings for Sophy, then he would be just as unpleasant in dealing with it as he would if he discovered he had come under suspicion. Marcus, who had a shrewd idea of what was going through his mind, raised an enquiring eyebrow, in response to which Adam offered hesitantly, "You don't need me to warn you about Charles, you know him too well, but I just want you to know that I shall never betray your confidence."

It was several moments before Marcus answered him, his expression unreadable as he looked at his cousin, saying at length, "My commanding officer used to say, 'Before you embark on a campaign, always make sure you know your own officers and men before you know the enemy's.' He was right," he nodded, "you're a good fellow officer, Adam."

"Well, since you know that," Adam smiled, "what about the campaign? After all," he pointed out, not unreasonably, "Sophy is as out of reach as the moon."

Marcus shrugged his broad shoulders, but his eyes clouded as he confessed, "I have no regrets about this particular campaign, but although I have long had the objective in my sights no attack has been attempted, and the devil of it is I don't know whether I shall end up the victor or the vanquished!"

Adam's knowledge of his brother told him that his cousin was doomed to disappointment; Charles never relinquished what was his, but as it was clear Marcus knew this as well as anyone Adam refrained from mentioning it, so after draining his glass he returned to the vexed question of his brother's probable intentions. "Y'know Marcus, about Charles; I hope to God we're wrong in this!"

The sombre tone of Marcus's voice was reflected in his eyes. "You don't wish that any more than I do, I assure you." He did not need to have his own part in this affair spelled out. He knew perfectly well how it would appear should their suspicions be confirmed, but the same held true if they were eventually proved wrong. To be instrumental in either the downfall or attempted discrediting of a man whose wife he himself was in love with was not something he felt particularly good about, useless of course to tell the gossipmongers that his motivation had stemmed from the purest of motives and not simply from a desire to win his cousin's wife at any cost.

Unfortunately, there was no time for more as the door opened and George walked in, still looking considerably ruffled. Staying only long enough to exchange a few words with him Marcus made his way to his aunt's sitting room to wish her goodnight to find that Amelia, who seldom joined her mother-in-law in her sitting room, was comfortably established there, sitting gracefully on an upright chair, her eyes sparkling at the sight of him. Fondly chastising him for neglecting them in favour of more manly pursuits, she smiled archly up at him, saying provocatively, "Shame on you, Marcus! I had never thought it possible that *you* of all people would prefer to linger over a glass of port with Adam rather than spending time with us. Or was it brandy?" she teased. "Yes, I can see it was," she smiled vivaciously in response to the rueful look in his eyes.

"Please accept my humble apologies," Marcus smiled as he bowed over her hand, "for my deplorable lack of taste in choosing my company."

"Very well," Amelia smiled coyly up at him, her eyes appraising as she took in every inch of him, "we shall forgive you on this occasion, *but*," she added playfully, "I warn you, we shall feel hardly used if it happens again."

Marcus smiled politely at this before turning to his aunt, wishing her a fond goodnight and kissing her affectionately on the cheek.

"Goodnight, Marcus," Charlotte smiled. "Come and see me again soon."

"You may be sure of it," he nodded, then, moving across to Sophy, said politely as he punctiliously raised her hand to his lips, "Sophy."

"Goodnight Marcus," she nodded, her eyes holding his as she felt his fingers reassuringly press her own, a slight tinge of colour creeping into her cheeks.

Sophy was not the only one who felt downcast at his departure. Charlotte too missed his reassuring presence and was vexed that there had been very little opportunity to have a private talk with him. It was a pity Amelia should have come into the sitting room when she did because Charlotte had hoped to have a moment or two alone with him following the early departure of Reverend Handley to talk about her granddaughter and to seek his advice as to what she should do if Jenkins's efforts proved futile, which was how it was beginning to look, but she had not wanted to discuss anything of this nature in front of Amelia. She had no qualms about discussing her granddaughter with her nephew in front of Sophy, but Amelia, whose views on this particular subject were far from compassionate, was entirely different.

Not only that, but there was Sophy to consider. Charlotte knew that Marcus would not leave without saying goodbye and therefore fully expected him to come to her in her sitting room where he also would expect to find Sophy. Charlotte had no need to question the integrity or behaviour of either her nephew or her daughter-in-law, but it would have been quite wrong for her to have attempted to prevent Amelia from remaining in order that they could have a few moments together. Unfortunately though, Amelia missed very little, and whilst Sophy had not behaved in a way which could open her up to criticism there *had* been that telltale tide of colour!

Charlotte sincerely sympathised with the predicament they were in, and even though she knew beyond any doubt that their feelings had never been demonstrated, human nature being what it was no reliance could be placed on keeping pent-up emotions in check indefinitely. The more she considered the matter the more convinced she became that a little separation may well be what was needed; nothing drastic, but perhaps Sophy would benefit from a visit to her brother Timothy, especially now as his wife, following several miscarriages, was expecting what they fervently hoped would be their first child! It would at least give Sophy and Marcus sufficient time to allow their emotions to cool as well as for their own protection. As far as Charlotte was concerned she could think of nothing better than these two people, both of whom she dearly loved, spending the rest of their lives together; unfortunately though, things were not that simple. There were too many considerations to be taken in to account. For one thing, had Charles seen that revealing flush of colour in his wife's cheeks he would instantly have read its significance for precisely what it was, and she knew Charles could be relied upon to take it very badly. That her son remained in ignorance of what was happening did not entirely surprise her. In her opinion he never accorded Sophy the respect or recognition she was due, and whilst Charlotte had no doubt that he fully asserted his rights as a husband, he certainly never paid any heed to her as a woman. If he did, he would undoubtedly see what she had known for some considerable time. Providing Sophy was dutiful he considered there was no cause to question her fidelity to him; at the moment this was certainly true, but given time, particularly if Charles continued to treat her in the way he did, then it would be an easy step for Sophy to turn to the man who, despite his outward show of composure, unquestionably adored her.

Then of course there was Amelia. Charlotte could only hope that she had read nothing amiss in Sophy's reaction; after all, she did have a tendency to be rather shy and more than once this had manifested itself in such a way, but with Amelia one could never quite tell what she had picked up on, but it would be foolish to take chances unnecessarily. Naturally, Charlotte would have to be careful how she approached Sophy. She loved her daughter-in-law very much and would do nothing to hurt or embarrass her, but if she was to be protected from denunciation and Charles's anger, then it was very necessary. From the very moment that Marcus and Sophy had discovered their love for one another Charlotte had always been able to rely on her nephew's discretion and impeccable behaviour towards Sophy, but Charlotte realised all too well that sooner or later even his strong will would break under the strain of holding his emotions constantly in check. She would have to think the matter over, but even before she had wished her two daughters-in-law goodnight she had already conceived a plan she believed would serve the purpose perfectly.

*

Having consumed more glasses of brandy than he had intended George's temper had considerably mellowed by the time he joined his wife upstairs, and any lingering irritation he may have had died the instant he laid eyes on Amelia. She may strictly adhere to the codes of mourning in her dress but in the privacy of her room she totally abandoned any pretensions to convention. Her nightdress and negligée, a recent purchase she had been quite unable to resist and which had been delivered only that morning by her dressmaker, were neither modest nor respectable, and even in George's slightly inebriated condition they appeared rather provocative. Not that he was complaining, mind you! Not at all! Unhappily, however, he would never be brought to see that she was not wearing them for his benefit, but as he had by this time completely misread the meaning of her attire it was going to take Amelia some time to make him realise that he had grossly erred in his assumption.

She had no intention of allowing him to make love to her even though she could plainly see that this was what he wanted. It took time as well as patience to convince him that she was not in the mood for his fumbling advances, and by the time she had finally dissuaded him her feigned headache had become a reality. Not only that, but George's ability would never match his ardour, especially now following what she suspected had been the consumption of several glasses of Nantes brandy. Unfortunately, George had never been able to hold his liquor; it not only loosened his tongue and prompted him into even more careless utterances but rendered him acutely susceptible to the amorous side of his nature, a circumstance Amelia was all too familiar with.

It was impossible for her not to draw comparisons between George and his brothers, and of course his cousin, all of whom were devastatingly attractive, and although there would never be another man for her but Charles she was honest enough to admit that under different circumstances she could quite easily succumb to Marcus's many understated charms. She understood perfectly well why Sophy had fallen in love with him, in fact Amelia would have to be blind not to recognise and appreciate his manifold qualities not to mention those harsh good looks, but it was not simply his handsome face that attracted her. Marcus possessed an air of unassuming masculinity which was all the more potent because of his unawareness of it and this, coupled with his excellent physique and that aura of hidden strength, all added up to an irresistible combination that acted on her sex with devastating effect.

She had no doubts whatsoever that Marcus would prove an excellent lover and regarded it as a great pity that he had set his heart on Sophy. Not that she would be unresponsive! Not at all. Amelia had caught that fleeting look of recognition between them this evening and the flush of colour which flooded Sophy's cheeks when he had held her hand and briefly brushed her fingers with his lips, and whilst she knew that nothing had occurred between them, Amelia found herself almost envying Sophy their inevitable coming together. Amelia instinctively knew that what they shared would live forever, and because Marcus was the kind of man he was, not only would he never even consider amusing himself elsewhere while he waited for the woman he loved but would remain very much in love with her for the rest of his life. Marcus, a man of old-fashioned and impeccable manners who punctiliously observed all the social courtesies, would not even have considered ignoring her flirtatious behaviour much less think the worst of her for it, but although Amelia had enjoyed their brief verbal encounter the gleam in his eyes had not been for her!

Of course, Charles was faithful to her too, if he were not then she would know it. Amelia had often wondered how she would feel if she ever discovered he had a connection elsewhere and how she would manage without him in her life. He had never told her he loved her, and whilst she had come to accept this the very thought that he no longer wanted her was so painful she had to stifle the little sob which rose in her throat. It had not escaped her notice that Charles had not been himself recently, and although he never subjected her to the same treatment he handed out to Sophy he had never confided in her. Of course, it filled her with a great sense of achievement to know that she alone had the power to take away that dark forbidding look, but on the one and only occasion she had ventured to ask him what was wrong he had merely kissed her, telling her there was nothing for her to worry about before proceeding to make passionate love to her. Amelia was under no illusion where Charles was concerned; he was by no means perfect, possessing more than his fair share of faults, but in spite of them she loved him and it was because she loved him and had become so attuned to his every mood that she instinctively knew something was wrong, but whatever was troubling him he obviously had no intention of telling her and as she struggled to find the answer she fell asleep, his name a soft sigh on her lips.

The object of her thoughts, in happy ignorance of the suspicions that were building up around him, kept his second assignation in Green Park the following afternoon with Ted Knowles, his mood very much lighter, a circumstance that did not escape his confederate's notice. Having reached the point of no return Charles looked upon his forthcoming actions as no more than self-preservation. There was no possible way he could raise five thousand pounds plus the interest Linas Webb would demand, and since that enterprising gentleman had politely but categorically refused to hand him back the jewellery on trust, Charles considered he had no other option available than the one he was about to embark upon. What had seemed an insoluble problem had now become nothing more than a minor irritation. Providence it seemed was smiling kindly upon him at last and he would be a fool not to take the one and only opportunity it was offering him. Of course, the beauty of it was that not only did it rid him of a thorn in his flesh but it gave him much-needed time to redeem the jewellery and, which was the prime attraction as far as he was concerned, it absolved him of all blame; a consideration he could not afford to overlook.

Ted Knowles had given his client's predicament a tremendous amount of thought, but upon learning what he actually had in mind he had to admit that Charles Harrington was as knowing a body as he had ever clapped eyes on! In Ted Knowles's expert opinion nothing could be better than the method his client had devised to rid himself of his problem, in fact it was nothing short of perfect, and so lost in admiration was he that all he could do was remove his bowler and scratch his head, his eyes wide with awe.

"I see it meets with your approval," Charles mocked.

Ted Knowles nodded. "Cudn't 'ave cum up with anythin' betta meself!"

Charles did not doubt it, pointing out with sardonic politeness, "Attractive though your options were, they were hardly guaranteed to ensure anonymity."

"Ah," Ted Knowles nodded knowingly, "you'm the one wi the 'ead."

"Thank you," Charles mockingly inclined his head.

"O'cus," Ted Knowles pointed out, "the thing is, 'ow's best ter do it?" Rubbing his chin reflectively, he said slowly, "O'cus, yer'll be wontin' it quick an' quiet-like, nuthin' ter draw attenshun." He sensed rather than saw the frown descend onto Charles's forehead and, enlarging on his theme, said meaningfully, "At the same time o'cus, there'd 'ave ter be sumbudy ter see it, ter prove it *wos* an accident."

Charles, who had already realised the necessity for a witness, perhaps even several, said sharply, "I am not a fool, Knowles; I am aware of that fact."

Ted Knowles, bearing all the signs of the onset of a severe cold and who had been growing steadily colder, rubbed his gloved hands together, marvelling at how his client seemed totally impervious to the steady drop in temperature. "O'cus," he supplied helpfully, blowing on his fingers, "the best thing 'ud be ter wotch the gerl, get ter know 'er ways like before decidin' 'ow best ter do the thing."

"I agree," Charles nodded, "but that will take time, and since I do not have an abundance of that particular commodity at my disposal, I shall have to forgo the usual preliminaries."

Apart from the fact that Charles's accomplice was firmly of the belief that the open air, especially on a raw, cold evening such as this, impaired the brain's capacity to think, he was beginning to feel the effects of his cold and longed for something warm and invigorating, preferably in front of a roaring fire, so taking it upon himself he suggested, "'Ows about you an' me talkin' it ova, ova a glass o' sumthin' warm. I knows the very place."

Charles could well imagine the type of establishment he had in mind and the suggestion was not at all favourable. He may have to rely upon this vulgar individual to assist him in carrying out his plans, but he did not trust him and certainly not enough to accompany him to a hostelry where he was probably known to any number of like-minded persons. It was unfortunate that he had had to resort to using Ted Knowles in the first place, but since he had he much preferred to deal with him on his own terms rather than his. Not only had Charles no wish to have his pockets felt or, worse, finding himself in a position whereby control was wrested from him, but it suited him far more to settle things here and now, but since Ted Knowles appeared to be having some difficulty in concentrating on the matter in hand, Charles reluctantly agreed to his suggestion. Having to content himself with his associate's affronted denial of holding any ulterior motives, he finally agreed to meet his co-conspirator at an establishment where he was assured of complete privacy and a good fire. Against his own better judgement Charles agreed to meet him later that evening, leaving Green

Park with nagging doubts as to the wisdom of allowing himself to be coerced into visiting a hostelry which, apart from the unsavoury location, was most probably a haunt for all the rogues in London!

The best one could say of Ted Knowles's habitual watering hole was that the landlord stocked an excellent cellar, but to one of Charles's fastidiousness not even this prospect was enough to induce him into stepping foot across the threshold again after this visit. To his knowledgeable eye 'The Black Swan' was clearly open house to all the lower elements of society, and since it was not his custom to associate with coal-heavers, women who offered their ample wares to anyone who would buy them or anyone else equally as vulgar, his presence caused him as much annoyance as it obviously caused them amusement and curiosity. The acrid smell of stale beer mingled with tobacco smoke was as offensive as the company and he devoutly trusted his new-found acquaintance would not keep him waiting in such a foul atmosphere for long. But fortunately for Charles within seconds of his arrival, Ted Knowles, who had been on the watch for him from his vantage point at the counter, caught sight of his tall and immaculately dressed person looking haughtily all around him and immediately pushed his way through the rowdy throng towards him. Ignoring his cheerful greeting with barely concealed antipathy, Charles allowed himself to be ushered into a private parlour, adamantly refusing to partake of any refreshment, much preferring to get on with the business in hand.

Charles may loathe his recently acquired acquaintance with every fibre of his being, but his knowledge and expertise in his own particular field, however questionable, were nevertheless precisely the kind of talents Charles needed. Within the space of three-quarters of an hour the two men had reached a calculated agreement, Ted Knowles accepting without question the responsibility of arranging the details of Charles's infallible scheme, more than happy to undertake whatever was necessary to honour his obligations as well as taking care to ensure that no wind of blame attached to his client, leaving Charles with nothing to do but await the terrible news of the girl's demise with as much patience as he could muster. The meeting, having begun quite amicably, soon began to take on a very different hue as both parties held reservations about certain aspects of it. Charles, whether he liked it or not, was totally dependent upon his confederate for the successful outcome of his scheme, and whilst he had every reason to believe that the result would be all he desired he was not overly pleased when Ted Knowles informed him that it would be necessary for him to bring in a third party. Immediately Charles looked wary, his eyes narrowing as he enquired further about this unknown individual. "Who is this man?" he asked abruptly. "I take it he is reliable?"

"Now lookee 'ere," Ted Knowles nodded, "if this 'ere thing is ter cum orf right, then Bill's the very man ter mek shua it does."

"It had better, Knowles," Charles warned. "You are not being paid to fail."

"There's no need ter fret yerself ova Bill," Ted Knowles assured him. "Fer one thing, 'e's as close as a clam, an' fer anotha," he pointed out, "'e's as gud a man fer this job as yer'll eva find." He received such a sceptical look from his client that he felt impelled to say, "Bill ain't no gabsta; 'e'll do the job fer yer right an' tight, no queshuns asked."

"You had better be right, Knowles," Charles told him coldly, "the fewer people who know about this the better it will be. I shall not take it kindly if what we have discussed leaks out."

"It won't," Ted Knowles told him. "Bill's dun more than one job that's needed ter be 'ushed up!"

Charles eyed his associate with a sardonic eye. "You really are to be congratulated on your choice of friends. Useless, I suppose," he mocked, "to recommend you being a little more discerning when you cultivate acquaintances in the future!"

It was on the tip of Ted Knowles's tongue to tell his client that it was all very well for him to scoff at his friends but it was his friends who were going to help him get rid of his problem, but thinking better of it he muttered something to which Charles was taking absolutely no notice. The truth was he had had enough of his acquaintance for one day, not to mention his distasteful surroundings, and was therefore in no mood to tolerate either any longer, so when Ted Knowles raised the question burning in his breast he was met with such a look that he swallowed. As his client's view of the financial arrangements unfortunately did not correspond with his own he was far from happy and allowed his annoyance to show.

Charles, quite unperturbed by the ugly which had descended onto Ted Knowles's face, quashed any hope he may have had of receiving something on account by demanding, "You surely do not expect to be paid before the job is done?"

"Well, as it 'appens," Ted Knowles told him, his colour darkening perceptibly, "I did think…"

"I have told you before, Knowles," Charles reminded him coldly, "you do a great deal too much thinking."

"That's all very well," Ted Knowles replied belligerently, his fists clenching suggestively at his sides, "but Bill'll wont 'is sher up frunt fer a start!"

Charles saw the huge paws clench and was neither impressed nor intimidated, merely allowing his gaze to travel contemptuously to the angry face staring mutinously up at him. "By all means make the attempt, if you think you can," Charles sneered, "but before you allow your inclinations to get the better of you, I think perhaps there is something you ought to take into consideration."

Ted Knowles looked wary, his eyes narrowing sharply. "An' wot'ud that be?" he asked suspiciously, watching his client take fresh stock of his surroundings with barely concealed loathing.

Indicating the door which led into the bar room with a nod of his head, the sound of raucous laughter clearly audible, Charles smiled disparagingly at his co-conspirator. "You do not appear to keep very good company, Knowles," he told him ominously. "It would be a pity, don't you think, if the landlord were to receive a visit from Bow Street," his eyes narrowing dangerously. "I am very sure they would be most interested to learn of the illicit activities which take place here," glancing significantly towards the door, "with your compliments, of course," he bowed mockingly. "I do not think your acquaintance, Benbow I think you called him," he raised a questioning eyebrow, "would take kindly to the notion of having to hand over his profits and, I make no doubt, the somewhat dubious contents of his cellar, over to the law, not to mention a spell at Her Majesty's pleasure."

Ted Knowles went as white as he had a moment ago been red, his voice wary. "Yer wud'nt dare!"

"You underrate me," Charles told him unpleasantly. "It would not do your reputation any good once it became known that you had turned tail on your friends, and be under no illusion," he warned menacingly, "I should ensure they knew it."

"They'd neva believes yer," Ted Knowles told him, not liking the way things were going, but felt all was not lost as he threw down what he believed to be his trump card. "I'd tells 'em all I knows, ah," he nodded, "an' the Peelers!"

"And what would you tell them?" Charles purred, eyeing him narrowly.

"That yer'd bin plannin' ter gets rid o' the wench," Ted Knowles nodded, his eyes suddenly wary at the ugly look which crossed Charles's face. "'Sides," he added in an attempt to give weight to his threats, "they'd know it's true; your man saw me at your place."

"You really think they would believe you?" Charles asked confidently, his smile far from pleasant, giving Ted Knowles pause for thought. "I very much doubt it," Charles shook his head. "I, my dear Knowles," he informed him, "apart from being a pillar of society, am a most law-abiding citizen, whilst you, forgive me for putting it so bluntly," he mocked, poking him in the stomach with the tip of his cane, "are a most unsavoury individual. So much so," he told him menacingly, "that no officer of the law would take your word against mine." After allowing sufficient time for this aspect to penetrate his confederate's brain, he withdrew the tip of his cane. "I hope I have made myself clear." Pulling on his gloves, Charles smiled thinly across at Ted Knowles, saying ominously, "I warned you before about the futility of crossing me, and if you think you can blackmail me you really are wasting your time. Your visit to my place of business was nothing other than a mere enquiry about my niece, and should you be misguided enough to elaborate on this to the authorities they will, out of necessity, demand to know how you know so much, a circumstance," he smiled ominously, "which I think even you will have difficulty in explaining. You shall get paid," he told him, "handsomely I assure you, but only when the job is done." Ted Knowles opened his mouth to speak but Charles forestalled him, saying dangerously, "If this fails because you or your so-called *friend*," he said with heavy sarcasm, "bundles, or discloses any of what has passed between us, you can not only say goodbye to any remuneration, but can look forward to enjoying Her Majesty's hospitality for some considerable time to come." Having reached the door he turned round, his voice hard and merciless, leaving Ted Knowles under no illusion. "Do not, under *any* circumstances, underestimate me. I shall not take it kindly if you betray me. Do not give me cause to warn you a third time."

Ted Knowles's first impressions of Charles Harrington in that he was dealing with no dupe as well as being a most dangerous man to cross, had undergone no change during the course of their dealings to date. He knew perfectly well that Charles Harrington was more than capable of informing against him and would have no compunction whatsoever in doing so. No one would ever doubt the word of a man like Charles Harrington as opposed to one such as himself, and unless he wanted to face the Queen's Bench as well as forgo what undoubtedly promised to be an ample reward for his services, he had no choice but to acquiesce. It went very much against the grain with Ted Knowles to acknowledge defeat much less to owning himself beaten and it certainly rankled to know that, for once in his life, he did not have the upper hand, but for all that he was astute enough to realise that Charles Harrington, by virtue of his standing in society, certainly held a much stronger position than himself, but the day would soon come when their positions would be reversed. At the moment Ted Knowles could not prove anything to Charles Harrington's detriment much less openly accuse him of planning his niece's death, but once the job was done then the possibilities were endless, and his client, despite his fine words, would soon be brought to see that not even he was above being blackmailed! In the meantime however, Ted Knowles could not afford to have the law poking their noses into Joe's business.

Ted Knowles's association with the landlord of '*The Black Swan*' was both profitable and of long duration; in fact, they had been cronies for a good many years and he knew as well as anyone that Joe Benbow's activities were very definitely on the shady side of the law. Yes, Bow Street would certainly be interested in Joe Benbow! For one thing, they would undoubtedly be interested to learn that not only did he take delivery of illegally imported wines and spirits but was also known to relieve some of his more questionable acquaintances of extremely suspect goods. Nor would they look too kindly upon Joe's habit of turning a blind eye to the women who plied their trade under his roof, freely supplying them with their 'mother's ruin' or whatever tipple took their fancy in return for a percentage of their earnings. Ted Knowles was the first to admit that Joe was as good a man as any to have in your corner, but he knew how to deal with someone who informed against him. More than once Ted Knowles had been privileged to see how his crony had dealt with a snitch or someone who had not honoured his side of a bargain, and he for one was none too eager to swell their number, having no desire to be on the receiving end of Joe's particular brand of punishment. Having to own himself floored on all points was something he was not used to but having been given no choice other than to accept Charles Harrington's decision about deferred payment, Ted Knowles tossed off his brandy before going home to nurse his worsening cold before setting his mind to the forthcoming task.

However much Charles disliked the idea of a third party being involved in his affairs, he nevertheless instinctively knew that Ted Knowles and his unknown confederate, neither of whom were in a position where they could afford to come to the notice of Bow Street, would not only do everything that was required of them without question but not allow their tongues to wag. Indeed, so confident was he of this that he gave the matter no more thought as he strolled round to his club to join a party of friends, arriving home just after midnight. His plans, which had been most carefully arranged with his confederate, left Charles with nothing more to do than to wait until the news of Alexandra's tragic accident was brought to them. As he leisurely climbed the stairs he gave no thought to the rights or wrongs of his scheme to dispose of his niece, on the contrary he was filled with an overwhelming sense of relief to know that he had staved off denunciation, buying himself precious time in which to redeem his sister's jewellery.

Chapter Eleven

George had no more liking for his mother's notion of having Alexandra live with her than Charles did, but when faced with her unexpected determination he failed to see what could be done. This did not mean that he had come round to the idea, nor did it prevent him from remonstrating with her daily as to the imprudence of having a stranger in the house because that was precisely what she was, not to mention her deplorable background, but it was noticeable that his belligerent warnings were becoming less forceful. Like Charles, George could not understand what had made their father change his mind about his will at the last moment, but as Jenkins had assured them of the document's legality as well as their father's sound mind, he was reluctantly growing to accept the unsatisfactory situation regarding Alexandra's inheritance.

Of course, he had been shocked at the disclosure, but that had been nothing compared to the shock of discovering his father's betrayal of what was his rightful due. To have the reins of power snatched out of his hands at the last minute had stunned him, and even now he was still furiously angry at being deprived of what he had always considered rightfully his. He would never be brought to believe that Charles had not engineered the whole thing, but he was nevertheless slightly mollified to know that Alexandra's recognition had toppled his brother's self-assurance where he had failed time and time again. Never would George forget the look of pure triumph on Charles's face when Jenkins had read out that shocking clause; it would be imprinted on his memory forever, and if it took him a whole lifetime he would pay Charles back for serving him such a trick. How he would achieve this George had no precise idea as yet, all he did know was that Charles would be made to pay for his part in the affair. Charles's armour appeared impenetrable, which only served to exacerbate his own temper even more when he considered that nothing he did seemed to dent it. All the same, it gave George some satisfaction to know that his brother's feathers had been very much ruffled by Alexandra, a circumstance he lost no opportunity to remind him of. It was his unshakeable belief that it was about time his family realised that as the eldest he was entitled to some respect, but since his mother was showing alarming signs of being more than capable of acting on her own initiative and disregarding his advice, and his brothers were totally ignoring his position and authority, his temper was becoming just brittle as that of Charles.

Mind you, he supposed he should have expected nothing else from either, but as far as Adam was concerned not only did he fail to grasp the enormity of the situation but treated it as casually as he did everything else, and on the several occasions George had attempted to explain the implications of their father's will to him it had been obvious that he may as well have saved his breath for all the notice Adam took. George was at a loss to understand what was keeping his youngest brother in town. According to him it was not, as he had originally supposed, Lily Southam, but if she was not the attraction, then who or what was? Having had his nose snapped off twice already for enquiring into the reason George was in no hurry to repeat the experience, but the more he saw of Adam the more convinced he became that he was up to some mischief. Regrettably, marriage had done nothing to improve his careless ways, and although George had at first wondered if Adam had married Isabel Marsden out of pique or from a blatant disregard for her father's wishes, allowing his temper and frustration to get the better of him and had since come to regret it, it had become increasingly obvious that he had wronged him. The marriage may not have been at his instigation or had his support, much less his blessing, nevertheless George had been acutely embarrassed when he had come upon Marsden the other day in Bond Street. Despite Adam's assurances that he and his father-in-law had worked out their differences and that he had even gone so far as to accept the marriage, from the look on Marden's face and his icily cold acknowledgement, George very much doubted it. He could only guess at what game his brother was playing, but whatever it was he was taking absolutely no notice of him whatsoever, and any attempt on his part to find out what he was up to was met with either a grin or a sharp rejoinder that it was none of his business.

Naturally, he liked Adam, who, in general, was rather even tempered and amiable, but he had many faults, not the least being his total disregard for appearances. To George's constant dismay, his youngest brother's worst fault was his unhealthy habit of hobnobbing with stablehands and the like and since Matthew, whether from perversity or an adamant refusal to give in to the bullying tactics of the developers, had, by his intractable stubbornness, not only ensured that forty-two Brook Street was one of the very few town houses in London who could still boast to having their own stables, but had virtually encouraged Adam's unseemly habit of fraternising. It was beyond George's comprehension how anyone could so far forget themselves as to spend so much as a minute indulging in conversation with the lad who cleaned your tack, but Adam it seemed had no such qualms. Everyone liked Adam, his cheerful insouciance and careless manners endearing him to even the lowliest servant, and all he had to do was smile for them to drop everything and attend him. Only this morning for instance, George had caught sight of him chatting away to old Jem as calm as you please, just as though they were old friends!

As far as Adam was concerned Jem was a friend; not only had he been with the family ever since he could remember, even putting him on his first pony, but he was a very knowledgeable fellow. More than once he had tipped him the wink about a sure thing at a race meeting or which prizefighter to put his money on, but this morning their conversation had nothing whatever to do with sporting activities.

Jem Davis had no liking for Charles, he had little cause to, he was none too keen on George either if it came to that, but Adam was a different kettle of fish altogether, and what he asked for Jem made sure he got. "The poultice'll do the trick," Jem assured him, running a knowing hand over the bay gelding which Adam had had to leave in Jem's care while he had been residing in Yorkshire. "Jus' give it a couple o' days more."

Adam nodded. "Thanks Jem."

"'Ow's the missus?" Jem asked conversationally, rubbing his hands down his leather apron.

Not at all put out by such familiarity, Adam grinned, "Fine as fivepence."

"Ah," Jem nodded, "'er's a grand lass. Rememba the day yer got shackled," chuckling to himself. "A rare set out that was. Thought the old guvna was gonna throw a fit the way he took on so!"

"Wasn't it just!" Adam laughed. "Although," he added a little defensively, "anyone would have thought I'd committed a crime!"

"Eva since yer was a nipper," Jem reminded him proudly, "yer've got yerself into some fine scrapes."

"And you got me out of most of them," Adam smiled, running a hand over his horse. "A pity you won't come to Yorkshire with me, though," he remarked.

Jem ran a hand through his grizzled hair. "Yer knows I can't, Guvna," he shook his head, "not w'ile the missus is 'ere."

Having come to Brook Street as Charlotte's personal groom upon her marriage, Jem's loyalty to her was absolute and no power on earth would prise him away while she was alive. He had an attachment to her which went far beyond his duties, and although she no longer rode he ensured her carriage was always ready for her whenever she needed it, dropping whatever he was doing so he could drive her wherever she wanted to go.

"I know," Adam acknowledged, "and it's good she has you to watch out for her."

"I al'as will," he told Adam firmly. "A real lady, yer mother. Al'as 'as a good word for everybody. More than can be said for sum," adding pugnaciously, "and although I dain't 'old with wot the master did over yer sister and poor Josh, I will say 'e was al'as fair."

Eyeing his disrespectful henchman with an indulgent eye, Adam grinned, "You seem mighty keen for a set-to this morning. Who's put your nose out of joint?"

"An' as fer you, young master," Jem told him as sternly as his fondness would permit, "yer not too old ter 'ave yer breeches dusted!"

Adam laughed, straightening himself up. "Well, if you think you still can you are perfectly welcome to give it a try."

"Give over," Jem grinned. "Fer one thing I ain't as young as I was when I used ter set yer straight."

"Running shy, are we?" Adam smiled, recalling fond memories.

"I ain't *never* run shy!" Jem exclaimed indignantly, the laughter suddenly dying in his eyes as he caught sight of Charles entering the stable yard, sitting astride a black thoroughbred that appeared to be every inch as unpredictable as its rider. "Bin in the park I expect," Jim grunted, giving the nod to his young apprentice. Waiting only for him to get out of earshot he bit out, "'Ope 'e's ridden off 'is temper!"

"I doubt it," Adam replied, watching his brother dismount before thrusting the reins into the lad's hands. "It will take more than a ride in the park to do that."

"Wot's up with 'im anyway?" Jem asked. "'E's bin in the sulks for weeks now!"

It was not like Charles to take a ride in the park mid-week, but, clearly, he had felt the need to do so this morning. However, if his intention had been to ride off his temper, then from the look on his face it had obviously failed in its object. Charles could not see his brother from where he was standing, and Jem, heaving a sigh of relief as he watched Charles stride straight into the house without venturing inside the stable, made no attempt to hide his feelings. "As nasty a piece o' work as I've eva seen," he told Adam candidly.

Adam secretly agreed that Charles did nothing to make himself agreeable, and certainly not to those whom he considered beneath him, but he felt it incumbent upon him to remind his childhood mentor that he was talking about his brother.

"I knows 'e is," Jem grunted, "but I still says it. As sharp a tung as yer'll ever find." Turning away from the door he looked up into Adam's face, saying with a frankness that would not have been tolerated by many, "It's no use sayin' I likes 'im, 'cus I don't, an' never will, an' if yer wants ter get rid o' me all yer 'as ter do is say so."

"Don't be an idiot!" Adam exclaimed irritably, gripping his shoulder. "But I would advise you to say nothing like this to anyone but me."

"I ain't no fool," Jem nodded, "but since yer've given me the nod to says wot I think, then I will. 'E don't treat folk proper, not likes yerself, nor 'e don't give us the time o' day, 'cept when 'e wants sumthin' or give us a rakin' down, an' then 'e finds 'is tung quick enough!"

Adam had always known that Jem had no love for his brother, in fact he doubted if any of the servants had, but this was the first time his old friend had ever really given vent to his feelings, and whilst Adam knew he ought not to have permitted it he believed that it was perhaps far better out of his system rather than being allowed to grow and fester.

Staying only long enough to reiterate his warning to Jem, Adam made his way back to the house to find Charles, having changed his clothes, was on the point of leaving. After exchanging a few words with his brother, Adam strolled into the dining room to ponder his next move over a lengthy and substantial breakfast. He knew Marcus was right in that they had no proof Charles was contemplating anything even remotely illegal, and as things stood at the moment no one could possibly accuse him of anything; besides which, as far as Adam knew, it was no crime to resent the contents of a will, even your father's! Short of following Charles around twenty-four hours a day in the hope he would provide them with the evidence they needed, Adam failed to see what else could be done, but as this was physically impossible he had to resign himself to the frustration of waiting for something to happen. Unlike his cousin, waiting was not his strong point. He hated having to wait upon events, much preferring to be up and doing and going out to meet whatever came along head on. He had never lacked courage, but he did tend to lack the foresight which characterised Marcus as well as his patience in carefully sifting through the facts. From the moment Adam had begun to suspect that Charles was concocting a plan of some kind to disinherit Alexandra he had not paused long enough to consider that Charles may need an accomplice to assist him, much less who he may be.

Marcus, on the other hand, had given this a great deal of thought. He knew that whatever Charles was planning he would need help, if for no other reason than to protect himself. He would not run the risk of acting in the matter personally, and although the planning would be his he would make quite certain that someone else carried it out. It would of course have to be someone he could rely on to follow his orders without question, but more to the point someone who would not let his tongue run away with him. Marcus was not overly familiar with Charles's circle of friends, but he felt it reasonably safe to assume that his cousin would not approach any one of them for assistance and this being so the only feasible conclusion as far as Marcus could see was that Charles would have to look elsewhere for a confederate, which in turn meant that he would be forced into employing help. His collaborator would naturally have to be a man who possessed little or no scruples and one, moreover, who would not be subjected to attacks of conscience about what he was asked to undertake, which of course meant that his services would have to be bought, and these would not come cheap. There were any number of places where such men could be hired, but Marcus suspected that his cousin had not had to look very far. In some strange way this unknown personality seemed to be inextricably linked with Alexandra herself, and unless he was very much mistaken he felt sure that the connection tying them together was Silas Jenkins.

Marcus easily acquitted him of being anything other than totally honest, which meant that his cousin's association with this unknown personality had come about by either innocent or accidental means. Events over the recent past had been quick and unexpected to say the least, and if memory served him correctly his uncle had instigated a search for his granddaughter in complete secrecy, which meant that he alone knew the identity of the man he had hired to find her. In view of Sophy's disclosure about her visit to Alexandra, Silas Jenkins had had to locate her somehow, and from what Marcus had managed to discover prior to this visit, his search had proved unsuccessful which meant that somehow or other he had managed to obtain her direction, and it followed therefore that Silas Jenkins would have had no alternative but to acquire this from the man Matthew had originally hired. If this was indeed the way of it, then Silas Jenkins had, by some means, managed to discover his identity. From what Marcus had been able to make out there had been nothing amongst his uncle's papers relating to the man and Silas Jenkins of all people would be in a position to know. How then, would one set about finding him? Had Marcus been in Silas Jenkins's position and faced with a task which was rather daunting to say the least, especially when he considered the animosity of his late client's family, he would, out of necessity, be forced to resort to the time-honoured method of placing an advertisement in the newspapers. Marcus could not recall having seen such an announcement and he was confident that no one else had either otherwise it would most certainly have been commented on; it followed therefore that the advertisement must have been placed in a newspaper no member of his family would be likely to read. Since he had no idea when it would have been inserted, he could see little point in wasting precious time by searching for it and considered the most logical step for him to take next was to pay Silas Jenkins a visit.

Not having expected him, Silas Jenkins received his late client's nephew with some surprise; quite at a loss to understand what had brought him here today.

"It is good of you to see me," Marcus smiled as he shook hands. "I know you must have a lot of calls upon your time."

Silas Jenkins was not the only one to succumb to Marcus's attractive smile, hastily assuring him that he was honoured. Partly because Marcus consulted the same solicitor his father had and also because of his time abroad with his regiment, Silas Jenkins had had very few dealings with Matthew's nephew, even so, from the little he had seen of him he struck him as being a man of calm good sense. Mrs. Matthew Harrington, he knew, not only relied upon his judgement and trusted him implicitly but had a great fondness for him, and Silas Jenkins could not help wondering if this visit was on her behalf, but when he eventually discovered the purpose of what had brought him here today he was very much taken aback, quite unable to think what he could possibly want with Ted Knowles.

As Marcus had no intention of taking him into his confidence, at least not at this stage, partly because he knew he could well be wrong in his thinking about Charles's intentions but also because he had no desire to raise alarm bells unnecessarily, he merely shrugged, saying calmly, "It is no great matter, but I should be obliged if you could furnish me with his name and direction."

Silas Jenkins eyed him closely, growing increasingly uneasy as he wondered what was in the wind. "I am, of course, in possession of both," he nodded, adding hesitantly, "although why you should be enquiring after him is more than I can tell."

"It is merely a private matter," Marcus assured him.

"Forgive me," Jenkins apologised, "but whilst I accept that you are at liberty to consult whomsoever you wish, I fail to see what you could possibly want with this man other than in connection with your late uncle's estate. In which case," he pointed out, "I can neither promote nor condone it."

"Nor would I wish you to," Marcus surprised him by saying.

Silas Jenkins's eyes narrowed as he looked at the inscrutable but determined face opposite him, totally confused. "But I thought…"

"I have no reason, much less the desire, to discuss my late uncle's affairs with anyone," Marcus told him firmly. "That would be quite wrong and well outside my jurisdiction."

Silas Jenkins was relieved to hear this but he was still feeling rather perplexed and could not help regarding it as a pity that he did not know Marcus Ingleby better because if he did, then perhaps he would not feel quite so uncomfortable. "Then why…?"

"I am afraid," Marcus smiled ruefully, "that I am going to have to ask you to trust me."

Silas Jenkins pursed his lips. "Please, do not misunderstand me," he shook his head, "I should, of course, be quite happy to do so if I knew the precise nature of your business with him."

Marcus acknowledged the justification of this comment, regarding it as quite understandable in the circumstances, but he was as disinclined to open his mind to Silas Jenkins as he was to discussing his late uncle's affairs outside the family. Not only that, but as things stood at the moment everything was purely supposition and Marcus knew he could be considerably wide of the mark about Charles's intentions and the last thing he wanted was to voice his feelings, but since Silas Jenkins had made it quite clear that he was not prepared to release any information without a very good reason for doing so it was therefore with extreme reluctance that Marcus took him part way into his confidence. It was not something he was either eager or happy to do but given Jenkins's stance there seemed to be no other way of getting him to release the information he had asked for, not that Marcus could really blame him for exercising caution, after all as far as Jenkins was concerned he was something of an unknown quantity, but there was no disguising that diligent professional's horror upon hearing the carefully worded reason for such an extraordinary request.

Silas Jenkins instinctively knew that Marcus had not told him the full sum of his suspicions and certainly not the identity of the supposed perpetrator, but it was enough to shock him into exclaiming, "Good God! You cannot be serious, surely? I realise that her inclusion in your uncle's will was not universally received, but that any one of them should try to deprive her of her inheritance is too incredible!"

"I assure you," Marcus told him truthfully, "that no one wishes to have my concerns proved wrong more than I do, but if I am right, then steps must be taken to prevent it from happening."

"I agree," Jenkins concurred, but he was still deeply shocked by what had been disclosed to him. Then, after a moment's deliberation, asked, with more optimism than he felt, "I suppose there is no possibility that you could be wrong?"

"There is every possibility!" Marcus admitted. "But, surely, you must see that it has to be looked in to?"

Silas Jenkins did see and he was greatly perturbed by it, saying despondently, *"Never,* in all my years of legal practice, have I come across anything like this! Of course," he sighed, "I knew how it would be when Matthew instructed me to insert that codicil, but he would have it his way in spite of my earnest representations for caution." Then, as if something had suddenly occurred to him, he asked warily, "I don't quite understand though; why are you involving yourself in this?" Without giving Marcus time to respond he pointed out, not unreasonably, "Strictly speaking, your uncle's affairs are not your concern."

Having anticipated this question, Marcus replied steadily, "I quite agree, but if I am right and Alexandra does stand in danger of being deprived of her inheritance, then I for one would much prefer to deal with it as quietly as possible. You will agree, I am sure," he nodded, "that no possible good could result from presenting this matter to the authorities, besides," he pointed out firmly, "I have no intention of allowing this to come to my aunt's ears, and I shall do everything in my power to protect her and prevent her from discovering what I believe to be true."

As this aspect of the matter had not previously occurred to him, Silas Jenkins had to acknowledge the sense of it, and having by this time somewhat recovered from the initial shock of Marcus's confidences he had to admit that he was right. Upon reflection, Silas Jenkins knew that nothing would be more disastrous than putting this whole affair before the police, and even if he acted in the matter himself it would still create embarrassing questions. After only a few moments of debating the dilemma confronting them, he relented to Marcus's request, saying resignedly, "The man who presented himself to me called himself Ted Knowles. I must warn you, however," he cautioned, "that this individual is not at all the type of man I would place any degree of trust in, indeed, I was quite shocked to discover what kind of man your uncle had employed," he swallowed. "Unfortunately, however, my dealings with him were rather forced upon me; I hope I have no need to tell you that in the normal course of business I would never have consulted him. Regrettable though it is," he confessed, "I am afraid to say that my own efforts to locate the girl proved fruitless, indeed, I found myself in the disagreeable position of having to carry out my responsibilities to your late uncle in any way I could." Not for the first time during the past half hour or more he found himself coming under intense scrutiny from his visitor, disconcertingly aware of how those brown eyes had a way of penetrating deeper than one would like. After absently tidying some papers on his desk he raised his eyes and offered tentatively, "Unfortunately, I found myself with little choice other than having to place an advertisement in the newspapers requesting this man to get in touch with me."

"And?" Marcus prompted, crossing one long leg over the other, clearly indicating to Silas Jenkins that he was going nowhere without the information he had come for.

Marcus Ingleby may possess a far more amiable disposition than George and Charles but Silas Jenkins, like many before him, was beginning to realise that he was not the type of man to be fobbed off. Even so, he had been Matthew Harrington's legal adviser for a good many years and he still looked upon it as his duty to serve his late client's family with all the discretion and diligence at his command, and even though there may be storm clouds gathering he nevertheless felt impelled to impress upon his visitor the need for caution.

"I am aware," Marcus acknowledged, "that you are naturally hesitant to divulge anything relating to my late uncle's estate, but I should not be here now unless I thought it necessary."

Torn between the sense of Marcus's reasoning and his own professionalism, Silas Jenkins weighed the argument carefully. His knowledge of Mrs. Matthew Harrington's nephew may be limited but there was something about him which told him he could be trusted and it only took a matter of seconds before he made up his mind to do just that. Retrieving Ted Knowles's calling card from his desk drawer he handed it over to Marcus, saying, "I would, however, advise caution in your dealings with him."

After eyeing the card with its florid legend dispassionately, Marcus put it into his pocket, neither his face nor his voice giving anything away. "Thank you. By the way, I may as well have the girl's direction while I am here."

Silas Jenkins eyed him closely for several moments, then, as if thinking better of arguing the point, scribbled it down on a sheet of paper and handed it to him, commenting, "I trust you know what you are doing?"

"I do," Marcus replied calmly. "Incidentally," he said conversationally, "I trust you found Alexandra well."

"So," Jenkins nodded, eyeing Marcus sharply, "Mrs. Charles Harrington told you about her accompanying me?"

"Yes," Marcus nodded, his tone somewhat condemnatory, "she told me."

Jenkins sighed, reading the silent accusation perfectly. "Believe me," he told him truthfully, "had there been any other course open to me I would have taken it. I am perfectly well aware of your cousin's views on this matter," he nodded, "and whilst I realise how displeased he would be if he knew that his wife had accompanied me on a visit to the girl, given the circumstances I was faced with no alternative." After clearing his throat, he said, somewhat defensively, "I am fully aware of the awkward position in which I placed Mrs. Charles Harrington, but this matter of acquainting the girl of her inheritance had already been allowed to drift for far longer than it should, and whilst I know perfectly well that it has not found favour with certain members of your family, I could not permit it to drag on indefinitely." He then went on to further explain, "From what I have been privileged to see of Mrs. Charles Harrington as well as Harris's confidences to me about the unfriendly reception the girl received upon her visit to Brook Street, it therefore seemed sensible to enlist her aid as she appeared, with the exception of yourself, to hold no animosity towards the girl. Do not forget," he reminded him, "I represented the Harrington family, and bearing in mind the ill feeling towards her followed by her hasty departure from Brook Street, I formed the impression that she would be none too eager to see me, which is why," he told him, "I thought that if Mrs. Charles Harrington were to accompany me it would not only go a long way to reassuring the girl but also that she would perhaps be the only one Alexandra would probably take notice of."

"Which apparently she did." Marcus cocked a knowledgeable eyebrow.

"Yes," Jenkins nodded, adding, "at least it was due to Mrs. Charles Harrington's representations that she promised to give consideration to Matthew's bequest as well as thinking very carefully about her grandmother's wish to have her residing with her in Brook Street. The position now," he sighed, "is that she requires time to consider the matter further, although what there is to consider I don't know," he commented, shrugging his narrow shoulders. It was impossible to read his visitor's thoughts, but for some reason he felt it incumbent upon him to stress his duties as his late uncle's legal adviser and that he was perfectly justified in doing whatever was required of him to bring matters to a favourable conclusion.

Marcus had no cause to question his diligence, only his wisdom in involving Sophy, but deeming it prudent to say no more on this he merely rose to his feet and reiterated his thanks.

"I don't know what you expect to discover from this man Knowles," Jenkins shook his head, "but I would advise you to tread carefully. I gained the very strong impression that he is far more than the private detective he purports to be, and by no means as genial as he appears."

"I shall bear that in mind," Marcus nodded.

"Just one more thing," Jenkins forestalled him, "whoever may be at the back of what you seem to regard as some kind of plot to disinherit the girl, then I have to tell you that I for one find it impossible to believe that a member of your family, no matter how much they may deprecate that codicil in Matthew's will, had so far forgotten themselves by discussing affairs to those who have clearly furnished Ted Knowles with as much information as he appears to be in possession of. Indeed," he confessed, "I was most surprised, not to say shocked, at the extent of his knowledge regarding your family's affairs, particularly the girl's expectations."

"In other words," Marcus supplied, not in the least surprised, "he obviously has an informant and one, moreover, who enjoys considerable trust within the family."

Jenkins nodded. "That is my own belief, yes."

To Jenkins's surprise Marcus did not seem at all perturbed by this unsavoury aspect of the case. "If this Ted Knowles character is the kind of man I take him to be," he pointed out placidly, "then I should certainly expect him to rely heavily upon people in privileged positions, whether they form part of a domestic household or not. They would, I suspect, feature as an integral part of his activities or, at least," he added, "the more illicit of them."

Silas Jenkins eventually said goodbye to his visitor with very mixed feelings. He may not be as familiar with Marcus as he was with his cousins, but Jenkins had seen enough of him to say that he did not strike him as being a man given over to exaggeration or making mischief, and therefore if he was involving himself in something that was really no concern of his, then either he had seen something he himself had not or he had stumbled upon something which could in all probability land the Harrington family knee-deep in scandal.

Marcus may not have named Charles as the one who had come under suspicion, but Jenkins failed to see how it could be anyone else. George, he knew, was all wind and bluster, and as for Adam he was so blatantly unconcerned and blasé about things that at times Jenkins had wondered if he was capable of taking anything seriously. No, if something was going on he would lay his life that Charles was at the back of it, but what this may be exactly Jenkins could only hazard a guess. If Marcus was right, and Jenkins had the sneaking feeling that he was, then he could expect a pretty uncomfortable time in the none too distant future. At the moment though, his hands were tied and he could only hope that Marcus was wrong, or at least able to nip whatever it was in the bud before the whole family was plunged into disaster. Not for the first time Jenkins found himself pitying the girl whilst at the same time wishing she would hurry up and make up her mind. For the life of him he could not understand why she was dragging her feet over this. Whatever she may feel for her grandfather, surely, she could see that what was being offered her was far better than what she had now. Nevertheless, despite his frustration he was prepared to keep his word to Mrs. Charles Harrington and not press the girl for her answer, but he devoutly trusted that she would not take too much longer in coming to a decision.

But Alexandra had by no means come to a decision about her windfall any more than she had about accepting her grandmother's invitation to stay with her. Silas Jenkins may look for an early response to his visit, but in view of the enormity of what she was expected to consider, then he was destined to disappointment. She could not deny that thirty thousand pounds was an enormous sum of money, far more than she had ever thought of and certainly quite unlooked-for. Not only would it take her away from a life which she had never really accustomed herself to but it would mean the end to what she could only describe as an intolerable existence. Then, of course, there was her mother's jewellery. This, more than the money, had come as a tremendous shock. Her mother had never spoken about her jewellery, in fact there was so much she had kept to herself, and although Alexandra had no idea how the collection was made up or how much it was worth, she did know that there were certain members of her family who bitterly resented her grandfather leaving her anything at all. She did not need it pointing out that she would be a fool to throw her good fortune away, if for no other reason than it was hers by right but also because it would enable her to maintain herself without the need for further financial worries.

There was no doubting Sophy's integrity, on the contrary she was both sincere and genuine and, apart from her grandmother, Alexandra believed that she was the only one who wished her well. Sophy's arguments had been sensible as well as just, and in her heart, Alexandra knew she was right. Her reluctance stemmed from knowing that to accept her inheritance meant that she not only forgave her grandfather but would be virtually betraying her parents. Not even during their most straitened times had her mother gone cap in hand to her father begging for forgiveness and asking for assistance; and for her now to walk into a life which her grandfather had made possible by virtue of that bequest, a life which he had cruelly denied her mother, made her feel the worst kind of traitress. Balancing practicalities against emotion was never easy, but for Alexandra it seemed impossible. Sophy had said that her mother would have wanted her to take what her grandfather was offering, but instead of making her decision easier it seemed to make it all the more difficult. Even if she did take Sophy's advice Alexandra knew perfectly well what her reception in Brook Street would be; and from what she had seen of her newly acquired relatives she did not think she was up to coping with their barely concealed animosity. Emotionally she was far too vulnerable to manage successfully their blatant hostility and contempt, and in view of this decided that, for the time being at least, she would be far better leaving off making her decision for a while longer.

Alexandra's opinion of her family was not misplaced. Ever since the reading of Matthew's will the bequest to his granddaughter had caused nothing but anger and resentment, and Emily, who had still not reconciled herself to Edward's paltry sum, bitterly resented the girl. She was at a loss to understand what her father had been thinking of when he had added that codicil to his will and could only conclude that he must have suffered some kind of temporary insanity because as far as she could see nothing else explained his behaviour satisfactorily. Her father's ultimate recognition of the girl was nothing short of an insult to the whole family, but for her part she would never acknowledge her! Despite her numerous attempts to dissuade her mother from having the girl stay in Brook Street when she was eventually found, Emily's entreaties fell on deaf ears. To her surprise her mother was proving a force to be reckoned with; not that she shouted or lost her temper like her father, but in her own quiet and unassuming way she was showing a determination which almost bordered on stubbornness. It seemed the more one remonstrated with her about the imprudence of what she was planning the more she was digging her heels in; and certainly nothing to date was having the slightest impact on her. Emily's fruitless efforts to bring her mother to her senses had left her with no other course open to her but to enlist Charles's help. Of course, she had not really forgiven him for his behaviour towards her on the day of her father's funeral but deciding to put this to one side in favour of more important issues she was confident that he would know how to put a stop to all this nonsense. All the same, she had to own up to some astonishment in that, considering his attitude about the whole affair, Charles had not yet managed to turn his mother away from her fixed intention.

Emily had no way of knowing about the plans her brother had set in motion but having witnessed his annoyance and representations about the girl, it did seem a little odd to her that he was apparently not doing enough to stem her mother's ridiculous ideas. As Charles's views ran parallel with her own where Alexandra was concerned, Emily found his sudden and inexplicable submission quite confusing, in fact she was astonished that he appeared to have shrugged off any responsibility to the family about the girl, seemingly having finally come round to the idea.

"My dear sister," Charles told her coldly, "I have no more liking for this idea of my mother's than you do, and as for the girl's inheritance I believe I have made my views on that perfectly clear, but in view of my mother's obvious determination in this matter I fail to see what else any one of us can do." Her insistence that he must not let the matter rest, was met with the icy reply, "When I require your advice on how to deal with family affairs be sure I shall ask for it. In the meantime," he recommended sharply, "I would strongly advise you to concentrate on your own." Leaving Emily to read into this whatever she liked Charles abruptly left the room, leaving her to gasp her indignation.

Charles knew the direction of his mother's thoughts very well, but although he too was surprised by her unexpected resolution he also knew that her ambition would never be realised. Before long Alexandra would be nothing more than a fleeting memory in their lives; a momentary diversion which would prove to be as transient as the blinking of an eyelid. He believed he had expressed his views as well as his disapproval as often and as strongly as he could, in fact so vehement had his arguments been that his mother clearly knew them by heart, but since he was a man who wasted neither his time nor his breath on lost causes, he deemed any further remonstrations as being quite futile. If Emily felt the need to say anything further then she was perfectly welcome to do so and, as for George, whose favourite pastime was listening to the sound of his own voice and giving advice which was as unwanted as it was banal, he was more than capable of speaking for the rest of them. The brat had caused Charles too many problems for him to feel guilt or remorse over instigating her permanent removal from their lives, in fact as far as he was concerned he would not mourn her passing.

Charlotte had weathered the disapproving storm of her family's opposition extremely well so far, but the effects of constantly fending off their arguments were beginning to tell. It had not escaped Sophy's notice that her mother-in-law was looking far from well, indeed she was suffering an inordinately high number of headaches recently which were causing her grave concern. She knew Charlotte would not allow her to call in Doctor Rowley, not only because she did not like him over much but because she refused to acknowledge the frequency and severity of them any more than she acknowledged the way her nerves jumped at the slightest sound or the way she winced at the overexuberance of her two young grandsons whenever Amelia permitted them downstairs before dinner with Nanny Bishop. Although Sophy would have felt very much better if Charlotte would at least consent to talk to Doctor Rowley, she nevertheless shrewdly suspected that her mother-in-law was most probably suffering the effects of too much family friction. Sophy herself was conscious of the need to sometimes escape their feuding and fully sympathised with Charlotte's desire to be alone, but as this was nothing more than an idyllic dream, she too had to make the best of things.

Having appeased her daughter-in-law by promising to think about seeing Doctor Rowley if her headaches persisted, Charlotte set her mind to the far more important task of how to bring about Sophy's visit to her brother and sister-in-law without arousing suspicion. Charlotte knew Timothy to be a kind-hearted young man and one, moreover, who was extremely fond of his sister, and from this standpoint at least she knew he would not disappoint her.

Emily, deciding to make yet another attempt to bring her mother to her senses since it seemed that Charles had washed his hands of the whole affair, walked unceremoniously into her sitting room just as she was in the middle of composing a letter to Timothy, but believing her errand to be of far more importance than her mother's correspondence as well as still bristling with indignation at her brother's abruptness a moment ago, imperatively demanded to know whether she still intended to make the name of Harrington a laughing-stock.

The mere thought of yet another confrontation made Charlotte close her eyes on a despondent sigh; she had endured enough recently without her children adding to her worries, and was therefore in no frame of mind to listen to her daughter's further reproaches. Laying down her pen she turned her head slightly, saying with a quiet firmness which seemed to have no effect upon Emily whatsoever, "If by that you mean am I still of the same mind, the answer is yes. Once Jenkins has found Alexandra I have every intention of renewing my invitation to her to stay with me for as long as she wishes."

In her desire to prevent her mother from realising her ambition Emily entirely failed to see the strain on her face or the tiredness behind the smile, saying sharply, "I should never have believed you thought so poorly of us as to humiliate us in this way!"

"Any humiliation brought to this family was done years ago," her mother informed her wearily. "The inclusion of my granddaughter to its ranks will not add to it, on the contrary," she said simply, "it will absolve it."

Emily's cold eyes sparkled with indignation. "My father did the only honourable thing under the circumstances!"

"And what do you know of the circumstances?" her mother enquired, rising slowly to her feet. "You were a mere child when it happened."

"That's hardly the point," Emily bit out. "Elizabeth disgraced us; condemned us for all time!"

A little smile played at the corner of Charlotte's mouth. "A somewhat melodramatic statement, don't you think?" Clearly Emily did not think so, and Charlotte, determined to put a stop to this ridiculous charade said, as considerately as she could, "Falling in love is not a crime, Emily."

"For heaven's sake, Mamma!" Emily cried. "He was a servant, a mere stablehand!"

Her mother paused for several moments, regarding her daughter thoughtfully, asking at length, "Do you think your sister was any the less happy for that?"

Emily eyed her mother with barely concealed horror, exclaiming, "You actually *approved* of it!"

"No mother could want such a connection for her daughter," Charlotte admitted truthfully, "but emotions do not always behave to order. Naturally, I wanted Elizabeth to make a good marriage, not the one your father had in mind for her, however, but neither did I want her marriage to be at the expense of her happiness." Emily scoffed at this, but Charlotte continued as if there had been no interruption. "Marriage is for life, Emily. It cannot easily be undone simply because one discovers too late they have made a mistake. To spend one's life in close proximity to a man you do not love is no pleasant thing."

Judgemental and proud by nature, Emily could neither enter into her mother's sentiments nor understand them. She totally disregarded the fact that she was fortunate her husband had been of her own choosing and that her father, albeit after looking carefully into his background and circumstances, had finally accepted Edward Machin into the family without demur.

Charlotte may not entirely approve of wearing one's heart on one's sleeve but at the same time a little display of affection never came amiss, but with Emily it was almost impossible to tell to what degree she loved her husband, her undemonstrative nature prohibiting her from showing any feelings of love or tenderness. Charlotte was completely at a loss to account for her daughter's rather prudish streak as well as her bigoted attitude, even so, she knew it was these unattractive qualities which prevented her from having the slightest understanding of her sister's behaviour.

It was otherwise with Sophy. She may not wear her heart on her sleeve but she was more than capable of love and tenderness. Charlotte would not go so far as to say that Sophy would turn her back on everything for love, but she fully understood human nature and what had made Elizabeth accept her banishment and give up her life for the man she loved. Charlotte disliked drawing comparisons between those whom she loved, but as she looked at Emily, a picture of righteous wrath, she found it virtually impossible not to do so. It would never so much as cross Emily's mind to give her all to a man as Elizabeth had done, and since it was useless trying to explain it or her own feelings towards her granddaughter, Charlotte allowed Emily to talk herself into a one-sided argument which eventually resulted in her frustrated retreat from the sitting room.

The hostile reaction of her offspring may distress and sadden her, but it had in no way deterred Charlotte in her determination to put right a terrible wrong; a wrong which Matthew had automatically inflicted on Alexandra the moment he had disowned her mother. Charlotte realised perfectly well that she could not replace those lost years any more than she could undo the traumatic events Matthew had set in motion over twenty years ago, but no matter what it took she was going to do everything in her power to make up for the unnecessary deprivation her granddaughter had endured.

Since receiving that first letter from Silas Jenkins the only other communication Charlotte had had from him was a brief note expressing his sincere belief that the search was almost at an end, but since that had been over a week ago with no sign of anything resulting from it, she decided that the only course open to her was to enlist Marcus's help. She knew it would not be denied her, and although there had been little opportunity for her to have a private word with him over the past week or so, she promised herself a few moments alone with him next time he called.

Chapter Twelve

Had Charles the least idea that Ted Knowles's cold had taken priority over the matter in hand he would not have been so complacent, but so severe was the chill that had descended upon his confederate that he was forced to keep to his bed for two whole days. Even to raise his head from the pillow caused the room to swim violently around him, and his landlady, never before knowing her most lucrative tenant to take so ill, could not be dissuaded from visiting Mr. Ponson in order to purchase some of his beneficial powders. Eventually though his chill loosened its grip, but it was close on a week before he was able to venture out and then only for short periods of time as his resultant weakness and the continued cold weather proved too much for him. Nevertheless, neither of these inconveniences prevented him from setting his mind to the job in hand. Armed with a fortifying glass of Joe Benbow's best brandy, far better in Ted Knowles's opinion than those repulsive powders from Mr. Ponson, and wrapped in a shawl in front of the fire, he methodically began to lay the foundations of his plan of campaign.

It was unfortunate that he had no way of knowing Alexandra's routine but, like Charles Harrington, he felt it reasonable to suppose that she would not be overly burdened by social engagements, which would probably have taken her to goodness only knows where. He further supposed that for most of the time she kept to the house and that any outside activity would be local, which, considering her straitened circumstances, seemed more than likely. Unfortunately though, it did make it rather difficult to get her to a venue of his choosing without arousing her suspicions, which was vital given that the success of the scheme depended solely upon this one circumstance.

Unhappily, this was proving to be the biggest stumbling block to his plans and, having discarded one idea after the other on very practical grounds, he consequently found himself forced into adopting measures which he knew full well Charles Harrington would most strongly disapprove of. His client had been by no means pleased to learn that he had brought in a third party, and although he had eventually been brought to see that Bill Ryde was an indispensable addition to their number if the thing was to come off right, Ted Knowles doubted very much whether he would look upon using his wife to further his ends in the same way. It was all very well for Charles Harrington to dictate terms, but he was not the one having to work out the intricacies of their plans any more than he was to execute them, and therefore Ted Knowles had no doubt whatsoever that his client would fail to realise that the only way of coaxing the girl out of the house was under the innocent guise of meeting someone who was already known to her.

Not only would she adamantly refuse to meet his client at any time but the same went for himself, their last encounter still vivid in Ted Knowles's memory, but since he had no idea who her circle of friends and acquaintances were, assuming of course she had any, who could possibly prove useful, he had been faced with no alternative but to recruit the services of one who would raise no suspicions in the girl's mind; a lady she already knew and clearly trusted. He knew full well that Charles Harrington would have no liking for it, but if nothing else he would surely appreciate the irony!

Of course, Ted Knowles could not take it for granted that Mrs. Charles Harrington would do as he wanted, but in view of her visit to the girl in company with Silas Jenkins, and not forgetting what his most reliable informant had told him about her kindness and generosity, he had the sneaking suspicion she would; even so, he was not one to enter into a venture blindfolded. Charles Harrington had told him that he always tested the water first, well, so did he, and reaching for several sheets of notepaper and a pen, began the first stage of his campaign.

Ignorant of the role Ted Knowles was creating for her, Sophy was enjoying an agreeable couple of hours with her sister-in-law, looking anything but a conspirator in a forthcoming plot. Out of her husband's company Sophy was certainly more relaxed. With no constraints upon her she was virtually animated, her lively sense of humour and keen intelligence apparent to all who saw her. Jane, whose keen eyes missed very little, noticed the difference in her sister-in-law when Charles was not around, and although she loved her brother she was not blinded to his faults or the adverse effect he had on her, and secretly thought that Sophy should never have married someone with such an autocratic disposition. Charles had never confided in her, but long association with him was more than enough to tell Jane that he had never liked having his hand forced, and therefore his marriage to Sophy had been a constant source of irritation to him. Be that as it may, however, it did not prevent him from feeling bitterly disappointed in that after nearly three years of matrimony no children blessed their union.

Sophy could not explain her barren state any more than Jane could and it worried her more than she ever owned about their childless marriage. Certainly, there were no obvious reasons to account for it, and although she had never given up hope there were times when it seemed as if motherhood was going to be denied her. The fact that she did not love Charles was beside the point; she was failing in her duty to her husband, and the longer time went by without any sign of her conceiving a child the more impatient Charles became. She had inwardly winced at his silent condemnation when Henry had called to tell them of Jane's safe delivery of a son, and when Emily had made her announcement yesterday it seemed nothing else was needed to set the seal on her despondency. Charles may not love her but even so his scarcely veiled references to her own inadequacy had hurt, but not by a word or gesture did Sophy let him see it or how very conscious she was of her unfortunate situation. She was also very conscious of the fact that more than once of late she had been forced into banishing from her mind the pleasing picture of being married to the man she loved more than life itself and presenting him with a child conceived out of love and not duty, but the inner glow which had coursed through her as a result of these imaginings had been all too fleeting, leaving her with the painful knowledge that this could never be.

Jane had not the slightest inkling that Sophy was in love with her cousin, but it did not take much to see that all was not well with her. Naturally, Jane knew the circumstances surrounding Sophy's marriage to Charles, and whilst she may consider her brother to be the wrong type of man for her, she had hoped, in spite of his resentment over the way he had been coerced into marrying Sophy, that they would grow into a comfortable relationship, if not based on love then on mutual understanding and friendship. However, it had struck Jane more than once of late that this was not so and that her sister-in-law, in spite of her determined efforts to the contrary, was not as happy as one would think. At first, she had put this down to the fact that Sophy had as yet not conceived a child, but more recently she had begun to suspect that Sophy's unhappiness clearly stemmed from other causes. What these were Jane had no idea, but apart from the fact that Sophy would never contemplate discussing Charles or her marriage with anyone, she would shrink from disclosing her innermost thoughts and would not welcome any invasion of them. All the same she liked to think that Sophy knew she could confide in her should she ever choose to do so, but until then all Jane could do was sit and wait in anxious silence and pray that whatever was troubling her sister-in-law would speedily resolve itself.

Jane was not alone in this wish. Sophy too wanted nothing more than to have her troubles resolved, but she was realistic enough to know that they never would be. It was not only her failure to give Charles a son which was causing her anxiety but the tormenting knowledge that she was destined to go through life married to a man she did not love. Too late to tell herself that she ought never to have agreed to her parents' wishes so unquestioningly, and the pain this belated acknowledgement brought would doubtless serve as adequate testimony to her easy acceptance in the years to come. Before her lay an uninviting future, desolate and meaningless without Marcus beside her. It was useless to deceive herself into believing that as time passed she would grow accustomed to life without him or that she would be able to school herself into behaving dispassionately towards him. Honesty compelled her to admit that the more she saw of Marcus the harder it was becoming to feign indifference; if all he had to do was look at her for her heart to pound in her breast or touch her hand for her to want to melt into him, give herself body and soul to him, then how could she possibly survive the years ahead? Occasionally, Sophy had wondered whether it would be far better to go through life without ever being subjected to the upheaval of love, to remain in ignorance of the pain and despair it could leave in its wake. And yet never to experience its overwhelming joy was a deprivation no heart should suffer. Perhaps if her marriage was more bearable, if Charles treated her differently, then she would not yearn for what was just tantalisingly out of reach, but deep in her heart she knew it would make no difference to her love for Marcus.

She had come to realise that one could not dictate the course of one's emotions any more than one could ignore them, but even if by some miracle the opportunity arose whereby she could stop loving Marcus at a stroke, she knew she would not take it. She knew too that there was no possibility of Charles ever granting her a divorce, not simply because he could not bear the stigma and scandal which would ensue, but to step aside for his cousin to take his place would be an insult he would neither forgive nor ignore.

It was not so much a question of fighting her emotions but trying to hide how they made her feel so that no one would see how agonisingly in love with Marcus she was. It was so very difficult to pretend she had no feelings for a man who meant more to her than life itself when only to hear his voice set her pulses racing and her heart somersaulting. She knew perfectly well that she could not prevent him from visiting his aunt, to do so would not only be extremely awkward but also foolhardy, but unless she wanted to alert Charles to the truth she had to try to make sure that she was in Marcus's company as little as possible. She could see no point in deliberately courting disaster, and even though the thought of not seeing him quite so often tore her apart, common sense told her that it was nevertheless very necessary.

From the beginning she had accorded Charles all the respect and loyalty due to him as her husband. The fact that he had not returned either of these made no difference. His affair with Amelia was something Sophy could do nothing about, even so, the idea of her doing likewise with Marcus was so repugnant to her that she never so much as considered it. The vows she had taken nearly three years ago bound her to her marriage, and whilst Charles's treatment of her was hardly what she had expected, to turn her back on those solemn words would be tantamount to betraying the very sanctity of the marriage service. Charles, on the other hand, cared nothing for the solemnity of the vows he had taken. As far as he was concerned they signified nothing more than a means to an end. He had no intention of terminating his ties with Amelia, on the contrary he had never even so much as contemplated ending a liaison which gave him so much pleasure and satisfaction.

*

Charlotte's letter to Timothy had done its work well, and her exclamation of surprise upon hearing the results of her efforts was so genuine that no one could possibly have accused her of being its instigator. Having fully expected Charles to raise objections to the visit, Sophy was somewhat taken aback by the eagerness with which he encouraged it. Having meddled in his affairs once he was none too eager for her to do so a second time, and when she received Timothy's letter inviting her to journey into Kent for a long overdue stay, Charles had put forward no opposition, urging her to write her acceptance without delay.

Unaware of his co-conspirator's indisposition, Charles could only wait with what patience he could muster for the news which would signal the end to his problem. By now his mood hovered dangerously between ominous calm and biting sarcasm, a circumstance which every member of the household was fully aware of. With the exception of Amelia, it seemed that no one escaped his acid tongue; even George, not so adept at dealing with his brother, appeared reluctant to cross verbal swords with him. As far as Charles was concerned Timothy's invitation had arrived at a most opportune moment. Since Ted Knowles had so far not shown his hand in the affair Charles was more than anxious to know what the devil was holding him up, the matter in hand taking far longer to conclude than he had anticipated.

It was not only because Sophy had not seen Timothy and Annabel for some considerable time which accounted for her looking forward to the visit but also because it was a means of escaping from an atmosphere which was so overcharged and oppressive that the slightest thing was guaranteed to spark off another painful scene. Sophy did not need it pointing out that Charles's temper was dangerously balanced at the moment, she was all too aware of it, but although she failed to discover the cause of it she was far too relieved at his endorsement of her visit to her brother to question it further. She was still convinced in her own mind that the root of Charles's annoyance stemmed from Alexandra's inclusion in Matthew's will, but since she was in no position to delve into matters which Charles clearly did not want her to be involved in, all Sophy could hope for was that her worries were unfounded or that they would resolve themselves in time. Charles may dislike the idea of his father making a last-minute inclusion in his will in Alexandra's favour, but although Sophy knew that he was more than capable of doing something to prevent her from enjoying her inheritance it never so much as crossed her mind that he would go so far as planning her demise to ensure it.

Had Sophy the least idea of what was going forward she would not have been making preparations for her departure with so much enthusiasm. As it was, the only cloud on her horizon was the prospect of being so far away from Marcus, but as she had not seen him since receiving Timothy's letter she had not been able to tell him. As she was reluctant to leave without saying goodbye to him she had at one point briefly toyed with the idea of writing him a note advising him of her imminent trip, but it had only taken her a matter of a few moments to see how foolhardy this would be, and therefore she could only hope that Marcus would call in Brook Street before she left in two days' time. That this wish went completely against her decision to see as little of him as possible only proved to her how unstable her emotions were and how irrationally she was behaving, but then love was all these things; it could not be rationalised or even understood, and by the time she had talked herself in and out of excuses she knew it must be true.

Charlotte, having kept a discreet but watchful eye on her daughter-in-law, had accurately assessed her see-sawing emotions and was more than ever convinced that her letter to Timothy had been written just in time. She knew that Sophy would never intentionally betray Charles, but Charlotte knew perfectly well that when emotions were running high one's sense of equanimity was sometimes lost sight of. Sooner or later Sophy would give herself away; a little gesture perhaps or an unthinking word would leave her lips before she could prevent it and the truth would be told, leaving her exposed to Charles's anger.

Unfortunately for Charlotte, who remained in total ignorance of Ted Knowles's existence, she had failed to include him in her calculations when considering Sophy's predicament. Having recovered sufficiently from his sickbed to set his plans in motion he was unwittingly about to overturn

Charlotte's intervention on Sophy's behalf by the simple expedient of an ingeniously worded letter.

Unlike Amelia, Sophy never breakfasted in her room, and as it was Harris's custom to put her correspondence beside her place at the breakfast table she was rather surprised when he discreetly slid an envelope into her hand, whispering conspiratorially as he did so, "Pardon, Mrs. Harrington, but I have been asked to give this to you, personally."

Glancing from the envelope up into Harris's impassive face Sophy questioned, "For me! By whom?"

"*That,*" he emphasised, "I could not say, the young person who delivered it being quite unknown to me."

Shaking her head bewildered, Sophy asked, "When did this arrive?"

"Quite early," Harris informed her, keeping a watchful eye on the door.

"How odd!" Sophy exclaimed, turning the envelope over.

"*Most* irregular!" Harris concurred, adding by way of explanation that as it was his custom to ensure Mary had put a light to the fire as well as checking that Ellen had laid the table to his satisfaction, he had been on the point of returning to the kitchen when the sudden clanging of the bell stopped him in his tracks. He further explained that the young lad who had thrust it into his hand clearly had no intention of divulging his own identity or that of the author. "In fact," Harris informed her disgustedly, "he ran off the moment I took it from him." This sort of behaviour was not at all to his liking or what he was accustomed to but feeling he had discharged his duty as best he could and without anyone being the wiser, he walked discreetly over to the heavily laden sideboard in order for Sophy to read her correspondence in private.

The writing on the envelope, which had by now become rather mangled, was quite unknown to her, and since none of her friends or acquaintances were likely to send her notes in such a surreptitious manner, Sophy was at a loss to understand who her correspondent could be. It was not until she had torn open the envelope and retrieved the single sheet of notepaper, her eyes quickly scanning the hastily written lines, that she realised her hands were shaking. All thought of breakfast left her, but Harris, whose devotion to duty would not allow him to leave the dining room until every member of the family had breakfasted, hovered discreetly in the background, waiting to serve her with whatever took her fancy. Having no desire to satisfy his curiosity, Sophy folded the sheet of paper back into its creases, returned it to the envelope and deposited it safely into the pocket of her skirt before informing Charlotte's faithful retainer, in a voice which she knew must be her own, that she required nothing but a poached egg.

To Harris's way of thinking Mrs. Sophy had had the appetite knocked out of her. Not only had her face turned alarmingly pale but her eyes had taken on a guarded expression which had not been there before, but doing as she asked he placed the solitary egg in front of her, watching her heroic attempts to swallow every mouthful. Unless he was very much mistaken she was doing everything possible to prove to him that the content of that letter had not knocked her for six.

It may not have knocked her for six precisely, but the urgency of it gave her cause for grave concern. When she had said goodbye to Alexandra ten days ago Sophy had certainly not gone away with the impression that she would come to a decision in so short a time. Her new-found niece may not want for sense, indeed she would eventually realise that what was being offered her was far better than what she had been accustomed to, apart from being hers by right, but she did not forgive easily and Sophy knew that Alexandra would certainly give the matter a lot of thought before arriving at a decision. As much as it pained her, Sophy could not help thinking that Alexandra was more than capable of prolonging her answer in some misguided attempt to make her grandmother suffer a little for all the years of hardship endured by her mother even though she had acquitted her of all blame and, if this was indeed the truth of it, then something quite drastic must have occurred to induce her to write that letter, especially when Sophy considered its urgently expressed plea. A second reading of it in the privacy of her room did nothing to dispel her fears any more than it explained away her questions, and Sophy knew that these would only be answered by keeping the appointment Alexandra had so earnestly requested.

Sophy's forthcoming visit to Timothy was instantly forgotten as she pondered the problem posed by that letter. There could of course be quite a simple explanation attached to it, but, somehow, she did not think so especially when she considered the almost furtive manner in which it had been delivered; not even Alexandra's intense dislike of her maternal relations could possibly account for it!

Then of course there was Charlotte to consider. Marcus was quite right when he said she would have to be told something sooner or later, after all it was unjust to keep her in the dark about her granddaughter's whereabouts, not to mention the visit she herself had paid her in company with Silas Jenkins, and Sophy could only hope that after her meeting with Alexandra this morning she would be in a more favourable position to do so. Sophy still believed that until Alexandra had come to a definite decision it would be too cruel to fill Charlotte with false hopes; hopes that stood every chance of being dashed, and that would surely be worse than anything! All Charlotte knew at present was that Silas Jenkins was still doing everything possible to locate Alexandra, and whilst her mother-in-law seemed to be accepting this well enough Sophy saw the distress she attempted to hide and consequently felt nothing short of a traitress to deny her the news she desperately longed for; she was to feel it even more when she informed Charlotte, with a casualness that totally belied her anxiety, that her mother had sent a note requiring her attendance for several hours.

After eyeing the weather thoughtfully for some minutes followed by several more in considering how best to reach her destination without attracting attention, Sophy eventually decided to walk down Bond Street to the corner of Oxford Street where she could easily pick up a hackney to take her to the appointed meeting place. If she asked Harris to call one up for her it could easily bring forth questions she would rather not answer particularly given that her mamma lived within walking distance of Brook Street, and neither could she risk hailing a hackney too near to home in case anyone saw her; the last thing she wanted was for this to come to Charles's ears, the mere thought making her feel quite sick. It was imperative she do nothing to advertise her errand thereby giving the servants something to gossip and speculate over as well as cutting down the risk of being spotted by an acquaintance, and therefore her careful preparations to reduce the likelihood of either of these eventualities arising included putting on the heavily veiled black hat which she would never wear under normal circumstances. It really was quite hideous, and for the life of her Sophy could not even recall the reason for her purchasing such a monstrosity in the first place but telling herself that it was perfect for her needs as not only did it suit her state of mourning but it also ensured a certain amount of anonymity, besides which, it had the added advantage of protecting her face from the wind which, this early in March, was bitingly sharp.

Nevertheless, she could not prevent the flush of guilty colour staining her cheeks when she ventured downstairs to find Harris staring open-mouthed at her astonishing appearance before recollecting himself as well as his duties and opening the door for her, silently congratulating himself on deducing the contents of that letter with almost unerring accuracy, shrewdly guessing that Mrs. Sophy was on an urgent, not to say secretive, mission. It was perhaps unfortunate that Farley, Charles's punctilious if somewhat ingratiating valet, had caught sight of his employer's wife leaving the house dressed in a way he could only describe as heavily disguised. He may not have been a member of the household for as long as Harris, a mere two years in fact, but he was well enough acquainted with the goings-on in the family to make him instantly suspicious. Unfortunately for him, however, he had found no friend in Harris, who looked upon his colleague as being nothing more than an upstart. Almost from the beginning Farley had the knack of always managing to turn up in a part of the house where he had no need, such as now, and upon his smooth-tongued enquiry as to where Mrs. Charles Harrington was bound he was met with a haughty look from Harris and a pointed reminder that it was not his place to ask.

Unaware of the interest shown in her activities, Sophy made her way down Bond Street towards Oxford Street without running into any one of her friends or acquaintances, relieved that Charlotte at least had accepted the excuse she offered for going out so easily, but unfortunately her relief was short-lived. Having just crossed Oxford Street where she had flagged down an oncoming hackney, Sophy could hardly believe her eyes when she saw Adam strolling towards her on the opposite side of the street. The fact that he was engaged in conversation with a man who was totally unknown to her made no difference; for one awful moment it seemed to her that her heart had stopped beating, and the gasp of fright which left her lips was so painful she felt quite sick. She knew she had no need to fear Adam, but she could see little point in favouring him with her confidences; besides which, she had no wish to be the cause of creating a rift between him and his brothers should her errand leak out.

Anxious in case he should look up and see her, Sophy quickened her step to conceal herself from his line of vision, arriving at the spot where the hackney was waiting for her a little discomposed, almost stumbling as she hurriedly climbed up into the vehicle, questioning the wisdom of her errand as she did so. In her efforts to assist Alexandra she was opening herself up to all manner of trouble, and she could only hope that matters would be speedily settled because she doubted her ability as well as her nerve to constantly fabricate reasons or excuses.

The last time Sophy had visited Regents Park was over six months ago when Charles had escorted her and a party of friends to watch a balloon ascension, but unlike then the park was not overcrowded, for which she was heartily thankful. Not only did she feel extremely apprehensive but decidedly conspicuous, and as she walked down Broad Walk towards the Royal Zoological Gardens where Alexandra had said she would meet her, Sophy hoped that she would not have to wait too long before her niece arrived. Already the sight of a tall and unaccompanied lady dressed all in black and heavily veiled into the bargain, was causing no small amount of interest to passers-by. Only a few yards from the entrance to the Zoological Gardens, discreetly set a little way back from the pathway, was a seat, and because she had no way of knowing how long she would be required to wait, she sat down to await Alexandra's arrival.

One by one the minutes ticked by until almost twenty minutes had passed with no sign of her. Suddenly attacked by a nagging doubt that she had misread the time, Sophy retrieved the single sheet of paper from her bag to peruse the hastily scrawled lines for a third time.

My dear Sophy,

I am writing this letter in haste and have entrusted someone I know to deliver it to you. There is no one else I can turn to. If you would consent to meet me at the entrance to the Zoological Gardens in Regents Park this morning at fifteen minutes to twelve o'clock I will explain everything. As my only friend, I am confident you will not only forgive the presumption but offer me all assistance. You are the only one I can trust. Please, do not fail me!

Yours, Alexandra.

Sophy had not mistaken the time nor had she misinterpreted the urgency, but unfortunately there was nothing she could do except anxiously sit and wait until the full meaning of it could be explained. Twenty minutes soon became thirty until a full hour had passed without any sign of Alexandra. By now Sophy's anxiety had increased to such a pitch that she found it impossible to sit any longer. Agitatedly rising to her feet, she stepped a little away from the seat to eagerly scan the various approaches to the Zoological Gardens, but although there were several people in view there was no sign of Alexandra. Numerous reasons for her failure to come flitted into Sophy's mind, but in view of the letter's content somehow none of them satisfied her.

To her growing dismay and embarrassment, she had, over the last ten minutes or so, become self-consciously aware that her continued presence had aroused the curiosity of a park keeper and was not altogether surprised when she saw him approach her, politely enquiring if he could be of any assistance. Assuring him that his services were not required and that she was certain her friend would not be many more minutes, Sophy saw, to her acute discomfort, that his expression took on a singularly knowing look, leaving her in no doubt as to what he was thinking. It was quite obvious that he believed she was waiting for a man, definitely not her husband, which in turn clearly signified an illicit assignation. Beneath the black veil her face flamed, taking small comfort from knowing that he could not obtain a clear view of her face. After what seemed like an eternity he slowly walked back to his post leaving her prey to all manner of doubts and uncertainties, but his continual glances in her direction only served to make her feel more conspicuous than ever.

After waiting a full hour and a quarter it was evident that Alexandra was not going to keep the appointment she had so urgently requested. Sophy knew it was useless to wait any longer and decided that there was nothing else she could do other than retrace her steps along Broad Walk and to make her way home. It was when she was approaching the gates to the park that the idea of going to Hoxton to find out what was happening crossed her mind, but it only took her a matter of moments to realise that this was not the answer. For one thing, Alexandra may not be in and her landlady may have no idea where she had gone or when she was likely to return. Sophy could not afford to waste time on a journey to Hoxton simply on the off chance that Alexandra may be at home, any more than she could walking around looking for her, and it was equally out of the question for her to remain here any longer; already her continued presence had excited too much curiosity.

There had to be a reason for that letter as well as Alexandra's failure to show herself, but although Sophy had no reasons to account for either she was firmly convinced that something was dreadfully wrong. Why would Alexandra write her an urgent letter, have it delivered in such a way, then fail to keep the appointment? It did not make any sense. Sophy had seen enough of her niece to know that once having set her mind to something she would not be easily diverted, but clearly something must have occurred to prevent Alexandra from keeping the meeting with her.

It gave Sophy no comfort to remember her own situation and the restrictions put upon her abilities to offer assistance, and painful though it was she had to admit that she was not in a very good position to help the girl. At the same time, she could not just sit back and do nothing. That Alexandra needed help was certain, but what she personally could do without alerting Charles to the fact had Sophy in a puzzle. She knew it would be useless to confide her concerns to George, not only because he could not be relied upon to keep such news to himself but also because his attitude towards Alexandra was just as prejudiced as his brother's. She could approach Adam of course, but Sophy was rather reluctant to involve him in something which could well cause a rift between him and his brothers should it ever leak out that he had tried to help her in a matter on which they strongly disapproved. It was a pity that Timothy lived so far away because even though he may not be able to do anything practical to assist her she knew she could go to him with her worries without fear of betrayal.

But there was another whom she knew she could go to for advice with equal confidence, a man who would neither ignore her plea for help nor betray her. Although her decision to go to him ran counter to her resolution to see as little of him as possible, this matter of Alexandra was of far more importance than her own feelings, and hurriedly emerging from Regents Park Sophy hailed an oncoming hackney, briskly requesting the driver to take her to an address in Knightsbridge, not pausing to consider that Marcus may not be at home.

Chapter Thirteen

From the looks of it, it seemed to Sophy that the heavy clouds were finally going to give way to the sun, which had been struggling all morning to show itself. It was extremely doubtful whether it would maintain its supremacy for long, but by half past one its weak, pale rays were filtering through the window of Marcus's drawing room, picking out the rosewood half-moon table on which reposed a china cupid. Caught in its path lay the pale blue Aubusson carpet, its intricate yet delicate pattern momentarily brought to life, the fragile dart of light continuing its way to the fireplace over which hung a portrait of Imogen Ingleby.

No solid Victorian trappings could be seen in this room; everything from the floor to the ceiling depicting the graceful elegance of over fifty years ago, but whilst everything else in the house had moved with the times this drawing room had remained unchanged by the prevailing mode. As Sophy waited for Webster to inform his employer of her arrival, she took a moment to admire her surroundings but it was not long before her attention became irresistibly drawn to that portrait, relegating the importance of her errand and how this unannounced visit could be interpreted to the back of her mind, struck by the likeness between mother and son. Only faint traces of her brother could be seen in the face looking serenely down at her, her sweet expression making it impossible to believe that Matthew could have been in any way related to this woman whose whole demeanour exuded a tranquillity her brother had lacked. It was easy to see from whom Marcus had inherited his calm good sense and even temperament and Sophy was conscious of a deep sense of loss in not knowing her.

Her attention, at first caught by the image looking calmly down at her, was now firmly held and so intense had her study become that she entirely failed to either see or hear the door open and Marcus enter the room, totally unaware that she was no longer alone. Not until a quiet voice, as familiar to her as her own, said, "She *was* beautiful, wasn't she?" did Sophy become aware of his presence.

*

His interview with Silas Jenkins may have been more successful than he had anticipated, but nevertheless he regretted the necessity of having to confide as much as he had to him. Unfortunately, however, he had been faced with little choice as that astute man of law had made it quite clear that he was not prepared to divulge any information unless he had a valid reason for doing so. Marcus fully acknowledged that Jenkins's caution was perfectly justified, but it had nevertheless been with considerable reluctance that he had had to take him part way into his confidence and Marcus could only hope that he had not opened himself up to a future charge of slander, his refusal to openly accuse his cousin affording him little solace.

Charles may have no compunction in doing whatever he considered necessary to achieve his own ends but his name as well as his integrity were so far unsullied, and if Marcus could not prove his suspicions then it would be he and not Charles who would find himself publicly condemned for bringing into disrepute a man who was not only his cousin but a respectable pillar of society.

Like Sophy, Marcus was having to rely on Silas Jenkins's discretion and professional integrity, and whilst he had no grounds to doubt either, Marcus was nevertheless in a situation he neither liked nor desired. Being in possession of Ted Knowles's direction only meant that he had scaled the first hurdle, not that he was on the right track. Marcus knew there was every possibility that he was totally wrong in thinking Charles had employed this man to ensure the successful outcome of whatever he was planning, if indeed he was planning anything at all, which was by no means certain, but as far as Marcus could see Ted Knowles was the most likely candidate for the post. In any event if he was to discover exactly what Charles may be planning he had to begin somewhere and Ted Knowles was as good a starting point as any.

That instinct which had served him well during his military career was once again doing its work and unless it was playing tricks on him now it was telling Marcus that time was of the essence. If he was right, then Charles would not prolong the proceedings by dragging his feet any longer than was absolutely necessary, in fact Marcus was pretty sure that his accomplice was already in receipt of his instructions and only waiting for – waiting for what? Marcus contemplated this as the hackney carriage made its slow and ponderous way through the busy streets towards Knightsbridge, his agile brain going over all the possible permutations available, but since these were many and varied he decided to waste no more time in considering them.

He was firmly of the opinion that the only way the pieces to this puzzle would become clear was by paying Ted Knowles a visit and Marcus promised himself an interview with him before the day was out. This resolve, whilst going some way towards putting things into some kind of perspective, did nothing to make him feel any better. He was by no means proud of the thoughts that plagued him, and whatever his feelings towards his cousin no one wanted to be proved wrong more than he did about what he suspected to be true. If his intuition was not playing him false, then Marcus could not reconcile it with his conscience to sit back and ignore it. He had not needed Silas Jenkins to remind him that his uncle's affairs were not his concern, he knew it well enough, but an innate sense of justice refused to allow him to turn a blind eye to the possibility that Alexandra stood in danger of being denied what was rightfully hers. Of course, Marcus fully appreciated that that added clause in Matthew's will had come as a tremendous shock to them and naturally they would require time to adjust to it, but he could neither understand nor sympathise with their prejudice any more than he could with their belief that the girl should forgo her inheritance simply because her mother had behaved in a way they considered reprehensible. However, he had every hope that, given time, they would come to accept the inevitable. He would not go so far as to say that they would ever look upon her as one of the family, indeed she was more than likely to be subjected to all manner of verbal injustices, but even he doubted their bias could last forever.

He could not say the same for Charles, however! Marcus knew his cousin had never reconciled himself to the fact that his mother's marriage to Matthew Harrington had instantly deprived him of the life his maternal relatives took for granted, and his overwhelming pride had never allowed him to forget the disparity between them. It had irked him all his life and his attempts to adopt the aristocratic lifestyle they enjoyed by right had resulted in an expenditure which his father had adamantly refused to continue financing. Matthew had been a wealthy man, but it had not come easily; years of hard work and long hours as well as sound and wise investments, which had yielded immense rewards, had been the secret of his fortune. He had been quite happy to pay his sons a generous quarterly allowance in return for their participation in the business, but he had been neither inclined nor prepared to maintain his sons in a life of indulgence at his expense. Matthew may have been prepared to assist Charles with some of his more pressing obligations, even giving him extra financial succour when required, but his attendances at prestigious race meetings in company with several young aristocrats with whom he had been friends since his days at Eton, required Matthew franking Charles far more often than he was prepared to allow. Exasperation at his son's mounting costs had finally resulted in him refusing to come to his aid any further, his decision bringing about that disastrous ultimatum.

Charles's personal finances may be required to frequently support more than they could adequately bear, but Marcus did him the justice to own that in business he was entirely scrupulous. The more he considered the matter the more convinced he became that something quite untoward must have occurred which had put Charles's finances under an intolerable strain, and even though Marcus had no idea what could possibly have arisen it must have been something that required a rather hefty sum to defray and one, moreover, for which he could not apply to his father. Adam's concerns in that his brother could well have used Elizabeth's jewellery to offer him much-needed financial relief, however distasteful the thought, would, without doubt, be looked upon by Charles as being a far better prospect than going cap in hand to George, the very thought of which would make him recoil, or to himself for that matter. Marcus gave his cousin credit in believing that he had fully intended to amend the discrepancy eventually, but from the looks of it, it would appear that circumstances had intervened to prevent this. It was incredible to believe that Charles, by no means lacking in intelligence, had actually done something which he must have known would not go unnoticed indefinitely. If this was indeed the case, and Marcus failed to see how it could be otherwise, especially when he thought of Charles's rigid attitude ever since the reading of Matthew's will, then it went a long way to explaining his dark forbidding humour of late as well as his unreasonable anger over Sophy's innocently spoken words.

So lost in unpleasant thought was he that Webster, whose unobtrusive entrance had gone unheard, found it necessary to cough twice in order to gain Marcus's attention. Webster, who had been with the Ingleby family for many years, knew Mr. Marcus well enough to say that something had obviously occurred to bring that slight frown down onto his forehead, but upon informing him that a lady had called to see him and was at this very moment awaiting him in the drawing room, he saw the frown lift and an arrested expression enter his dark brown eyes.

"A lady?" Marcus questioned, looking up into Webster's impassive face.

"Yes, sir," Webster nodded. "Mrs. Charles Harrington." Unlike Harris, Webster had no idea that Mr. Marcus looked upon Mrs. Charles Harrington as anything other than his cousin's wife, but he was nevertheless quick to notice that fleeting expression which had entered his eyes, and unless he had misread the signs he was certain that Mr. Marcus was by no means displeased at her unexpected visit, but having discharged his duty Webster left the study as quietly as he had entered it.

Marcus was certainly not displeased, on the contrary he was delighted, but so unexpected was her visit that he could do nothing other than sit and stare at the door which had just closed behind his very precise butler, unable to believe that what he had just been told was true and not merely his imagination playing tricks on him. As Sophy had never yet honoured his home with her presence either in company with his aunt on her visits or with Jane when she had called upon him, he knew that something must have happened to bring her here now.

But upon entering the drawing room instead of finding Sophy pacing agitatedly up and down as he had fully expected, he saw her standing in front of the fireplace looking intently up at his mother's portrait, and not until he spoke did she become aware that she was no longer alone.

Sophy had no idea how long Marcus had been standing there watching her but upon hearing his voice she turned round, her eyes flying to his, revealing her uncertainty, and her face, delicately tinged with colour, betrayed how mindful she was as to how this unannounced visit must look. Hastily adjusting the veil of her hat which had fallen a little forward onto her shoulder with suddenly nerveless fingers, she managed, "Yes. Yes, she was; very beautiful." Then, after casting another quick look up at the portrait, said, none too steadily, "You're very like her."

"Thank you," Marcus nodded. "I take that as quite a compliment."

Sophy seemed to hesitate as if considering something, then said with perfect truth, "I wish I had known her."

Marcus's eyes held hers as he fully agreed with this. "So do I. I know you would have liked her; everyone did so. Unlike Matthew, she drew everyone to her. My father adored her, which is why he had that portrait done. I believe he paid quite a considerable sum for it, but he considered it well worth it. He would often come in here and look at it, just as you are now." He took a halting step towards her, saying, without the least degree of sentimentality, "This was her favourite room and the only one I have not altered in any way. I hope you like it as much as I like seeing you in it."

Even though this was touching very perilous ground Sophy's heart, which had long since given itself up to him, beat so fast she could hardly breathe, and her defences, if such one could call them, not very stable at the best of times, were, at these words, in imminent danger of collapsing. For one wonderful moment, she could so easily have forgotten her fears for Alexandra and the reason she was here and happily give herself up to the unconcealed warmth in Marcus's eyes, but clamping down on this very pleasurable inclination with every ounce of strength she could muster, said, as steadily as she could, "I daresay you must be wondering what it is that brings me here?"

"The reason will keep," Marcus shrugged as though it was of no importance. "For the present," he told her, "I am happy just to see you here."

Hovering just beneath the surface of these pleasantries ran a current of highly charged emotions; so strong were they in fact that Sophy was in grave danger of giving in to them, but managing to overcome the growing urge to surrender herself to her inclinations said, with more truth than poise, "I know I really ought not to be here, but you see there was no one else I could turn to." When he made no reply to this the dreadful suspicion crossed her mind that she had completely misread his previously offered services and knew one awful moment of panic. Inexplicably feeling the need to defend herself, Sophy faltered, a little apprehensively, "You... you may remember that... well, you... you *did* say that should I ever need any help I... I may rely on you."

"I remember," Marcus nodded, trying to ignore the overwhelming urge to fold her in his arms.

"Yes... well," Sophy began, quickly lowering her eyes to the gloves she was pulling nervously through her hands before raising them to fix her attention on an invisible point behind his head, "I... I wondered if..."

"If I meant it?" he broke in gently. She nodded, anxiously holding her breath. "You must know I did," he told her in a voice which considerably relieved her mind but did absolutely nothing whatsoever to help her maintain her composure.

For one incredibly reckless moment Sophy was conscious of wanting to cast herself into his arms – arms which she knew would welcome her willingly – but fighting this impulse said, with sudden shyness, "I really ought not to be here. I know now I should not have come."

Marcus was as aware of the tension existing between them as she was and that no matter how polite the words they uttered nothing could disguise what they felt for one another, but at this his eyes danced with irrepressible humour. "So it would seem," he remarked amusingly, indicating her hat with its heavy veil with a nod of his head. "I had no idea a visit to Knightsbridge warranted such a disguise! Are we such doubtful characters in this part of town that you dare not let it be seen you have ventured amongst us?"

Amelia would have known precisely how to respond to this light-hearted raillery, especially from such a devastatingly attractive man as Marcus, but instead of responding in the same light-hearted spirit, Sophy could only blush and stammer her renewed apologies for intruding on him unexpectedly, reiterating that she should not be here.

"But you are here," Marcus reminded her softly, taking hold of her agitated hands in a firm warm clasp, "and I have no intention of letting you leave until you have told me what it is that has brought you here, but before you do so," he urged, "allow me to show you into the study, there is a fire in there and you will find it far more comfortable than here."

Without giving her time to demur he led the way across the hall to a medium-sized room bearing all the hallmarks of being a very masculine domain and one, moreover, in which he clearly spent most of his time, and before she realised it had allowed herself to be persuaded to stay. Under different circumstances Sophy would have appreciated the subtle richness of her surroundings, but even though she was preoccupied with worrying over Alexandra as well as trying to not think of what Charles would say if he could see her, she was not so lost to the fact that Marcus's presence seemed to dwarf the room, making her even more aware of him than ever.

Her trust in him was implicit and her decision to turn to him for help had been purely altruistic, knowing that if something had indeed happened to Alexandra he was the only one who could possibly help her, but even in the midst of all her mixed up thoughts and emotions Sophy was conscious of the feeling of having come home, but resolutely forcing everything but the issue at hand to the back of her mind, his suggestion that she sit down by the fire was, like his offer of refreshment, hastily declined. Since Marcus was no inexperienced youth in the throes of a first love affair, Sophy's obvious desire to keep this visit as matter-of-fact and as brief as possible in no way upset him, accepting her refusal with unruffled calm. However, it did not take much to recognise that she was deeply disturbed and whatever the cause it was clearly a matter on which she could not approach Charles. Again, that unerring instinct told Marcus that it was in some way connected with Alexandra, and whilst he delighted in Sophy's visit the idea that it was perhaps a most opportune moment for her to call increasingly grew on him. It could well be that what she had to tell him may well be linked to his own forthcoming dealings with Ted Knowles.

But the story she poured out, disjointed though it was, was not quite what Marcus had expected. If his quick appraisal of this morning's events was right, then Charles was certainly wasting no time, and his earlier assumption about his cousin's accomplice already being in receipt of his instructions was not only correct but made Marcus rethink his own line of approach with Ted Knowles. Marcus could well understand Sophy's anxiety and was moved to think that she trusted him enough to come to him. Whilst he acknowledged the cunning stroke of genius in using Sophy in their schemes he lacked the appreciation which had clearly inspired her inclusion. Even before he had read the letter she held out to him, he was convinced that whoever the author was it was certainly not Alexandra, and he was therefore more than ever determined to foil what he guessed was carefully laid plans before they came to fruition.

He knew beyond doubt that Sophy, although she obviously suspected something was very wrong, had no idea as to the extent of Charles's almost certain involvement. Marcus was sufficiently well acquainted with his cousin to know that no matter how dire the circumstances his wife was the very last person he would confide in, and for this reason he had no desire to deliberately malign Charles to her by implicating him in something which was as yet unproven as well as deeming it wise not to tell her about his visit to Silas Jenkins which would necessarily mean explaining his reasons for doing so. Sophy was already quite distressed by this morning's events, and Marcus certainly had no wish to increase her worries, but he nevertheless felt impelled to question the letter further, saying calmly, "I take it you can verify the handwriting as being Alexandra's?"

"Verify it!" Sophy repeated, her eyes widening at this.

"As I have never seen a sample of her handwriting," Marcus pointed out, "I for one could not say with any degree of certainty that she penned this letter herself."

As this aspect of the case had not previously occurred to her, Sophy could only stand and stare in disbelief, shaking her head, bewildered. "Well, I... I naturally assumed she had written it. I never considered it to be otherwise."

"Of course not," Marcus nodded. Someone else had clearly assumed too, having a pretty good idea as to what her response would be upon receipt of such an urgently expressed letter, and in so doing had played a masterstroke. "You say it was delivered this morning?" he confirmed, his seeming calm admirably concealing his growing concern.

"Yes," Sophy nodded. "Harris handed it me when I went down to breakfast. He said that he had been asked to give it to me personally."

Marcus's brain was racing, but pressed gently, "And he had no idea who it was who delivered it?"

"No," Sophy shook her head. "When Harris questioned him he just ran off."

Marcus, perusing the letter again, nodded absently, and Sophy, who was by this time quite alarmed by the unexpected turn of events, asked, "What does it all mean, Marcus?"

"I'm not surely precisely," he admitted pensively, raising his eyes from the single sheet of paper in his hand, his brow creased in thought. "May I keep this?"

Sophy nodded. "But if Alexandra did not write it, then who did? And why?"

"I don't know," Marcus said meditatively, "but the more I consider it the more convinced I am that she did not write it. Had she have done so, doubtless she would have kept the appointment. As it is," he told her, "I am sure of nothing, but I promise you I aim to discover the truth."

Rather alarmed, Sophy laid an unsteady hand on his arm. "What are you meaning to do?"

"Nothing whatever for you to worry about," Marcus soothed, smiling reassuringly down at her, covering her cold hand with his warm one.

"But I do worry," Sophy told him. "I don't know why exactly, but I am so afraid that something dreadful has happened. I am certain she was prevented from meeting me."

"Assuming, of course, she did write it," Marcus reminded her. He saw the troubled look in her eyes and clasping her hands in his, smiled warmly. "You must not worry about this. Indeed," he assured her, with more confidence than he felt, "it will most probably turn out to be nothing as dire as you imagine."

"Oh, I do hope so!" Sophy cried.

He hated to see her like this and wanted nothing more than to take her in his arms and kiss away her doubts and fears, but managing to subdue this he said, with more optimism than truth, "Nothing has happened." She smiled mechanically, and he asked, "Will you do something for me?"

"Anything," she promised, returning his clasp.

"Will you leave this entirely in my hands?"

"Yes, of course," she nodded, "but you have not yet told me what it is you are meaning to do."

"I thought you trusted me," he reminded her gently.

"You know I do," she told him earnestly.

"Then do so now," he urged. "I promise you no harm will come to Alexandra, or to you; I give you my word."

She was much comforted by this and found it quite a relief to lay her troubles onto his shoulders, but her relief was short-lived as she recalled with vivid clarity the excuse she had offered her mother-in-law to account for her absence today, a little ashamed to know that her lie had been believed without question. "Poor Charlotte!" she exclaimed. "Should anything happen now I believe the shock would be too great for her. I dislike lying to her," she admitted, "and when I left her this morning, telling her I was going to visit Mamma, I felt such a traitress; I almost gave in and confessed everything."

"I am glad you didn't," Marcus said quietly. "Not that I advocate deceit," he shook his head, "but you were right when you said that no good could come from building up her hopes only to have them dashed down; it would be too cruel." Sophy nodded her agreement to this. "Whilst I agree she has to be told the truth, and soon," he told her, "for the time being, or at least until Alexandra has had sufficient time in which to consider matters, I think it best if things remain as they are."

"Yes," Sophy sighed, "I know you are right, but it is so very cruel!" she exclaimed. "If you could see her Marcus; know the agony she suffers as I do."

"I do know," he told her, his voice suddenly harsh. "I have seen the pain and the sadness and know that she receives no support except your own."

"I do little enough," Sophy shrugged helplessly. "To be honest," she confessed, "there are times when I feel afraid to show any kind of support at all. The hostility towards Alexandra is such that the slightest mention of her is sufficient to raise a storm of protest."

"I am afraid that sooner or later they are going to have to accustom themselves to the fact that she is going to be a part of their lives whether they like it or not," he pointed out. "What concerns me though, is that you and my aunt are having to bear the brunt of it all."

"They will never be brought to accept her, Marcus," Sophy told him despairingly. "Their resentment is very real."

"So is Alexandra," he nodded. "She cannot be swept under the carpet because they don't like her."

"I know," Sophy agreed, "but I have to confess that I fail to see how it will end, and whilst I hope for Charlotte's sake that she will realise her wish and have her granddaughter live with her, it will not be easy for either of them."

"And what about you?" Marcus asked softly. "If Charles ever discovers the part you have played in Alexandra's reinstatement he will take it very ill."

Sophy knew it, and the thought made her tremble, but summoning up a smile she dismissed it as only a slight possibility. "I have been very careful," she told him, considerably heartened by the warmth in his eyes.

Marcus bit down his anger, not for the first time wondering what the devil her parents had been about when agreeing with Matthew to tie her to such a man as Charles. Marcus looked down at her bent head, his eyes expressing all he was in no position to demonstrate. "Everything will turn out all right," he told her in a deep voice. "Haven't I promised that no harm will come to Alexandra – or to you?"

From the moment Sophy had received that letter she had not known a moment's peace of mind. It was not simply because she had been forced to lie to Charlotte to account for her absence this morning or the knowledge that Charles would be furiously angry if he ever discovered her errand but also because she had no idea what could possibly have happened to prompt Alexandra to write to her, pleading with her to meet her at the Zoological Gardens and stressing the urgency not to fail her. Without her being aware of it the tension inside her had steadily mounted, increasing unbearably when Alexandra had failed to keep their appointment; horrendous possibilities for her failure to show herself reared their heads, Sophy's nerves reduced almost to breaking point. To all intents and purposes, she owed her new-found niece no favours whatsoever, but it was not in her nature to ignore a cry for help any more than it was for her to harden her heart to someone less fortunate than herself, but, now, upon hearing that deep voice assuring her that everything would be all right and knowing in her heart she could rely on him totally, Sophy felt the tension leave her body, bringing with it the inevitable result. Tears of immense relief sprang to her eyes, but despite her strenuous efforts to hold them at bay, they began to fall unheeded down her cheeks, causing her to hurriedly search for her handkerchief. "I'm sorry," she apologised with a travesty of a smile. "I don't know why I am behaving like this. You must be thinking how very stupid I am."

"No," Marcus shook his head, his voice a caress, lovingly wiping away her tears with a gentle finger, "I think you are adorable."

Her soft skin tingled where his finger had lightly touched it, and that expectant flutter which had invaded the pit of her stomach the moment she had alighted from the hackney carriage at the thought of seeing him resurfaced, and when his hands came to rest gently on her shoulders Sophy looked up from the folds of her handkerchief, immediately realising her error as she saw the unmistakable look in his eyes.

"Oh, my darling, please don't cry!" Marcus begged hoarsely. "I can't bear to see you like this."

Sophy sensed rather than saw him bend his head to kiss her, and she made no effort whatsoever to avoid it. It was hardly a kiss at all really, so light and fleeting that it was over in an instant, but the warm touch of his lips on her own had the effect of making her heart yearn for more and provocative enough to arouse all her dormant needs and desires causing something between a cry and a sob of need, which she was powerless to prevent, to leave her parted lips.

Marcus had only intended to comfort her, to let her see that he understood her fears and she was not alone, but the moment his lips touched hers he experienced such a surge of need that anything remotely resembling altruism died. He supposed he should have known better than to think he could simply offer her much-needed comfort and support and not be affected by the touch of her; too late to chide himself for a fool! Having kept his emotions on a tight leash for so long it had really been too much to expect that such a feather-light touch would suffice. The inviting warmth of her lips, promising everything he had ever dreamed of, had been sufficient to open the floodgates to his needs and desires, intensified by that sob of aching recognition which had left her throat. A cry of need he was as powerless to resist as she had been to suppress, immediately banishing everything but the most masculine of demands and the longing to explore the kiss further. He had known for a long time that he held her heart, but it was not until now that he saw her need of him was as urgent as his own. More than once he had caught glimpses of the emotions she kept hidden, but never had he seen her like this, all the love she bore him clearly visible on her face, her eyes looking up into his with so much warmth and love that it took his breath away, and in that instant all restraint deserted him. *"Sophy!"*

Her name left his lips on an agonised groan, and later, when Sophy looked back on this moment, she would never be able to say with any degree of certainty whether she walked into his arms or he pulled her into them; all she knew was that she was where she wanted to be, being held so tightly that she could hardly breathe. From the moment his lips covered hers all restraint disappeared, kissing one another with a hunger far too long denied to be held in check another instant, their love and need of one another so great that the intensity of it frightened and excited her at the same time. Sophy had never considered herself capable of feeling like this, certainly her experiences with Charles had not evoked anything remotely like it, but when Marcus's demands intensified they drew from her such unfamiliar cries of pleasure that she could not believe they came from her. She knew now she had yearned for this, ached for the intimacy they were now sharing, but even though she had sometimes allowed herself, in moments of despondency and wretchedness, to wonder what it would be like to have Marcus make love to her, not one of her wildest imaginings had prepared her for how he would make her feel just by holding and kissing her. Gradually his impassioned assault on her mouth eased into something resembling hypnotic seduction, and utterly unable to resist it Sophy pressed herself even closer into him whereby he slowly, and quite deliberately, reduced her into a state of unreserved capitulation, rendering her incapable of standing without the support of his arms.

Knowing this would never happen between them again, Sophy eagerly received his drugging kisses, tasting and savouring them like a fine wine, trying to banish the unwelcome thought that she would soon be returning to her husband. She supposed this recollection should have had the effect of bringing her to her senses but it merely served to heighten her need of the man whose arms crushed her to him. Somewhere in the far recesses of her mind elusive fragments of her mother's denunciation of love hovered, but in the overwhelming joy of knowing that the man she loved was as moved as herself, she was easily able to ignore them.

After what seemed an aeon of time Marcus reluctantly released Sophy's lips from the confinement of his, but as if unwilling to let her go he held her tighter still, burying his face into the softness of her neck, her skin tingling from the touch of his lips, and although she never wanted this moment to end she knew it must, but this recognition did nothing to prevent her from feeling rather bereft when he gently eased himself away from her, cupping her flushed and glowing face in his trembling hands to look searchingly down at her.

"I never meant that to happen," he told her hoarsely, "but since it has I do not regret it, nor am I going to apologise for it."

Laying the palm of her hand tenderly against his face, her thumb gently brushing his tinted cheekbone, she smiled, saying huskily, "There is not the least need for regrets or apologies." A soft contented sigh escaped her as he pressed his lips into her soft palm. "In fact," she told him a little shyly, "I am glad it's happened because you see, I have been wanting you to kiss me for a *very* long time." All the love he had for her was there in his darkened eyes, but her own clouded a little as she said despondently, "But Marcus, it must never happen again – it can't."

It was several moments before he spoke, reminding her gently, "Unfortunately, one's emotions do not always behave to order, nor," he added, "can they be kept under control indefinitely; as we have just proved!"

She sighed. "I know," then, moving a little away from him, as if by doing so it would make what she had to say easier, "but you must promise me, Marcus."

"How easy that would be if I didn't love you," he stated simply, a rueful smile twisting his lips. "As it is," he told her, "I love you more than life itself, and to make you a promise which I know I can no longer offer any guarantee of keeping would be unforgivable."

"You *must*, Marcus!" she told him urgently, her eyes pleading. "You must help me. It would be different if I were free to love you but I'm not. I have a husband."

Marcus's eyes suddenly hardened. "A man who neither loves nor deserves you!"

"It makes no difference," she told him, her voice trembling. "I may not love Charles but he is my husband, and I will not betray him."

"I know," Marcus sighed resignedly, knowing her too well to think she would be capable of doing anything different, "and I would not expect you to." He hesitated as if choosing his words very carefully. "The last thing I want is to coerce you into doing something which would be totally unacceptable to you, but at the same time I am both human and honest enough to admit that loving you the way I do I cannot promise what happened a moment ago will not happen again." Sophy raised a protesting hand for him to stop, but disregarding it he asked, his voice raw, "Do you have any idea how you make me feel? How I have to constantly strive to hide the love and need I have for you? *I love you, Sophy*! I never thought it was possible for a man to a love a woman as I love you!" Without giving her time to respond he took several halting steps towards her. "Your loyalty to Charles is commendable, but if he loved you, made you happy, you would not be here now and I would not be fighting the overwhelming need to kiss you again! A need I might add, which you have enjoyed as much as I."

"Please, Marcus, don't!" she begged. "We must not say these things."

"Why not?" he demanded. "We both know they're true." Sophy shook her head, trying to find the words to refute this but could not, knowing in her heart that every word he had said was all too true. "Do you imagine I am happy with the way things are?" he asked urgently. "That I enjoy deceiving Charles? Nothing would give me greater pleasure than to tell him about us."

At this her face turned white, her eyes dilating with fear as she stared at him. "No! No, you mustn't!" she cried frantically. "Please, Marcus," she pleaded, "promise me you won't tell him."

A shaft of pain shot through him, and taking hold of her hands he said reassuringly, "You must know that I would never do anything to hurt you," he felt the relief escape her, but pointed out gently, "but how much longer this situation can go on, I don't know. Not only does it make me feel as though what we share is tainted but something to be ashamed of."

"But it isn't like that!" she exclaimed, aghast.

"No," he acknowledged, "I know, but this deceit is not at all what I like or am accustomed to. I have kept my tongue solely for your sake and not from any consideration for Charles."

Dissimulation of any kind was abhorrent to Marcus. Indeed, it was one of the many qualities Sophy admired in him, and it hurt her now to see the effect this enforced deceit was having on him. That he was adopting such a pretence to protect her only increased her distress, but no matter how hard she tried she could find no solution to a situation which was becoming more unbearable day by day. The palliative she had offered herself had long since failed to ease her conscience; Charles's indifference and cold politeness were no excuse for the mental and emotional deceit she was playing on him, although this was the first time she and Marcus had ever demonstrated their feelings for one another or even spoken of them, but even though her love for him would never die she could at least try to contain it. "Supposing you did tell him," she said unhappily, "do you think it would prompt him into granting me a divorce?"

Marcus shook his head, his eyes broodingly sombre. "We should be living in a fool's paradise to indulge that hope. We both know that Charles would never sanction such a thing."

Despair, frustration and a feeling of sheer hopelessness engulfed her all at once, and removing her hands from his she walked over to the window to stare blindly out of it, her eyes sparkling with fresh tears, but managing to overcome the urge to give in to them, she resolutely held them back before turning round to face him. "Oh, Marcus!" she cried in a choked voice. "I can think of no greater joy than to spend the rest of my life with you, but if I allowed myself to give in to my inclinations I should not be betraying Charles, I would be betraying myself and I could never live with the guilt; it would stay with me forever until it eventually killed our love."

"Oh, Sophy!" Marcus rasped, closing his eyes on an agonised sigh. "You must know that I don't want you as my mistress but as my wife! I know we have never discussed our feelings, much less marriage." He shook his head. "How could we with things standing the way they do? But you must know it is my dearest wish to make you my wife. Only tell me that this is your wish too and I shall be reasonably content." A stifled sob escaped her. "Oh, my darling!" he begged, striding towards her. "Please don't cry; I can't bear seeing you so unhappy."

"I'm sorry," Sophy cried, "it's just that I love you so very much. I am so unhappy when I am not with you." Totally disregarding her previously voiced wishes he took her back into his arms and held her close against him. "I want nothing more than to spend the rest of my life with you," she told him, her words rather muffled against his shoulder, "but I cannot, *dare* not allow myself to think of it; I should go mad if I did!"

Gently lifting her chin with an unsteady forefinger for her to look up at him, Marcus told her in a voice raw with emotion, "I love you, that's all I know, and just the thought of spending the rest of my life without you in it is more than I can bear." Then, lowering his head, he kissed her long and lovingly, so much so that for the next few minutes all other considerations were forgotten.

"Please try to understand, Marcus," she said huskily when she had sufficiently recovered her breath, resting her head comfortably against his shoulder, "it's not merely because two wrongs don't make a right."

"So," he said slowly, easing himself a little away from her to look down into her face, "you know about that?"

She did not pretend to misunderstand him. "Yes, I know," she nodded. "I have known almost from the moment it began."

"I admit I have often wondered whether you did," he said gently.

"Of course," she managed, summoning up a smile, "Charles is very discreet, but a woman can always tell; even those of us who don't…"

"Love their husbands," he supplied soothingly.

She nodded. "Not that it signifies, of course!" she managed. "A wife is not supposed to know." A twisted little smile touched her lips. "It doesn't hurt, not at all! I daresay if I loved Charles it would be very different." A deep sigh racked her body as she slowly eased herself out of his arms. "It merely serves as a constant reminder as to why he married me."

A multitude of emotions engulfed him, but the anger he felt over Charles's dismissive treatment of her outweighed everything else; so much so that he was forced into taking several moments to bring it under control. It was seldom Marcus lost his temper, but the thought of Sophy being subjected to his cousin's contemptuous indifference could always be relied upon to do nothing to promote cousinly love. Frustration and an overwhelming sense of impotence to offer her relief or assistance flooded through him. Left to himself, Marcus would take her away from the unbearable life she was enduring, to love and protect her from a man who cared nothing for her, but this was impossible. Not only because she would never consent to such a thing but deep in his own heart he knew he could not do it. To do so would be an ungentlemanly act, opening her up to public condemnation and vicious criticism. No man who loved a woman as he loved her would put her through such a despicable ordeal. "I wish to

God there was something I could do other than just stand helplessly by merely watching what passes as your marriage!" he exclaimed, frustrated.

"There is nothing you can do, Marcus," Sophy said simply, almost resignedly. "There is nothing either of can do."

"I refuse to believe that!" he exclaimed vehemently.

"You must," she urged, her heart aching. "We both must! Charles may not love me any more than I love him, but he will never grant me a divorce, the very thought of which would make him recoil. Then there's George!" she pointed out, not unmindful of his feelings. "Whether he knows about the affair I don't know, but I often think Charles would much rather things remain as they are than subject himself to the stigma of a divorce. Not only that," she told him, "but as far as he is concerned I belong to him, and he will never let me go. The sooner we accept that the better."

"You will have to forgive me if I don't give George much thought," Marcus dismissed. "If he can't see what's going on under his very nose then his feelings for Amelia must be tepid indeed. As far as we are concerned," he told her, "I tell you now that if you think for one moment I am happy to calmly sit back and accept a situation which, quite frankly, must be as unacceptable to Charles as it is to us, then you could not be more wrong."

"Believe me, Marcus," Sophy said sincerely, "if a solution to this predicament presented itself I would gladly take it, but there is none. We have to accept it – for both our sakes!"

In spite of himself Marcus smiled at this. "I am not afraid of Charles."

"I know," Sophy nodded, "but I am afraid for you."

"There is not the least need, I promise you," he smiled. "I am quite capable of taking care of myself," adding softly, "and of you," looking tenderly down at her.

She wanted him to take care of her and for a brief moment allowed herself to dwell on the thought; it was certainly an agreeable one and one she had often permitted herself to envisage, but it would not do to indulge it any more than it would the daydreams which constantly teased her mind, especially now when her resolve was at its most vulnerable and the man she loved was standing so near to her that a single step would take her back into his arms. She could think of nowhere else she would rather be, and the mere thought of being held against his strong hard body and to feel his lips on hers was so pleasurable that for one faltering moment she almost gave in to her better self, but calling upon every ounce of mental strength she possessed she somehow managed to resist the temptation to walk into them.

Marcus, whose own defences had proved to be no more secure than Sophy's, was acutely aware that his resistance was in imminent danger of crumbling at the foundations, and strove, with the same resolve as the woman without whom his life would be entirely meaningless, to channel the conversation onto safer ground. The courteous exchanges which followed may not have given the onlooker cause to draw certain conclusions, but both knew they merely cloaked the emotional undercurrents lying just beneath the surface, but by the time Sophy got round to telling him about her impending departure into Kent she was at least more in control of her emotions.

Marcus had always been aware of the close relationship which existed between Sophy and her brother Timothy, and it gave him some comfort to know that at least she would be spared any harsh treatment at his hands. Even so, to go just one day without seeing her was like a lifetime, but three weeks would be equivalent to an eternity! That he would miss her went without saying, but Marcus forced a smile for her sake. "I believe it is quite some time since you last saw him."

Sophy nodded, more composed now. "Yes. Although we have exchanged letters it will be nice to see him and Annabel again."

"Of course," he replied mechanically. "I understand she is expecting their first child."

"Yes," Sophy smiled, firmly banishing the thought of her own deficiencies in this area. "It was such a lovely surprise to receive his letter inviting me down," she told him as cheerfully as she could, "and you know how much he means to me."

"Yes, I do," Marcus acknowledged, his eyes holding hers. "I also know how much you mean to me." Giving her no time to respond to this, he said earnestly, "I realise you haven't seen Timothy in quite some time and this visit is perhaps long overdue, but at the same time I shall miss you more than I can say. Brook Street is never the same when you are not there."

Even though she hated leaving Charlotte to carry the burden of her family's animosity alone, Sophy longed to get away from the discordant atmosphere of Brook Street into a more carefree and relaxed environment such as was prevalent at Timothy's, but somewhere at the back of her mind she was conscious of the thought that perhaps, with Alexandra's affairs being somewhat uncertain, now may not be the best of times to journey into Kent. Even though she knew she could leave the matter of that letter entirely in Marcus's hands she could not help but worry and this, added to the fact that she would not see him for three whole weeks, slightly marred her pleasure at seeing her brother and sister-in-law.

She knew there was no hope or future for her and Marcus, and although she was resolved in her aim that what had happened between them must never happen again, just seeing him or hearing his voice rendered her unhappy and lonely existence in Brook Street more bearable. Such was the battle raging between her heart and mind, the former in danger of succumbing to what the latter strongly argued against, that she lowered her eyes as she deliberately took her time in pulling on her gloves to try to steady herself, managing at last, though not very convincingly, "Three weeks will soon pass, Marcus."

"Yes," he nodded, firmly clamping down on the impulse to take her back in his arms, an impulse he knew she would not resist, but fought the temptation for her sake, "and, hopefully," he added, striving for a lighter note, "when you return I shall have discovered the mystery of that letter."

She looked up at that. "The letter? Oh, yes," she nodded, "I was forget… I mean," she said hastily, "I hope so."

"My darling," Marcus cried raggedly, knowing precisely what she was going through, "this unbearable situation will not last forever, I promise you," taking hold of her hands and raising them to his lips.

She failed to see how it could be remedied, but if nothing else it was something to cling to in the dark days which loomed ahead. Refusing to allow him to request Webster to summon up a hackney for her, she left almost immediately with Marcus's kisses still burning on her lips and his assurances ringing in her ears, momentarily pushing the thought that she had left home over three hours ago to the back of her mind.

But good fortune it seemed was smiling down on her because the only one she encountered upon her return home was Adam, who, apart from a teasing but far from complimentary comment about her hat, made no attempt to ask her where she had been. Sophy had not forgotten the fright he had given her earlier when she had almost stumbled upon him in Oxford Street, but as she looked upon him almost as she would a favourite brother, she was easily able to forgive him, and as she made her way upstairs to tidy herself and discard the hat she vowed she never wanted to see again, she could not help wishing that the rest of his family were as likeable as Adam.

Chapter Fourteen

From what Farley had told him of Mrs. Charles Harrington and the brief glimpse he himself had of her, it came as no surprise to Ted Knowles to discover that she had kept the bogus appointment in Regents Park. Nor was he surprised to learn that she had had not the slightest inkling that she had been followed every step of the way or that her long and fruitless wait for Alexandra had been unobtrusively witnessed. Indeed, he would have been astonished if she had. Not only had he personally trained his young apprentice in all the arts pertinent to his calling but had done so to a standard which would defy the closest scrutiny. In happy ignorance of the more than casual interest in the affair of another party, Ted Knowles was easily able to dismiss the intelligence of Mrs. Charles Harrington's detour to a house in Knightsbridge prior to returning home as being totally unrelated to the matter in hand and not even worth the mentioning in his report to his client. Totally unaware that a man of equal resource as himself was determined to foil whatever scheme he was hatching, he eagerly continued to put forward his best endeavours to conclude his plans, confident that they were progressing just as they should.

Ted Knowles was equally confident of Charles Harrington's favourable response to the detailed account of the morning's activities and his next and final step to conclude this matter which his young friend delivered into his clerk's hands later that afternoon. It was all very well for his client to issue instructions then wash his hands of the whole affair as he waited for the tragic news of the girl's demise to reach him, but Ted Knowles believed he had assessed Charles Harrington's character well enough to say that he was more than likely to take exception to something or other and come back with accusations that he should have been kept informed, such as using his wife for one thing! Ted Knowles had no doubt that Charles Harrington, once his initial annoyance and disapproval had burnt itself out, would fully appreciate the delicate touch of irony in using his wife as a pawn. After all, who would question the word or integrity of a woman of her standing? Of course, it would be a terrible thing for her to witness such a dreadful accident, but having done so who in their right mind would doubt her evident shock, much less credit her husband as being its instigator?

Ted Knowles had not erred in his assumption. Charles was not at all pleased to receive a written report, as far as he was concerned the less put down on paper the better, and he was certainly far from pleased that such a delicate communication had been delivered into Perry's hands. He would much prefer to keep his dealings with Ted Knowles as far away as possible from such an industrious underling, even though Charles knew that Perry would never dare to open a communication clearly marked for his personal attention. Charles, who had hoped that this matter would have been dealt with by now, was neither concerned nor sympathetic with Ted Knowles's explanation in accounting for the delay in dealing with this affair, but he was certainly relieved to know that by this time tomorrow his problem would be finally out of the way.

But even though this was what he wanted he was by no means certain about the witness his accomplice had nominated in tomorrow's tragic events, and he could only assume that Ted Knowles had taken it upon himself to punish Sophy for going against her husband's wishes and paying a call on the girl. Charles had every intention of dealing with Sophy's meddlesome interference and her sheer defiance in going against his wishes, but he much preferred to deal with her in his own way and in his own time rather than having his hand forced. He would certainly have something to say to Ted Knowles on this point! Nevertheless, Charles was compelled to admit that the more he considered it the more attractive the idea became and that nothing could possibly serve the purpose better, in fact after only a little further thought he was eventually forced to concede that perhaps this was the idea behind Ted Knowles's thinking in the first place. Not only was the timing perfect, bearing in mind Sophy's departure the day after tomorrow, but it would teach her to mind her husband better in the future, as well as providing him with the perfect alibi. Who would dare to question his wife, much less draw conclusions from it? Everyone who knew her, knew her to be without malice and that it would be very like her to befriend a girl in Alexandra's circumstances, and her horror at witnessing so ghastly an accident would be so genuine that it would never enter anyone's mind to point the finger at him. Charles knew perfectly well that an accident had to be seen as such, and although he had never even considered Sophy as a possible witness, Ted Knowles's strategy had turned out to be a real stroke of genius. Charles was quite certain that she would not tell him about receiving that letter any more than she would about her fruitless wait in Regents Park, and although he would never forgive her duplicity where the girl was concerned, he had to own that her predilection for her company was proving very useful.

It certainly seemed as if Providence was continuing to smile down upon him, for which he was heartily relieved, because although he was not the type of man to admit defeat he had nevertheless experienced one or two moments recently when he had begun to think he would never be rid of the girl. This, coupled with the length of time Ted Knowles was taking to plan and execute her demise, had resulted in his patience being tested to the limit, but now, at long last, all the annoyance and frustration he had suffered seemed to have left him, in fact so confident was he in the inevitable success of tomorrow's events that he arrived home that evening in a very different frame of mind to when he had left it.

As far as Sophy was concerned the change in her husband's mood was met with relief, especially when she considered how she had spent part of her day. She may have fooled Charlotte into believing her story about visiting her mamma, but had Charles been in the same mood this evening as he had been for weeks past and had decided to question her again about her day's activities she would have been quite unable to answer him without giving herself away. When Sophy had turned to Marcus for help her motivation had stemmed from knowing that he was the only one she could turn to and not from any desire to have him make love to her. That kiss may not have been planned but she supposed she should have known it to be inevitable, if not today, then soon. It was very easy to tell herself that it would never have happened if her nerves had not been so overwrought, but this was a sop she refused to offer her conscience. The plain truth was she had wanted him to kiss her, and now, no more than then, did she feel ashamed or harbour any regrets over how she had happily surrendered herself to his kisses. The unforgettable feeling of being in Marcus's arms had been the sweetest and most wonderful experience of her life and one she longed to repeat. There was no denying that nothing in her so far well-ordered existence could compare with that shared intimacy, but, somehow, she had to hold on to her determination in never allowing it to happen again. Yet she was honest enough to admit that she was far too vulnerable to place very much reliance on this well-meaning but rather weak resolve. Until the advent of Marcus in her life Sophy had grown accustomed to the daunting prospect that love was most probably going to be denied her. Not that this was anything unusual, after all most wives did not look for love in marriage and, as for their husbands, it seemed they viewed it in a far more practical light, exercising their rights whilst seeking their pleasures elsewhere.

Prior to her marriage, her life had followed the prescribed pattern of parties, balls and the theatre as well as other social events which were considered an integral part of the world she had been born into. She had naturally enjoyed the light-hearted flirtations the young men of her acquaintance had embarked upon with her, but she could certainly not lay claim to having any amatory experience. Nevertheless, she had seen at once that her husband was a most adept and skilful lover and, had she loved him, then no doubt his experience would have been welcome, as it was, she had no desire to benefit from it any more than he was to demonstrate it to her. Sophy accepted it as perfectly natural that Marcus was not without experience, but when he had kissed her he had employed none of the arts of lovemaking she knew he must possess. His kisses had stemmed from love and an uncontrollable need and, even now, several hours later, she could still feel the warm touch of his lips on hers and the wonderful sensations he had aroused inside her, sensations she had never known existed, much less stimulated by her husband.

Although dinner that evening was no different to any other she had sat through, it was nevertheless an experience she was in no hurry to repeat. No one looking at her could possibly have accused her of being deeply in love, evincing none of the telltale signs, but it had not occurred to her that there was a radiance about her that no amount of self-discipline could dispel, and if, once or twice, Charles directed one of his searching looks at her, she was far too taken up with her own thoughts to wonder at the reason.

Amelia, no stranger to the aftermath of passionate lovemaking, had taken one look at her sister-in-law and knew instantly what had brought about that subtle change in her and the soft warm glow to her eyes. Not Charles, certainly! Sophy may say she had been paying a call on her mamma if she chose, but a visit to one's mamma did not make one glow like that, and the temptation to tease her a little was irresistible. "I trust you found your mamma well?" Amelia enquired politely.

As Amelia rarely enquired about her visits to her mamma, this perfectly harmless question considerably startled Sophy, but she somehow managed to reply with a calmness she was far from feeling, "Yes; very well, thank you."

"No doubt she charged you with all manner of messages for Timothy?" Amelia smiled, her eyes alight with amusement, fully aware of her sister-in-law's discomfiture.

"Yes," Sophy nodded, feeling the lie stick in her throat.

"I daresay, of course," Amelia continued inexorably, "that your sister was pleased to see you. She is so seldom to be seen in town that your visit must have been a welcome diversion for her."

"My sister, as you know, is unfortunately rather shy, for which her stammer is largely responsible, and finds it difficult to be at ease in company." This at least was true, but Sophy was certainly struggling to combat Amelia's sudden and unaccountable interest in her family and her supposed visit to see her mamma in particular, an interest which held every likelihood of exposing her if she was not careful.

"Precisely!" Amelia nodded. "I can understand why she enjoys your company."

"I certainly hope so," Sophy replied, her appetite rapidly deserting her.

"I am sure she does! Amelia exclaimed. "After all, it must be a somewhat dull existence for her."

"I am certain she does not find it so," Sophy managed, relieved that the conversation appeared to be taking a slightly safer turn. Unfortunately, however, her relief was destined to be short-lived.

"I fail to see how it could be otherwise," Amelia remarked. "I realise of course," she pointed out cunningly, "that it must be quite dreadful to be afflicted with such an impediment; rather debilitating in fact, but it is nevertheless a great pity that her affliction has prevented her from finding a husband."

"She has never intimated that she is anything other than content," Sophy told her, eyeing the dishes in front of her with distaste.

"I daresay she feels impelled to say so," Amelia argued, enjoying herself immensely, "but you and I know that her situation is not an enviable one."

"I have no doubt it has its compensations," Sophy offered.

"I fail to see what they could be!" her sister-in-law exclaimed, shaking her head, mystified. "Although," she commented innocently, "I am often amazed at the number of people who seem to prefer the single state. Marcus, for instance! Now, one would suppose that he would have gone to the altar long since, but here he is at thirty-seven and still unmarried. Now, why do you suppose that is?"

"I really have no idea," Sophy managed, not daring to raise her eyes from the food on her plate, feeling every mouthful would choke her.

"Well, I certainly can't find anything to account for it," Amelia shrugged, bewildered. "Of course, it is a thousand pities about his leg, but I fail to regard that as an impediment. In fact," she remarked, "I daresay there are any number of women who would look upon it as merely adding to his attraction."

"He could certainly give a woman everything she wants," George put in, helping himself to another portion of creamed mushrooms. "Financial security is not to be sneezed at, and Marcus, leg or no leg, is hardly short of the readies!"

"Precisely!" Amelia nodded, willing to overlook her husband's contribution. Pausing only to cast a look at Sophy from under her lashes, she threw down her trump card with all the air of one who had made a sudden and startling discovery. "Do you know, a thought has just occurred to me! Do you suppose it to be possible that Marcus has never married because he has a secret lover? Someone, perhaps, quite ineligible?" Then, with a magnificent display of shock, gasped, "My goodness! You do not think he is in love with a married woman, do you?"

If ever Sophy wanted the ground to open up and swallow her, now was the time. Not only did she feel physically sick but she was convinced that she was being intently scrutinised by several pairs of eyes. She was not, of course, but in her overwrought state of nerves she felt her love for Marcus was emblazoned on her forehead for all to see.

Fortunately, she was rescued by George who exclaimed, almost choking on his food, "What! Marcus, pining for a lost love! Nonsense!"

"Why is it?" Amelia demanded sharply, irritated that her prey had got away. "In fact," she pointed out, "the more I think about it the more likely it seems."

"Well, that's where you're wrong!" George dared to contradict, pointing his fork at her. "The very idea of Marcus shunning the female sex for such a reason is absurd. Why," he remarked recklessly, "I daresay he has had any number of women in keeping! In fact," he nodded, "he probably has…!"

"I don't think it," Adam broke in, mindful of Marcus's confidences, wondering what on earth had got into Amelia to put forward such a suggestion. "Besides," he added, casting a discreet glance across the table at Sophy, "it is neither right nor proper to be discussing Marcus's affairs in this way."

Amelia, realising she had taken it as far as she dared, reluctantly allowed the subject to drop, but she was nevertheless quite satisfied with her evening's work.

"Adam is right," Charlotte said disapprovingly, "but it is certainly not the kind of topic I approve of."

George hastily begged pardon before continuing his inspection of the serving dishes laid out on the table in front of him.

Sophy's deepening colour had not escaped her mother-in-law's notice, which is why she had deemed it time to call a halt to a conversation which, left unchecked, would in all probability cause no end of trouble. Charlotte was as annoyed as a woman of her placid temperament could be over Amelia's mischief making and could only guess as to what her motive could be. Charlotte had accepted Sophy's reason for her absence today without question, after all she was not her keeper, but she was no fool; just one look at Sophy's face had been enough to inform her that something other than the company of her mamma and sister, if indeed she had paid them a visit, had brought about such a distinct change in her. Clearly, Amelia had seen it too and had made it her business to try to make mischief, and Charlotte could only be thankful that in a little over thirty-six hours Sophy would be safely tucked away in Kent without any more such incidents arising.

Apart from a few disinterested comments, Charles had sat through dinner in a state of apparent boredom. In truth, he was pleasantly contemplating a trouble-free future from now on. With the girl out of the way, obviating the need to remove his sister's jewellery from Mercers' vaults, he could plan the redemption of those items at present in Linas Webb's possession at his leisure whilst at the same time considering how best to curb his wife's sudden and unaccountable venture into disobedient independence.

Sophy's determination to befriend the girl may be assisting his plans as well as affording him much-needed protection against accusations of personal involvement in her demise, but he by no means liked the idea of her believing that she had succeeded in hoodwinking him. Charles realised of course that the shock of witnessing such a dreadful accident would be no pleasant thing for her, which should be punishment enough for her duplicity, nevertheless, he wanted the satisfaction of making her aware that he had discovered her secretive behaviour and it would not be tolerated. She would be made to mind her husband better in future! Of course, he was still rather vexed at the length of time it had taken Ted Knowles to get things moving, looking upon his claim of succumbing to a severe cold as the reason for the delay as being no excuse, even so, his communication had been quite illuminating, in fact he had omitted not the smallest detail in the strategy he had arranged for Alexandra's sudden and tragic exit from this world before twenty-four hours were out. He had also been quite explicit about Sophy's part in the affair, and Charles, closely watching her across the dinner table was, for now at least, happy to allow her a brief moment of triumph as she basked confidently under the misapprehension of fooling him.

Having overcome the main hurdle to the scheme by creating a cunningly contrived exchange of letters between Alexandra and Sophy, neither of whom had the least idea they were in correspondence one with the other, to ensure the girl would leave her lodgings and proceed to a venue without arousing her suspicions, Ted Knowles had certainly hit the mark. Thanks to his report Charles knew about the second letter Sophy had received this afternoon, supposedly from Alexandra, apologising for not keeping their appointment today and arranging another for tomorrow. Obviously, Sophy was labouring under the belief that he was in ignorance of what was going forward between herself and the girl, and he took malicious satisfaction from knowing that far from helping the brat she was assisting in her permanent removal. He could only hazard a guess as to whether Sophy, in view of the girl's failure to show herself today, suspected the letters to be bogus; he personally doubted it, but the look on her face was giving no indication that the authenticity of the letters was troubling her, indeed she evinced no sign of partaking in any collusion at all. For the first time then, Charles found himself wondering what else she may be keeping from him, but it was not until Amelia's provocative comments a moment or two ago that he began to wonder more particularly about his wife. Certainly, she had given him no cause to suspect her of having a lover, for one thing it was totally against her principles and for another she would be too afraid of him discovering it. Now though, he was not so sure. Undoubtedly, she had always been dutiful, never once repulsing his advances, but never deliberately encouraging them either. He could not deny that she was very beautiful, and even though he may find Amelia's seductive charms far more to his taste it was not difficult to see what it was about Sophy that other men would find attractive – like Marcus for instance!

Marcus's wealth had always been a thorn in his flesh, Charles knew it always would be; he envied him that so much it would always impair his feelings towards his cousin, but his amatory affairs were no concern of his. If Marcus preferred the single state, then so be it, after all it was not such a rare thing for a man of his cousin's age to be still a bachelor, and his reasons for remaining one were something Charles had never so much as contemplated. But Amelia's words had set him thinking. To his well-trained eye Sophy had definitely reacted to Amelia's remarks. There had been no mistaking the wary, not to say scared look which had entered her eyes, nor the way her cheeks had flooded with colour. The idea may seem preposterous, but the more he considered it the more likely it seemed. However reluctantly, he had to acknowledge that Marcus was indeed a very handsome man and one whose whole bearing was guaranteed to please the ladies, but unlike himself Marcus had a tendency to be rather old-fashioned, quite gallant in fact. He was certainly the kind of man who, having fallen deeply in love, would remain faithful to the lady of his choice, and if that lady happened to have a husband it would be quite characteristic of him to accept the situation with chivalrous good grace.

Charles had always known that his cousin and Sophy got along extremely well, but never had he found it necessary to look deeper than the friendliness which existed between them or the common link they shared through Timothy. Charles was forced to acknowledge that Sophy could well be the kind of woman who would appeal to his cousin. He undoubtedly liked her, that much was obvious, and it was not long before past incidents came to mind, infinitesimal perhaps, but he found himself re-evaluating their relationship. If memory served him correctly there had been several instances when Marcus had come to her aid, and even, on occasion, rising to her defence, deflecting his own anger towards Sophy against himself. In short, the instinctive actions of a man in love.

Suddenly Charles found himself looking at her in a very different way, finding it incomprehensible that he had not read the signs which had been right under his nose more accurately until now. It was not his imagination which told him how her eyes lit up or how her whole being seemed to come alive whenever his cousin was around. Most assuredly, he could not recollect the same response being afforded to himself, and this knowledge, coupled with her duplicity over the brat, together with his own lack of awareness, made him furiously angry. The fact that he himself was engaged in a very agreeable extramarital liaison with his brother's wife, which in turn placed Amelia in a most suspect light, made not the slightest difference. That his wife should dare to harbour thoughts and feelings for a man other than her husband was not only unacceptable but insupportable. His marriage may have been entered into through financial expediency, but Sophy *was* his wife and he would certainly not tolerate such behaviour from her. Of course, there was not a shred of proof that his wife and cousin were having an affair, but the seed having been sown refused to go away. For the first time since he had married Sophy, Charles began to look more closely at the woman he had made his wife. At no point did he take into consideration that his own autocratic temperament as well as his indifference could quite easily have contributed to what he regarded as his wife's surreptitious behaviour in addition to possibly pushing her into the arms of a man who clearly appreciated her qualities far more than he did, assuming of course she was having an affair with Marcus. Charles may have to accept his cousin's visits to Brook Street when he came to see his aunt, but he was certainly not prepared to accept or overlook the possibility that these cloaked a far more personal reason. He would certainly have to keep a closer eye on Marcus!

To Sophy's overstretched nerves dinner seemed interminable, and she could only be thankful to Adam and her mother-in-law for bringing to a speedy conclusion a conversation which had been as unexpected as it was unwelcome. Amelia seldom enquired into her activities much less showed any interest in her family's well-being, and her reason for doing either this evening was inscrutable. Sophy had often wished that relations between her

269

and her sister-in-law were friendlier but on the several occasions she had made the attempt towards a closer understanding between them Amelia had refused the gesture. Their relationship therefore, had continued in a polite sort of indifference, neither seeking nor demanding any deeper commitment. Sophy would like to think that Amelia's intention this evening had been to make just such an attempt, but, somehow, she knew it was no such thing. There had been a look; an indefinable air about Amelia which filled Sophy with foreboding and no matter how hard she tried she could not dismiss it. It was almost as though Amelia knew about the state of affairs existing between herself and Marcus and had deliberately set out to expose it, but how this could be she did not know. Sophy was ready to swear that she had not said or done anything to alert her sister-in-law to the truth, on the contrary she was so very protective of her secret. As for Marcus, apart from those unguarded moments when he had inadvertently allowed his feelings for her to show, he treated her with the same courtesy he afforded his aunt and the rest of his female relations, giving no one cause to think that he looked upon her as anything more than his cousin's wife who just happened to be the sister of a long-time friend. It could well be, of course, that Amelia knew absolutely nothing at all but was merely amusing herself at someone else's expense, in which case Sophy felt she was worrying unduly, even so it would be foolish to take such an assumption for granted especially when she considered the intimacy she shared with Charles, after all it would be to Amelia's considerable advantage to pour forth her suspicions into his ears.

Since Charles had made no contribution to the rather sensitive topic Amelia had introduced into the conversation or given any indication that he had taken any notice of it, Sophy had no way of knowing what his thoughts were about his cousin's amatory affairs. He had certainly directed one or two searching looks at her, but as these had not been followed up by remarks of any kind it was impossible to say with any degree of certainty the reason behind them. His mood may have mellowed considerably since this morning, but this did not necessarily mean he was any nearer to enjoying her company than he ever was. Sophy supposed that by now she should have grown accustomed to his indifference and the almost dismissive glances he cast at her, but in view of Amelia's reckless words Sophy could only regard his searching looks this evening with increasing unease.

If she thought that by retiring early she could assemble her thoughts into some kind of order, she was mistaken. Sleep had never been farther away, for which she had to thank such an eventful day. Unlike Amelia, who had brought her own maid with her to Brook Street upon her marriage to George, Sophy managed perfectly well with the assistance of Ellen, a young woman who would willingly have dispensed with her other duties solely to wait on her permanently, but this evening Sophy much preferred to manage for herself and kindly informed her that she would not be needing her tonight. Ellen's cheerful face fell but recognised at a glance that Mrs. Sophy wanted to be alone so, after bobbing a brief curtsey, closed the door quietly behind her. Fervently hoping that Charles would not come upstairs to enquire as to the reason why she had retired so early, Sophy sat for some time in front of her dressing table mirror, looking blindly at the pale reflection staring back at her. She could only guess what the outcome of this tangle would be, but she had no need to guess her husband's reaction if he discovered her recent contact with Alexandra, not to mention her dealings with Marcus, the thought sending a cold shiver down her spine. There was no denying that it would be a tremendous relief to let down her guard during her stay with Timothy and Annabel; to know that she need not be afraid of saying or doing anything which could possibly bring retribution down on her head; only the knowledge that she would not see Marcus marring her pleasure in the forthcoming trip.

In the meantime, however, there was her meeting with Alexandra tomorrow when, hopefully, she would be in a position to convey good news to Charlotte. Retrieving the folded sheet from the pocket of her skirt, which had been delivered in the same surreptitious manner as the first, Sophy read for the second time the few hastily scrawled lines which did not quite dispel her fears.

Dear Sophy,

I hope I am forgiven for failing to meet you today, but if you will be so good as to meet me tomorrow at 12 o'clock in Park Street just opposite the Hanover Gate entrance to Regents Park, I will explain everything. Again, I beg of you not to fail me.

Yours as ever,

Alexandra.

Sophy had no way of knowing whether Alexandra had penned this letter herself or not, and although she was mindful of Marcus's doubts she could not help but respond to the plea it contained. It had occurred to her that she ought to advise him of this latest development, but since she could not leave the house again today in order for her to call upon him without questions being asked as to where she was going at this late hour and sending him a note was equally as impossible for the same reason, there was nothing else she could do other than wait until tomorrow when hopefully he would call in Brook Street and she could speak to him prior to her meeting with Alexandra. Sophy needed no reminding that she was balancing on a knife edge, but if tomorrow's meeting proved successful, then the chances were very good that Charles need never know of her involvement. She knew Marcus would never betray her, and as for Alexandra her dislike of Charles was such that she would never give him the time of day let alone tell tales to him about his wife. This reasoning went some way to easing the turmoil in her mind, and when she eventually pulled the bed covers over her she fell into a deep sleep almost immediately. Had she the least idea that Charles was aware of her recent activities and, also, that at this precise moment the author of that comprehensive report as well as those letters was standing in the library about to pour into his ears her visit to Marcus, she would not have closed her eyes at all!

*

Not surprisingly, it was some little time before Marcus could banish the sweet taste of Sophy's kisses lingering on his lips, but in view of what she had confided to him he had to somehow put aside the memory of those pleasurable moments when he had held her in his arms to deal with a situation he instinctively knew was about to come to a head. He was absolutely convinced that Alexandra had not written that letter, in fact he would lay any odds that she knew nothing whatsoever about it, which meant that Ted Knowles, or whoever it was Charles had hired to work on his behalf, had already set their plans in motion, but to what end still remained uncertain.

If Marcus was right about the jewellery, then Charles would do anything rather than risk denunciation and scandal, but that he would go so far as involving Sophy came as something of a surprise. Of course, it could well be that Charles's accomplice was most probably using her without his knowledge for his own devious ends, which, if he was the type of man Marcus took him to be, seemed more than likely. Charles may not love Sophy but it was extremely doubtful whether he would contemplate using her in such a way, and Marcus vowed he would make the responsible party sorry he ever dared to treat so callously a woman whose very life meant more to him than his own. It was impossible to try to fit her role into a sequence of events which were unknown to him, but he promised himself that before very long he would uncover the truth.

His feelings towards Charles may be very far removed from cousinly, but it never so much as crossed Marcus's mind that his cousin was capable of murder, whether brought about by accidental means or not, and he wondered whether his intention was simply to try to buy Alexandra off. But then, if Charles was experiencing difficulty in finding the money to redeem the jewellery, or at least certain pieces of it, then how could he possibly raise sufficient funds to tempt Alexandra into relinquishing the claim she had on her grandfather's will? She may not know the full value of her mother's jewellery, but she was no fool and must surely realise the sum total to be considerable. If she did allow herself to be persuaded into accepting Charles's offer to renounce her claim on the money and the jewellery, she would doubtless make him pay through the nose for it. Once again Marcus found himself going over old ground, but still the question persisted to plague him. For the life of him he failed to see how Charles, obviously unable to restore those items to the collection, could possibly raise sufficient money to buy Alexandra off? No! Marcus was more than ever convinced that there was far more to it than this and knew the answers lay with Ted Knowles and no other, and however obnoxious he may prove to be Marcus had to see him without any further loss of time.

But when, later that afternoon, he arrived at the address in Waterloo, it was to be met with the intelligence that Ted Knowles was not at home. Upon stressing the urgency of his visit Marcus was derisively informed, "It always is!" but Mrs. Tate, recognising a gent when she saw one, began to realise that her tenant's clientele was apparently becoming more select. It seemed that her tenant was clearly moving up in the world and since she had long cherished hopes of reaching a closer understanding with him, felt it behoved her to do all she could to ensure that his visitor did not take his business elsewhere. In view of this she relented sufficiently to say that if he would care to call back in a little while Mr. Knowles may well have returned. With this Marcus had to be satisfied, hoping that his second visit would prove more successful.

He was a patient man and one, moreover, who did not act rashly, but the delay in speaking to Ted Knowles only served to increase his anxiety. Marcus was as certain as man could be that time was running very short, and in view of that letter to Sophy, and bearing in mind her departure into Kent the day after tomorrow, he was more than ever inclined to think that he had little over twenty-four hours to get to the bottom of things. Unfortunately, however, until he had spoken to Ted Knowles there was nothing he could do but accept the delay with as much patience as he could muster. Marcus may hold several pieces of the jigsaw puzzle but, so far, the picture remained unclear, and that letter to Sophy, far from elucidating matters, only served to make them even more incomprehensible.

It was logical to assume that if Sophy had received a supposed letter from Alexandra, then she too must have received one allegedly from Sophy, clearly indicating that a meeting between the two was being arranged, but for what purpose remained a mystery. If his original idea of Charles attempting to buy the girl off was true, then Marcus failed to see the need for bringing Sophy into it. He knew his cousin well enough to say that if this was indeed what he had in mind then he would make sure no one, least of all his wife, would know anything about it, but Sophy's inclusion totally tore that theory to shreds. For the moment then, he could only speculate where Sophy fitted into the scheme of things, but he promised himself that before the day was out he would discover the truth one way or the other. No one looking at him as he alighted from the hackney carriage and strode into the house would have dared to doubt it; his face, as Webster later informed the housekeeper, was most forbidding.

*

But if Marcus could find no explanation neither could Alexandra, who, having read Sophy's letter several times, was at a loss to understand what could possibly have happened to induce her to write so urgently to her. Several possibilities sprang to mind only to be discarded, and after realising that if something had happened to her grandmother as she had at first thought, she would surely have been informed of it by Silas Jenkins and not an aunt by marriage, and certainly not in such a way. It had occurred to her that Sophy was most probably pressing her for a decision regarding her grandfather's will, and even perhaps for an answer regarding her grandmother's invitation, but not even such valid reasons as these could fully explain Sophy's entreaties not to fail her. Sophy did not strike her as being of a dramatic turn of mind, on the contrary she gave the impression of going about things in a quiet, rather shy way, and if she did happen to stand in need of urgent assistance or advice, perhaps even require a shoulder on which she could unburden herself, Alexandra knew that she would not be the one to whom Sophy would apply. It never so much as entered her head that far from writing the letter Sophy was in complete ignorance of it, as she was of the two which had been sent to Sophy in her name, and therefore decided it was useless to speculate further as to its meaning; doubtless it would all be fully explained tomorrow. As it happened, however, Alexandra was not averse to meeting Sophy again; in fact, prior to the letter's arrival this afternoon she had been wondering how best to get in touch with her as she had now made up her mind regarding her grandfather's will. Had Alexandra the least idea of what awaited her tomorrow, she would not have been so eager to meet her new-found aunt!

Her decision to take Sophy's advice and accept the bequest had been more difficult to make than one would have thought, but several things had tipped the scales in favour of it. Alexandra supposed that no one would ever know why her grandfather had suddenly changed his mind and included her in his will; perhaps it was guilt and remorse after all, or nothing so noble, but whatever it was it in no way altered her feelings towards him. But Sophy had been a persuasive advocate. She had said her mother would have wanted her to live the kind of life she herself had only briefly enjoyed before it was taken away from her, and that it was only natural she would have wanted her daughter to enjoy it too, besides which, it was hers by right.

From what Alexandra had seen of her grandmother she could readily believe that she had had no hand in her mother's eviction, and whatever her feelings she had to admit that what was being offered her was a far better prospect than the one she now faced. She had never been able to accept the drudgery which passed as her life, and she was human and honest enough to admit that she hated the way in which she was forced to live. In spite of what she told her grandfather she wanted the life her mother had been denied. She wanted to escape from a world of mend and make do, of having to resort to the most menial of tasks to make ends meet; to have a roaring fire on a bitterly cold day without having to eke out her small supply of fuel and so many things she found insupportable. She was woman enough to want to be admired, after all she was not unattractive. She wanted to enjoy life; to go to parties and the theatre, to look and feel attractive in the kind of clothes she knew Sophy would wear when not in mourning and not to have to keep repairing the few things she had, already so threadbare from numerous launderings. But most of all, she wanted desperately to leave a neighbourhood of deprivation and poverty, where the very air she breathed was distasteful, and although she had made a few friends since she had come to Hoxton, it did not prevent her from acknowledging that she had very little in common with them, so much so that she knew she would never really be one of them.

It had been from sheer necessity that she had come to this locality. On the death of her mother she had been obliged to leave the cottage on the Maybury estate and, with only a few shillings in her purse, she had known that she had no choice but to seek a roof over her head as cheaply as she possibly could. She was not entirely sure whether to be grateful or not to the boot boy's kindly offered suggestion that she come to Mrs. Drew's, but poverty was a hard master and Alexandra could not afford to pick and choose where she would live, nevertheless, Mansion Gardens, whose name did not live up to the dilapidated reality which met her eyes, was, whether she liked it or not, to become her home for however long she could afford it. She had never realised just how many men were out of work or how ragged children, playing in the filth-ridden streets, seemed to be denied the most basic education; and where women, desperate for money, seemed prepared to do anything to put food on the table and keep the bailiff away from the door. She could only hope that her parents would forgive her, but somewhere deep inside her she knew they would not despise her for accepting a new life from the very man who had deprived them of theirs. Other than Sophy and her grandmother, Alexandra had no wish to associate herself with the rest of her family, but as this would most probably be unavoidable residing in the same house, she decided not to allow this to weigh with her.

*

Unfortunately for Marcus, his second visit to Waterloo proved as fruitless as the first, and no persuasion of his would induce Mrs. Tate to allow him to step inside to await her tenant's return. Upon asking her where Mr. Knowles was most likely to be found she told him that she did not know and, furthermore, it was not her habit to keep tabs on her tenants. A further enquiry as to his probable haunts proved just as useless, but she was a fair-minded woman and unbent sufficiently to suggest that if he would care to leave his name and direction she would tell Mr. Knowles, and no doubt he would be in touch. There seemed to be nothing else Marcus could do at the moment, and after handing her a card he pulled out of his wallet he doffed his hat and bid her good afternoon.

He had briefly toyed with the idea of waiting for Ted Knowles to return from a discreet vantage point across the street, but since Mrs. Tate had more than one tenant and Marcus had no idea what he looked like, apart from which it could be hours be before he returned, he decided against what would most probably turn out to be an unprofitable venture. As all Marcus had to go on was nothing more than conjecture, it could well be that he was allowing himself to think the worst over nothing more serious than a severe attack of pride. After all, Charles was exceptionally proud and surely a few chance words uttered in the heat of the moment did not necessarily denote anything sinister, but Marcus's instincts, which had never yet proved him wrong, were so strong that he could not dismiss them and knew that if he allowed them to pass unheeded he would be brought to regret it. But more than this there was that letter to Sophy, which surely proved they were more than suspicions. Unable to shrug off his growing concerns he knew he had to try again to speak to Ted Knowles no matter how late the hour, and upon returning home Marcus wrote a few lines to his old friend Anthony Merpin offering his apologies for cancelling their dinner engagement that evening, and Webster, upon being asked to ensure that the note he was handed was delivered straightaway merely nodded his head, concealing his surprise as well as his curiosity. Amusing company though Anthony was, Marcus's business with Ted Knowles had to come before a dinner engagement, even with such an old friend as Anthony, and although Marcus experienced a twinge of guilt over letting his friend down at the last minute he could not regret it, and so, at fifteen minutes to seven o'clock, he climbed into the antiquated vehicle which Webster had summoned up for him, setting out on his third visit to Waterloo.

Ted Knowles was not only confident in his own abilities but never even gave a thought to the possibility that he was being tracked down by a man of equal resource and determination as himself. He would have been astonished to know that by the mere handing over of his card to Silas Jenkins pieces of the jigsaw he had put together were being assembled by the very person Mrs. Charles Harrington had called upon prior to returning home earlier today, a visit he had chosen to ignore on the grounds of it being totally unconnected to the matter in hand. Unaware that he was standing on the brink of defeat, it was therefore without the least suspicion that Ted Knowles read the calling card Mrs. Tate had given him, bearing only the name *Marcus Ingleby*. He did not know of anyone by that name, but upon being informed that he had already called twice, stating the matter was urgent, he had no doubt that his visitor would call again, rubbing his hands together expectantly. If what Mrs. Tate had said was true, then whoever this Marcus Ingleby was he must be desperately in need of assistance, and Ted Knowles was just the man to provide it – for a price!

He had certainly not expected this Marcus Ingleby to call again today, but if he found it necessary to pay a visit at ten minutes past seven o'clock in the evening it must be important, and desired Mrs. Tate to show him up, wondering which one of his many services his visitor required. Of course, it was a pity that a new client was seeking him out at this precise moment when he was already heavily preoccupied, but business was business and he was not prepared to turn it down, and it was therefore with a beaming smile that he greeted his visitor.

Marcus's face betrayed none of his feelings to the man who surged forward with his ham-like fist extended to him, in fact Ted Knowles was everything he had expected him to be, and merely took the hand offered, enquiring, "Mr. Knowles?"

"Ay," he nodded, "that's me."

"How do you do?" Marcus smiled politely, taking the measure of him straightaway. "I feel I owe you an apology for calling so late. I hope my visit is not inopportune?"

Ted Knowles smiled and, after eyeing him speculatively for several moments, assured Marcus that new business was never inopportune. He may have marked Marcus down as a well-breeched cove, but there was something about him that warned Ted Knowles to tread warily and that in this tall, broad-shouldered man he was dealing with no fool and, from the look of quiet determination on the strong handsome face, which suggested he was perfectly capable of handling his own affairs without the assistance of such as himself, he could not help but wonder what had brought him here. Marcus did not strike him as being the kind of man who would need his particular services, and in view of this Ted Knowles's eyes narrowed suddenly but reassured his visitor that it was never too late to do business.

"I shall not take up too much of your time," Marcus assured him, "but I believe you may be able to answer one or two questions I have."

This was a totally new experience for Ted Knowles. He was the one who usually asked the questions, and he was not altogether pleased to find that for once the boot was on the other foot. There was nothing in Marcus's demeanour to suggest he was in any kind of trouble which would automatically put him at a disadvantage requiring him to adopt a conciliatory attitude, on the contrary he appeared to be fully in command of the situation and quite prepared to remain until he got what he came for. Ted Knowles was ready to swear that he had never before set eyes on this man, but he could not rid himself of the feeling that there was something vaguely familiar about him, but as this would no doubt come to him eventually, he merely eyed his visitor, saying warily, "Queshtuns, yer say!"

"Yes," Marcus nodded, casting a cursory glance around the room, noting that although the carpet and furniture were old and shabby everything was spotlessly clean.

"An' wot might they be?" Ted Knowles asked cautiously, rubbing his chin thoughtfully.

"Nothing too taxing, I hope," Marcus smiled, but there was nothing friendly in the smile.

"Such as?" Ted Knowles prompted, scanning his memory in an effort to try to place this man.

Marcus smiled, noting the guarded look which had entered those blue eyes and knew that his instincts had not misled him in that this man was without any doubt his cousin's accomplice. "Merely that I believe you had occasion, some while ago, to find a young lady on behalf of a client."

Ted Knowles's eyes narrowed even more, eyeing Marcus cautiously before saying, "I find lots o' things fer lot's o' people."

"I do not doubt it," Marcus agreed affably. "However, something tells me you know the young lady to whom I refer."

Ted Knowles knew very well, but for the life of him he failed to see this man's connection with her. "Wot's yer int'rest in 'er?" he asked suspiciously.

'That," Marcus smiled, "is something which need not concern you. Suffice it to say," he informed him with dangerous calm, this man's callous usage of Sophy very much at the forefront of his mind, "that my dealings with her will not wait upon your convenience."

For the first time Ted Knowles felt unsure of his ground. It had not taken him long to see that he was not dealing with a man who harboured a dark secret or one who needed discreetly extricating from a delicate situation, but with a man who knew precisely what he wanted and was determined to get it. He much preferred dealing with people he had some kind of hold over, to dangle their secrets over their heads until he had their undivided attention, but the man looking down at him with such calm indifference made him pause. His plans regarding the girl were already in motion, and even if he was in a position to rescind them he would not. For one thing, it would do his reputation irreparable harm if it ever became known, and for another he did not fancy being on the receiving end of Charles Harrington's retribution should it not go ahead as planned. On the other hand, of course, he was none too eager to cross this man either, who, despite his civility and apparent ease, looked to be in no very good humour and pretty useful with his fives into the bargain! What was needed was for him to play for time. The first thing he had to do was to ascertain the reason for this man's enquiries, not that he looked to be any too forthcoming, but it could well be that if he played his cards right this interview may not turn out so very ill after all.

"Alrite, Guvna," Ted Knowles conceded. "Now, wot did yer say 'er name wos?"

"I didn't," Marcus replied smoothly, eyeing him with intense dislike. "In fact," he pointed out, "I do not think you need reminding of it. I feel sure you know it already."

"Ah," Ted Knowles smiled, nodding his head appreciatively, "you'm a knowin'un. I says ter meself as soon as I clapped eyes on yer, 'Ted,' I says, "ere's as knowin' a body as H'ive eva seen."

Charles must be desperate indeed if he trusted this man to help extricate him from a potential scandal. For himself, Marcus would not trust him an inch, and if it was the last thing he ever did he would bring this obnoxious individual to book. "You are wasting time," Marcus told him. "Did you or did you not locate the girl?" Upon receiving an assenting nod, Marcus asked, "Have you communicated with her since?" He saw the shuttered look descend over the pale blue eyes and knew his instincts had not erred. When Ted Knowles made no effort to answer Marcus took several steps towards him, saying, with a distinct edge to his voice, "I think I must warn you that I am in no mood for your delaying tactics. I should be obliged to receive your answer."

Ted Knowles knew the voice of authority when he heard it, but he was still very reluctant to divulge information. However, in view of the steely look in those brown eyes he decided his best course of action, for the moment at least, was to prevaricate. He shook his head. "No, but 'er gran'pa wos none too 'appy 'er 'adn't shown 'erself. 'E asked me ter go back an' see 'im ter mek shua I'd told 'er."

Knowing his uncle, Marcus felt sure that this was most probably true. "So," he said purposefully, "you are saying you did not visit her again." Ted Knowles shook his head. "Have you had occasion to communicate with her since on other matters?"

"Wy shud I?" Ted Knowles shrugged, realising that he was not going to find it as easy as he thought to bluff his way out of this interview.

"I can think of several reasons," Marcus told him. "Well?" he prompted.

For one who was accustomed to dealing with people who stood in no little awe of him, even going so far as to entreat his help, it was a considerable shock to Ted Knowles to learn that this man, far from placating him, was actually making demands. Charles Harrington may be a dangerous man to cross, indeed his punishment for failure would be ruthless, but Ted Knowles knew that he still held the upper hand simply because his assistance was needed and, which was more to the point, he was privy to his secrets, which could be put to good use whenever it suited him. But this man clearly had nothing to hide much less something to fear, and consequently it made him far more dangerous than Charles Harrington could ever be. To Ted Knowles's annoyance he was the one who was having to placate and for one of his domineering disposition it sat very ill on his shoulders, but he was also consumed with curiosity. Who was this man? And why was he so interested in the girl? He was determined to find out. Marcus Ingleby was unquestionably a gentleman and unless Ted Knowles mistook the matter, which he doubted, he had a distinct military bearing, which meant he was more than capable of taking care of himself and one, moreover, who was used to command. It was going to be no easy task to discover what his interest was in the girl, but Ted Knowles knew more than one way of skinning a rabbit. In the meantime though, his visitor was waiting for an answer to his question. "I ain't set eyes on the wench since," he told him, knowing that this at least was true. "An' as fer getting' in tuch wi' 'er, wy shud I? Ain't no reasun wy I shud!" he lied glibly.

To his dismay, he watched Marcus stroll around the room with almost nonchalant ease, taking in every detail of his cosy little domicile, his glance eventually coming to rest on the table upon which lay several sheets of discarded notepaper he had not yet got round to disposing of, knowing a moment of panic as he anxiously watched those gloved fingers pick up a number of the crossed out sheets. Too late to berate himself for being stupid enough not to have got rid of them sooner, but then, how was he to have known he would receive a visitor whose sole interest was the girl? His feeling of panic increased as he watched with pending doom while Marcus scrutinised the sheets.

"So," Marcus mused, "you have not communicated with the girl," eyeing his host with unqualified dislike. "If that is so, then how do you explain these?"

He couldn't, but since he had to prevent this man from finding out the truth Ted Knowles merely shrugged before making a hasty attempt to reach the table to gather up the remaining sheets to throw them onto the fire, only to find himself prevented from doing so by Marcus's cane being pointed at him.

"Not so fast, my friend," Marcus halted him, crushing the half dozen sheets in his hand.

"'Ere!' Ted Knowles cried, his face growing a deeper shade of red. "Wot's yer game?"

"My game," Marcus told him firmly, "is to discover certain facts, facts which I believe will not only prevent a most unpleasant occurrence but will also ensure certain parties coming under the full glare of the law."

Ted Knowles, who liked being threatened with the law no better than he liked this man who was for the moment calling the tune, lunged forward in a wild attempt to snatch those incriminating practise sheets out of his hand, but a nicely timed movement of Marcus's foot resulted in him falling backwards, stumbling into a chair and momentarily winding him. It was several moments before Ted Knowles recovered his breath, during which his adversary had enough time to examine the handwriting more closely, finding it to be identical to that on the letter which had been addressed to Sophy and which was presently safely tucked away in his study. Putting the sheets of notepaper into his inside coat pocket, Marcus then waited for Ted Knowles to get his breath back, watching unmoved as the huge hands gripped the arms of the chair in a futile attempt to regain his feet, his efforts wasted as the tip of Marcus's walking cane was pressed into his stomach, keeping him lightly but firmly pinned in the chair. Ted Knowles did not need to be told that this man was holding his temper on a very tight rein and that it would go ill with him if he refused to cooperate. One look at those hard and unforgiving eyes was enough to tell him that it would afford his persecutor immense satisfaction to knock him senseless, at total variance to the tone of perfect affability in his voice. "Now you and I, my friend, are going to have a little talk."

"Wot about? I ain't got nuthin' ter says ter yer," Ted Knowles snarled, eyeing Marcus with something akin to loathing, breathlessly pointing out that he had no right to come here and treat him like this.

"I would strongly advise you to be very careful what you say," Marcus warned. "I am in no mood for the likes of you."

Having had sufficient time to gather his scattered wits, Ted Knowles began to think it behoved him to play ball for a while, even though the thought of having to do so went very much against the grain. He was expecting Davy any minute, and surely between the two of them they could adequately deal with this man.

"This morning," Marcus informed him, just as though he was chatting to an old friend, "a letter was delivered to a certain lady, requesting her to keep an appointment in Regents Park, an…"

"Well?" Ted Knowles growled. "Wot's that ter me?"

Ignoring the interruption as if it had not occurred, Marcus continued, "An appointment which turned out to be bogus."

"I dunno wot you'm talkin' about!" Ted Knowles said gruffly, keeping his ear cocked for Davy.

"You wrote it," Marcus accused.

"I *neva!*" Ted Knowles barked, keeping a wary eye on the walking cane, unwelcome recollections of Charles Harrington doing precisely the same thing coming involuntarily to mind.

"Oh, but you did," Marcus smiled, "and these discarded sheets prove it. How very careless of you to have kept them," giving him a gentle prod in the stomach with the tip of his cane. "You really should have disposed of them sooner." He eyed Knowles coldly, but his voice remained perfectly affable. "Now, what I want to know is: what are your instructions and who is paying you?"

Ted Knowles could not believe this was happening to him, much less how this man had got wind of him. He knew Charles Harrington would never have said anything to give the game way, which left him with only one conclusion. Someone had betrayed him, but as he was presently in no position to discover the traitor's identity he would have to wait a while before he could deal with this rather unpleasant aspect accordingly. Right now though, he needed to train all his energies on how to get out of this fix in which he found himself. "I dunno wot you'm talkin' about," he shot out, a pulse beating alarmingly at his temples and his hands forming into formidable fists.

Marcus saw those huge paws clench and was ready for him whenever he made his move. Ted Knowles obviously knew how to use his fists, but for a man of his bulk his movements would certainly be less swift than his own, not that Marcus fell into the trap of underestimating him. Ted Knowles may be less agile than himself, but for one who considered himself cornered he would put up a very good fight. "I am waiting," Marcus reminded him.

"I keeps tellin' yer," Ted Knowles bit out, "I dunno nothin' about no letta."

"Please do not make the error of misunderstanding me," Marcus warned, the impulse to land him a flush hit having to be strongly curbed. "You seem to be forgetting, Knowles, that I hold the evidence in my pocket, so you may as well accustom yourself to the fact that I have no intention of leaving here until you tell me what I want to know."

The heavy jaws worked feverishly and the bull like face took on an alarming shade of purple, his eyes spitting out hatred to the man who seemed to be in no mood to take his word. "Damn you!" he barked, his attempt to stand up being thwarted by a delicate nudge of the cane.

"Please, do not force me to use violence," Marcus advised him, his eyes glinting. "You, my friend," he said without the smallest semblance of friendliness in his voice, "have been busy making plans, and that letter to Mrs. Charles Harrington and these discarded sheets on which you rehearsed what you would say to her and, from the looks of it, what the girl would say to Mrs. Charles Harrington in her supposed letter to her, forms part of them."

Heaven help him, but he would find the one who had betrayed him! "Plans! Wot plans?" Ted Knowles thundered, itching to get his hands around that throat.

"That," Marcus inclined his head, "is what you are going to tell me."

Where the devil was Davy? He should have been here by now! It went very much against the grain with Ted Knowles to have to play for time, but until Davy arrived he failed to see what else could be done but bluff his way out of this incredible predicament. "'Ow can I tells yer wot I dunno?" he asked. "Be reasunable, Guvna."

"I am always reasonable," Marcus told him, "except when it comes to individuals like you who make a profit out of the misfortunes of others. Now," he bit out, "enough of this time wasting. These discarded sheets in my pocket bear the same handwriting as on the letter which was delivered this morning to Mrs. Charles Harrington." Not for the first time he saw the flash of recognition on Ted Knowles's face at the mention of Sophy's name. "I see the name is not unfamiliar to you," he remarked. "Now, why should that be, I wonder?"

That he of all people should find himself in such a situation as this was incredible. He, who had always been so careful and planned everything in painstaking detail, should end up being pinned to a chair by a man he had never known existed until about twenty minutes ago! For the life of him Ted Knowles could not understand how this man came to be in possession of his name and direction, but if it was the last thing he ever did he would return the compliment in full measure. "I ain't neva 'eard o' nobudy o' that name."

"You really will have to do better than that," Marcus shook his head. "Unless, of course," he suggested, "you prefer to talk to a police constable at Bow Street. In either event," he promised, "I shall arrive at the truth."

"Wy you…!" Ted Knowles made a sudden lunge out of the chair, his huge hands making for Marcus's throat, but he was ready for the attack and sent Ted Knowles sprawling backwards with an excellent right to that massive jaw. But Ted Knowles could take a knock or two and came back almost immediately with a charging head thrust to the stomach, sending Marcus back against the table with him grappling on top of him, attempting a right to the head which only missed its mark by the quickness with which Marcus managed to push Ted Knowles off him and reverse their positions. It was obvious to Marcus that his opponent was used to a scrap or two and knew how to handle himself, if not with pugilistic nicety then with the instincts of a man determined to win. Ted Knowles was a big man to tangle with, but just when Marcus had him in his grip, an unexpected blow delivered with tremendous force struck him from behind, knocking him senseless, a black chasm opening up before him before he slumped in an inanimate heap to the floor.

Davy Wilkins beamed triumphantly as he looked down at Marcus's motionless form on the floor, his hands clenching at his sides ready to finish him off, but the small cudgel he had so effectively used had been more than enough to ensure that his boxing skills would not be needed; not that his meagre skills would have done him any good as Ted Knowles knew very well. Compared to the man on the floor, who carried three times Davy's weight, he would not have stood much of a chance; even Ted Knowles had to acknowledge that he had been no pushover.

It took several minutes for Ted Knowles to get his breath back, his huge chest heaving from an exertion he had not experienced for quite some time, but eventually he was able to speak, gasping to Davy that he look through his pockets. No sign of life emanated from Marcus while this task was being carried out, and after handing his mentor their contents Davy listened in shocked silence at his bitter recital of what had happened; strenuously denying any collaboration with the enemy on his part.

"I knows that, lad," Ted Knowles growled, burning the incriminating evidence which had been fished out of Marcus's inside coat pocket, "but sumone's tried ter stitch us up gud an' propa!"

"But 'oo'd do such a thing?" Davy demanded incredulously, his faith in Ted Knowles implicit.

"I dunno, Davy lad," Ted Knowles mused, wincing as he tenderly touched his chin, discounting his associates at 'The Black Swan', which left the hapless Farley, Charles's somewhat ingratiating valet, "but I'm gonna find out. Now tho," he said briskly, "let's tek a luk in 'ere shall we?" indicating the wallet Davy had removed from that impeccably tailored coat, revealing two callings cards and several five pound notes, the sight of which made Davy's eyes glisten. "That's inuf o' that lad," Ted Knowles warned. "You jus' rememba, I ain't no tea leaf an' nitha are you!"

"But Guvna…!" Davy exclaimed, the sight of so much money almost proving too much for him.

"Don't yer 'Guvna' me," Ted Knowles admonished. "Ain't I tawt yer no betta than ter filch?"

Watching his mentor restore the wallet, complete with the bank notes, to Marcus's pockets, Davy asked, "But 'oo is 'e, Mr. Knowles?"

"A body 'oo knows too much lad, that's 'oo. Wot we've gotta do is ter shift 'im, an' 'e's no light weight. 'E'll be out cold for a while yet, thanks ter you lad."

"Yer means 'e knows everythin'?" Davy asked, his sharp face contorted in surprise as he looked up from the still figure on the floor to Ted Knowles.

"'E knows inuf," Ted Knowles nodded. "But first I wonts yer ter go an' see Joe. Tell 'im I 'ave sumthin' I wonts 'im ter keep 'is eyes on." Davy nodded, his light brown eyes darting warily to Marcus's lifeless body. "'E'll be no truble. Now, 'urry up lad; there's not much time."

Davy nodded and, after fitting his cap on his head, made his way to the door but was forestalled when told him sharply, "Mek shua 'er downstairs don't sees yer." Looking down at the inanimate figure lying on the floor at his feet, slightly mollified with the result of Davy's punishing blow, Ted Knowles now found himself with the problem of having to discover who this man was and where he fitted into the picture but, more to the point, how much he knew.

There was no question of keeping this surprising turn of events to himself; like it or not Charles Harrington would have to be told. It could of course be that they were acquainted with one another, which may well go some way to explaining things, but since Ted Knowles could not be sure if this Marcus Ingleby had confided his thoughts to anyone else, he could not afford to take any chances. Once he had him safely housed in Joe's cellar he would be able to breathe a bit more easily and knew he would be safe there while he visited his client. That Charles Harrington would be far from pleased was certain, but Ted Knowles could not help thinking that he would be even less pleased if he was not kept fully informed of what was going on. All he could do now though was await the return of Davy.

Chapter Fifteen

Since Adam's protracted visit seemed to indicate that he had indeed reconciled his differences with his father-in-law, the only cloud on Charlotte's horizon where he was concerned was that it was a pity Isabel was not with him. She was of course delighted to have her youngest son at home, but she could not understand why he appeared to be in no hurry to return to his young bride and could see no reason why he was delaying his departure. That he loved Isabel was evident, and if Charlotte needed further confirmation on this point she only had to think of the letters he had written during his stay to put any doubts on that score to flight. From what she could see his continued presence was not due to any problem with the marriage, but as he was putting forward no explanation in defence of his remaining in Brook Street, she was beginning to grow a little uneasy.

Since Adam could hardly tell his mother what was in his mind he had taken refuge in prevarication, and even though the reasons he put forward to account for his extended stay sounded lame even in his own ears, he considered it far better than telling her the truth. Having turned down his cousin's advice about returning to Yorkshire, he was not at all sure whether to feel disappointed or not to know that so far no good had come from his self-imposed stay. He had had no precise idea what he expected to happen, but that something was in the wind he felt sure. As far as he was able he was keeping a watchful an eye on his brother as was humanly possible. Naturally, there were very practical reasons why he could not follow Charles around twenty-four hours a day, not the least being that he was no fool and would surely wonder why his youngest brother had a sudden and unaccountable predilection for his company. But from what Adam had managed to discover to date Charles had done nothing more sinister than taking a stroll round to his club, and certainly nothing which could possibly substantiate the vehemence of his words to Sophy or the attitude he was adopting towards Alexandra.

It was just as Adam was on the point of coming to think that not only himself but Marcus as well had totally misread Charles's display of fierce resentment that something quite unexpected occurred to rekindle his belief. Having sat through dinner wrapped in his own thoughts, he had played very little part in the various discussions which had been exchanged, and although he sympathised with Sophy over the awkward position Amelia's carefully constructed comments had placed her in, other than a reasonable disclaimer at George's remarks about his cousin's amatory affairs, Adam considered the less said about it the better.

As his mother and Amelia had removed to the drawing room and Sophy had retired earlier than usual stating that she had a severe headache, and George, declining to spend the remainder of the evening with his brothers on the grounds of an engagement with a friend, Adam had ample opportunity to broach the matter of Alexandra to Charles over a glass of something invigorating. But even before he had managed to get his brother into the library much less decide how best to approach him on such a delicate subject, the clanging of the bell was heard followed seconds later by Harris entering the dining room. Informing Charles in a voice completely devoid of emotion as he handed him the calling card on a silver salver that he had a visitor and one, moreover, who seemed impervious to the lateness of the hour as well as being under the impression that he would not be turned away, he waited patiently for him to say something.

From the expression on Charles's face it was obvious to Adam that the caller was not only known to him but most unwelcome, and after what seemed to be an inner struggle Charles offered a curt apology to his brother before following Harris out of the room. Had Charles not been so angry he would have realised that his confederate's arrival on his doorstep had been forced upon him through the direst necessity, but no sooner had Harris closed the library door behind him leaving the two men alone than Charles gave vent to his feelings, honouring his visitor with a brief and derogatory denunciation of not only his intellect but flagrant stupidity in coming here.

Having already suffered a gross invasion of his home as well as his person, Ted Knowles was pushed to the limits of his endurance by this scathing attack, belligerently informing his client that it was not of his choosing he had come here tonight, and if he did not want to hear what he had to say then it was all one to him.

Somewhere in the pit of his stomach Charles knew without being told that Ted Knowles had brought bad news; nothing else could account for him tracking him down at home. Eyeing his unwelcome visitor with barely concealed loathing, he bid him say what he had come for, but this invitation, delivered in an icily cold voice, was hardly encouraging, and Ted

Knowles, not liking the look in his client's eyes, swallowed hard and, after taking a deep and resolute breath, embarked on his tale. Not until he had come to the end of it did he mention to Charles about his wife's detour to an establishment in Knightsbridge, explaining to his client that he had not looked upon it as important at the time, but in view of this evening's events he thought he had best mention it because he could not help but wonder if he may know this Marcus Ingleby and, if so, could he be the person Mrs. Harrington had called upon and who was now currently imprisoned in Joe's cellar? "'Cus if 'e is," Ted Knowles pointed out helpfully, "I'd say it's 'ow 'e cottuned on ter things in the first place!"

Whatever Charles had expected it was certainly not this, and there was no denying that the disclosure came as a severe shock. Ted Knowles had known that he would not receive this news with open arms but he had not expected to find his client almost paralysed by it. The plain truth was that Ted Knowles's revelation was nothing short of a body blow, especially about Sophy's visit to see his cousin, Charles's brain momentarily too numb to comprehend what he had been told, but gradually the paralysis began to ebb away and it was not long before he was able to take in the damning significance of this evening's events.

He was not a man given over to panic, but for one awful moment Charles was conscious of an overwhelming sense of despair as the thought of inevitable exposure and disgrace, the very things he had been strenuously trying to avoid, loomed large before him. However, his anger soon banished everything but an urgent desire to save himself and rescue what seemed to be the dying embers of his plans as well as demanding of the man standing uneasily in front of him as to why, bearing in mind the so-called accident was set for tomorrow, he had not seen fit to enlighten him of his wife's visit to Knightsbridge in his handwritten account. Upon being patiently informed a second time by Ted Knowles that it was not until this evening's unprecedented events that he realised her detour might have some bearing on things, Charles honoured him with a comprehensive denunciation of his intelligence as well as his failure to grasp the enormity of his wife's actions, interspersed with a string of expletives which, although they considerably relieved his feelings, they by no means provided him with the answer as to how to deal with his cousin, a man who could bring all to ruin.

Upon learning that Marcus had taken a hand in the affair and that Sophy had purposely delayed returning home to call in Knightsbridge to see him, not only proved to Charles that her relationship with his cousin went deeper than he had thought but that his carefully laid plans were in danger of breaking down. Other than knowing that Marcus knew of the letter received by Sophy, Charles could only guess as to the extent of his knowledge, but why she had delivered it into his hands and to what end he was not entirely sure. According to Ted Knowles she had kept the bogus appointment in Regents Park, then realising the girl was not going to show herself she must have made the decision to visit Marcus prior to returning home to confide the whole to him. Charles may not fully see the reason for this, but that she was closer aligned to his cousin than he had supposed was certain. He knew perfectly well that Sophy would never tell him about that letter, to do so would mean having to make a confession about her visit to the girl in company with Silas Jenkins but also because she would know what his reaction would be, after all had he not made his views regarding the brat clear? Since Sophy did not know that the letter had not been written by Alexandra, Charles failed to see why she had felt the need to consult his cousin and, having done so, why Marcus should then have paid Ted Knowles a visit to question it.

As far as Charles was aware Marcus had no idea of Ted Knowles's existence, particularly as the search for the girl had been conducted in complete secrecy, and therefore Charles was at a loss to understand how his cousin had come to know about him. To his way of thinking it seemed that the only possible answer was that Silas Jenkins must have furnished his cousin with Ted Knowles's name and direction, but even supposing this was the case it did not explain why Jenkins should have done so. There was absolutely no reason Charles could think of to account for Marcus's interest in Ted Knowles because if memory served him correctly Silas Jenkins had only met him once when he had responded to that advertisement he had inserted in the newspaper as a last resort to finding the girl. As no member of his family knew who their father had employed and no mention of him was found amongst his papers, Silas Jenkins, no more than the rest of them, had ever heard of Ted Knowles let alone suspect that he would later contact himself regarding the girl. Charles knew his dealings with Ted Knowles had been conducted with the utmost discretion, and he failed to perceive the slightest chink in their plan's armour which could possibly have given them away, but somehow or other Sophy and his cousin were not only aware of their plans but had made it their business to involve themselves.

It was pointless deceiving himself into thinking that they were acting from pure guesswork. Like Ted Knowles, Charles could not help but think that something or someone had alerted them to what was going on, and although it was vital he discover how they came to be in possession of so much information regarding what he had arranged for the girl, if he was to come out of this unscathed the first thing he had to do was to determine just how much they knew, but at all costs he had to prevent them from investigating further. At first, it had been his intention to speak to Sophy there and then, but only a moment's thought was sufficient to tell him that this was not the answer, especially when he considered the role she was to play in tomorrow's events. No, he would deal with her later!

Ted Knowles, who had been staring at the heavy opulence around him with wide-eyed interest, brought his gaze back to rest on his client's saturnine face, glad at least to have Marcus Ingleby's identity explained. He fully sympathised with his client's dilemma, but whilst he had no stomach for turning tail on a job the more he thought about it the more it seemed to him that nothing but trouble would result from this one. Upon suggesting they put their plan back a few days, or at least until they could discover how his wife and cousin came to be in possession of so much information, Charles shook his head, adamantly refusing to alter the schedule of events in any way, knowing full well that even a few days may prove critical as no dependence could be placed upon the girl not coming forward to claim her inheritance. As it was clear his client could not be persuaded into changing his mind, Ted Knowles, who had no objection about going ahead, nevertheless felt it incumbent upon him to point out the added difficulties his cousin's intervention had created, not to mention the unexpected part his wife was playing over and above that designated for her and the uncertainty of her intentions.

"'E means truble," Ted Knowles pointed out forcefully, his chin still extremely tender from the brutal contact with his prisoner's fist, the recollection bringing a martial light to his eye. "H'if you'm not careful," he warned Charles, "'e'll ruin everythin'; then the fat'll be in the fire! Best deal wi 'im now, before 'e can say or do anythin'."

There was no misunderstanding his meaning, and even though he was already skating on rather thin ice Charles was not unappreciative of its merits, and it did not take him long to concede that Knowles was right. If Marcus was not dealt with he could cause all manner of trouble, the thought bringing a deep frown down onto Charles's forehead. Everything may pay point to an informer, but no one knew better than he did just how astute Marcus was, and irrespective of whether he had been alerted to the truth by an unknown party or his involvement stemmed from nothing more than some instinct or other, Charles could not afford to run any unnecessary risks and jeopardise everything he was working towards by deluding himself into thinking that Marcus could be persuaded into turning his back and leaving him to get on with things.

Ted Knowles saw his words go home and knew from the look on Charles's face that he was coming round to his way of thinking. Of course, it was all one to him whether he disposed of one or more obstacles, but Ted Knowles was rather hoping that Charles Harrington would leave Marcus Ingleby to him. He would take great pleasure from paying him back for the sledge-hammering earlier on. "Let me 'ave a tuch at 'im, Guvna," Ted Knowles urged, his huge paws gripping the rim of his hat expectantly.

"No," Charles said slowly, turning his gaze upon him. "This requires careful thought, and not just a little finesse. I shall deal with my cousin."

"Very well, Guvna," Ted Knowles shrugged, disappointed. "Altho I mus' say I wos lookin' forward to…"

"I daresay," Charles broke in, "but that pleasure will be mine." He was conscious of no cousinly feelings or remorse over his forthcoming dealings with Marcus; only the vital need to save himself from disgrace and ruin, and if this meant getting rid of a slip of a girl who threatened his peace of mind and a man who had never failed to rouse a streak of jealousy in him, then so be it. There was no room in his calculations for sentiment; matters had progressed too far for that. Trust Marcus though to involve himself in something that was no concern of his! Even so, Charles could not help wondering whether his cousin had had no idea that something was going forward and would have remained in ignorance of the whole affair had it not been for Sophy's visit! But it was all conjecture for the present. But how astute Amelia was in recognising the signs which he had incredibly missed! Just how close was the relationship between them? And when did Sophy begin to feel the need to turn to him and confide in him? Charles's shapely hands closed into fists and his eyes narrowed as he contemplated the two of them in league against him, his anger equally divided between the two of them, but first things first. "You have him at *The Black Swan*', you say?" he said meditatively.

"Ah," Ted Knowles grinned, "'e's safe inuf there. Trusst up like a chickin 'e is; Joe'll see 'e won't get away."

"I hope not," Charles warned menacingly. "Now, listen. I want you to return there and stay with him until I arrive."

"Righto, Guvna," Ted Knowles nodded. "Er… wot about the missus?" he asked warily, jerking his thumb towards the door.

"She need not concern you," Charles dismissed. "She will play her part tomorrow as arranged, and then you may leave her to me. I shall join you at *The Black Swan*' as soon as I can, where I shall have much to say to my enterprising relative."

Since this did not seem to be the time to remind his client about financial remuneration, Ted Knowles merely nodded, but was rather inclined to take exception to the way Charles personally escorted him off the premises. "Jus' as if I'm a commun tea leaf!" he expostulated, his mumblings going unanswered as Charles closed the front door firmly behind him.

Upon hearing the library door open followed seconds later by the front door opening and closing, Adam filled two glasses with some of his father's excellent malt which had been brought into the dining room earlier by Harris, fully expecting Charles to join him once his caller had left. But when, ten minutes later, he put in no appearance, Adam strode into the hall to be pulled up short by the sight of his brother coming out of the library with a note in his hand which he held out to Harris with curt instructions to ensure it was delivered immediately to Sir Michael Overton. Adam, who knew that his brother had arranged to meet Sir Michael later at his club, wondered what could have arisen to render it necessary to cancel their engagement, but before Adam could question this he saw Charles nod his head towards the stand whereupon Harris removed his overcoat and assisted him into it before handing him his hat, gloves and cane, with the promise that he would make sure the note was delivered. It was clear from the look on Charles's face that whoever his unexpected visitor was he had obviously not been the bearer of good news, in fact, Adam would go so far as to say that his brother bore all the signs of one who had suffered a severe shock, but from his expression it was quite evident he was in no mood to answer questions or offer explanations to account for his sudden departure, much less his destination. As Adam had never made the error of falling into the same trap as George, he was by no means overawed or disconcerted by Charles's acid tongue any more than he was by his temper, and the only effect his brother's cool reply had on him in response to his polite enquiry if anything was amiss, was a shrug of the shoulders.

It was not until Harris had seen Charles out of the house that Adam began to wonder more particularly into the reason for his brother cancelling his engagement with Sir Michael then going out hard upon the heels of his recently departed visitor. It seemed most unlikely that a business acquaintance would come to see him at this hour, and although several possibilities for Charles going out so unexpectedly presented themselves to Adam, none of them seemed very plausible, but somewhere at the back of his mind he could not help wondering if it was in some way connected with Alexandra. Of course, it could well be he was allowing his imagination to run away with him and just because Charles had sent a note cancelling his engagement with Sir Michael followed by his unexpected departure after his late visitor had left, may have nothing whatever to do with her, but something Adam could not quite define told him that something did not feel quite right, and no matter how he tried he could not dismiss it. It was then that he took the sudden decision to follow Charles, considerably startling his mother's faithful retainer by briskly requesting him to get his overcoat, disappearing into the dining room for just long enough to finish his drink before returning to the hall to shrug himself into it. As it was patently obvious that Harris was agog with curiosity and Adam could not enlighten him, although he would have been hard put to do so considering he had no idea himself what was going on, he put on his hat and gloves with a casualness which totally belied his concerns as well as making Harris want to box his ears, and that mischievous grin, which he knew from experience foretold trouble and did not fool him in the least, made him wonder what was going on. However, as Adam seemed intent on keeping his own counsel, Harris was obliged to be content with his own assumptions and, after handing Adam his cane, let him out of the house and quietly closed the door behind him, his mind awash with conjecture as he made his way back to his own downstairs domain.

Even though the time which had elapsed from Charles leaving the house to his own hasty departure was a matter of minutes, Adam could only hope that he would still be within sight of his brother. He was quite convinced that Charles's unknown visitor had not only been responsible for him cancelling his engagement but also his hurried exit, and for reasons Adam could neither explain nor understand he sensed that this evening's events were going to prove decisive. He could not argue with Marcus's reasoning when he said that more than suspicions were needed to accuse Charles of making plans to deprive Alexandra of her inheritance and that they could in all probability be doing nothing more than indulging their imagination by reading more into his resentment than was actually the case, but surely the unexpected arrival of his late caller and his reaction to it discounted that!

As luck would have it, just as Adam had descended the last step he caught sight of his brother's tall figure strolling across Bond Street towards the other half of Brook Street in the direction of Hanover Square, where he knew Charles would easily pick up a hackney. The idea of spying on his brother was not something Adam contemplated with relish, in fact the whole idea left a rather nasty taste in his mouth, but since this evening's unlooked-for events bore all the signs that something rather dubious was going on, then he could not sit back and simply ignore it. Whatever twinges of conscience smote him as he followed his brother he reconciled it with the palliative that it was not only his duty to do everything possible to prevent a probable disaster befalling them but also to protect his mother from discovering that one of her children had done something which was probably not only outside the law but would ensure the name of Harrington was besmirched forever.

Having no very clear idea of what would happen when their destination was reached or what he would be called upon to do, Adam decided his best course of action was to wait upon events. After following behind at a discreet distance for several minutes, he eventually saw his brother hail a hackney and waiting only until he had climbed inside and the conveyance had turned the corner, Adam quickened his step to where another vehicle had just come into view. He had a very shrewd idea of what was going through the driver's mind when he was told to follow the carriage in front, and from the expression on his face it seemed as if nothing this exciting had happened to him in a long time. Leaning forward in his seat Adam could see they were travelling east along Oxford Street towards Holborn, eventually turning right into Kingsway in the direction of The Strand. He wondered if their destination was perhaps Waterloo, and when they eventually crossed Waterloo Bridge he was sure of it. He was not overly familiar with this part of London but as he looked about him for possible landmarks he saw that the driver was heading down Waterloo Road and could not help wondering where his brother could possibly be going. After a few minutes the pace noticeably slackened and almost immediately the driver turned left, then, after some little way, turned right, where, halfway down, he pulled up outside what was clearly a public house and, turning round, informed his fare that the front vehicle had stopped and the occupant alighted. Adam, doing likewise, asked if he had seen where the passenger had gone and was told, "'E's gawn in *The Black Swan*'. Consumed by curiosity at these stirring events he then asked Adam if he would like him to wait, but upon being told that it was not in the least necessary for him to do so he shook his head, offering a nasal warning to Adam to take care he did not get his pockets felt, pocketing the coin tossed up at him before whipping up his horse and driving away.

The Black Swan', a three-storey building standing on the corner of Birch Street and Dove Walk, bore all the hallmarks of being a hostelry which Adam would never have thought to be the kind of place his brother would patronise, as well as being an establishment every kind of disreputable individual headed for, and was beginning to regret his dismissal of the hackney driver. From what he could make out in the dim light given off from the gas lamps, the immediate area surrounding *The Black Swan*', with its dirty cobbled streets and terraced houses, though run down and shabby, was not as bad as he had at first thought, but the noise blending with the raucous laughter which emanated from within served to heighten the depressive atmosphere which hung over the place.

Outside in the doorway stood a man in a muffler, a pint of beer in one hand and the other fastened around the waist of a woman of unkempt appearance and indeterminate age, whose half-hearted attempts to wriggle free fooled no one. In the middle of the street a group of children were laughing as they teased a stray dog with a stick, only one taking no part in this torment, but standing to one side with a wary eye cocked on the door the of *The Black Swan*'. Adam, looking all about him in dismay, was just about to enter *The Black Swan*' when the boy suddenly darted across the cobbles and pushed past him in an attempt to take a peep behind the smoked glass door, only to be cuffed around the ear by the man in the doorway, his nasal, "Get art of it!" adding to the depressing scene which met Adam's eyes.

The sight of Adam, following hard upon the heels of that other swell, created no small stir. The children, breaking off from their teasing of the dog, who took the opportunity to run away, stared curiously at him before inching nearer in the hope of largesse, and one or two passers-by turned their heads in his direction, wondering what the likes of him was doing here, while the two in the doorway eyed him up and down, the woman startling him with a suggestion that made him shudder and her companion give out a guffaw.

Adam had no need to see the customers of 'The Black Swan' to recognise the type of establishment he had entered, and like Charles he visibly recoiled at the smell of stale beer and tobacco smoke which lingered in the air, the firmly closed windows affording no outlet or relief from either of these offensive odours, quite at a loss to know what could possibly have brought his brother to such a place.

Joe Benbow's customers were used to seeing all manner of people within the precincts of their watering hole, but it was not often they had the pleasure of welcoming someone as well dressed or as obviously well blunted as Adam and, like his brother minutes before, his progress to the bar was rather slow. Dexterously managing to extricate himself from more than one feminine suggestion as to how he could spend his time as well as his money, he finally reached the counter with the sound of their coarse laughter ringing in his ears.

Joe Benbow had spotted Adam's tall figure the moment he had walked in, but, somehow, he did not strike Joe as being a man on the lookout for a bit of the common, nor did he have the appearance of being an officer of the law; which, considering his guest in the cellar, not to mention some of his more illicit activities, would not be at all surprising. A man in his position could not be too careful, mind you, it would take a bit of doing to pull the wool over his eyes! Up to every move on the board he was, even so, it would not do a mite of harm to tread careful. Nudging Albert, busy pulling pints next to him, Joe nodded in the direction of Adam who, at that moment, was trying to evade the faded charms of Annie.

Albert, who had long since come to the conclusion that Joe's more illicit ventures would bring the law in on them sooner or later, eyed the newcomer with a well-trained eye, expertly assessing that this well-breached swell, whoever he was, was no fastener. Like Joe, Albert did not think he had anything to do with the other swell at the moment enjoying the sparse comforts of the cellar, and since nothing else came to mind he could only shrug his ignorance.

Wiping his hands on a grimy towel Joe walked to the end of the counter where Adam had managed to forge a space between two men intent on discussing the rival merits of cocks they had a mind to back in a forthcoming fight. Joe Benbow, a tall, well-built man in his late forties, not only boasted a pair of broad muscular shoulders but a pair of arms with biceps which bore adequate testimony to the fact that he must have been quite a formidable bruiser in his day. The pale grey eyes, running rapidly over Adam, asked him what he wanted in a voice that made it perfectly clear that the likes of him were not welcome in his hostelry.

It had taken no more than a cursory glance around the bar room to see that there was no sign of his brother's tall figure amongst the noisy crowd, and as Adam was unaware of what kind of a relationship existed between Charles and the landlord he had no wish to ask after him and run the risk of spiking his guns at the outset. If Charles was indeed setting plans in motion, then 'The Black Swan' was certainly the place to come if he wanted to hire help, but whether the landlord was a party to it Adam had no idea. If he was, then Adam had no desire to alert him to the fact that he was on to him. On the other hand, if the landlord was innocent of any involvement Adam could see no point in causing an unnecessary stir, which would more than likely bring the law down on him. If his suspicions were correct, then the last thing he wanted was to start a hue and cry, which would clearly lead to questions being asked.

Upon being asked a second time what he wanted, Adam stared at the slightly scarred and weather-beaten face warily eyeing him with barely concealed horror. The mere thought of partaking of refreshment in a place where the bar slops had obviously not been cleaned up for goodness only knew how long and the condition of the glasses could not be trusted, was so repugnant to him that he shuddered. However, it was apparent that the landlord clearly expected him to say something, and after a few seconds of thinking of a suitable reply, offered lamely that he was waiting for someone. Since Joe Benbow failed to see what the likes of him would be doing waiting for someone in his establishment he eyed Adam closer still. Joe did not think he had anything to do with the swell in the cellar, and since the gent who had come in only a few minutes earlier had made no mention of a third party joining him, as well as Albert's expert testimony that he was no fastener, Joe was able to dismiss Adam with a shrug.

So far Joe had managed to avoid a brush with the law, priding himself in keeping one step ahead of them, and he was determined to keep it that way. It had taken him a long time to establish himself and gain the trust of his clientele, and although his dealings would not take too much scrutiny, up to now he had evaded the interest of Bow Street, and that is how he wanted it to remain. He had no objection to accommodating someone in the cellar, but it seemed that Ted Knowles had got himself into pretty queer company, and if his old crony wasn't careful this latest escapade could well turn out nasty. However, Joe did not think there was anything to worry about from this young sprig, even so, he was mightily glad when he saw Adam eventually leave his premises.

Joe would not have felt the same, however, had he have known that far from leaving his disreputable hostelry his unwelcome visitor had merely taken up an observation post across the street. As it was impossible for Charles to just simply disappear, he had to be somewhere inside 'The Black Swan', possibly in a back room or private parlour, but in any case, he would have to come out again and when he did Adam was conveniently situated to see him. By now it was well after quarter to ten but even though the gas lamps gave off only a dim light he could see quite clearly the comings and goings from his vantage point across the street. Fortunately for him his continued presence occasioned no comment, but the frequent necessity of having to dart up an entry between two houses to escape detection was beginning to make him feel like jack-in-the-box. A constant stream of people came and went, leaving Adam in no doubt that 'The Black Swan' was a haunt for all the rougher elements of society. He was quite convinced that Bow Street would most certainly find it a worthwhile experience to pay the landlord a visit, doubtless he associated with every thief and cutthroat in London. By quarter past ten, what had begun as a drizzle a short time ago had turned into a heavy downpour, ensuring that emergence from the entry would mean a thorough soaking, but since no one had arrived or left during the past ten minutes Adam had so far remained reasonably dry, if uncomfortable.

If anyone had told him earlier that he would be standing in a cold and draughty entry keeping vigil on a public house which was suspect to say the least, Adam would not have believed them, and it was only his sense of family duty which kept him there, but by quarter to eleven, with no sign of his brother, he had come to the conclusion that more positive action was required. Whatever Charles was doing in there it was taking the devil of a time, and apart from the fact that Adam was sick and tired of darting in and out of the entry he was growing steadily colder; a little activity therefore would certainly not come amiss. Since he could see little point in entering 'The Black Swan' by way of the front door, which would definitely set the landlord thinking, he decided that his best course of action was to gain entry to the premises through the back entrance. After ensuring that no one was in sight, Adam left his hiding place to make a stealthy reconnaissance of Joe Benbow's backyard.

Chapter Sixteen

Opening his eyes to a pounding head and the uncomfortable sensation of being bound hand and foot, Marcus had a vague recollection of a stunning blow being delivered to the back of his head. He knew it would be useless to attempt to free himself. Whoever had tied his wrists and ankles to the chair had certainly known their business, and other than cutting the ropes there was no possible way they could be worked loose. It was several minutes before his eyes were able to focus clearly, but gradually the mists began to clear and he was able to take stock of his surroundings.

From the looks of it he appeared to be enjoying the bare, cold comforts of a cellar, and unless he was mistaken the ramp which ran from the cracked tiled floor to the flat wooden doors at the top told him he was in the cellar of an ale house. It was quite large, but unfortunately the low ceiling offered no escape for the obnoxious fumes from the oil lamp burning fiercely on the wooden table. Over to his left he could see half a dozen barrels of ale, and around the walls, stacked precariously on top of one another, were numerous kegs of cognac and wine on which he shrewdly guessed no duty had ever been paid. Broken chairs and cooking vessels were strewn untidily wherever there was an available space, giving the impression that everything which no longer had a use eventually found its way here. In one corner, looking in imminent danger of collapsing, a shelf sagged under a formidable array of bottles of all shapes and sizes, their labels long since obliterated with a generous coating of dust. The smell of beer, intermingling with the sickening fumes from the lamp, hung nauseously in the air, the whole scene one of oppressive gloom.

But it seemed that none of these discomforts bothered Ted Knowles, sitting astride a chair opposite him, watching his prisoner with a more than ordinarily close eye. This well-breached swell had given him food for considerable thought, so much so that by the time he entered the cellar he was feeling so belligerent that it would have given him tremendous satisfaction to have dealt with this interfering busybody there and then, but mindful of his client's warning that he was not to lay a finger on him, he had to content himself with venting his spleen in some well-chosen words to the vacant air, none of which made him feel very much better. His jaw still felt extremely tender, not to mention the discomfort of a loose tooth, and it annoyed him beyond bearing to know that the man responsible for both was here in front of him tied to a chair and he could do nothing to him. Davy's blow had certainly ensured that he would be out cold for some considerable time, but Ted Knowles had not expected him to remain unconscious for the better part of two and a half hours and was more than a little relieved when he eventually began to show signs of coming round. It was not only Charles Harrington who would be far from pleased if anything happened to his cousin at this stage of the game, Joe too would not take it kindly to finding himself with a corpse on the premises.

To Ted Knowles's dismay, his prisoner was giving no indication that he was suffering any kind of discomfort from the ropes which bound him to the chair or that his head was throbbing painfully from the blow it had received. Instead, and quite to Ted Knowles's surprise as well as his growing frustration, he remained as calm as though this was an everyday occurrence. In truth, he was hoping that Marcus would try something, that way he could easily excuse any violence on his part, but the only thing he did was to ask for a drink of water.

Eying the glass into which his guard poured the water from the earthenware jug on the table, Marcus was barely able to conceal his distaste, but his mouth was extremely dry and it was with the utmost reluctance that he accepted the unpalatable fact that beggars, unfortunately, could not be choosers. At first Ted Knowles wondered if he was playing off some trick, glancing suspiciously at the prisoner, but one look at that pale face was enough to tell him that he must be feeling like the devil, nevertheless, he felt it wise not to take any chances and it was therefore with extreme caution that he held the glass to Marcus's lips, having to suppress the overwhelming urge to throw it over him.

"Thank you," Marcus said politely. "It was somewhat difficult for me to do myself." Ted Knowles grunted, and Marcus said with the same infuriating ease, "I take it you are the one responsible for my being here and tying me to this chair?" When his guard made no reply, he inclined his head in acknowledgement. "Please, accept my compliments on an excellent piece of work."

Not in the least mollified by this tribute, Ted Knowles merely grunted again, refraining from telling him that it had been no easy matter to carry someone of his height and weight down two flights of narrow stairs before bundling him into a hackney to convey him the short distance to *The Black Swan*', and that the excellent piece of work had taken the efforts of not only himself and Davy but another crony as well.

"You must be getting paid handsomely," Marcus remarked conversationally. "Assault and abduction are very serious offences, not to mention the plans you have hatched for the girl."

Ted Knowles shot him a wary look tinged with loathing, but as the question of abduction had not yet entered into his thoughts, the mention of it clearly disturbed him. Rankled, he snarled, "You shut yer mummer, or I'll shut it fer yer!"

"Taking advantage of a man in my position is hardly fair," Marcus pointed out calmly. "However, I will let that pass and remind you instead of the penalties attached to a crime of this nature. Of course," he added, "you may be aware of them already, but I doubt the man who is paying you will enjoy the sparse comforts of a prison cell."

It was plain that this aspect of the matter had not previously occurred to Ted Knowles, and he was visibly shaken by it. "Wot yer mean?" he asked suspiciously, cocking a wary eyebrow, his heavy jaws working as he considered this.

"I should have thought it was plain enough," his prisoner shrugged, pressing home his advantage. "However, if you are prepared to take the blame as well as the consequences while he remains free of the law, then that is entirely your own affair, but if I were you I should start giving the matter serious thought."

Ted Knowles had never been one to shrink from a task merely because of unpleasant consequences, especially if the money was right, but when he had entered into this affair it had been on the understanding that no repercussions would rebound on himself. His plan had seemed foolproof, but now it was taking on a very different complexion altogether. It was all very well for Charles Harrington to instruct him to go ahead, but now this relative of his was taking a hand in the game things were beginning to look very different indeed, and no more than the next man did he want to face the Queen's Bench let alone having to spend the next few years in a prison cell, if the truth about the girl's so-called accident became known. His prisoner could not possibly know what they had planned for her, but the fact that he had come this far, whether on guesswork or not, certainly proved that he was more than capable of discovering the truth, and once he did that then not only could he say goodbye to his hard-earned reward but most probably his freedom as well. His position was an unenviable one. If he let this man go and rescinded his plans regarding the girl he would have to answer to Charles Harrington, and Ted Knowles was honest enough to admit that he did not relish the kind of retribution he would hand out. On the other hand, if he carried his plans through to the bitter end he could easily find himself answering charges of abduction and conspiring to commit murder, and not one penny of the money promised him would do him a mite of good.

Marcus had a very shrewd notion of the thoughts going around in Ted Knowles's head, and watched in expectant silence while he pondered his predicament, but if Marcus wanted to persuade this obnoxious individual into releasing him it would require very adroit handling. Thick skinned Ted Knowles may be, but a fool he was not, and although it took him a little time to comprehend his prisoner's meaning it gradually began to dawn on him what he was trying to do. A knowing look suddenly entered his eyes, clearly informing Marcus that the doubts he had tried to instil into his mind had fallen wide of the mark, his confident nod of the head signifying that his prisoner would have to get up pretty early to catch him napping! Of course, he appreciated Ingleby's attempts to sway him into releasing him, but he was not so gullible. Charles Harrington had assured him that he would deal with his meddlesome relative himself and then his wife, which meant that he could not possibly be held responsible for what happened to either of them, and as for abduction – why, Ingleby would not be here to lay a charge against anyone! With the fear of the Queen's Bench fast receding, Ted Knowles's habitual buoyancy and confidence returned, and the look of near triumph he threw at Marcus was enough to tell him that his gambit had failed. It had been well worth the try however, but he knew it was pointless in pursuing this tactic, and instead set his mind to other lines of attack.

Unfortunately, his attempt to draw Ted Knowles out about what they had planned for Alexandra and when failed, but that it was imminent was patently obvious. Marcus was still not quite certain where Sophy fitted into the scheme of things but that she formed an integral part of it, he was convinced. He was also convinced that that bogus letter had been a dummy run; but a dummy run for what? And why? His overseer was giving nothing away, but it was his guess that she had been designated to act as a witness of some kind or, failing this, to unwittingly lure Alexandra to a destination for some reason or other. Whether her inclusion had Charles's blessing or not Marcus could not say, but knowing his cousin's dismissive attitude towards her anything was possible.

The pounding in his head was gradually diminishing but his body felt extremely stiff from being in one position for so long, and his wrists, expertly tied behind him to the back of the chair, were exceedingly sore, and his right leg had begun to throb painfully. He had no way of knowing how long he had been here, but it was obvious Ted Knowles had to have help in moving him, and since it would have been somewhat perilous to carry a body through the streets without attracting attention, the indications were that they would have had to convey him here in a hackney or, which was quite possible, they did not have to carry him too far from where he had been brutally knocked out in Knowles's sitting room. But just as Marcus was about to question this enterprising individual he heard a door being opened behind him followed by a firm tread descending the five well-worn stone steps which led down into the cellar. He had no need to be told who had just joined them, but immediately Ted Knowles was on his feet and striding towards him where a brief and low-voiced discussion followed. Marcus could distinguish very little of what was being said, but no sooner had Ted Knowles hurried up the steps and closed the cellar door behind him than he heard Charles walk slowly up to him and, half turning his head, mockingly apologised for not rising to his feet.

"I trust you are not too uncomfortable, Cousin," Charles enquired, eyeing his surroundings with shuddering distaste before flicking dust off the corner of the table with his handkerchief.

"I was beginning to wonder when you would show yourself," Marcus remarked, watching his cousin perch himself on the edge of the table, swinging one elegantly tailored leg back and forth.

"I am sorry if I kept you waiting," Charles ironically apologised, removing his hat and placing it beside him on the table next to his cane, "but I had not anticipated the unexpected pleasure of playing host to you this evening," removing his gloves.

"If it comes to that," Marcus acknowledged, inclining his head, "I had not expected the pleasure of being your guest this evening, but then," he pointed out, "I was not given the opportunity to decline your most novel invitation." He could well imagine his cousin's chagrin upon being told of his involvement in the affair. He knew Charles well enough to say that he would not have been at all pleased in having his hand forced, necessitating the need for him to show himself, and even though he appeared to be his usual calm and poised self it was clear from the tautness around his mouth and the over bright glint in his eyes that he felt very far from both.

It was several moments before Charles spoke, his expression unreadable as he searched Marcus's face. "You know, Cousin," he sighed, "you have put me to *quite* an inconvenience."

"At least I have accomplished something," Marcus acknowledged, no trace of his growing anger visible on his face.

"A minor accomplishment, I assure you," Charles dismissed.

"Indeed!" Marcus exclaimed.

"My dear Marcus," Charles sighed, "you know, you really ought to refrain from meddling in what does not concern you."

"For your sake, or mine?" Marcus asked.

"If I may be permitted to point out," Charles said politely, admirably concealing his annoyance, "*you* are the one ignominiously tied to that chair, not I."

"A minor inconvenience, nothing more," Marcus assured him.

"You are either an optimist or a fool to think so," Charles drawled. "Again, I feel compelled to remind you of certain facts. Since you have elected to involve yourself in my affairs you must therefore accept the consequences of your meddling. Not only has your interference placed you in a most disadvantageous and unenviable position but your efforts, which I assume are to thwart my dastardly schemes," he mocked, "are not only a waste of time but entirely futile. You see, Cousin," he drawled confidently, "apart from myself and Knowles and his equally scurrilous friends upstairs," he pointed out, "no one knows you are here!"

"A trump card indeed!" Marcus smiled, his eyes glinting with a look Charles had never seen before.

Anyone who had served with Major Ingleby, or indeed anyone who knew him well, would have registered the danger signs straightaway, but Charles, a stranger to them, merely ignored them, saying, "I am glad you appreciate that because it will save me the necessity of having to expand on it."

"Your consideration is most touching," Marcus acknowledged sardonically, "but I feel you may find it rather more difficult to rid yourself of me than you anticipate."

"You crow too loudly for a man in your position," Charles told him coldly.

"Nevertheless," Marcus remarked, "you would willingly exchange yours for mine I'll be bound."

"*My* position," Charles told him firmly, "is not irremediable, whereas yours, I am sorry to say, *is*."

"Really!" Marcus exclaimed sceptically. "I should have thought the opposite were true."

"No, no," Charles shook his head, leisurely rising to his feet, surveying his surroundings distastefully, "allow me to disabuse your mind of that at least. You see, Cousin," he said confidently, "by this time tomorrow I shall be rid of a most bothersome obstacle, and little though you may relish the thought there is nothing whatsoever you can do to prevent it. Although," he confessed, "I must own that your involvement had not entered into my calculations."

Well, if nothing else, Marcus at least had the answer to one question! Whatever Charles had in mind it was clearly set for tomorrow, although whether the obstacle he referred to was that codicil in his father's will or the girl herself remained unclear, but if Charles's aim was to overturn that clause or deprive Alexandra of her inheritance then surely none of them would be here now! But vital though it was for Marcus to glean as much information as he could, he was nevertheless forced into frustratingly reassessing his position. If he was going to prevent whatever plan had been hatched from going ahead, because nothing would convince him that Charles's aims where Alexandra was concerned were in any way avuncular, he had to find a way of getting out this cellar, but since he was securely bound hand and foot to this damned chair and Ted Knowles was hovering outside within call of he knew not how many like-minded cronies, it was not going to be easy. "I almost feel as though I should be offering you an apology," Marcus remarked with deceptive politeness.

"There is not the least need," Charles assured him, waving a languid hand. "I am quite prepared to overlook the niceties on this occasion."

"You are too kind," Marcus mocked, making yet another attempt to try to work the ropes loose around his wrists, even though he knew his efforts to be futile.

"Not at all," Charles inclined his head, "after all, good manners cost one nothing, don't you agree?"

"Oh, quite!" Marcus agreed.

"I knew you would understand," Charles replied smoothly, his eyes glinting. "It makes things so much easier, don't you think? Especially when one is to be told of the... er... well, how shall I put it?" He raised a satirical eyebrow. "The fate that awaits them."

"I am all eagerness to know the fate that awaits me," Marcus remarked. "Although," he pointed out, "I think I can hazard a very good guess as to what you have in mind."

Charles eyed his cousin speculatively. "You always were astute, Marcus," he acknowledged, "but you will have to forgive me when I say that it is a trait I have never appreciated, and never more so than now when I consider your interference."

"I didn't think you would," Marcus smiled with infuriating calm.

"I am glad it affords you amusement," Charles commented coldly. "Enjoy it while you may."

"You know, Charles," Marcus mused, "I really had no idea you possessed a turn for the dramatic."

Whatever it was Charles had been about to say he clearly thought better of it. "I don't, but I do possess a strong sense of self-preservation, which your arrival on the scene has somewhat jeopardised, and to which I take great exception. It has become expedient therefore, to remove you. Regrettable, of course," he smiled thinly, "but quite necessary."

Marcus eyed his cousin for several moments, realising for the first time just how ruthless he actually was and that whatever had brought him to this point it was decidedly far more serious than he had ever supposed. Charles may have experienced more than one financial crisis in his life, but in the end he had always known that his father would come to his rescue even if that assistance ultimately carried Sophy as the price tag. But only sheer desperation could have driven him to the point where he was prepared to take such monumental risks. Marcus did not need Charles to enter into precise details about what he had planned for him, he knew as well as his cousin that to release him would be an act of gross stupidity, especially as he could not afford to allow any of this to become public knowledge, which surely proved beyond any doubt that the obstacle he had spoken of was Alexandra. "You will forgive my curiosity, I know," Marcus said conversationally, playing for much-needed time, "but am I permitted to enquire how you intend to achieve my removal?"

"By all means," his cousin replied affably, "after all, it is the least I can do." A cloud descended onto his forehead as if a thought had suddenly occurred to him, and when he eventually spoke his voice was silky smooth, but Marcus was quick to note the underlying irritation Charles was not quite able to suppress. "I promise you, Cousin, I have every intention of doing so, after all," he shrugged, "how very ill-mannered it would be of me not to, but before I do so I should be most interested to learn what alerted you to my... er... plans? You see," he told him simply, "I laid them so very carefully. I left nothing to chance."

"Why, *you* did, Charles!" Marcus told him calmly, shocking his cousin into stunned silence.

"*I* did!" he repeated when he had overcome his astonishment, momentarily forgetting his wife's involvement in his affairs, but it was noticeable that some of his self-confidence had deserted him. "How?" he asked warily.

"You know, Charles," Marcus pointed out conversationally, "it has been

306

my experience that if you do not wish anything to become known you keep it to yourself."

Charles's eyes narrowed, fearing a trap, but felt impelled to ask, "In what way did I betray myself?"

"By the simple means of allowing your temper to override your judgement." Marcus waited only long enough to see the effect this had on his cousin. "Had you not been so vehement in expressing your sentiments regarding your father's will or voiced your dislike of Alexandra beyond what was naturally expected, I should have been none the wiser, and certainly not here now bound hand and foot to this chair." When Charles made no reply to this, Marcus continued, "Of course, your biggest mistake was making such an issue of Elizabeth's jewellery. Had you not have done so I doubt very much if I would have suspected anything at all."

Charles had turned quite pale at this, but managing to regain sufficient command over his voice, said, "This is nothing but guesswork."

"Until now, yes," Marcus acknowledged. "Unfortunately for you, however, my being here merely confirms those suspicions as fact. My visit to your enterprising accomplice was nothing more than a shot in the dark, but the very fact that he found it necessary to bring me here after I had been knocked senseless from behind, proves beyond doubt something is going on and that he is implicated in your plans and afraid I shall discover what they are."

Marcus may not have mentioned Sophy by name and her visit to him with that letter but Charles knew perfectly well that without her interference all of this could have been avoided, certainly his cousin could never have connected him with anything no matter how strong his suspicions. Now though, he was facing an entirely different situation altogether and found his anger and resentment equally divided between Marcus and his wife.

Charles had a lot to thank Sophy for! Until her visit to Marcus with that incriminating letter followed by his visit to Knowles, he had been simply turning things over in his mind, certainly he had nothing on which he could accuse him. Marcus may suspect him of anything he liked but no court of law would condemn anyone without sufficient evidence. But now, thanks to his wife's meddlesome interference and that inept and bungling Knowles, his future prospects were beginning to take on a very different outlook. Obviously, Knowles had lost his head and panicked and even though Marcus still had no idea what was planned for the girl he knew enough to be dangerous. From the moment Knowles had told him of Marcus's visit and the charade which followed, Charles had known immediately that he could not afford to let him go free. He knew his cousin too well to think his silence could be bought, and since he was determined to do everything possible to prevent his plans from going ahead Charles was faced with little choice but to deal with Marcus in the only way which would guarantee his silence. It was of course regrettable that he found it necessary to adopt such drastic measures, but when faced with the damning consequences of denunciation it was certainly expedient. Charles may have no love for his cousin, even less so now when he thought of his connection with Sophy, but nevertheless he was honest enough to admit that if any other solution presented itself he would gladly take it. He had no need to be told the seriousness of his situation or the enormity of what he was contemplating for Marcus, and should it ever become known that he had instigated the death of his niece as well as his cousin the consequences would be damning.

Charles position was certainly awkward. If he spared the girl now he would be faced with the consequences of explaining away the fake items of jewellery as well as the condemnation of his family and friends, and the scandal which would ensue was too horrendous to contemplate. On the other hand, if he went ahead with his plans it would mean that he would have to deal with Marcus, and since he could not be bought or persuaded into turning a blind eye, much less going along with it, it really did seem that only one option was open to him. Whichever way Charles looked at it he was in too deep to withdraw now, but if he played his cards right he had every reason to believe that no repercussions would rebound on himself. Surely, if one accident could be arranged, so too could another! After all, no one knew anything about his plans for Alexandra except himself, Ted Knowles and his crony, and although Marcus was still in the dark as to precisely what he had in mind for her it was safe to assume that no one knew of his visit to Ted Knowles or that he was now safely tucked up in Joe Benbow's cellar. Charles could only hazard a guess as to whether Sophy knew of his cousin's visit to Knowles, but since she would soon be brought to mind him better in the future he did not allow himself to worry unduly over this. As for the rest, Charles had no doubt at all that the landlord of this disreputable establishment would have no objections to housing his guest for a while longer, at least until after tomorrow! It really was a constant source of comfort to him to know that his faith in human nature had not erred. How easily people would sell themselves for the right price!

His irrevocable course being set, Charles could breathe more easily, confident that nothing now could possibly interfere with his plans. He knew without question that Ted Knowles and his cronies would not be averse to undertaking one more task, and even more certain that they would keep their mouths shut. The likes of Ted Knowles may be proud, even eager, to display their talents, but Charles knew too that they would not want them to come under the watchful eye of Bow Street. Having assured himself of total anonymity and that there was no possibility of him being implicated in anything, he eyed his cousin thoughtfully, then, with a return to his drawled confidence, said, "You have been greatly inconvenienced, Cousin, but you really have only yourself to blame."

Charles's resurgence of self-assurance was not lost on Marcus, but since it behoved him to do all he could to extricate himself from his manacled position he drew a bow at a venture. "I am glad you have confidence in your accomplice. I can, of course, only speculate as to what it is that has brought you to the point where you feel you need to embark on such a drastic course of action, but whatever it is, it is clearly of the utmost importance to you, and this being so," he smiled, "I would say that Knowles is hardly the type of man to be relied upon. If he were," he pointed out reasonably, "he would not have lost his head and I should not be here now."

But Charles was not going to be provoked so easily. He realised what his cousin was attempting to do and was not unappreciative of his efforts, but the time had come to end any hopes he may have of being released. "Do not waste your eloquence," he advised, "it will not serve you. My plans are far too advanced to be rescinded now."

"Am I allowed to ask what these plans are," Marcus asked with sardonic politeness, "and why you have found it necessary to go to all these lengths merely to persuade the girl into relinquishing her claim on your father's will, which, I assume," he shrugged, desperately trying to discover what he had planned for Alexandra, "is what all this is about?"

The look he encountered was unmistakable. It told him more than any words could have, but it shocked him to the very core of his being. Having discounted the theory that Charles was hoping to buy the girl off on the grounds of lack of funds, Marcus had failed to come up with another one other than that his cousin was probably trying to talk the girl into accepting something which fell far short of her inheritance. As this in turn had raised the question of where Sophy fitted into it, he had been forced to admit that he had no satisfactory explanation whatsoever to account for her inclusion. It had at one point crossed his mind that Charles, knowing Alexandra's hostility towards her family and to himself especially, had realised that he would be the last person she would wish to talk to and by arranging that meeting between her and Sophy he was allowing his wife to persuade the girl into meeting him with a view to discussing his father's bequest to her. Plausible though this theory was it too had been discarded, if for no other reason than if Charles simply meant to talk to the girl he would not have found it necessary to deceive Sophy by sending her that bogus letter arranging an equally bogus appointment. The same went for Ted Knowles.

Had he been simply employed as a bona fide agent then there would have been no need for him to have reacted to his own visit in the way he did, resulting in him being hit senseless from behind before bringing him here.

However, in view of his cousin's announcement regarding the dire plans he had in store for him, Marcus had briefly wondered whether Charles had arranged for the girl to be kept hidden somewhere until she relinquished her claim on his father's will or perhaps even be shipped abroad somewhere to disappear without trace, after all this would not be too difficult a task, but at no time had he ever so much as thought that Charles meant to harm the girl. But that one look had proved beyond any doubt that this was precisely what he intended, and from what he had already told him it was planned for tomorrow.

More than most did Marcus know of Charles's dread of scandal, and yet here he was on the very brink of creating one, the repercussions of which would far surpass anything which had brought him to this point in the first place. In his desperation to save himself from humiliation and disgrace he would doubtless be prepared to take any number of risks, and although Charles could only hazard a guess as to how much he knew, it did not take much intelligence to realise that his cousin could not afford to allow him to leave here and jeopardise everything he was striving for by reporting his findings to the police.

Never having made the error of underestimating his cousin, Marcus had always believed that if ever Charles found himself in a corner he would be a most dangerous man. When he had cautioned Adam about not letting Charles know that he had come under suspicion he had not exaggerated, but it came as a profound shock to discover that not only had he grossly underrated his cousin but had misread his own instincts. Marcus was to doubt them even more as he listened in appalled silence to Charles outlining his plans for the girl's demise, growing ever more frustratingly aware of the impotence of his position and the futility of trying to free himself. He had known from the outset that Charles could not afford to let him go and run the risk of him reporting his intentions to Silas Jenkins or the authorities as either would be enough to denounce him, but it now looked certain that Charles was fully intending to honour him with a similar fate to that which clearly awaited Alexandra, but it was extremely doubtful whether it would be carried out here. The landlord of 'The Black Swan' may be disreputable but he would not be such a fool as to have a death on his hands, and therefore it was almost certain he would be moved to his place of execution.

"What is it, Cousin?" Charles enquired politely, when he had come to the end of his description of forthcoming events, considering his cousin's shocked faced. "You seem to be experiencing a little difficulty."

"Good God!" Marcus exclaimed at last. "You must be mad!"

"No," Charles mused, as if giving this his full consideration. "I see no reason why you should think I might be."

"You don't seriously expect to get away with this?" Marcus demanded incredulously.

"Oh, but I do," Charles replied with unimpaired calm. "In fact, I foresee no contingency to expect otherwise." He smiled, a cold and cynical parting of the lips which sent a shiver down Marcus's spine. "Of course," he pointed out, "I was at first in quite a dilemma as to how to set about disposing of the girl without incriminating myself – a most important consideration you understand," he inclined his head, "but once having done so all that remained was to ensure that the tragic accident which would befall her should be seen as being precisely that." He saw the look of horror on Marcus's face and, quite unmoved by it, commented dispassionately, "I realise, of course," he shrugged, "that accidents come in all guises, but one *does* have to be realistic; after all, it would not do to arrange a 'questionable' accident, and who knows better than you and I, Cousin," he remarked matter-of-factly, "how horses are prone to shy at the least provocation. It has always seemed to me somewhat incomprehensible how the most docile of them can suddenly bolt for no apparent reason." He eyed his cousin speculatively for a moment or two before pointing out practically, "Of course, one must feel some sympathy for the poor man who is trying to bring the terrified animal under control. It can be no easy matter to negotiate a busy thoroughfare with an untried horse. Only think of his dilemma and the futility of attempting to steer a bolting animal away from the hapless victim standing immobile with fright on the pavement! A terrible thing to happen to one, don't you agree?" he raised an eyebrow. "But, after all," he sighed mournfully, "even a poor hackney driver has to earn a living." After subjecting his surroundings to another contemptuous review, he brought his gaze back to rest on his cousin. "You do realise of course, that your stay here will have to be extended, but that you are here at all is quite your own fault. You see, Cousin," he reproved on a deep sigh, "not only have you made it necessary for me to come to a place which is really not at all to my taste, but you have forced me into taking an action which is not only outside of my calculations but really quite repugnant to me."

Marcus raised a sceptical eyebrow at this, commenting sardonically, "I suppose you would have preferred it if I had merely sat back and let you get on with it."

"Infinitely!" Charles agreed. "But as I have already pointed out, this habit you have of seeing far more than is good for one is really quite irritating and one, moreover, which has not only placed you in a most disagreeable position but has rendered it prudent for me to embark upon a course which I would much rather have not."

"I suppose I should be grateful for your reluctance," Marcus mocked.

"Yes, I think you should," Charles replied, giving the matter some thought.

"Well, since my days are obviously numbered," Marcus shrugged fatalistically, "would it be too much to ask if you could enlighten me as to why you found it necessary to use Elizabeth's jewellery in the first place?"

"Not at all," Charles replied affably, "after all, it is the least I can do, especially when I consider all the effort you have expended on the girl's behalf."

But his dispassionately delivered recital, instead of stirring his cousin's sympathy only served to confirm his belief as to just how cold and determined Charles actually was. Marcus found it incredible that the purchasing of some amatory correspondence had resulted in the planning and imminent execution of a cunningly contrived accident. He was not entirely sure which sickened him the most; Charles's apparent lack of concern over bringing about the death of a girl whose only crime was to be made a beneficiary in her grandfather's will or his total lack of remorse. "And all this because of a few paltry letters!" Marcus shook his head, his voice echoing his disbelief.

"Oh, I should hardly call five thousand pounds paltry, Marcus!" Charles cried, aghast.

"It makes no difference what you call it," Marcus told him. "It is certainly not worth a girl's life! Surely to God you can see that?"

Apparently, he could not. "So, you must see, Marcus," Charles shrugged, "there is no way I can allow the girl to take possession of the jewellery. Once that collection is removed from its hiding place it will not be long before the deception is discovered, and I shall be utterly disgraced."

"Rather that," Marcus returned coldly, "than the girl's death on your hands!"

"Well, I daresay that must depend upon one's point of view," Charles replied matter-of-factly, "and, of course, the weight of one's purse."

"You must have been desperate indeed to have embarked upon such a course," Marcus remarked.

"I was," Charles nodded. "The cost of literary endeavour it seemed was more than I had bargained for. Suffice it to say," he commented, "I have not made the same mistake again!"

For the past half hour and more Marcus had been conscious of an ever-growing desire to inflict pugilistic punishment on his cousin, but as this wish for the moment could not be fulfilled his impotence to carry it out merely served to exacerbate his frustration. It was seldom he felt such anger as he did now, and it took him a little time to convince himself that this was not the moment to let his feelings override his common sense. If this mess was to be resolved and without creating the devil of a stir, then it could only be achieved with a clear head and not one clouded by anger and disgust.

He had always known that Charles was no fool, on the contrary he was most astute, but it had occurred to him that in his cousin's determined efforts to stave off exposure he had totally lost sight of the inevitable consequences resulting from his plans. Whether they were successful or not Charles was certainly putting himself at risk by the associates he had employed to assist him. They may not be any too eager to come to the notice of Bow Street, but they would know that Charles would not be either, and therefore he was laying himself wide open for blackmail. Should his plans fail he faced certain exposure once the jewellery was in Alexandra's hands as Marcus felt it reasonably safe to assume that her dislike of Charles would be more than enough to prompt her into taking the matter further, which would doubtless be followed up by a none too pleasant court case and a probable prison sentence following hard upon its heels. If his plans succeeded, then he stood in very real danger of being blackmailed by his confederates in return for their silence and should Charles refuse to pay the chances were very good that they could well inform against him anonymously to the authorities, ensuring the blame fell entirely on his shoulders. The police would, out of necessity, investigate the allegations put forward against him which would inevitably lead to Charles facing his trial, not for inciting or conspiring to commit murder which would bring a sentence of penal servitude in its wake but for murder, in which case no power on earth could prevent him from going to the gallows. Whichever way it went there would be no stopping the scandal which followed and the name of Harrington would be damned forever.

Alexandra did not deserve what Charles had planned for her any more than his aunt deserved the condemnation of her world or the ostracism of society, and Marcus was therefore determined to do all he could to protect them both, and if this meant trying to placate Charles into rescinding his plans he was quite prepared to do it. If he could persuade his cousin into allowing him to redeem those two pieces of jewellery on his behalf and to cancel his plans for tomorrow, then he would guarantee never to speak of it to anyone, but when this suggestion was put forward, it was instantly rebuffed. "Don't be a fool, Charles!" Marcus urged. "It is not too late.

Forget these plans of yours and accept my offer. For once in your life can't you swallow your damned pride?"

Charles, who had all this time been contemplating the tip of his cane, looked up at this, but the look in his eyes told Marcus that his plea as well as his offer were as unwelcome as they were unwanted. "Your generosity is overwhelming, Cousin," he drawled, "but you will have to forgive me when I say that I am not wholly convinced that your motive is entirely altruistic." After removing a speck of dust from his sleeve he pointed out, "You seem to be labouring under a misapprehension, several in fact. In the first instance, not only am I determined to prevent the girl from having the jewellery, for reasons which I have already made abundantly plain," he inclined his head, "but the mere thought of her receiving thirty thousand pounds plus the added indignity of having her reside in Brook Street is so repugnant to me that I am quite prepared to do anything to prevent such a dreadful prospect. No, no, Cousin," he shook his head when he saw the effect these words had on Marcus, "I can see how you would dearly love to plant me a facer, but I am afraid you will have to content yourself with wishful thinking."

"You hate the girl that much?" Marcus asked, astonished.

"You will never know how much," Charles stated simply. "For my mother even to contemplate housing a brat from the gutter is quite beyond my comprehension, indeed," he shrugged, "I am quite surprised by her stubborn insistence in this matter."

"I pity you," Marcus told him sincerely.

"An emotion entirely wasted on me, I assure you," Charles dismissed.

"So I see," Marcus nodded. "Although why I should have expected otherwise I don't know, after all you have certainly exhibited none where Sophy is concerned. To put her through the ordeal of witnessing such a terrible accident is an act of sheer cold-bloodedness!"

Charles's eyes glinted dangerously and his voice was ominously smooth. "Ah yes, Sophy," he mused. "I am glad you have mentioned her, Cousin, because it brings me to one of those other misapprehensions I spoke of. Much as it pains me, I do have to confess to being extraordinarily obtuse where the two of you are concerned."

How Charles had discovered what they had both tried so hard to hide Marcus did not know, perhaps Ted Knowles had picked up on something during his scurrilous dealings on his cousin's behalf, but he was not sorry it was out in the open at last. Even so, Marcus had to do all he could to protect Sophy from her husband's anger. "I am not going to lie to you by saying I don't love Sophy, I do, more than you could possibly know, but she has never betrayed you."

Charles's lips thinned, but he held onto his temper. "It really makes no difference," he shook his head. "Sophy is *my* wife and will remain so – until death do us part."

"Even though you don't love her!" Marcus bit out.

"Love!" Charles scorned. "My dear Marcus, what on earth has that to do with it? I am her husband, and once you are no longer around to distract her not only will Sophy learn to mind me better but behave in a manner which befits my wife."

"My premature exit will serve two purposes therefore," Marcus acknowledged.

Charles bowed. "Precisely!" Then, as if bethinking himself of something, said, "I daresay you are wondering how I know about you and Sophy. It is not, I am ashamed to say, through any awareness of mine, you were most careful there, were you not?" he pointed out. "But you see, Cousin, what my charming wife failed to realise was that her movements today were observed. You may disparage my friend Knowles," he told him, "but you must confess that in this at least he outwitted you." Without waiting for Marcus to respond to this, he continued, "Of course, as soon as he told me about Sophy's visit to an establishment in Knightsbridge immediately following her fruitless wait in Regents Park, I knew instantly whose house it was, the same as I knew that you had later recognised the handwriting as being that of Knowles." His eyes narrowed as he looked down at his cousin, his voice dangerously thin. "It was a pity he had not got round to disposing of those practise sheets," he shrugged, "really quite careless of him, but had you not elected to involve yourself in my affairs the urgency for him to do so would not have arisen any more than he would have found it necessary to take an action which, regrettably, leaves you in a most unfortunate position." His lips compressed into a thin ugly line. "It seems you and Sophy have been extremely busy of late regarding my affairs."

"Sophy knows nothing of this," Marcus assured him. "She merely sought advice; advice for which she knew she could not apply to you."

"I have no doubt at all that your advice was admirable," Charles mockingly inclined his head, "but your part in this affair has come to an end. However," he raised an eyebrow, "there *is* one thing you have not explained."

"Really?" Marcus enquired, raising a questioning eyebrow. "And what might that be?"

"Only that I should be interested to learn what it was that put you onto Knowles."

Not wishing to involve Silas Jenkins, Marcus merely eyed his cousin steadily. "Let us just say," he shrugged, "the fact that I did so merely goes to prove how unreliable an accomplice he is."

Had Charles been given more time in which to extricate himself from his predicament he would most certainly not have applied to Ted Knowles for assistance, nevertheless, he doubted even he would have been stupid enough to advertise his interest in this affair and, totally acquitting Sophy on the very practical grounds that she had never even heard of him, Charles was left with nothing but conjecture. He may not know of that meeting between his cousin and Silas Jenkins, but having recognised a long time ago that Marcus saw far more than was good for one, there was no telling what he had picked up or from whom, but since his cousin was clearly not going to enlighten him, Charles bit down his impatience and merely shrugged, saying, "Very well, have it your way if it affords you amusement, not that it really matters because you are going nowhere to tell anyone anything." Marcus merely nodded his head in acknowledgement, which considerably rankled his cousin, but once again Charles bit down on the anger rising inside him, saying, with more calmness than he felt, "Your er... what shall I call it? Ah yes, your untimely end will not only ensure that but it will serve the purpose where Sophy is concerned. Unfortunately," he remarked, picking up his hat and gloves, "I shall have to delay your very necessary fate for the time being. As you will no doubt appreciate, I have a lot of calls upon my time at this present, but fear not, Cousin," he smiled thinly, "I shall not forget you are here."

"I never thought for a moment that you would," Marcus inclined his head.

It seemed for a moment that Charles was going to say something, but instead he put on his hat and gloves and, after picking up his cane, slowly walked away, pausing only briefly to turn round before ascending the steps and tapping his cane on the door, in answer to which it was hurriedly unlocked and, without a backward glance, he left the cellar.

His anxious wait over, Ted Knowles looked hopefully up into his client's face, the grimness around his mouth not lost on him, and wondered what had passed between the cousins, but as it was clear he was not going to be told, he waited instead for his instructions. It was disheartening to know that for the time being at least he was to do no more than keep an eye on the prisoner, and to ensure that no one other than himself or Joe go anywhere near him. Ted Knowles may be longing to pay Marcus back for that brutal attack on his jaw, but he was not so unsympathetic to the fact that he may by now be hungry, as he was himself, and ventured to ask what he should do about it.

"By all means take him something," Charles dismissed, adding with wry humour, "after all, a condemned man is usually granted a last meal. By the way," he drawled as though a thought had just occurred to him, "I would strongly recommend you take that fellow Benbow with you. My cousin it seems, is more than a match for you." On this parting shot he turned on his heel, striding leisurely down the dim and dusty passageway which led to the front of the premises, his whole bearing patently contemptuous of not only his surroundings but the company he was being obliged to keep.

Since nothing was to happen to the guest in the cellar for the time being, Ted Knowles deemed it about time he quenched his thirst with a drop or two of Joe's best brown ale, after all he had more than deserved a little something, especially after what he had been through tonight! Before settling down to enjoy Joe's hospitality though, he thought it best to make sure Ingleby was still securely tied to the chair, but one look was enough to tell him that he would not be going anywhere, and it was therefore with a clear conscience that Ted Knowles locked the cellar door and hurried along the passageway to Joe's cosy little parlour in Charles's wake, deciding to let his prisoner wait for something to eat a little longer. Besides, it would not do him any harm to ponder his future. It was surprising what an empty stomach would do!

Charles, having turned round upon hearing the bolt of the cellar door being shot, was confident that his cousin would be secure enough until he had time to consider his fate; in the meantime, however, he was only too eager to shake off his surroundings as quickly as possible. It was perhaps as well that Charles had no idea that at the precise moment he stepped out of the front door onto the pavement Adam had just slid unobtrusively into Dove Walk, the brothers missing sight of one another by seconds.

Chapter Seventeen

Adam's emergence from the entry having gone unnoticed, he darted across the street with one eye fixed firmly on the front door of 'The Black Swan', and as no one appeared on the scene to mar his progress he was more than relieved to have successfully scaled the first hurdle in his reconnaissance of the premises. Unfortunately, the one and only gas lamp located on the corner of Birch Street and Dove Walk, a dingy side street that ran parallel to the side of 'The Black Swan' which served as delivery access for the dray, to which the evidence on the cobbles testified, was only bright enough to give a good light for a couple of feet all the way round until the next gas lamp several hundred yards further down Dove Walk, which opened out onto what appeared at this distance to be a more frequented road. Turning into Dove Walk, he began to walk down the grimy street, soon out of the light's orbit and into almost total darkness. From his preliminary survey, it seemed there was no easy access into the back yard of 'The Black Swan', and on first looking at that ten-foot high wall which ran nearly the whole length of Dove Walk Adam knew that even for one of his height it was not going to be easy to scale, especially with that row of coping stones running all along the top.

By now he was soaking wet, but the rain, which had not abated, at least ensured that no one would be likely to venture out from any of the run-down terraced houses opposite, and even though no one had entered this back street from either end he kept well within the wall, his dark overcoat providing adequate camouflage. He had no precise idea what he would do once he had gained access much less what he would find, but with characteristic optimism he decided to wait and see what came along. All he was certain of was that Charles had come here for a reason, and whatever that reason was it was taking the devil of a time to deal with. To Adam's way of thinking 'The Black Swan' was most definitely not the kind of hostelry his brother would ordinarily patronise, but obviously he had found it necessary to come here tonight, and this visit, following hard on the heels of his unexpected visitor earlier not to mention cancelling his engagement with Sir Michael Overton, had to mean something, convincing Adam that his own surreptitious entry was vital. Of course, what he would say or do should he run across his brother inside was another matter; trying to explain away his reason for following him would no doubt be as difficult as it would be embarrassing.

The force of the rain and the inadequate light rendered visibility poor, and it was several minutes before he could accurately make out that the dark shadow just ahead of him was in fact a beer barrel. At any other time, Adam would have questioned the reason for it being left outside the yard, especially in such close proximity to the padlocked gates, but he was far too relieved to find such a conveniently placed piece of apparatus to hand, which meant it should be a fairly simple matter for him to scale the wall, providing of course it would take his weight. Unfortunately, his problem was not knowing what was on the other side, but as there was nothing else for it but to trust to luck he could only hope that he would have a clear and unimpeded descent. After another searching look up and down the street to ensure he was quite alone, he tested the ability of the barrel to take his weight by placing his hands on the top and pressing down with all his strength, relieved to find that it was sturdy enough for what he wanted. Having moved it a few feet further away from the gates he was easily able to climb on to its flat round surface to enable him to peer all around the dark recesses of Joe Benbow's back yard, but although Adam's vantage point gave him a clear view in all directions there was no way he could see into the far shadows, but if nothing else he could at least make out that there was nothing at the base of the wall to obstruct his descent. Darting a quick look up and down the street to make sure it was still deserted, he strategically placed his hands on top of the wall, carefully avoiding the coping stones, before heaving himself up to allow him to throw one leg then the other over the wall, hanging quite still for some moments in order to listen for any sound which would signal he was not alone, but as none came to his ears he let go of the wall to drop the several feet which separated him from the ground, dusting himself off before peering into the gloom all around him.

It was some little time before his eyes accustomed themselves to the darkness all around him, but gradually he was able to see his path to the back door, thanking Providence that Joe Benbow had not seen fit to set a dog to guard the rear of the premises. Moving stealthily forward, carefully avoiding the empty barrels, packing cases and piles of rubbish which had been scattered all over the yard without any kind of order, Adam hurried past the securely padlocked doors covering the ground entrance to the cellar to where half a dozen stone steps led up to the back door, disheartened but not at all surprised to discover it was firmly locked against him. As forcing an entry was impossible, he descended the steps to stand looking up at the rear of the premises in order for him to obtain a wider view in case another mode of entry presented itself, but as the only two windows he could see were out of reach and quite unattainable, he had to try to find another way in.

It was while he was studying the layout and considering how best to gain entry that he was suddenly jerked out of his absorption by the sound of scraping bolts being pulled back followed by the turning of a key in the lock, both of which sounded abnormally loud in the night's stillness. Having already considered the possibility of someone seeking to gain access to the yard at this late hour as unlikely, it came as something of a surprise to realise that this was precisely what was happening and immediately Adam began to look around him for a suitable hiding place, taking refuge in the dark recess where the side wall of the steps met the wall of the building, pinning himself flat against it. Holding his breath as he waited to see who came out, he eventually saw a small wiry figure walk down the steps carrying what looked to be a crate stuffed with bottles, instantly recognising the man the landlord had addressed as Albert striding across to the far end of the yard until he reached what looked to be a lean-to. Stepping away from the wall to stretch his head out sufficiently for him to see what Albert was doing, it was with relief that Adam saw his back was turned towards him as he made room to stack the crate securely and so, without any hesitation, he decided to take the opportunity unexpectedly offered him and, with lightning speed, raced silently up the steps and into 'The Black Swan'.

Having succeeded in gaining entry, he found himself in a dimly lit and narrow passageway with solid doors on either side. He knew the one on the left to be the cellar, but as Albert would most probably notice the bolt had been pulled back Adam had to find another hiding place. As he had no way of knowing who or what he would find behind the other door he had little choice but to slip into the narrow recess immediately to his left at the side of the back door, almost falling over a mop and bucket which had been left there. After what seemed like an eternity but was in fact only a couple of minutes, the sound of footsteps approaching met his ears and knew Albert was coming back, pressing himself as far into the shadow of the recess as he could. It was while Adam was pressed against the wall that he saw with horror his wet footprints on the floor, coming to an abrupt halt almost where he was standing and could only hope that in the dim light Albert would not notice them. He did not, but to Adam it seemed to take him an extraordinarily long time to lock and bolt the door behind him. Not until his footsteps had retreated down the passageway and the door leading to the front of the premises had been closed behind him did Adam leave the recess, carefully looking in the direction Albert had gone to ensure there was no possibility of him returning, then, quietly walking down the passageway towards the cellar, he silently pulled back the bolt before turning the key which was still in the lock, opening the door with his shoulder pressed firmly against it to reduce any scraping on the stone floor. He had no precise idea what he would find, but whatever it was it was certainly not to see his cousin tied to a chair, and the sight of Marcus, securely bound hand and foot, came as a considerable shock, exclaiming incredulously, *"Marcus!"*

Upon hearing the bolts being pulled back and the key turned in the lock followed by the door being pushed open, Marcus automatically assumed that Ted Knowles had returned, but upon hearing his cousin's voice he turned his head as if to convince himself he was not imagining it, momentarily as shocked as Adam. *"Adam!"*

"What in God's name...!" Adam exclaimed, not stopping to descend the stairs but vaulting over the rail, hurrying forward.

"I don't know what it is that brings you here," Marcus told him immensely relieved, "but thank God you are!"

Adam's eyes started from their sockets as he stared down at his cousin, looking as stunned as he felt. Several times he opened his mouth to speak but nothing came out, and it was not until Marcus said, "Just get me out of this damned chair!" was he jolted out of his stupor. Having assured himself that he had not stepped into a nightmare, questions began to pour off Adam's tongue as he searched hurriedly around the cellar for something suitable to cut the ropes, but as nothing came to hand he resorted to picking up the jug sitting on the table and smashing it on the floor, the sound almost deafening in the confined space of the cellar as the shattered pieces scattered everywhere. Marcus, keeping an eye on the door, could only hope that the sound of the jug breaking would not be heard above the noise coming from the bar room, but as no one came in he gave Adam the all clear before demanding to be told what had brought him here. Without looking up from his efforts on the ropes around Marcus's wrists he gave him a brief if rather disjointed account of the evening's events.

"I can imagine Charles's reaction to a visit from Ted Knowles," Marcus commented, failing to see who else his cousin's uninvited visitor could have been, continuing to keep one eye on the door while Adam continued to work on the ropes, his prehistoric tool proving rather unwieldy.

"Who's Ted Knowles?" Adam enquired, relieved to find that his strenuous efforts were beginning to take effect.

"Ted Knowles," Marcus explained, "is not only the most unscrupulous individual I have ever encountered, but unless I miss my guess he was Charles's unexpected visitor, apart from which," he further explained on a sharp intake of breath as Adam gave a final tug to the frayed rope around his wrists, "he is not only responsible for my being here but also to ensure that I remain so." Feeling the final tug of the ropes, it was with relief that he was at last able to flex his arms.

"Are you saying that Charles came here because this man Knowles informed him he had you tied up in this place?" Adam asked incredulously.

"Yes, I'm afraid so," Marcus nodded.

Adam swallowed, eyeing his cousin closely. "Just *what* is going on, Marcus?" he demanded, beginning to work on the ropes around his ankles.

Since Adam was unaware of the true state of affairs Marcus was by no means happy to have to be the one to inform him of what Charles had got himself into, but at the same time he had a right to know. But the cellar of an unsavoury ale house was not the place to make such a disclosure, besides which, Ted Knowles could return at any minute. "Unfortunately," Marcus told him, "there is no time for explanations. It's my guess Knowles has only gone for a drink and could be back any minute. If we are going to prevent a tragedy from taking place we have got to get out of here fast."

Adam looked up into his cousin's face, his own troubled and questioning as he demanded, "What do you mean, a tragedy?"

"Not now, Adam," Marcus shook his head. "Just get that rope cut so we can get out of here!"

It seemed at first as if Adam was going to argue the point, but upon being assured that everything would be explained later he resumed his work on the ropes until they finally gave way. It was with tremendous relief that Marcus was finally able to stand on his own two feet, taking a few moments to walk around the confined, if cluttered, space to get the circulation moving and to try to ease the throbbing in his leg.

Adam, who was by no means satisfied at being kept in the dark, asked tentatively, "Is your being here Charles's doing?"

Marcus took a moment or two to answer, but felt he owed his cousin something for arriving just in time. "Yes," he nodded. "I'm sorry, Adam."

Adam hesitated before pointing out, "I have a right to know, Marcus. This is my brother we're talking about."

"I realise that," Marcus acknowledged, "and I promise you I shall tell you everything, but not here. We have already lingered too long as it is. At any moment Knowles or one of his cronies could come back here; we do not have any time for talking."

With this Adam had to be satisfied and, after nodding his head, strode over to the steps and, taking them in two, stood with his ear to the cellar door to listen for any sound. When none came he gave his cousin the all clear. "Looks like we've got a clear run," he whispered. "Think you'll be all right climbing over that side wall?"

"Just show me the way," Marcus smiled, coming up beside him.

To their relief the door at the far end of the passageway leading to the bar room was firmly shut, the noise coming from the other side drowning out the scraping of the bolt on the rear door being pulled back. Emerging into the darkness they quickly made their way across the yard to the side wall where Adam paused to pick up a packing case, strategically manoeuvring it to assist their ascent. For men of their height the scaling of the wall and the drop on the other side to the pavement was achieved without any difficulty or loss of time, and as the side street was still deserted they speedily made their way towards the main road at the opposite end to *The Black Swan* totally unobserved.

Adam's actions this evening had been purely spontaneous. From the moment he had left the house in Charles's wake until now, the only defence he could put forward for following his brother and his stealthy entrance into the premises was the unwelcome feeling that something was dreadfully wrong. Of course, Charles could have visited *The Black Swan* for a perfectly legitimate reason but try as he did Adam could find none. That he had found his cousin imprisoned in the cellar had been the last thing he had expected, but that Charles had something to do with it was beyond doubt. From what Adam could make out this Ted Knowles character had visited his brother for the sole purpose of informing him that he had got his cousin safely tucked away. Nothing else could possibly account for Charles visiting such an unsavoury place. The question was, where was Charles now? Conjecture and speculation ran riot in Adam's brain and his entreaties to Marcus to be told what the devil was going on were met with nothing but a shake of his head and the promise that all would be explained later. Since nothing would move his cousin Adam was obliged to contain his impatience as best he could and to wonder uneasily what his brother would do next.

Marcus had every intention of telling his cousin the truth, but the middle of the street was no place to disclose such a shocking and distressing piece of news. Not only that, but to linger unnecessarily was dangerous, knowing it was only a matter of minutes before his escape was discovered. So far, they had been lucky, there was no sense in pushing it. If he was right, Ted Knowles had merely joined his cronies in order to refresh himself. He would not leave his prisoner long on his own, and to remain in too close a proximity to *'The Black Swan'* was courting trouble. If they were to prevent a tragedy from occurring there was no time to waste in hanging around discussing what had already happened. The important thing now was to reach a place of safety to plan the next move.

Having by this time arrived at a more frequented thoroughfare without encountering any late wayfarer or desperate person intent on Marcus's recapture, they were fortunate to come upon a stationary hackney carriage. Rousing the sleepy driver perched on the box with a brisk request to carry them to Knightsbridge, they climbed into the antiquated vehicle quite oblivious to the fact that the sight of two gents, who looked rather dishevelled to say the least, had aroused his curiosity as well as his doubts as to their ability to pay the required fare. But upon arriving at their destination Marcus was in fact able to defray the charges, surprising not only the driver but himself as well, having fully expected to find himself the lighter of his wallet.

Upon opening the door to his employer and cousin, Webster betrayed none of his surprise at their appearance, but it was plain to the meanest intelligence that they had been up to something, and although he was far too well-trained to ask any questions he would have given a month's pay to know what they had been up to. Marcus, accurately reading the rampant curiosity behind the impassive face, had no intention of confiding anything so delicate to him, but mindful of the loyalty he had always given him he eased Webster's disappointment by thanking him for waiting up and telling him that he would not be needed again. With this Webster had to be satisfied, and after closing the study door behind the two men he made his way to his own quarters, his mind awash with conjecture.

Adam was not so easily put off, demanding to be told what was going on the instant they were alone, but the story which unfolded was not quite what he had expected. The news that his brother had not only removed two items of his sister's jewellery for financial gain and had them replaced with copies but also that he had set plans in motion to kill Alexandra under the guise of an accident, was a devastating shock. Gone was the insouciance which characterised him, his face pale and taut as he digested the enormity of what he had been told. *"My god!"* he exclaimed at length, "it's even worse than I thought." Tossing off the whisky Marcus had handed him, he said a little unsteadily, "Surely he doesn't expect to get away with it?"

"I am afraid he does," Marcus told him, his calm voice going some way to steadying Adam, whose hands shook perceptibly as he attempted to come to terms with his cousin's disclosure. "He left me in no doubt of his intentions."

Staring down into his empty glass, Adam uttered, "He must be mad!"

"No," Marcus shook his head, "not mad, just desperate; and it is this desperation which has driven him on and will continue to drive him until all the obstacles which can denounce him are out of the way."

"It's incredible!" Adam cried, unable to hide his shock. "All of this," shaking his head, "for the sake of a few letters he once wrote!"

"You will find that they signify a great deal more than that to Charles, I promise you," Marcus told him, draining his own glass.

"They're certainly not worth a girl's life!" Adam bit out.

"I quite agree," Marcus concurred. "I do Charles the justice of saying that I firmly believe he had every intention of returning the originals at some point, the fact that he has not done so can only be through lack of funds, which," he nodded, "is partly the problem now. However, if you think you can persuade him into accepting the redemption of those pieces either by my agency or your own on his behalf, then certainly do so. Perhaps your powers of persuasion are greater than mine."

"I doubt it," Adam shrugged, helping himself to another whisky. "We have got to stop it, Marcus," he said firmly, swallowing the fiery liquid. "From what you have managed to discover there is no time to be lost."

"All Charles saw fit to tell me was that the accident is to take place tomorrow; where and when is anyone's guess, and I am afraid," Marcus told him resignedly, "he was not prepared to disclose either. It would appear therefore," he explained, keeping a close eye on his cousin's use of the whisky decanter, "that since I said goodbye to Sophy this afternoon our friend Knowles saw fit to compose another letter. We can only assume the contents, but I would say it was probably along the lines of a supposed apology from Alexandra. I am only conjecturing here," he admitted, "but perhaps something to the effect that if Sophy would meet her tomorrow she would explain the reason why she had not kept their meeting today as well as explaining why she had an urgent need to talk to her. The girl in turn would also receive a letter, supposedly from Sophy, requesting she meet her at an appointed place. Both women wondering what the other wants to talk about, having no idea they have been exchanging letters. It's very clever. Neither of them realising that this supposed exchange of correspondence is merely a deviously clever ploy to lure the one to her death while the other is there to act as a witness. Ingenious!" he acknowledged.

"*Ingenious!*" Adam cried. "It's downright criminal!" Then, as if a thought had just occurred to him, he said, "Yes, but what I don't understand is, if Sophy showed you the first letter why has she not showed you the second one?"

"Obviously because there has been no opportunity for her to do so," Marcus replied calmly. "There is no way we can say for certain what time the second letter arrived, but I would speculate late this afternoon. From what Charles told me," he explained, "Sophy's bogus appointment in Regents Park was merely a trial run to establish that she would in fact meet Alexandra. Apparently, Knowles had Sophy followed to make sure she had complied with the letter. Having been assured that she had, a dress rehearsal if you like, then he would assume it was safe to write her a second letter in preparation for the real thing. Remember," he told him, "Sophy would not have arrived home until mid-afternoon, which means that Knowles's accomplice could not have reported back to him straightaway. It also explains how Charles got to know about the letter in my possession; Knowles's crony apparently reported every one of Sophy's movements, including the visit she made to me."

"Well, if you are right," Adam exclaimed, "and it seems most likely that you are, then we can't just sit here doing nothing! We have got to act now."

"And what do you suggest we do?" Marcus enquired, raising an eyebrow. "If we knew where or when the supposed accident is scheduled to take place we could do something, but we don't, and if Charles or Knowles did not volunteer the information while I was their guest in that cellar I doubt very much if either of them are suddenly going to experience a change of mind. No," he shook his head, "if we do anything at all, especially on the spur of the moment, we could most probably make bad far worse. Whatever we do it has to be given serious thought."

"Then you give it serious thought!" Adam shot at him. "But I'm not sitting here while my brother does his best to put a rope around his neck!" Suiting the action to the words he strode over to where his overcoat lay on the back of a chair, but even before he had picked it up his cousin had covered the distance between them and gripped his arm like a vice.

No one knew better than Marcus that acting under the influence of anger and shock, a powerful combination especially when fuelled with alcohol, only resulted in disaster. He was a seasoned campaigner and knew that only carefully laid plans would ensure the success of this particular campaign and not the impassioned actions of a madcap young hot head who would most likely bring all to ruin through going off half-cocked. It took him several minutes to impress upon Adam the need for caution and the futility of doing anything in the heat of the moment. Marcus was not unmindful of his cousin's concerns over his brother's plans and he would have given anything to have spared him, but if a disaster was to be averted and without creating any scandal, only calm and logic would win the day.

Having succeeded in bringing Adam to a calmer frame of mind, Marcus put forward the semblance of an idea which had been taking shape in his mind for the past half hour or so, and Adam, apart from putting the odd question, finally accepted the sense of what his cousin was saying, but for the life of him he failed to see how it could be executed successfully, foreseeing all manner of obstacles.

Ted Knowles meanwhile, considering the enormity of tomorrow's forthcoming events and Charles Harrington's expectations resulting from them, was certainly taking a long time in refreshing himself with Joe's best brown ale. Had his client been privileged to have seen him he would most definitely have disapproved of such flagrant dereliction of duty, but as his prisoner was perfectly safe in the cellar with no hope or means of escape, he was able to disregard the urgency of returning to keep his vigil. Compared to the cold comforts of the cellar Joe's snug little parlour was far more inviting, and by the time Ted Knowles had consumed several tankards of the nicest drop of ale he had ever tasted he was well under the mellowing influence they had evoked and was therefore easily able to persuade himself that after all he had been through today he more than deserved this little respite. Besides, it would not do his prisoner a mite of harm to ponder his predicament a little.

Joe Benbow may have no qualms about using his cellar for illicit purposes, after all most of his activities were conducted well outside the boundaries of the law, but he had an uncanny instinct when it came to judging people and from the moment he had set eyes on Charles Harrington he had taken him in dislike. He could not base this on anything specific but there was something about him which warned Joe Benbow that prolonged association with him could well bring trouble down on his head, and this alone made him cautious. Ted may say what he liked about being able to handle him but Joe wanted no Peeler poking his nose in his place and the sooner this business was over the better he would like it. It was not his place to tell Ted how to conduct his affairs, but he was by no means easy about leaving that swell unguarded in the cellar. He may be tied as safe as houses to that chair but Joe had seen enough of him to know that he was more than capable of taking care of himself as well as finding a way out of his predicament. When Ted had sent Davy to ask him to get his cellar ready he had been quite happy to oblige him and no questions asked, but since then Joe had given the matter some profound thought and had arrived at the conclusion that it was perhaps safer in not knowing the full extent of what was afoot. Should anything happen while he was playing host he had no need to be told that Ted's accomplice would find it far easier to extricate himself from what Joe knew was something damned havey-cavey as well as absolving himself of all blame than he would. A man in Charles Harrington's position would carry far more weight with the authorities than someone like himself and no law officer would be likely to question the integrity or word of a gentleman of Charles Harrington's standing, whereas he would instantly be looked upon as not only a liar but a most suspect individual. It was therefore with a strong sense of self-preservation that he reminded his crony of his responsibilities regarding the prisoner, and although at first it seemed as if Ted was going to prove awkward he soon began to realise that Joe was right.

Wiping his mouth on the back of his hand Ted heaved himself out of his chair, walking with remarkable steadiness towards the door, pausing only to tell Joe that he did not need him to remind him of what he had to do. Joe merely looked sceptical, shrugging his powerful shoulders with the retort that if that was the case then why was he still here in his parlour, before returning to the bar to evict the last of his customers. Had Ted Knowles the least conception that his prisoner had an accomplice he would not have been so complacent, but as this possibility had never even so much as crossed his mind, it was in a mood of considerable well-being that he strolled down the dimly lit passageway towards the cellar.

Totally confident in the infallibility of his plans and the quickness with which he had dealt with Marcus Ingleby, Ted Knowles foresaw no cloud on the horizon, added to which he was in for a nice little earner when this job was done, but the unexpected sight of the cellar's half open door came as something of a shock. He was convinced that when he had left Charles Harrington he had securely locked and bolted it behind him, and for several bewildering moments he was at a loss to account for it. His heart began to beat uncomfortably fast but managing to push the worst of his fears to the back of his mind he nudged open the door, his eyes almost bulging from their sockets when he saw the empty chair and the cut ropes lying on the floor, but of Marcus Ingleby there was no sign. Ted Knowles stared round the cellar in disbelief, panic welling up inside him as he realised the significance of his disappearance, and the sensation that the ground had been kicked from under him made him feel sick. He had no idea how his prisoner had managed to escape, much less how he had been able to cut the ropes. Apart from the fact that he had been securely tethered with no possibility of getting free, he himself had checked his pockets and found no implement on his person capable of cutting anything. It was then that his eyes fell on the jagged fragments of the jug scattered on the floor, instantly explaining how the ropes had been cut. Somehow Ingleby must have manoeuvred himself into a position which had enabled him to knock the jug off the table, using one of the pieces to cut through the ropes. But even though this sounded feasible enough Ted Knowles could not so easily explain away how his prisoner had managed to open the cellar door, especially when he was ready to take his dying oath that he had secured the bolt.

It was while he was pondering the mystery of his prisoner's escape that Joe joined him, his expression a nice mix of shock and satisfaction. "I 'nowed 'ow it 'ud be," he shot at Ted Knowles. "Yer can neva trusts a swell!" Rounding on his crony he said bitterly, "Aimin' too 'igh, Ted Knowles; that's wot yer've dun, an' see wot's cum of it. I don't say I mindid yer usin' me cella 'cus I dain't, nor I ain't gonna say that I blames yer fer tryin' ter mek a few extra bob, 'cus I ain't, but what I *dus* say is this sort o' thing ain't in my line. Mind you," he confessed, scratching his head, completely forgetting Adam's visit earlier and how he could have some bearing on matters, "beats me 'ow 'e's got out. Trussed up like a chickin 'e wos."

Ted Knowles had endured more than enough today without Joe adding to it, but his crony's unsympathetic outburst was the last straw, and when Albert arrived on the scene a few minutes later a lively argument was in full swing. Not until their vocabulary of insults had been exhausted did they notice he was there, but no sooner did Joe lay eyes on him than he demanded to know if he had seen anyone when he went outside earlier.

"Dain't see a soul," Albert shook his head. "Gawn 'as 'e?"

"O'cus 'e's gawn!" Joe said irritably. "Yer don't thinks we'd be 'ere arguin' the toss othawise, dus yer?"

Peering over their shoulders to take a look into the cellar Albert pulled down the corners of his mouth, no more able to understand how the prisoner had escaped than his two cronies, and since he too had apparently banished Adam from his mind he could only repeat that he had seen nothing.

"It don't mek an 'aporth o' diffrunce wetha yer did or yer didn't," Joe bit out. "'E's gawn 'an that's all there is to it!" Looking down at Ted Knowles, who bore all the appearance of having been stuffed, he said pointedly, "Thing is, wot yer gonna do now? 'Is nibs'll 'ave ter be told; an' from wot I've sin of 'im 'e ain't gonna be any too pleased wen 'e 'ears about this little capa."

As he had not yet got round to thinking about Charles Harrington, Joe's reminder hit Ted Knowles like a body blow. It was useless to deceive himself into thinking that this night's adventure could be kept from him. Unless a miracle occurred whereby his prisoner could be recaptured he had no choice but to brace himself for the unpleasant task and its none too pleasant consequences. No reliance could be placed on Marcus Ingleby keeping his mouth shut; only one word from him in the right quarter would be enough to bring every law officer in London down on them. Ted Knowles did not need to have Joe reminding him of what Charles Harrington's reaction would be, he already knew and the knowledge made him feel sick. What he had to do was somehow try to salvage the situation and prevent a complete disaster, but his bemused brain was unable to come up with anything even remotely resembling a feasible plan. What he needed was something warm and invigorating, but immediately found his way to the bar blocked by Joe's massive frame.

"Yer've alreddy 'ad one pull too many," Joe told him, "an' if yer thinks that a ball o' fire will do the trick, then yer fer an' far off!" An ugly look crossed Ted's face but he was no match for Joe, who pointed out practically, "'Sides, standin' 'ere arguin' the toss ain't gonna do yer no gud. Wot yer needs ter do is ter think o' sumthin' ter tells yer fancy frend, and I don't see 'im bein' any too pleased to 'now that 'e's gawn," indicating the prisoner's vacated chair.

"If I 'nows anythin'," Albert put in helpfully, "'e'll 'ave bolted fer 'ome."

Joe gave him a withering look. "O'cus 'e 'as!" he exclaimed irritably, "but 'e's 'ardly likely ter let Ted in so 'e can bash 'im ova the 'ead agen!" Albert begged pardon, saying he was only trying to be helpful. "Well, yer ain't," Joe told him unkindly. "Anybudy can see 'e's gawn. An' if that's the best yer can do Albert Lynch," he added, "it'd be best fer yer ter say nuthin'!" Bringing his gaze back round to Ted Knowles, he said, "It ain't no manna o' use standin' there with a gormless luk on yer face. 'E's gawn an' that's all there is to it, and yer've itha got ter find 'im dubble quick an' get 'im back 'ere or find sumthin' ter tells 'is nibs."

But Ted was not listening. He had to admit that he had no liking for the task of informing Charles Harrington of tonight's setback, but if the plan formulating in his ever-fertile brain came off, then he could deal with his prisoner and the girl in one fell swoop. Of course, it would take a little time to work it all out properly but at least he had the rudiments of an idea, and as he was of a permanently optimistic nature he had every hope that it would all work out perfectly, and the beauty of it was Charles Harrington would not be blamed at all! Surely, that would raise him in his client's esteem!

Joe knew that look in Ted's eye from old, and unless he was very much mistaken he was up to something, but after this latest turn up Joe was not at all sure he wanted to know what it was. Even so, he did not like to think that his old crony was heading for trouble, but since he was giving nothing away he could only hope that Ted would not do anything stupid.

Without giving Joe any satisfactory explanation of what he intended to do, Ted simply told him that there were things he had to sort out and would see him tomorrow.

It was not up to Albert to tell Joe how to run his place but using the cellar to truss up a swell was asking for trouble! If he did not know better he would think Joe had taken leave of his senses, not to mention Ted, who, apart from always having had an eye for the main chance, seemed incapable of turning down the opportunity of making money. But since neither of them would ever listen to him Albert merely kept his fingers crossed that no wind of tonight's fiasco would come to the attention of certain members of their clientele. Just a whiff of a Peeler poking his nose would do untold damage to Joe's reputation, but since his opinion was never asked for or wanted he merely went about his business. Nevertheless, when he unbolted the front door to let Ted out he would not have been at all surprised to have found the place surrounded by fasteners!

Chapter Eighteen

Setting aside Marcus's duplicity regarding the true nature of his feelings towards Sophy and Charles's own humiliation at being obliged to let it go unanswered in the manner he would have liked, there had never been any love lost between the cousins. Nevertheless, despite the urgency to settle his affairs without any repercussions rebounding on himself and without any further loss of time, Charles was most reluctant to take the irrevocable step of putting an end to his cousin's life. Like Ted Knowles, Charles knew that if he allowed Marcus to go free no dependence could be placed on him keeping his mouth shut simply because he was far too honest and honourable to turn a blind eye to what was after all cold-blooded murder, even if it did come under the guise of an accident, and since he could not be kept a prisoner indefinitely and no other practical solution had presented itself, there really did seem to be no other alternative but to dispose of him. Charles certainly had no regrets about getting rid of the girl, nor was he conscious of any feelings of remorse, but he could not pretend that by dealing with his cousin in the same carefully contrived manner he could look upon it in quite the same way.

Ever since Silas Jenkins had read out that disastrous clause in his father's will his temper, always rather uncertain, had fluctuated dramatically, but during the last few days Charles had been given every reason to believe that at long last his problems were well on the way to being solved. Unfortunately, the discovery of Marcus's involvement in his affairs had put quite a different complexion on things. Whilst Charles still had every confidence in the successful outcome of his plans he could not deny that what, up until a short time ago, had been a foregone conclusion, had suddenly become tinged with doubt. Anger had enabled him to conduct that interview with some semblance of dignity and pride, and whilst he could congratulate himself on the impeccable way in which he had not only dealt with Marcus but concealed his innermost feelings from him, he could not hide the truth from himself.

The shock he had experienced upon discovering his cousin's involvement, culminating in that visit to Knowles followed by his incarceration, had been tremendous. Marcus's intervention had been the last thing Charles had expected or needed, and to discover that he had been working against him all this time had rendered it necessary for him to seriously contemplate taking drastic action. He had been so close to resolving his difficulties without anyone being the wiser or exposing himself to public condemnation, but even though he had every confidence in dealing with this unlooked-for eventuality it was a circumstance he could well do without.

It afforded him some consolation to know that Marcus's situation was far from enviable, locked in that cellar with the daunting prospect of what awaited him. This should have been sufficient to weaken his cousin's resolve, but the minimal amount of satisfaction Charles derived from this was unfortunately rather short-lived as he recalled that instead of begging or entreating his release on promises of silence, Marcus had exhibited all the appearance of one who was completely in control of himself and one, moreover, who had every faith in his ability to ultimately foil any plans. Given the opportunity Marcus would certainly do all he could to ruin everything he was working towards, he was more than capable of it, and Charles knew he would be a fool not to recognise this fact and to act upon it. Admittedly, his cousin had made that generous offer but he would rather die than accept such a gift from the man he resented and envied more than any other, besides which, it would provide Marcus with a most convenient tool which he could use against him at any time should he ever choose to do so. Not that Charles envisaged such an act of revenge from his cousin; Marcus was nothing if not a gentleman, whose honour and integrity would not allow him to sink to such depths, but in view of his own recent discovery regarding the true nature of the relationship between Marcus and Sophy, Charles could not afford to take this assumption for granted. He may not love Sophy but she was his wife, and he for one was determined she would remain so.

His cousin's death, apart from ensuring Sophy's future fidelity, would also rid him of possible consequences arising in the future should Marcus decide to show his hand. Regrettable though it was, it was certainly very necessary to dispose of Marcus. Charles knew that if he allowed him to go free, even with his assurances of keeping silent and turning a blind eye to imminent events, he would never know a moment's peace of mind; always wondering what his cousin was going to do and when. No reliance could be placed upon the word of a man whose back was against the wall, especially one whose very code was grounded in truth and integrity! He could not afford to indulge in sentiment or to allow their relationship to cloud his judgement. Reluctant he may be to instigate his cousin's demise, but he was practical enough to realise that it was most certainly expedient. The only question mark was how best to set about it, although he had no doubt that Ted Knowles knew any number of desperate persons ready to oblige him! Charles needed time to consider how best to achieve his cousin's exit from this world. It certainly could not be arranged in haste, to do so would be madness. There could be no loopholes or room for error in carrying out such a vital task. Marcus was by far too clever and astute to be caught out by an inadequately laid scheme, carried out by equally inadequate persons! His cousin's death could leave no room for doubt but, more vital still, no suspicion of blame must fall on him! Fortunately, however, Charles had a little time left to him to consider how best his cousin's death could be brought about, and unless Ted Knowles bungled things he should be safe in Joe Benbow's cellar until tomorrow.

Bungled! Suddenly his parting words to Knowles came involuntarily to mind. Knowles had already bungled. He had mismanaged a situation that a child could have dealt with. Of all the incompetent idiots! A more generous man than himself may say that in defence of his confederate there had been no way he could have foreseen that he would receive a visit from Marcus, but had he destroyed those incriminating practise sheets Charles knew he would be facing an entirely different situation. Sophy had obviously shown that letter to Marcus, allegedly written by the girl, but without those discarded sheets he could never have connected it with himself. Marcus must still have that original letter in his possession, and it was by far the most incriminating piece of evidence against him! Knowing Marcus, he would not have been such a fool as to take it with him on his visit to see Knowles, which meant it was safely locked away somewhere; at all costs, Charles must retrieve it! As it was, not only had Knowles just scraped through the whole thing due to the timely intervention of one of his cronies fortunately coming to his aid and knocking Marcus senseless, but it had placed him in a most delicate position.

No! Knowles was no match for his cousin. Sooner or later he was bound to find a way out of that cellar, and once that happened there would be no way he could avert the consequences. Charles had put his trust in Knowles only to find it misplaced. Marcus was right about that at least! No, he could place no reliance upon an associate who had already bungled. To do so would be an act of gross stupidity. There seemed then, to be no alternative but to take matters into his own hands. Not until his cousin was permanently out of the way would he know any peace of mind, but first, he had to retrieve that vital piece of evidence in his cousin's possession. Once he had that safely on his person he could deal with the Marcus. First though, he had to discover where he kept it hidden, but considering the hopeless position his cousin was in, Charles did not envisage too much difficulty in prising the information out of him, especially when he knew that Sophy would suffer for his lack of cooperation.

At no point did Charles even consider that Marcus was working hand in hand with an accomplice much less his own brother, who had only minutes before assisted his cousin to escape. Confident that he was on the point, if not of killing two birds with one stone, then at least obtaining that incriminating letter, Charles called to the hackney driver to take him back to where he had come from. The instruction was instantly met with an expletive quickly followed up by a bitterly delivered retort to the effect that he wished folks would make up their minds where it was they wanted to go. Ignoring this with the contempt it deserved, Charles checked his inside pocket and, having reassured himself of its contents, sat back in pleasant contemplation during his return journey to 'The Black Swan'.

It was at this precise moment that Joe Benbow was giving it as his opinion that he would see himself ditched before he got involved with another swell again, to which Albert fully concurred. Joe hoped that tonight's shindig would be a lesson to Ted. It was all very well rubbing shoulders with the toffs but when push came to shove they would look to themselves, and unless he was very much mistaken this little venture Ted was heavily involved in was bound to lead to trouble. It stood to reason that one way or another someone was going to have to pay the piper for tonight's fiasco, and Joe had a very strong feeling it would be himself. The minute a Peeler shoved his nose round the door he could say goodbye to his profitable little business. If that swell did not go to the Runners for this night's work he would own himself astonished.

Albert, fully agreeing with every one of Joe's embittered grumblings, took it upon himself to tell Joe that he had known all along how it would be, but when, about fifteen minutes later, an imperative knock was heard on the front door, so convinced was he that they were being besieged by Bow Street that he spilled his pint. Joe, darting a wary glance across at him, rose cautiously to his feet, but as no official cry accompanied the knocking he felt it safe to assume that whoever was demanding admittance it was certainly no law officer.

Having found it necessary to return to such a lowly establishment as 'The Black Swan' was bad enough, but to be kept standing on the doorstep under the amused and curious eye of the hackney driver fuelled Charles's anger to fever pitch, so much so that when Joe finally opened the door he instantly delivered himself of a pithy demand to know what the devil had taken him so long.

Finding Charles Harrington on his doorstep and not an officer of the law, Joe was too relieved to take any notice of the string of descriptive expletives which left his lips, but when he finally came to the end of his expressively phrased sentiments to demand an immediate interview with his cousin, Joe began to wonder if it would not have been better after all to find the whole of Bow Street on his doorstep than Charles Harrington. From the looks of it, his unexpected visitor was in no mood to receive bad tidings, but as it was obvious that he had come back for a reason and he was not going to leave until he had done what he had set out to, Joe had little choice but to tell him of the stirring events which had recently taken place. There had not possibly been enough time for Ted to seek him out to tell him the bad news himself, which meant he would have to do it for him, something Joe by no means felt inclined to do. Charles's brown eyes narrowed into slits of anger as they stared menacingly at him and the grim thinning of his lips made Albert heave a sigh of relief in that he was not the one to break the news to him. But Joe was not so easily overawed. He was not afraid of Charles Harrington, in fact he had no doubt of being able to deal with him in one blow, but there had been enough trouble tonight without asking for any more. Since there was no point in beating about the bush, he told Charles Harrington that it was no manner of use asking to see the swell in the cellar because he had gone. Upon being ominously asked to repeat what he had just said, Joe went over the events of the last half hour or so again, but upon seeing the ugly look that crossed Charles Harrington's face Joe felt it prudent to add that it was not a particle of use asking him how the swell had escaped because he couldn't tell him, in fact, it had him fair bamboozled!

Had Albert been asked to give an opinion he would have said that Charles Harrington looked for all the world as if he had been pole-axed. It was no less than the truth. Acknowledging his cousin's ability of finding a way out of the cellar at some point was one thing but to learn that this was precisely what he had done and so soon after he had left him, was quite another. It was a devastating blow, to which the shocked incredulity on his face bore adequate testimony.

Joe's descriptive explanation about tonight's events certainly raised questions; not the least being where was Ted Knowles when it happened? And how had Marcus managed to open a door which had been securely bolted on the outside?

Relieved to be able to answer the first of these enquiries at least, Joe explained that Ted had only grabbed a few minutes to partake of refreshment, but, sadly, he could offer nothing in the way of the prisoner's escape. "Ferly sent me ter grass it did!" Joe exclaimed, scratching his head.

"Very likely!" Charles snapped, pushing Joe unceremoniously aside as he headed for the cellar.

Unfortunately, the empty chair and discarded ropes told him very little more than they had Ted Knowles, but unlike his accomplice Charles realised that unless his cousin had performed a miracle he must have had help in getting away. He had seen for himself just how securely tied Marcus had been to the chair, and whilst Charles had not failed to notice the jagged remnants of the jug scattered on the floor, he had read far more into the scene than Knowles apparently had. Marcus must have had help, nothing else could possibly explain his escape satisfactorily, and certainly not how he had managed to unbolt the door from the inside, but for the life of him Charles could not imagine who it may be. Marcus had a wide circle of friends and acquaintances, but Charles was ready to swear that his cousin would not have enlisted their help; to do so would mean confiding his suspicions to them, and that was something he would never do. No! The accomplice must be someone closer to home.

Contemptuously dismissing Albert on the very reasonable grounds that he would never have the nerve to do anything like this, and Joe Benbow because he had far too much sense to do something that could possibly bring the law down on him, Charles was forced into the unwelcome task of mentally scanning the possible candidates who would be likely to offer his cousin aid. However time consuming this task, it was imperative he discovered the identity of Marcus's collaborator; at all costs he had to avoid another loose end! Too many things had gone wrong already without the added worry of another interested party, but no matter what it took he had to discover who his accomplice was; under no circumstances could he disregard it!

He did not need to have the implications of Marcus's escape spelled out, Charles knew perfectly well that there was every likelihood of him taking his information to the authorities at some point. Come what may he had to prevent this from happening! If his calculations were correct, then based upon his own knowledge of his cousin he would not do anything immediately. Marcus was a thinker, and one who studied a problem from every conceivable angle, and he would no doubt give this one more than ordinarily deep thought. He may not bear the name of Harrington but everyone knew of his connection with it, and whilst Marcus was at heart an honest man whose every feeling revolted at deceit and dissimulation, he would not be quite so eager to bring the name into disrepute any more than he would be in a hurry to bring it under the full glare of official scrutiny. As far as Charles could make out, Marcus had been gone for about twenty minutes, and unless he had grossly underestimated his cousin he was fairly sure that he would have made his way straight home to cogitate on tonight's events and to consider his best course of action. That Marcus would remove himself from his affairs and let him get on with his plans was indulging optimism too far! The frown on Charles's forehead deepened as he pondered his predicament. Having returned here for a specific purpose, he was by no means pleased to learn that his sole aim in coming back could not be carried out.

He stared at the scene in front of him with narrowed eyes, his brain racing as he considered the possible reasons and explanations to account for his cousin's escape and the unfortunate position it had placed him in. Having considered this eventuality was one thing, but it by no means lessened the shock of discovering that his worst fears had been realised. Marcus was certainly full of surprises! Of one thing though Charles was certain, and that was this unexpected turn of events had rendered him acutely vulnerable to attack. Somehow, he had to regain his lost position, and without any undue loss of time. The frown furrowing his forehead deepened even more as he pondered his next move. With his cousin safely locked in the cellar he had held an unassailable position reinforced with strong bargaining powers, but now that was gone! Or was it?

Charles's frown lifted as he contemplated the idea which had been hovering on the periphery of his consciousness for the past few minutes in more detail, gaining merit with every second that passed, so much so that when Joe joined him in the cellar several minutes later it was to find his crony's accomplice with something close to a smile on his lips. Charles at last had something to smile about. Providence, it seemed, was continuing to smile on him by showing him another, and by far safer, way of extricating himself from his difficulties. In fact, so perfect was the idea which had miraculously struck him that he could not conceive why he had not thought of it before. But first, he had to seek out his inept confederate. Although Ted Knowles had already bungled what should have been a quite simple affair, unfortunately Charles was in the position whereby he could not delay matters by seeking another accomplice. Like it or not he was stuck with Ted Knowles, and reluctant though Charles was to admit it, he needed his help if he was to avert a complete disaster. However, in view of the ultimate outcome of what he considered to be an infallible tactic to induce a change of mind in his cousin, he was quite prepared to overlook Ted Knowles's previous ineptitude. The smile broadened. What a fool he was not to have seen what had been staring him in the face before now! But all was not lost. Providing Ted Knowles did everything he was told, Charles foresaw no problems to mar such a watertight strategy. And it was such a brilliant strategy. He would not only be rid of the girl as arranged tomorrow with no possible suspicions falling upon himself but it would also obviate the necessity of disposing of his cousin. Honest though Marcus was, there was a way his silence could be bought after all! "Where is Knowles now?" he enquired of Joe without even turning his head.

"'E's gawn," Joe told him, eyeing his crony's accomplice warily.

"Obviously," Charles drawled sardonically, "but *where* has he gone?"

"'Ome I wud think," Joe shrugged. "Why, does yer wonts 'im?"

"You know," Charles sighed, "you really must cure yourself of asking the obvious. Of course I want him!" he bit out. "Though not, I hasten to add, because I desire his company above all others."

Joe, to whom this smooth and malicious eloquence was somewhat unintelligible, merely scratched his head, looking at Charles with a rather blank look on his face.

"God grant me patience!" Charles cried, exasperated. "Don't just stand there, man!" he snapped. "Go and tell Knowles I want him here immediately."

As this form of address was more in line with what Joe was used to, he hurried out of the cellar, setting up a cry for Albert as he did so.

As nothing remained for Charles to do other than await the arrival of Ted Knowles, he sauntered into the stuffy bar room with all the air of one under sufferance, only the knowledge that he could not possibly fail now rendering his stay bearable. Having neither the time nor the inclination to listen to Joe's description of Albert's voluble reluctance to being used as an errand boy, Charles merely inspected the condition of a chair before gingerly sitting down on it, crossing one leg over the other, completely ignoring his host by demanding some paper and a pen. Joe, who was not accustomed to such contemptuous treatment of his hostelry, took one look at that cold and implacable face and instantly thought better of uttering the blistering words hovering on the tip of his tongue, merely shrugging his broad shoulders as he went away in search of these commodities.

Meanwhile, Ted Knowles's brain was working at fever pitch, so much so that by the time he arrived home the idea that had come to him was beginning to take shape, the resurgence of his natural buoyancy marred only by the thought that Charles Harrington would be bound to accuse him of shirking his responsibilities by not informing him immediately of his cousin's dramatic escape from the cellar. However, it had taken Ted Knowles only a few minutes to realise that it would be far better to break the news to his client if it was followed up by a plan of action rather than simply trying to give a good account of himself. Naturally, there were one or two minor points to his scheme which would require a bit more thinking out, but he was convinced that after a drop or two of Joe's best brandy he would be in a fair way to tying the whole thing up as neat as you please. Joe's illicitly acquired cognac may have cleared his brain regarding his schemes but it in no way brought him any nearer to liking the thought of telling Charles Harrington about his cousin's escape, but Ted Knowles consoled himself with the thought that at least the confession would be far easier for him to swallow when he knew of his contingency plans. He could well imagine Charles Harrington's reaction upon learning that his cousin was as good as dealt with and without any repercussions rebounding on either of them, and as for the girl – well, that would still go ahead as arranged!

Of course, it still puzzled him how Ingleby had managed to escape. 'The Black Swan' was not an easy place to get in and out of without being seen, but somehow or other he had done just that. Mind you, he would not enjoy his freedom for long! It was surprising how even such a clever swell as Ingleby could be duped with a cunningly contrived ruse! All Ted Knowles had to do now was to decide which one of his cronies could be trusted to take on such an important job, it would not do for this to go wrong, but just as he was counting one or two possible candidates off on his fingers he heard, much to his surprise, hasty footsteps on the stairs, coming to an abrupt halt outside his room. Almost immediately the door was thrust open and Albert, looking flushed and angry, crossed the threshold, still far from pleased at having been obliged to come out at this early hour of the morning, for it wanted only two minutes to half past midnight, to run an errand like a schoolboy, and not until his vehement grumblings had ceased did Ted Knowles get to hear the reason for his unexpected visit.

The news that Charles Harrington had returned to 'The Black Swan' and discovered Ingleby's escape for himself, was rather daunting to say the least. He could not understand what could possibly have caused him to return, but as it was obvious that Albert was under strict instructions to find him and take him back to 'The Black Swan' without any loss of time, Ted Knowles knew he dared not refuse to go. No more than Albert did he appreciate being treated like a schoolboy, even so, he was conscious of a strong feeling of self-preservation and the urgent need to absolve himself of all blame. He had a fair idea that his client would not be in the best of humours and was beginning to think that his precipitous flight from 'The Black Swan' only served to put him in the worst possible light. The fact that he had a very serviceable plan to put forward suddenly seemed to be of no importance, and as he hurried beside Albert through the damp and deserted streets back to 'The Black Swan' the best he could hope for was that Charles Harrington had not decided to dispense with his services thereby having to forgo his hard-earned reward.

But to Ted Knowles's astonishment and relief, this punishment was not forthcoming, but there was no mistaking the anger on Charles Harrington's face or the cold contempt in his eyes, but apart from a scathing attack on his abilities and the promise of dire consequences should he bungle again he had miraculously been given another chance to redeem himself. No one could accuse Ted Knowles of lacking nerve, but upon being ordered to account for his lack of devotion to duty thereby allowing something of this magnitude to occur under his very nose, was no easy thing. Ingleby's escape was something to which Ted Knowles could put forward no suitable explanation, and upon being required to endure at least ten minutes of listening to a severe denunciation of his intellect as well as his capabilities, he had wisely decided that now was perhaps not the right time to put forward his ideas, electing instead to hold them in reserve for the time being. It could well be that at some point in the none too distant future they could come in very useful, especially if his client's new scheme failed, which it could quite well do, especially when he considered the kind of man they were dealing with. He knew perfectly well that he had been lucky in coming out of this evening's fiasco with a whole skin, and although he could not afford to have anything else go wrong, he was shrewd enough to realise that the only reason he had been let off so lightly was because his client had something else in mind, for which he needed his help. The prisoner's escape had been most unfortunate, but he was not entirely to blame for it, and when he pointed this fact out to Charles Harrington it was met with the cold reminder that he had been left solely in charge, and if he was not responsible, then who was?

Charles, who was in no mood to listen to Ted Knowles's further explanations about his need of refreshment, eyed his accomplice with aloof disdain, coldly informing him that he would thank him to refrain from offering any further excuses. "I am in no mood for them, besides which," he added nastily, "enough time has been wasted thanks to your inept bungling!"

Ted Knowles was just about to argue this point when he caught sight of Joe's warning glance and, merely shrugging his shoulders, asked belligerently what it was his client wanted him to do. Having listened with scarcely concealed scepticism to the bare outline of the new scheme for dealing with Marcus Ingleby, Ted Knowles was still of the unshakeable belief that his own plan was the only answer, and after several minutes of profound thought he was still of the opinion that his client's scheme stood every chance of dying a death.

As far as Joe was concerned, who had been of the opinion for some time that no good could possibly come from kidnapping and murder, the scheme just put forward by Charles Harrington was a masterstroke of genius. The beauty of it was, as far as he was concerned, it brought no trouble to his establishment in the shape of law officers, a consideration he could not afford to overlook.

Ted Knowles, however, had very different views on the subject, and upon being handed the letter which Charles had written earlier to his cousin with instructions that he was to deliver it straightaway and then personally accompany him back here, Ted Knowles stared incredulously, daring to say that he could not see his cousin going anywhere with him. "Not afta wot's 'appenened," he pointed out. "Stans ter reason 'e wudn't trusts me ter even walk down the street wi' me."

Apart from this very reasonable argument, he had had enough of Marcus Ingleby to last him a lifetime and the only thing which would make a further meeting between them acceptable to him was for him to be able to pay him back for his brutal treatment. It seemed to him that this notion of coercing Ingleby by means of emotional blackmail needed far more looking into than he had at first thought. Charles Harrington's idea was all very well, but whilst it ensured him protection it left himself far too exposed for his liking. Even supposing Marcus Ingleby did keep his mouth shut to save the family from being plunged into scandal, which Ted Knowles did not think at all probable, it left him wide open for trouble. He had no fancy for coming to the notice of Bow Street and since his overriding concern was one of self-preservation, this new plan of Charles Harrington's callously disregarded his safety. His client could say what he liked, but this plan of his, apart from being too one-sided for Ted Knowles's liking, offered no guarantees where Ingleby was concerned. It was all very well for Charles Harrington to talk about this being a far better idea than doing away with his cousin, but it was certainly not too promising as far as Ted Knowles was concerned. The Harrington family may come out of this untainted but it stood to reason that somewhere along the way someone was going have to pay for it, especially if it ever became known that the girl's death was not an accident after all! The Peelers may be taken in by the words of a swell, but they would certainly not be any too willing to listen to his side of things, and this being so he was left with no choice but to make certain arrangements to protect his interests by taking out some personal insurance. After all, what Charles Harrington did not know would not hurt him, and anyway this way was far better, as he had known it would be from the outset!

Ignoring his comments, Charles told him haughtily, "You are not being paid to think, Knowles. You will take that letter to my cousin, the content of which will ensure he accompanies you. I do not expect you to keep me waiting," adding nastily, "I have already wasted far too much time this evening through your inadequate efforts, and I am in no mood to be kept hanging around any longer than is absolutely necessary. Besides, I have had my fill of this establishment!"

Pushing the letter into his pocket Ted Knowles nodded, promising to deliver it and return with his cousin, by no means confident in Marcus

Ingleby's compliance as his client apparently seemed to be, but since his opinions were neither wanted nor welcomed he did not spend much time worrying over it. Nevertheless, he would have given anything to know what was in that letter because from what he had been privileged to see of Marcus Ingleby it would have to be pretty good to induce him to accompany the man who had been responsible for that knock over the head.

Had Charles Harrington been privileged to have seen his accomplice's movements upon leaving 'The Black Swan' he would not have been quite so complacent, and it was perhaps as well for his peace of mind that he knew nothing of the slight detour he made prior to making his way to Knightsbridge. The dingy little side street down which Ted Knowles turned was far from salubrious, giving the distinct impression that every unsavoury individual known to Bow Street must live in one or the other of the houses which made up the shabby and run-down terrace. Clearly no stranger to this grimy back street, located only a few hundred yards from 'The Black Swan', Ted Knowles trod purposefully up the cracked path of number fourteen and knocked on the door, quite certain of a response even at this unseasonable time of the morning. He did not have long to wait before the door was cautiously opened, revealing a burly looking individual whose whole appearance bore all the hallmarks of a bruiser. Not at all put out by a demand to know if he was alone, Ted Knowles assured him he was and, after a quick and furtive look all around him, the occupant pulled open the door just wide enough to allow Ted Knowles to step inside.

Not having anticipated his cousin's unexpected return to 'The Black Swan', Marcus was of the belief that Ted Knowles would not linger long over advising him of his escape, and he did not envy him the task. Charles would not be at all pleased to discover that the man he had set to guard him had let something as serious as allowing him to escape to happen, and he could well imagine the anger and frustration he would feel knowing that his cousin was at large and armed with damning and incriminating information. Charles would have no way of knowing what he would do or when, and therefore this uncertainty would most probably push him into doing something quite uncalculated, and if Marcus knew his cousin whatever he decided to do he would waste no time.

Adam had been thinking along the same lines, but if Charles had no idea what Marcus would do or when, having no idea his own brother was in league with his cousin, then they in turn had no idea what he would do, which placed them in an equally impotent position because they could set no plan in motion to counteract Charles's next move. Unfortunately, Adam had been unable to come up with anything better than Marcus's idea of removing the girl from her lodgings and keeping her safely hidden until the danger was over. Of course, Adam did not exactly relish the thought of disturbing people at this hour of the morning and could all too easily envisage the scene as they awakened the household in the early hours, attempting to explain away their unexpected arrival without disclosing the reason behind it. But be that as it may, he was forced to admit that it did seem to be the only way of thwarting his brother's plans as well as ensuring the girl's safety. The only drawback as far as he could see was the girl herself, and upon being asked the reason for his sudden frown, said, "You say you've only met the girl once?"

"Yes," Marcus nodded, "the day your father died. Why?"

"Then what makes you think she will trust either of us enough to come with us? After all," Adam pointed out reasonably, "she's never laid eyes on me before, and she was certainly not visiting my father because she wanted to. My understanding is that there was hostility on both sides."

"I shall just have to try to convince her that I am in earnest," Marcus said firmly, adding, "but do not forget, her hostility was aimed more at Charles."

"Well, in that case," Adam nodded, after giving it some thought, "if you think you can persuade her into leaving her bed at this hour of the morning, although what possible reason we can give without telling her the truth I don't know, we had better be making tracks."

But Marcus was given no opportunity to respond to this as the sudden clanging of the bell broke the silence. Whoever it was demanding admittance at half past one in the morning certainly seemed determined to remain on the doorstep until it was answered, and from the number of vigorous tugs on the pull it seemed more than likely to wake the whole household into the bargain.

In view of Charles's earnest desire to secure anonymity, it had been a little difficult to speculate on what his next move would be. He could not risk taking a hand himself for fear of exposure, and unless he reverted to the rather dubious efforts of Ted Knowles it certainly seemed to his brother and cousin that his options were somewhat limited. Knowing Charles as well as they did it had never so much as crossed their minds that he would track Marcus down at home, but since the unlooked-for visitor could not be anyone else, this unexpected strategy took them both a little by surprise.

Adam, suspecting his brother's visit to mean only one thing, warned his cousin to be careful, but Marcus had no such suspicions. Charles may have been forced into coming here through necessity, but he was not so lost to common sense that he would attempt to murder him under his own roof. By no means satisfied with the way his cousin brushed this possibility aside,

Adam pointed out that since his brother obviously considered himself to be at the point of no return, no guarantee could be placed on him thinking rationally. Marcus agreed to it, but he remained adamant in the view that no matter how desperate Charles was he was not so lost to all reasoning that he would attempt anything so rash. With this Adam had to be content, leaving him with nothing to do but frustratingly kick his heels in the study while Marcus opened the door to his fate.

As far as Ted Knowles was concerned his client had been calling the tune for far too long, and from what he could see of it things were not looking any too promising. Nevertheless, he knew of no reason why he should forgo his just rewards for services so far rendered, and he was therefore quite prepared to go along with his client's newly formulated plan whilst at the same time setting his own in motion to protect himself. For reasons best known to himself, his client had obviously had an unaccountable change of heart where his cousin was concerned, and although he had a very good idea of what the outcome of their forthcoming meeting would be he was quite willing to humour Charles Harrington by going along with his revised intentions. Even supposing he did discover the counter plans he had set in train to deal with Ingleby once and for all Ted Knowles could not see him railing against them, especially when no accusing fingers would be pointed in his direction when the tragic news of his cousin's death became known. To all intents and purposes Marcus Ingleby would be reported as being the innocent but fatal victim of a robbery committed by person or persons unknown, and this, surely, should be enough to reconcile Charles Harrington!

Fully expecting to open the door to his cousin, Marcus was considerably taken aback to find himself face to face with the man who was not only responsible for that crashing blow to the back of his head but also his recent incarceration. The instant he had opened his eyes in that cellar to find Ted Knowles sitting guard over him Marcus had promised himself the pleasure of paying him back for his efforts, but to discover him on his doorstep within so short a space of time of his escape, was not at all what he had expected. The initial shock having worn off, he was left with the overwhelming urge to send Ted Knowles sprawling down the steps, even more so when he was clearly showing no signs of discomfiture or embarrassment over their previous encounter, and therefore Marcus's struggle to contain this desire was all the more difficult.

The look on Marcus's face should have been sufficient to warn Ted Knowles that he was treading on very thin ice and that he could count himself fortunate he was still standing on his own two feet, but his exceptionally thick skin coupled with a natural buoyancy meant that these signals simply bounced off him.

Marcus felt not the slightest inclination to invite him to step inside, but since his unlooked-for visitor had clearly asked the hackney driver to wait and was, to his dismay, looking interestedly in their direction, he deemed it wise, if not desirable. If Ted Knowles experienced any awkwardness at meeting his recent captive he was certainly giving no indication of it, in fact, he looked as unperturbed as though nothing had happened, or, indeed, was going to happen, merely doffing his hat and smiling, "Evenin' Guvna; or mornin' I shud say!"

He was without doubt the most objectionable individual it had ever been Marcus's misfortune to encounter, and whilst nothing would give him greater satisfaction than to plant him a flush hit, he knew that this was not the solution. Ted Knowles had come here for a specific purpose and gratifying his understandable inclinations would not discover what it was, apart from which there was more at stake than his own feelings. Marcus, ignoring his greeting as well as his genial admiration over his escape with a curt demand to know his business, Ted Knowles gave him a brief account of what had followed once his disappearance had been discovered. "Ferly sent me ter grass it did!" he told him, scratching his head. "'Owd yer do it, Guvna?" he asked, genuinely interested. "Trussed up like a Chrismus terkey, yer wos!"

Unfortunately for him, his host was in no mood to appreciate either his interest or his easy dismissal of what had taken place earlier, cutting short his untroubled remarks with a peremptory order to hand over the letter he had been asked to deliver. The poor quality of the envelope and the two folded sheets of paper inside certainly did not belong to Charles, but the smoothly composed words most certainly did. Considering the perilous position Charles was in, Marcus could only marvel at the self-assured, even confident message the letter contained, but he could not help wondering what exactly was going through his mind and what he hoped to achieve by this latest approach. Whatever it was he must be fairly convinced it would succeed, but Marcus's attempts to draw Ted Knowles out failed, either because he had been warned to say nothing or, which Marcus thought more likely, Charles had not taken him into his confidence, for which Marcus could not entirely blame him. Ted Knowles was hardly the type of man he himself would trust to undertake something of such magnitude, having allowed himself to be caught napping once it was more than probable to be the case again.

Scanning the sheets again in case he had missed something, Marcus's second perusal of it merely confirmed his original view that, as usual, Charles was being deliberately mysterious.

Cousin,

Permit me to be the first to congratulate you upon your remarkable escape. I can, of course, only speculate as to how you achieved so incredible a feat, but I assure you I am quite lost in admiration when I consider your infinite resource and enterprise and offer you my sincere compliments. Needless to say, I am most interested to learn how you accomplished what I had believed to be an impossible task and look forward to hearing all about your breathtaking escape when next we meet, which, I am sorry to say, will be rather sooner than you anticipated.

Naturally, I sympathise with your feelings towards our mutual acquaintance, but providing you do as I ask I promise you that after this evening, or should I say this morning? – there should be not the least need for your paths to cross again.

I feel sure you will agree that despite our last, and most regrettable meeting, we should be able to overcome our difficulties in a manner befitting gentlemen and, to this end, I have every confidence in your good sense by accompanying our friend to 'The Black Swan' where I shall be awaiting you. I must apologise for not being able to suggest a more salubrious venue, but you will agree to its being able to provide us with a certain amount of privacy.

I trust there is no need for me to impress upon you the extreme delicacy of the situation or the consequences which will result should you decide not to accept my invitation.

Painful though it is, I feel I must remind you that there are others who will suffer from your refusal.

Yours,

Charles

Marcus's eyes narrowed as he pondered the letter. Apparently, his cousin had had a change of heart about doing away with him, but what he intended as an alternative remained to be seen. If he wanted to find out what Charles had in mind, as well as trying to avert a catastrophe, he knew he had no choice but to accompany Ted Knowles, a man he neither liked nor trusted, but he owed it to Alexandra to do all he could to protect her. "I understand I am to accompany you," he stated coldly.

"That's it, Guvna," Ted Knowles nodded. "'Ackney's alredy waitin'."

Marcus eyed him closely. "You seem to have taken my acceptance for granted."

Ted Knowles rubbed his chin reflectively. "Well, as it 'appuns, Guvna," he explained, "sumone else tuck it fer grantid."

"My estimable cousin, no doubt," Marcus supplied.

"That's it, Guvna," Ted Knowles nodded, relieved that he was not going to argue the point. "Look'ee 'ere, Guvna," he said audaciously, "no 'ard feelins about earlia."

"I suppose you think that is sufficient?" Marcus bit out.

"Dang me!" Ted Knowles exclaimed, disgusted. "And I dain't even filch yer pockits!"

"I suppose you expect me to be grateful for that?" Without giving him time to respond, Marcus said curtly, "Wait here."

Turning on his heel he headed for the study where Adam instantly pounced on him, impatiently demanding to know what the devil was going on. The warning glance he received from his cousin was enough to tell him that he did not want to let Ted Knowles know anyone else was in the house, and it was therefore in a fierce whisper that Adam demanded to know what, in the name of all that was wonderful, was he doing here instead of Charles? But after reading the letter Marcus handed him he stared aghast before saying, "You mustn't go, Marcus! It's a trap."

"Perhaps, but I must go," Marcus dismissed, shrugging himself into his damp and rather dishevelled overcoat.

"Then I'm coming with you," Adam said firmly.

"No, you are not," Marcus shook his head. "You will be of far more use to me by following behind. Give me five minutes, and then make your way to *The Black Swan*. I know," he nodded, seeing the look of horror on Adam's face, "I assure you, I have no more wish to return there than you have, but it seems your brother is not going to give me the opportunity of choosing another venue. When you arrive there," he told him, "you do not come inside. I am afraid," he said apologetically, pulling on his gloves, "it means you having to make further use of that entry." A smile touched his lips at the look of pure aversion which had descended onto Adam's face. "A horrifying thought, I know, but at least I shall know where you are should I need you; I shall find a way of signalling you if I do. Under no circumstances," he stressed, "do I want your involvement known at this stage."

"That's all very well," Adam pointed out, "but Charles is going to know the part I have played in this sooner or later. Far better sooner!" he stated unequivocally.

"At the moment," Marcus told him, "Charles believes he only has me to deal with, and that's how I want it to remain for the time being. Hopefully though, we can settle matters without the need for me to call in reinforcements," inclining his head significantly at Adam.

"Keeping me in reserve, eh!" Adam grinned, by no means happy about this new development.

"If you like," Marcus nodded. "I have no way of knowing what Charles has in mind," he admitted, "and until I do we must put the girl's safety before anything; which means that for the time being she will be far better off at home than whisking her away."

Following another word of caution from Adam, Marcus rejoined Ted Knowles who had whiled away the time by studying his surroundings appraisingly, by no means troubled by the counter-plan he had set in motion, deeming it all in a day's work. Upon seeing Marcus emerge from the study and stride into the hall Ted Knowles put his hat on his head and opened the door, following Marcus down the steps of the house and into the waiting hackney.

As it was obvious to the meanest intelligence that his companion was in no frame of mind to make conversation, Ted Knowles slipped into contented silence, pleasurably dwelling on the successful outcome of his carefully laid schemes and his hard-earned reward. From time to time he glanced sideways at Marcus, but as his face was mostly in shadow it was impossible to read his expression. Even so, it did not take much to see that he was not in the most amiable of tempers, and Ted Knowles, usually a most loquacious individual, made no attempt to break the silence, but whiled away the journey by wondering how his client had passed his time; not a little relieved when the hackney eventually pulled up outside '*The Black Swan*'.

Charles, far from impressed with his surroundings and the unsavoury company he was being obliged to keep, devoutly trusted that he would never again be called upon to come anywhere near this locality, and to this establishment especially. He had every faith in his cousin, knowing full well that he would comply with his request, and upon seeing him walk in with Ted Knowles a confident smiled crossed his lips, making his wait worthwhile.

Across the space which separated them the cousins eyed one another steadily for several moments, but it was Charles who broke the silence. "Marcus! How good of you to join me."

"You left me with very little choice," Marcus replied coldly, walking further into the bar room, his eyes hard and unyielding as they held his cousin's, totally dismissing Joe and Albert, who viewed the forthcoming interview with mixed feelings.

"Well, that was the general idea," Charles conceded.

"You must forgive me if I do not share your humour," Marcus mocked, glancing fleetingly across at Joe and Albert, not at all sure they liked such dismissive treatment, "but your choice of venue is not at all to my taste. I have had my fill of this establishment."

"I sympathise entirely," Charles assured him, "but necessity, Marcus," he told him smoothly, "does not always leave one too much room for manoeuvre."

"Well, now that I *am* here," Marcus said shortly, keeping a watchful eye on Ted Knowles, "may I enquire as to the reason, or do you intend to keep me guessing?"

"Always to the point, are you not, Cousin?" Charles mocked, his eyes glinting. "Whatever my faults," he inclined his head, "I am not so ill-mannered as to bring you all this way without explaining why; although," he raised an eyebrow, "I should have thought no explanation was in the least necessary considering the unfinished business between us."

"I had a feeling it was not merely to discuss my escape," Marcus commented dryly.

"I have every intention of discussing such a feat with you," Charles informed him smoothly, "but you must know, Marcus," he said affably, "eager though I am to hear how you accomplished it, there *is* something of more moment I need to talk to you about."

"I thought perhaps there was," Marcus nodded, removing his hat and gloves.

"What a pleasure it is to deal with a man whose intelligence corresponds precisely with my own," Charles drawled mockingly. "I cannot tell you how wearisome it is to be constantly obliged to explain my meaning." When Marcus made no reply to this, Charles offered politely, "Please, do sit down. I cannot vouch for the cleanliness of the chairs in this establishment," he apologised, glancing disparagingly round at Joe and Albert, "but we may as well make ourselves as comfortable as possible."

"I do not intend making a long stay, Charles," Marcus informed him. "I can listen equally well standing." He cast a brief look in the direction of the landlord and his crony before bringing his gaze back to rest on his cousin. "I should prefer it, however, if our conversation could be conducted without an audience."

Charles glanced at his associates, all of whom were experiencing varying degrees of apprehension as they witnessed this polite exchange between the two men who, as anyone but a fool could see, clearly had no love for one another. "You need not be afraid, Marcus," he assured him. "You would be surprised how deaf, dumb and blind they can be when they choose."

Marcus's face looked grim, but as Charles clearly intended to conduct this meeting right here and now, he said brusquely, "If you insist on discussing what I deem to be an extremely delicate matter within hearing of those whose discretion is patently questionable, so be it. What is it you want, Charles?"

Charles's lips thinned, but when he spoke it was still in that smoothly ominous tone. "I should have thought there was no need to ask that."

"You must forgive me," Marcus replied with sardonic politeness, "I appear to be a little obtuse. No doubt the result of a most unusual evening. Quite enough to dull the intellect, wouldn't you say?"

Charles was rankled by this, but managing to hide it, said calmly, "You do yourself an injustice, Cousin. At no time would I ever accuse you of that. However, I have not invited you here on a whim, but to tell you that I now find it no longer necessary to... er... what shall I say? – ah, yes, put an end to your existence. You see," he pointed out confidently, "I discover that there is not the least need to do so."

"Indeed!" Marcus exclaimed. "I am relieved to hear it."

"I knew you would be," Charles smiled.

"Although," Marcus told him with quiet confidence, "there was never the least likelihood of your schemes to rid yourself of me succeeding."

Charles's eyes narrowed, but he felt compelled to ask, "Oh, why not?"

Marcus smiled, saying with perfect composure, "I think I could have roused myself sufficiently to thwart your efforts." Without giving his cousin time to respond, he pointed out reasonably, "Of course, it does raise the question as to what you intend as an alternative. I think you will agree that that is a rather important consideration from my point of view."

"Naturally," Charles concurred, determined not to allow his cousin to gain the upper hand, "but consideration, Cousin," he pointed out, "works two ways. For instance, you must realise that I cannot possibly allow you to impart what you know to the police."

Marcus took time in answering this, saying at length, "It is your turn to be under a misapprehension, Charles. At no time was that my intention," Charles looked his surprise at this, but ignoring it, Marcus continued, "though not, I hasten to add, out of consideration for you. For my part, I would willingly leave you to face your accusers, but that would mean others would suffer irreparable harm because of you, and it is those whom I wish to protect. However," he added inexorably, "it *is* my intention to frustrate your plans for tomorrow, and I will do so by whatever means at my disposal."

As Joe and Albert had no idea what was going to happen tomorrow they merely exchanged significant glances, but Charles had certainly not expected such resolution as this, although he supposed he should have done considering his cousin's chivalrous nature, not that it altered a thing! He had still his trump card to play, after which, Marcus would sing a very different tune. *"Very noble!"* Charles drawled. "But you see, Cousin, you have overlooked one little thing." Apart from a raised eyebrow Marcus made no response to this. "Do you honestly believe for one tiny instant, that I shall have nothing to say about your meddlesome interference? No, no, Marcus," he shook his head, "like you, I think I could exert myself sufficiently to prevent any intervention on your part. It behoves me, therefore, to disabuse your mind of any hopes it may cherish of interfering in my plans."

"If you think you can buy me off," Marcus warned him, "you are quite wrong."

"Not with money, no," Charles conceded, "but there are other means of tender."

"No inducement you could offer me makes your scheme any more acceptable to me," Marcus stated unequivocally, "any more than it would persuade me to ignore it."

Charles appeared to give this careful consideration, after which he said softly, "You seem very sure of that, Cousin."

"I am," Marcus replied implacably. "I am not for sale, Charles, at any price. I thought you would have known that."

Charles's eyes narrowed, but undeterred said, "You wrong me, Cousin, I do indeed know it, but I am afraid you cannot have considered the consequences of such a rigid stance. Allow me to point them out to you."

"You're wasting your time, Charles," Marcus told him. "Whatever consequences ensue from this, you are the once facing them."

"Do you think so, indeed?" Charles raised a questioning eyebrow, a malicious glint in his eyes. "I wonder," he mused. "Of course, you could be right," he acknowledged, "but somehow I don't think so." He eyed his cousin to see what effect his words had had on him, but apart from a slight narrowing of the eyes, he made no attempt to speak. "Have you noticed, Marcus," he remarked conversationally, "how busy the town is becoming with traffic of late? Indeed, I marvel how people ever manage to cross from one side of the street to the other without mishap. It is a constant source of concern to me, especially when I consider how often Sophy goes abroad on foot."

There was no mistaking the meaning behind the subtlety, and for one awful moment Ted Knowles thought Marcus was going to kill his cousin where he stood. Such a blaze of anger shone in those eyes that Ted Knowles doubted if even his intervention could prevent a murder from taking place. Never had he seen such fury on a man's face before, and he could only wonder what was preventing him from using those purposeful fists clenched at his sides.

Marcus did indeed experience a moment of unrestrained anger when he could have willingly murdered his cousin and to the devil with the consequences, but his common sense eventually managed to overcome this overwhelming urge, telling himself that not only was Charles not worth going to the gallows for but it would inevitably lead to the kind of scandal he was trying desperately hard to avoid.

The anger still burned in Marcus's eyes but Charles was more than a little relieved to see it gradually diminish as well as those purposeful fists unclench. He was no stranger to the pugilistic art and had even been known to give a good account of himself, but should his cousin decide to use his fists on him he was certainly in no mood to extend to him any of the professional courtesies which usually accompanied such an exchange. He may be of equal height to his cousin but Charles was physically no match for a man who could give him at least a stone or more, and he knew a moment of heartfelt relief when the danger point had passed. He could not deny that he had experienced a most uncomfortable few minutes, but the truth was he had known the moment the idea had first come to him that Marcus, despite his anger and revulsion, would comply in the end; after all, he was dealing him a hand which left no room whatever for manoeuvre. Charles knew that Marcus would like nothing more than to lay him out cold, but he knew too that it was the thought of Sophy which prevented him from carrying out this wish. So long as he dangled his wife in front of his cousin Charles knew he was safe, and fully protected against any repercussions. Marcus may rail against the idea of having to turn his back and keep silent, but so long as he knew Sophy stood in the firing line resulting from any input of his, he would not say or do anything to interfere, either now or in the future.

The white heat of Marcus's anger may have died down but he was still conscious of the very strong desire to inflict the utmost punishment on his cousin, but managing to control it, he cried, *"You wouldn't dare!"*

"Are you prepared to gamble Sophy's life on that chance?" Charles asked, his confidence returning now the danger of physical retribution had passed.

"I prefer your original proposal to this," Marcus bit out, his voice ragged.

"I daresay you do," Charles acknowledged, "but you must agree that this one is far better."

"Then you are alone in that belief," Marcus told him grimly.

"I am confident that should suspicion for your death have fallen upon me I could have adequately dealt with it, but this way obviates that risk. Besides," Charles pointed out reasonably, "why create a question mark when it can so easily be avoided?" Pouring himself a glass of Joe's best cognac, brought up earlier from the cellar by his reluctant host, he took a generous mouthful, the fiery liquid putting new life into him. "All I ask," he sighed, "is that you forget all about my plans for the girl and, of course, the events leading up to them and, in return, I give you my word that no harm will come to Sophy."

"And if I refuse?" Marcus demanded, his eyes accusing.

Charles returned the look. "You won't," he shook his head. "You see, Marcus, I know you better than you know yourself. Apart from the fact that you are too much the gentleman to do anything else, you love Sophy too well to put her life at risk."

"You have it all worked out, don't you?" Marcus asked coldly.

"Let us just say that having considered all the options this is by far the better one," Charles commented smoothly, unaware of Joe's silent agreement.

"For whom?" Marcus demanded disgustedly.

"For all of us I should have thought, for you especially," Charles informed him, draining his glass, "after all," he shrugged, "being alive is better than being dead."

Marcus shook his head in bemusement. "You really don't understand, do you?"

"I am glad to say I don't," Charles told him. "Being noble is all very well, but it can render one exceedingly uncomfortable. I think you will agree that life is a far better prospect than the alternative."

"At what price, Charles?" Marcus demanded. "You expect me to sell my honour and integrity and to live in comfort with it! Well, you may be able to do so, but I cannot."

"Such histrionics over a chit of a girl!" Charles scorned.

"Call it what you will," Marcus ground out, "but unlike you I had rather by far have no life at all than to live it dishonourably!"

"And what of Sophy's life?" Charles reminded him softly, still supremely confident of his cousin's ultimate capitulation. "Are you prepared to sacrifice her for a spawn's brat whom you have only laid eyes on once? Well," he demanded, "are you?" When Marcus made no reply to this, Charles smiled. "No, of course you are not. Like it or not, Cousin," he said confidently, "you will say and do precisely nothing."

The look of triumph in his eyes fuelled Marcus's anger and, worse, his impotence. He knew perfectly well that Charles would have no compunction in sacrificing Sophy to secure his own ends, just as Marcus knew that he in turn would do everything in his power to protect her.

"You know, Marcus," Charles said smoothly, "despite your high ideals and talk of honour and integrity, you too are for sale – just like the rest of us!"

It was an inflammatory remark, guaranteed to rouse anger in the most placid of men, as Charles knew very well, but even though the look he encountered from his cousin told him that Marcus would like to make him eat every word, he knew he stood in no danger of physical retribution. Sophy was not only his insurance policy but a protective shield, and Charles was quite prepared to exploit both to protect his interests and to ensure the successful outcome of all his efforts. Marcus may hate him as well as himself for the impossible position he had been forced into, and whilst Charles realised that his cousin could only be pushed so far, he was nevertheless more than happy with the outcome of this meeting.

Ted Knowles, who had witnessed the interchange between the cousins with growing interest, could only marvel at Marcus Ingleby's self-control, but, unlike Charles Harrington, he placed very little reliance on the continuance of his cousin's agreement. Whatever his feelings towards Marcus Ingleby, Ted Knowles had recognised instantly the type of man he was, and although he had been coerced into turning a blind eye for the sake of protecting the woman he clearly had strong feelings for, he placed no guarantee on him continuing to do so. Charles Harrington, clearly convinced that his gamble had paid off, was, or so it seemed to Ted Knowles, content to trust his cousin's word as well as his integrity, but it was his experience that integrity could very easily backfire, and he was now more than ever convinced that his plan to take care of Marcus Ingleby was the only sure way of ensuring his silence. A man like that could not easily ignore his conscience any more than he could his own personal code of honour, which, apparently, was so far unsullied. It would be an extremely hard pill for him to swallow to sit back while he knew the girl was on the point of being put out of the way and he could do nothing about it. No! That was asking too much for a man like Ingleby and, unless Ted Knowles was very much mistaken, his silence would not last very long! More than ever, he knew his solution was the only one, and he had no doubt that, in time, should Charles Harrington ever discover the truth, he would be brought to see he was right.

Neither Joe nor Albert had understood very much of the subtly smooth conversation which had just taken place, but it did not take much for them to see the animosity which existed between the two men, but as it was becoming increasingly obvious that no bout of fisticuffs or, worse, was to be enacted on the premises, they both heaved a tremendous sigh of relief. Joe had no doubt that he could handle any number of combatants, but the less trouble in his place the better he liked it. He could not afford to have the Peelers at Bow Street shoving their noses into his premises!

"You will admit, Cousin," Charles said provocatively, "that there *was* one inducement, after all!"

It was several moments before Marcus could trust himself to speak, but eventually he managed to say, his voice somewhat strained, "So it would seem."

"Do not take it so much to heart, Marcus," Charles advised. "After all, what is the girl to you?" When Marcus did not reply, he said, "There is not the least need to reproach yourself; you did everything possible to save her, and whilst I am at a loss to understand the reason why, I *do* understand your motives for finally letting events take their inevitable course."

Marcus was breathing hard, his anger a tangible force he found hard to suppress, but he did manage to achieve some semblance of calm, saying with a sincerity his cousin could not mistake, "Then understand *this*, Charles; should any harm come to Sophy, I hope *you* will understand *my* motives when I take the inevitable course of putting a period to *your* existence!"

Charles acknowledged this with a slight inclination of the head, saying, "In that case, it behoves us both to behave like gentlemen and keep our promises." Eyeing his cousin in some amusement, he said, "But something tells me you don't feel like one."

"I don't," Marcus ground out, "and loath though I am, I shall keep my promise – for as long as you do."

"I am glad we understand one another," Charles nodded, "after all, it would do neither of us any good to break our word."

"Your subtlety is commendable," Marcus pointed out, "but I don't like threats, no matter how you coat them. Let it be enough that I am aligned to your dirty crime, rendering myself an accessory before and after the fact."

"You take far too gloomy a view, Marcus," Charles remarked lightly, "but if it helps you at all, simply look upon your agreement as protecting the family; after all, Sophy especially will be eternally grateful."

"You must forgive me for not applauding your tactics," Marcus said sardonically, "but your devious methods rouse no admiration in me."

"I am prepared to forgive anything," Charles told him affably, "providing, of course, you keep your word."

"I have given it," Marcus bit out, his eyes cold and hard. "Let that suffice."

Charles bowed his head. "Thank you, Cousin; you are too kind," he mocked. Then, as if a thought had suddenly occurred to him, he said, "Ah yes, I knew there was something else."

"More demands?" Marcus enquired derisively.

"Not a demand, precisely," Charles replied smoothly, "I prefer to call it a request."

"Your requests are nothing if not unique. What is it?" Marcus demanded.

Pausing only to remove a speck of dust from his sleeve, Charles said conversationally, "You have, I believe, a certain letter in your possession; a letter which, unless I am very much mistaken, was handed to you by Sophy earlier today, or should I say yesterday?" he raised an enquiring eyebrow.

"What of it?" Marcus dismissed, eyeing his cousin narrowly.

"Let us just say," Charles said softly, "that I should feel far happier if that letter were in my possession instead of in yours."

Marcus smiled for the first time, not his usual friendly smile but one of pure self-satisfaction which made Charles cautious. "I daresay you would," he acknowledged, "but I am not prepared to give it to you."

"You're refusing?" Charles said dangerously, determined to get his hands on that letter.

"You surely do not expect me to calmly hand it over to you, do you?" Marcus mocked.

"Oh, but I do," Charles told him softly.

Marcus eyed him squarely, his voice taking on an inflexible note. "That letter remains with me, Charles, and, *this* time, no inducement you could offer me would make me relinquish it." Charles had never heard his cousin speak in this tone before, and it gave him pause for thought. "You have sunk lower than I thought any man could by using his wife as a form of insurance to protect himself, well," Marcus told him unequivocally, "I too have taken out some insurance, though not for myself. You have disregarded Sophy's feelings as well as her life with a callousness I had not thought possible, even from you, but that letter will ensure her permanent safety, and if I ever discover that you have harmed her in any way, I shall have no hesitation in using it against you."

At no point had Charles considered this possibility but he knew his cousin well enough to know that he would do precisely what he said, and if this meant confessing his own part in the affair, he would do so. "You too, it seems, have thought of everything," he said, the edge to his voice unmistakable.

"When one is dealing with a fox one must think like one," Marcus told him. "You are not the only one to plan and scheme, Charles. So long as I hold that letter, which, however tenuously, links you to the girl's death, Sophy is safe, so too is my aunt as well as the name you bear, which, apparently," he derided, "means no more to you than the life of one whom you should wish to protect above all others."

"And what of you?" Charles demanded, by no means pleased that his cousin intended to hold on to that valuable piece of evidence, which, however flimsy, could do him immeasurable harm.

"Me?" Marcus raised a questioning eyebrow. "Believe it or not, Charles, I would much rather produce that letter than live with the knowledge of what I have done tonight."

"You're a fool, Marcus!" Charles told him irritably. "The girl's not worth it."

Marcus looked his sickening disgust. It was not difficult to see what had driven his cousin to this point. Even if Alexandra had not been mentioned in her grandfather's will and those precious items of jewellery were not an issue, the very thought of her residing in Brook Street was more than Charles's pride and arrogance could bear, and whilst Marcus was not proud of his own actions he was nevertheless able to take some small comfort from knowing that his decision to keep silent had stemmed from motives which were far purer than his cousin's. Even so, the nasty taste in his mouth would not go away, and he knew it never would as well as knowing that he would have to live with his decision for the rest of his life, deriving no consolation from the fact that he had been emotionally coerced into it. "Obviously not to you," he bit out.

Still far from happy about that letter, Charles had to accept that no persuasion of his would induce Marcus to hand it over, and whilst he may not like the idea of having it held over his head he was sufficiently confident in his cousin's word to be certain that it would never see the light of day providing he kept to his side of the bargain. By now it wanted only a couple of minutes to two o'clock, but he could not call an end to the evening without questioning his cousin's escape.

Marcus had expected this, but he could see little point in divulging Adam's part in it. Charles would take it very ill if he knew his brother had been working against him with his cousin, and since it was not Marcus's desire to set them against one another he failed to see what possible good would come from it. If Adam felt the need to tell Charles the truth then that had to be his decision, but now the whole sorry business had been uneasily settled between them, Adam's role had effectively ceased.

"Come, Cousin," Charles urged, "confess, you had help. Do not bother to deny it," he shook his head. "I saw Knowles bolt that door myself. You could not possibly have opened it."

Marcus smiled, infuriating his cousin by saying dismissively, "Put it down to my infinite resource and constant endeavour, just as you commended me in your letter."

Irritated by such a response, Charles said impatiently, "This is no time for humour, Marcus. You must acknowledge that a third party is likely to bring all to ruin."

"Set your mind at rest, Charles," Marcus told him, heading for the door. "No one is going to expose you – unfortunately. Your little venture is safe enough. *Now*," he said with finality, "I am going home. Whether I shall be able to sleep is another matter. Although," he admitted, "I doubt I shall ever sleep again knowing what I have agreed to tonight! But come what may, I have had my fill of this place; enough to last me a lifetime!" On which parting note he left the premises.

Chapter Nineteen

Trying to summon up a hackney at quarter past one in the morning was not the easiest thing Adam had ever done, but after walking through the damp and deserted streets of Knightsbridge for the better part of ten minutes, he eventually came upon a vehicle parked at the corner of Cromwell Road and Queen's Gate. The driver, a sullen-looking individual who had decided it was time to go home, stared down at Adam with a ruminating eye before saying churlishly that he was taking no more fares tonight. Adam's promise of making a journey worth his while was met with an instant demand to see the colour of his money first. Reluctant though Adam was to take out his wallet in the middle of the street, he knew there was really no alternative. Having satisfied himself that the gent had adequate funds to honour his promise, he jerked his thumb towards the vehicle, whereupon Adam climbed inside, silently cursing all hackney drivers.

For the second time within the space of a couple of hours he found himself keeping watch outside 'The Black Swan', and so profound was his antipathy of the place that he devoutly hoped he would never set eyes on it again. Nothing of the activities going on inside were visible through the clouded glass of the windows, and since everything appeared fairly quiet at the moment he prepared himself for another lengthy vigil. The air was uncomfortably damp and chill and raising his coat collar did nothing to help but at least it was no longer pouring with rain, and even though the draughty entry was as unpleasant and uncomfortable as Adam remembered it, it at least afforded him protection in case his brother left first or, even perhaps, in company with Marcus, as it would not do for Charles to catch sight of him.

Since Marcus had told him he was not to show himself unless he signalled for him to do so, Adam could do no more than wait for such a sign or the eventual sight of his cousin leaving the premises. As it was he had to wait almost an hour before Marcus emerged from 'The Black Swan', during which time Adam had wondered what was going on inside. He had seriously toyed with the idea of going against Marcus's orders by going over to find out what was happening, but only a little thought was enough to tell him that he could most probably make bad worse by doing so. Nevertheless, upon seeing his cousin finally leaving the premises Adam was conscious of a feeling of relief to know that his services had not been required after all, in fact, having reflected a moment he supposed it was far better for the business to have been transacted as quietly as possible rather than running the risk of bringing the law down on them and creating an out and out scandal.

Charles had obviously decided to remain a little longer as Marcus was quite alone when he came out of 'The Black Swan', spotting Adam immediately huddled inside the entry, inclining his head for him to join him. It did not take much to recognise the grim look on his cousin's face, clearly indicating that the news was not going to be good, but since the middle of the street was not the place to discuss something of this nature, and certainly not within the immediate vicinity of 'The Black Swan', Adam managed to refrain from pressing him with questions. Not until they arrived at Waterloo Road did they slacken their pace sufficiently to hold any kind of conversation, and although Marcus would have preferred to wait until later to discuss it, he was fully aware that he owed Adam an explanation of some kind.

Whatever Adam had expected to result from the meeting between his brother and cousin it was certainly nothing like what he was hearing, and for several stunned moments he walked beside Marcus in a state of shocked silence. Adam had detected the guilt in every word his cousin had uttered but given the circumstances he failed to see what else Marcus could have done. His position was certainly unenviable, but Adam supposed if he had been placed in the same situation he would have done precisely the same thing. He knew without any doubt that had there been a viable alternative Marcus would have taken it, although knowing his cousin as well as he did Adam would go so far as to say that he would have much preferred it if Charles had stuck to his original idea rather than holding Sophy as well as his integrity to ransom with a proposal that was as despicable as it was unbearable. Charles had certainly done his work well, knowing that the ultimatum he had put forward could not have been turned down. Adam had always known his brother possessed a ruthless streak and an inflexible determination, but that he should go to these lengths surprised even him. Charles must be desperate indeed to adopt this tactic but having finally gained his cousin's promise to leave well alone he obviously considered he had nothing to fear from him.

Adam wondered what Marcus would do now, although to his way of thinking there seemed to be nothing he could do, or himself for that matter. Adam had seriously toyed with the idea of rescuing his niece himself, but only a very little thought was sufficient to tell him that his hands were just as tied as his cousin's because should his brother's plans be thwarted by either of them, then it would be Sophy who would pay the ultimate price for their intervention on Alexandra's behalf. Not only that, but it would be opening Charles up to all manner of things, if not from his confederates then certainly from the police as Adam failed to see how it would not come to their notice, and all their efforts to avoid a scandal would have been for nothing, and for his mother's sake if nothing else, he was determined to do all he could to try to prevent his brother from ending up on the end of a rope. Adam did not judge or condemn his cousin for what he had agreed to, after all, his brother had given him no other choice, but he only wished that matters had not come to this point.

By now they had crossed Waterloo Bridge heading in the direction of The Strand where they could most probably pick up a late hackney. Thankfully, the damp streets, if not deserted, were frequented by only a handful of passers-by who, whether from apathy or being in a state of inebriation, took no notice of the two men whose appearances were anything but presentable. In view of Marcus's disclosure, they both walked on in silence, wrestling with their own thoughts; the one shocked at discovering his brother's involvement in something which could only be described as criminal, and the other biting down on his vexation over the despicable agreement he had made. As luck would have it, they found a lone hackney at the corner of Wellington Street and The Strand and, after giving curt instructions to take them to Knightsbridge, they climbed into the antiquated vehicle to sit back against the squabs, both men not daring to think of the outcome of tomorrow's planned events.

Marcus's thoughts were not very elevating. Charles had held him to ransom with Sophy's life, and he was man enough to want to protect her. Marcus gave his cousin credit for keeping his word, but whilst this should have eased his conscience, it did not. It was true that he had only met Alexandra once, but Charles was quite wrong when he said that he owed her nothing. How could one sell her life for that of another? How could one possibly dismiss her as of no importance? Marcus thought of her mother, Elizabeth, and felt sickened at the part he had been forced to play. Yet how could he have done otherwise? Sophy meant more to him than life itself; she was life – his life! Without her everything was empty and meaningless. Yet how could he face the woman he loved after what he had done? He had not only sold his honour and integrity but had disregarded every code by which he lived, and the guilt he was already experiencing was like a lead weight. Somehow there had to be a way of saving the girl and protecting Sophy whilst at the same time averting the devil of a scandal, but try as he did he could think of nothing which would serve the purpose. It was not until a chance remark made by Adam, who had begun to find the silence oppressive, that a solution came to him.

Relieved to see the frown lift from his cousin's forehead and the severity leave his face, Adam produced a somewhat tentative smile, asking hesitantly, "Are you all right, Marcus?"

"Never better!" Marcus smiled, gripping his arm. "Thanks to you."

"Me?" Adam echoed, surprised. "Why, what have I done?"

"More than I can ever repay," Marcus told him, the relief emanating from him like a physical force.

Fortunately for Adam's overstretched nerves, they were soon set down outside Marcus's house, barely able to hold back the number of questions he wanted to put to him until they got inside. As Marcus expected, Adam's reaction to what had passed between himself and Charles was one of profound shock, and he did his best to answer his questions without wounding him even more. Adam may not share a thought in common with his brother, but the discovery of his involvement in a crime which, should it ever become known, would inevitably end with him facing the gallows, was something he could not contemplate without acute pain. Despite their differences, they *were* brothers; bound together by an invisible bond which was as intrinsic as it was impossible to ignore. For Adam's sake as well as the girl's, Marcus had to make the attempt to prevent the very worst from happening. Charles may well sever all ties for what he was planning, but that, surely, was far better than ending his life on the scaffold!

"Pluck up; all's not lost," Marcus smiled, gripping his shoulder.

Reluctant though he was, Adam had to acknowledge that his brother had been exceptionally clever in dealing with a situation which anyone else would have given up for lost. Charles had never been one to give up easily on anything and, in Marcus and Sophy, he had found the perfect pawns for manoeuvring himself into an unassailable position. Marcus's character had been used against him with devastating effect, knowing that he would do nothing to jeopardise Sophy's life, for which Adam could not blame him, but as far as he could see they could not help the one without risking the other, and no matter how he tried he failed to share Marcus's unexpected optimism in that all was not lost.

Accurately reading his thoughts, Marcus smiled, the heavy burden of guilt removed and, after draining his glass and refilling it, suggested they sit down. "Nothing can be done until the morning."

"I fail to see how anything can be done at all!" Adam told him candidly. "Or are you by any chance thinking of your earlier idea of removing the girl from her lodgings tonight?" raising a questioning eyebrow. "Because if you are," he shrugged, "I fail to see how that will answer."

Marcus shook his head. "Having had time to reflect upon it, I don't think that would be a very good idea, after all. I think she will be far safer where she is tonight than anywhere else. Besides," he pointed out realistically, "there is nowhere I can take her. I cannot possibly take her to a hotel without questions being asked, and she can hardly go to Brook Street to your mother without the whole sorry story being told, and since I cannot offer her shelter under my own roof for obvious reasons, she will just have to remain where she is."

"Then what *are* we going to do?" Adam asked, beginning to realise that effecting a rescue was not as easy as he had thought.

A slight frown creased Marcus's forehead as he considered something, then, after what appeared to his cousin to be several minutes of deep mental absorption, surprised him by asking, "What time does Charles usually take breakfast?"

"About eight o'clock," Adam shrugged. "Why?"

"And what time does he usually leave to go the brewery?"

Again, Adam looked his surprise, answering cautiously, "No later than nine o'clock. What *is* all this, Marcus?" he demanded.

"We get Sophy and the girl away, of course," Marcus replied calmly.

Adam stared at him. *"Get them away!* What the *devil* do you mean?"

"Well, it was you who put the idea into my head," Marcus told him.

"I did? When?" Adam asked curiously.

"On the way here in that hackney," Marcus reminded him. "Had it not have been for you I doubt I should have thought of it."

Adam seriously doubted this. His cousin's thinking so far had been pretty well accurate. "Well, I'm not sure I remember what I said precisely," Adam confessed, "but whatever it was I'm glad I did, or, at least, I think I am, but remind me; what did I say?"

"Only that you hoped you would never again have to go junketing about in a hackney at dead of night," Marcus told him.

"But what did that signify?" Adam asked, shaking his head.

"From what Sophy told me earlier today, 'junketing about' was the very phrase Emily used only a couple of days ago when she told her about her visit to Timothy's," Marcus explained, setting several logs onto the fire.

"I still don't understand," Adam said, eyeing his cousin closely.

"The day after tomorrow," Marcus reminded him, "Sophy goes to stay with Timothy and Annabel. Well, I am going to arrange for her to go a day earlier, only she won't be alone." He paused just long enough to see the effect this had on his cousin, who, after all the shocks and surprises he had endured, was looking rather ragged. "As soon as Charles leaves for the brewery tomorrow you must get Jem to bring your mother's carriage round to the front of the house, then, after the luggage has been bestowed, he will drive Sophy to the girl's lodgings. I am afraid," he sighed, "I shall have to leave Sophy to fabricate some tale to your mother to account for her departure to Timothy's a day earlier than planned, but given the circumstances," he shook his head, "there is no help for it." He saw the deep frown crease Adam's forehead. "Believe me, Adam," he told him frankly, "if another solution presented itself I would take it, but there is none. I don't like deceiving my aunt any more than you do, much less asking Sophy to lie on my behalf to her, but, like you, I am determined to do everything I can to prevent my aunt and Alexandra from ever knowing the truth. As far as *you* are concerned," Marcus told him, "you are merely accompanying Sophy and her maid to the railway station to see them and their luggage safely installed into a compartment, but instead of accompanying Sophy to Alexandra's lodgings I want you to purchase four train tickets to Maidstone then bring them here in readiness; the less time we waste the better. I feel certain," he smiled, "that you can persuade Jem to say nothing to your mother about Sophy's detour to Hoxton."

Adam almost dropped his glass, staring incredulously across at his cousin as if he could not believe what he had just heard. He had every faith in Jem, but it was not this faithful retainer that concerned him. "It will *never* work!" he exclaimed, shaking his head.

"Yes, it *will*," Marcus nodded. "Sophy dare not leave the house until after Charles has left at his usual time; under no circumstances must any of us give him cause to suspect that something is going forward."

"We're cutting it pretty fine as it is," Adam reminded him, having given it some thought. "We not only have no idea what time the accident is scheduled to take place tomorrow but we don't even know where!"

"I know," Marcus agreed, "but the more I think about it the more likely it seems that this so-called accident is not scheduled to take place before midday."

"We can't know that for certain." Adam shook his head.

"No, of course we can't," Marcus acknowledged, "but think, Adam; if you were planning something of this nature you would want to ensure that as many people as possible saw it, which means that every one of them will corroborate Sophy's story. You must agree," he nodded, "that there are far more people abroad at midday than early in the morning."

Adam, who had been doing some mental calculations, offered, "Then working on that premise, we have about three hours to get Sophy and Alexandra away."

"Precisely!" Marcus concurred. "Obviously, Sophy knows the venue of her supposed meeting with Alexandra as well as the time, but since we can hardly disturb her at this hour of the morning to discover either, all we can do is speculate and try to plan around it. But in any event," he shrugged, "nothing can be done until Charles has left the house."

Adam looked doubtful and shook his head. "Charles is no fool, the moment he returns home and discovers Sophy has gone as well as being informed, which he no doubt will be, that the accident has not taken place, he is bound to know you have hatched the whole."

"When I agreed to Charles's dirty little bargain," Marcus told him, "I had made the unforgivable error of not realising the deeper significance that letter in my possession represented; instead, I used it, regrettably, not to prevent a tragedy from occurring but just to protect Sophy."

Even now he could not believe he had been fool enough to overlook the full value of such a vital piece of evidence when he had agreed to Charles's demands, but having given it deeper thought he believed it may well work out better this way than he had any right to hope for. By allowing Charlies to believe, if only for the time being, that he was going along with his schemes it would, if nothing else, grant him precious time in which to ensure the safety of Sophy and the girl.

Adam, wondering whether his cousin was suffering a delayed reaction of some kind from his knock over the head, eyed him warily, asking tentatively, "How could you have used it differently? I don't see what other purpose it could have been put to. Don't forget," he reminded him, "it's not in Charles's hand."

"No," Marcus agreed calmly, "but it definitely links him with the plan he and Knowles concocted, and if my assessment of our obnoxious friend is correct, should things become a little too uncomfortable I don't think he will take much persuading about turning evidence against Charles."

"I don't know," Adam said thoughtfully. "I can't see Knowles opening himself up."

"That's where you're wrong," Marcus said firmly. "The likes of Ted Knowles are confident enough on their own ground, but they have no desire to come to the notice of the police and, unless I have grossly misjudged him," he nodded, "Knowles would much rather save his own skin than anyone else's, besides which," he pointed out, "I would stake quite a substantial wager that he has not yet received a penny for his efforts, and a man like Knowles won't swallow that easily."

"But this letter," Adam argued, "I still don't see how you can use it against Charles!"

"Don't you see, Adam?" Marcus urged. "I told Charles that so long as I hold that letter, proving beyond doubt that it is in Knowles's handwriting and implicating them both in the girl's death, that it was Sophy's insurance policy."

"Yes, well?" Adam pressed.

"It can still be used as such," Marcus told him, "but instead of protecting Sophy *after* the girl's death it can also protect her *before* it, the girl too. Think, Adam," he urged again, "Charles may be furiously angry over the fact that I have got them both away to safety, but so long as he knows I have that letter safe and that I shall be perfectly prepared to use it should he have other ideas about the girl after all, or," he nodded, "he attempts to seek revenge on Sophy, there is very little he can do without exposing himself."

Adam shifted in his seat. He had no objection to playing his part in tomorrow's forthcoming events, but he nevertheless felt impelled to point out one very important point which had clearly escaped his cousin's attention. "This is all very well, but we are gambling an awful lot on Charles doing what we want him to."

"I realise that," Marcus acknowledged, "but when one considers the enormity of the plans he has set in motion as well as his eagerness to have his part in the affair kept secret, I cannot see him changing his routine, to do so could only raise questions he would much rather not have to answer, indeed," he shrugged, "he cannot answer them. Whatever else Charles may be, he is no fool."

Adam nodded and, after digesting what his cousin had just said, concluded that his strategy seemed to be the only likely way of averting the disastrous consequences resulting from the dire state of affairs facing them. "What do you want me to tell Sophy? Although," he added candidly, "no matter what we tell her it's going to be the devil of a shock for her to discover her husband's involvement in something of this nature."

"I know," Marcus sighed, wishing he could shield her from such a disclosure. "She may have suspected for some little time that something is very wrong, but for her to learn the full extent of her husband's perfidy will be extremely distressing. Unfortunately there is no way the truth can be withheld from her." Emptying his glass, he told Adam, "What I want you to do is to take a letter to her. You must make sure she gets it first thing in the morning. I will explain everything as far as I am able and, also, tell her what I want her to do."

"What *do* you want her to do?" Adam asked, still not sure how they were going to get away with it.

"You will agree," Marcus stated calmly, "that the girl trusts Sophy, which is just as well, because she will have to go to her lodgings and persuade her into going away with her for a short time. I have every faith in Sophy concocting some tale or other, even explaining away their supposed exchange of correspondence, but under no circumstances can we tell the girl the truth, either now or in the future. It may take Sophy a little while to convince her, after all she is bound to be still rather nervous of the Harrington family, but having done so she will wait for her to pack a few belongings, after which Jem will bring them here and I shall then escort them down to Timothy's. I can't see him turning his sister away because she has arrived a day earlier than arranged, nor, for that matter, Alexandra; not when he knows the situation. As for you," Marcus smiled, "when you leave here tomorrow you will return to Brook Street. Jem will return there after he has taken us to the railway station." He smiled a little ruefully. "I am afraid it will mean leaving you to deal with Charles. When he discovers that Sophy has gone into Kent one day early as well as the accident not having taken place after all, he is bound to know it's more than coincidence, but since he knows nothing of your involvement I can't see him suspecting you for either."

Adam nodded his agreement to this, but he felt impelled to question him on a certain point. "You're going to tell Timothy what's happened?" not at all certain he liked this idea.

"I shall have to." Upon seeing the doubtful look on Adam's face, Marcus assured him, "You needn't be afraid, I know Timothy; he's no gabster. It's only right he should be told the truth, besides," he pointed out, "he's bound to question Sophy about Alexandra, and I have no wish to cause a rift between them by withholding the facts from him or placing Sophy in the position where she feels she has to lie to her own brother to protect Charles."

Adam gave this his full consideration, after which he said, "Very well, I agree. I don't know Timothy as well as you do, in fact, I don't think I've ever met him above two or three times in my life, but I trust your judgement. However," he said firmly, "under no circumstances must George or the others get wind of this; m'mother especially."

Marcus agreed to this. "Naturally. For one thing, George cannot be trusted to keep his mouth shut, particularly when he is out of temper or had one brandy too many; and, as for my aunt, most definitely not." He shook his head. "I agree with what you yourself said not long ago in that she would never sustain the shock of knowing that one of her children had engineered something as despicable as this!"

"Yes, but," Adam shook his head, a little confused on several points, "well, what I mean is, how long can Alexandra remain at Timothy's? Then there's Jenkins. Isn't he waiting for her to come to a decision about things? M'mother too," he pointed out, "she's hoping to have Alexandra stay with her once Jenkins finds her!"

Marcus sighed. "I accept there are certain aspects to which I have no answers at this precise moment, but we shall just have to cross these bridges when we come to them. The important thing right now is ensuring the girl's safety, Sophy's too, not to mention Ellen who looks after her. The last thing I want is Ellen to be interrogated by Charles as to what she knows of this business, perhaps even dismissing her, and neither do I want Sophy to be in Charles's line of fire when he discovers the truth. Hopefully, though, by the time she returns to Brook Street in three weeks' time, or whenever she feels up to returning, he will have cooled down."

"Yes, I've been thinking about Charles," Adam nodded, still not entirely convinced that he would calmly accept this new development. "To be quite frank with you, I can't see him going tamely along with it."

"I don't see Charles going tamely along with anything," Marcus nodded, "but given the circumstances I can't see him doing anything else; not unless he wishes to put a rope around his neck! Whether he likes it or not his hands are tied; he cannot afford to act openly in this himself, and if he decides to call my bluff about that letter and goes after them regardless or even tries to arrange something else to rid himself of the girl, it will certainly raise questions he cannot afford to answer."

"Damn it, Marcus!" Adam exclaimed. "He'll be ready to murder you for this!"

"Very probably," Marcus agreed unperturbed, "but you must admit that his position is most awkward."

"I daresay it is," Adam acknowledged, "but aren't you forgetting our friend Knowles? Charles may not be able to work openly in this, but he only has to drop a word in his ear!"

"You can leave Charles and Knowles to me," Marcus told him firmly, a martial light in his eyes. "Charles has been having his own way for far too long; it's time someone else took the game in hand."

Adam was still not quite convinced. He knew his brother too well to believe that he would calmly sit back and accept something like this, but from the look on his cousin's face he did not think Charles would be in any position to say anything very much at all. "But even supposing this works out," he stated reasonably, "it still leaves Charles in the position of having to find the money to redeem the jewellery. What I mean is," he pointed out, "if he could not lay his hands on sufficient funds in the first place, how the devil can he do so now?"

"I shall just have to persuade him into allowing me to become his benefactor," Marcus said affably.

Adam had always liked his cousin, indeed, they got along extremely well, and he had never had the least difficulty in understanding why he was so well liked and respected. Marcus was not a man given over to panicking in a crisis, on the contrary he was calm and reassuring and one whom you knew could be approached for help in times of trouble; nor was he one to puff off his own abilities or successes, even so, it had more than once occurred to Adam that beneath Marcus's placid and easygoing ways there ran a hint of steel which was as inflexible as it was daunting. Charles may have turned down Marcus's offer once already, but Adam had no doubt at all that he would be given no opportunity to do so a second time. When faced with Marcus's fait accompli, intimidating enough for anyone, Adam would have thought, his brother would soon be brought to see that, resentful of Marcus though he was, he was going to have to eat humble pie merely to save himself from disgrace and scandal, even a walk to the scaffold! "He's not going to take too kindly to that," he told him, tempting fate by raising his glass in premature congratulation.

"Most probably not," Marcus shrugged, having refilled his glass and returned the salute. "I can't help feeling, however," he inclined his head, "that he would take to a prison sentence or, if his collaborators have their way if he doesn't pay them blood money, the gallows, even less kindly!"

Adam shuddered at the thought. "It doesn't bear thinking about."

"Then don't think about it," his cousin advised kindly. "Charles may want to tear me limb from limb for what he calls my meddlesome interference, but even he will agree that it is far better than the end he was lining up for himself."

Marcus may not have said anything, but Adam knew perfectly well the high price he was paying for his brother's salvation; and not just in monetary terms. For a man of his cousin's affluence, redeeming a couple of items of jewellery was neither here nor there; the real cost of saving Charles from his own destruction was the irrevocable loss of the woman he loved. There would be no possibility of claiming her as his own, Charles would see to that; his thanks would not run to relinquishing Sophy to the man she loved. Charles's nature was neither generous nor forgiving, and it would be characteristic of him to despise Marcus for what he had done rather than offer him thanks of any kind. Knowing his cousin though, he would not mind this so much, but losing Sophy would tear him apart; being separated from the woman he loved, knowing that she would never be his, was the real price he was paying to save Charles and the family from disgrace and scandal. It was a painful subject and one Adam knew his cousin would not readily discuss, even with him, but despite this he could not help commenting upon it. Marcus accepted this in his customary calm fashion, but Adam saw the sombre light in his eyes and wished to God there was something he could do other than offer meaningless platitudes. "I'm sorry, Marcus," he offered lamely.

"So am I," his cousin replied, an odd inflexion in his voice. "But in the words of Charles," he said undemonstratively, briefly raising his eyes from the letter he was composing, "I must look upon it as 'protecting the family'," his expression telling Adam that the topic was closed; not to be reopened. Finishing off his drink, Marcus continued with his letter to Sophy, but by the time he had come to the end of it, comprising four sheets, he believed he had covered all the salient points. He would have much preferred to tell her the distressing truth face to face, but for her to follow his instructions he had to explain the reason in more detail than he would have liked. He did not think she would be overly surprised to learn that Charles had been playing such a dangerous game, even so, it would still come as a tremendous shock. He was determined that no one other than themselves should ever know the truth; Charles may be the author of his unenviable destiny, but no possible good could come from acquainting the family of his plans for Alexandra. Unfortunately, there was no way Marcus could keep the truth from Sophy, but he trusted her enough to be assured that she would tell no one of what had been going forward, and he could only hope that nothing would occur to mar their escape.

Chapter Twenty

Sophy awoke the following morning to the sound of rain beating hard against the window pane and to the surprising discovery that Charles had not been to bed. Although he seldom advised her of his private arrangements, she knew he had an engagement with Sir Michael Overton after dinner at his club, and although she had not expected Charles back until late, she nevertheless found his absence rather perplexing. She did not allow herself to worry unduly over it, however, telling herself that there was most probably a perfectly reasonable explanation to account for it, but that Charles's failure to come home last night was in any way connected with Alexandra never so much as crossed her mind. However, upon her arrival downstairs a short time later to find Adam anxiously awaiting her in the hall with a letter from Marcus, Sophy experienced such a feeling of foreboding that her hands visibly shook.

The contents of Marcus's letter left her in no doubt that matters had progressed to a point where she failed to see how they could be halted, and whilst he had only lightly touched upon his incarceration, the information he had gleaned from Charles was sufficient to tell her that his dealings were far more serious than she had ever supposed. It certainly explained his fluctuating temper over the last few weeks, but so horrified was she to learn of the drastic measures he had been prepared to adopt to prevent the truth from coming out, it made her feel faint with sickened disgust. She certainly looked dreadfully pale, and it seemed that only by clinging to the banister rail was she able to stop herself from falling into a crumpled heap at Adam's feet.

No one looking at Adam would ever have suspected he had been up half the night and had, in fact, had little more than three hours' sleep, but for all that he was looking remarkably refreshed and wide awake, especially after consuming a substantial breakfast. He knew Sophy was not the kind of woman who was prone to falling into fits of hysteria or having nervous spasms, but nevertheless he was genuinely concerned at the effect Marcus's letter had had upon her. She may not have fallen into hysterics, but it was only by a determined effort that she forced herself to stay calm and remain standing on her feet. Her hands were far from steady as she returned the sheets to their envelope, and so grateful was she for her brother-in-law's proffered arm and gentle words of comfort that she could have defied anyone in his defence as he escorted her into the dining room.

Any appetite she may have had deserted her, considerably surprising Harris, who, having just come in to serve her, was informed that she was not hungry. Adam, correctly interpreting his expression, dismissed him with a knowing look and nod of the head before taking it upon himself to pour her a cup of tea with a reminder that starving herself was not going to do any good. Sophy refused his tempting, but she drank the tea gratefully. He only hoped George would not come down just yet; the last thing Adam wanted was for his brother to start asking probing questions, which he surely would after one look at Sophy's ashen face. He fully agreed with Marcus in that no one other than themselves must know the truth, and although George meant well he could be very indiscreet upon occasion, especially when he was anxious or in a temper, and particularly after imbibing too much. Under no circumstances must he discover the truth! But how Marcus intended to cover it up Adam did not know, especially if they failed in saving the girl.

"Where is Charles now?" Sophy asked. Her voice, though strained, was perfectly calm. "He did not come last night."

"I don't know." Adam shook his head truthfully, unable to explain his brother's failure to come home having been under the impression that when he finally left 'The Black Swan' he would return straight here. "Are you sure he did not come back here?"

Sophy nodded. "Quite sure. Although," she pointed out reasonably, "having read Marcus's letter I can well understand why."

Adam nodded, but Charles's unaccountable failure to come home had put quite a different complexion on things. "I know Marcus intends to get the two of you away to Timothy's today; are you prepared to do as he asks?" he queried, not unmindful of the awkward position she was in. Even so, until they knew Charles's whereabouts they could hardly set about making preparations for their journey; it would not do for Charles to suddenly arrive home as they were on the point of leaving.

"Oh, yes," Sophy nodded, "quite prepared," her eyes rather sombre. "Compared to Alexandra's life," she told him, "nothing else is of the least importance; not even my loyalty to Charles."

Adam seriously doubted whether his brother deserved any loyalty at all. Even during the short period of time he had been here, he had seen enough of Charles's behaviour towards Sophy to know that he treated her with a kind of disdainful indifference she did not deserve. Charles may have been coerced into marrying her by his father, but she had never given him cause to warrant such cold contempt, and that she should now, after all she had learned, still think of loyalty towards him, proved her commitment to a marriage which, quite frankly, should never have taken place at all. Keeping these reflections to himself, however, Adam remarked candidly, "You know, it amazes me how Charles managed to keep something of this magnitude to himself! After all," he commented reasonably, "it's not as though he had been planning an afternoon picnic!"

Sophy, who had been thinking along the same lines, confessed, "I knew something was wrong; but never this! What could have possessed him?"

Adam was no coward, but he was honest enough to admit that he much preferred his cousin to be the one who did the explaining, but unfortunately for him he was not here, and as Sophy clearly needed answers of some kind now, he tried his best to oblige her. Not having been privileged to see the letter before Marcus sealed it, Adam was thankful to learn that his version of events more or less ran faithfully to it, and since he had no wish to be the one to cause her further alarm or distress, he was able to heave a sigh of relief. He was not afraid of Charles and, unlike George, he had never felt the need to either pander to his moods or to defend himself, but Adam was nevertheless conscious of feeling some wariness when he thought that Charles could arrive home before Sophy had managed to leave. Trying to explain to his brother what he would undoubtedly regard as suspicious to say the least, was not something Adam contemplated with any relish and, in view of this, attempted to impress upon Sophy that time was of the essence.

She agreed to this, adding also that Marcus was quite right in that it was far better for her to see Alexandra alone. She may not have taken Marcus in aversion, or herself for that matter, but she was still far too wary of her newly acquired relations to feel comfortable in their presence. Fortunately, Sophy's own luggage was ready and only needed to be brought downstairs, and as Adam had promised her that he had already spoken to Jem who had assured him that his mother's carriage would be at the front door in plenty of time, it seemed that her only concern was how to explain her departure a day earlier than arranged. Charlotte would certainly find it difficult to understand, and, as for Charles – well, perhaps she had better not think about him! To do so would undo any resolution she had. No matter what he had planned or how sickened she was by it, Sophy was still very wary of him. Slightly comforted by Adam's presence she rose to her feet, telling him that as she had a full day ahead of her and because it would most probably take some time to convince Alexandra, it was perhaps time she made a move.

Adam was still wondering what feasible explanation Marcus could possibly offer to satisfy all parties concerned when the clanging of the bell sounded. As it was far too early for morning callers and Charles would most certainly let himself in with his key so as not to acquaint the whole household that he had been out all night, Sophy and Adam looked at one another like children who had been up to mischief. Had they not have been so taken up with the matter in hand they would have laughed at one another's horrified expressions but considering the importance of what they had both recently discovered, the sounding of the bell seemed like a portent.

Although the door to the dining room was standing slightly ajar, nothing could be discerned from the subdued and rather indistinct conversation emanating from the hall, but when Harris re-entered the dining room with the news that two police officers from Scotland Yard were desirous of a word, they felt as if they had been turned to stone. It was Adam who found his voice first requesting Harris to show them into the study, after which he told Sophy to remain where she was and he would go and talk to them. She nodded, then watched him follow a somewhat bewildered Harris out in to the hall, feeling very much as though she had lost her only friend.

Adam's brain was awash with supposition; he could not begin to understand what had brought two police officers here, and so early. For one insane moment, he wondered if Charles had lost complete control of his senses and murdered Marcus in a fit of panic, but no sooner had this idea entered his head than he dismissed it as ludicrous. Adam then wondered if they had actually murdered the girl ahead of schedule, but this too was dismissed as totally unreasonable; his understanding was that as far as Charles was concerned every conceivable angle had been covered, even down to blackmailing Marcus into keeping silent and turning a blind eye, therefore obviating the necessity of doing something stupid enough to jeopardise his plans.

Like all the rooms in the house, the fire in the study had been lit some time before, but no heat was filling the room, the air still cold and unwelcoming. Whether this was due to Adam's own tension or simply because his two unexpected visitors were standing immediately in front of it, he was not sure. Waiting until Harris had closed the door behind him, Adam looked from one man to the other as if seeking enlightenment, asking what it was he could do for them.

"Mr. Harrington?" asked a deep voice, very much in the manner of a man who had bad news but was reluctant to impart it.

Adam found himself looking at a thickset, middle-aged man who stood no more than medium height, whose nose, for some obscure reason, forcibly reminded him of a bird he had once seen in a drawing, beneath which he boasted a black handlebar moustache which he had a habit of stroking from time to time with a thick forefinger. Despite the outward appearance of fatherly understanding, which Adam believed merely hid a hint of steel and a determination to do his duty by any means at his disposal, he had the distinct impression that this ability to put one immediately at ease was specifically calculated in order to allow people to unbend and talk quite freely.

But Adam felt very far from easy as he said, "Yes, I am Mr. Harrington, Mr. Adam Harrington. What can I do for you?"

"I'm Inspector Jarrod, sir," he announced, "and this here is Sergeant Daker."

Sergeant Daker touched his forehead, his helmet held firmly under his right arm, revealing a thick crop of red hair which emphasised his fresh and liberally freckled complexion. He was a tall and rather lanky young man whose whole demeanour echoed the fact that he was inordinately proud not only to be accompanying a man of Inspector Jarrod's reputation, but also that he had only recently received his promotion to sergeant.

"Would I be right in saying, sir," Inspector Jarrod asked with slow deliberation, "that you have a brother by the name of Mr. Charles Harrington?"

It seemed to Adam that his heart had suddenly stopped beating, but he managed to reply with perfect composure, "Yes, I have a brother of that name. Why do you ask?"

"Well, sir," Inspector Jarrod said, choosing his words carefully, casting a glance up at the sergeant, "I don't quite know how to tell you this, but early this morning Sergeant Daker here was on duty in Waterloo when he heard someone set up a cry for help." He paused, again looking up at his colleague. "Upon investigating, he came upon the body of a man who we have every reason to believe is your brother."

Adam felt sick, and only by holding onto the back of a chair did he seem able to remain on his feet. Inspector Jarrod saw him change colour, asking if he would like to sit down. Adam shook his head, inviting him to continue.

This was one part of the job Inspector Jarrod had never liked, even so, it had to be done. "Well, sir," he continued, "from the looks of it, it appears as though he had been set upon and robbed; his calling cards and wallet were gone. In fact, sir," he informed him, "not a penny piece was found on his person."

"That's right, sir," Sergeant Daker confirmed. "About six o'clock this morning it was when I found him."

Adam stared from one to the other, a glimmer of hope rising in his breast. "But if his cards and his wallet had been taken, how do you know the dead man is my brother?"

Inspector Jarrod cleared his throat. "The thing is, sir, Sergeant Daker here used to work a beat in Islington, where I believe you have premises," to which Adam nodded, and Inspector Jarrod explained, "well, sir, when you work a beat for a length of time you get to know the people; seeing them regularly and that."

"Well?" Adam demanded, his brain too bemused to think clearly.

"Well, sir," Inspector Jarrod informed him, stroking his moustache, "he got to know Mr. Charles Harrington, only to say good morning to or good evening, mind, whenever he saw him arrive at the brewery or in the evening when he left. Sergeant Daker has only been on the Waterloo area a few weeks, but as soon as he saw the deceased, he recognised him instantly." Adam swallowed, rubbing his forehead with a hand that visibly shook. "Of course, sir," Inspector Jarrod said cautiously, "I can't say what took Mr. Charles Harrington to such a locality, but I shouldn't have thought he would have had cause to transact any business there at that time of the morning."

How could Adam possibly tell him that that was precisely what his brother had been doing there? There were so many questions to which he had no answers, not the least being what was Charles still doing there at that time of the morning? "Waterloo, you say?" Adam repeated. "Where in Waterloo?"

"I shouldn't think you would know the place, sir," Inspector Jarrod said, "but it was down a side alleyway called...?" looking enquiringly up at his sergeant.

"Meadow Row, sir," Sergeant Daker supplied.

"No, I don't know it," Adam shook his head, which was perfectly true. It could, of course, have been one of the side streets he and Marcus had walked past on their way home last night, but he could not swear to it, not having paid much attention to the names.

"I realise, of course, sir, that this has come as a dreadful shock to you," Inspector Jarrod sympathised, "but do you have any idea what it was that took your brother to Waterloo last night?"

"No," Adam shook his head, "I am afraid I don't," hoping he did not look as guilty as he felt at this blatant lie.

"No idea at all, sir?" Inspector Jarrod cocked his head.

"No, none whatsoever, Inspector," Adam shrugged.

"But you did know he had left the house?" Inspector Jerrod commented.

"Yes," Adam nodded, "in fact, I saw him leave, but he did not tell me where he was going, and I did not ask him," catching sight of Sergeant Daker feverishly scribbling something in his pocket book.

"And what time was that, sir?" Inspector Jarrod queried.

"After dinner," Adam told him, "about half past eight or thereabouts."

"Is there anything else you can tell me?" Inspector Jarrod asked.

It was at this point that Adam bethought himself of Ted Knowles and the visit he paid here last night to see Charles. As far as Adam was concerned the less Inspector Jarrod knew about this obnoxious individual the better, but since there was every possibility he would question Harris about the events of last night, who, Adam felt reasonably sure, would tell the Inspector of his visit, he felt it behoved him to mention it as well as keeping as close to the truth as possible. It seemed to Adam that this mire Charles had got himself into was about to suck them all in, but since he could not withhold this information from the inspector he told him, with a calmness he was far from feeling, that his brother did have a visitor last night, who he was he could not say, but within minutes of his departure his brother had a message conveyed to Sir Michael Overton to cancel their engagement, after which Charles had left the house, to which Inspector Jarrod nodded his head to Sergeant Daker who immediately left the study to go in search of Harris.

"And what were your movements last night, sir?" Inspector Jarrod cocked his head.

"*My* movements!" Adam exclaimed, momentarily shocked. "Are you suggesting...?"

"I am not suggesting anything, sir," Inspector Jarrod told him calmly, "just trying to establish the facts."

"Well, if you must know," Adam told him, "I spent the evening with my cousin."

"And where did the two of you spend the evening?" the inspector asked.

"At his house," Adam nodded. Even though it was true that he had been with his cousin and he trusted Marcus to corroborate it, he knew he was giving the inspector a totally false interpretation on how they had spent last night. Like Marcus, Adam was totally honest, but under no circumstances must this extremely diligent police officer know the truth.

Once he did, then there would be no stopping the scandal, and Charles's name would be in shreds.

"I take it your cousin will corroborate this?" Inspector Jarrod cocked his head.

"Lord, yes!" Adam exclaimed, furnishing the inspector with Marcus's name and direction.

The return of Sergeant Daker curtailed any further questions, and Adam, holding his breath a hushed discussion took place between the sergeant and Inspector Jarrod, could only hope and pray that Harris had not read the name on the calling card Ted Knowles had handed him last night to give to Charles. Inspector Jarrod, informing Adam that although Harris had confirmed that a man had called last night to see his brother he could unfortunately not tell them who it was, not having read the legend on the card. Adam's heartfelt sigh of relief was short-lived when Inspector Jarrod said, "I'm sorry, sir, but although I have no wish to cause you any further distress, I am afraid there are certain formalities which have to be gone through."

"Formalities?" Adam repeated, his knowledge of these things rather vague.

"Yes, sir," Inspector Jarrod nodded. "I am afraid that someone will have to formally identify the body."

Adam instantly recoiled, but realising that it was necessary, asked faintly, "When? Now?"

"If you don't mind, sir," Inspector Jarrod said gently. "It's best to get this sort of thing out of the way as quickly as possible."

"Yes of course I will come," Adam nodded, "but, first, I must inform my family and, naturally, my sister-in-law." As if needing to explain himself further, he said, "You must know, Inspector, that my brother lives... I mean," he hastily corrected himself, "lived here with his wife."

"I see," Inspector Jarrod nodded. "I did not realise your brother was married, sir," he told him.

"Yes, he is... I mean, he was," Adam quickly amended, wondering how on earth he was going to break the news to his mother and Sophy.

"And you, sir," Inspector Jarrod enquired, "I take it you too reside here?"

"Well, no," Adam shook his head, "I'm only here for a short time," briefly explaining the reason for his temporary residence in Brook Street.

"I see, sir," Inspector Jarrod nodded. "Now, sir," he said quietly, "about

Mrs. Charles Harrington; if we may be permitted to speak to her."

Adam looked a little surprised. "Speak to her?"

"Yes, sir. If you could possibly…" he began.

"If you don't mind, Inspector," Adam told him, "I would much prefer to tell her myself."

"If you…" Inspector Jarrod got no further as the sudden and forceful opening of the door caused him to break off.

George looked from one to the other with a nice mix of incredulity and belligerence on his face. It had been something of a surprise to come downstairs to be met by Harris with the startling intelligence that two police officers had called and were at this very moment talking to Adam in the study. He would have plenty to say to Adam later! As the eldest he should have been notified at once, not left to find out just as he was on the point of having breakfast. Whatever these police officers had to say it should be said to him and not Adam.

Totally ignoring the inspector and his sergeant, George glared accusingly across at his brother, but paying no heed to it Adam merely introduced him to them before saying, "I am afraid, George, that they have come with bad news."

"Bad news?" George repeated, his colour darkening even more.

"Yes," Adam nodded. "It appears that Sergeant Daker here believes that the body of a man found dead this morning, is that of Charles."

George's mouth dropped open and his eyes bulged from their sockets as he looked from one to the other. "Dead!" he echoed. "Nonsense!" he growled. "There's been a mistake." Casting a glance at the clock on the mantelshelf, he said, "Charles is either upstairs or has left for the brewery by now."

"I am afraid not," Adam said quietly. "According to Sophy, Charles did not come home last night."

"I'm sorry, sir," Inspector Jarrod intervened, "but Sergeant Daker knows Mr. Charles Harrington and had no difficulty in recognising him," refraining from saying 'only just', the numerous blows to his face and head making him only just recognisable.

"The inspector wants one of us to formally identify the body," Adam told his brother. "I said I would go with them. Where is my brother now?" he asked, turning to Inspector Jarrod.

"He has been taken to the mortuary at St. Pancras, sir," he told him steadily.

Having been met by Harris, anxiously awaiting him in the hall, to the news that two police officers from Scotland Yard had called and were at this very moment talking to Adam in the study, filled George with fierce resentment. The reason for their unexpected visit was not of such importance as knowing that as head of the family he had not been notified immediately, but that Adam, who did not even live here, had taken it upon himself to oversee the interview. George's sense of ill-usage was so strong that his colour rose, instantly demanding of Harris the reason for him not advising him of their arrival sooner. He would not be set aside like a schoolboy; he suffered enough dismissive treatment at Charles's hands without Adam overriding his authority as well! Without waiting for Harris to either explain or apologise for the oversight George brushed him aside and entered the study in a state of considerable peevishness and, upon seeing his brother handling a situation which should have been his privilege as well as his right, made his jaws work feverishly. He eyed Adam accusingly, fully intending to take him to task for blatantly disregarding his position, but upon learning the reason for their visit, all thoughts of sibling rivalry deserted him. So shocked was he by the news that he momentarily forgot his feelings of self-importance as the full impact of what he had been told began to seep into his brain. Suddenly, there was no room in George's thoughts for raking Adam down, just a stunned shock which completely deprived him of speech.

For as long as he could remember there had been an ever-growing rift between him and Charles, which had, over the years, gone beyond healthy rivalry. So eager was he to topple Charles's confidence and superiority by any means at his disposal that it had developed into an obsession. He had not missed an opportunity to exert his authority or to remind Charles of the fact that he was the eldest and, as such, was entitled to the respect and adherence his age and position demanded.

Having over the years failed miserably to endorse himself, George had made the mistake of trying to emulate Charles but lacking his brother's finesse as well as his naturally smooth eloquence, it had merely resulted in him being made to look ridiculous. With apparent ease, Charles had unremittingly succeeded in arousing every kind of emotion in his brother except that of brotherly love. With no effort whatsoever, Charles had managed to bring out the worst in him and each time the animosity had deepened until it had developed into an extreme dislike one for the other which no amount of time would ever repair. Now though, none of this mattered; gone was the desire to outshine Charles. His brother was dead; that was all George could think of, and the realisation that he had finally got what he had always strived for, to come out on top over Charles, seemed like a hollow victory.

Inspector Jarrod, after looking from one brother to the other, finally addressed himself to Adam, repeating his suggestion that he speak to Mrs. Charles Harrington, but the unobtrusive entrance of Sophy at this precise moment prevented him from answering, and instead he attempted to gently shepherd her out of the study to the quiet solitude of his mother's sitting room, but to no avail.

Placing a cold hand on his arm, she said quietly, "It's quite all right, Adam. I have a feeling these police officers have brought bad news. Is it Charles?" she asked, looking up into his troubled eyes.

Adam nodded. "I'm afraid so."

Having recovered from his stupor, George turned to face his sister-in-law, his expression a mixture of sympathy and a determination to assert himself, but Inspector Jarrod, taking his measure straightaway, intervened before he could speak, saying calmly, "I take it you must be Mrs. Charles Harrington."

Sophy nodded, stepping further into the room. "Yes, I am Mrs. Charles Harrington."

"How do you do?" Inspector Jarrod smiled, taking her hand. "My name is Inspector Jarrod, and this is Sergeant Daker."

"How do you do?" she said faintly, looking at Sergeant Daker, who had touched his forehead respectfully.

"I am sorry to have to be the one to bring you such distressing news, Mrs. Harrington," Inspector Jarrod told her, "but I think you have already guessed the reason for our visit."

"Are you telling me that my husband is dead?" Sophy managed.

Inspector Jarrod sighed. "I am very sorry to have to inform you, Mrs. Harrington, that that is regrettably the case." Assisting her onto a chair, he said, "This has come as a dreadful shock to you."

"Yes, it has rather," Sophy replied faintly. "How did it happen?" she asked unsteadily, looking up into his face, her own alarmingly pale.

For one awful moment Inspector Jarrod thought she was going to faint, but as this did not happen, he said, "We have every reason to believe that your husband was set upon and robbed." After briefly explaining Sergeant Daker's role, he then went on to inform her that her brother-in-law had agreed to identify the body, but no sooner had the words left his lips than George, now fully in control of himself, belligerently argued against Adam being the one to carry out the identification.

Inspector Jarrod, no stranger to family feuds, had by now assessed

George's character and the importance he placed upon his position within the family to a nicety. After questioning him as to what he knew of his brother's movements yesterday evening, he was told, somewhat belligerently, that he was not his brother's keeper nor, for that matter, was he privy to his engagements and, what was more, he did not take kindly to being asked about his own movements, which, George nodded furiously, did not include following his brother around waiting for the right moment to kill him. After painstakingly assuring him that no such thought had entered his head but that he was merely trying to ascertain the facts, Inspector Jarrod cunningly avoided a painful scene by the adroit way he suggested to George that he believed his mother would rather hear the dreadful news of her son's unfortunate death from him than anyone else. Not surprisingly, this acted upon his lacerated feelings like a tonic, and after very little thought he was brought to see that this painful but necessary role was of far more importance than visiting a mortuary. Lingering only long enough to offer Sophy his sincere and deepest condolences, he went off in search of his mother to break the news to her as he believed only he could.

Sophy was not the only one who was relieved to see him go. No one knew better than she did about the bitter rivalry which had existed between him and Charles, but whilst she had every sympathy with him over his constant struggle to better his brother in any way he could, she was not so blinded to the truth that she could not see that George brought most of Charles's contemptuous disdain upon himself.

Charles, arrogant and insufferably proud, had always seemed invincible to her. At all times controlled and self-assured, with the strength of purpose to stroll confidently through life knowing precisely what he wanted and in no doubt of getting it, but the news just imparted left her shocked and incredulous. It seemed impossible that a man of her husband's eminence should have been so ignominiously done to death, and had she been a less generous woman she would have said he deserved it, but no such thoughts entered her head. She was deeply and genuinely grieved at what had happened, and totally at a loss to either explain or understand it. Whatever her feelings towards Charles she had never wanted this, and the news that he had been brutally set upon and robbed, left her confused and bewildered. Sophy could not imagine her smoothly sophisticated husband being taken unawares, but of course he must have been, otherwise the culprits would never have succeeded in overpowering him. To the uninitiated, his sartorial perfection was misleading; Charles was more than capable of defending himself, but irrespective of how many assailants had attacked him he must clearly have been set upon from behind, taking him completely by surprise.

The tactful and discreet questions put to her by Inspector Jarrod to try to account for her husband being in the vicinity of Waterloo and at such an hour, made it embarrassingly clear to Sophy what conclusions he and his sergeant had already arrived at. Had she not known the circumstances leading up to Charles's presence in such a locality as well as his affair with Amelia, she would no doubt be thinking very much the same as the inspector, but since he was clearly striving to avoid mentioning such a delicate topic outright and she could not enlighten either of them as to the real reason for Charles being in the neighbourhood of Waterloo, Sophy merely allowed them to think what they considered to be a foregone conclusion.

Like Adam, who did not need to have it spelled out what they were thinking about his brother's reason for being in Waterloo, Sophy was at a loss to understand why, having concluded his affairs, Charles had not left 'The Black Swan', if not with Marcus then almost immediately afterwards. It was incomprehensible to her how such a thing could possibly have happened much less how Charles could have been taken so unawares. According to Inspector Jarrod, his body had been found in an alleyway early this morning, but whether he had willingly gone down it or whether his body had been left there after the attack, he could not at this stage say. But her knowledge of her husband told her that he was far too clever and astute to be caught out by a trick, which made it even more inexplicable. Naturally, it put quite a different complexion on things regarding Alexandra. Unfortunately, there was now no possibility of her complying with Marcus's letter, but it could not be taken for granted that the plans Charles had set in motion would not go ahead.

This thought had also occurred to Adam, and that a message must be conveyed to Marcus as soon as possible. Not only had he a right to know about Charles's death, but something would have to be done about the girl. Whether Ted Knowles had been paid or not, he had set Charles's plans in motion to be rid of her, and even though Sophy could not possibly keep their appointment Adam was certain Knowles's associates would. If Alexandra was not notified about the unexpected turn of events which had rendered it impossible for Sophy to keep their supposed meeting, it was quite safe to assume she would arrive at the appointed venue without the least suspicion of what awaited her. It was also safe to assume that whoever Knowles had hired to carry out such a dirty deed would do so whether the delegated witness happened to be there or not, and should that happen, then God only knew what would result from it!

As there appeared to be nothing Sophy could say to assist the police with their enquiries, Inspector Jarrod tactfully suggested that perhaps it was time Adam accompanied them to St. Pancras. It was not something he was looking forward to, but since he could not expect Sophy to carry out such a dreadful task he braced himself for the inevitable, if not with fortitude then certainly with resignation.

After escorting Sophy to the drawing room with the promise that he would have a message conveyed to Marcus straightaway and that she was not to worry herself over Alexandra, he returned to the study to scribble a brief note which he handed to Harris on his way out, with instructions that he was to make sure his cousin received it immediately, and, also, he was to tell Jem that he no longer needed his mother's carriage. This faithful retainer, who had been given no reason for being asked questions about Mr. Charles by Sergeant Daker, and totally ignored by George upon his emergence from the study, was profoundly shocked upon being told by Adam that Mr. Charles had been found dead early this morning. As soon as Harris had ushered in the two police officers from Scotland Yard he had been consumed with curiosity as to what could possibly have brought them here, but the intelligence which Adam had just imparted to him was so far removed from what he had expected that he reeled in shocked disbelief. It was true he had no liking for Mr. Charles, in fact, he could not call to mind one member of the staff who did. As for Farley – well, it was virtually impossible to tell from his habitually closed expression what he did feel, but even though Harris had never taken to this ingratiating individual it had to be acknowledged that during the two years he had been Mr. Charles's valet he had had to put up with all manner of verbal abuse and had appeared to have coped with it remarkably well. No word of thanks had ever left Mr. Charles's lips for any service rendered him, accepting it as his right to expect every member of the household to adhere to his wishes as and when required of them. He inspired neither loyalty nor respect; but, for all his faults and autocratic temperament, Harris received the news of his death in stunned horror.

As expected, the tragic news spread through the household like wildfire; but nowhere was it received with more violent impact than the quiet solitude of the room Amelia shared with George. Having made his way there with the intention of breaking the news to his wife so that she could be on hand to render his mother all the assistance and comfort she could, it was perhaps as well that his own reaction was such that he failed to notice the effect the news of his brother's death had on his wife. Since their afternoon of passion had banished forever any thoughts he may have harboured about the state of affairs existing between Amelia and Charles, George read nothing more than a natural shock in her expression. He found nothing irregular in her white face or startled eyes to rekindle his suspicions, on the contrary he considered these outward signs of shock as being perfectly normal upon learning of the sudden death of a brother-in-law.

Amelia was far too well-trained in concealing her emotions to allow them to show above what was considered acceptable, but although she was somehow or other able to conduct herself in a manner which breached no codes of etiquette or raised questions in her husband's mind, she nevertheless had to strenuously fight the overwhelming nausea and giddiness which swept over her. She was glad that George seemed to expect no response to his outpourings, at least it gave her precious time to gain some control over her emotions. At the moment though, she did not think she could utter a word without giving herself away, and for the first time she welcomed her husband's inanities which, thankfully, required no response from herself. Reading into her nod that she would join him in his mother's room after she had finished dressing, Amelia stared blindly at the door he had quietly closed behind him.

She had no idea how long she stood dazedly at the foot of the bed, her left hand still holding one of the posters, her knuckles white from gripping its vital support. Despite the fire burning in the grate she felt icy cold, her creamy white shoulders convulsing in response to George's news, her undressed hair dancing from the violent movement. Strange how, even when racked with pain and grief, she could feel those long sensitive fingers playing in her hair, touching her skin with such deft strokes that it was almost as though Charles was actually here with her. If she closed her eyes she could see him; feel the passion they shared. Her body tingled in awareness, or was it memory? It was so real this sensation that she did not want it to end; she wanted it to go on forever. She wanted to feel him next to her, to reassure herself he was here with her, kissing her with such need and desire that everything else fell into insignificance. Only Charles could evoke such a passionate response from her; only his fingers could find the right spot to arouse her; only his lips could tantalise and excite her. Suddenly, she was warm again and reached out her hand to touch his face, bewildered to find he was not here. She opened her eyes; he was gone. He had not been here at all! Then she remembered. Charles was dead! She had imagined the whole. Tears stung her eyes before falling freely down her cheeks as she realised the awful truth; she would never see him again. She shivered, convulsive and uncontrollable sobs racking her body, cruelly and fiercely reminding her that never again would she talk to him or make love to him. It was over. It was unimaginable! Her legs seemed to be in imminent danger of giving way under her, and the throbbing in her head made her feel sick, but this was nothing compared to the unbearable pain of knowing that he was gone from her forever and that never again would she share with him those intimacies she would go to her grave longing and craving for. Sitting down on the edge of the bed she caught sight of her reflection in the mirror, hardly believing she was looking at herself, but the pale and drawn face which mocked her was nothing to the raging turmoil inside her or the emptiness around her heart, and not even burying her face into the feather quilt had the power to relieve her tormented spirits or erase Charles's handsome face from her mind.

But by the time she joined her husband and mother-in-law neither her pain nor her emotional outburst, which had racked her physically and emotionally, were visible. To all who saw her, except for Sophy, who had accurately guessed her reaction to Charles's death, Amelia was her customary controlled self; immaculately coiffured and dressed and perfectly poised. If, once or twice, her eyes clouded, or a catch in her voice made her pause momentarily, they were looked upon as nothing more than the understandable reaction from hearing such tragic and unexpected tidings. Sophy longed to comfort her, to tell her that she understood her pain and loss, but knew she dared not. Amelia would neither welcome nor want her sympathies, in fact, it was more than likely she would resent such an approach, especially from the wife of the man she loved. Sophy had always known that Charles had come between them, preventing any friendship from forming. Amelia was no fool, she would know better than anyone the true relationship between her and Charles, and therefore she was not likely to take kindly to her words of comfort. Sophy sighed. She knew it was useless to say anything. She could not pretend to have been in love with Charles, but his death was the last thing she had expected or wanted. The news was as much of a shock to her as it was to Amelia, and whilst Sophy could not admit to experiencing the same depth of devastating loss, it was nevertheless true to say that his death had left her in a state of numbed disbelief.

Had Amelia given any thought to the matter she would have seriously doubted George's ability to deliver such tragic news with the sensitivity it deserved, but to do him justice he performed the painful task with a calmness which would most certainly have surprised her. He may still bristle about Adam taking charge of a situation which he believed should rightly have fallen to him, but the truth was he was far too shaken to enact the role of head of the family. Having fully expected his mother to throw herself onto his chest in an uncontrollable fit if crying, George was somewhat relieved to discover that far from doing any such thing she received the news in a dazed calm, neither asking for details about her son's death nor the probable causes for it, merely accepting what he told her. Since he could not have enlightened her it was perhaps as well that she raised no questions, but once his own initial shock gradually began to recede he found himself questioning his brother's unfortunate end more closely.

Since revealing Charles's recent activities would serve no purpose, indeed, it would be quite fatal, Sophy could only hope that George would not take it into his head to bombard her with questions. Not only was she not up to answering them but to do so would merely lead to the kind of scandal they were striving hard to avoid, as no reliance could be placed upon him keeping it to himself.

*

The identification of Charles's body had been an extremely painful affair; indeed the sight of his brother's bruised and battered corpse had nearly proved too much for Adam. It certainly seemed as though whoever had set upon him had done so to such brutal lengths that his face was only just recognisable. Inspector Jarrod, although he fully agreed with the pathologist that the deceased's violent end had been the result of sustaining several severe blows to the head and face, almost certainly with a cosh of some kind or blunt instrument, he could not be entirely sure whether the attack had been carried out by one or more assailants.

"In fact," Inspector Jarrod told him once they were outside, "whoever is responsible for such an assault, they certainly know their business."

Adam, shocked and appalled by recent events, nodded absently, neither their commiserations nor explanations of procedure penetrating his consciousness. He had been only vaguely aware of stark white walls and covered bodies lying on top of long wooden trestle-type beds as he had struggled through the ordeal of identifying his brother. Nausea had welled up inside him but, somehow, he had managed to overcome this as well as the buzzing in his ears and the sensation that the room was swimming around him, and it was therefore not without a sigh of relief to eventually find himself outside in the fresh air.

After a brief word with Sergeant Daker, Inspector Jarrod turned to Adam, his hand gripping his shoulder, saying, not unkindly, "I'm sorry, sir, but it had to be done. Not very pleasant I know, but at least it is over now."

Adam turned an ashen face towards him, his voice not quite steady as he asked, "What happens now?"

"Well, sir," he was told practically, "the coroner will now call an inquest."

"An inquest?" Adam repeated faintly, raising an unsteady hand to his forehead.

"A coroner's inquest is compulsory in cases of violent or sudden death," Inspector Jarrod told him.

"Yes, of course." Adam shook his head, not just a little bewildered by sudden events.

Inspector Jarrod, who could see from Adam's face that the whole ordeal had taken quite a toll, said considerately, "I am not saying the inquest will reveal the identity of the perpetrator, but it will at least enable your brother's death to be officially recorded as murder," to which Adam nodded. "In the meantime, however," Inspector Jarrod told him, "we shall continue our investigations, and, hopefully, before too long we shall find whoever is responsible."

Adam looked down into the inspector's face, his own contemplative. "Tell me, Inspector, what are the real chances of finding those responsible?"

Inspector Jarrod fingered his moustache. "The truth, sir," he sighed, "unless someone witnessed the attack the chances are very remote. Cases like this seldom bring to light the assailant."

Adam nodded. "I thought so." Then, cocking his head, asked, "Is there anything else, Inspector?"

"Just one more thing, sir," Inspector Jarrod said, "about your brother being in Waterloo last night."

Adam was no fool; he knew precisely the connotations Inspector Jarrod placed upon Charles being in such a locality, but since he could not tell the inspector the identity of Charles's unexpected visitor last night without the whole sorry story coming out, Adam merely shrugged. "I am afraid I cannot tell you anything more than I have already, Inspector; I have no idea what took my brother to Waterloo last night."

Inspector Jarrod fingered his moustache for a moment, then, looking up at Adam, said tentatively, "I was, as you will appreciate, a little reluctant to question your sister-in-law too closely on what could possibly have taken her husband to Waterloo, but are you *quite* sure, sir, that you have no idea what could possibly have taken him there?"

"Quite sure, Inspector," Adam told him firmly, feeling the lie stick in his throat.

"Did he, perhaps," Inspector Jarrod suggested, "have friends in the neighbourhood or business acquaintances?"

"He may well, Inspector," Adam told him, "but as I told you earlier, I live in Yorkshire where my family have premises. I only came home to attend my father's funeral. It is only to be expected that I should know very little of my brother's activities or all his friends and acquaintances." As this seemed to satisfy Inspector Jarrod, he asked if there was anything further and upon being told that there was nothing more for the moment, Adam nodded and thanked him, finding his hand grasped in a painful but well-meaning grip before watching him stride down the street.

It was not in Adam's nature to dissimulate; but given the circumstances he could do little else. It may leave a rather nasty taste in his mouth, but once he revealed his brother's purpose there would be no stopping the furóre which followed. Charles would be utterly denounced and condemned with his reputation and that of the family in shreds. The name Harrington would not be worth the paper it was written on and, for his mother's sake if nothing else, Adam had to do all he could to prevent the truth from coming out. He supposed if Inspector Jarrod knew the truth he would find himself arrested for wasting their time or withholding vital evidence, but as there was nothing else he could do he would just have to ride the storm for a while longer. Like Sophy, Adam knew precisely the interpretation Inspector Jarrod and Sergeant Daker had placed on Charles's visit to such a district, and whilst nothing was further from the truth, this perfectly natural conclusion had to be preferable to the real reason. Society may look askance at such conduct, perhaps even leniently, upon the foibles of a man who sought his pleasures in such a way, but it would never be brought to accept attempted murder with the same tolerance. At least the obvious conclusion left Charles's name and reputation undamaged, and Adam for one was determined they should remain so.

Despite the rain, which had not abated, Adam decided to walk at least part of the way back to Brook Street, turning down several cries from expectant hackney drivers. After enduring such a gruesome experience as identifying his brother's body, he not only needed to be in the fresh air for a while after being in such a chilling and claustrophobic atmosphere, but to be alone with his thoughts before being faced with a barrage of questions from George. It was not simply because Adam was in no position to answer them but also because he was in no frame of mind to listen to what he instinctively knew would be a demand to know why he had been so callously disregarded when two police officers had descended on them. Adam was not unsympathetic, but since he was all too familiar with his brother's reaction to anxiety as well as the importance he placed on his own position, he was in no humour to put up with George's officious moralising any more than he was his attempts to assert his authority.

Adam knew that even though Sophy had not been happy in her marriage she was not so callous or unfeeling as to remain unmoved at the news of her husband's death, indeed, her face had echoed her profound shock and disbelief, and not even upon discovering that Charles had laid plans to rid himself of his niece, had rendered the news any more welcome to her. Adam, no more than Sophy, knew the circumstances surrounding Charles's death, but, like him, she did know about the events leading up to it, and whilst neither of them could reveal the truth her distress would not prevent George from firing questions at her in a strenuous effort to discover what Charles had been doing in such a locality. Inspector Jarrod may have played an exceptionally good hand in getting rid of George, but Adam placed no dependence on his brother's tact and diplomacy, indeed, he did not perform well under anxiety or shock, and this, coupled with what Adam knew would be a firm attempt to assert himself as head of the family by approaching Sophy for answers, was enough to hasten his return to Brook Street.

*

Adam's hastily scrawled message left Marcus momentarily bereft of speech, and totally at a loss to account for Charles's death. This devastating news was certainly unexpected, but by no stretch of the imagination could it be looked upon as coincidental. The police may have drawn premature conclusions, but Marcus was far from satisfied with their apparent reasoning. At no time had Charles's death entered into Marcus's calculations, and whilst he was firmly convinced that it was not unconnected with Alexandra, he entirely failed to see where it fitted in with the current sequence of events. Like Adam, he had supposed Charles to have left 'The Black Swan' not long after himself, but clearly something must have delayed his departure. Even so, this did not explain the tragedy which had followed. Having no idea what could possibly have happened all Marcus had to work on was speculation and pure guesswork, but he could not rid himself of the idea that somewhere along the way Ted Knowles had played a significant part, but to what end remained unclear. The more Marcus thought about it the less sense it made.

Ted Knowles may not be the kind of man he would place his trust in and, unless he had grossly miscalculated, he would say that Charles would not either if circumstances had been different, but Ted Knowles was no fool, on the contrary he was more than ordinarily astute, and he would not be so short-sighted as to rid himself of a man who could be made to pay handsomely for his silence any time it suited him. Ted Knowles would know perfectly well that Charles would not want their dealings to come to the notice of the police; only one word would suffice to bring Charles to ruin, and this being so it left him wide open for blackmail – and Charles would have paid! Under no circumstances would he want his part in this affair to leak out, and Ted Knowles would have had no compunction in holding such a threat over him. No, it would not suit Knowles at all to do away with such a golden goose, and one, moreover, which promised such golden eggs, yet his name was stamped all over Charles's tragic end.

A frown creased Marcus's forehead as he pondered the inexplicable death of his cousin, but no matter how hard he tried he could think of nothing to explain it. He thoroughly discounted the idea that Charles had been set upon and robbed as the police seemed to think, although he had to admit that the inference leading to this conclusion had been carefully planned in order that this was what they should think. Charles's death had been neatly arranged and carried out with precision by someone who knew precisely what they were doing, leaving no possible clue as to the identity of the person or persons involved. His cousin would certainly have put up quite a fight before succumbing to the onslaught, but whoever had committed such a brutal assault had clearly been well primed as to his movements, knowing full well where he would be. According to Adam's note, Charles's pockets had been well and truly emptied, but still Marcus did not believe that his cousin had been the victim of a random street robbery, and as his death could not be explained away satisfactorily in his own mind he began to question whether his cousin had been the intended victim after all, but had, in fact, been mistaken for someone else. Unfortunately, he did not have the time now to take these thoughts further as the question of Alexandra had yet to be dealt with, recent events having rendered his plans to get her and Sophy away no longer viable.

Since he had no idea as to the time or venue of Alexandra's meeting with Sophy when the supposed 'accident' was scheduled to take place, Marcus's main priority had to be the girl. He was not in the least surprised that Adam, finding himself unexpectedly confronted by two police officers from Scotland Yard with such devastating news, had forgotten to ask Sophy this vital question. There was no time to be wasted now by visiting Brook Street to obtain this information from Sophy, and whether Alexandra trusted him or not, Marcus was determined to get her away from her lodgings and into his aunt's safe-keeping, even if this meant forcibly removing her. Circumstances had rushed things along, but since providing Alexandra with sanctuary under his own roof was out of the question, he had no choice but to take her to Brook Street to her grandmother, whom he knew would welcome her willingly. He could not say the same for the rest of his relatives but given the extraordinary situation there really was nowhere else he could take her.

In view of Adam's hastily scribbled postscript, Marcus fully expected to find himself being questioned by Inspector Jarrod at some point today, as well as being asked if he could corroborate Adam's statement about having spent last night in one another's company. Marcus could well imagine his cousin's feelings of surprise upon being asked to account for his movements last night as well as his disgust at the interpretation the police clearly put on Charles's reasons for being in Waterloo, but if they were to keep the truth of this tragedy from leaking out Marcus knew the dissimulation they were perpetrating, however distasteful, was very necessary. Should the police so much as get a whiff of Ted Knowles, then it would not be long before the whole sorry story was known and, for Sophy and his aunt's sake, then, like Adam, Marcus was quite prepared to deviate from the truth just enough to throw the police off Ted Knowle's scent. Marcus had gleaned enough from his cousin's note to know that Harris had no idea who Charles's visitor was last night, which was just as well, but Marcus instinctively knew that before this unpalatable affair was finally over they were most probably going to have to do even more side-stepping if an out and out scandal was to be avoided.

Marcus may have no qualms about being questioned by this Inspector Jarrod, in fact, the sooner it was over the better, but he wished he had not chosen to call just as he was on the point of setting out on his visit to Hoxton to see Alexandra. Considering the urgency attached to this visit Marcus was extremely conscious of the time, and that every second he delayed in removing Alexandra from her lodgings to a place of safety was taking her one step nearer to her supposed 'accident', but none of his concerns for her safety and well-being were visible on his face as Webster showed Inspector Jarrod into the study.

Marcus, unconsciously echoing Adam's thoughts in that it was best to stay as close to the truth as possible, answered the inspector's questions without so much as arousing suspicion or doubt in his mind, but when Inspector Jarrod asked him to confirm if his cousin, Mr. Adam Harrington, had visited him last night as he had said, despite Marcus's firm assertion that he had he nevertheless devoutly hoped that this extremely diligent police officer would not ask to speak to Webster to verify it. He did not, much to Marcus's relief, asking instead, "And what time did your cousin leave here, sir?"

"Oh," Marcus shrugged, "about three o'clock or thereabouts," which at least was true.

Inspector Jarrod raised an eyebrow at this. "I see you made quite a batch of it!"

"Yes," Marcus confessed, a slight smile touching his lips, "I am very much afraid that we did," to which Inspector Jarrod nodded.

Marcus was not at all sorry when, following one or two more questions, he walked with him to the front door to show him out, but upon seeing Inspector Jarrod pause and look up at him he was not at all surprised to be asked, "Are you *quite* sure, sir, that you have no idea what could possibly have taken your cousin to Waterloo last night?"

"No," Marcus shook his head, "I am afraid not. You must know, Inspector," he told him, "that my cousin did not make me privy to his engagements," to which Inspector Jarrod nodded and, after shaking Marcus's hand, left.

Waiting only long enough to have a brief word with Webster, Marcus shrugged himself into his coat and, after donning his hat and gloves and picking up his walking cane, left the house to hail a hackney.

Chapter Twenty-One

Without doubt, Hoxton was unquestionably one of the most run-down areas in London, upon which not only society but prominent citizens had clearly turned their backs; either unable or unwilling to improve conditions which could only be described as disgraceful. Unfortunately, Marcus had no time to dwell on society's failings, the only important thing was to get Alexandra to safety, but as the hackney pulled up outside number eighteen Mansion Gardens he experienced the same sadness and disgust which had attacked Sophy, motivating him to an even greater determination to remove Alexandra from a place in which she most definitely did not belong. Instructing the driver to wait, he trod up the path and knocked on the door, aware of the curious stares cast at him from passers-by as well as from behind the torn and dirty curtains of the houses across the street. He was not surprised, the arrival on the scene of a stranger who was obviously a gentleman would naturally arouse their curiosity and, as he waited for the door to open, he vowed that no matter what it took he was going to remove his cousin's daughter from this dreadful neighbourhood.

As expected, Alexandra's reception of him, if not hostile, was certainly wary, but eventually Marcus managed to persuade her to allow him to step inside, shocked and appalled at the conditions in which she lived but putting these ills to one side he began by apologising for descending on her so unexpectedly and hoped that his visit was not inopportune, to which she told him it was not. After taking the seat offered him, Marcus went on to explain the reason for his visit, expressing regret for Sophy being unable to keep their appointment due to the sudden and tragic death of her husband. Alexandra was certainly taken aback by this news, but no matter how startled she was at hearing about Charles's untimely demise she could feel neither regret nor sorrow and made no attempt to express any. Marcus could not entirely blame her for this, clearly his cousin's attitude towards her still rankled, but whilst she had every sympathy for Sophy, Alexandra firmly believed that her newly found friend would be far happier without him, and she knew no hesitation in saying as much.

"I am afraid I really cannot comment upon that," Marcus told her, knowing it would be quite wrong in him to convey his own opinion, "but it would be neither right nor proper for either of us to remark upon it. Sophy is very distressed by the news," he told her, knowing that even though he had not seen her he felt he could say this in perfect truth.

"Please, offer my condolences to her," Alexandra said sincerely, for she had truly taken a liking to Sophy.

"Thank you. I should be happy to do so, of course," Marcus smiled, "but you can offer them to her yourself; you will be seeing her shortly."

"Seeing her myself?" Alexandra repeated, startled. "What do you mean? I thought you said she was unable to keep our appointment."

"She is, but I am not here solely as her advocate," he said calmly, "but, also, to take you to your grandmother."

Her eyes widened at this, her face slightly tinged with colour. "Take me to my grandmother?" she repeated, astonished.

"Yes," Marcus said kindly, not failing to notice the agitated movement of her hands as they rested on her lap. "You know very well that she wants nothing more than to have you stay with her, and your company, especially at such a time as this, would be of great comfort her."

"So, that is why you are really here," Alexandra mused at length, not quite able to keep the accusatory note out of her voice.

"*That* is why I am really here," Marcus confirmed gently, treating her very much in the same way he would a nervous colt. "Do not think for one moment that I do not understand your very natural reserve about renewing your acquaintanceship with your newly acquired relatives," he said sincerely, "I do, I assure you, but you and your grandmother are my main concern now."

Alexandra looked him over, her wide green eyes frank and appraising. He did not give her the impression of having an ulterior motive but considering she had only met him once in her life she was a little at a loss to understand why he had come here as her grandmother's representative. If her grandmother needed an advocate to act on her behalf, then surely Silas Jenkins would be the one to whom she would approach especially when Alexandra considered his previous visit to her and the question of her unsettled affairs. "My grandmother is one thing," she pointed out, "so too is Sophy, but the rest of them," she told him candidly, "are quite another! You were there that day I called," she reminded him, "you witnessed their reception of me; can you honestly see them welcoming me in Brook Street?"

"I wish I could attribute their behaviour towards you as merely stemming from the shock of discovering your existence," Marcus admitted truthfully, "but I cannot. I neither applaud nor uphold their treatment of you, indeed, it makes me quite ashamed, but whilst they cannot be ignored or disregarded, they are of no importance," to which she raised an eyebrow, "but your grandmother is," he told her steadily. "It is her dearest wish to have you stay with her for as long as you choose to do so. As for the rest of them," he smiled, "they will soon grow accustomed to you."

"Do you honestly believe that?" Alexandra asked doubtfully, "because if you do, you are more of an optimist than I am."

"Yes, I do," Marcus nodded, hating the lie he was giving her, but compared to her life it was a small price to pay. "Just give them, and yourself, a little time."

She eyed him warily, asking, "Did my grandmother enlist your aid rather than approach her solicitor, Jenkins? Or is it merely a case of you taking matters into your own hands?"

Marcus eyed her steadily, realising, and not for the first time, that Alexandra was no fool, but, also, that she deserved no less than the truth, yet to tell her the truth was impossible and, consequently, he had no alternative but to prevaricate. "As Sophy has done me the honour of reposing her trust as well as her confidence in me," he told her calmly, "I am aware of the visit she paid you a short time ago with Silas Jenkins and the reason for it, and that it had been decided, for the time being at least, that matters were to be held in abeyance until you had arrived at a decision. I know too that you were to meet her today, but for reasons I have already offered she is unable to keep that appointment. I came here to inform you of it whilst at the same time to try to persuade you into accompanying me to your grandmother." Feeling something more was needed to demolish the barrier he sensed was already weakening, he smiled. "I am exceedingly fond of my aunt," he told her sincerely, "indeed, I hold her in very great esteem. It is her dearest wish to have you with her. You met her only briefly," he said gently, "but you must have seen for yourself that she had no hand in what happened all those years ago, and no matter what her feelings your grandfather overrode them. She knows that what happened to your mother cannot be altered or wounds healed overnight, but she is nevertheless most desirous of your company; and if all that is required to bring this about is a little effort on my part, then it shall not be lacking."

There was no doubting his sincerity, and unless Alexandra's instincts had grossly erred she knew he was a man of his word and one to be trusted, so very different to his arrogant and insufferable cousin! In fact, Marcus's calm good sense, coupled with his attractive smile, to which she was by no means impervious, were already beginning to win her over, but some doubt still lingered. Her brief experience of her newly acquired relatives had not led her into believing they would receive her with the same eagerness as her grandmother and Sophy, and in a desperate attempt to delay her decision a little longer, said, "Sophy told me very much the same thing when she came here. She is, apart from my grandmother, perhaps the only one who would welcome me in Brook Street, either now or in the future."

"Sophy would dearly love to have you in Brook Street," Marcus told her truthfully. "You must know that she would be more than happy to see you safely installed there. I know too," he said sincerely, "that she would feel far more comfortable knowing you were away from this neighbourhood, as I would."

Alexandra rose hastily to her feet and took a turn around the confines of her room, torn between her stubborn defiance and the very human desire of wanting the comfort and luxury her inheritance as well as her grandmother could give her. Marcus too had risen but made no effort to move or speak, watching Alexandra pacing up and down in silence, knowing the struggle which was going on in her mind, but even if she should ultimately decide not to accept her grandmother's invitation after all, he had every intention of overriding that decision and removing her from these most unsatisfactory surroundings and the brutal fate which, whilst averted as far as today was concerned, could still await her.

Alexandra certainly did fight the inner battle going on between her head and her heart, but deep down she knew in which direction she would ultimately go, and if she needed anything to finally convince her she only had to look around at every dull and dismal detail of her life, heartily despising it. If she could endure such conditions, then, surely, she could do likewise with her relatives! Her visitor seemed genuine enough, and she already knew she liked Sophy, and since she had already come to terms with her newly acquired inheritance and Charles would not be there to ridicule and taunt her, she began to view the prospect of living in Brook Street with more hope.

But the residue of caution which naturally stilled lingered was soon dispelled as she looked at Marcus, recalling everything she had ever heard her mother say about him and all the efforts he had made to come to her assistance, as well as intervening with her grandfather. She remembered his kindness to her that day when she had called in Brook Street, something she would never forget, especially when she called to mind how she had been surrounded by opposition and open hostility, and as she looked at him now she saw for herself that Marcus was indeed the man her mother had always spoken of with affection. "Did Sophy tell you why she had written to me, asking to meet me?" she asked.

Marcus shook his head. "No, she did not." He hated the idea of lying to her, but he saw little point in alerting her to the truth.

"Well," Alexandra sighed resignedly, having given the matter some thought, "I suppose there is no harm now in telling you that I had already decided to take her advice, in fact," she told him, "I thought perhaps that was the reason she wanted to meet me." Marcus mechanically agreed to this, trusting Sophy not to deny it. "Well," Alexandra grimaced, "as you can see," indicating her surroundings with a sweeping hand, "I have not much to pack, and what I do have," she shrugged, "is not worth the trouble."

"It's no matter," Marcus said gently. "Just come as you are."

"You are very persuasive," she told him, "yet something tells me," she mused, her eyes alight with amusement for the first time, "that no matter what my decision you are determined to take me to my grandmother."

"I won't deny it," he smiled. "There is no way I am going to leave here without you; even if I have to carry you out kicking and screaming," to which she gave a choked little laugh. "You must know, as I do," he told her seriously, "that this is no place for you, and irrespective of your feelings towards your grandfather and all that has gone before, it is time you took your rightful place within the family. Like it or not," he said with a finality she could not mistake, "I intend to see that you do."

She considered this for a moment, knowing he was perfectly capable of forcibly removing her if she refused, but, more importantly, she knew there would not be the least need for him to do so; she was more than ready to go with him. "In that case," she smiled, "you leave me with little choice."

"You must know it is for the best," Marcus told her gently. Like Sophy, he saw the vulnerability behind the hardiness, and yet again found himself at a loss to understand the narrow-minded prejudice which had set in motion so much unnecessary heartache and pain. "Apart from your grandmother and Sophy," he told unhappily, "I cannot promise you a warm welcome in Brook Street, you know that as well as I do, but in time I have every expectation that all will be well."

Alexandra doubted it, but it was kind of him to say it. "Forgive me," she said with an irrepressible smile, "but I am beginning to see why Sophy likes you so much."

"Did she tell you so?" Marcus asked, raising a questioning eyebrow.

"No," she shook her head, "but I could tell."

Now that the moment had come for her to leave, Alexandra discovered that there were practical difficulties she had to see to before this could be accomplished, not the least being paying her rent, and since she had not yet been paid for the sewing she had done her pockets, she told him candidly, were quite to let. This, Marcus told her, was easy enough to solve, seeking out her landlady to pay her rent to date and to inform her that Miss Dawes, apart from one or two treasured items which had belonged to her mother, would not be taking anything with her, and therefore whatever she wanted from Alexandra's room she was quite at liberty to take, whereupon he escorted her off the premises where she soon found herself seated beside him in the hackney.

During the drive to Brook Street, Alexandra answered Marcus's few questions without any reserve, discovering, like Sophy, that he was a man she could place her trust in, and one, moreover, who made her feel quite at ease. Even so, it was clear to the man sitting next to her that she was trying desperately hard to banish the thoughts of what would most probably be a very mixed reception upon her arrival in Brook Street, and upon feeling his hand taking a warm hold of her cold one and giving it a reassuring squeeze, she summoned up a smile, leaving Marcus in no doubt that apart from no possible good resulting from telling her the truth she had more than enough on her mind as it was, especially as their destination drew ever nearer.

Even though Alexandra was grateful for his understanding and comforting presence as well as putting her at ease, nothing could quite dispel her apprehension. Her grandmother and Sophy may welcome her willingly, but as for the rest of them – well, perhaps she should not think about them right now. Marcus felt the small cold hand tremble in his and gave it another reassuring squeeze, knowing precisely what was going through her mind. It was going to take time on both sides for wounds to heal and hostilities to fade but considering the personalities of all parties concerned he held out very little hope of reconciliation in the immediate future. He had meant what he said when he told her that he was perfectly prepared to forcibly remove her from Mansion Gardens had she proved obstructive, and he would have known no compunction in doing so. It was not only because she deserved better than such a lowly establishment or to please her grandmother, but also because her life was still very much in danger. Alexandra knew Charles had not liked her, but it would astonish and shock her to learn that he had planned to have her put out of the way, and as Marcus sat beside her in the hackney with her hand trustingly tucked into his, he knew that had he stood by and allowed his cousin's plans to go ahead he would never have rid himself of the guilt; it would have stayed with him for the rest of his life.

Harris, opening the door to find Marcus and Miss Elizabeth's daughter on the step considerably startled him, but his years of training soon dispelled the look of incredulity on his face, but once having recovered from the shock Harris had to admit that he was pleased to see her. He could well imagine the furore which would follow once she entered the drawing room; they were all there, except for Miss Jane, but he could not see them receiving the girl any too kindly, especially when he remembered the last time she had come here.

He was not mistaken. George's jaw dropped and his face became suffused with indignant colour at the sight of her; Amelia, still reeling from the shock of Charles's death, eyed her with blatant hostility while Emily rose hastily to her feet, two spots of angry colour on her pale cheeks as she stared from Alexandra to Marcus with accusing eyes. Only Sophy and Charlotte showed any sign that she was welcome and, ignoring the protests from her family, rose to her feet and hurried across the room to where Marcus was standing beside her granddaughter, immediately embracing her, oblivious to the chorus of disapproval. "Oh, my dearest girl!" she cried between tears and laughter. "Is it really you?" she sobbed. "How happy I am to have you here."

Alexandra returned the embrace, relieved to know that one person at least loved and wanted her. "I wasn't sure you wanted me here," she told her unsteadily, "but Marcus assured me that you did."

"Want you!" cried Charlotte. "Oh, my dearest child, of course I want you here, and for as long as possible."

Sophy too had risen and crossed over to where they were standing, one hand taking hold of Alexandra's cold one and the other unthinkingly coming to rest on Marcus's arm. She warmly kissed her niece's cheek before telling her how pleased she was to see her, then, turning to Marcus, she smiled mistily up at him with so much love and gratitude that he had to strenuously fight the urge to take her in his arms and kiss her. "Thank you," she said fervently.

Before he could respond to this, George, having recovered from his stupor, demanded angrily, "What the devil do you mean by bringing *her* here? I *must* say, Marcus," he told him fiercely, "you have a damned nerve! Taking such a thing as bringing her here upon yourself."

"Someone had to," Marcus replied coolly, long having given up hope of George cultivating a little common sense.

"Really, Marcus!" Amelia exclaimed, her bosom heaving. "At no time would she be welcome here, but at a time like this it really is unforgivable of you! And as for *you*, Sophy," she admonished, "I can only say that I am *astonished* that you, of all people, should behave in a manner which Charles thoroughly deprecated!"

"I am quite aware of what my husband's views were," Sophy reminded her quietly, "but I really do feel the time has come to put aside these prejudices."

"Has it not occurred to you," Amelia pointed out, affronted, "that a girl of her sort is more than capable of taking advantage of your sympathies?"

"No," Sophy shook her head, "it has not occurred to me, indeed," she said truthfully, "I should be appalled if it had."

"Very well, then," Amelia replied very much in the vein of one who washed her hands of things, "have it your own way, but do not be surprised when you eventually discover that I am right."

"I doubt I shall make that discovery," Sophy smiled. "Should I do so, however, then you will be able to say, 'I told you so.'"

"I am glad you find this amusing," Amelia remarked coldly. "For my part, I find it particularly disgusting, but whilst I am prepared to accept your sympathetic motives I find it incomprehensible of you, Marcus," turning to face him, "especially when I consider Charles's views on this very point; views I must add, you have been aware of from the beginning!"

"Amelia is quite right," Emily shot at them, shrugging off Edward's hand on her arm. "How *dare* you bring her here!"

"I have merely carried out my aunt's wish," Marcus told them, quite unperturbed by the accusations being flung at him.

"Marcus is right," Charlotte told them quietly, releasing her granddaughter for a moment. "Since Jenkins apparently has had no success in finding Alexandra, Marcus has done it for me." She held out a warm hand to her nephew, never for one moment pausing to think how he had managed it. "You must have read my mind, Marcus; I have been meaning to speak to you about this." She swallowed, her whole face reflecting her joy, saying unsteadily, "I can never repay you for this, but – oh I *do* thank you, so *very* much!"

Marcus raised her hand to his lips. "No thanks are in the least necessary. It has been a very great pleasure to serve you," he smiled, "both of you."

George witnessed this display in patent horror, crying, "Surely, Mamma, you cannot seriously expect us to have her here?"

"Oh, but I do," Charlotte told them with more firmness than they had ever heard from her, "and I have no intention of allowing any one of you to drive her away. Your father recognised her at the end and made provision for her; I expect no less of you."

"Really, Mamma!" George exclaimed disgustedly. "If I didn't know better I could almost believe you had taken leave of your senses!"

"Alexandra is *my* granddaughter," Charlotte told him unequivocally, "and I intend to have her stay with me for just as long as it suits her, which," she smiled, turning to look at Alexandra, "I hope will be for a *very* long time."

"For goodness sake, Mamma!" Emily cried horrified. "Have you no consideration for us? Do you have any idea what people will say when they know you have her here?"

"I do not intend to give it any thought," Charlotte told her with blatant indifference, adding, not unkindly, "Emily, my dear, I am very mindful of your condition, but I do wish you would strive for a little conduct."

Emily blushed scarlet, throwing Alexandra a withering look, but undaunted by her mother's rebuke, shot out, "It is *this* brat who has no conduct," pointing an accusing finger at the young woman she adamantly refused to acknowledge let alone call niece. "Had she any decency at all she would never have shown her face here, and as for *you*, Marcus," she accused, "I am surprised that you dared to contradict our wishes and seek her out! Had Charles have been here you would not have done so, I assure you!"

Since Marcus could hardly tell her that had Charles been here Alexandra would most probably be lying dead by now he merely ignored her, turning instead to his aunt, saying pointedly, "I think, perhaps, you and Alexandra may wish to be alone."

Charlotte nodded her comprehension, but before she could take Alexandra upstairs to the privacy of her room, the drawing room door opened to admit Adam, his eyes starting from their sockets as he caught sight of a young girl with his mother's arm around her waist, knowing immediately who she was. "What the devil!" he cried.

"I don't wonder you stare!" Emily cried, misunderstanding the reason for her brother's exclamation of surprise. "Marcus has not only taken leave of his senses but has insulted us into the bargain!"

"Insulted us?" Adam repeated, astonished. "What the devil are you talking about, Emily?" he demanded.

"*That* is what I am talking about," she told him, pointing yet another accusing finger at Alexandra. "Marcus seems to think that this brat is…"

"I will have you know, Emily, that…" Adam broke off as he caught sight of Marcus's warning look, then, realising what he had been about to say, hastily corrected himself, saying, "I tell you this, Emily, unless you soften that tongue of yours you'll find yourself one of these days with the devil to pay!"

Emily's bosom rose and fell in indignation, casting her brother a resentful look, but with the timely intervention of Edward tentatively suggesting that the girl was not worth making herself distraught over, she let out a sob and dropped onto her chair, covering her face with her hands.

Adam, not unnaturally, was eager to know how his cousin had managed to effect Alexandra's rescue, but since now was not the appropriate time to fire questions at him, he merely surveyed the scene being played out in front of him with barely concealed impatience. Their dislike of Alexandra surprised even him; not only was it blatantly calculated to ostracise her but to one of his easygoing temperament downright insulting, and by the time Charlotte had taken her granddaughter upstairs he was beginning to wonder whether bringing her here had been the right decision after all. From what he could see of it she was going to be in for the devil of a time from one or the other of them and did not envy Alexandra her stay, but as there were other and far more important things to think about right now, he temporarily shelved the problem facing Alexandra to the back of his mind.

George, having recovered from the astonishment of seeing the girl, a young woman who, like Emily, he too adamantly refused to acknowledge or call his niece, turned his mind to the matter of his brother's death, instantly demanding of Adam if the body he had seen was in fact that of Charles. Adam was certainly shaken from the experience, indeed, he thought he would never forget it, but he bore George's barrage of questions remarkably well, informing him that it was undoubtedly Charles.

George, who had been through much this morning, was not at all sure which aspect upset him the most; the discovery that two police officers had arrived without him being informed of it until the last moment, the shocking news of his brother's death or the fact that Marcus had taken it upon himself to bring his disgraced sister's daughter here to Brook Street, but to have it confirmed that the body his youngest brother had seen was in fact Charles, killing at a stroke any hope an error had been made, seemed like the last straw. Words momentarily failed him, but upon being informed by Adam that there would be a coroner's inquest his eyes widened to their fullest extent. "Inquest!" he exclaimed, the very idea being quite repugnant to him. "I've never heard anything like it!"

"I understand from Inspector Jarrod that a coroner's inquest is normal practice in cases of sudden death," Adam explained.

Emily wept bitterly into her handkerchief, inconsolable and shocked, and although Adam had often considered his sister to be a cold-hearted creature he could not help feeling sorry for her at the loss of a brother with whom she had more in common than the rest of them.

George, still striving to come to terms with the realisation that his brother was indeed dead, looked questioningly at Marcus, demanding to know if he could shed any light on Charles's death.

"Since I was not present when it occurred," Marcus told him with barely concealed annoyance, "I fail to see how I could possibly enlighten you."

Undeterred by this sharply delivered reply, George pressed again, "Yes, I know, but I wondered if perhaps Charles had said anything to you."

"About what?" Marcus enquired, raising a questioning eyebrow.

"Well, I... er... well," George stammered, realising too late his error, "I just wondered if he may have mentioned his reasons for being in such a locality last night."

"Did you ever know Charles to advise me about his engagements?" Marcus asked curtly.

"No," George admitted, "I can't say I..."

"For *heaven's sake,* George, let it rest!" Amelia exclaimed irritably. "How on earth could Marcus or any of us know what happened when we were not there?"

George looked a little startled at his wife's unexpected outburst, but only a moment's reflection was sufficient to tell him that she had suffered a terrible shock and, after hastily begging pardon for his unthinking words, he went on to explain that he merely thought it mighty odd that his brother should be visiting in such an area.

"I daresay it is," Amelia replied, more composed now, "but there is little point in speculating. No doubt in due time the truth will be revealed. Until then," she recommended, "I think it best if we refrain from discussing it," following this up with the calmly delivered announcement that she would retire to her room for a while as she had a headache.

Sophy had no trouble in believing this. Amelia had been bearing her pain and loss remarkably well so far, but George's constant stream of questions and demands had eventually proved too much, indeed, she was herself succumbing to the need to escape them.

Emily, still sniffing into her handkerchief, said tearfully that she for one would never rest until the truth was known. "Poor Charles!" she cried. "It must have been dreadful for him. Only think of his surprise at being so suddenly set upon!"

"You must not distress yourself, my dear," Edward soothed, genuinely concerned for her mental well-being as well as the state of her health. Only minutes before the arrival of William, Charlotte's harassed young footman, bearing the tragic news, she had only just recovered from a most distressing attack of nausea, and such tidings, following quickly upon it, had given rise to her falling unconscious in Edward's arms. Naturally, the news of his brother-in-law's death had come as a reeling blow, not at all what he had expected to read in the note he was handed. It was impossible for him to calculate his thoughts at such a moment. Charles had always fascinated him, but he had overawed him too, making him feel quite insignificant and, on occasion, not even worth his notice. Nevertheless, Edward had secretly admired his brother-in-law and had tried his best to emulate him, but, like George, had failed, and although he was offering his wife stout support during this most wretched time, he could not in all honesty admit to feeling anything near the terrible loss Emily obviously expected him to feel.

"Something must be done to bring these murderous rogues to justice!" Emily cried.

"They will be," Edward assured her. "You may depend upon it."

"That may not be so easy," Adam pointed out practically.

"What do you mean?" Emily shot at him, her face unhealthily flushed.

"I think we can safely assume that whoever set upon Charles would have made sure there were no witnesses," Adam told her as gently as he could, not unmindful of her condition.

"Then some must be found," Emily declared angrily.

"I am afraid you don't quite understand," Adam told her.

"I understand that my brother has been brutally murdered," she bit out, rising to her feet, "and that someone must be made to pay for it." Scanning the faces of her relatives as if seeking enlightenment, she cried, "Why? It is so incredibly hard to believe! Why should anyone want to murder Charles? I simply don't understand it!"

"None of us do," George shrugged helplessly, having asked himself this question more than once since the tragic news had been known. "I assure you, I am just as astonished and in the dark as anyone."

"My poor brother!" Emily cried, wiping her nose on her already sodden handkerchief. "It is just impossible for me to understand. None of it makes any sense!"

Correctly interpreting Marcus's silent message, Edward tentatively suggested that she lie down for a while.

"I don't want to lie down!" Emily cried fretfully, resisting his attempts to escort her upstairs.

"Really, my dear," Edward urged, "I think you should. You have still not quite recovered from this morning."

"Very well," Emily sniffed, "if you think it best," allowing herself to be persuaded into leaving the drawing room, leaning heavily on her husband's arm as he escorted her out of the room.

Being of the firm opinion that women could not possibly be expected to bear such news with either equanimity or fortitude, George hesitantly put forward the suggestion that Sophy too may like to follow the example of her sisters-in-law by retiring to her room to rest.

"I am, of course, terribly shocked and distressed by Charles's death," she told him truthfully, "but I assure you I am not in the least hysterical, and that there is nothing I desire less than to lie down upon my bed."

George could readily understand her shock and distress but failed to believe her latter assertion, and he reiterated his belief that he felt sure an hour's rest would do her good.

For perhaps the first time Sophy found herself more in accord with Amelia than she could ever remember, and she could quite well understand and sympathise with her irritation a few short minutes ago. Sophy too found it extremely difficult to cope with George in his officious moods, but merely smiled, saying gratefully, "You are very kind, George. Indeed, I am most touched by your concern, but I much prefer to remain here."

Since she could not be moved and Adam and Marcus never took any heed of his advice or suggestions, George deemed it wise to excuse himself with as much dignity as he could muster on the pretext that he would go and see how Amelia was feeling. Had he have had the least suspicion that this was precisely what the three of them wanted he would not have departed so readily, but once the door had been closed firmly behind him the three conspirators sighed their relief.

"Thank God he's gone!" Adam exclaimed.

"It won't be for long, however," Marcus pointed out. "If I know Amelia, she will soon send him packing."

"Then we don't have much time," Adam stated. "Has Inspector Jarrod spoken to you yet?"

"Yes," Marcus nodded. "He came to see me just as I was on the point of setting out to see Alexandra," going on to tell him what had passed between them.

"I'm sorry I placed you in such a position," Adam apologised, "but I couldn't tell him the truth."

"No, of course you couldn't," Marcus assured him, "no more than I could."

"Do you think he believed you?" Adam cocked his head.

"I think so. I certainly hope so," Marcus smiled.

A frown touched Adam's forehead, asking, "What do you make of this business, Marcus?"

But his cousin's attention was momentarily fixed on Sophy's pale face. "One moment, Adam." Then, turning to Sophy, asked gently, "Are you quite sure you are up to discussing this? I am afraid the truth is not very pleasant."

She gave him a rather wan smile. "I already know so much, and although I am shocked and appalled at what I have learned, I have to know the whole truth."

Marcus squeezed her hand reassuringly. "I understand that," he said softly, "but there was so much I could not explain to you in my letter."

"I realise that," Sophy acknowledged, "but no matter how painful it may prove to be, I have to know the full extent of Charles's involvement."

"Very well," Marcus nodded, "it shall be as you wish."

But by the time he had come to the end of his account of the past twelve hours or so, so stunned and dismayed by the whole truth was she that she could not contain the sob which rose in her throat. Sophy was not at all certain which aspect upset her most; the fact that Charles had had every intention of putting an end to Marcus's life before uncharacteristically changing his mind by holding him to ransom, or his determination to murder Alexandra. "My god!" she cried, burying her face in her hands. "I can't believe it!"

"Not very uplifting I know," Marcus said grimly, "but his position was so desperate that he considered anything was preferable to being exposed as a thief."

"But Alexandra," she queried, "are you saying you told her what Charles had planned for her?"

"By no means," Marcus shook his head. "As far as she is concerned I have merely brought her to stay with her grandmother and to enable her to take possession of her inheritance. I saw no reason to enlighten her to the truth."

"She must *never* discover what Charles had planned for her," Sophy cried earnestly.

"She will never discover it from me," Marcus assured her, *"nor,* for that matter, will my aunt. Indeed," he said firmly, "no one other than ourselves must know of Charles's dealings."

"But the police?" she questioned. "Surely they will find out the truth!"

"How?" Marcus asked. "All they know is that Charles was in Waterloo last night. They have no way of knowing the reasons which took him there."

Sophy lowered her eyes and her colour deepened, saying hesitantly, "I believe they already suspect Charles's reasons for being in such a locality."

Marcus did not pretend to misunderstand her but, however unpalatable, the same thought had occurred to him; it was, after all, a natural assumption for the police to make, but taking hold of her hand he said gently, "I realise that thought is far from flattering to either of you, nevertheless, it has to be better than the truth."

Sophy nodded. "I know, and whilst I suspected that that was what was going through their minds this morning, I should have liked very much to have disabused them."

"I am afraid," Marcus said gently, "that if we are to keep this tragedy amongst ourselves we have no choice but to allow them to think whatever they choose, however undesirable."

"Yes, I know," she acknowledged a little sadly. Then, looking up at him said, "I haven't yet thanked you properly for all you have done this morning, but I do, so very much."

"There is nothing to thank me for," Marcus assured her, his eyes smiling warmly down into hers, reassuringly squeezing her cold hand as it rested in his warm one. "Once having read Adam's note I knew that our plans to get you both away this morning were no longer viable, and so my main priority had to be the girl. Since I could not waste time in coming here to establish the time and place of your meeting, I went straight to her lodgings."

Her fingers moved in his, but before Marcus could respond, Adam, who had been listening to their interchange with only half an ear, asked, "But what of Knowles? If this attempt on Alexandra's life didn't take place as planned, what's to stop him from trying again?"

"I think it most unlikely," Marcus shook his head, having given it some thought. "He's no fool. Without Charles's backing I cannot see him making another attempt."

"And what of George?" Adam wanted to know. "Apart from being far from pleased about bringing Alexandra here, he's going to want to know more about Charles's death and what he was doing in Waterloo."

"If I know George," Marcus smiled, "he is going to be far too busy exercising his authority to worry about Alexandra for very long, and as for Charles's death," he shrugged, "when he realises that no one can answer any of his questions adequately he will soon give it up."

Adam, still not quite able to banish the horrific picture of Charles's body from his mind, had, for some time, been turning over an idea in his head which would not go away, and mentioned the matter to his cousin. "Do you think Charles's death is in any way connected with Alexandra?"

"I am convinced of it," Marcus nodded, "but exactly where it fits in I have no idea. Unfortunately," he sighed, "I doubt we ever shall."

Adam, who sensed that Marcus had already some idea in mind about his brother's death but was disinclined to discuss it in front of Sophy, was obliged to accept this for the time being, but as he shrewdly guessed she wanted a few moments alone with his cousin, he excused himself by saying that he ought to go upstairs to see his mother.

Slipping her hand out of Marcus's comforting one, Sophy walked over to where Adam was standing, kissing him affectionately on the cheek, telling him that she did not know how she would have coped had he not been here with her this morning, to which he smiled and said it was nothing, nothing at all. Looking meaningfully at Marcus over her head, his eyes telling his cousin that he had not believed one word he had said about Charles's death, Marcus merely nodded comprehendingly, whereupon Adam left the drawing room.

"Did you mean that, Marcus," she asked earnestly, "about this man Knowles making no more attempts on Alexandra's life?"

"As sure as I can be," he told her truthfully. "It won't be long before the news of Charles's death becomes known. There is now nothing for Knowles to gain from her death, and if I know his type, he will want nothing more than to run for cover."

"I do so hope you are right!" she exclaimed fervently, wringing her hands.

"And I hope you are not going to sit here worrying about it," he chided gently. "There is not the least need for you to do so. All you need concern yourself with is that Alexandra is safe and that Charles's reputation is undamaged."

"And what of you?" she asked softly, gently taking hold of his hands to look at the marks on his wrists where the ropes had cut into them, raising her eyes to his.

"What of me?" he asked tenderly, his eyes looking warmly down into her own.

"I was horrified to learn that you had been locked in that cellar; you could have been killed, Marcus!" she cried, mentally shying away from the brutal images which crept into her mind.

"There was not the slightest chance of that happening," he assured her. "Charles may have considered his back to be very much against the wall, but I doubt even he would have taken that perilous step."

"But he could so easily have done," Sophy told him seriously. "No one knew Charles better than I and what he was capable of."

Marcus took hold of her hands, kissing their soft palms, saying gently, "My dearest Sophy, had Charles given in to such a temptation, I assure you I could have more than adequately taken care of myself."

She was not convinced and, suddenly, the tears she had tried so hard to control began to fall unheeded down her cheeks as she finally succumbed to all the various emotions brought on by this morning's events, comforted only by the strength of his arms as he wrapped them around her.

"I know you have had a terrible time of it," he said softly, "but it is over now. I am perfectly safe, and so is Alexandra."

"It could all have turned out so very differently," she sobbed. "Oh, why could not Charles have applied to me for help rather than embark on such a hazardous course?"

"I think you know the answer to that," he told her quietly. "Charles would not have applied to you for financial relief any more than he was prepared to accept my offer. He was far too proud."

"It seems incredible that he was prepared to go to these lengths all for the sake of some letters he once wrote!" she cried, aghast, easing herself out of his arms. "Surely they were not so important?"

"To Charles they were of paramount importance," he reminded her. "Do not forget, he had used some of Elizabeth's jewellery to raise the money to redeem them, but once he learned the contents of Matthew's will the whole thing blew up in his face. I don't condone what Charles planned," he told her, "but I *can* see how desperate he must have felt knowing his deception could be discovered at any moment. He had no way of knowing how long it would take Jenkins to find Alexandra, but even if he had it would have been quite impossible for him to raise enough money to redeem those pieces in time to avert disclosure."

"But where are those pieces now?" she asked.

"I wish I knew," Marcus confessed. "However, I think it is safe to say that whoever Charles employed to copy those pieces was very well known to him; under no circumstances would he risk taking them to someone he did not know or trust. From the looks of it," he speculated, "I would say that this particular jeweller, however skilled, is clearly not the most honest member of his profession, if he were, then he would not have even considered undertaking such a commission. Nevertheless," he told her, "he must be found and those pieces redeemed as soon as possible."

"You mean *you* will redeem them," she supplied, not at all surprised by this generosity.

"It will be a small price to pay for coming out of this business as well as we have," he told her. "I know Charles and I had our differences, and whilst I still cannot believe the lengths to which he went to not only rid himself of Alexandra, who he confessed to me was a humiliation to him, but also to free himself of his difficulties, there was no way I wanted his death. The least I can do is try to get those pieces back, not only for the girl's sake but his as well."

Sophy nodded, then asked, "Do you think the police will find whoever killed Charles?"

"Unless someone comes forward who witnessed it," he shook his head, "and I very much doubt anyone did, then I have to say it seems most unlikely," he admitted.

"This inquest," she queried, "shall we be required to attend?" her eyes troubled, thinking of the pain Charlotte had already suffered.

"I am afraid so, yes," he confirmed quietly.

"Poor Charlotte!" she sighed. "She has suffered enough."

"I know," Marcus acknowledged, "but I am afraid there is no way any of us can avoid the legal formalities attached to such things."

"I realise, of course," she conceded, "that the matter has to be gone into most thoroughly, but I am afraid that at some point the truth will come out, and Charlotte must be protected from that at all costs!" she told him earnestly. "She would never be able to bear the news that her son had been brutally killed because he had removed some of his sister's jewellery and replaced them with copies as well as what he had planned for Alexandra!"

Marcus shook his head. "I doubt very much that this will prove to be the case. Consider for a moment," he advised gently, "a man's body was found early this morning, seemingly the victim of a street robbery. Now, unless Knowles comes forward, which, quite frankly, I cannot see him doing, with evidence to the contrary, which, incidentally," he told her, "would clearly implicate him, the result of the coroner's inquest will simply be what the police already believe – a case of murder by person or persons unknown."

"But what if this man Knowles had nothing whatever to do with Charles's death?" she asked.

"I think you will find that he was heavily involved in it," he told her firmly. "I do not pretend to know how or why," he admitted, "but I would stake my life on that!"

"Oh, Marcus!" Sophy cried. "I know whoever killed Charles deserves to be punished for such a brutal crime, but I can't help thinking that his scheming was the cause of it, and yet," she confessed earnestly, "despite everything, I would hate to see his name sullied and his reputation torn to pieces because of it."

"I agree," Marcus nodded. "As to whether he deserves that," he sighed, "I don't know, but I for one intend to ensure his name remains untarnished."

"I know I did not love Charles," she confessed, contentedly resting her head against his broad chest, "but I never wanted his death."

"I know," Marcus soothed, folding her in his arms and kissing the top of her head, "neither did I. Whilst I accept it has rid us of obstacles preventing us from being together, I would give all I possess to have him alive."

"Am I wicked to still love and want you, Marcus?" she asked, raising her head to look up into his face. "Knowing that my husband is dead; brutally killed only this morning?"

"Wicked?" Marcus repeated. "My poor darling, of course you are not. You must not even think such a thing."

"I can't help it," Sophy confessed. "I love you more than I ever thought it possible to love someone, yet to do so seems terribly callous in the light of what has happened."

"One does not cease to love because of tragedy," he told her gently. "Emotions and feelings do not die simply because of circumstances."

"I couldn't bear to lose you now," she confessed, pressing herself even closer into him.

"You are not going to lose me," he assured her in a deep voice. "I am of the same mind now as I have always been and Charles's death has not changed that. As soon as your period of mourning is over, I intend to ask for your hand in marriage."

"And I shall say yes," she smiled up at him. Suddenly her eyes clouded. "What will people say, do you think?"

"They will say whatever they wish to," Marcus dismissed. "I for one have no intention of paying any heed to them, besides," he commented, "they will soon cease talking about us once another topic claims their attention."

"I suppose you are right," she nodded. "And Charlotte?"

"If I know my aunt," he smiled, "it would not surprise me to learn that she has been aware of what's between us from the outset."

Sophy laughed. "I have a feeling you are right." She was suddenly serious again and eased herself out of his arms. "But we must not forget Alexandra. She is going to find her stay here most uncomfortable. Naturally, I shall do all I can to make her stay a happy one, but you heard them yourself. They will never be brought to accept her, Marcus."

"They are going to have to," he said firmly. "However, I think my aunt may be well advised, after the funeral, to take Alexandra away for a while, at least until things have settled down here."

"I don't think they will ever settle down," she admitted, her eyes clouding. "They are so prejudiced against her that I can well imagine her life here being a terrible ordeal."

"We shall just have to ensure it does not come to that," he told her, adding, "but my main concern is for you. Naturally, you will have to notify Timothy of what has happened, but I would strongly recommend you remove to your brother's as soon after the funeral as possible. If nothing else, it will give you a respite from the animosity here."

Sophy agreed to it, but for now she was happy to forget the harsh realities which faced them, content to remain in Marcus's arms a while longer, all her cares and worries temporarily shelved as she welcomed his kisses with the same eagerness he was giving them; kisses she thought she would never receive again.

Chapter Twenty-Two

It was not to be expected that the sudden death of a notable businessman and unquestionable pillar of society like Charles Harrington would escape the notice of the newspapers for long. By the early afternoon edition, the story was printed on every front page. That his death had been a violent one, clearly the tragic result of a robbery, was in no doubt. Various sources were quoted as saying that the violence on London streets was becoming a national disgrace, and that no decent citizen was safe while such despicable acts went undetected. "What," one correspondent to the editor of a national newspaper vehemently demanded to know, "were the authorities doing about such vicious crimes?" It was a lengthy and accusatory letter, which, said the writer, echoed the views of many readers, but it left one reader especially reeling in numbed disbelief.

Ted Knowles cared nothing about the scandalous outcry regarding the increase in crime on London's streets, or that certain prominent personages were being called upon to render an account as to their unacceptable mishandling of criminals to date. Nor did the scathing denunciation of one distinguished Member of Parliament, bitterly animadverting on the disgraceful state of affairs when a law-abiding citizen like Charles Harrington could not walk the streets without fear of molestation, have the least effect on him. None of these outraged comments were of any concern to him, in fact, he read no further than the first half a dozen lines of the opening paragraph outlining in as much detail as possible the death of his client. Having fully expected to read the news of Marcus Ingleby's death, it came as a stunning blow to discover that far from being dead he was very much alive, and instead of lying on a mortuary slab his cousin was there instead. For close on ten minutes Ted Knowles's brain spun in incredulity and disbelief, made worse by the frustrating knowledge that today's plan of action had failed.

He had not needed Davy to tell him that neither Alexandra nor Mrs. Charles Harrington had kept their appointment at the Hanover Gate in Regents Park, the expression on his face told him equally as well. Bill Ryde, not the most patient of men, had angrily demanded of Davy what the devil Ted was playing at? Over an hour he had waited, and neither the girl nor that other mort had shown themselves, going on to belligerently tell Davy that if Ted thought he was going to get out of paying him just because the thing had not come off, then he was very much mistaken. He had kept his side of the bargain and shown up at the time Ted said and now he wanted his money, after all fair was fair because it was not his fault the thing had been bungled.

Davy's subsequent errand to Mansion Gardens in a frantic effort to discover what was going on proved quite disheartening, his repetitive banging on the knocker eventually eliciting the response from an irate Mrs. Drew that Miss Dawes was not in, no, nor likely to be ever again since her shot had been paid by some toff before going off with him as calm as you please in a hackney this very morning. Upon being informed of this unwelcome news Ted Knowles knew instantly who the toff was, and that Marcus Ingleby had played a hand in the game just as he had promised he would by doing everything possible to save the girl. How he had managed it Ted Knowles had no idea, but he had shown he was not a man who made false promises and how to pay him back in his own coin teased Ted's mind for some considerable time, but no matter how much it went against the grain with him to admit it, Marcus Ingleby had proved to be as good as his word as well as being a force to be reckoned with. Ted Knowles, who had no liking for having his schemes foiled let alone finding himself faced with two devastating blows one after the other, neither of which were his fault, was filled with fierce resentment, but before he could even begin setting his mind to assembling the wreckage or working out a suitable revenge for Marcus Ingleby, he had to find out the truth surrounding Charles Harrington's death.

Ted Knowles could not believe that Jack Dooney, as good a man as any to have in your corner, had misunderstood his instructions, but the more Ted Knowles thought about it the more convinced he became that his crony had made a monumental blunder. It hardly seemed possible, but there was no explanation as far as he could see other than Dooney had mistaken his man. The news of Charles Harrington's death had hit Ted Knowles hard and, loath though he was to admit it, he was a very frightened man; his late client's death was far too close to home for his liking. Nevertheless, Ted Knowles retained a sufficient measure of clear mindedness to prevent total panic from setting in, knowing that until he had spoken to Jack Dooney it was useless to speculate on what had gone wrong the other night.

Like most of his cronies, Ted Knowles found Jack Dooney's particular talents came in very useful on occasion, but they would also be of no small interest to Bow Street, which meant he kept his head down as much as possible. This suited Ted very well, but anyone seeking to transact business with him had to do so under cover of darkness. Jack Dooney's motto was, and always had been, as he now told Ted Knowles, "Say nowt, an' yer won't get found out."

"Yes, that's all very well, but..." Ted began belligerently, determined not to be diverted from his aim.

"An' *anotha* thing," Jack demanded angrily, "wot's yer mean by cumin' 'ere in broad daylight?"

"Neva mind that!" Ted dismissed. "Wot I wonts ter know *is*, wot 'appened t'otha night?"

"Yer knows wot 'appened," Jack snarled, taking a pull from the bottle conveniently placed at his elbow, his battered face taking on a pugnacious expression.

"That's just wot I *don't* know," Ted snapped, throwing a crumpled newspaper down onto the scrubbed top table, his thick forefinger pointing to the article on the front page, momentarily forgetting that his crony could neither read nor write. "Now p'raps yer'll tells me 'ow yer cum to topple the wrung cove," he demanded.

Jack Dooney may not be able to read or write let alone possess the sharpest intelligence, but he knew trouble when he smelled it. He also knew that Ted would not be here at eleven o'clock in the morning without a very good reason and, from the looks of it, that was precisely what he had got.

Jack Dooney, 'The Dynamo' as he had been called in his prime, had been one of the best prizefighters of his day. His footwork and the most punishing left imaginable had been admired and applauded by all the fanciers of the ring, hailed as the best they had ever seen. Envied by his opponents and emulated by aspiring pugilists, he had been the one to whom they had looked for scientific purity, his fame and impressive record ensuring heavy bets were placed in his favour. It was said by some that he surpassed even the great Jackson himself, whose boxing saloon in Bond Street had once drawn professionals and amateurs alike. From young hopeful to a master of his art in a surprisingly short period of time had augured well for a glorious future, but Jack Dooney's unfortunate inclination towards all games of chance, having on occasion been known to bet his purse on the longest of odds, and a propensity for drink, had resulted in him being constantly in debt, and his need of money soon exhausted the handsome purses he had earned, necessitating his return to the ring again and again very much against the advice of all who had his welfare at heart, finally resulting in one bout too many. It had become the rumour at fight venues that Dooney was not the man he had been and he would kill himself before he was through, arriving at the ring still unrecovered from the previous night's indulgencies. His antagonists and those who had bet heavily against him, went so far as to say that his brain was addled and that his habitual drinking sessions followed by a fight was something no man could do, but his urgent need of money had rendered it necessary for him to ignore his worsening physical condition by stepping into the ring once more. Onlookers shook their heads, wondering how much longer he could go on punishing himself by continually returning to the ring for an ever-dwindling purse. His lack of education, volatile temperament and his increasing consumption of drink not only made him unfit to fight but too much of a liability for the many employers who had taken him on when he could no longer endure the rigours of the ring.

Quite when his name and past glories had ceased to open doors for him no one knew, but his reputation had become so far removed from what it had once been that he had come to be looked upon as unpredictable as well as a liability. From supreme prizefighter to public house brawler had been a short step, and instead of the fanciers of the ring paying to watch him fight they paid for his drinks instead, certain of seeing a once great pugilist entertain an amused and deriding crowd, if not with scientific precision then certainly with sufficient pathos to make the initiated shake their heads in sorrow.

Always in need of money, though not to provide for a long-suffering wife and half a dozen children, but to keep him in the tipple Joe Benbow had long since refused to put on tick for him, he had slid easily into the practice of hiring out his fists for anyone with the means to pay for them. So lucrative was this new line of business, especially with the more unsavoury usurers attempting to recoup their outlay from defaulting clients, that he had acquired a favourable, if nefarious reputation amongst certain members of the criminal fraternity whose desire for anonymity and the need to keep a wide berth of the law was as earnest as his own.

Ted Knowles regarded himself as tolerant a man as any and one, moreover, who certainly did not begrudge a man earning a living any way he could, even if that meant doing someone else's dirty work for them, but when one paid for a job one expected it to come off right. What one did not expect, or need for that matter, was the wrong party being put away. He was still waiting for an explanation, but since Jack appeared to be in no hurry to offer one, he repeated his question, barely able to hide his frustration.

"I dunno wot yer talkin' about," Jack told him, shrugging his massive shoulders.

"I'm talkin' about the swell I paid yer ter see to," Ted bit out, suddenly remembering his crony's illiteracy.

"Oh, 'im," he shrugged, his grin exposing several missing teeth. "Yer've no need ter wurry yerself, I've sin ter 'im all right an' tight."

Ted Knowles let out an exasperated sigh. "Oh, yer've sin ter 'im all right!" he scorned, removing the bottle out of Jack's reach. "The only thing is," he told him nastily, "yer've sin ter the wrong cove."

Jack Dooney stared across at his crony with a look of blank astonishment, and for one irritating moment Ted Knowles thought he had not grasped what he had said and impatiently repeated himself.

The pale blue eyes, bloodshot and scarred, opened as far as they possibly could, staring myopically at his crony in dazed disbelief. "The wrung cove?" he repeated incredulously.

"The *wrung cove*," Ted confirmed disgustedly. "Now, wot I wonts ter know *is*; 'owd it 'appen?"

Jack gave this as much thought as was possible for a man of his limited intellect, but after several minutes of deep concentration he was still unable to find a reason for it, saying at length, "Yer told me that the swell yer wonted seein' to wud be leavin' Joe's and that I wos ter folla 'im 'till I finds the propa place ter sees to 'im; an' that's wot I did," he said firmly. "I gets there jus' as the swell wos leavin'."

"Wot time wos that?" Ted demanded, a startling thought occurring to him.

Once again Jack gave this question a lot of thought before shrugging, "I dunno, 'arf past two or thereabouts mebbe."

Ted Knowles pursed his lips as he cast his mind back to the other night, trying to remember everything that had happened to try to account for Dooney mistaking his man. Ted Knowles had no difficulty in recalling the conversation which had taken place between the cousins, nor, for that matter, the undercurrents lying just beneath the polite surface. Their gentlemanly conduct may have gone over the heads of Joe and Albert, but he had been quick to detect the true feelings which existed between them. Mind you, if what he had picked up from their conversation was only half true, then he was not at all surprised at the animosity between them. He had at one point fully expected Marcus Ingleby to lay his cousin out, but having somehow managed to master the impulse, clearly thinking better of it, he had eventually been brought to agree to his cousin's ultimatum. If Ted

Knowles remembered correctly the conversation had then turned to the letter in Ingleby's possession and finally his escape, and whilst that letter was something Ted Knowles would have to turn his mind to it was not of such importance as the colossal blunder of Charles Harrington's death. To his recollection both men had lost and gained ground in the encounter, but in the end the honours had unquestionably gone in his client's favour. If memory served Ted Knowles right that had been the end of the discussion, whereupon Ingleby had left 'The Black Swan', that would be about quarter past two or round about and Charles Harrington did not leave until about fifteen minutes or so later, enjoying Joe's excellent brandy too much to be in a hurry to leave.

Gradually the mists began to clear, and before long Ted Knowles realised just what had happened, but discovering the answer to the puzzle also brought with it the unpalatable realisation that he as much as his crony was to blame for identifying the wrong man. He had made two unforgivable errors when imparting his instructions to Dooney and berated himself now for his stupidity in behaving like a veritable novice. First, he had totally misjudged the length of time the meeting between the cousins would take, and although he had not expected them to leave Joe's together, especially considering the far from friendly relations which existed between them, he had then followed this gross error up by miscalculating how long Charles Harrington would linger in order to finish off the bottle of cognac Joe had brought up for him earlier. But, which was even worse, he had failed to take in to account that when he had described Marcus Ingleby he could just as easily have been describing Charles Harrington. Admittedly, Ingleby was by far the bigger built of the two, but both were exceptionally tall men and, which had completely escaped his usual quickness, both were immaculately and expensively dressed, each wearing dark overcoats over their impeccably tailored clothes.

As far as Jack Dooney was concerned, Ted had a more than accurate picture of his part in the affair. Clearly, he had mistaken the hour, although why Ted should expect his crony to tell the time when he could only mark his name by a cross he did not know. If he knew anything about it, it had been more a case of guessing the time rather than telling it, and this, unless he was very much mistaken, coupled with the amount of drink Jack must undoubtedly have consumed, would have rendered it impossible for him to know precisely what time he arrived at 'The Black Swan', let alone being able to identify a certain party leaving it. If Charles Harrington had left Joe's immediately after Ingleby then he would still be alive now, admittedly so too would Ingleby, but that surely would be far better than the wrong man being put out of the way!

Ted Knowles knew it was useless to try to question Jack further, not only because it was doubtful if he could remember but, also, from the looks of the empty bottle on the table it seemed very much as though he had been drinking most of the morning and no sense would be got out of him. Ted Knowles made ready to leave but not before demanding the contents of his late client's pockets.

"Wots that yer say?" Dooney asked warily.

"'And 'em ova," Ted demanded, holding out an imperative hand.

"Ah, you'm a knowin' 'un," Dooney grinned, reluctantly delving into his trouser pocket to pull out the wallet together with a signet ring and a watch and chain. "But thay cud cum in mighty 'andy thay cud."

"Oh, thay'd cum in 'andy all right an' tight!" Ted scorned. "Thay'd be inuf ter meks sure that every Runna in Bow Street 'ud cum 'nockin' on yer door. Don't yer knows that anybudy found wi' these on 'em is as gud as 'ung?"

As this aspect of the case had not previously occurred to him, Jack Dooney tossed Charles Harrington's belongings onto the table, then, digging a hand into his other trouser pocket, pulled out the cunning little pistol which Charles had had made specially for him by Reilly in Oxford Street, tossing it onto the table, eyeing his crony with resentment at having to hand over such a useful haul.

Ted Knowles eyed the pistol in some surprise, not having expected his late client to carry a weapon upon his person but tucking it into his pocket with the intention of throwing it in the Thames at the earliest opportunity together with the rest of his possessions, he then flicked through the contents of the wallet. "Yer've forgotten sumthin' ain't yer?" Ted said sharply, raising his eyes from the empty wallet in his hands.

"Wots that?" Jack shrugged.

"The money," Ted said firmly. "Let's 'ave it, Jack," he demanded, holding out his massive paw.

"There wos none," Dooney dismissed, reaching out for another bottle.

"Don't lie ter me," Ted warned. "A swell like that 'ud 'ave sum readies on 'im."

"Well 'e dain't, see," Jack told him belligerently, daring Ted to argue the point, still unable to believe that a very timely means of financial gain had come his way.

Ted knew that he was lying and had in fact most probably taken the money to supply him with a few more bottles, but since Dooney could not be moved into confessing his theft Ted irritably pointed out that he had not been told to filch the cove's pockets for his own personal gain, bearing in mind he had already been paid for his expert services, but to make the job look right. Jack shrugged, and Ted, realising that he would not budge on the subject, left.

Discovering the reason for such a monumental mistake was one thing, but it in no way made Ted Knowles feel any more comfortable, on the contrary he was treading on very thin ice, and not only where Ingleby was concerned. Bill Ryde, who clearly expected to receive his money even though the job had not come off, was not the type of man who would wait too long for what he believed was his due to be handed over, but as things stood right now, not having been paid for his own services to date, Ted Knowles knew that coming up with the readies was easier said than done. The contents of Charles Harrington's wallet would have come in mighty handy. Bill was not a man to be balked and, come what may, he would expect his money. Perhaps Ingleby could come in useful there!

Had Dooney identified the right party and had the girl met with the accident that had been arranged, Ted Knowles knew that there would have been no way any accusing finger could have been pointed in his direction for either tragic incident. Although he was furiously angry to learn that neither had come off, the first because the girl and Mrs. Charles Harrington had failed to show themselves, thanks to Ingleby, and the other because Dooney was a fool, he would by now be sitting on a nice little earner with no repercussions rebounding on himself. Unfortunately, Ingleby was still alive and the girl safe and sound, leaving him wide open for attack, a completely new experience which Ted Knowles was by no means happy about. When he had set out to rid himself of Marcus Ingleby it had been in the belief that his death would be looked upon in the way he had predicted in that the authorities would be of the unqualified opinion that the deceased had been the unfortunate victim of a brutal robbery committed by person or persons unknown, but to be faced with such a ghastly mistake as the wrong party being put away had not been in Ted Knowles's calculations at all. It made not the slightest bit of difference telling himself that his plans had gone wrong through no fault of his own, the fact remained they had, but whilst the authorities may well believe what he had hoped they would, he knew there was one man who would not – Marcus Ingleby! He was far too astute to be taken in by such a story; he would know that there was far more to it than appeared on the surface, and unless Ted Knowles was very much mistaken he knew that this thorn in his flesh would know precisely where to look for the culprit.

Despite the differences which had existed between Charles Harrington and Marcus Ingleby they *were* cousins, carrying the same blood and family ties, and Ted Knowles had come to know Ingleby sufficiently well to realise that he would certainly look beneath the surface and delve into the affair until he arrived at the truth. Ingleby was no fool; far from it! In view of recent events he would soon put two and two together and know that his cousin's death was no coincidence; he may even know that it was he who had been the intended victim and not his cousin. Once he concluded all of this, there was absolutely nothing to stop him from taking the information to Bow Street, especially now that there was nothing to prevent him from doing so. Ted Knowles knew he was perfectly safe where the girl was concerned, if for no other reason than he did not think Ingleby would frighten her by telling her just how close she had come to death, and then there was no evidence against him to prove he was involved. Should matters come to this point, it would merely be Ingleby's word against his own. Unfortunately, Ted Knowles soon found himself disabused of this comfortable theory as the unwelcome thought of that letter in Ingleby's possession came forcibly to mind. If he had been frightened before, he was even more so now; when faced with a man of Ingleby's background and reputation what court of law would take the word of a man like himself? This unpleasant thought made Ted Knowles swallow uncomfortably. There had to be something he could do to avoid coming face to face with the Queen's Bench and, horrendous thought, probably ending up by having his neck stretched.

But Ted Knowles was nothing if not resourceful, his ever-fertile brain seemingly capable of great inventiveness when a situation became desperate, and now it came into its own again; so much so that by the time he arrived back home the seeds which had taken root had grown into a foolproof scheme. Marcus Ingleby had proved once before that he could be coerced, well, Ted Knowles was going to put that to the test again; he would make Ingleby a proposition he would find impossible to turn down.

*

The news that Charles Harrington had been murdered within so short a time of leaving his hostelry, made Joe Benbow sweat. Naturally, he could not prove who was responsible for it but he would lay his life that Ted had had something to do with it. Ted had been having some deep doings recently and proving mighty cagey about them too, but this arrangement he had had going with Charles Harrington, whatever it was, seemed pretty serious to him. Joe could only look on and be glad he was well out of it as it all seemed very havey-cavey to him, which the recent illicit use of his cellar proved!

The more he thought about it the more likely it seemed that someone had gone to a great deal of trouble to dispose of Charles Harrington, and unless Joe was grossly mistaken the whole dirty business seemed very much like the handiwork of Dooney. Whether this was the case or not, Joe nevertheless heaved a tremendous sigh of relief to see that no mention had been made of 'The Black Swan' in any of the newspapers, even so, it was still far too close to home for comfort. The more he set his mind to it the more bewildered he became. He wouldn't like to think that Ted had had a hand in it, but his crony had never had any liking for being told what to do, and Charles Harrington had been mighty prone to giving his orders. Even so, it seemed a pretty flimsy reason to do away with a cove; but no matter which way Joe looked at it, it made no sense to have Harrington put out of the way especially as, according to Ted, he was still waiting for his money. Joe had known from the beginning that Ted was up to something dubious, but in the light of Harrington's death he was more convinced than ever that the less he knew the better it would be for him. All the same, he could not help wondering how it happened. Charles Harrington may not have been so powerfully built as the man he had come to learn was his cousin, but even so he had struck him as being more than capable of taking care of himself and, no matter how contemptible, he could not help but arrive at the conclusion that whoever had set upon him had taken him from behind. Joe may not have liked the man, but he did not hold with dirty tricks like this, and he was therefore ready to swear that Harrington never had the time to defend himself.

Joe was perfectly right. Having succeeded in bringing his cousin round to his way of thinking, Charles had been more than pleased with the outcome of their second meeting. It was a pity his cousin took such a serious view of things, but, be that as it may, he had gained his objective and had celebrated his success with several glasses of cognac. "I must compliment you on your excellent cellar," he told Joe, adding, "although I very much doubt it has paid duty!" Joe shuffled uncomfortably, and Charles laughed. "Do not be afraid," he said affably, "your secret is safe with me." Then, turning round to Ted Knowles, said meaningfully, "I shall look forward to receiving good news tomorrow, but please," he said almost painfully, "do not put yourself to the trouble of bringing it to me personally." Ted Knowles did not pretend to misunderstand him, but had Charles not been so relieved at his cousin's agreement to turning a blind eye, albeit reluctantly, he would have seen the preoccupation on his accomplice's face. Having no idea that Ted Knowles had set plans of his own in motion to deal with Marcus once and for all, Charles completely misread this, saying sharply, "It had better work, Knowles. I shall not take it kindly if it fails."

Jolted back to the matter in hand, Ted assured his client that it was as good as done. "There's no need to fret yerself," he told him, affronted.

"I hope not," Charles warned. "You are not being paid to fail –

remember that."

To Albert's disgust, Charles made no attempt to pay for his refreshment, seeming to take it for granted that it was on the house, but if he expected Joe to remind their unwelcome visitor of his financial obligations he was wrong; Joe had no intention of requesting payment even though it went very much against the grain with him to see good cognac being handed out free of charge. The truth was he was too eager to see the back of Ted's acquaintance, and therefore did not intend to delay his departure by asking for payment which he knew full well would not be forthcoming.

He was right. Charles had no intention of paying for the finest glasses of cognac he had ever drank, and without even offering Joe a word of thanks he put on his hat and gloves and, following a final warning to Ted Knowles, left 'The Black Swan' twenty minutes after his cousin in the most leisurely fashion.

The night was cold and damp, rendering it necessary for Charles to turn up his overcoat collar, but he was not so much bothered about the weather any more than he was about walking along the streets at this hour of the morning trying to find a late hackney; his only thoughts were for tomorrow and the successful outcome of his plans. Ted Knowles, apart from naming the individual he had hired to carry out the 'accident' as Bill, declining to offer a surname, not that Charles wanted to know, but he felt reasonably sure that whoever he was he was undoubtedly possessed of the same criminal tendencies as Knowles.

It went without saying that he was looking forward to a prosperous future resulting from tomorrow's so-called accident, and whilst Charles still looked upon it with complete detachment, a cautionary note had crept into his thoughts. Marcus had given him his word that he would keep silent, and Charles believed he meant it if only for Sophy's sake, but somewhere at the back of his mind there lurked the nagging thought that his noble and quixotic cousin may, for some ridiculously chivalrous reason, decide to break his word. He pondered this possibility as he walked along, his shadow keeping in perfect step in the dim light from the gas lamps, unhelpfully offering no response to his burning question. Could he trust Marcus to honour his promise? He was convinced he could. His cousin may have pledged his word with the utmost reluctance but having given it he was far too much the gentleman to either retract or renege on it. Admittedly, Marcus could use it against him at any time, and although this could not be entirely ruled out it seemed most unlikely, if for no other reason than Marcus, possessing a very different code of honour to Ted Knowles, or to himself for that matter, would shrink from the very idea of doing anything so ungentlemanly. No matter how tiresome these noble virtues were,

Charles had to acknowledge that they did have their uses; especially when they could be used to such good effect by turning them against one's personal code of honour. His cousin's involvement in his affairs was, to put no finer point on it, extremely annoying, and although his incarceration had been a most regrettable incident, he had to admit that, all in all, he was rather well satisfied with this evening's events and foresaw no obstacle to ruin his plans or his trouble-free future.

Walking confidently on, unaware of the stealthy approach from behind by Jack Dooney, Charles saw he was nearing a junction with a main road and was hoping that once he was in a more frequented thoroughfare he would find a late vehicle to convey him home. For a man of Jack Dooney's ungainly bulk he moved with surprising swiftness and agility, his light-footedness enabling him to gain on his quarry without him being aware of it. The first Charles knew that he was no longer alone was when he heard the sound of heavy breathing close behind him, but before he could even turn round to see who it was, something resembling a band of steel closed round his neck like a vice, momentarily surprising him into immobility. The arm closed tighter, gradually choking the breath out of him, his desperate attempts to reach the small but serviceable pistol in his inside pocket as useless as his strenuous efforts to remove that arm. He found himself being easily hauled backwards along the pavement for several yards, his stunned brain only just managing to register the fact that he was being effortlessly dragged into what appeared to be a dark alleyway. His throat felt on fire and his head seemed likely to burst open from the fierce pounding. Several times he tried to cry out for assistance but no sound emanated from his swelling throat, his chest heaving painfully with every breath he drew.

Jack Dooney knew it was only a matter of moments before his victim succumbed to suffocation but remembering his instructions he dug his free hand into his jacket pocket, pulling out a small heavy cosh which he brought crashing down onto his victim's head. Charles knew no more; falling to the ground with a heavy thud. Time and again that cosh accosted Charles inanimate form, his head and body brutally assaulted, the blood from these ugly wounds oozing out onto the wet cobbles. Returning the vicious weapon to his pocket, Dooney rifled through Charles's pockets before dragging his body even further into Meadow Row, the dark recesses of this narrow and dingy alleyway ensuring it would not be discovered until it was light. Pausing only to catch his breath, Dooney left the alleyway as quietly and as stealthily as he had made his approach, congratulating himself on as easy a job as he could have wished for.

*

It would be a long time before Adam would forget seeing the results of

Dooney's handiwork and, as he told his cousin when he called on him the following morning prior to their visit to Silas Jenkins, he thought the memory of Charles's battered body would haunt him forever. "My god, Marcus!" he shuddered. "It was horrible. I barely recognised him." He shook his head, saying fervently, "I hope and pray to God that I never again have to see anything like it!"

Having been a soldier for most of his adult life, Marcus was no stranger to death or to experiencing the sickening reality of identifying the mangled corpses of men who had once been loyal friends and comrades, their distorted features embedding themselves in his memory for all time. How much more horrifying to identify one's own brother's disfigured body! He knew words were quite unavailing at a time like this, but he responded to Adam's devoutly expressed plea with sympathetic agreement, whilst at the same time trying to turn his mind away from the mental images locked in his mind of Charles's body lying cold and battered on a mortuary table.

"What do you think will happen now?" Adam asked, pouring himself a much-needed cup of coffee.

"I should think that very much depends on the coroner's inquest," Marcus told him, "but of one thing we *can* be certain," he nodded, "and that is I doubt very much whether the perpetrator of such a vicious crime will be identified."

Adam looked down at the coffee in his cup in considerable thought, and Marcus, knowing his cousin too well, asked, "What's wrong, Adam? I know you have something on your mind other than your natural shock over Charles's death."

A little smile played at the corner of Adam's mouth; Marcus had always seen too much. "As a matter of fact, there is," he confirmed, finishing off his coffee.

"What is it?" Marcus encouraged, believing no good would be served by bottling things up.

Adam drew a deep breath before saying, "I know we touched upon this yesterday, but I wish I knew where this Knowles character fits into Charles's death. For something like this to happen at such a moment goes beyond coincidence."

Marcus had been thinking along the same lines himself ever since he had learned of his cousin's death, and he could not argue against the sense of this. "As I told you yesterday, I have no doubt at all that our friend Knowles had a hand in it, in fact," he pointed out, "I am very sure he planned the whole thing."

Adam shook his head. "But why? What could he possibly hope to gain from his death? It just doesn't make sense!"

"What happened yesterday morning makes perfect sense," Marcus told him calmly, "if you accept the premise that Charles was not the intended victim."

Not unnaturally, this statement took Adam by surprise, staring at his cousin as if he could not believe what he had just heard. "What do you mean?" he asked, dumbstruck. "Of course Charles was the intended victim!"

"Not 'of course'," Marcus shook his head, "but 'unfortunately'." He saw the look of incredulity cross Adam's face. "We have assumed, or, rather," Marcus corrected himself, "we have been led to believe that Charles was set upon and robbed."

"Which he was!" Adam exclaimed, not at all certain what his cousin was driving at.

"Precisely!" Marcus nodded. "But you yourself have said that Charles's death, coming at such a time, could not be coincidence."

"Well, it can't!" Adam cried. "The odds against that would be tremendous."

"Yes, they would," Marcus agreed. "Which leads me to question why he was disposed of in the first place."

"Just what are you driving at?" Adam asked, his eyes searching his cousin's face.

"We both agree that Knowles had a hand in the affair," Marcus explained, "in fact, we believe he planned the whole thing."

"He must have," Adam said firmly. "Who else could it have been?"

"Quite!" Marcus nodded. "We also know that the question as to why he should want to rid himself of Charles cannot be adequately explained away, but we do know that he entered into this affair with Charles for monetary gain and no other reason. Whether he has been paid or not is anyone's guess, but what we *can* say for certain is that Knowles is not only resourceful but extremely avaricious." Pausing only long enough to finish his coffee he continued, "Charles needed help in getting rid of the girl, and neither of them it seems were overly concerned how it was achieved. Above all else, Charles wanted to keep this enterprise a secret; at all costs, he could not allow it to come to the notice of the police. Knowles would know this and being a naturally greedy man with no scruples whatsoever he would no doubt have considered the possibility of bleeding Charles dry at some point in the future. The opportunities were endless, and the fear of Knowles exposing him would have been too horrendous for Charles to contemplate.

Knowles is no fool; there is no question of him doing away with Charles and cutting off the flow of money he knew Charles would have paid him for his silence."

"So?" Adam pressed.

"So," Marcus inclined his head, "it is for this reason that I am firmly convinced that Charles was mistaken for the real victim."

"The *real* victim!" Adam repeated, aghast. "What do you mean? If not Charles, then who *was* the real victim?"

Marcus eyed him steadily, a look in his eyes Adam had not seen before, saying, quite unmoved, "I believe I was."

Adam's jaw dropped. *"You!"* he exclaimed, almost dropping his cup.

"It makes far more sense than it being Charles," Marcus offered. "I can, of course, only speculate on the thinking behind it, but I believe I have hit upon the reason to account for Knowles's counter-plan."

"Well, it's more than I have!" Adam told him, wondering how many more shocks he could expect to receive before this ghastly nightmare was over. "What conceivable reason could he have?"

"The fear of exposure," Marcus supplied. "Consider, Adam," he advised, "Charles and Knowles were on the point of committing murder, and prior to my arrival on the scene they believed they were going to get away with it. As far as they were concerned it was their secret, then I came along and spiked their guns. Charles was forced into taking drastic action, that is to say, getting rid of me – another unfortunate victim!" he commented sardonically. "Then, for whatever reason, Charles thought better of resorting to such a violent solution with one so subtle he knew it could not fail."

"He held you to ransom with Sophy," Adam supplied grimly.

"Precisely!" Marcus nodded. "Thanks to Knowles, he had discovered the true state of affairs between us and decided to use it against me. Charles knew me well enough to be certain that I would do nothing that could possibly put Sophy's life at risk, offering me an ultimatum I would find impossible to refuse."

Adam, who had risen from his chair to begin pacing up and down, his head awash with everything that had happened, suddenly came to a halt, turning to face his cousin. "But having given your word Charles must have known you would not break it."

"Charles knew that, certainly," Marcus agreed, also rising, "but Knowles did not. For all he knew I could have been simply playing for time and, once having left 'The Black Swan', there was nothing to stop me from going straight to the police."

"But that doesn't tell us much!" Adam dismissed irritably. "If Knowles had arranged your death, when could he have done it? He could not have known your response to Charles's ultimatum beforehand!"

Marcus acknowledged this, but explained, "When Knowles came here bearing Charles's letter with instructions for me to accompany him back to 'The Black Swan', I tried to pump him for information, but he was not forthcoming. I assumed, quite wrongly I see now," he admitted, "that he knew nothing of what Charles had in mind, but he must have done. Charles must have told him just enough to get him to do what he wanted, but as we have already said, Knowles is no fool; indeed, he is very astute, and it would not have taken him long to assimilate the facts. Let us suppose," he argued, "that Charles told him about his idea of holding me to ransom and that he believed he could coerce me into going along with their plans, or, rather," he corrected himself, "he could render it impossible for me to do anything other than turn a blind eye."

"Well?" Adam urged.

"Unlike Charles," Marcus told him, "Knowles would have no way of knowing that, having given my promise, I would keep it. *Remember*," he emphasised, "Knowles is a great believer in self-preservation, and saving his own skin means more to him than saving anyone else's. No more than Charles would he want their enterprise to be made known. My guess is," he nodded, "that our friend Knowles was forced into making unexpected contingency plans on the spur of the moment. I believe that at some point after leaving 'The Black Swan' and immediately prior to visiting me, he must have sought someone out to arrange putting an end to my existence. Whoever it was, it had to be somebody he knew and trusted and one, moreover, who would have no qualms about hiring himself out for such a dirty job. As to how Knowles's confederate came to mistake Charles for me, I don't know," he shrugged. "It could have been any number of reasons; but that he did so, I am convinced."

Adam, having listed to his cousin's theory with intense concentration, rubbed his nose reflectively, eyeing him thoughtfully before saying cautiously, "There's an awful lot of *ifs* there, Marcus, but I have to say," he admitted, "it makes perfect sense."

"There is, of course, every possibility that I am totally wrong," Marcus conceded, "but having given the matter a considerable amount of thought, I fail to see what other answer there could be to account for Charles's death."

"I don't suppose there is any way we can prove any of this, is there?"

Adam asked hopefully.

"Not a chance, I'm afraid," Marcus shook his head. "Besides, even if we had proof we could not use it."

Adam looked his disgust. "It sticks in my throat to know that after all Knowles has done he gets to walk away as free as a bird. The man deserves to be hanged!"

"It would be a fitting tribute, certainly," his cousin acknowledged, "but I am afraid we shall never see him receiving his just rewards." He paused only long enough to put his empty coffee cup down on the table, saying, "Unless I am very much mistaken, Knowles is as much aware of situation as we are. He knows perfectly well, or so I should have thought, that even if we had the evidence to prove him guilty a hundred times over, we can never use it against him. To do so would mean divulging Charles's part in the affair as well."

A none too pleasant look crossed Adam's handsome face, telling his cousin more than any words could that it would give him tremendous satisfaction to take the law into his own hands to ensure Knowles got what he deserved. Marcus was not entirely surprised at this, indeed he would have been astonished if Adam did not wish to seek retribution for his brother's death, but Marcus was not inexperienced in handling young men of Adam's stamp, and was more than capable of damping his very human desire for revenge should the eventuality arise. He was not unsympathetic to Adam's very natural need to make Knowles pay for his crimes, but had Charles not taken it upon himself to embark on such a dangerous mission in the first place, he would not now be lying on a mortuary slab, but as Marcus was by far too generous and kind-hearted to kick someone when they were down, he merely spent the next few minutes listening in compassionate silence as Adam put forward various ideas for Knowles's punishment. Not surprisingly, this delayed emotional outburst did not last long, and by the time he had reached the end of it Marcus not only knew his cousin would feel very much better for it but that there was no possibility of him putting in to execution any of the ideas he had angrily suggested, which, from Adam's rueful expression, he knew himself to be highly impractical.

"I'm sorry, Marcus," he apologised, a little shamefaced. "I don't know what you must be thinking of me, but I…"

"You know what I think of you," Marcus cut in, gripping his shoulder. "You are understandably upset and angry over everything that has happened, but little though either of us relish the thought of Knowles getting away with his crimes, there is absolutely nothing we can do about it other than accept the situation as best we can, distasteful and repugnant though it is."

Adam knew this was true, but since there was nothing they could do to bring Ted Knowles to justice, then, like Marcus, he had to content himself as best he could with knowing that at least Charles had escaped public condemnation. Even so, he could not help owning to Marcus that he was astounded to know that his father, as astute a man as you would ever find, had used someone as cunning and devious as Ted Knowles because he felt sure that had he known the kind of man he was he would never have been allowed to cross the threshold.

Marcus, who had been thinking along similar lines himself, was at a loss to understand how Matthew could have allowed himself to be so easily taken in by a man he personally would not trust an inch. There had been much in his uncle he could not like, not the least being his overbearing behaviour towards his wife and Elizabeth as well as his predilection for liking things his own way, bringing about that travesty of a marriage between Charles and Sophy, but in business Marcus had never known his uncle put a foot wrong, in fact, he was a hard-headed businessman and one who knew precisely what he was doing. For a man to take his father's backstreet brewery and turn it into what was nothing short of an empire required not only an indomitable will but a drive and a determination which could not help but command his respect, which made Matthew's decision to use someone like Ted Knowles even more inexplicable. Were it not for the devastating events of recent weeks, Marcus would have said that Matthew could be forgiven for making what was nothing short of an uncharacteristic error of judgement because he doubted even his uncle would be so Machiavellian as to use the services of a man like Knowles with the deliberate intention of causing so much havoc.

*

Silas Jenkins was a patient man, but as the days slipped by his tolerance was fast receding as he frustratingly contemplated the question of how to induce his late client's granddaughter into hastening her decision. It was all very well for Mrs. Charles Harrington to say Alexandra must not be hurried but apart from the fact that Charlotte was pressing him for a speedy conclusion regarding her granddaughter, the finalising of Matthew's affairs was already long overdue.

Having been out of town over the last few days on business, it was only this morning that Silas Jenkins learned of Charles Harrington's death the day before, his clerk thrusting the newspaper into his hands almost as soon as he had walked through the door. To say the news was a devastating shock was a gross understatement, but even before he was fully able to take in all he had read, Marcus and Adam were announced. Jenkins was naturally relieved to see them and knew instantly what had brought them here, but although he was glad to see that George had not accompanied them, a man who, without any effort whatsoever, possessed the unhappy knack of turning a tragedy into a drama, he felt impelled to ask if he would be joining them later. Upon being informed by Adam that due to Charles's sudden and unfortunate death it had been necessary for George to visit the brewery at Islington to attend to affairs there, which, considering what he and Marcus had to disclose to him, was just as well, Silas Jenkins merely nodded his head.

He was, of course, relieved to learn of Alexandra's eventual reconciliation to her newly found status and that she was already safely installed in Brook Street with her grandmother. This welcome news was certainly a heavy weight off his shoulders, but although the news of Charles's death was a devastating shock to say the least, this was nothing compared to the horror he felt upon hearing of the events immediately preceding it.

Jenkins had not forgotten Marcus's previous visit and the concerns he had raised, and although he had not mentioned Charles as the likely offender, indeed, he had cast no aspersions on anyone, Jenkins had instinctively known that if something underhand was going forward then the chances were very good it would be Charles who would engineer it. His own feelings towards Charles aside, Jenkins had never believed him capable of such infamy. The removal of some of his sister's jewellery to borrow money on and then have them copied so no one would be any the wiser was a despicable act of deceit in itself, but that he should go so far as to plan the murder of his own niece, under any guise, was too base even to contemplate. Jenkins had known from the moment he had read out Matthew's will that Charles had no intention of making himself agreeable to the girl, but he had never for one instant suspected the awful truth lying just beneath the surface of his resentment and animosity; or that it would lead him into planning her death. That Charles had considered himself to be in a desperate situation could not be argued, but it certainly did not lead Jenkins into using this as an excuse for justifying such unspeakable behaviour, much less condoning it. He supposed the only saving grace to come out of the whole affair was that the girl was safe, but it in no way made it any more acceptable to him, indeed, he was deeply and profoundly shocked at what had been disclosed.

When he had cautioned Matthew about revising his will to include his granddaughter he had done so with the best of intentions, knowing from experience how something of this nature could so easily lead to discontent if suddenly thrust upon an unsuspecting family, but even though Jenkins had had no idea at the time what far-reaching consequences the new will would have, upon reflection he was honest enough to admit that, in that revised document, had lain the seeds for what followed. Nothing could possibly justify Charles's actions, but the fact remained he was now lying dead on a mortuary slab with no hope of the culprits being apprehended and brought to justice. Like his two visitors, Jenkins was firmly convinced that Ted Knowles was unquestionably implicated in it, but even though he shared their distaste at the thought of a scoundrel like him getting away with kidnapping, inciting the murder of his client's cousin, the fact that it had backfired with horrendous results being quite beside the point, and arranging the death of a girl whose only crime was to be a beneficiary in her grandfather's will, he failed to see how he could be brought to account for his crimes without bringing the name of Harrington into shame and disrepute. He was neither a vindictive nor a vengeful man, but he had to admit that it would give him tremendous satisfaction to see Ted Knowles hang from the nearest gallows; besides which, it was no more than he deserved.

However, Jenkins had to acknowledge that Marcus and Adam were right in that this fitting end to Ted Knowles's nefarious career could never be realised without divulging Charles's part in the business, and since it was their wish as well as his own to save Mrs. Matthew Harrington any pain or embarrassment he was reluctantly forced to accept that no other course was open to them. He fully concurred in their desire to keep the matter between themselves and that under no circumstances must George get wind of it as, unfortunately, he could not be trusted to keep such explosive and damaging news to himself. Charlotte, of course, must never know the truth about her son's recent activities or that his involvement in such a devious scheme had more than probably brought about his brutal death. Mrs. Charles Harrington would naturally not want her husband's crimes to be broadcast, and Jenkins accepted without question her continued silence on such a painful and distressing issue. As far as the police was concerned, he could only hope that they would continue to think along the same lines as they had thus far. He may not precisely relish the thought of withholding vital evidence from them regarding such a serious matter as murder, but on this particular occasion he had to admit that unless they wanted Charles to be branded as a thief and a would-be murderer, he had no choice other than to deny any knowledge of his dealings. He could not pretend to be anything other than shocked and appalled by all he had learned and the deceitful path he was being forced to tread to protect the Harrington family, but he was realistic enough to know that no good could possibly come from telling the truth.

"I realise how distasteful all of this is to you," Marcus acknowledged, genuinely grieved at the deceit they were all having to employ, "but I fail to see what else we can do."

When Silas Jenkins made no reply to this, Adam, feeling something more was required, said sincerely, "I assure you, I am very conscious of what is being asked of you in order to protect my mother and family, but as my cousin has just pointed out, there is nothing else we can do but keep this tragedy amongst ourselves."

Silas Jenkins pulled down the corners of his mouth, his eyes sombre and his face echoing his revulsion. "I can only say," he said at length, indicating the newspaper on his desk with a wave of his hand, "that the only redeeming feature is that the newspapers have not got wind of the truth. Should they ever do so," he nodded significantly, "there will be nothing any of us can do to protect your family. However," he sighed, "I am, as you say, finding this whole affair most distasteful, indeed, I find it impossible to comprehend, but I hope I am realistic enough to accept the facts for what they really are." Looking straight at Adam, he said, "Disclosing your brother's activities may be the right as well as the moral thing to do, but, like you, I believe no good could come from revealing the truth to the police." Adam hardly knew what to say to this generosity, and merely nodded his head in heartfelt thanks. Silas Jenkins nodded, then, looking straight at Marcus, asked, "What reliance do you place upon Knowles keeping his mouth shut? My experience of him has not instilled me with any great hope of his silence."

Adam looked at his cousin, who instantly replied, "Knowles would have to be a fool if he doesn't know, as we do, that he cannot go to the police with information about Charles without revealing his own part in the business, any more than we can divulge information about him without exposing Charles." A slight smile twisted his lips as he informed his listeners, "It is, I believe, what an American acquaintance of mine in India would call a Mexican stand-off."

As neither his cousin nor Silas Jenkins had ever heard such an expression and one could not enlighten the other as to its meaning, Silas Jenkins coughed. "Yes, well, whatever it is called, I don't trust Knowles. Perhaps he won't go to the police for the reasons you stated," he acknowledged, "even so, I have a most unpleasant feeling that we have not heard the last of him."

"By that I take you to mean he will attempt blackmail?" Marcus cocked his head, unperturbed.

"That's *precisely* what I mean," Jenkins nodded vigorously, "especially if, as you seem to think, he has not yet received any payment."

"And what, exactly, leads you to this conclusion?" Marcus asked calmly.

"Because I saw enough of him to know that a man of his persuasions would not scruple to do anything," Jenkins told him candidly, "no matter how devious, which, you will agree, has already been more than adequately demonstrated!"

"I have every expectation of him making the attempt," Marcus replied placidly, taking Jenkins a little aback. "In fact," he pointed out, "I thought I should have received his demands by now."

"You thought…!" Jenkins began, words momentarily failing him. "I don't understand," he shook his head. "How could you possibly have expected such a thing?"

"Because like you, I know Knowles; perhaps more so," Marcus commented meaningfully, "but I also know that any attempt he makes will meet with disappointment."

"You seem very sure of that," Silas Jenkins said, his eyes narrowing.

"I am," Marcus nodded.

"But you can't possibly know what he will demand in advance!" Jenkins cried bewildered.

"On the contrary," Marcus told him, "I know precisely what he will demand."

Jenkins's eyes narrowed. "Money?"

"Money, certainly," Marcus acknowledged, "but what he really wants is that letter."

Jenkins's eyes narrowed even more as he gave this some thought. "But that letter on its own, surely," he shook his head, "is not enough to condemn him!"

"No," Marcus agreed, "it's not, but it certainly implicates him; something which Knowles will be very much aware of, especially as it is in his handwriting. Should that letter ever be produced to the police it will certainly give rise to questions being asked, questions which Knowles cannot possibly answer without the truth coming out. He knows, as we do," he nodded, "the significance of it and what it would mean to him should I ever decide to use it against him."

"You really think it will serve?" Jenkins asked at length. "Do not forget," he reminded him, "any counsel worth his salt could easily discredit it on the reasonable grounds that it could have no bearing on the case whatsoever, in fact," he nodded, "they could argue that it could just as easily relate to any number of matters."

"Very true," Marcus conceded, crossing one long leg casually over the other as though this aspect of the case was totally irrelevant, "but Knowles will not know that. He could neither employ legal counsel for the reasons we have already mentioned any more than he could explain it away if subpoenaed to attend court." Adam was equally as impressed with this line of reasoning as Silas Jenkins, but before either of them could respond Marcus continued, "That letter proves Knowles had a reason to write to Mrs. Charles Harrington, and the only reason he could possibly have, bearing in mind that he is quite unknown to her as well as the family, is that he was part of Charles's schemes in the furtherance of his ends to kill the girl." He paused momentarily, his attractive smile dawning as he saw the look of scepticism on Silas Jenkins's face. "Yes, I know," he acknowledged, "it is a pretty thin argument to put before a court of law, but Knowles, knowledgeable though he is, will be in no frame of mind to examine the requisites demanded by the legal system. If I am any judge," he pointed out, "Knowles will be far too relieved to get away with a whole skin to think about the legal aspects and just what a flimsy hand we really hold."

"I can't fault your reasoning, in fact," Jenkins admitted, "all you say is quite true, but have you considered the possibility that Knowles, given the kind of man he is," he nodded significantly, "could quite well call your bluff?"

"Whilst I agree that is a possibility," Marcus conceded, "I cannot see Knowles doing anything so rash. Remember, he's avaricious, not a fool. He is also a big believer in self-preservation, and I would hazard a very good guess that he has no intention of going anywhere near Bow Street either now or in the future. He knows, as we do," he nodded, "that should he do so, although what conceivable reason he could have escapes me, by revealing the truth about Charles's activities he will merely be opening himself up to questions he cannot possibly answer without incriminating himself and the part he played in recent events."

"Yes," Jenkins nodded, "I tend to agree with you." He paused momentarily as a thought just occurred to him, his lips pursing. "Of course," he frowned, "he could well present his demands to Mrs. Charles Harrington in the hope of forcing your hand through her. Have you considered that possibility, I wonder?" he asked, raising a questioning eyebrow.

"He won't." Marcus shook his head. "That does not mean to say the thought will not have occurred to him," he acknowledged, "especially as he witnessed Charles's attempts to coerce me into turning a blind eye to their plans by holding me to ransom with her life, but I think we can safely take it that as I am the one holding that letter I shall be the one he approaches."

"Yes," Jenkins nodded, having given it some thought, "you are very probably right. Even so," he sighed, "it is a most unpleasant business!"

Adam, devoutly trusting that Jenkins and his cousin were wrong in their convictions that Knowles would attempt blackmail, could only hope that they had seen the last of this man, a man he had no hesitation in deeming to be a most devious and underhand individual.

Marcus, however, had no such hopes, in fact, he was a little surprised that Knowles had not paid him a visit before now, but sooner or later he would show himself and, when he did, Marcus was more than ready for him, in fact, he looked forward to the eventual meeting.

Chapter Twenty-Three

The coroner, having read out the results of the post-mortem asserting that Charles Harrington's death had resulted from a vicious and brutal beating, presided over the inquest in a quiet and dignified manner, during which the identification of the body was formally noted together with the date and approximate time of death, concluding at the end of the hearing, having consulted with the men who made up the coroner's panel, by announcing that the death of the deceased as being 'murder by person or persons unknown'.

It had been a painful ordeal for all concerned, the coroner's questions being intrusive and to the point, so much so that George, upon being asked by that estimable official if he could shed any light on why his brother had been in the vicinity of Waterloo at such an hour, replied irritably that instead of putting ridiculous questions which none of them could possibly answer he would, in his opinion, be better employed in finding the culprits instead of wasting precious time and upsetting every member of his family into the bargain. Not unnaturally, this reply was met with a nicely worded rebuke, instantly followed up with the reminder that he was not conducting this inquest for his own amusement but to try to discover certain facts which would help reveal the truth surrounding such a tragic affair and, hopefully, help bring the perpetrators to justice. George begged pardon, but he was by no means reconciled to the morning's proceedings, and by the time they returned home so belligerent was his mood that Adam, still not fully recovered from the shock of seeing the battered and disfigured corpse that had been his brother, found George's repetitive questions and observations too much to bear. It was therefore with a sharpness no one had ever yet heard from him that he told his brother the coroner had only been doing his job and, furthermore, he would be doing them all a very great favour by refraining from commenting upon something which none of them could shed any light on, and which he was not the only sufferer. As expected, George took instant umbrage to this, but since it was apparent that this was not only Adam's view he relapsed into sullen silence.

However, a few days later when Charles's body was finally released for burial and the funeral arrangements could proceed, nothing it seemed could prevent George from taking sole charge and planning his brother's obsequies. Charlotte, whose only solace was her granddaughter, was more than willing to allow him to do whatever he thought best and, since she considered arguing with him to be not only debasing the solemnity of the proceedings but not worth the effort, George threw himself into the arrangements with gusto. In fairness to him, however, he did spare a thought for Sophy's feelings; after all, he supposed, in his more reasonable moments, that she had more right to make the arrangements than anyone, enquiring of her if she had any views or special wishes regarding the details of her husband's funeral. She had, but when she put forward her ideas he argued against them on several grounds until she too was more than happy to allow him to have his way.

The inclusion of Alexandra into the household was certainly timely where her safety was concerned, but her presence was by no means looked upon as a happy event by her relatives. Sophy did all she could to ensure her stay in Brook Street was as smooth and as untroubled as possible, but she could not pretend that Alexandra's arrival was anything other than an embarrassment to her in-laws, who seemed to be labouring under the belief that they were the laughing stock of London. However much Sophy condemned this, she had to admit that it was perhaps as well that, for the most part at least, Alexandra remained either in her own room or in her grandmother's sitting room, seldom joining the rest of her family.

Sophy knew Marcus was right when he said that his aunt would be well advised to take Alexandra away for a while after the funeral because although she appeared to be coping well with the snubs she received whenever she ran across one or the other of them in the hall or on the stairs, Sophy could not deny that it was far from comfortable for her and could see no happy ending to her stay in Brook Street. It had crossed her mind that Charlotte's sister, living a solitary but seemingly contented life in her spacious five-bedroomed house in Hertfordshire since the death of her husband seven years ago, would most probably be more than happy to accommodate them for as long as it suited them. Having maintained a regular correspondence over the years as well as exchanging gifts on birthdays and at Christmas and, on the odd occasion, paying one another short visits, Sophy believed that this could well be the answer to their difficulties.

During the brief space of time Alexandra had been with them, their friendship had progressed and strengthened and, as the days passed, it seemed to be well and truly cemented, and Sophy, informing her that a shopping expedition was called for, looked forward to the promised treat as much as she did. Understandably, this could not take place until after Charles's funeral, but since Alexandra had nothing but the clothes she had arrived in, Sophy, somewhat hesitantly despite their flourishing friendship, made the offer that, if Alexandra liked, she was perfectly happy to donate one or two things she no longer wore, if she could undertake one or two vital alterations. Fortunately, the suggestion met with her niece's approval, and after only two or three days Alexandra found herself with a newly acquired, if borrowed, wardrobe.

Unlike her sister-in-law, Amelia was by no means eager to associate with her niece, a relationship she adamantly refused to acknowledge, making it patently obvious that, having made her feelings quite clear on the subject already, she had no intention whatsoever of making Alexandra welcome, much less wanted. Sophy, saddened and disheartened at this, had finally been brought to accept, after making several attempts to try to reconcile Alexandra and Amelia, that there was nothing she could do to change her sister-in-law's rigid stance, it was therefore with a heavy heart that she gave up any hope she may have had of any kind of communication taking place between them and, like Adam, was beginning to foresee the future as anything but a happy one.

Amelia, still trying to come to terms with Charles's death, was certainly in no frame of mind to recognise a girl whose very presence in the house filled her with disgust, but since Alexandra seemed perfectly content to live virtually separately to the rest of them, their paths seldom crossed. As it was useless to bring Charlotte to her senses where the girl was concerned, Amelia decided that she for one was certainly not going to waste either her time or breath by attempting any further protest, and if George continued to persist with a topic on which his mother had grown quite immune, then so be it. For herself, there were far more important things to occupy her mind; not the least being Charles's funeral tomorrow.

The mere thought of witnessing his coffin being lowered into the ground, finally and irrevocably reminding her that she would never see him again, was so painful that she had at one point seriously considered not attending. As this plan could not realistically be adopted without occasioning comment, she knew it would be necessary for her to draw upon all her strength and emotional reserves to help see her through what she could only envisage as being a most distressing day, and she hoped that George would be far too taken up with his own feelings to notice what effect the proceedings may be having on herself. So far, she had managed to hide her tormenting pain behind an aloof façade which fooled everyone except her sister-in-law, whose generous nature had several times prompted her to make an approach of some kind to Amelia, but on each occasion Sophy had changed her mind at the last minute, familiarity with Amelia telling her that it would not be well received. It was therefore with considerable surprise that Sophy discovered Amelia had decided to seek her out.

Having put the finishes touches to a bowl of yellow roses in Charlotte's sitting room, the heavily perfumed blooms having been brought round by Henry on behalf of Jane only half an hour earlier in the hope that they would help to raise her mother's spirits, Sophy had just stepped back to view her efforts when the sound of the door quietly opening made her turn round. Fully expecting to see Alexandra or Charlotte, Sophy was a little taken aback to see Amelia standing on the threshold, her eyes widening in surprise, her sister-in-law seldom coming to the sitting room since Alexandra had arrived in Brook Street. Despite Amelia's immaculate appearance, nothing could hide the strain on her face or the emptiness in her beautiful blue eyes, and Sophy, her ready compassion roused, had never felt so sorry for anyone in her life. Amelia's pain was acute, the loss of the man she loved leaving her distraught and desolate but knowing quite well that nothing she could say or do would ease her suffering, Sophy strove for words suitable enough without sounding stupidly mundane.

"I have always admired your way with flowers," Amelia told her in a brittle voice, closing the door behind her before walking further into the room. "You really must let know your secret one day."

"Such beautiful flowers display themselves," Sophy smiled.

"You must not be quite so modest," Amelia chided gently. "You have many talents. Indeed, I have often thought so."

Not knowing quite how to respond to this, Sophy said, "I thought you were still laid down upon your bed."

"I was," Amelia nodded, accepting that her arrow had missed its mark, "but I found I could not sleep."

"I'm sorry," Sophy said, genuinely concerned over sister-in-law. "Is there anything I can get you?"

"No," Amelia shook her head, "thank you." Taking several awkward steps around the room, restlessly picking up and putting down various pieces of china or whatever lay near to hand, it was obvious to Sophy that her sister-in-law was no longer the poised and self-assured woman she was accustomed to seeing. She also had the distinct impression that Amelia wanted to say something to her, but either because she did not know how to or was reconsidering the wisdom of doing so, Sophy could only wait as she watched in some concern while Amelia moved rather ungainly around the room, seemingly in no hurry to say what she had come for.

After what seemed to Sophy several tense minutes, Amelia turned to face her, saying uncertainly, "As a matter of fact I came down here to speak to you. I am glad to have found you alone."

"Alexandra is upstairs with her grandmother," Sophy informed her, realising that Amelia must have known this before coming downstairs; she would not have come to the sitting room otherwise.

"She appears to have quite taken over this room," Amelia commented disparagingly, her glance skimming over a miscellany of items belonging to Alexandra which she had left behind.

"I believe she feels more comfortable here," Sophy explained, not that it needed explaining. Amelia was as aware as she was that Alexandra was all too conscious of the hostility towards her, and since Amelia hardly ever entered this room since her niece had been using it, it seemed to be her only haven from the barely concealed animosity aimed at her.

"I daresay!" Amelia dismissed. "But she would be doing us all a very great favour if she brought her visit here to a close, if for no other reason than we should all of us be far more comfortable. Well, except perhaps for you and Charlotte."

Sophy sighed. It was pointless trying to take up the reins in the girl's defence; nothing she could say or do would alter their feelings, even so, she could not help saying, "Surely, she cannot be blamed for what her mother did."

"Her mother," Amelia pointed out coldly, "in case you had forgotten, brought disgrace on her family by running off with a servant, and a stablehand at that! I can only agree with Emily," she added unkindly, "in that Matthew must have been suffering from acute senility to even think of making provision for her!"

"Can't you try to accept her, Amelia?" Sophy urged, her hazel eyes reflecting her sadness. "If Matthew could find it in him at the last moment to acknowledge her, could not you?"

"Unlike you, Sophy," Amelia informed her matter-of-factly, "mine is neither a generous nor a conciliating nature." She looked Sophy over. "You're a fool, Sophy! Oh, I mean that in the nicest possible way," she assured her, "but surely you can see that the girl is merely taking advantage of your kind heartedness."

"You have it quite wrong, Amelia," Sophy said gently. "She is doing no such thing."

Amelia shrugged. "Very well, have it your own way, but I warn you," she pointed out, "you will soon find yourself regretting the day you and Charlotte ever welcomed her here. However," she shrugged again, "I did not come here to talk about the girl."

"No," Sophy shook her head, "I had a feeling you did not."

"No," Amelia repeated quietly, eyeing her sister-in-law closely. "As it happens," she told her, "there is something I need to say to you, Sophy."

"Why don't we sit down and make ourselves comfortable?" Sophy suggested, instinctively knowing what was on Amelia's mind.

"No," Amelia shook her head, "I would much rather stand, besides, what I have to say will not take long," averting her gaze as her long slim fingers caressed a yellow petal which had dropped from its bloom.

Sophy had long since realised that this conversation would take place sooner or later, and since Amelia seemed determined, or so it seemed, that it should be now, she decided to make it a little less awkward for her, surprising her sister-in-law by saying calmly, "I think I know what it is you wish to say to me."

"You do?" Amelia replied warily, eyeing her sister-in-law guardedly, beginning to wonder whether a confession was such a good thing after all.

"Yes," Sophy nodded. "It's about you and Charles, isn't it?" she said steadily.

Amelia considered her sister-in-law thoughtfully for a moment or two before saying slowly, "So, you *do* know."

"Yes, I know," Sophy confirmed, her tone neither condemnatory nor resentful. "I have known almost from the moment it began."

Amelia nodded her acceptance of this. "I have often wondered whether you did," she said slowly. "Yet, you never said anything. Why?"

"What was there to say?" Sophy replied resignedly.

"Plenty, I should have thought," Amelia offered, unable to understand how Sophy could have accepted their affair in silence all this time.

"Had I loved Charles, perhaps I would have," Sophy confessed, "but even then," she sighed, "I doubt he would have taken notice of it."

Amelia looked at her sister-in-law as though she were seeing her for the first time. "It seems I have misjudged you," she said meditatively. "And I thought we had been so very discreet."

"You were," Sophy nodded, "but I am sure you will agree that for some inexplicable reason a wife can usually see through discretion."

"So it would seem," Amelia mused, the rose petal crushed between her slim fingers. "How you must despise me," she stated matter-of-factly, neither flinching from this prospect nor hurt by it.

"No, I don't despise you," Sophy assured her, never having felt so sorry for anyone before as she did now for Amelia. "There is no reason why I should."

"No reason!" Amelia exclaimed incredibly, taking a hasty step towards her. "I was having an affair with your husband! Surely that is reason enough?"

Yes, it was. But Sophy knew all too well how it felt to be in love; how every second you were away from the man you loved was a torturous pain. She could not condemn Amelia for succumbing to temptation; after all, how secure would her own defences be if she lived in such proximity to Marcus every day? It would be so easy for her to judge and pronounce sentence upon her sister-in-law, but Amelia would be punished enough in the days and years to come, knowing that never again would she experience the joy of being held in the arms of the man she loved. Sophy's tender heart could not harden against her and add to her sentence, and even though their affair had not been what she had expected to result from her marriage to Charles, she was far too conscious of her own secret longing and the overwhelming need to be with Marcus to judge her. Lovers were not blessed with caution, having to steal their intimate moments when they could; hadn't she been guilty of that? Under different circumstances Amelia would be right in thinking she had cause to despise her, but although Sophy had given Charles loyalty as well as the respect due to him as her husband, she had not loved him; or he her. It had more than once occurred to her that Amelia and Charles had been meant for one another; indeed, they certainly shared more than she and Charles had done and certainly more than Amelia obviously did with her own husband for that matter. "How can I possibly despise you when your only crime was to fall in love?" she asked simply.

Looking up into her sister-in-law's face without a trace of her usual indifference, Amelia acknowledged, "Well, I suppose if I am honest I really don't deserve that, but nevertheless I thank you for it." She paused, a slight smile twisting her full and generous mouth. "You may not believe this, Sophy," she told her truthfully, "but I have often wished that you and I could have been friends; but Charles always came between us."

"I should have liked that," Sophy told her genuinely. "I still would."

Amelia grimaced. "The truth is, I was jealous of you being married to the man I loved, knowing that you did not love him or he you." She heaved a sigh, shrugging her shoulders. "Unlike you, Sophy, I am far too selfish and self-centred to think of others, especially when I want something. You see, I am not as generous or as understanding as you are. I wanted Charles more than I ever wanted anything or anyone in my life before, and I was too much in love with him to even give your feelings a moment's thought."

"I daresay," Sophy managed, "that there are times when all those who love feel the same degree of selfishness."

"All except you, it would seem," Amelia remarked, not unkindly.

Sophy's eyes flew to her sister-in-law's face, the colour flooding her cheeks. "What do you mean?" she asked in a stifled voice.

"Oh, come, Sophy!" Amelia smiled. "Do you really believe that I am unaware of what you and Marcus feel for one another?" Sophy felt her colour deepen and Amelia laughed, a gentle and not altogether unsympathetic sound, totally alien to what Sophy knew of her. "I can see you are wondering how I know," she remarked as Sophy shook her head in futile denial. "Unlike Charles, who, surprisingly enough," she nodded, "had failed to see what was directly under his nose, I have seen how you blush a little whenever Marcus is around even though you try very hard not to, then, of course, there is a way you have of lowering your eyes or averting your glance as though he means nothing to you when, in fact, the very opposite is true. I have seen too those looks which pass between you on the occasions your eyes have met, and however silent and unnoticeable to those around you they are so very eloquent. You see, I too am most astute," she nodded. "But, unlike me," she added truthfully, "despite your feelings for Charles, you took your marriage vows very seriously and have honoured them admirably," she applauded. "I also know that, again unlike me, you were not tempted into betraying your husband. In fact," she pointed out, "you would shrink from embarking on an affair; whereas I knew no qualms whatsoever in doing so."

Sophy's eyes flew to those blue ones, half expecting to see a hint of malicious satisfaction, but there was none. Her breathing seemed suddenly a little laboured as she strove to refute what Amelia was saying. "I really..."

"There is no need to be embarrassed on my account, I promise you," Amelia told her truthfully. "You see," she grimaced, "being no stranger to the emotion, I am afraid I recognised the signs straightaway."

"Really, I..." Sophy began, feeling suffocated.

"Do not be alarmed," Amelia shook her head. "I am neither shocked nor disapproving, but if it is of any consolation at all I also know that however much you want to be together you have never discussed an affair, let alone embarked on one. How do I know this?" She raised an eyebrow. "Because I know *you*, Sophy and, as for Marcus," she shrugged, "he is by *far* too much the gentleman to put such a suggestion to you. Oh, I confess he is very discreet," she acknowledged appreciatively, "in fact, so careful is he not to do anything which could possibly alert one to his feelings that one could be forgiven for thinking he feels nothing whatsoever for you, but no matter how keen he is to protect you not even Marcus can always hide his feelings. I have seen the way he looks at you when his guard is momentarily down, and I am afraid," she smiled, "it is all too evident."

Sophy's cheeks were flooded with colour, in fact, she felt suffocated at the thought of her sister-in-law knowing so much. Having kept her secret locked in her heart for such a long time, it was a dreadful shock to discover that it was known to the woman with whom her husband had had such a long and, apparently, happy liaison.

Amelia had a very shrewd idea of what was going through Sophy's mind, and said, with rare sincerity, "You need not be afraid that I shall speak of this to anyone, I shan't. However," she shrugged, "since I am baring my all, for perhaps the first and last time, you may as well know that I had every intention, at some point convenient to myself, of telling Charles about you and Marcus." She paused, looking at her sister-in-law with a touch of defiance. "*Now* tell me that you don't despise me and still wish us to be friends. If you can," she nodded, "then you are indeed more of a friend than I deserve. You see, Sophy," she pointed out, without any malice whatsoever, "no matter how unpalatable the thought, you and I share one thing in common; we both harbour a secret and, as it happens, the same secret. You were not in love with your husband any more than I am with mine. We both yearn for another man. You, however, can still fulfil your desires, I cannot."

"Oh, I don't know what to say!" Sophy cried, covering her face with her trembling hands.

"Well, as you said yourself a moment or two ago; what is there to say? Oh, the case is not so rare, I assure you," Amelia told her realistically. "*Your* case is not so desperate that it cannot be remedied," she told her. "*I* on the other hand," she commented, "have no such hopes. I shall, of course," she shrugged, "continue with the farce of being George's wife; although the prospect is not one I am looking forward to with any marked degree of pleasure. To spend the rest of my life with a man I find extremely boring and tedious, listening to his endless inanities, is really more than I can bear, but I tell myself that it could be worse," she sighed. "The truth is," she confessed, "my only consolation is my beloved sons. Indeed, without them I doubt I could get through the remainder of my days."

Sophy swallowed the uncomfortable lump in her throat, saying unsteadily, "It is true that I love Marcus; I always have, but that I should want my future happiness at the expense of Charles's death and your sorrow is very far from the truth."

"I know it is," Amelia nodded, for once in her life thinking of someone other than herself. "But there are times when we have to accept what fate has given us. You have been given the opportunity to begin your life anew, and you would be a fool if you did not take it." She paused, looking down at the band of gold on her finger, saying quite dispassionately, "One would think that I would love and revere the man who placed this ring on my finger, but the truth is I do not and never shall. I have nothing but contempt for my husband. That shocks you, doesn't it?" she commented. "I'm sorry," she grimaced, "you must forgive me, but I see no reason why there should be any pretence between us."

"But George loves you," Sophy managed, her mind unable to take in all that had passed between them.

"Yes, I believe he does," Amelia conceded at length, having given it some thought. "What a pity I cannot return it. I wonder though," she mused, "whether he would still do so if he knew that tomorrow I shall be saying goodbye to the only man I have ever loved and would willingly have put in his place?"

"I realise, of course," Sophy said faintly, "that tomorrow is going to be a dreadful ordeal for you. I just want you to know that I shall understand if…"

"That is very kind of you, generous too," Amelia broke in hurriedly, not at all convinced she felt better for her confession, "but I hope I shall have sufficient command over my emotions not to allow them to overspill. That would be dreadfully vulgar, don't you think?"

Sophy could think of nothing to say in response to this, but felt compelled to ask, "Why have you told me all of this, Amelia?"

"Why?" Amelia shrugged. "I really don't know; although they do say that confession is good for the soul!" she grimaced. "No," she shook her head, "that's not the reason. I suppose the truth is that I like you too much to go on deceiving you. Believe it or not," she told her, "I have a great regard for you. Indeed," she added, as near to friendliness as was possible, "I wish I could be more like you, but I know I never shall. You see, Sophy," she acknowledged honestly, "I have none of the virtues and qualities which you possess. I wish I had, but if I strove to acquire them from now until the day I die I should never succeed." She paused, eying her sister-in-law unflinchingly. "To be honest with you, I envy you more than you will ever know." A twisted smile touched her lips. "Now *there's* a confession, if you like!" Sophy looked her embarrassment and Amelia went on, not unkindly, "There is no need to be embarrassed, I have merely spoken the truth."

Deeming the interview to be at an end, she crossed over to the door, then, as if a thought had suddenly occurred to her, she turned, saying, "For what it is worth, you deserve Marcus, and whilst I have to say that, with the obvious exception of Charles, he is the most devastatingly attractive man of my acquaintance, he is by *far* too much the gentleman to suit my tastes."

"You are very kind," was all Sophy could think of to say, her mind in a daze.

"Not at all," Amelia shrugged, "but I am going to give you some advice, Sophy; whether you take it or not is entirely your own affair. Perhaps you think I am the wrong one to be offering advice; well, you may be right, but marry Marcus just as soon as you can. Do not live the rest of your life in regret. Take your happiness while you can; it is taken away from us all too soon," on which parting note she left the sitting room as quietly as she had entered it.

It was a long time before Sophy left the seclusion of Charlotte's sitting room. She was naturally pleased that at long last she and Amelia had reached a relatively amicable agreement, yet shocked and quite appalled that she had discovered her secret. Sophy believed her when she said she would tell no one, but that she was aware of her feelings for Marcus was more than she could bear. She was still struggling to accept the fact that Charles too had discovered the truth and had blackmailed Marcus because of it. It left her wondering who else knew, and the colour flooded her cheeks at the thought that her deepest longings were common knowledge. It seemed that one could not keep a secret no matter hard one tried, but she supposed she should have expected Amelia to see the truth, after all she missed very little.

Charles had never pretended to love her. Indeed, he had more than once made it perfectly clear that he resented having to marry her because of financial or any other reason urged upon him by his father. It was therefore some comfort to know that Charles's feelings would not have been hurt by the discovery that his wife was in love with another man, it would have been the knowledge that the other man was his own cousin which would have done the damage. His pride would undoubtedly have taken a severe denting from this, but his heart would have remained quite untouched. The fact that he had been prepared to use her feelings for such a despicable act proved that he was not interested in anything but his own needs, and Sophy could only thank God that she had not loved him; to have done so would have been to open herself up to an unbearable heartache. She was pleased that a new understanding had developed between herself and Amelia, and whilst her confession may have surprised her, it merely went to prove just how well matched she and Charles really were. Had Sophy known that Charles's associate was working out ways and means to achieve his financial ends by attempting to blackmail Marcus, she would have been in no doubt that Charles and Ted Knowles also were extremely well matched.

*

As Marcus had fully expected Adam's hope that Ted Knowles had gone to ground was mere wishful thinking, and he was therefore not at all surprised to receive a visit from him midway through the afternoon on the day before Charles's funeral. Webster, entering the study bearing the expression of one who had just undergone a severe trial, sincerely hoped that his employer would show this coarse and vulgar individual the door without any undue loss of time.

"Where is he now?" Marcus asked, scanning the florid legend on the card Webster had just handed him, a strange light entering his eyes.

"Well, sir," Webster informed him in a tone of exculpation, "not liking the idea of putting him the drawing room or the rear sitting room and not knowing what else to do with him, I have left him standing in the hall."

"Well, I certainly know what I should like to do with him," Marcus said severely. "Unfortunately, however, the laws of this land will not permit it."

"Sir?" Webster said, bewildered.

"It doesn't matter," Marcus shook his head. "Show him in will you please, Webster?"

"Very good, sir," he nodded, unable to account for his employer's comment or what this vulgar individual was doing visiting a gentleman's home.

Ted Knowles would have been more than happy to have told him given half the chance, instead of which he had been left to kick his heels in the hall like someone of no importance. Well, he would show this Marcus Ingleby whether he was of no importance or not before he was through; see if he wouldn't. He had embarked on this venture in good faith, fulfilling his every part of the agreement. Not only had he expended considerable time and effort over this business but had endured physical and verbal abuse into the bargain and, on top of all of this, he had not yet received a penny for his trouble. Ted Knowles easily discounted that five pounds from Silas Jenkins as well as the roll of soft from Charles Harrington on the first evening as nothing more than out-of-pocket expenses and, according to his reckoning, he was due for payment in full.

It was, of course, unfortunate about his client's death but it was not his fault that Dooney had mistaken his man, and, after all said and done, it was only fair that he should come out of this with something. Ted Knowles had seen enough of his late client's cousin to know that he was a well-breeched

450

swell and one who could more than afford a little something for his trouble, besides which, not only had he earned it but Ingleby would not be any too pleased should the truth slip out about his cousin's recent activities. In his estimation, his silence was worth paying for and, in any case, it was no more than he deserved after all the trouble he had been to, not to mention a gross invasion of his home as well as his person, to which his still-tender jaw bone more than adequately testified. Any man who lived in a house like this in one of the best parts of town would not miss a bob or two, in fact, if he played his cards right he could live as high as a coach horse for as long as it suited him.

This pleasant daydream was rudely interrupted by Webster emerging from the study to inform him in a dispassionate voice that Major Ingleby would see him now. Nodding his head, Ted Knowles strode across the hall and through the door Webster was holding open for him, winking at him as he passed, confident of a profitable outcome to his interview.

His host, making no attempt to vacate his chair to greet him, lounged at his ease, seemingly quite unmoved by his arrival. With his long legs stretched out in front of him and his elbows resting comfortably on the arms of his chair with his chin propped up by his entwined fingers, was surely not the attitude one would adopt under the circumstances.

The truth was that Marcus's relaxed pose had the effect of putting Ted Knowles on the defensive, and his confidence, which, up until now, had been steadily mounting, began to subside slightly, and although he was the one with the ammunition guaranteed to put fear into the heart of his victim, for some inexplicable reason he felt totally unarmed. "Aftanoon yer 'oner," he nodded, gripping his bowler.

"Good afternoon, Knowles," Marcus returned smoothly, making no effort to rise to his feet. "I have been expecting you."

"Yer 'as?" he asked warily, surprised at this.

"Most certainly." Marcus inclined his head. "Although," he told him, "I must confess to having looked for you before now."

"Yer neva!" Ted Knowles cried, his eyes narrowing, fearing some trick. This was certainly not the way he had visualised the interview to commence, especially as he had been of the belief that his visit would take Ingleby completely by surprise, but in view of what he had just said, it would appear this was not the case. However, it was still early days and Ted Knowles felt sure that once Ingleby had heard the full sum of what he had come for, he would soon be only too eager to give him whatever he wanted in return for his silence about his cousin. All the same, there was something in that hard and unrelenting gaze which warned him to tread carefully, realising that his carefully rehearsed opening lines would have to undergo some modification.

"But of course," Marcus replied easily. "You may be surprised to learn, Knowles, that not only have I been expecting you but I also know the reason why you are here."

"Yer can't do," he shot out, astonished, taking an involuntary step forward.

"I assure you, I do," Marcus told him, his eyes glinting.

"'Ow?" Knowles demanded, his eyes protruding in disbelief.

With slow deliberation Marcus rose to his feet, walking leisurely round the desk until he was standing immediately in front of his disagreeable visitor, towering above him. "How?" he repeated, raising a supercilious eyebrow. "Because I know you, Knowles, that's how. I know you for the obnoxious and devious individual you are."

"'Ere, that's slanda, that is!" Knowles warned, not taking kindly to his character being called into question.

"Not slander, Knowles," Marcus said smoothly, "the truth. You are a blot on decent society and one, moreover, who deserves the full penalty of the law."

Ted Knowles looked up at him with venomous dislike, wanting nothing more than to send him sprawling to the floor, but his recent pugilistic encounter with him told him that this would be easier said than done, and this time there would be no Davy to offer him assistance. Calling his bluff, he said, "Yer can't thretun me wi' the law; I knows too much."

Marcus eyed him steadily. "And what is it you know, precisely?"

"Ah!" Knowles nodded, rubbing his nose with his forefinger. "That's got yer stumped right inuf!"

"You misjudge the case, Knowles," Marcus told him. "You have nothing whatsoever to take to the police, and should you ever be misguided enough to pay them a visit, I have no doubt at all that they will find you a most interesting individual, so much so," he said pointedly, "that they will doubtless be more than happy to house you for a very long time."

Ted Knowles turned a little pale at this, knowing it to be no less than the truth, but as it was not his intention to visit Bow Street either now or in the future, aiming to give the place an extremely wide berth, he was able to put this unpalatable thought to the back of his mind and turn his attention to the reason he was here. From the look on Ingleby's face, however, convincing him that it would be wiser to accede to his demands was not going to be as easy as he had at first thought. Nothing would give Ted Knowles greater satisfaction than to be able to knock him senseless, but as he had already discounted this pleasurable thought for very practical reasons, he decided instead to adopt more subtle methods of persuasion. Having been blessed with an extremely agile brain and most persuasive tongue, he realised that if he was going to obtain that incriminating letter as well as filling his purse he had no choice but to employ more conciliatory measures.

Unfortunately for him, however, Marcus gave him no time to put this new line of approach into effect, forestalling his opening menaces by saying, "You came here today in the full expectation of holding me and my family to ransom, but in this respect you have grossly erred. You see, Knowles," he informed him with relish, enjoying the moment as a just and fitting reward for his recent incarceration, "not only do you hold a very poor hand with which to bargain but you have overlooked the fact that I am not prepared to pay you a penny, and if, which I believe to be the case, you are also endeavouring to obtain a certain letter at the moment in my possession, not only have you mistaken your man but in your unscrupulous attempts at blackmail you have failed to take in to account that even if I don't hand over what you demand, there is nothing whatsoever you can do about it."

Ted Knowles's eyes narrowed and his colour darkened at this, not liking the way things were going. When he had planned to extort money as well as that letter out of Marcus Ingleby he had fully believed that he would prosper, especially holding such a trump card. Naturally, he had been prepared for delaying tactics of some kind or, failing this, a game of bluff, but he had not expected to be faced with such calm assurance, and this alone made his temper rise. "I'll keep mum," he shot out, "neva!"

Unperturbed by this, Marcus merely shrugged, saying with infuriating indifference, "As you wish," adding smoothly, "but I feel it only fair to warn you, however, that should you decide to say anything to anyone about recent events you will be making a great mistake."

"Fer you, yer mean," Knowles retorted, his fists clenching suggestively. "It wudn't suit you at all, wud it? I cud do you an' yer family a lot of 'arm if I opened me mummer."

"I am confident that our reputation is well enough established to deflect anything you could possibly say," Marcus told him firmly.

"Ah!" Knowles nodded, steadily growing more confident, delivering what he thought to be a trump card of no mean order, guaranteed to break down any final resistance. "But is it strung inuf ter shrug orf attemptid merder?" When Marcus made no reply Knowles believed he had hit the mark at last, pressing this home by saying in a voice nicely mixed with threats and persuasion, "It'ud luck gud in the papers, wudn't it? 'Ow'd yer think 'is ma 'ud feel ter reed that 'er son 'ad planned ter do away wi' 'is own neece? Terribul shock fer 'er, it'ud be. Dow't 'er'd eva recova from it. Wot, wi' the Runners knockin' the door and people knowin' everythin'! It don't ber thinkin' on." He shuddered theatrically.

"I agree," Marcus said affably, strenuously fighting the urge to send him sprawling, "it would be a most distressing and painful ordeal for all of us, but for you especially."

"Me?" Knowles repeated in surprise, at a loss to understand how it would affect him.

"But of course," Marcus nodded, raising an eyebrow. "I should have thought that a man of your intelligence would have realised that." He paused, eyeing his visitor closely. "I must say, however, I am really quite surprised that a man of your infinite resource and, dare I say it?" he smiled not very pleasantly, "– many talents, has failed to take in to account the fact that your position, especially in view of this new but not very imaginative enterprise, is rather delicate to say the least. You really must, in the future, when embarking on such a course as this, be more aware of what ground you hold. The fact that you have not realised what is patently obvious is really quite astonishing."

"Realised wot?" Knowles asked suspiciously, fearing a trap, missing the touch of irony Marcus could not resist. "My name ain't 'Arrington."

"No," Marcus shook his head, devoutly thankful for this, "but you see, Knowles," he informed him, "should you decide to take such a reckless step, the police will, out of necessity, want to know how you come to be in possession of so much information, which, in turn, will automatically lead to the events prior to my cousin's death being disclosed." He smiled, a none too pleasant smile which told Knowles that he was fast losing ground. "I hate to be the one to point this brutal fact out to you," he mockingly apologised, "but I do not think that a man of your questionable character will be able to convince them of the purity of your motives or that you are merely acting as a good citizen by doing whatever you can for the benefit of justice."

"'Ere," Ted Knowles barked, taking several steps towards his immovable host, "wot yer tryin' ter pull?"

"I am not trying to pull anything," Marcus told him evenly. "I am simply pointing out that by threatening me with your intention of going to the police if I do not do what you ask, not only are you wasting your breath but you will be opening yourself up to probing questions; questions, I might add, which you cannot possibly afford to answer, especially when it comes to the murder of my cousin."

"Wot's that ter me?" Knowles growled, swallowing an uncomfortable lump which had suddenly appeared in his throat.

"I was rather hoping you could tell me," Marcus replied quietly.

"*Me?* Wot can I tells yer?" Ted Knowles shrugged. "I dunno nothin' about it."

"Now, why don't I believe you?" Marcus mused, wanting nothing more than to give him his just rewards right here and now instead of having to ignore the impulse. "You must admit that his death, brutally executed, is quite inexplicable, indeed," he shrugged, "one might almost say coincidental coming at such a time, not that I believe in coincidences," he informed him.

Ted Knowles, who was by now beginning to wish he had not decided to come here after all, swallowed nervously and gradually began to take several backwards steps towards the door. He supposed he should have known that Ingleby was not the type of man to be bought or bribed in any way but having already witnessed one such attempt he had been brought to believe, quite wrongly he knew now, that he could be bought again. There was a look of implacability on Ingleby's face which boded no good for him, and he was honest enough to admit that if he had stopped and considered the matter more carefully instead of simply looking as to how much money he could extort out of him, he would have known that his position was not strong enough to bargain on. It was a pity about that letter, mind, but even though he knew precisely what Ingleby thought of him and that he would like nothing better than to personally escort him all the way to Bow Street with that written evidence, he knew there was no fear of him doing so any more than there was of him using it against him, and since the possession of it was not worth the trouble, especially if he did not want to be on the receiving end of those suggestively formidable fists, or, worse, he had no choice but to wait expectantly to see what fate Ingleby had in mind for him.

Since he had resigned himself to saying goodbye to that letter as well as the idea of extracting money from him, Ted Knowles decided that what he needed to do was play for time, not only to enable him to get out of here in one piece but to evade the question about his client's death, but from the looks of it Ingleby was apparently not prepared to let him leave here until he had some answers. Ted Knowles knew that he had no proof on which to accuse him, in fact, when he considered the matter there was absolutely no reason to account for him wanting Charles Harrington put out of the way at all, and this reasoning, although it was all he had on which to base his defence, was in actual fact no less than the truth. Marcus Ingleby was an intelligent and clever man, and, surely, he could see that his cousin's death would not have suited him at all. No one was more sorry than he was about Charles Harrington's tragic end, in fact, he had still not quite recovered from it, but even though it was obvious to the meanest intelligence that Ingleby would like nothing better than to see him receive the full penalty of the law for his cousin's death, the truth was that he had nothing to go on but suspicion, and no man, surely, could accuse another of murder on such insecure grounds. Be that as it may however, he knew he was treading on very thin ice and no matter what he told himself should Ingleby ultimately decide to go to the police after all, he knew he would have a lot of explaining to do because no matter which way he looked at it he had set plans in motion to get rid of Ingleby, the fact that his cousin ended up being got rid of instead did not alter the fact that he had arranged it. Deciding that calling his bluff was really the only way out of this, Knowles told him with as much sincerity as he could muster, "I knows what you'm thinkin', but I dain't lay a finga on yer cusun. No reesun wy I shud."

"I am not a fool, Knowles," Marcus told him coldly. "I know you would not have sullied your own hands with such a dirty crime any more than you were prepared to with the girl, but a man of your unsavoury reputation knows any number of like-minded individuals to do it for you, which," he informed him, "is precisely what you did." He looked down into Knowles's red face with cold inflexibility. "Understand me, Knowles; I know you planned my death and the reason for it, and that whoever you employed to carry it out mistook Charles for me."

"It's a lie!" Knowles cried, not very convincingly, keeping a wary eye on those fists. From the looks of it, Ingleby would like nothing better than to send him crashing to the floor, but even though he had so far held onto his temper there was no saying how long he would be able to keep it check, and he knew he could do nothing but await his fate as best he could.

"We both know it is not," Marcus bit out. "Please, do not insult my intelligence by denying it."

"Yer can't prove it," Knowles shot out, his palms beginning to sweat.

"No, I can't," Marcus acknowledged. "No court of law would ever accept your guilt on supposition alone."

Knowles heaved a deep sigh, but he was not out of the wood yet. "Wot yer gonna do?" he asked cautiously.

"Well now," Marcus mused, looking thoughtfully down at him before asking ominously, "what would you do in the same circumstances?"

"Well, then?" Knowles prompted, not unhopefully.

The mere thought of Ted Knowles walking away from his crimes unpunished was quite repugnant to Marcus, indeed, it went against everything he believed in, and even though he was forced to accept this most unsatisfactory state of affairs he was very far from happy with it. However, there was one thing he could do and it would give him tremendous satisfaction as well as going some way to rewarding him for his efforts. "I will tell you what I am going to do, Knowles," he said softly, considerably startling him when he unexpectedly grabbed hold of the lapels of his coat with his right hand and virtually lifted him off the ground as he pushed him against the wall with no effort whatsoever, his eyes cold and hard. "Understand me, Knowles," he warned dangerously, "if ever I see your face again you will be wishing I had not. If you so much as open your mouth about any of what has occurred recently, I shall have no compunction whatsoever in taking that letter to Bow Street." Knowles shook his head and spluttered something quite unintelligible, but Marcus got the gist of it. "If you think for one moment that I am bluffing and would not dare to do so to protect my cousin, you could not be more mistaken. You are a most devious and unsavoury individual, Knowles, who, compared to me, would not be believed, and after the police heard my side of the story I assure you that Charles will come out of this as white as snow, while you my friend will face the full penalty of the law. Do I make myself clear?" Knowles nodded and Marcus released him, dusting off his hands as though they were contaminated. "I would strongly recommend you, Knowles," he warned, "to make every effort to keep out of my way because should our paths ever cross again I promise you, you will not enjoy the encounter."

"I've got yer," Knowles choked, feeling as though he had been mauled.

"I hope so. In fact," Marcus further warned, "I think you ought to remove yourself from London for a while. As my cousin was once kind enough to remark, one never knows what mishap may befall one."

Knowles, who did not need to have his meaning spelled out, began to back away towards the door, only to find himself stumbling over a chair as he did so, but even before he had time to straighten up, Marcus's left hand took hold of his arm in a vice-like grip, pulling open the study door with the other, purposely propelling Knowles into the hall.

"I'm goin'," Knowles assured him hastily. "There's no need to fret yerself."

"I know you're going," Marcus said firmly, "and I intend to make sure you do," opening the front door on the words and thrusting his unwelcome visitor through it and out of the house.

Marcus may have had his differences with Charles, but his death was the very last thing he had wanted and, like Joe Benbow, he shrewdly guessed that his cousin had been given no time to defend himself. That his brutal murder had been a case of mistaken identity made no difference to the fact that it had been coldly and deliberately calculated, and whilst he could not prove that Ted Knowles had had a hand in it Marcus knew it as surely as if he had made a confession under oath and wholly deserved the full penalty of the law for his cousin's death as well as for orchestrating the murder of Alexandra under the innocent guise of an accident.

Marcus was neither a violent nor an aggressive man, but it had taken great self-restraint on his part to keep from knocking Ted Knowles senseless, but however gratifying this would have been he firmly believed the purpose had been served by threatening him with Bow Street because despite Ted Knowles's bluff bravado upon being manhandled out of the house, Marcus saw enough to tell him that he was sufficiently frightened to ensure they had seen and heard the last of him. He doubted Knowles would be setting up shop again in London under any guise, although a man of his resource and enterprise would find it a relatively easy matter to begin his dirty trade somewhere else.

It appeared that Ted Knowles's desire to suddenly absent himself from such a dangerous locality was infectious. Marcus, informed by Adam later that evening that Farley had quite unexpectedly made a hasty departure, only served to reinforce his suspicions that he had been Knowles's informant. Considering how much knowledge Knowles had acquired about the family, it went beyond all reasoning to suppose that he was acting on gossip and guesswork; someone within the household must have been keeping him well informed. Marcus easily acquitted Charles of divulging anything about his family's affairs; he had been far too proud for that, and since every one of the servants had been with the family a long time, excepting Farley, it certainly seemed that he was the most likely candidate. His precipitate and unexpected flight from Brook Street surely proved that! Apart from Adam, Marcus had told no one about Farley's almost certain part in the affair, small though it was; once questions were raised about one member of staff it could so easily lead to a most unpleasant situation, and therefore both cousins received the news of his flight with the same surprise as everyone else, offering one or two possible reasons to account for it. Harris, who had never liked him, was personally of the belief that Farley, upon discovering his employer's sudden and tragic demise, had taken the opportunity to vacate what must have been a most unenviable post in Charles's service to seek other and far more congenial employment.

This certainly seemed to be the general opinion, and George, declaring that the scoundrel had even had the nerve to demand a reference as well as his wages before leaving, said that he had never liked the fellow by half anyway, always seeming to turn up in a part of the house where he had no business.

Marcus, who had had every intention of taking Charles's valet to task for his confidences to Knowles in exchange for monetary gain, suspected that the arrival of two officers of the law making enquiries about Charles's death had given him a fright. No doubt he had considered it wise to make his escape before his minor role in the tragedy was discovered. After only a very little thought, Marcus realised that it was perhaps better this way; after all, the chances were Farley would have denied any accusation and there was always the possibility that he could have turned the tables on him by approaching George in a desperate attempt to bluff his way out of trouble. Should that have happened, Marcus knew there would have been no way he could have kept the truth from him; if nothing else, George could certainly be relied upon not to keep such damaging news to himself. Adam, having listened to Marcus recounting his meeting with Ted Knowles over a glass of something warm and invigorating in the study, fervently expressed his hope that he was right in that they had finally seen the last of him, but as it seemed that all either of them could now was trust that all possible leaks of recent events had been covered and dealt with, they eventually joined the rest of their family at the dinner table.

Adam, who felt he had been on a roller-coaster of emotions over the last week or so, mentally prepared himself for tomorrow; his brother's funeral, apart from being the last thing he had expected to attend when he left Yorkshire, was something which could not be anything other than a terrible ordeal. Whatever disgust or horror he felt about Charles's despicable actions, it could not be denied that they had evidently brought about his untimely death, but despite his feelings of shock at the extent of Charles's scheming, Adam could not view his brother's demise as anything but a tragic waste of life, and Marcus, accurately reading his thoughts, knew that words of any kind at such a moment would be totally inadequate and that only time would help ease the pain around Adam's heart.

Chapter Twenty-Four

The early spring sunshine flooded the cemetery. Although a sharp wind was blowing and depriving the mourners the benefit of its mild warmth, it was not unduly cold. The leaves on the trees rustled in the breeze, a soft, delicate sound which contrasted sharply to Reverend Handley's penetrating voice, his rheumatic fingers continually being obliged to prevent the pages of his Bible from flicking over. Occasionally, the sound of one of the horses neighing intruded on the ear but ignoring this as well as his innermost feelings, Reverend Handley went doggedly on, determined to do full justice to the solemnity of the occasion. Whatever his thoughts he kept them admirably to himself, delivering his sermon with painstaking diligence, devoutly trusting he would not be struck down by divine intervention for uttering words he felt sure would have held little meaning to the deceased, his only hope being that the good Lord would forgive Charles his sins. Like his late father, Charles Harrington had seldom attended church, only doing so when his presence was unavoidable, but considering himself to be a generous man the persistent cleric afforded him the same respect as he would have to any of his parishioners.

Charlotte was under no illusion where her son's sins were concerned, having for a long time been fully aware of his imperfections, but as she stood beside the prepared ground none of his faults seemed to matter. Beneath her veil her eyes flickered in a vain attempt to stem the flow of tears, but after several minutes of strenuously trying to hold them back they started to fall unheeded down her face, her gloved fingers unsteadily wiping them away with her handkerchief. The loss of yet another son and in the same inexplicable circumstances, left her bemused and quite at a loss to understand how either of their deaths could have happened. Since she could find no answers to her many questions, she could only hope that after such eventful careers they were now both at peace. She was not alone in her recollections.

Emily and Jane, standing side by side, each had their own thoughts and memories of the brother, who, despite his autocratic temperament and insufferable pride, could, on occasion, be quite approachable and not unkind. Jane, nearer in age to Charles than her sister, was neither ignorant nor blind to his faults, and whilst she could not condone them she could forgive them. They had never really been very close, and since her marriage even less so, but she supposed Charles would always remain something of an enigma to her. She knew Henry was convinced that his death was not quite as straightforward as they had been led to believe and knowing something of her brother's character and temperament she was forced to acknowledge that her husband was probably right. It seemed that Charles had been endowed with the unenviable gift of alienating people without any apparent effort, and although she had been one of the very few to escape this far from attractive side to his nature it was not one of his more endearing qualities.

Emily wept bitterly, inconsolable and grief-stricken at the loss of one whom she secretly admired, even adored, and who had been more in tune with her than any of the others. Although there had been times when she had argued fiercely with him, his death had left an enormous gap in her life. She could not accept it any more than she could understand it, and she could only hope that the perpetrators of such a vicious crime would be caught and brought to justice, receiving the full penalty of the law.

Standing beside his wife with a look of complete and utter disbelief on his face, George stared down at his brother's coffin as one in a daze. From childhood, they had been bitter enemies, one always trying to better the other, and whilst he would never forget Charles's unbearable conceit or his scarcely concealed contempt, he could not deny that life would never be quite the same without him. Having tried for years to put Charles in his place once and for all, it was incredible to believe that never again would he see his brother or feel the need to defend himself.

Adam was as torn as a man could be, easily remembering incidents from years past when, as a boy, he had looked up to and idolised his older brother, not only as a fountain of knowledge but as someone he could aspire to and emulate. It was surprising how easily half-forgotten memories came to mind; not the least being of how, as a small boy, he had constantly followed him around, often since marvelling at Charles's forbearance upon being persistently dogged by an adoring younger sibling who had been forever demanding to be told what he was doing or where he was going. As Adam grew older his adoration died a natural death, but they had always maintained a kind of affectionate indifference which placed no demands on either of them. Charles's only downfall had been his overwhelming pride and the burning resentment he had felt at not being the first born as well as being deprived of the status held by their maternal cousins. Never having experienced either of these needs himself, Adam had never quite been able to understand his brother's two most earnest regrets, but George, himself fired with an equally burning passion, had often been at odds with him. He himself had never found it necessary to pander to Charles's moods or answer to him for his actions, but he had often wished that things had been different between his two older brothers. That George had played his part in bringing so much of Charles's contempt upon himself could not be argued, but whilst Adam could have found it in him to not only overlook this far from attractive trait in his brother but to forgive it, the mere thought of what he had recently planned for his niece had the effect of banishing any of his finer feelings. Looking now at the prepared ground in front of him he experienced a rare surge of anger. Charles's death had been virtually self-induced, and whilst he would give anything to turn the clock back Adam had to admit that what he was witnessing was nothing short of poetic justice. This acknowledgement however, did nothing to ease the pain around his heart.

Despite having braced herself for this moment with every ounce of strength and fortitude she possessed, beneath Amelia's black veil the strain clearly showed. Her tormenting pain cut into her like a knife and only the thought of her beloved sons rendered the future without Charles worth living. It was impossible to imagine the future without him; to know that never again would she see him or speak to him, that in the long days and nights ahead there would be nothing but her store house of precious memories to sustain her. Never again would she feel the strength of his arms around her or feel his body next to hers and the sound of his heartbeat keeping perfect time with her own. She tried to tell herself that this empty space where her heart used to be would heal, that in time this devastating pain would go away and she would think and feel again, but she knew it was not true. There was no solace for her, nothing to look forward to except George; poor, inadequate George! It was a daunting prospect. For her life had now ended, and although she would continue to do all things she had always done there would be no joy or sweetness; nothing on which she could build her hopes. Only the knowledge that she had her boys helped to sustain her; life would certainly be an empty shell without them. A stray tear slid silently down her cheeks, followed by another and another until she could no longer stem the flow, her heart in despair at the loss of the man she would never cease to love.

Sophy caught the movement of Amelia's hand as she raised it unsteadily to her eyes, relieved that George had not seen this open display of grief as he would surely read it for what it was, his attention solely fixed on the two men lowering his brother's coffin into the prepared ground. Sophy swallowed, saddened and heavy-hearted at what was happening, not quite able to comprehend that it was her husband in that ornate oak casket. It was impossible for her to assess her thoughts at such a moment, just as it was equally impossible for her to believe that they were standing here today paying their final respects to a man who had left an everlasting impression on all who came in to contact with him. It seemed that only Amelia had been privileged to see his better side, the more human side of him, whilst for the rest of them he had, at one time or another, subjected them to his contempt and disdain. From the very beginning of their marriage Sophy had been wary of him and, more recently, even afraid of him. There had been very little friendliness between them and not even the pretence of any rapport. She had been dutiful and loyal, never doing or saying anything which would run counter to her husband's wishes, but all to no avail. She could have endured her loveless marriage if only he had tried to accept it, but he had railed against it from the outset, only his desire for a son rendering it as well as herself acceptable to him.

Had it not have been for his carefully contrived plans regarding Alexandra Sophy could, even now, find it in her to forgive him, but the despicable means he had adopted in his determined efforts to save himself from denunciation and scandal killed at a stroke any generous instincts she had. She would not easily forget how close Alexandra had come to losing her life or what Charles had planned for Marcus until he had come up with his new and equally scurrilous scheme for his salvation, and she could not help but wonder if he would have really gone through with his plans to kill his cousin had it not have been for Adam coming to Marcus's assistance.

That Charles had approved Ted Knowles's usage of her in the affair proved his contempt for her, but this was a small matter when Sophy compared it to knowing that her husband had been prepared to sacrifice the lives of two people, one of whom meant more to her than life itself; something she could not contemplate without sickening disgust. There could be no question that Charles's death had come about due to his underhanded arrangements, and far from taking consolation in knowing that he had finally received his just punishment for all he had done, it grieved her to know that his brutal and premature end had effectively been brought about by his own hand when things could have been so very different. But what might have been was as irrelevant as recrimination was pointless. Charles had chartered his own course and had paid the ultimate price for it, but somehow this thought brought her no comfort nor did it give her any satisfaction to witness the consequences of his actions or to know that his violent death could be looked upon as atonement for his crimes, on the contrary it saddened and distressed her, and Sophy mourned for him.

The solemnity of the occasion may not have instilled in Marcus the need to either deny or retract his differences with Charles, but it certainly intensified his regret over the futility of recent events. He could quite well understand his cousin's dilemma; after all, five thousand pounds was an awful lot of money to recover what was, theoretically speaking, one's own property. Whoever the lady was who had enjoyed Charles's patronage, she had certainly placed a substantial value on her worth, and whilst Charles was, to all intents and purposes at least, a wealthy man, he had suffered a staggering blow upon receiving her demand. Far from being the wealthy man she had clearly believed him to be, the facts were very different, and her offer to sell those letters back to him had placed his cousin in an impossible position. Under no circumstances would Charles have applied to him for relief, and most certainly not to George, and for reasons Marcus could only guess at, Charles had not requested assistance from Matthew either, leaving him with very few if any options. His ultimate decision to take the irrevocable step of using some of his sister's jewellery had sown the seed for what had followed, and although his own recent offer had been genuinely made Marcus supposed he should not have been surprised when Charles had turned it down.

Of course, Charles could not have known that his letters would be used against him, and whilst Marcus could excuse the folly of writing what must have been a set of rather amorous love notes, he could neither condone nor approve his method to redeem them. As long as Elizabeth's jewellery went unmentioned and no efforts were made to remove them from their resting place in Mercers' vaults, Charles had been relatively safe, with very little chance of his deception being exposed, but the moment Silas Jenkins had read out that catastrophic clause in Matthew's will, the whole thing had threatened to explode in Charles's face. His subterfuge to cover up their removal by putting fake ones in their place had eventually escalated into attempted murder. Marcus could only hazard a guess as to whether doing away with Alexandra had been Ted Knowles's idea or his cousin's, but in either event he had been deeply involved in the planning of it, but, at no time, had either of them made any effort to draw back or call a halt to the proceedings.

As far as he was concerned, Charles had decided to blackmail him instead of putting an end to his life. Marcus had no way of knowing with any degree of certainty whether his cousin would have gone through with it or not, but that he had even considered such a step proved how desperate he had regarded his position. He knew all too well that should the story of Charles's dealings ever leak out there would be some who would look upon his death as nothing short of just and fitting punishment, but, for himself, Marcus considered his cousin's violent end to have been not only unnecessary but a terrible waste of life; and one, moreover, capable of far more good than he ever evinced.

Henry, who had attended this solemn occasion merely for his wife's sake, had no more liking for his brother-in-law than he had had for his father-in-law. The truth was that apart from Charlotte and Marcus he had nothing in common with his in-laws, although he was quite prepared to reserve judgement where Adam was concerned. The news of his brother-in-law's death had come as a dreadful shock, not at all what he had expected to hear, and although he was not an unfeeling man and regretted the whole affair, Henry had to confess that he had never liked Charles from the moment he had first been introduced to him. It seemed to him that there was more to Charles's tragic and brutal death than met the eye, but since nothing had come to light to substantiate this, although whether deliberately suppressed or merely overlooked he could only hazard a guess, he supposed that the whole truth would never be known.

Having been informed by Jane that George had taken complete charge of the funeral arrangements, Henry had accepted this as perfectly natural as well as easing the burden on Charlotte and Sophy but knowing something of the feud which had existed between Charles and George he had been rather taken aback, upon arriving in Brook Street, to see that he had spared no expense when arranging his brother's obsequies. No fewer than six gleaming black horses had been hired to pull the carriage conveying Charles's coffin, on top of which George had positioned, in pride of place to the others, a huge wreath of pure white roses, bearing a legend which could have led the uninitiated to believe that they had enjoyed a far closer relationship than they had. Henry could only conjecture the reason for this public show of grief and affection, but for a man of his integrity and openness he found George's extraordinary behaviour quite nauseating. None of these thoughts, however, were voiced, not even to Jane, but he himself would have thought better of George had he kept the cortège as small and dignified as possible.

But George was more than content with his arrangements, believing that anything less would have constituted a rather shabby affair, especially when he considered that his brother bore a name which was regarded with respect. Had he been asked if there was another and more personal reason for such a show, he would have categorically denied it.

"Quite a turn out this, wouldn't you say?" Henry remarked in a quiet aside to Marcus when they later made their way back to the waiting carriages.

"Perhaps." Marcus inclined his head slightly, not having given it very much thought considering recent events.

"I can only hazard a guess as to George's reason for it," Henry commented, "but I should have thought a smaller, more quiet affair, would have been better."

"Why do you say that?" Marcus asked, looking anxiously down at Henry, a slight crease descending onto his forehead.

"Well, for one thing," Henry told him, "they were hardly the best of friends; this set out give quite a different impression."

Marcus, conscious of an intense feeling of relief at this, had, for one awful moment, wondered if he had heard something about Charles's activities, but was thankfully spared from answering as Edward caught up with them, offering his own opinion as to the whole tragic affair.

The strain of the morning clearly showed on Charlotte's face, and instead of accompanying her family into the drawing room upon returning home she went straight to her sitting room where she was joined soon afterwards by her nephew.

"I was hoping you would come and join me before Jenkins reads Charles's will," she smiled, the lines around her eyes and mouth more pronounced than usual, showing just how tired she really was. "I must confess to a little unease when I think of what it may contain. All I can hope for is that it holds nothing inflammatory. You know what George is," she pointed out, "and right now I do not feel I can cope with an emotional outburst."

Marcus had no difficulty in believing this, suggesting she remain quietly here instead as no one would be surprised or offended if she did not join them in study for the reading.

"I know," she sighed, "and if I had any sense or feelings of self-preservation, that is precisely what I would do, but I cannot."

He did not press her, but said in his calm way, "I am sure George will realise that."

"I hope so," Charlotte sighed, "but you know as well as I do that no reliance can be placed upon him holding his tongue, especially when he is upset; and should Charles's will contain anything untoward I have every confidence in George exercising no restraint whatsoever."

Considering George's reaction to Matthew's will Marcus had no difficulty in believing this, but since he had never known his cousin exercise tact or discretion, let alone restraint, he envisaged the reading to be anything but uneventful, and were it not for his aunt's appeal earlier that morning for him to be present, not because either of them thought for one moment that Charles had bequeathed him anything, but merely to give her much-needed support, he would certainly not do so. Left to himself, he would much rather wait for his family in the drawing room, but his aunt was far too vulnerable to be alone with her warring offspring as not only George but Emily too were more than capable of rendering the ordeal somewhat harrowing. Keeping these reflections to himself he asked after Alexandra, not at all surprised at her absence from church this morning. She may be on excellent terms with Sophy and his aunt but not even this would induce her to attend the obsequies of a man whose dislike of her had been as profound as her dislike of him.

"It seems that you and Sophy are the only ones I can talk to without being asked how much longer Alexandra is likely to remain here," she told him. "Nevertheless, she is a great comfort to me."

Marcus moved over to the fireplace and stood with his back to it, looking down at his aunt's diminutive figure sitting as upright as ever in her favourite chair, his eyes narrowing slightly. "Just give them a little time," he advised with more confidence than truth. "They will soon become accustomed to her being here."

She smiled up at him but shook her head. "I don't think so, and neither do you, although it is just like you to say so, but we both know they will never accept her."

Marcus did not need this reinforcing, he knew it perfectly well and suggested, "Have you considered going away for a while? Perhaps it is what you both need."

She nodded. "It has occurred to me, in fact," she told him, "I have been wondering whether to take her stay with my sister."

Memories of an awe-inspiring dowager sprang to mind, and he could not help but wonder whether Alexandra would take to such a redoubtable old lady even though he knew that beneath her formidable façade lay a heart of gold, but keeping this thought to himself he said, a little cautiously, "It *could* answer."

"As you know," she explained, "she has been a widow for several years, and although she has a most forthright manner her bark," she smiled up at her nephew, whose face echoed his recollections of her, "is far worse than her bite."

"She terrified me to death!" Marcus exclaimed, not quite able to hide the smile in his eyes.

"Yes, of course she did," Charlotte nodded with mock sympathy, "so much so that you still keep in touch with her."

"Purely selfish motives, I assure you," he smiled, his eyes alight with amusement.

Unable to resist his smile, Charlotte responded to this light-hearted raillery, after which she admitted, "I know that she can be quite a handful at times, nor have I forgotten the occasions when, as children, you were, all of you, subjected to her sharp tongue, but she has a most generous nature beneath that stern exterior and, as you know, we have always got along extremely well, but although she was never blessed with children herself she is not unkind. Perhaps in a few days I will write to her."

As no other alternative suggested itself, Marcus was brought to see that this did indeed seem to be the only practical solution to the difficulties facing them. "I think you may be right," he agreed, adding provocatively, a smile playing at the corner of his mouth, "providing, of course, you do not expect me to escort you."

Charlotte smiled, having not the least difficulty in understanding why Sophy had fallen in love with him; she herself was conscious of just how irresistible his attractive smile was and how his sense of humour could easily undo one's resolve. "As if I would *do* such a thing!"

He responded in the same good-humoured vein by reminding her of the many instances, which he swore were still vivid in his memory, to substantiate his reasons, but even though she laughed at his attempts to raise her spirits, it was becoming increasingly obvious to him that her thoughts had strayed a little, her eyes staring unseeing in front of her.

"Strange," she said wistfully, "how a mother never expects her children to pre-decease her, but I have lost two of my sons; first Richard and now Charles, and both in the most inexplicable of circumstances!" She looked enquiringly up at her nephew. "You would tell me if there was more to Charles's death than I have been told, wouldn't you?"

"Of course," Marcus nodded, hating the lie he was giving her, "but his death, however tragic, was nothing more sinister than him being in the wrong place at the wrong time."

"I can't quite understand it," she shook her head. "What was he *doing* in Waterloo, and at such an hour? According to George," she shrugged helplessly, "he does not think that Charles had any business acquaintances or personal friends in the neighbourhood, but then, considering the animosity between them it is hardly surprising that George would not know." Thankfully, Marcus was spared having to answer this as she quickly followed it up with, "Do you think the police will find the ones responsible?"

"I would like to think so," he told her with feeling, still far from reconciled to the unpalatable fact that Ted Knowles and his band of cutthroats would never be brought to justice, "but I am afraid that unless someone witnessed it, it seems unlikely."

Charlotte considered this for a moment or two, then nodded her head in acceptance, but her eyes were clouded and troubled as she raised them to his. "Did he suffer much pain?"

Since his own opinion was that the first blow would have been sufficient to render Charles senseless, he was able to tell her in all honesty that he believed he did not.

"I am so glad," she told him, relieved. "I could not bear to think that he did."

"None of us would," Marcus assured her. "It was a most regrettable tragedy," he told her truthfully.

"Both my sons' deaths were regrettable tragedies!" she cried. "First Richard and that ridiculously old-fashioned and stupid duel he took part in; goodness only knows why he felt such a need! And now Charles." She summoned up a smile but her eyes remained sombre. "Oh, I know Charles had his faults, not the least being his insufferable pride and arrogance, and his behaviour towards Sophy was not at all what I would expect from one of my sons, indeed," she confessed, "there were times when I positively disliked him," she swallowed, "but he was my son, and I loved him."

"You don't have to tell me that," Marcus said quietly, "I know you did."

"He was so like Matthew," she stated simply, "in more ways than one; more so than George, in fact. Indeed," she acknowledged, "Charles was more like his father than any of them. I often think the similarity between them was the cause of their many disagreements."

"I should imagine so," Marcus nodded, knowing more about the root cause of their arguments than she evidently did. He knew perfectly well that his aunt was not unaware of how Matthew had more than once come to Charles's assistance, but Marcus had no doubt at all that she had no idea just how much of a mess his personal financial affairs were in or of Matthew's growing exasperation with them. He and his cousin may not have seen eye to eye most of the time, but no power on earth would induce him to alert his aunt to the truth. "But despite their disagreements," he reminded her gently, "they rubbed along together remarkably well."

She agreed to this. "You are right, of course. It was a constant source of amazement to me how, after a long and heated argument, they could still converse quite amicably." She paused, her eyes clouding momentarily. "Poor Amelia," she sighed, "she is going to miss him dreadfully."

Marcus eyed her narrowly. "Amelia?"

"But of course!" Charlotte nodded. "You must know, as I do, that they were far closer than they had a right to be."

"I had no idea you knew about that," Marcus said, a slight inflexion of surprise in his voice.

"My dear Marcus," she smiled, "my opinion may seldom be sought, but I have eyes in my head. Of course," she acknowledged, "neither Charles nor Amelia confided in me, but it did not take much to see the way things were between them. Indeed," she nodded, "it had often occurred to me how well suited they were." She sighed. "I can only be thankful that George never knew, had he have done so the animosity between them would have been far greater than it already was."

It was becoming increasingly clear to Marcus that his aunt, whom he had always known to be far more astute than her family had any idea of, did in fact see far more than even he had thought. He had always had a deep and genuine affection for her, holding her in the greatest respect and admiration, but he would have sworn that Charles's affair with Amelia had gone unnoticed by her. Clearly, it had not done so, which only served to confirm his belief that she was by no means ignorant as to the true state of affairs between him and Sophy. Something in the way she was looking at him now told him she knew exactly what he was thinking.

Rising to her feet with the aid of his proffered arm, Charlotte looked steadily up into his face for a few moments before saying gently, "You are very like your mother, so much so that despite your differences with Charles you can still find it in you to be generous towards him." When he made no reply to this she told him, "I miss her very much, you know. She was my dearest and closest friend long before she ever became my sister-in-law." She smiled knowingly up at him. "I think Imogen would be well satisfied with the woman you have chosen to set in her place."

Marcus did not pretend to misunderstand her, in fact, she merely confirmed what he had suspected for some little time. "I wondered whether you knew," he smiled. "There were times when I was convinced you did, and at others," he shook his head, "I was not so sure. Although," he smiled, "why I should have ever doubted it I don't know, especially in view of what you have just disclosed."

"Oh, my dear Marcus!" she cried, squeezing his arm. "Of course I knew. You forget," she reminded him, "I saw the two of you together in this very room during your convalescence. Had others been privileged to have seen you as I did, they would have been in do doubt that the two of you had fallen deeply in love."

"And how do you feel about it?" he asked, confident of her answer.

She did not disappoint him. "It makes me very happy," she told him sincerely, "but even if it didn't," she remarked, "something tells me you would not care too much for that. And that is how it should be," she nodded. "Happiness is not easily come by, and when it does come our way we should do all we can to hold onto it."

"I intend to," Marcus said firmly.

"You love Sophy very much, don't you?" Charlotte stated simply.

"Yes," he confirmed quietly, "very much," his eyes holding hers. "But you must not think that she betrayed Charles, she did not."

"There is no need to tell me that," Charlotte shook her head, "I know she did not." She thought a moment, then, looking up at him, enquired, "Did you know that it was I who instigated Sophy's visit to Timothy?"

"No," Marcus shook his head, an arrested expression entering his eyes, "although," he confessed, "I suppose I should have." He eyed her closely, a gleam of pure amusement lurking beneath the surface. "I am given to wondering though, why you did not take such pains over Amelia by instigating a visit to her brother Giles?"

Without a moment's hesitation Charlotte replied calmly, "Amelia is well able to take care of herself, and whilst I have no wish to see her unhappy or hurt in anyway, Sophy is a very different matter."

"I quite agree," he acknowledged, "but a less generous man than I," he told her with a laugh in his voice, "would take this as meddlesome interference."

She patted his cheek. "Most probably, but I did it with the best of intentions," she told him, briefly explaining her reasons for doing so. "I may not always like what my family do, and ordinarily I would never interfere, but I am extremely fond of Sophy, and knowing her as well as I do I realised that it was only a matter of time before Charles would have seen what I already knew, indeed," she admitted, "I must own to some surprise that he remained in ignorance of it." She paused before saying tentatively, "You know as well as I do that should he have discovered the truth, he would have taken it very badly, and Sophy, unfortunately, would have been subjected to even harsher treatment than she already was."

As this had long been a major consideration for him, especially knowing that there was nothing whatever he could do to protect her from her husband's anger and retribution, Marcus had had to live uncomfortably with his impotence and growing frustration with what patience he could. He may not be able to tell his aunt that Charles had in fact eventually discovered the truth without disclosing his recent actions, but Marcus could not deny that she was quite right about what would have been in store for

Sophy. Charles may not have gone so far as to send her away for a time on the pretext of a sudden indisposition or for the state of her nerves to keep the two of them apart, but he would most certainly have ensured that no further meetings would have taken place between them on the occasions he came to visit his aunt. In fact, Marcus would not have put it beyond Charles to stipulate that his visits to Brook Street cease, and if he wanted to see his aunt then she must visit him. Should this have happened Marcus would have had no choice but to comply with such a demand, not because he was either overawed or afraid of his cousin, but simply for Sophy's sake.

"I know I can rely on both you and Timothy never to tell her, it would only embarrass her," Charlotte said quietly, breaking into his none too pleasant thoughts.

"I shall never do so," he promised, his eyes reflecting all he was feeling.

Charlotte saw his lips compress and knew precisely what he was thinking. "You know, Marcus," she said gently, "I am not unaware of the position you were in, but you know as well as I do that Charles would never have sanctioned a divorce."

"I know," Marcus sighed, "and since the alternative would have been as repugnant to Sophy as it was to me, I was left with nothing to do other than having to stand by knowing there was nothing I could do to help ease her situation. I have never felt so useless in my life before!"

"There was nothing you *could* have done," she told him gently. "Unfortunately, not even your love for Sophy had the power to come between a man and his wife."

"I know," Marcus sighed, "and that is why I am determined to do everything in my power to make her happy from now on."

Charlotte nodded, but a slight frown creased her forehead. "Have you mentioned marriage to Sophy at all?"

"Yes," he nodded, "but I have not offered her a proposal if that is what you mean. How could I," he shrugged, "when she was not free to receive one? But it is what she wants too."

Charlotte nodded. "I cannot deny that the two of you are perfectly suited," she told him truthfully, "indeed, I can think of no two people who deserve one another more than you and Sophy, but Marcus," she reminded him gently, "whilst I shall be the first to dance at your wedding, no formal offer of marriage can be made to her until she is out of mourning."

"I am as aware of that as you are, believe me," he told her. "I too know the codes and conventions by which we have to live, and that if I followed my natural inclinations and ignored them I should condemn her in the eyes of society forever. For myself," he told her unequivocally, "I care nothing for the gossip which would follow our immediate marriage, but to subject Sophy to such condemnation would be unforgivable. I love her too much for that." A slight smile touched his lips. "You need have no fears," he assured her, kissing her cheek, "having waited this long to make Sophy my own, I think I can wait a little longer. I would do nothing whatever to compromise her." Charlotte squeezed his hand, and he said, "Although Sophy does not need her brother's consent to remarry, she would very much like his blessing, as I would, so, in true chivalrous style," he smiled, "in twelve months' time I shall present myself to Timothy, whereupon I shall romantically plead my cause for her hand."

Charlotte laughed at this, as he had intended her to, but she knew that beneath his light-hearted raillery to wait a further twelve months for the woman he loved would seem like an eternity. "I realise it is going to be difficult," she acknowledged, "but I cannot see Timothy withholding his blessing, and even though you cannot yet formally ask Sophy to marry you, I feel quite sure that Timothy will not deny you his permission to visit her because I know," she told him, "from what Sophy has said to me, that it is her intention to stay with him and Annabel when this is all over for a couple of months at least. In the meantime," she asked, "what are your plans?"

Marcus instantly looked a little rueful, a smile playing at the corner of his mouth. "Well," he sighed, "the first thing I must do is to pay my uncle a long overdue visit. I am afraid I have neglected him shamefully. He would be the first to admit, however, that he is quite happy and, certainly, more than capable of looking after the business, and whilst this is perfectly true," he acknowledged, "the fact is he is not getting any younger, but now that I am largely conversant with things, I really think it is about time I took a lot more responsibility onto my own shoulders."

"Of course, I do understand," Charlotte nodded. "When do you intend leaving for Yorkshire?"

"As soon as I possibly can." A mischievous twinkle entered his eyes, fond memories coming to mind. "I daresay I can expect a rare dressing down when I do show my face; and in the broadest of Yorkshire too!"

"I hope he doesn't scold you too much," she smiled.

"I can't vouch for that," Marcus grinned, "but I admit it will be good to see him again." Whereupon he escorted her out of the sitting room to join the rest of the family for luncheon.

Although Sophy was sitting directly opposite Marcus at the luncheon table she was unfortunately granted no opportunity to speak privately with him but felt herself to be more than adequately compensated by the silent messages she read in his eyes every time he looked across at her.

Amelia had not missed those unspoken exchanges which passed between them, and she knew a moment of intense pain. Charles had looked at her in just such a way, telling her more than any words possibly could. She envied Sophy the love she shared with Marcus and their future together, and although she did not begrudge her the happiness and fulfilment she knew would be hers, it nevertheless all went to emphasise the emptiness of the days and years which depressingly loomed ahead of her. This gloomy prospect did nothing to raise Amelia's spirits or her appetite, pushing her plate away with barely concealed distaste. Her part in what passed as conversation over luncheon was minimal, speaking only when directly addressed, but as she was only vaguely aware of what was being said, this was hardly surprising. Predictably, George monopolised whatever conversation did take place, introducing one mundane topic after another, but it was not until he touched upon the subject nearest to his heart did Amelia's mind focus more closely on what was being said. Having forborne to mention the matter burning in his breast for as long as he possibly could, George, finally finding it impossible to refrain from raising the issue any longer, considerably shocked that diligent professional sitting opposite him by his direct question.

Silas Jenkins, appalled by such forceful tactics as well as George's lack of consideration, was rendered acutely uncomfortable, tactfully suggesting that he hold it in abeyance until Charles's will was read out after luncheon. Unfortunately, tact and restraint were not George's strongest points, and in his determination to receive an answer to his question, he repeated it. Silas Jenkins looked warningly across at him, but upon seeing it was going unheeded, whether deliberately or not he could not tell, looked beseechingly at Adam and Marcus, silently entreating their assistance. But it was Charlotte who unexpectedly came to his rescue by gently reminding George that the luncheon table was not the place to discuss it, to which he hastily begged pardon before relapsing into sullen silence. Unfortunately, his silence was not destined to last for long.

Charles's Last Will and Testament was by no means the foregone conclusion everyone had expected it to be, not the least being Sophy, who, upon learning that he had more than adequately provided for her by stipulating that she was to receive fifteen percent of his share of the business, stared aghast at Silas Jenkins as if to assure herself she had heard him correctly. He confirmed that she had, but since this was not the time to discuss it she refrained from questioning it further. She supposed she should have been relieved to know that he had made some provision for her but knowing her late husband she felt more inclined to attribute his generosity to depriving his brother rather than ensuring her financial comfort. Charles had made no secret of the fact that he knew perfectly well what his elder brother had always hankered after – full control of the business – but even from the grave it seemed Charles was determined to deny George, and not for the first time had used her to achieve his ends. As Charles could not possibly have foreseen his own untimely end, Sophy, like Silas Jenkins and everyone else, could only guess as to what had prompted her husband to make changes to his will; changes that were guaranteed to create precisely the kind of furore Charles must have known they would.

Like Matthew, Charles had ignored Silas Jenkins's advice when, only a few days after the reading of his father's will he had informed him that he wished to make changes to his own. Upon discovering the full sum of those changes Silas Jenkins had looked horrified at his client, hardly able to believe the instructions he had received. As Charles had had very little personal money to bequeath, he had left fifteen percent of his share in the brewery to his wife and the other eighteen percent to Adam, increasing his share to fifty-one percent, not even leaving George with so much as one percent to give him even a decent portion much less a majority share, wiping out his authority at a stroke. Totally disregarding Silas Jenkins's sincere and earnest pleas in that to leave his share in the brewery between Adam and his wife would not only wipe out any influence George had on the board of directors his father had set up but would be bound to cause trouble, and that George would take it very badly, to which Charles had merely smiled, a cold thinning of the lips that left no room for argument. "Precisely!" Silas Jenkins had remonstrated with Charles, only to be told, "You will please allow me to decide how best to dispose of what is mine." His tone had been implacable, and Silas Jenkins, knowing when he was beaten, had simply nodded his head in reluctant acceptance.

George's reaction to such an inflammatory bequest came as no surprise to that long-suffering professional, in fact, it was precisely how he had known it would be; George's face was suffused with angry colour and the accusations which left his lips concise and to the point. Upon being advised to calm down he rose to his feet with such force that his chair almost fell over; looking accusingly from Silas Jenkins to Sophy and finally to Adam, whose face clearly echoed his shock and amazement, his older brother demanding to know what trick they were playing. "Naturally," George conceded, eyeing his sister-in-law doubtfully, "I should like to absolve Sophy of all blame, but there has been some dirty work done in this business, and I aim to discover which one of you it was," incorporating Silas Jenkins in this sweeping statement, "who persuaded Charles into making these changes to his will."

"I *really must protest!*" Silas Jenkins cried, deeply offended, attempting to impress upon George that no one had persuaded his brother into doing anything. "Your brother made his own decisions," he stressed, wiping his spectacles nervously.

"Of course he did!" Adam exclaimed, but his denials that he knew absolutely nothing about Charles's plans to leave more than half his share of the premises at Islington to him were furiously dismissed as lies, quickly followed up with the accusation that he had worked his way into his brother's good graces by cajolery and deceit. "You'll take that back!" Adam bit out, his face pale and grim, rising hurriedly to his feet.

"I'll take *nothing* back," George barked. "I have often wondered what was keeping you here, and now I know!"

"You must be out of your senses if you think that I could possibly want to take over Charles's share of the business. For God's sake, George!" Adam exclaimed. "Why should I want it? And how the devil do you think I could run it miles away in Yorkshire?"

Under different circumstances the expression which crossed George's face would have been rather amusing, but the moment was too serious for amusement, and Sophy, surprised and quite bemused over the unexpected turn of events and more than a little hurt over George's barely concealed accusations, felt the need to escape this overcharged atmosphere and silently left the study.

Marcus watched her leave without making any effort to either detain or follow her, knowing she much preferred to be alone, but Charles's revised will had certainly come as a shock. Marcus could understand George's amazement and disbelief upon hearing such a bequest, but that he should dare to fling scarcely veiled accusations at one who was unquestionably innocent of any deceit annoyed him, and he promised himself a word with George before he left. Charlotte, deeply distressed, rose stately to her feet, quietly informing her relatives that she had the headache and would retire to her bedchamber, thanking Silas Jenkins for his services before following Sophy out of the study.

It soon became apparent to George's audience that Charles's reasons for changing his will were finally beginning to seep into his stunned brain. In his earnest desire to attain what he had always believed to be rightfully his, George had not even considered for so much as a second that Adam, like Sophy, was not only innocent of the charges he had flung at him, but totally ignorant of what Charles had planned. Had George paused for only a moment to consider the contents of his brother's will, he would have realised at the outset that this had been his way of finally and maliciously attempting to get the upper hand. Never having recovered from the shock of his father's will depriving him of full control this devastating bequest had been the last straw. It never even entered his head that Charles would take their feuding to the grave with him by removing at a stroke his ultimate authority, believing that at long last he had got what he had always wanted. Gradually, George began to accept Adam's forceful but sincere denials of any collusion with Charles, and after only a moment's consideration George began to see that not only had he made a fool of himself but had completely attached the wrong interpretation to Charles's final and supreme insult. Embarrassment quickly followed George's explosive attack on his brother, rendering it necessary to offer him an apology, hoping that his acknowledgement of his offence would be accepted by Sophy as generously as it had been by Adam.

George's uncontrolled outburst made Amelia mentally writhe in anger and frustration, although she supposed she should not really have been surprised at his behaviour. It really did seem to be expecting too much of her husband to exercise restraint or waiting to discuss an issue of this nature at a more convenient time, preferably without an audience. For her part, she did not care who took over from Charles; the only important thing as far as she was concerned was that the man she loved was dead.

It had been a most unpleasant scene and one which left everyone feeling uncomfortable and not a little awkward, but thanks to Adam's good sense, the matter was later amicably settled by enquiring of Jenkins whether he could, if he wished, turn the eighteen percent share which had been bequeathed to him by Charles over to his brother by way of a deed of gift. This assurance having been given, Adam was then pleased to be able to tell George that he could have his eighteen percent share and welcome, a gesture which, although it may have mollified him, also went to rekindle his antipathy towards Charles which had, over the past few days, begun to wane.

Having been informed by Jenkins that her percentage, providing of course it was what she wanted, could easily be negotiated, Sophy accepted George's apology with the fervent wish that she hoped this was now the end of the matter, adding further that she was quite prepared to come to some arrangement as Jenkins suggested, even forgoing her share, if it ensured that there were no more arguments. Whilst she could understand George's anger and resentment, the whole affair had nevertheless upset her very much, and she could not quite absolve Charles of having deliberately planned what he must have known would be a most uncomfortable situation.

Marcus, by no means as easy to placate as Sophy, made his cousin aware that he regarded his attitude towards her as quite unforgivable. "You were a trifle high-handed there, were you not?"

"I am sure I don't know what you mean, Cousin," George blustered, conscious that he had been at fault.

"Next time you decide to hurl accusations," Marcus advised him coldly, "I would recommend you consider well before you speak."

"I merely spoke the truth," George defended himself, by no means pleased at having his actions commented upon. "Besides," he asked, "what is it to you?"

Quite unperturbed by this direct question, Marcus said coolly, "You have upset people who are very dear to me. You have exhibited neither consideration nor understanding for the feelings of those whom you should have wished to protect from any further distress."

George opened his mouth to refute what he knew to be the truth, but the unexpected entrance of Amelia made him think better of it. She eyed him knowingly, not needing to be told that once again he had allowed his tongue to overcome his judgement, and she was not at all surprised when he brushed past her in a state of considerable belligerence as he left the drawing room.

"You must not think that I was deliberately eavesdropping," she told Marcus, "but George, you must admit, does have a rather penetrating voice." When Marcus made no reply to this, she grimaced, saying conversationally, "You know, it is of great mortification to me to know that my husband has neither sense nor tact."

"I am sorry you overheard such an exchange," Marcus apologised, not unmindful of Amelia's feelings.

She gave a shrug of her shoulders. "Your efforts to bring him to some kind of awareness are appreciated, but quite wasted I assure you. For myself," she confessed, "I have long since resigned myself to the fact that tact and discretion are really quite beyond him." On this parting statement Amelia made a dignified exit, leaving Marcus with the firm conviction that the sooner his aunt and Sophy removed themselves from this house, the better.

Adam's feelings as well as his pride had suffered a stinging blow by his brother's accusations, telling Marcus that he would never have thought George could be fool enough to believe, even for so much as a second, that he could possibly want the added burden of Charles's share of the business.

Never having given any thought to the contents of his cousin's will, Marcus had automatically assumed that Charles would bequeath most of his share to George and more than likely leave Adam and Sophy equal halves of the remainder; that he had not done so, whilst something of a surprise, did not come as a bombshell to Marcus as it had for the rest of them.

Whilst he regarded George's outburst and resultant accusations as unpardonable, he could nevertheless appreciate his feelings upon discovering that his brother had dealt him one final and cruelly humiliating blow.

"What an idiot!" Adam exclaimed. "Fancy George believing I was in cahoots with Charles!"

Marcus eyed his cousin thoughtfully for several moments, not unsympathetic to his lacerated feelings, but deciding that no good would be served by fuelling his anger, said calmly, "As to why Charles felt the need to make amendments to his will so soon after your father's death, I can't say," he shook his head. "His last-minute change of heart was certainly ill-advised, but I suppose we should have prepared ourselves for something like this."

"To think that at the very end he still craved a desire to oust George!" Adam exclaimed, horrified. "I know there's never been much love lost between them, but I never suspected something like this! And Sophy!" he cried. "One can only imagine what Charles had stipulated for her in his original will, but that he should have placed her in such a position is unforgivable! It beats everything!"

Given the modest state of Charles's personal finances, Marcus had no doubt at all that he had made a far less attractive bequest to Sophy in his original will, but that he should have done something so blatantly callous surprised even him, however, deeming it wiser to say nothing further on this point, he said encouragingly, "Forget it. It's over. George has now more or less got what he wanted, and I have no doubt at all that Sophy is more than a little relieved to feel that she no longer has such a burden to carry. You can do no more here," he smiled, patting Adam on the shoulder. "Go home to Yorkshire and Isabel, who, I have no doubt at all, is already wondering what has become of you." Marcus, dismissing his cousin's thanks, told him the sooner he put everything out of his head the better. "We can't change any of it, no matter how regrettable. We shall all of us have to live with it the best we can."

Adam nodded, then, having bethought himself of something, frowned. "Yes, but what about Lizzie's jewellery? What I mean is," he shook his head, "we can't just leave those pieces in the hands of some unknown villain."

"You can leave the question of the jewellery to me," Marcus assured him. "I have no intention of leaving those pieces in the hands of those to whom they most definitely do not belong!"

"Yes, but," Adam pointed out reasonably, "you don't even know who

Charles took them to."

"No," Marcus agreed, "I don't, but surely a man of his unscrupulous ethics must have come to someone's notice before now."

Adam's offer to remain in town a few days longer to assist his cousin to track him down, although appreciated, was immediately vetoed, promptly followed up with his reiterated advice about him returning home to Isabel. Adam, after only a moment's thought, nodded his head, then, after agreeing to this, thanked Marcus again for all he had done, then, shaking hands with his cousin, renewed his invitation to visit them when next in Yorkshire.

"That will be sooner than you think," Marcus smiled. "I am on the point of visiting my Uncle Lionel, so be prepared to receive me very soon."

"I shall look forward to it," Adam grinned. "So too will Isabel." A final handshake and he was gone, to pack his bags and inform his mother that he would be leaving for home the following morning.

His departure, midway through the next day, left Charlotte and Sophy feeling quite bereft; the house would certainly seem empty without him. Naturally, Charlotte realised that he could not extend his stay any longer, and although she would miss him she was all too aware of Isabel's claims upon him. Sophy, with something very close to a tear in her eye, wished him a fond farewell accompanying it with her heartfelt thanks for his support. Self-consciously shrugging off her gratitude, he told her rather sheepishly that thanks were not in the least necessary, adding with a mischievous grin that he looked forward to dancing at her wedding. Unsteadily holding him to this promise, Sophy returned his hug before watching him stride down the steps and into the waiting hackney, not for the first time feeling as though she had lost a very dear friend.

Fortunately for Charlotte and Sophy they were kept far too occupied to remain downcast for long. The acquisition of an entire new wardrobe for Alexandra kept Sophy busy for several days. As shopping expeditions to Bond Street were out of the question due to her recent bereavement, her favourite dressmaker was requested to visit the house bringing with her such suitable items of clothing for her young niece. Watching Alexandra try on the many outfits afforded Sophy as much pleasure as her niece, more than once finding herself having to exert considerable restraint in resisting some of the very fetching dress patterns which that deft but astute dressmaker had brought with her in the hope of tempting her long-standing and valued client to have made up but which would certainly not have suited her present state of mourning. Alexandra, seeing that Sophy was trying hard to resist that artiste's persuasions, added her own to them, the result being that Sophy, telling herself that just one or two things would not hurt, finally succumbed to temptation.

Having lost that painfully thin sharpness it could be easily seen that Alexandra was indeed very beautiful, and her natural grace coupled with everything her mother had taught her, would no doubt catch her a suitable husband one day, to which she laughingly agreed, but nothing, not even her new stylish appearance, had the power to bring her into favour with her relations. Emily, upon a visit to Brook Street to see her mamma, not the first she had made since her brother's funeral, pointedly ignored the young woman she adamantly refused to call a niece, but whilst she managed to refrain from being downright rude, she could not resist uttering the snide little remarks that were guaranteed to let Alexandra know that she was no nearer being a part of this family than she ever was. Edward, who was beginning to gain a little confidence in himself now that Matthew and Charles were no longer around to either intimidate or overawe him, felt it safe to give his opinion in that the sooner the girl took herself off the better, but whilst this show of support pleased Emily it left Sophy not only feeling saddened and disheartened but uncertain as to whether her brother-in-law's freely expressed views stemmed from domestic expediency or from a firmly held belief that Alexandra was indeed the embarrassment his in-laws thought.

Amelia, who was still of the opinion that Alexandra had done an excellent job in worming her way into her grandmother's affections by stealth and guile as well as cunningly taking advantage of Sophy's generous nature, made no effort whatsoever to hide her hostility or to acknowledge her. She was of the same mind now as she had always been, but since Charlotte appeared determined to keep the girl with her and Sophy refused to believe that she had been most carefully and craftily used, Amelia washed her hands of the whole affair, and it was therefore with barely concealed relief that she learned of Alexandra's imminent departure into Hertfordshire, devoutly trusting she would remain there.

Having already received his sister's telegram informing him of the tragedy and that her visit would have to be postponed, the newspaper articles reporting on Charles's death were not the shock to Timothy they would otherwise have been. Sophy did not need Timothy to tell her that his feelings towards Charles had been far from friendly; she had always suspected that there had never really been any love lost between them, but she accepted her brother's sincere commiserations in the same spirit with which he had given them.

It was not his dislike of Charles which had prevented him from attending the funeral but the false alarm of what had been thought to be a miscarriage for Annabel, not the first she had experienced since the start of her pregnancy. As far as Timothy was concerned his wife's health and well-being were far more important to him than attending the funeral of a man he had never liked, and although he had never once intimated his feelings to Sophy he had nevertheless apologised for his absence with the same affection and consideration he had always afforded his sister. Her response to his letter had resulted in a direct reply including the earnest wish that she come into Kent as soon as possible for however long she chose to stay. Sophy was of course delighted at the prospect of visiting them, but the news of Annabel's problematic pregnancy caused her grave concern, hastening her departure.

Charlotte too had received good news from her sister, inviting her and her granddaughter, '...or should I say my great niece?' she had added in brackets, to pay her a visit just as soon as she could possibly arrange it. Alexandra was naturally pleased to learn that she was about to escape from the claustrophobic confines of Brook Street, and secretly knew the heartfelt desire of never wanting to return. Except for her grandmother and Sophy, she kept her distance from the rest of the family as much as possible, but it was only to be expected that she would run across one or the other of them from time to time. For herself, she cared nothing for their dislike of her, after all it was entirely reciprocated, but she knew it upset her grandmother and even though it went very much against the grain with her to either conciliate or hold out olive branches she had nevertheless made several attempts to forge an understanding of some kind, but as these were coldly and pointedly ignored, she gave up trying. Unconsciously echoing Sophy's thoughts, Alexandra could not help wishing that the rest of her family were as likeable as Adam, because although she only laid eyes on him now and then it was as plain as a pikestaff that he was as different to the rest of them as anyone could be.

In an unlooked-for show of courtesy and consideration where Alexandra was concerned George offered to escort her and his mamma into Hertfordshire, but as his niece had no more desire for his company than he really had for hers, this generous, if somewhat suspect proposal was turned down by both ladies. The truth was Alexandra would rather have walked every inch of the way than accept his escort, and she was therefore rather relieved when her grandmother had said she would much prefer to travel in her own carriage driven by the devoted and careful Jem rather than the prospect of undertaking a journey by train. Charlotte was secretly relieved that her granddaughter preferred her own luxurious if outdated mode of transport to that of a steam locomotive; never having been on one in her life, distrusting their safety, she could look forward to her journey without any fears of meeting with an accident of some kind. As George could not afford to spend too much time away from the brewery, his brother's death having increased his burden of responsibility, travelling by road would have taken up by far too much time, apart from which he really did not want to have anything to do with his niece if he could possibly help it, he was only too pleased to give way to his mother's wishes.

Now that affairs were more or less settled, Marcus knew he could not delay his journey into Yorkshire any longer, and by mid-morning on the day following Adam's departure from Brook Street he was boarding the train for York at King's Cross railway station, having briefly broken his journey for just long enough to bid his aunt goodbye and to express the wish that she and Alexandra have an enjoyable stay in Hertfordshire.

Any hopes Marcus may have had of having a few moments alone with Sophy before he left were instantly put to flight as Emily, taking it into her head to pay her mother an unexpected visit at the very same moment as her cousin, rendered any chance of a private word with her out of the question. Charlotte, whose efforts to draw her daughter out of the sitting room to allow her nephew and daughter-in-law a few minutes alone proved futile as Emily, who stood in no little awe of her cousin as well as hating the thought that she could possibly appear to disadvantage in his eyes, seemed determined to absolve herself of any prejudice or lack of feeling by explaining to Marcus her reasons to account for her behaviour towards Alexandra, attributing it to the shock of her father's death quickly followed by that of her brother and her present condition. As all Marcus wanted to do right now was to take Sophy in his arms and kiss her, his cousin's self-exculpatory confession was not only ill-timed but wholly insincere, but Emily, in complete ignorance as to the true state of affairs existing between her cousin and sister-in-law, either because she did not want to appear in a bad light to her cousin or whether to prove to her mamma that she was not above admitting a fault, was still exonerating herself of any wrong-doing as she heard Marcus say it was time he was leaving. Good manners prevented him from telling Emily what he really thought about her behaviour as well as compelling him into accepting her company to the front door with further explanations tripping off her tongue as she did so, but despite her confession something told him that she was not in the least repentant. Over her head his eyes met Sophy's, and whilst it was small consolation for not being able to take her in his arms and kiss her goodbye, what he saw in those hazel depths went some way to making up for it.

Sophy was indeed sorry not to have been granted so much as five minutes alone with Marcus, and Charlotte, who had no qualms in leaving the two of them together, did not want to alert her daughter to the truth just yet, but to have attempted to divert Emily to grant them a few minutes alone would have made her instantly suspicious. Charlotte could therefore do nothing more than watch helplessly as Marcus and Sophy bid one another a polite goodbye in the hall, neither of them giving Emily the least cause to suspect just how difficult their parting was. Emily, totally unaware that she had thwarted a tender goodbye, walked calmly back to the sitting room with her mamma while Sophy, following resignedly behind, wondered when she would see Marcus again. Happily for her, however, he had, immediately upon his arrival in Yorkshire, wrote to her saying how sorry he was not to have been granted a moment alone with her prior to his departure, but hoped to be back in London in time to escort her to Timothy's.

Unfortunately, his business took far longer to transact than he had envisaged and he wrote to advise Sophy that he would, regrettably, not be back in town to see her safely transported into Kent. She was naturally disappointed but did not mind too much as she would have Ellen to keep her company on the journey, happily telling herself that they would have the rest of their lives together, and this pleasant thought, stubbornly refusing to go away, occupied her mind during the train journey into Kent the day after Charlotte and Alexandra had left for Hertfordshire.

Like Alexandra, Sophy was conscious of the need to escape from Brook Street with its all too unpleasant memories and overcharged atmosphere, and in her eagerness to leave all of this behind her she set out on her journey in a mood of considerable excitement and buoyancy. So far removed from her state of mourning was her relief on leaving the home she had shared with her husband that had her mamma have witnessed her smiling face she would most certainly have given her a sharp reminder of her recent bereavement. As it was, she was far too indisposed to see her daughter set off on her trip to Timothy's, but had, somewhat magnanimously, allowed Harriet to do so with instructions to tell her sister that her mamma, whose state of nerves were such that her doctor deprecated her leaving the house quite yet, hoped that a stay in the country with her brother and sister-in-law would soon restore her to equanimity which, sadly, could not be said of herself. If Harriet saw anything in Sophy's demeanour to suggest that she was feeling anything but unhappy or distressed she made no comment, but as she loved her sister very much Harriet would never have dreamed of informing against her to her mamma, but simply kissed her affectionately and told her to give Timothy and Annabel her love.

Arriving at Maidstone only minutes before Timothy's carriage came into Sophy's view, there was barely time for her to ensure that their luggage had been collected by a porter, but upon seeing the familiar face amongst a crowd of strangers she immediately forgot everything as he jumped out and hurried towards her, hugging her with brotherly fervour, her reply to this a mixture of laughter and tears. It was wonderful to see him again after so long, catching up on all the news and gossip as they trotted at a sedate pace along the country lanes, the smell of blossom wafting deliciously into the carriage through the open windows.

End House, a red-bricked Queen Anne building, which, if all Sophy had ever heard was true, boasted quite an interesting and varied history, was situated about five miles south of Maidstone, nestling on the edge of the village of Church Warping, two miles to the north of Royal Tunbridge Wells. Timothy was naturally very proud of the improvements he had made to the house and estate, telling his sister that he could not wait to show her around, excitedly informing her that she would hardly recognise the place from when their father was alive.

It had been nearly twelve months since she had last seen her brother and sister-in-law, but whilst Timothy had changed hardly at all she could barely hide her surprise at the sight of Annabel. She had lost weight and tired easily and her recent false alarm had taken its toll, rendering her nervous and anxious, the slightest sound making her jump. Her pretty face, alarmingly drawn and pale, reflected the strain of what was proving to be a difficult pregnancy.

Her excitement at presenting her husband with their first born in four months' time had been tempered by the distressing and severe bouts of nausea which had attacked her almost from the beginning as well as having experienced the stressful ordeal of two false alarms of a miscarriage, and as she later confided to Sophy when they were alone on her first evening, her greatest fear was that she may lose yet another baby. Sophy did her best to soothe her fears, but as these were very real to her convincing Annabel that everything would be all right took time and all Sophy's powers of persuasion. There was no denying that Annabel was extremely distraught, but by the time Sophy eventually left her laid down upon her bed she appeared quite calm and inclined to sleep, and as Sophy believed in the benefits of this old and trusted remedy, quietly closed the door behind her and joined her brother downstairs in the cosy library situated at the rear of the house, a wonderfully cluttered and untidy room.

Timothy, having just finished his after-dinner glass of port, rose to his feet at her entrance. "How is she?" he asked urgently, his concern etched into every inch of his face.

"Better," Sophy was pleased to inform him. "She is asleep, and I think if she is not disturbed will remain so until the morning."

He nodded, but it was clear that he too was feeling the strain of Annabel's pregnancy, and his concern over her well-being and their unborn child was poured into his sister's ears. She did not mind. Sophy was pleased that he found himself able to confide in her, knowing that he would feel the better for it. The likeness between brother and sister was not in their features so much as in certain facial expressions and mannerisms, and whilst each of them were tall, she was slender and by far more graceful in her carriage and movements than her brother, whose lean physique clearly evinced a masculine energy and strength. Where her eyes were a warm hazel his were a darkish brown, and instead of possessing his sister's rich auburn hair he had to be content with a rather nondescript light brown, which was as unruly as hers was elegantly confined.

Having inherited the estate in Kent from his father, Timothy had settled easily into the life of a country gentleman, but unlike his patriarch he was liked and well respected by his tenants. No one who had known the late Roland Lessington could ever remember him so much as passing the time of day with one, let alone rolling up his sleeves and giving a helping hand at busy times like harvesting. Roland Lessington had been a wealthy man whose business interests had covered a wide field, ranging from heavy investments in the manufacturing industries in the midlands and the north to rich and fertile lands in the south; all of which had brought him enormous profits. It had been through his shrewd investments which had brought him into contact with Matthew Harrington, their growing financial partnership finally resulting in what Timothy personally believed to be a catastrophic marriage between his sister and Charles Harrington. Roland's widow, never taking the trouble to hide her dislike of country life, had only ever set foot in the house half a dozen times, much preferring the sophisticated elegance of the house in Mayfair which she shared with her unmarried daughter.

Timothy had always been very fond of his younger sister, Harriet, as well as regarding it as a great pity that her affliction not only rendered her acutely uncomfortable about venturing into society very often but making it necessary for her to remain at home with their opinionated mamma. Elspeth Lessington may frequently be heard to bemoan the fact that she still had a daughter on her hands, who, it seemed, was destined never to take a walk down the aisle, but as she all too often relied on her own frail, though imaginary, constitution and delicate state of nerves, to ensure that her offspring danced continual attendance on her, her undutiful son knew perfectly well that she enjoyed his sister's constant pandering to her wishes too much to be without her. He knew too that should the day ever dawn when Harriet did announce her intention to marry, his mamma could certainly be relied upon to argue against it on several points, but it could not be denied that her unceasing claims on Harriet did nothing to help her either overcome her affliction or to meet a personable young man.

But however fond he was of Harriet it was his youngest sister, Sophy, with whom he was closest, indeed, he was more in tune with her than any other member of his family. From childhood, they had always been friends, having many interests in common and sharing the same sense of humour, and as they grew older, even though they formed their own circle of friends and acquaintances, he had nevertheless kept a brotherly eye on her. It had therefore been to his dismay when he learned of his father's intention to marry her to Charles Harrington, a man who, from the moment they had first met, Timothy had taken in dislike, his autocratic temperament leaving him no doubt that he was far from being the right kind of man for his sister. It was not for him to question his father's decisions regarding either of his sisters, but even though Sophy had passed the age of her majority and was at liberty to dictate her own affairs, it came as no surprise to him when she had not argued against the marriage; being dutiful as well as loyal, his father, treating a connection with the Harrington family as nothing more than a financial arrangement, had played heavily on these qualities.

Sophy had never spoken of her marriage but knowing her as well as he did there was no need for any confessions or confidences. On the few occasions Timothy had been in their company he had witnessed enough to know that his sister was far from happy in her marriage, and the frustration and impotence he had felt on being unable to do anything about it, only served to increase his dislike of his brother-in-law.

Sophy was not unaware of his feelings, but always reluctant to inflame them, she kept her own counsel, and seeing no point now in resurrecting the past or Charles's behaviour towards her, concentrated her energies on turning Timothy's mind from Charles's conduct to Annabel. She wished there was more she could do to help other than sit and listen sympathetically to the difficulties of her sister-in-law's pregnancy and was just wondering what she could possibly do when Timothy asked her how she felt about remaining with them until the baby was born. "I realise, of course," he told her, "that you may have other things planned, but since you can't further them until your period of mourning is over, we would like you to stay here. Annabel likes you, indeed, she loves you very much, you have always known that," he smiled, "apart from which, you seem to have a calming effect on her."

As Charles's widow, Brook Street would always be her home, at least until such time that she ever remarried, but since returning there was something she was by no means inclined to do and resuming residence with her mamma, even as only an interim measure, had its disadvantages, Timothy's suggestion found instant favour with her. "If you think I can be of some benefit to Annabel," Sophy smiled up at him, "then, of course, I should be delighted to stay."

"Only if you are sure," he warned. "I do not want you to think that we are imposing on you."

"You're not," Sophy assured him. "Nothing could please me more."

"Well, that settled, then," he smiled, his relief written on his face.

"I shall do all I can to help," she promised him. "Of course, never having been in Annabel's situation, I can't promise to be of any real practical help."

"Just being here will do her the world of good!" he nodded.

And so it proved. During the days which followed Annabel grew more relaxed, even content, and all her tension and fears seemed to leave her. Endorsing the doctor's instructions that she rest as much as possible, Sophy encouraged her sister-in-law to sit outside now that the weather was beginning to improve and, with a shawl around her shoulders and a blanket across her knees, Annabel felt more like herself than she had for some considerable time. It was becoming noticeable that the colour was returning to her cheeks and her appetite, waning alarmingly over recent weeks, was starting to pick up again.

So pleased was Timothy with Annabel's improved state of health that he told his sister when they were alone one afternoon that he had never seen her looking better. "I can't tell you the difference it has made having you here. She seems to mind you more than Doctor Powell." He hesitated a moment before saying tentatively, "I could, however, say the same of you. You're looking more like the sister I once knew since you have been here, or is it, perhaps," he smiled, "your correspondent?" looking from Sophy's slightly flushed face to the letter in her hand which had been delivered that morning. "I have no wish to pry into your private affairs," he assured her earnestly, "but I could not help noticing that the handwriting on the envelope is the same as on the one you received last week – and on the one the week before."

Sophy could not deny that over the last few weeks she too had begun to feel the benefit of those lazy afternoons sitting beneath the warmth of the early May sunshine, sheltered from the wind by the yew hedge which surrounded the small and secluded garden which Timothy had had specially created for Annabel. Sophy had not realised until now just how tired and tense she had been and how the strain over the last month or so had taken away some of her sparkle, but those relaxing hours she had spent with Annabel, doing nothing more strenuous than reading a book or setting a stitch at her embroidery, had certainly had a beneficial effect on her. She wondered what her brother would say when she told him that her revitalised appearance was not only attributable to long lazy days spent in the heart of the Kent countryside but to a very human and far more personal reason as well as the pleasurable prospect of what lay ahead for her and Marcus.

She held Timothy's searching gaze, not the first one he had directed at her since her arrival, her eyes smiling up into his with a mischievous look he recognised only too well. He had not seen that look for a long time, since before her marriage to Charles in fact, and he waited in silence for her to tell him what was on her mind. She could not, of course, confide what Charles had planned for Alexandra to him, although her reluctance to do so was not merely to protect his reputation. The story was not hers alone; it involved others who may prefer to keep recent events to themselves. She knew she could trust Timothy not to divulge it to anyone, but she was disinclined to tell him something which would only serve to feed his already deep dislike of his late brother-in-law. Such an unpleasant and painful episode could never be totally forgotten, but in time Sophy had every reason to hope that it would naturally diminish in significance until fading into the background of her memory where it belonged. She eyed her brother, wondering whether to tell him about her and Marcus and how they hoped to marry at some point in the future following her period of mourning. He would have to be told some time, besides, she did not like keeping it from him. She did not think he would mind, after all he had known Marcus for a long time, and although their paths had gone diverse way since leaving Oxford, she knew she liked him.

Timothy, watching the various expressions flit across his sister's face, shrewdly suspected that she wanted to tell him something and, unless he was very much mistaken, he felt sure that it had a lot to do with her letters, or, to be more precise, her correspondent, so, deciding to put an end to her agony of indecision, asked her if something was wrong. Encouraged by his smile, Sophy took a deep breath and haltingly explained who the letters were from and the reason for them, trying to read his thoughts as she did so. Although Timothy believed in certain standards of behaviour, especially where the women in his family were concerned, Sophy knew him to be neither judgemental nor unfeeling, and therefore looked for a not unfavourable response to her confession.

He may not have been displeased at her disclosure but he was nevertheless quite surprised by it, and for several moments he found himself looking at his sister in a completely new light. However, honesty compelled him to admit that he could easily see why she had fallen in love with Marcus; he was a very personable man and, compared to Charles Harrington, a far better candidate for his sister's hand. He easily acquitted her and Marcus of conducting an affair behind Charles's back but he nevertheless felt it incumbent upon him to question Sophy further. She may be of an age whereby she did not need approval or guidance, being her own mistress, but he would hate to think that she had mistaken her feelings. Her response to this, however, was categorical, and by the time she had left him he was convinced that her feelings for Marcus were genuine and not merely a case of finding his company more agreeable than that of her husband.

Nevertheless, Timothy had the feeling that there was something she was not telling him. Although he had dismissed the idea of her indulging in an affair behind Charles's back, he could not rid himself of the thought that her relationship with Marcus went far deeper than the result of their being thrown together during his convalescence, but refraining from pressing her he had assured her, in reply to her question, that he would have no objection to Marcus visiting her, and whilst he would happily give them both his blessing as well as his approval, he felt it only right that he speak to Marcus privately first. As Timothy watched Sophy through the window on her way to join Annabel in her sheltered haven, it struck him that whilst he was certain his sister had not mistaken her heart, he could not rid himself of the feeling that she had not told him everything as well as being somewhat relieved when her confidence came to an end.

Sophy was indeed glad to have scaled the hurdle of informing her brother about her feelings for Marcus and their wish to marry eventually, but she sensed he was far from convinced that she had told him everything. It had been impossible for her to do so, however, and although she hated to deceive him she shrank from imparting such a dreadful confession to a man whose very life was grounded in truth and integrity; a confession which would have done nothing to bring about a change in his feelings for the man his sister had not long buried.

Chapter Twenty-Five

From Marcus's letters Sophy learned that affairs at the mill had rendered it necessary for him to remain in Yorkshire for longer than he had thought, but had, whilst there, taken the opportunity of spending several enjoyable evenings with Adam and Isabel, both of whom sent her their warmest wishes. As Marcus intended to break his journey into Kent to visit his aunt in Hertfordshire he could not say at this juncture precisely when he expected to be with her, but he hoped it would not be too many days distant as he longed to see her again.

His visit was sooner than she had expected, arriving at End House within ten days of receiving his last letter, taking her unaware one afternoon as she sat alone in the small garden, Annabel having gone for a carriage drive with Timothy. The book Sophy had started reading two days before had long since begun to pall, and just as she was on the point of consigning it back to Timothy's library shelf the sound of footsteps approaching on the gravel drive which skirted the yew hedge made her look up. She could hear Timothy's voice as well as Annabel's, and there was another, deep and distinct and as familiar to her as her own. Sophy could make out very little of what they were saying, but that was not important. She held her breath expectantly until eventually they turned the corner into the garden, her book falling to the ground forgotten as she rose hurriedly to her feet, her face suddenly lighting up with a glow her brother had never seen before. She looked from one to the other, a little bemused, until Timothy broke the spell by saying cheerfully, "We have brought you a visitor, Sophy. We came upon him as we turned into the driveway just as he was alighting from a carriage."

"Marcus!" she cried, her impulse to run into his arms having to be strenuously checked.

"Sophy," Marcus said quietly, his voice not quite steady as he raised her hand to his lips.

She could feel the strength of his fingers, her own trembling in his, her face delicately flushed. "I... I..." she faltered faintly, shaking her head. "It... it is so *good* to see you."

If Timothy had any lingering doubts where Marcus and his sister was concerned the look on her face when she had seen him and the way they were looking at one another now, immediately put them to flight; there was no doubt in his mind that they were very much in love. The unspoken messages which passed between them, their eyes not quite able to hide all they felt, told their own story, and Timothy, who had every faith in Marcus behaving just as he ought towards Sophy, experienced no qualms, even though he did perhaps hold her hand a little longer than he should!

Marcus knew from Sophy's letter, which he had received just before he left Yorkshire in response to his last one, that she had not told Timothy anything about what had occurred over recent months but had confided the truth to him about the two of them. Marcus fully understood why she had done so, but nevertheless he felt it incumbent upon him to speak to Timothy himself and sought for a way to get him on his own at the earliest opportunity for him to do so. As it happened it was Annabel who provided it for him. Smiling up at Marcus, she apologised for having no refreshments ready but would arrange for something to be brought out to them as soon as possible, then, looking at Timothy, suggested he show Marcus around the place and the improvements he had made while they were waiting, and since her husband needed very little encouragement to show off several years' laborious work, this found instant favour. Leaving the ladies seated beneath the shade of a heavily blossomed lilac tree, unaware that Annabel had cleverly manoeuvred the situation for her to ply Sophy with questions, Timothy strolled away with Marcus.

As soon as the two men were lost from sight, Annabel, having heard Timothy speak of his friendship with Marcus Ingleby, immediately gripped Sophy's arm, insisting that she tell her everything. "I know Timothy made me promise him that I would not mention it to you, but Sophy you *cannot* be so cruel as to keep it from me!"

Sophy laughed. "There is really very little to tell."

But Annabel would not be put off. Sophy was not entirely surprised to learn that Timothy had told Annabel about her and Marcus, and whilst she had no objections to her knowing it would not do for her to learn the truth about Charles, and therefore considered it prudent to leave out certain aspects of her story.

Upon hearing Sophy's edited version of events, Annabel clapped her hands ecstatically. "Oh, it is *so* romantic!" For her part, she had no difficulty in understanding why her sister-in-law had fallen in love with Marcus; compared to Charles he was a far better proposition for someone as gentle and kind as Sophy. She had only met Charles about half a dozen times and she had never liked him, in fact, she had been a little afraid of him and had not envied Sophy being married to him, but this she wisely kept to herself.

Sophy, listening to her sister-in-law with only half an ear, could still not quite believe that Marcus was here. It seemed so long since she had seen him and found it almost impossible to realise that she was not dreaming. She had no doubt whatsoever that he would tell Timothy about Charles's recent activities, in fact, she hoped he would, because then it would prevent her from having to lie to him or, which was infinitely worse, deceive him should he ever question her.

It had been quite a while since the two men had met, the last time being almost twelve months ago when Timothy had paid a brief call on his sister during a flying visit to town and Marcus happened to be in Brook Street at the time. Naturally, Timothy was eager to catch up on all the news since then, after which Marcus listened with keen interest to Timothy, whose pride in his estate was patently obvious, and it was therefore some time before Marcus could forge the opening to tell him about his feelings for Sophy and their hopes for the future as well as his cousin's far from commendable undertakings. Timothy was inordinately proud of all he had achieved since he had inherited the property from his father, so much so that he got quite carried away as he explained how much work had had to be done before they could even begin preparing the ground to either grow crops or graze cattle. Marcus, genuinely interested as well as very much impressed by what he saw and heard, complimented Timothy with a sincerity that brought something close to a boyish grin to his lips, however, it was not until they had left the formal gardens at the rear of the house behind that Marcus was finally able to tell Timothy about himself and Sophy.

Had the opportunity presented itself he would have told Timothy precisely how things stood before now, but circumstances having intervened to prevent him from doing so he was more than a little relieved to finally discuss it with him. As Marcus was not a man who liked shelving his responsibilities, much preferring to be the one to do his own explaining, he eyed Timothy squarely, saying directly, "You must know I would have been here sooner were it not for the fact that I have been in Yorkshire on business."

Timothy understood the requirements of business only too well, having been indoctrinated into its importance by his ruthless and determined father at an early age, and easily acquitted Marcus of hiding behind Sophy's skirts. Timothy liked Marcus very much, he always had; he was honest and trustworthy and a man of the utmost integrity, nevertheless, he felt impelled to ask some pretty pertinent questions, questions he found impossible to put to Sophy.

Marcus fully understood his concerns, but although he commended Timothy on his natural desire to protect his sister he knew he could not answer his questions without telling him about Charles's recent dealings, and he decided that the only way to explain everything to Timothy's satisfaction was to tell him the truth.

Whatever Timothy may think about his late brother-in-law he had never once believed him capable of doing anything like what he was hearing, and when Marcus came to the end of his not very edifying account Timothy stopped dead in his tracks. "*Good God!* He must have been out of his senses!"

"One could be forgiven for thinking so," Marcus concurred, "but the whole thing was planned and executed with clear mindedness and precision."

"But surely to God he did not honestly think he was going to get away with it!" Timothy cried, aghast.

"I am very much afraid that he did," Marcus told him. "At no point did he even contemplate failure or that something could go wrong to foil his plans. My intervention," he pointed out, "was regarded as nothing more than a mere setback." Timothy shook his head in horror and disbelief, his eyes staring incredulously up at Marcus, who explained, "So desperate was he to avoid the truth coming out about the deception he had perpetrated with Elizabeth's jewellery that he was fully prepared to go to any lengths and, as I have already said, he was not loath to using either myself or Sophy to achieve his ends."

It was apparent to Marcus that Timothy was struggling with several emotions, not the least being an overwhelming anger over Charles's callous and cold-blooded usage of his sister. "I can't believe that he had the nerve to use Sophy for such an infamy!" Without waiting for Marcus to respond, he cried savagely, "*My god,* if he hadn't met his end when he did I would have killed him myself!" He raised a shaking hand to his forehead. "I cannot believe he thought so little of her, or of you for that matter. To think that he was prepared to keep you tied up in that cellar then do away with you!" He was clearly overcome. "Thank God Adam came along when he did!"

"His timing was certainly opportune," Marcus remarked with feeling.

"Yes." Timothy nodded his agreement. "Then, if all that was not bad enough," he cried horror-struck, "he blackmailed you with Sophy's life! It is beyond all comprehension," still unable to take in the enormity of what he had heard. "That he should go to such lengths to cover up something he had no right to do in the first place goes beyond all reasoning."

"I am afraid that as far as Charles was concerned reasoning never came into it," Marcus told him. "At all costs, he had to avoid the truth coming out about those two pieces he had removed and substituted with copies. Once Alexandra took possession of her mother's jewellery it would only have been a matter of time before the deception was discovered. There was absolutely no possibility of Charles finding such a sum to redeem them in so short a time."

"What beats me," Timothy shook his head, bewildered, "is how he managed to find someone prepared to make copies of them, and," he nodded, "loan him sufficient money to recover those letters."

"I am in no doubt whatsoever that it was someone already known to Charles; he would not have taken the risk of going to a reputable jeweller, indeed," Marcus shook his head, "no respectable jeweller would have touched such a job."

"A Cranbourn Alley merchant!" Timothy supplied knowingly.

"It would seem so," Marcus nodded. "In any event, he must be found and those pieces recovered."

"Yes, but that's not going to be an easy task," Timothy pointed out, "unless, of course, there was something amongst Charles's papers."

Marcus sighed. "Not being privileged to have seen any of his papers I can't say, but I doubt he would have been fool enough to leave something so incriminating for anyone to see. No," he shook his head, "I am convinced that this man Charles employed was someone well-known to him; most probably they had transacted business together before." They had by now walked round to the front of the house, but Timothy, still reeling from the shock of Marcus's confidences, stopped, looking thoughtfully down at the ground, his hands dug deep into his pockets. "He has to be found," Marcus told him, "but time is running out. At the moment, Alexandra appears to be in no hurry to even want to see them, indeed, when asked by my aunt before they left London if she would like to she said no, which is just as well," he sighed, relieved, "but sooner or later she will, if for no other reason than curiosity, and once that happens it will only be a matter of time before those two pieces are identified as copies. Unfortunately," he sighed again, "it was not possible for me to try to track down this man before I left for Yorkshire, but upon my return to town that is the first thing I must do. According to my aunt when I paid her a visit before coming here," he explained, "they seem to be pretty well fixed in Hertfordshire for some time yet, which, hopefully," he nodded, "will give me time to try to find this man and redeem those pieces."

"That's quite a mammoth task," Timothy sighed, "but I wish you luck," frustratingly kicking the ground with a well-shod foot. "Even so, finding one man amongst goodness only knows how many capable of such underhanded work is going to be the devil of a job! I would offer my services gladly," he told him truthfully, "but whilst Annabel is still far from well I must admit that I would prefer to remain within reach of here. Nevertheless," he added sincerely, "if there *is* anything I can do, I hope you will let me know."

"You may be sure of it. However," Marcus confessed, "I hope it won't come to that. What is it?" he asked, seeing a frown suddenly crease Timothy's forehead.

"Well, it has just occurred to me," he told him thoughtfully, "even supposing you do find this man and recover those pieces, how are you going to return them to Mercers' vaults without anyone knowing? What I mean is," he nodded, "you don't bank there yourself, and since you were not named as an executor to either Charles's will or your uncle's, how will you manage it?"

"I can't," Marcus smiled ruefully, "which is why I shall just have to rely on Silas Jenkins for that; no one is going to question Matthew's solicitor."

Timothy nodded, then, looking up at Marcus, mused, "So, Charlotte and the girl are in no hurry to return to Brook Street. Well," he conceded truthfully, "I can't say I blame them. The last time I was there the place was like a damned mausoleum, excepting your presence, of course!" he grinned.

"It can be a little oppressive," Marcus smiled, "but I think the main reason my aunt is happy to remain with her sister for the foreseeable future is because Amelia and George are still set against the girl, and Emily," he sighed. "Despite what she told me in order to account for her behaviour towards Alexandra, I am afraid there is no getting away from the fact that she will never be brought to accept her, in fact, whenever Emily visits her mother she makes no effort whatsoever to hide her dislike."

"They are going to have to accept her at some point," Timothy pointed out, "after all," he shrugged, "it *is* Charlotte's home, and they can't remain in Hertfordshire forever."

"I agree," Marcus acknowledged, "but according to my aunt, Alexandra is enjoying the attentions of the male population between the ages of twenty and thirty-five far too much to want to leave," he smiled. "However,

I do share my aunt's view in that it is a little too soon to be making any decisions in that area, although," he smiled, "Alexandra is more than capable of making up her own mind."

"Well, from what you have told me about the girl," Timothy said reasonably, "I think you are right." He looked up at Marcus, asking seriously, "Do you honestly believe that your aunt and the girl can be kept in ignorance of what happened?"

"How can they possibly get to hear about it?" Marcus asked. "Had the events of the past couple of months come to George's ears then I would have to say there was every likelihood of it, especially when you consider that he can never keep anything to himself, but I shall never tell them and neither will Sophy or Adam, and as for Jenkins, most definitely not. We are agreed that no good could possibly ensue from either of them knowing."

Timothy nodded his head in agreement, but it was apparent that something else was troubling him, and asked, "About this man, Knowles?"

"What about him?" Marcus cocked his head.

"Well, it's all very well saying you've seen the back of him, but a man like that could quite easily make things very awkward."

Marcus nodded. "I agree, but he does not want his part in the affair to come to light any more than we do ours. Do not forget," he reminded him, "a man like Knowles cannot afford to have anyone delving into his affairs, which, I am convinced, will not tolerate too much scrutiny any more than will those of his crony at *The Black Swan*'. I saw enough of him to feel reasonably certain that should Knowles decide, for whatever reason, to visit Bow Street after all, then the police will be the least of his problems!"

"Well, perhaps you're right," Timothy conceded doubtfully, "but I hope for your sake he *does* take himself off!"

"Believe me," Marcus told him with feeling, "you don't wish that any more than I do!"

Timothy accepted this, but it was apparent that something else was on his mind, and in response to an enquiring lift of Marcus's eyebrow, said hesitantly, "About you and Sophy. You must not think that I am not pleased about the two of you because I am, more than I can say, in fact," he remarked candidly, "I never did understand or approve of my father's wish for her to marry Charles, but why did neither of you say anything to me?"

"What could we have said?" Marcus replied calmly. "Whilst Charles was alive there was no hope of a future for us because there was no way he would ever have granted Sophy a divorce, and should she have filed for one the chances were very good that it would not have been granted; the results of which would have been disastrous for her, but even if she had not applied for a divorce there was no likelihood of her position improving, and should anything have leaked out about the two of us Charles would have taken it very badly, and Sophy was already enduring enough from him."

"I don't mind saying," Timothy told him frankly, "I am glad she is out of that marriage."

"No more than I am," Marcus said firmly. "Knowing there was nothing I could do other than helplessly stand aside and watch what passed as her marriage to Charles did nothing to endear him to me. All the same," he said earnestly, "I never wanted Charles's death just so I could marry her."

"There's no need to tell me that," Timothy shook his head, "I know you didn't, but you must admit," he nodded, "that had he lived your future together looked extremely bleak." Marcus nodded, and Timothy, unconsciously echoing Adam's thoughts, felt it reasonably safe to say that had Marcus redeemed those pieces, not only to save the girl but Charles's reputation as well as his life, his thanks would not have run to relinquishing Sophy, but as Timothy had no doubt that Marcus was as aware of this as he was he refrained from mentioning it and merely smiled, saying, "I know Sophy needs neither my permission nor approval to marry whomsoever she wishes, but I want you to know, for what it is worth, that once her period of mourning is over, I shall have no objections to you asking for her hand in marriage, *nor*," he grinned, patting Marcus on the shoulder, "shall I object to you visiting Sophy while she is here."

Marcus shook his hand, smiling. "Thank you. I know Sophy will appreciate that, as I do." Timothy nodded. "You need have no fears for your sister," Marcus assured him. "My only desire is, and always has been, to make her happy, and I shall do so by whatever means in my power."

"Even if I hadn't known you all these years and that you are a man of your word," Timothy told him, "I only have to look at Sophy's face to know you already do!" Then, giving Marcus his promise that what he had told him about Charles would go no further, they began to make their way back to the sheltered garden.

Annabel, delighted to hear of the romance which had sprung to life and been kept a secret all this time between her sister-in-law and Marcus, a man she instinctively knew she liked even though she had never laid eyes on him before, invited him to sit beside her upon his return to the garden with her husband, unable to hide the conspiratorial look in her eyes as she smiled up at him. Timothy, drawing his sister a little to one side told her what had passed between himself and Marcus, and Sophy, relieved that he knew the truth at last, heaved a sigh of relief in that she would no longer have to go on deceiving her brother.

Marcus, declining their invitation to remain at End House overnight, having already arranged accommodation at '*The Crown*' in Maidstone, gratefully took up their offer to dine with them, remarking to Sophy in an amused aside as she entered the house on his arm, "I get the feeling that Timothy is going to ask me about my prospects!"

The look she gave him was not lost on Timothy walking behind them with Annabel on his arm, realising in that moment that even if he had the power to forbid their marriage he would not do so. He had never seen his sister so happy, and even though no offer of marriage could yet be put forward, he was genuinely pleased for her.

Dinner was served early, a relaxed affair which placed no demands on anyone, and Sophy, in between talking to Annabel and responding naturally to comments or questions by either of the two men she loved most in the world, was simply content to sit and look at Marcus as he and Timothy conversed easily on any number of topics; so very different to the strained atmosphere which had prevailed over the dining table at Brook Street. Annabel, whose imagination had taken flight upon learning of their romantic love story, could not help casting periodic glances from one to the other, observing with satisfaction the looks which were frequently exchanged between them, her mind busily making plans even before she rose from the dinner table.

Having spent a most happy and agreeable day it was with reluctance that Marcus said it was time he was leaving, to which Timothy immediately sent word to the stables to bring the carriage round to the front door in ten minutes to drive his guest back to Maidstone. Thanking them for their hospitality, Marcus then bid them goodnight and, after raising Annabel's hand to his lips, was left to have a private word with Sophy, the first they had had since he arrived.

She was naturally pleased to hear news of Charlotte and Alexandra, but fully agreed with Marcus that it was far too soon for Alexandra to be making plans about her future. "I have no doubt, though," she smiled up at him, "that she has very definite views on what she wants."

"I agree," Marcus nodded. "I have seen enough of her to know that she will not be pushed into doing something she has no mind for."

"But about her inheritance?" Sophy queried. "Are you really saying that she has no wish to see the jewellery?"

"Apparently not, at least for now," he nodded, "but she will, which is why my first task on returning to London must be to try to find this man who holds the originals."

"But isn't that going to be rather difficult?" she asked anxiously.

"I have no doubt it will have its setbacks," Marcus conceded, "but he must be found."

"And if you do find them and get them back," she asked, looking concernedly up into his face, "how will you return them?"

"I am afraid I shall have to rely on Jenkins to do that," he told her. "I could not possibly return them myself. It would be different if I banked at Mercers or if I had been appointed as executor to Matthew's will, or even Charles's will come to that, but as I have not, then my reason for visiting the vaults would immediately be questioned, and that," he pointed out, "would not do at all."

"No, of course not." She shook her head. He saw a slight frown suddenly descend onto her forehead, asking gently if something was wrong. "No, not wrong precisely," she said slowly, "it's just that... well, was Timothy very angry about what Charles had planned?"

"Let us just say," he told her, "that he was profoundly shocked, which," he nodded, "is really quite understandable."

"Yes," she sighed, "I knew he would be, but, Marcus," she urged, "Annabel must never know," she said firmly. "I love her very much, but the fewer people who know the better."

"Timothy will not say anything to anyone," he assured her, "not even to Annabel."

"Oh, it's all so dreadfully deceitful!" she cried, wringing her hands. "But what else can we *do*, Marcus?"

He took hold of her hands and drew her a little to him. "Nothing," he said gently. "It has been a most painful and regrettable affair, and whilst I hate the deception as much as you and Adam, I am afraid there is nothing we can do but accept it as best we may."

"Yes," Sophy sighed, "I know, but it has all been so very distressing."

"Yes, it has," Marcus agreed, "for all of us, but whilst we cannot deceive ourselves into thinking that we shall be able to forget what has happened in a hurry, we must take what comfort we can from knowing that Alexandra is safe and Charles's reputation is intact."

Sophy nodded, but her eyes clouded a little. "I know, but I wish..."

"I know what you wish," Marcus said softly, comfortingly squeezing her hands, "and you do not wish that any more than I do, but we must keep in mind that whilst all our efforts were not enough to save Charles they did ensure his name would remain untarnished."

"Oh, I know," she agreed fervently, "and despite everything I am glad of that, but I... oh, Marcus," she cried, "I could not have borne any of it without you!"

"Couldn't you?" he asked, his voice a caress.

She shook her head. "No, any more than I can now bear the thought of not seeing you as often as I should like for twelve whole months!"

"I see," he said slowly, looking warmly down at her. "In that case," he smiled, "it is just as well that Timothy has given me permission to visit you whenever I wish, isn't it?"

"He... he has?" she asked a little breathlessly.

"Mm," he nodded.

"I... I didn't think he would object," she faltered, "but I am so glad!"

"So am I," he said relieved, "but he's going to watch us like a mother hen."

"I know," she nodded, "but you must not blame him for that, Marcus."

"I don't," he shook his head. "In fact," he admitted, "if I were in his shoes I should feel just as protective towards my sister, no matter how honourable her intended's intentions were. However," he confessed, drawing her closer to him, "speaking as the man who loves you and is aching to make love to you, it's going to be unbearable knowing that my future brother-in-law is keeping a close on me and, to make matters worse," he conceded in a deepening voice, "is the agonising thought of having to wait another twelve long months before I can make you my wife."

Sophy looked up at him, all the love she had for him shining in her eyes, confessing a little guiltily, "I know it is; I feel it already."

Marcus laughed, a deep throated sound which sent a quiver of excitement running through her, then, drawing her into his arms, said, a little throatily, "So, you feel this waiting to be unbearable too, do you?"

"Yes," she said huskily, "because you see, Marcus, I love you so very much."

The only response he made to this was to hold her so tightly against him and kiss her with such need that not only did she believe her ribs would crack but that her lips would be bruised for days, but as these were mere irrelevancies she willingly gave herself up to his demands until, gradually, the urgency of his lips eased into long and loving kisses which made her melt even closer into him. Even though she and Charles had never been in love she supposed she should not be feeling like this, especially so soon after his brutal death, but the truth was there seemed to be nothing she could do to stop this overwhelming love and need she had for the man whose arms were crushing her to him. Somewhere at the back of her mind she was so very conscious of how easy it would be for her to give in to her emotions, and when Marcus hoarsely pressed against her lips, *"I love you, Sophy,"* she could only hope that she would have the strength of purpose to wait for the day she longed for and not surrender to the tempting of her heart, which, as she knew only too well, was very susceptible to him.

It was with a deep sense of loss that she finally bid Marcus goodnight, his kisses burning on her lips long after he had left, consoled only by the thought that Timothy had raised no objections to him visiting her.

*

That first visit by Marcus was the forerunner of others, although his regular trips to Yorkshire, quite often necessitating lengthy stays, rendered it impossible for him to see Sophy as often as he would have liked, and whilst Timothy had no objection to him seeing his sister, he nevertheless deemed it to be his duty to keep a watchful eye on the happy couple. Annabel, when finally venturing downstairs having been safely delivered of a healthy son, had watched her husband's clumsy attempts to ensure his sister was not alone for too long with Marcus, with fond indulgence. She could quite easily understand Timothy's very natural concern, but she had nevertheless considered it prudent to gently remind him that they were not in the least likely to do anything reprehensible. He knew she was right, but it did not prevent him from feeling in some sort responsible for his sister.

Marcus may want to make love to Sophy with every fibre of his being, but far from wishing to steal a few moments with her for this purpose, he had instead very definite plans for this very special moment in their lives, and he was therefore able to witness his future brother-in-law's efforts with an amused eye.

Chapter Twenty-Six

When Marcus had set himself the task of seeking out Charles's disreputable jeweller, he had known it would be no easy matter to track down one man among many capable of such work. If his suppositions were correct, then he doubted this discreditable individual conducted his illicit dealings amongst those ethical exponents of their art in Hatton Garden, but after only a very little thought he had every reason to believe that his search may not prove as daunting as he had originally supposed.

Although he had never lost hope of placing his ring on Sophy's finger, Marcus was honest enough to admit that there had been times when he had come to believe this joyous and longed-for day would never arrive, but although their marriage may be some little way in the future, he had every intention of bestowing something very special on the woman without whom his life would be entirely empty and meaningless.

*

Cornelius Royston, a man his father had recognised as a master of his craft and from whom he had often commissioned special pieces of jewellery for his mother, fortunately still traded from his premises in Leather Lane in that most notable quarter of town and knowing he could rely on this man to create something exceptional for the woman he loved and adored, Marcus had no hesitation in paying him a visit. It could also be that at some point during his transactions with him he could forge an opening which might help him in his search.

Cornelius Royston, upon seeing Marcus's tall figure enter his place of business, greeted him with unalloyed pleasure, shaking him warmly by the hand before ushering him into his private back room with instructions to his son that he did not wish to be disturbed. As expected, it was not many minutes before Royston was happily recalling fond memories of how, as a boy, Marcus had often accompanied his father when he had come to

503

choose something that little bit special for his mother, interspersing these reminiscences with recounting amusing anecdotes, ending by saying how sorry he had been to hear of his accident. "But look at you now, Mr. Marcus!" he smiled, his pale blue eyes twinkling. "Well I *never!*" He shook his head.

"I see *you* haven't changed, Royston," Marcus smiled.

"Well, as to that, Mr. Marcus," he grinned, patting his thickening girth, "I wouldn't like to say." Marcus laughed. "Now," Royston nodded, "what is it you would like me to do for you, Mr. Marcus?"

"I would like you to make a *very* special necklace, Royston," Marcus nodded, "for a *very* special lady."

The pale blue eyes lit up. "Ah, I see." He nodded indulgently: "And the lady?" he urged tactfully, raising an enquiring eyebrow.

"Exquisitely beautiful," Marcus smiled, knowing perfectly well what Royston was thinking, "and, I am pleased to say, shortly to become my wife."

Upon hearing this Royston clapped his hands together ecstatically before shaking Marcus vigorously by the hand. "My *warmest* felicitations, Mr. Marcus!" he offered genuinely. "Allow me to wish you very happy."

"Thank you, Royston," Marcus smiled, once again having his hand enthusiastically shaken.

"*Now,*" Royston asked, the romantic in him coming to the fore, "do you have something specific in mind or, would you, perhaps, like me to show you our design plates?"

"Actually, Royston," Marcus said thoughtfully, "I *was* thinking of pearls; three rows, held together by an emerald clasp."

"An *excellent* choice if I may say so, Mr. Marcus!" he exclaimed, whereupon he rose to his feet and, pulling out a key on the end of a chain from his pocket, he unlocked the huge safe behind him, removing from one of the shelves two covered trays. Placing them almost reverently on the desk, he sat down and carefully removed the black felt covering of one of the trays to expose a myriad of pearls, one of which he picked up and, after eyeing it closely for a moment, handed it to Marcus. "You see," he said, "that lustre; that unmistakable iridescent sheen? Now, if you take this glass," he told him, handing him a magnifying eye glass, "look at the pearl and tell me what you see."

"Looks like irregularities of some kind," Marcus observed slowly, after scrutinising the pearl for several moments before looking up.

"Now, look at the others," Royston suggested, sliding the tray towards him, "tell me how they compare to the one you have just looked at."

"The same," Marcus said at length, having looked closely at them. "A slight differing in size and shade, perhaps."

"I see you have an eye, Mr. Marcus," Royston said appreciatively. "They are real saltwater pearls, which is why they differ somewhat in size and shade."

"They're beautiful, Royston," Marcus acknowledged, fingering the pearls, imagining them around Sophy's neck.

"Ah yes, Mr. Marcus," Royston nodded. "The finest saltwater pearls I have ever seen; far superior in quality than freshwater pearls, but, sadly," he shook his head, "a little too expensive for most people."

Marcus looked up from the pearl he was still holding, a smile lurking at the back of his eyes. "The lady is worth it, Royston," he said meaningfully, to which that astute man of business nodded comprehendingly.

As Marcus was admiring the pearls resting in the palm of his hand Royston uncovered the second tray, his forefinger running carefully over the uncut emeralds lying in their bed of soft fabric in front of him, picking one out and then another, which he looked at in turn through his eyeglass, finally handing one over to Marcus. "Exquisite, aren't they?" he raised an eyebrow. "Of course," he commented, "emeralds have many inclusions," he informed him, "imperfections you may call them, due to the way they are grown, but the richer the green, like these, the more expensive the stone, but I believe," he told him, "well worth it, indeed," he informed him, "they are much sought after, and the ancients, or so I understand, believed they encouraged good health and, if I may be permitted to say so," he smiled, "love."

"Exquisite, indeed!" Marcus admitted, holding it up to the light.

"Such perfect stones," Royston pointed out, "would splendidly complement such beautiful pearls as these."

"What about the cut, Royston?" Marcus enquired.

"Well," he replied, "it is usually best to do an octagonal cut for an emerald." Marcus raised an enquiring eyebrow at this. "Oh, yes, Mr. Marcus," Royston nodded. "You see, it not only helps the stone to retain its weight but also its colour."

Marcus nodded, then watched as Royston drew several quick sketches to show how the pearls and the emerald could be worked to their best advantage and, after about half an hour, the design had been agreed with Royston assuring him that he would cut the emerald himself. Upon being told by Marcus that he also wanted him to design a ring to celebrate their betrothal, Royston immediately exclaimed, "Diamonds, Mr. Marcus! I have the *very* thing, direct from Antwerp less than a month ago." Removing a velvet purse from the safe, he carefully opened it up and let fall onto his palm one solitary stone; a diamond of perfect clarity and colour. "Three carats, Mr. Marcus!" he told him in a rapt voice. "Have you ever seen a stone of such perfection?"

Marcus could not say that he had and, holding it up against the light, saw for himself, with the aid of Royston's eyeglass, that no inclusions could be seen; it was unquestionably flawless. "It's beautiful, Royston!" he breathed softly.

"Yes, it is," Royston sighed pleasurably. "If you look carefully, Mr. Marcus," he suggested, pointing a knowledgeable finger, "you will see that it requires no cutting; I bought it from Van Buden already cut, indeed, this particular cut is very much in vogue and most sought after with its shallow pavilion and more rounded shape with different arrangements of facets; beautiful!" he sighed. "Of course," he said, almost apologetically, "the higher the carat weight the…"

Marcus could not deny its beauty and, handing him back the diamond, smiled and, inclining his head, said significantly, "I can only repeat, Royston, the lady is worth it."

"I take it then," Royston raised an eyebrow, "it must be twenty-two carat gold?"

"Yes, Royston," Marcus nodded, "I am afraid it must."

The finer details having been worked out and decided upon, Marcus, knowing Sophy's finger size with unerring accuracy, made ready to take his leave, commenting as he rose to his feet, "My father was right about you, Royston."

"Indeed, Mr. Marcus!" he raised an eyebrow.

"Yes," Marcus smiled, speaking no less than the truth. "He always said you dealt in only the finest stones and gems."

"Ah," Royston nodded reminiscently, "your father knew a good stone when he saw one, Mr. Marcus, and, if I may say so, it was a pleasure to do business with him."

"I recall him saying once," Marcus remarked casually, hating the deceit he was playing on him, but considering what was at stake he knew he had to take advantage of this opportunity if he was to try to locate Charles's disreputable jeweller, "that you could tell an imitation from an original stone by merely glancing at it."

Cornelius Royston coloured slightly. "Well, that might be a slight exaggeration," he shrugged, "but," he conceded, "even though I *do* say so myself, one close look would be sufficient." He sighed. "It is a sad truth, Mr. Marcus," shaking his head, "but there are any number of imitation pieces around. I've had many a one cross my path," he confided, "some of them really excellent pieces of work too, but they have not got by me!"

"I imagine it would take great skill to copy a piece of jewellery," Marcus remarked interestedly.

"Oh, great skill," Royston told him firmly. "It involves a lot of work, but although they would pass a cursory inspection by someone who did not know their business, they would not get by a jeweller worthy of the name."

"Are there many disreputable people around who do this?" Marcus asked incredulously.

"Oh, yes, Mr. Marcus!" he confirmed, not at all surprised by Marcus's horror at such a thought. "Though not, I am happy to say, anyone of my professional acquaintance. No," he shook his head, "you would have to look elsewhere for a man capable of such despicable counterfeiting. Although," he confided, having suddenly recalled an instance to mind, "I *do* remember now there being just such a one; not two streets away in Turnmill Street it was, Mr. Marcus; been with Rutger for several years he had, honest as the day's long, or so old Reinhold Rutger thought, until he discovered he had been creating fake necklaces and such like and substituting them for the real ones which had been taken in for repair or a clean; oh, not distinctive pieces mind, only selected ones, if you know what I mean? And the poor customers not knowing a thing about it!"

"Good God!" Marcus cried, genuinely shocked.

"Yes, indeed, Mr. Marcus," he nodded, having no difficulty in fully understanding Marcus's feelings. "Don't think old Reini ever recovered from it."

"I don't wonder at it!" Marcus exclaimed.

"No," Royston sighed. "Poor Reini, and, of course," he said sadly, "to make it worse, the villain absconded before anything could be done to apprehend him."

"You mean he was never caught?" Marcus asked, genuinely surprised.

Cornelius Royston could do no more than shrug helpless shoulders. "No, I am afraid not," he told him regretfully. "Quite taken in by him was Reini, but although it goes against the grain with me to say it," he sighed reluctantly, "he *was* an artist, no question about it, Mr. Marcus; he could cut a stone with such delicacy and precision that it was a pleasure to watch him do it, but, then," he nodded shrewdly, "men like Leonard Webbley know how to ingratiate themselves!"

Whoever Charles had employed could certainly be called an artist, but whether this Leonard Webbley was the man who had created the imitation necklace and bracelet for his cousin remained to be seen, but if nothing else it was a name, and, surely, it had to be worth a try in attempting to track him down. Should it transpire that he was not his cousin's disreputable jeweller, and he stood every chance of not being, then he could well know of him or, at least, point him in the right direction. Marcus had no liking for using Cornelius Royston in such a devious way, but if the use to which Charles had put his sister's jewellery, culminating in the devastating trail of events which had followed, were not to be revealed at this stage, there was little choice open to him, besides which, it was only right that the originals were returned to the collection.

"The police never found him?" Marcus queried.

"No," Royston shook his head sadly, "unfortunately, they did not. However," he sighed, "I did hear that a man resembling him set up business elsewhere; Clerkenwell I think it was," he nodded, "or was it Islington?" he mused. "It was one or the other I am sure, but, of course, you know how rumours spread, Mr. Marcus?"

"Yes, I do," Marcus concurred, his brain racing. "And Mr. Rutger?" he queried politely. "Is he still in business?"

"Oh, yes," Royston nodded, "but not for much longer I fear. No son to take over, you see," he explained sadly.

Marcus replied suitably to this and, after remaining a few minutes longer, shook his hand and left, armed with more information than he could ever have hoped for. Clerkenwell; just a step from Islington where Charles had conducted his business. It could not be coincidence, surely!

*

Leonard Webbley, having deemed it wise to change his name after being unexpectedly discovered carrying out his underhanded sideline at Rutger's, had, for the past five years or so, conducted a gainful and law-abiding little jewellery business under the name of Linas Webb. This did not mean he had totally abandoned all the skills that he had deviously put to regular use and which had come to such an ill-timed end, not at all! Indeed, his skills had still been put to very good and profitable use since he had come to Clerkenwell, and since those of his clients who commissioned him to put whichever devious skill to use on their behalf were as eager for anonymity as much as himself it had proved most lucrative.

He had, of course, heard of the sudden and tragic death of Charles

Harrington, and although he had been somewhat taken aback at the news he had come to believe that since no one had been party to the transaction other than themselves, those precious pieces in his possession were now his sole property. Unfortunately for him, however, the unexpected arrival of Marcus Ingleby at his premises soon put this belief to flight.

Marcus's enquiries at half a dozen or so clock and watch making businesses, for which the area was renowned, had brought forth no favourable response about a Leonard Webbley much less his whereabouts, but just as he emerged from yet another premises with no promising news, if not discouraged then fast coming to the conclusion that he had been totally wrong in his assumption, he caught sight of the name '*Linas Webb – dealer in second-hand jewellery*' over the top of a door just across the street bordering a narrow alleyway. They were the same initials certainly, but, surely, that was nothing more than coincidence? Even so, he could not ignore it especially if there was the slightest chance of gleaning anything from this Linas Webb which may help him in his search, apart from which he could not totally dismiss his supposition that Charles's unscrupulous jeweller conducted his business in this locality; it was too close to the brewery to be merely chance!

The tinkling of the doorbell brought Linas Webb immediately into the front of the premises from his back room, standing behind the counter warily eyeing his tall and impeccably dressed visitor, unable to think what the likes of him was doing in his little backstreet shop. He may advertise himself as dealing in second-hand jewellery, but he knew as well as anyone that all the goods on show, excepting for those discreetly housed in his safe, were nothing more than cheap trinkets. Linas Webb had never laid eyes on this man before and the name on the card handed him was quite unknown to him, but, like Ted Knowles before him, he had the very strong feeling that he was vaguely familiar and, unless he was very much mistaken, he had the sneaking suspicion that this man boded no good for him. Denying all knowledge of anyone by the name of Leonard Webbley with a nonchalant shrug of his narrow shoulders, he handed Marcus back his card fully expecting him to leave, but upon seeing him make no effort to vacate his premises he asked if there was anything else he wanted, quite taken aback to hear him repeat his question.

Unless Marcus's instincts were misleading him, and he was certain they weren't, he sensed he had finally found the man with whom Charles had transacted business and this Linas Webb and Leonard Webbley were one and the same person, and if he remained here all day, Marcus was determined to leave with those two items of jewellery. He could only hazard a guess as to how Charles had come to meet this devious individual in the first place, but that he had done so he felt certain. Upon having his enquiry denied a second time Marcus drew a bow at a venture, saying, quite politely, "It would appear I am mistaken, even so," he frowned, as if in an effort of memory, "I could have sworn from Mr. Rutger's description that I had at last found Mr. Webbley."

Upon hearing the name of his past employer, Linas Webb's thin and sallow face paled and the slate grey eyes narrowed, but he was not going to be tricked into admitting his identity. Since he had no reason to connect this man with his late client or those precious items safely tucked away in his safe, he failed to see what he could possibly want with him. He had at first wondered whether Mr. Rutger had hired a private detective to track him down in a final attempt to bring him to justice, but one look at the swell standing in front of his counter put this idea to flight; no private detective would be wearing clothes which, unless he was very much mistaken, had Savile Row written all over them. Again, like Ted Knowles before him, Linas Webb saw the futility of either trying to trick this man into believing he had made a mistake or to try to bluff his way out; he was neither stupid nor blind and knew that whoever this Marcus Ingleby was, he was definitely no tec, much less a dupe, not only that, but from the looks of him he was going nowhere until he had some answers. Nevertheless, he had to do all he could to convince this man that he was mistaken, the last thing he wanted was to be faced with the law much less to handing over his precious hoard. Shaking his head and shrugging his shoulders, he said, "Who'd yer say?"

"Rutger," Marcus repeated, "Reinhold Rutger."

"No," Linas Webb shook his head again, "ain't neva 'eard of 'im eitha."

"Mm," Marcus pondered, "strange, that."

"Oh?" Linas Webb queried, his eyes narrowing even more.

"Yes," Marcus nodded. "You see, Mr. Leonard Webbley was in Mr. Rutger's employ until about five years ago when, after being discovered conducting his own illicit dealings on the premises, he just simply disappeared." He raised an eyebrow. "Turnmill Street?"

"No," Linas Webb shook his head again, "can't 'elp yer."

"Well," Marcus sighed, inclining his head, "I can't say I am not disappointed that you are not he because you see, you fit the description admirably."

"Well," Linas Webb grimaced, hoping he looked and sounded as nonchalant as he tried to appear, "I can't 'elp it if I look like someone else, can I?"

"No," Marcus agreed affably, "you cannot."

"Like I say," Linas Webb shrugged, beginning to relax, "I can't 'elp yer. Wish I could."

"Mm, that certainly is a pity," Marcus said with credible disappointment, "but," he sighed, "if you are not Leonard Webbley and have no idea of his whereabouts, I see no point in taking up any more of your time."

"Don't menshun it," Linas Webb shrugged. "I... er... I take it yer've bin askin' around?" he queried, his eyes watchful.

"Yes," Marcus smiled, "but, alas, I have drawn a blank everywhere I have been. It would seem," he shrugged, "that this Mr. Webbley has, indeed, disappeared, after all!"

"Well," Linas Webb hunched a shoulder, "sorry I can't 'elp yer." He would stake his life that he had never seen this man before, but the feeling that he looked vaguely familiar would not go away. For one awful moment he wondered if he was acting on behalf of a friend with whom he had transacted business, but even though he very soon discounted this idea he was nevertheless consumed with curiosity, and, cocking his head, asked, "Er, wot is it yer wont 'im for?"

Marcus eyed him steadily, but the only answer he vouchsafed to this was, "Thank you for your time," inclining his head before heading for the door. Then, as if suddenly bethinking himself of something, he turned, saying, with credible forgetfulness, "Oh, by the by, I almost forgot," he smiled, "I take it those items Mr. Charles Harrington left in your care are still safe?"

"There's no need ter fret yerself ova them sparklers. Safe as 'ouses they..."

"It is an old trick," Marcus mockingly apologised, walking back to the counter, "and yet, surprisingly," he raised an eyebrow, "it *never* fails."

"So," Linas Webb mused, rubbing his chin, angry with himself for falling into such a trap, "that's wot yer doin' 'ere, is it?"

"*That* is what I am doing here," Marcus concurred.

Linas Webb looked at the determined face in front of him, realising the futility of denying any knowledge of Charles Harrington and their business arrangement. Even so, he felt compelled to ask, somewhat cautiously, "Wot's yer int'rest in 'em?"

"I want them back," Marcus said calmly.

Linas Webb's eyes stared incredulously at the man opposite him as one dumfounded. "Wont 'em back?" he echoed.

"Oh, didn't I tell you?" Marcus asked surprised, raising an eyebrow.

"They belong to my family. You see," he informed him, "when you took possession of them in return for the copies you made and the money you handed over for your client to borrow on, you effectively received stolen goods. The necklace and the bracelet were not his property to dispose of."

Providing the price was right it had always been Linas Webb's policy never to ask questions or poke his nose into the affairs of others, and his transaction with Charles Harrington had been no different. He had had no idea whether the jewellery belonged to him or not, as far as he was concerned a deal had been struck to the satisfaction of both parties and, to his way of thinking, that agreement was still binding, and therefore he was not prepared to hand over anything to this man without the agreed sum, plus the interest, in exchange. However, when he pointed this fact out to Marcus, a circumstance which appeared to make no impression on him whatsoever, Linas Webb became quite argumentative, stating that if he thought for one moment he could walk into his place of business dictating terms then he would very soon discover his mistake. "And *anotha* thing," he nodded, "I'm an honest..."

"You are very far from that, I assure you," Marcus interrupted coldly, "so, shall we dispense with all of this?" not impressed in the least. "I know you for what you are, Leonard Webbley; now," he inclined his head, "if you choose to call yourself Linas Webb that is entirely your own affair, but it does not alter the fact that you are a most devious and underhand individual, and whether you like it or not you may as well accept the fact that I am not leaving here without those two pieces of jewellery, and," he warned him, "if you think you are going to receive a penny in exchange you could not be more wrong." An ugly look crossed Linas Webb's face upon hearing this, but without giving him time to speak, Marcus continued purposefully, "Do not misunderstand me, Webb; I am in no mood for the likes of you. Now, as far I see it, you can either do as I ask or I shall be obliged to report the theft to Bow Street." He saw the alarm enter those slate-grey eyes at the mention of the police. "I am not at all certain how you stand from a legal point," Marcus inclined his head, "but I should have thought that receiving stolen goods, especially when placed alongside your dealings with Rutger, a man who would have no difficulty whatsoever in recognising you, I assure you, would surely be enough to bring serious charges down upon you and, I have no doubt," he nodded, "a prison sentence."

The thin face paled at this and, like Ted Knowles, Linas Webb found himself unable to believe he was in the position in which he now found himself, especially having entered in to the transaction with Charles Harrington in good faith. Eyeing Marcus with something akin to loathing, Webb made a determined stand to defend himself, after which he belligerently argued that he had no right to come here and threaten him with the law, to which his visitor was taking absolutely no notice.

"What you did to Rutger was not only criminal but quite despicable," Marcus told him coldly, "and if I had my way you would, even now, face the full penalty of the law, but I am here on my own behalf which is to reclaim what is my family's property. The choice is yours, Webb," he told him firmly, the steely look in his eyes telling him that he meant every word, "you can either hand over those pieces and forgo the money and that is the end of the matter or, if you refuse to do so, I shall ensure you lose your freedom. Which is it?"

Linas Webb, when confronted with a man of equal determination as that of his late client, had, within a very short space of time, realised he was wasting his breath. Despite his vehement arguments that he had entered in to the transaction in good faith and therefore should not be expected to forgo what was his rightful due, just one look at that implacable face told him that further argument was entirely useless. He had no idea how this man was linked to Charles Harrington or what had put him onto the business in the first place, but he shrewdly suspected that he would not tell him if he asked. He bitterly resented having to hand over those valuable pieces in return for not even a penny piece, but neither had he any desire to have his affairs scrutinised by Bow Street any more than he was to have his past career resurrected and he certainly did not want to go to prison, but although parting with the necklace and the bracelet would cost him a severe pang as well as leaving him out of pocket, he had to grudgingly admit that it was better than the alternative. Nevertheless, it was with the utmost reluctance, not to say resentment, that he agreed to hand them over.

It was just as he was about to walk into the back premises when Marcus forestalled him, saying, "Please, do not make the error of attempting to escape by way of the back door. If you put me to the trouble of coming after you, I promise you," he warned, "you will not enjoy the experience."

A look of pure loathing was the only answer Linas Webb made in answer to this, but when he returned a few minutes later so belligerent was his mood that he threw the drawstring purse down onto the counter with such force that it almost slid onto floor. Without a word, Marcus opened the purse to check the contents and, upon seeing that the necklace and bracelet were intact, he returned them to the purse and put it into the inside pocket of his coat.

In a last-ditch attempt to receive something in return, Linas Webb growled, "The least yer can do is offer me somthin'."

Marcus eyed him steadily, saying coldly, "I have made you an offer, Webb; be thankful I am a man of my word!" upon which he left the premises.

*

Silas Jenkins, relieving Marcus of those items of jewellery with the same relief he had experienced upon having them reluctantly thrust at him by Linas Webb, was thankful to be able to see them securely deposited in his safe until he could return them to Mercers' vaults. "However much it pains me to say it," Jenkins confessed to Marcus, "it seems that your cousin knew some pretty suspect individuals!"

"So it would seem," Marcus reluctantly agreed.

"Tell me," Jenkins asked, leaning forward on his elbows, "do you place much reliance on this Webb character keeping silent?"

"Yes," Marcus nodded. "He is in no hurry to have his identity uncovered and his past career made public, not to mention the police finding his current premises worth a visit."

"It seems to me," Jenkins sighed, "that Bow Street could do no better than paying Knowles and Webb a visit; I have absolutely no doubt that both would be more than worth their while!"

"I've no doubt," Marcus agreed, "but should they ever do so," he told him realistically, "then everything we have been striving for will have gone for nothing!"

*

The police may find a visit to either man well worth their while, but as far as finding the person responsible for Charles's death was concerned they had, unfortunately, drawn a blank.

Inspector Jarrod had realised at the outset that this was going to be no straightforward case, but as he later reported to Sophy, surprising her one afternoon by turning up quite unexpectedly at End House, that the chances of finding the perpetrator of such a vicious crime looked remote, much less making an arrest. Unless she, or one of her brothers-in-law, could give any indication as to what had taken her husband to Waterloo that night or if he had had an engagement with someone who could be questioned, then without witnesses he advised her, it seemed they would never know the truth surrounding her husband's death.

After only a very little reflection, Sophy supposed it was perhaps better this way because once Inspector Jarrod discovered the reason for Charles being in Waterloo that night, it would not be long before the whole truth came out. She could not condone what Charles had done with regards to removing some of his sister's jewellery from Mercers' vaults or what he had attempted afterwards to cover it up, but she could understand how desperate he must have felt, and whilst it was not in her nature to lie and dissemble, especially in a matter as serious as this, she could see no good resulting from the facts being made known. She could only hope that this was now the end of the matter and that Alexandra would never get to hear the truth about her mother's jewellery and the subsequent series of events which had followed. It seemed her only remaining concern was whether Marcus would manage to find Charles's disreputable jeweller or not, surely no easy task when one considered, no matter how sadly, how many discreditable jewellers there must be who were capable of such underhanded work. It was therefore with relief that she received Marcus's letter informing her that he had been successful and that those pieces were now with Silas Jenkins. He had not gone into any detail as to how he had managed it, but Timothy's own opinion was that when faced with the unenviable option of either having to answer to the law for what was nothing short of theft or returning them to their rightful owner with no questions asked, the choice was surely a foregone conclusion!

Sophy may not have loved Charles, but her sorrow over his death was very real and she could not prevent herself from thinking that it was a terrible waste to throw one's life away with such careless disregard. Her thoughts often turned to Amelia, wondering how she was managing to cope without the man she loved, knowing perfectly well that George would never fulfil her expectations, much less take the place of the man she had loved and lost. Timothy did all he could to direct Sophy's thoughts onto a different track and, with Annabel's unwitting help, succeeded, if not entirely, to encourage her in putting the past into perspective.

It would be untrue to say that Sophy could not wait for her period of mourning to come to an end, but she nevertheless awaited the day with eager anticipation. She remembered all too well Charles's proposal of marriage and the reasons behind it, and whilst it may not have been the cold and brusque offer one would have expected in the circumstances, it was certainly made with an unwillingness which boded ill for their future.

Sophy knew that Marcus was an old-fashioned man at heart who observed all the courtesies and which accounted for his impeccable behaviour towards her, but it was impossible for her to misinterpret the look in his eyes whenever he came to see her, realising that his codes of conduct were struggling against his very human needs. She herself was conscious of her own needs and desires and knew moments when she could have thrown restraint to the winds, but clamping down on these with every ounce of strength she possessed she finally managed to see out her period of mourning.

Unfortunately, Sophy did not see Marcus for several months following her emergence from this conventional expression of loss, his hastily written letter advising her that due to his uncle having sustained a fractured left leg resulting from a fall, it was not now possible for him to leave Yorkshire to visit her. This was almost immediately followed up with another telling her that he would come and see her as soon as he possibly could, but as things stood at this moment he did not envisage it to be for some little time. She was disappointed but perfectly understood and filled her time until she saw him again with entertaining her nephew.

*

It had been a wet October, but Sophy could not help thinking that the countryside was at its best clothed in autumn colours; the rich reds and varying shades of gold intermingling with the fading green, helping to brighten up the damp scene all around her. Having taken the opportunity on the first dry day for over a week, she spent the early part of the afternoon pushing her nephew around his inheritance in his perambulator, pointing out items of interest to which he was taking absolutely no notice.

Deciding that Peter had had enough of looking at his future estate, she slowly began to make her way back to the house, reaching its shelter just as it started to come on to rain and, handing him over to his nurse, Annabel enjoying an afternoon rest, Sophy went up to her room to remove her hat and coat. It was just as she raised the brush to tidy her hair when she heard Timothy tapping on her door informing her that Marcus was here and wishful of seeing her. Her hand stilled in mid-air, and her heart, which up until now had been behaving quite normally, suddenly began to beat rather fast while her stomach turned heartwarmingly over. She had no need to look at her reflection in the mirror to know that her colour was considerably heightened, but hastily placing the hairbrush down onto the dressing table she hurried across the room on legs which were far from steady, flinging open the door to find her brother standing just outside telling her in a conspiratorial whisper that Marcus had arrived about twenty minutes ago and was waiting for her in the drawing room. She knew from the expression on Timothy's face the reason for Marcus's visit and looked expectantly up at her brother, her eyes reflecting her joy, but apart from a knowing grin and a brotherly kiss on her cheek she got no more out of him and waiting only for him to step aside she quickly made her way downstairs to the drawing room.

Standing with his arms behind his back looking abstractedly out of the window on to the damp landscape, Marcus turned immediately at her entrance, noting with unashamed appreciation her transition from black to a soft shade of blue. For several moments Sophy could neither move nor speak, and for some reason she could not explain or understand she felt suddenly shy and nervous, her breath stilling in her lungs as she saw the love in his eyes as he looked at her across the space that separated them. She knew precisely what had brought him here, but although she had longed for this moment now that it had arrived she could think of nothing to say. Swallowing an unexpected lump which had formed in her throat she took a hesitant step forward, her face delicately touched with colour, saying, a little unsteadily, "Timothy told me you had come to see me and that I should find you in here."

It was a moment or two before Marcus spoke, his eyes taking in every beautiful inch of her, hardly able to believe that at long last he could ask for the hand of the woman he loved. "He told me I may speak to you," he told her meaningfully.

Sophy swallowed nervously, trying to steady her unruly senses. "I... I trust your uncle is now better."

"Much better," Marcus told her, knowing precisely how she was feeling. "His doctor assures me he will live forever. I certainly hope so."

"I do hope so too," she smiled. "I am so glad he is better."

"So am I," he nodded, demolishing what little composure she had by saying, "but however much I mean that, I know he will forgive me when I say that it does not make me half so glad as I am to be here now, on the point of asking the question I have been wanting to ask you for a *very* long time."

Sophy found her unexpected shyness inexplicable. How could one possibly feel so shy with the man one loved?

Marcus knew perfectly, however; he himself was conscious of their love and need for one another. "It seems like an eternity since I saw you last," he told earnestly. "I have missed you so much, more than I can say."

"And I you," her voice quavering a little. "I have looked forward so much to seeing you again."

Marcus smiled, a heart stopping smile which made her draw in her breath, then, taking several halting steps towards her, his eyes saying far more than words, he took her hands in his, raising first one and then the other to his lips. "Sophy, you know why I am here."

She nodded, her breath suddenly constricting in her lungs. "Yes, I know."

He looked down at her, still unable to believe that the moment he had longed for was finally here. "You know," he smiled ruefully, "I had a speech all prepared for this moment, but now," kissing her hands, "I can't bring one word of it to mind."

"Y-you can't?" Sophy faltered, looking lovingly up at him, her fingers trembling in his.

"No," he said softly, shaking his head, "not one, which means," he said a little unsteadily, "I am left with nothing to say but Sophy, my darling, will you make me the happiest man alive by consenting to become my wife?"

It was several moments before Sophy could speak, her emotions threatening to overcome her, but raising her eyes to his, mistily glowing with the love she had for him said, in a voice which she knew must be her own, "I can think of no greater joy than being your wife. It is the dearest wish of my heart."

After kissing her fingers, he released her hands to allow him to remove from his inner pocket a small square box which he had not long collected from Cornelius Royston, opening it with slightly trembling fingers to reveal a diamond solitaire ring resting on a bed of white velvet. "Will you wear this for me, Sophy?" he asked gently.

She stared mistily down at it before returning her gaze to his face. "It is the most beautiful ring I have ever seen!" she said huskily. "I shall never take it off," she promised. She removed the band of gold already on her finger and put it into her pocket, then, holding out her left hand watched as Marcus reverently slid his ring into its place, its diamond glinting in the light from the fire. Somewhere at the back of her mind Sophy recalled the ring she had just removed which had been placed on her finger without any feelings of love or tenderness, but this was different; it was a symbol of Marcus's love.

He raised her left hand to his lips, his thumb gently stroking the finger on which he had just placed his ring. "I love you, Sophy," he told her in a deep voice. "I always have. I love you more than life itself!"

She gave him a tremulous smile, admitting huskily, "I love you too, and although I don't quite understand what it is I have done to deserve you, I am so *glad* you love me!"

Something like an agonised groan left his throat at this, but deciding no words were adequate to express his feelings he drew her urgently into his arms and kissed her, not at all gently, but the excited shudder of her body as he held her against him and her irresistible response to his kisses, meant that it was quite some time before his lips released hers. At no time had Marcus intended to either abuse Timothy's trust or give full rein to his emotions, but although he knew that the mere feel of her body against his own did nothing for his self-control, just having Sophy in his arms was an exquisite joy. Being fully aware that her brother's drawing room was not the place to give in to his desires, Marcus eased himself a little away from her, but one look at her glowing face with her eyes darkened by desire and her lips parted invitingly he found himself quite powerless to resist kissing her again. It was just as his kisses began to deepen, causing her to melt deliciously into him and his arms to tighten around her, that the sound of a burned through log on the fire collapsing into the bottom of the grate penetrated his consciousness, resulting in him gently easing himself away from her, but when they joined Timothy and Annabel in the small sitting room a few minutes later to tell them what they already knew, the newly betrothed couple were not at all sure whether to be glad for the interruption or not.

From that moment on Annabel's thoughts and conversation, with the natural exception of her baby son and the approaching Christmas season, centred around their forthcoming wedding, and nothing could prevent her from throwing herself into the preparations with gusto in between arranging the Yuletide festivities. There seemed to be nothing Sophy could do but go along with the flow and prepare her trousseau, but since this was a most enjoyable occupation she did not take too much persuading to discuss such important matters as her dress. In the midst of all this, she had several times wondered what Marcus had in mind for their honeymoon, but not all her coaxing could wheedle it out of him; he had merely smiled, saying that he was keeping it as a surprise.

The only thing as far as Sophy could see to mar her happiness was telling her mamma of the true relationship between her and Marcus. She knew it was not going to be easy and had several times pondered how best to tell her, but taking Timothy's advice she refrained from doing so until her period of mourning was over. Now that it was she knew she could not postpone it any longer, and therefore nervously put pen to paper in the hope that she could explain everything satisfactorily. She was not at all sure whether to be glad that she had vetoed Marcus's wish that he be the one to tell her or not, but knowing her mamma Sophy felt it reasonably safe to say that she would take great exception to being told of something like this from someone other than her daughter, even her prospective son-in-law. It was a far more difficult letter to compose than she had anticipated but eventually it was finished to her satisfaction, and as Timothy irrepressibly told her, "If this doesn't make Mamma stir from that mausoleum of a house in Mayfair, nothing will!"

It may not have stirred her into visiting her daughter, but it certainly moved her sufficiently to write her a letter, expressing in the most shocked terms, that she was unable to believe something of this nature had been going on without her being aware of it. It was apparent to her offspring that it was not the relationship which had displeased and shocked her so much as not having been advised of it before now.

"She'll come round," Timothy told Sophy. "After all, what can she do?"

Timothy was found to be right. Following a series of letters to Sophy, it was becoming apparent to her son and daughter that each one was less forceful and condemnatory than the one before, reluctantly coming to accept what she considered to be really quite reprehensible. Sophy was indeed relieved to learn that her mamma was coming round to the idea, but when she informed her of her decision to be married from her brother's home and that the service was to be conducted at the parish church in Church Warping, it had brought forth another letter, demanding of her daughter why this so-called marriage of hers, if all was as above board as she had said, could not be conducted in town, in a proper church, instead of an out of the way place no one had ever heard of as well as giving all her acquaintance the idea that it was nothing more than a hole-in-the-corner affair. However, upon discovering that nothing would move Sophy, she immediately wrote to her daughter stating that she had not thought she would have so little consideration for her state of nerves but, then, she supposed she should have looked for nothing better from a daughter who appeared to be totally lost to all reasoning. A journey into Kent, she wrote, was not at all what her doctor would approve of, which, she said tartly, was the reason she had not visited them over the Christmas season, but since it was apparent that Sophy was determined to have her way, irrespective of her mamma's health, she would travel down with Harriet, trusting that no ill-effects would result from this exertion.

"Which means," said Timothy, resigned but by no means eager, "she will be descending upon us before we can turn round!"

Charlotte however, had no objections or complaints to put forward about Sophy's wedding arrangements, and informed her in a lengthy letter that she could hardly wait to travel down into Kent with her granddaughter to witness such a long awaited and happy occasion and, accepting Timothy and Annabel's kind invitation to stay at End House for as long as they chose, happily announced that they would look forward to it. Having enjoyed her nephew's company and that of his Uncle Lionel over the festive season in Hertfordshire, Charlotte had seen all too clearly what Marcus could not quite hide in that he was awaiting his forthcoming marriage to Sophy with the same eagerness as Charlotte had no doubt Sophy was to him. It would certainly be a very happy day, and whilst Charlotte still mourned the loss of a son whose death continued to remain incomprehensible to her, she could not deny that her nephew was far more deserving of Sophy than Charles had ever been.

The excitement of working on her wedding dress with Annabel may have been a real pleasure as well as a labour of love, but it left Sophy's mind too free, and every now and then her thoughts turned to that other wedding nearly four years ago and all that had followed it. At no point had Charles even tried to reconcile himself to their marriage, and she felt quite certain that even had he known that she knew of his affair with Amelia, it would not have prompted him into ending it. Sophy may not have loved him, but she could see how their relationship could have been more harmonious than it was, but since he had had no desire for the marriage in the first place he had at no time made even the slightest show of pretence that he was, if not blissfully happy, then at least reasonably content. His treatment of her may not have been physically brutal, but there was no denying he more than adequately compensated this by the dismissive and contemptuous way he spoke to her; her thoughts and feelings were of little or no consequence. She could, even now, if not forgive him for his callous disregard of her, then at least attribute it to his natural arrogance, but she only had to think of what he had planned for Alexandra and how he had determined to deal with Marcus, and any generosity of spirit she had left her; all the same she had never wanted his death. She had meant every word she had said to Amelia in that she had not desired her own happiness at the expense of Charles's life and her tragic loss, but as Timothy realistically pointed out, circumstances and events had been beyond her control and any intervention on her part would not only have been regarded as unwelcome but would not have changed any of it.

Naturally, it was impossible to constantly dwell on something which had not only been outside of her control to prevent but beyond her power to alter in any way, especially when one was only days away from what one had longed for, for so long. As the wedding preparations were all in hand and the happy event drew near, if Sophy was not able to entirely banish her memories she was at least able to correctly evaluate them and put them in their proper place.

She was disappointed but not altogether surprised to receive a note from Amelia offering profound apologies on behalf of herself and George for declining her kind invitation, but due to both her sons succumbing to measles at the same time, she was sure Sophy would understand the very natural concern of their parents to be with them at this most distressing time. Sophy did, of course, but she could not help wondering if there were far more human and personal reasons to account for it. She was sorry they would not be attending but accepted her sister-in-law's reason for their absence. Her invitation to Emily and Edward had been for Charlotte's sake rather than her own, and she was therefore conscious of feeling no regret upon receiving their politely worded letter declining the invitation for reasons which Emily did not go into, but Sophy was genuinely pleased that Jane and Henry would be attending. It would be good to see Isabel and

Adam again and she was pleased that Marcus had asked him to be his supporter at the wedding. It was a pity there was insufficient room at End House to accommodate them, but since it appeared they had no objection to putting up at *'The Crown'* in Maidstone the same as Marcus, which was not that far away, Sophy would at least have a little time alone with her sister-in-law, Timothy promising to send the carriage to bring Isabel to End House for a visit so she and Sophy could enjoy a good gossip together.

Her mamma, having decided to descend on Timothy and Annabel days ahead of schedule, totally ignoring Harriet's anxious protests that they would not be in any way prepared for their early arrival, shrugged this aside with the quelling announcement that as the mother of the bride she had a right to be with Sophy and to give her the benefit of her advice and experience. To her offspring this was more in the way of a taking a perverse delight in criticising and disapproving of everything that had been arranged for the happy day, finally rounding off her catalogue of grievances by telling Harriet, in a voice which bordered on the reproachful, that never would she have believed to see her one daughter going to the altar for a second time whilst her other had never once received an offer of marriage. As expected, this resulted in a burst of tears from her unmarried daughter and vexation from the other, whilst Timothy, raising exasperated eyes to heaven, took the edge off his temper and frustration by enjoying a vigorous gallop.

Charlotte had, of course, met Sophy's mamma on many occasions, but she had never quite understood why it was that she seemed to take a delight in her numerous, if imaginary, ailments. She had often thought that if Elspeth Lessington spent as much time concentrating on her children, especially poor Harriet, as she did pandering to her purported fragile health and delicate state of nerves, which she ruthlessly used to either excuse or exonerate her for doing precisely what she wished, she would do very much better.

During the past two weeks End House had been a hive of activity, Timothy's faithful but hard-pressed butler barely leaving the hall before the sound of the bell pull came again, signifying the delivery of yet another gift. The small sitting room, which had been turned over to housing the many presents, was now so full to overflowing with not a table or chair with any more available space, that Annabel, laughingly telling Sophy that she did not know where she and Marcus would put the half of them when they returned from honeymoon, was nevertheless conscious of a deep sense of sadness at the thought of saying goodbye to her sister-in-law. But no one looking at Annabel's smiling face as she softly entered Sophy's room the night before her wedding would have had the least guess of the gap her departure would leave in her life.

Sophy, expecting the tap on her door to signal the entrance of her mamma to either complain about Charlotte taking things upon herself or giving her opinion on something which she did not approve, was relieved when she saw who it was. Sophy, regarding her sister-in-law as a very dear friend, smiled at her entrance and, hugging her knees as she lay back against the pillows, feeling ridiculously like a young girl again, with Annabel curled up beside her, enjoyed a pleasurable hour or so exchanging feminine confidences and talking and laughing about nothing very serious.

Chapter Twenty-Seven

Sophy awoke the following morning to the delicious feeling that something wonderful was going to happen, and to an overwhelming sense of well-being. Through the open window the early spring sunshine filtered in, promising yet another lovely day and, somewhere inside her, was the pleasurable thought that the day she had long awaited had finally arrived. The truth was she had hardly slept at all, only falling into a light sleep as the dawn began to break. She could not remember ever experiencing this light and giddy sensation before, making her feel like a young girl on the threshold of life, promising so much. As she lay back against the pillows, her eyes wandering towards the bright blue of the cloudless sky outside, her stomach fluttered on a ripple of anticipation and excitement, her pulses racing at the thought of what lay ahead. Several times during the night she had had to pinch herself to make sure she had not imagined everything or that she was merely taking part in some beatific dream, but as she glanced across to where her wedding dress was hanging up, a delightful confection of ivory-coloured gauze over satin, she knew it was no dream.

Today she would join herself to Marcus irrevocably and unreservedly, and the thought made her tremble. It was hard to believe that at long last she was going to marry the man she loved, had loved almost from the very moment she had set eyes on him and, yet again, Sophy could not help but wonder what she had done to deserve such happiness. So lost in thought was she that she entirely failed to hear the cautious opening of the door and the silent entrance of Charlotte carrying in her breakfast tray. Upon seeing who it was Sophy let out a sigh of relief, guiltily conscious of not wanting it to be her mamma. She loved her mamma, of course, but it seemed that every time she saw her a fresh complaint left her lips; if it was not disagreeing with the wedding arrangements it was to issue another protest about something Charlotte had done or a task Annabel had failed to do as she had particularly asked her to. No words of encouragement had left her mamma's lips and certainly no expressions of joy or the hope that she would be happy. Confiding in her mamma was something Sophy had always found impossible to do, and she was therefore glad that her final confidences would be shared with the woman who had made her life in Brook Street so much easier, and one whose only desire was to wish her well.

Waiting only until Charlotte had plumped up the pillows and placed the tray resting on the wicker bridge across her knees, Sophy leaned forward and kissed her cheek. "I thought you were Mamma."

"Your mamma," Charlotte informed her, far more relaxed than Sophy could ever remember, "is still in her room. From what Annabel told me a moment ago when I met her on the stairs, it appears that she will remain there for some little time yet."

"Oh," Sophy nodded, hoping her parent would not choose today to contract a sudden indisposition! "You do not think...?"

"No, I do not," Charlotte said firmly, not pretending to misunderstand her. "If you think that she would miss today of all days, you are mistaken. Nothing would keep her away. Now," she nodded briskly, "I have no wish to hurry you, but it is eight o'clock already and you are to be married at eleven. If you do not wish to meet your future husband looking as though you have been scrambled head first into your clothes," she smiled, being in no doubt that if Marcus could see her right now with her long hair cascading halfway down her back and such a radiant look on her face, he would have no fault whatsoever to find, "I suggest you eat your breakfast."

"I really don't think I could eat a thing," Sophy confessed, leaning back against the pillow with her arms behind her head.

"Yes, you can," she was told firmly.

"Well, perhaps just a little," Sophy nodded, "but I really am not very hungry."

"You will feel better when you have eaten something," Charlotte told her.

Sophy picked up her napkin, her eyes widening in surprise a she saw lying hidden beneath it an oyster-shaped green leather case with a white envelope sitting just beneath. Raising enquiring eyes to Charlotte, who merely shrugged her innocence, she watched Sophy open the envelope with trembling fingers to retrieve a single sheet of paper, its half a dozen or so lines written in a strong masculine hand. Having read its contents, Sophy handed it to Charlotte, who, having promised Marcus only a couple of days ago that she would make sure Sophy received the necklace and the note this morning, was a little hesitant to read what promised to be a private love note, but Sophy, looking upon her as far more than her mother-in-law, felt she could not keep such happiness all to herself, and insisted she read it.

My Darling Sophy,

It seems like an eternity has passed since I saw you last, and then only briefly, even though it was only a few short days ago. I can barely contain my impatience at seeing you again when I finally make you mine. I long to see you and hold you in my arms, but until that joyous moment I send you this token of my love and eternal devotion and hope it will hold a place in your heart as you do, and always will, in mine.

My Undying Love,

Marcus

Charlotte raised misty eyes to Sophy, moved by what she had been privileged to read, but she was not attending. Held reverently in the palms of her hands was a treble row of pearls, their clasp a brilliant emerald stone which sparkled vibrantly as it lay in the sun's path. A sob left her throat as she held the necklace up, transfixed by the translucent sheen and exquisite lustre of those pearls. Charlotte, who had been shown the necklace by Marcus to see if she thought Sophy would like it, stared anew at such perfection. She could not begin to calculate its value, but Sophy, no such thoughts entering her head, regarded it as a gift of love and not one of monetary worth.

"Oh, Charlotte! It's beautiful," Sophy cried in a throbbing voice. "Look."

Without question they were the most beautiful pearls Charlotte had ever seen, not to mention that emerald, and could quite well understand Sophy's feelings upon receiving such a declaration of love from the man who had long held a place in her heart. She herself was conscious of a lump forming in her throat, but since it would do no good for either one of them to succumb to tears and emotion, Charlotte swallowed hard, saying, "It's exquisite. Shall you wear it today?"

Sophy, momentarily deprived of speech, nodded vigorously. Even had those pearls not been the exact colour of her dress nothing would have prevented her from wearing them. Her breakfast forgotten, Sophy pushed the wicker bridge away and climbed out of bed, hugging Charlotte, saying between tears and laughter that she never thought she could be so happy, not because of the necklace but because Marcus loved her.

"I know he does," Charlotte confirmed quietly, returning her hug, "very much indeed. You know, Sophy," she said gently, "I am not unmindful of the way Charles treated you, but that is over now. You will not be subjected to anything like that with Marcus. He loves and adores you."

Sophy sniffed. "I know, and I love him."

"You have waited a very long time for this day," Charlotte reminded her softly, "and it is understandable that you should be feeling a little nervous."

"You must be thinking I have run quite mad!" Sophy shook her head, all thoughts of breakfast forgotten.

Charlotte did not, but by the time Ellen came in to prepare Sophy's bath she was feeling much calmer and, for the remainder of the time left to her, her room was invaded by a steady stream of well-wishers. Alexandra, being the last to enter, fell into tears, hiccupping, "I am s-so happy f-for you." Alexandra, who had indeed grown into a very beautiful young woman during the time she had been with her grandmother, had enjoyed more than one cosy chat with her favourite aunt, proudly telling her of her many conquests in Hertfordshire. It was obvious from her confidences that although she enjoyed their attentions none of them were in the least likely to find permanent favour with her. Her plans, she had told Sophy, were quite uncertain, but perhaps in a little while she would discuss them with her grandmother. In the meantime though, her conquests and plans were forgotten as she entered in to the spirit of the morning before being taken away by Annabel.

Before she realised it, Sophy was at last alone with Timothy, waiting for their carriage to arrive. He had no qualms about handing her permanently into Marcus's care, knowing that at long last she had the happiness she deserved. "Nervous?" he asked softly, squeezing her hand as they were about to leave the house.

"A little," Sophy confessed, "but it's a nice kind of nervousness."

He laughed, kissing her cheek before assisting her into the carriage. Soon they were being set down at the church, and Timothy, giving her hand a reassuring squeeze, began to walk her down the aisle to where Marcus was standing waiting for her.

She would never be quite able to say for certain how many people had flocked into the small church at Church Warping, but, or so it seemed to Sophy, that she was surrounded by a sea of people. All she would ever be able to recollect with any certainty was that she only had eyes for the man who stood, apart from Adam, head and shoulders above everyone else. There was no mistaking his soldierly bearing, solid and dependable, whose grey cut-away tailcoat and neatly arranged neck-tie, reflected a military smartness without a hint of flamboyance.

Not all her mamma's arguments, and there had been many, had induced

Sophy to wear a veil or a hat in place of the flowers threaded through her hair, lovingly and cleverly arranged by Annabel, each one perfectly matching the small bouquet she carried. Her dress, a modified version of one her grandmother had worn many years ago and which she had kept and proudly shown Sophy as a child, had also come under her mamma's censure. It was one thing to see the dress hanging innocently up, but quite another to see Sophy wearing it. The skirt, not so full and billowing as the original, was nevertheless, in her mamma's eyes at least, suggestive, floating in a cloud of gauze over satin around her ankles, but which became Sophy's tall figure admirably, had made her mother stare in frank disapproval and shock. The fact that a piece of gauze had been sewn all around the off the shoulder neckline to gather in a collar of satin at the throat, shamefully omitted on the original, had made not the slightest difference. No lady, in her mamma's view, would be seen in such a garment; and that bodice, far too tight and provocative for decency, was an outrage! She dreaded to think what people would say when they saw it!

As no one else shared this moralistic opinion, and the look in Marcus's eyes told her precisely what he thought of it, Sophy was easily able to banish any qualms her mother's criticism may have raised. Nothing could have complemented that treble row of pearls to better effect, and as she came to stand beside her bridegroom, unashamedly showing his love as he looked down at her, she knew her mamma's strictures meant very little when compared to the unmistakable adoration of the man she loved. Every word she solemnly uttered came from the heart and reflected the love she had for the man whose eyes never left her face, and whose own responses clearly echoed the depth of feeling which threatened to overwhelm him.

Having for so long waited for this moment, even doubting it would ever happen, Marcus could still not quite believe it was finally here and that he was about to place that narrow band of gold on Sophy's finger. There could well have been only the two of them there in that ancient church, its aura embracing them with something so special they did not want to share it with anyone. His kiss, a delicate touch against her lips, was more a reverent vow than a passionate declaration and, in that instant, Sophy knew that what they shared would never die.

From the moment she came out of the church into the sunlight until she bid everyone farewell following the wedding luncheon, everything had passed in a kind of blur. She had only a vague recollection of what she had said or to whom she had said it, her only clear remembrance being that Marcus was never very far from her side until the moment they went upstairs to their respective rooms to change their clothes. Sophy did recall her mamma conferring favourable praise on the necklace Marcus had bestowed on her as well as commenting on his excellent taste, but it seemed that not even these merits had the power to take her mind off that dress, to which she was still far from reconciled, but as she was the only one who held this view Sophy did not allow it to either mar or deflate her happiness, but it was Harriet's tears and her reply to her own assurance that one day she too would be preparing for her wedding which almost undid her. "Oh, no," Harriet shook her head, kissing her sister affectionately, "y-you see, I am n-not b-beautiful like y-you, S-Sophy."

Not until she was seated beside Marcus in the open carriage was Sophy able to pause for breath, saying, rather guiltily, that she could not remember whether she had said goodbye to this person or not, he had simply taken hold of her hand, smiling reassuringly, "I said it for you."

She was relieved, but confessed, "I am afraid that I can recollect very little of what happened once we left the church."

"Providing you remember what took place *inside* it," he said in a deep voice, "nothing else matters."

She looked up at him, promising huskily, "I shall never forget it."

An open carriage was all very well on such a beautiful day as this, but it lacked the privacy Marcus would have liked to respond suitably to this, therefore rendering it impossible for him to do anything more than to slide his left arm around her waist and his right hand to clasp hers. "If you do," he teased quietly, lightly brushing her parted lips, "I shall take the greatest of pleasure in reminding you."

"You haven't yet told me where you are taking me," she told him unsteadily, as conscious as he was of Timothy's groom on the box.

"For the next three weeks," he whispered in her ear, "I am looking forward to having you all to myself, and, I believe, I have found the very thing which will ensure we are not disturbed."

"It sounds wonderful," she breathed contentedly, "but what have you planned?"

"All in good time," he told her softly.

She could get no more out of him and decided that whatever it was he had arranged for the next three weeks he was determined to keep it as a surprise until the very last moment. His arm still encircled her waist while the other clasped her hands, and as this was the only intimacy permissible to them in an open carriage, apart from occasionally passing a comment about something they saw on their drive, they sat in contented silence until their destination was reached.

It was almost six o'clock by the time they arrived at Whistable, but due to the press of traffic it took a while to reach the harbour. Sophy, still bewildered as to what Marcus had in store for her, looked wonderingly all around her as she alighted from the carriage before casting a questioning look up at him. A fairly strong wind was blowing and the vessels at anchor, all privately owned apart from two pleasure cruisers, were bobbing rather vigorously up and down. She cast another enquiring glance at Marcus, who merely smiled as he took her arm to escort her up the gangway of a yacht secured to its moorings on the quay. The captain, a weather-beaten man his early fifties, welcomed them aboard before a steward escorted them into a large and elegantly furnished saloon which would not have looked out of place in a Grosvenor Square mansion house, leaving Sophy to stare incredulously at her luxurious surroundings, momentarily lost for words.

Never having been on a yacht before she had not known what to expect, but nothing had prepared her for the elegant sophistication of the room in which she found herself. The heavy brocade curtains draped gracefully around the portholes and the thick pile carpet, which was a perfectly matching shade of green, made her almost afraid to walk on it. Rich mahogany furniture, clamped to the floor, shone in the glow from the crystal drop chandeliers which hung from either end of the ceiling, with wing chairs and sofas sedately resting against the walls. The steward, taking it for granted that they wanted to see the rest of the yacht, took them on a tour of what Sophy could only describe as a floating home. The dining room, an elegant apartment decorated in blue and gold with an oval table and six chairs, caused her eyes to open to their fullest extent but felt some relief in that the small sitting room adjacent to it, a burst of deep yellow and gold, did at least have the appearance of being cosy, but it was the master and guest bedrooms, connected by a dressing room, which made Sophy turn a laughing eye up at Marcus. She had no doubt at all that the other bedroom was seldom, if ever, used, and Marcus, responding to the laughter in her eyes with an amusing grin, almost proved too much for her self-control.

Waiting until they were back in the main saloon and the steward had left did she ask, between laughter and exasperation, "Marcus, will you *please* tell me whose boat this is and what we are doing on it?"

"*The Neptune,*" he told her with perfect gravity, "belongs to a friend of mine who has generously offered her to us for as long as we want it."

"Who is this friend?" she asked, removing her hat and gloves.

Marcus's eyes lit up. "He is," he told her with a laugh in his voice, "Alistair Renfrew McLaughlin McGregor, The Most Noble, The Marquis of Lomand."

She stared at this. "My goodness!" she exclaimed faintly, looking about her in renewed awe. "He *owns* this?" she raised an eyebrow.

He nodded. *"This,* a very imposing mausoleum in Cavendish Square, a hunting box in Leicestershire and a very attractive house in Argyle."

She was impressed. "I see. Does he, I wonder, own anything else?"

"Several things, actually," Marcus smiled, "but it is his string of race horses of which he is most proud."

"I see," she said slowly. "Was he at our wedding?" she queried guiltily. "Because if he was," she confessed, "I can't recall meeting him, although," she pointed out, not without a laugh in her voice, "with a name like that I can't see how I could have forgotten!"

"No," Marcus smiled, shaking his head, his eyes brimming with laughter. "According to Alistair," he told her, "he has recently made the acquaintance of a most exquisite creature from whom, or so he assured me, he cannot bear to be parted."

Sophy laughed, a happy sound which made him take hold of her hands. She looked up at him. "I know precisely how he feels, and I am quite prepared to forgive him."

Marcus brushed her hands with his lips. "Of course," he said meaningfully, "it is most unfortunate that she is *quite* ineligible to meet his mamma." Sophy nodded her understanding, her mouth forming an 'Oh'. "She tells him that now his poor papa is no longer alive he owes it to his name to meet a respectable young female and get married," he smiled, adding, "but since his affairs are usually of violent but short duration, I don't think his mamma need worry too much."

She laughed again, not at all shocked. "Where did you meet him? He sounds wonderful."

"To the ladies he is certainly wonderful, generous too, but to those of us who know him well he is the best of friends. We served together in India," he explained, "and although we do not see each other very often now we do run across one another in town from time to time. In fact," he told her, "I came upon him a few months ago when he invited me to dine with him at his club. As soon as he learned of our forthcoming marriage nothing would do for him but to offer us *The Neptune'.* Don't you like it?" he asked, squeezing her hands.

"Like it!" she gasped. "It would be difficult not to."

Marcus considered this a little before saying cautiously, "Mm, perhaps a little too ornate for my taste, but it is the perfect hideaway, wouldn't you agree?"

She did, but could not refrain from remarking, "I cannot help but wonder though, just how many ineligible females this Most Noble friend of yours has entertained on '*The Neptune*'.

This thought had already occurred to him, and even though he knew Sophy was no prude he had deliberately refrained from commenting upon it. "I've wondered that too," he told her quietly, "but if the thought of it upsets you at all, it is not too late, we can find a hotel in town or…"

Sophy shook her head. "Of course, not. I would not hear of it. It was a most kind and generous gesture of his to offer her to us," kissing his cheek, her smile one of pure mischief. "It doesn't matter how many females, *ineligible or otherwise*," she pulled a face, "he has entertained here; it does not affect us. What has happened in the past has no bearing on the present or our future."

Marcus did not envy Alistair his affairs, for himself there was only one woman, there always had been and there always would be, and he thanked God for his good fortune. He was agonisingly aware of how close he had come to losing her and the mere thought of spending the rest of his life without her was too horrendous to contemplate. He was just about to take her in his arms when the steward returned to inform them that the captain was just on the point of setting sail, and they would lay anchor that night a few miles down the coast in a sheltered harbour.

Deciding against changing for dinner, which was served about an hour later, they found themselves sitting down to a rather sumptuous affair, rounded off by a bottle of vintage champagne thoughtfully provided by their absent host. Whatever Webster may have thought about his surroundings neither Marcus nor Sophy knew, his face as impassive as ever, but to Marcus's well-trained eye he rather thought that his old retainer considered '*The Neptune*' an extravagant luxury which was not at all to his taste. After finally removing the covers and ascertaining that they required nothing further, Webster bid them both a very good night, keeping his thoughts and reflections to himself. He had been Marcus's butler and valet for a good many years, and therefore he would have been grossly offended not to have accompanied him on this trip, but it seemed to him this Most Noble Marquis friend of his, whoever he was, had some very peculiar notions, to which the bedroom arrangements were adequate proof.

Apart from the swell beneath them rhythmically flapping against the hull, which Sophy appeared to deal with extremely well, everywhere was quiet and still. It seemed to her that the whole crew could well have deserted them, but so well-trained were they that they were able to carry out their tasks efficiently and unobtrusively as they sailed to the anchorage.

"We shall remain here tonight," Marcus told her when dinner was over, "then, in the morning, we will weigh anchor." He looked down at her, his eyes warm and dark as he drew her into his arms. "All you have to do," he said softly, kissing her forehead, "is tell me where you wish to go. Where do you fancy?" he smiled, holding her tighter. "The South of France? Italy?"

Folding her arms around his neck, Sophy smiled mistily up at him, saying softly, "As long as we are together, I don't care where we go."

A ragged sigh left his throat, telling her in a deepening voice, "It's not important right now," bringing the palm of his hand to rest against her cheek and gently stroking it with his thumb, "there will be plenty of time to decide in the morning." It was just as he was about to kiss her when a discreet tap on the door made him pause. The steward, far too used to his noble employer's affairs to just walk in unannounced, waited for the invitation to enter, whereupon he presented the captain's compliments followed up by a request that Marcus join him on the bridge. He nodded, then, after escorting Sophy to the master bedroom, said softly as he left her, "I shan't be long."

Ellen, who had travelled down with Webster and all their luggage before the wedding luncheon had ended, was carefully hanging her clothes in the fitted wardrobe when Sophy entered. Eternally grateful that she had been taken off domestic duties to tend to Mrs. Sophy permanently, from whom a cross word nor a rebuke for some oversight had ever been heard to leave her lips, bobbed a curtsey at her entrance. It was impossible not to like Mrs. Sophy, for whom Ellen could not do enough, and if anyone were ever to ask for her opinion she would have to say that it was about time she had some happiness and, from the looks of it, she had finally found it.

It was, of course, exciting to be on a boat and, understandably, Ellen could not resist taking a sneaking tour of it earlier, but the opulence which met her eyes, never having come in her way before, had made her gasp in astonishment, and whilst she could not claim a liking for the rich crimson colours which had been used to decorate the bedroom apartments, she was quite prepared to overlook it in the face of such a wonderful adventure. After hurriedly putting the remaining dresses in the wardrobe she then helped Sophy to undress before unpinning and brushing her hair, all the time talking animatedly about the events of the day, to which Sophy nodded and laughed, given no opportunity to respond, but eventually Ellen paused for breath long enough to allow Sophy to thank her for her efforts, after which she bid her goodnight, telling her that she would ring for her in the morning when she was ready, to which that happy young lady bobbed a curtsey and left.

Sophy had no idea where they were anchored but the swell had subsided considerably and, walking over to the porthole, pulled back the curtains to see the moon dancing on the water and, over to the left, just about visible, was the unmistakable sight of the white chalk cliffs which made up the

Seven Sisters. It was an eerily beautiful scene, and suddenly long forgotten childhood stories of smugglers bringing their illicit cargo ashore came to mind. It had all sounded very romantic, but of course it had been no such thing. According to Timothy the trade had virtually died out, although some still did attempt to defraud the Customs and Excise.

Apart from the breeze catching the rigging and the gentle movement of the boat nothing seemed to be stirring, and if it had not been for the sound of Marcus moving around in the dressing room next door and his low-voiced conversation with Webster, Sophy could almost have believed that she was the only one on board. A fluttering of excitement invaded the pit of her stomach as she thought of him in the adjacent room, gradually increasing until her whole body tingled in anticipation, barely able to breathe while she waited for the connecting door to open. Eventually, she heard the door leading onto the walkway open and Marcus wish Webster goodnight, then, within seconds, she saw the handle being turned on the door to the master bedroom and waited expectantly as it opened and Marcus walked in, catching her breath at the sight of him, watching him walk towards her on legs which, all of a sudden, seemed remarkably unsteady, his dark blue brocade dressing gown emphasising his height and broad shoulders, making her feel rather small and vulnerable yet longing to be in his arms.

For almost a full minute neither of them said anything, their eyes saying all that needed to be said, hers a little shy and expectant, his warm and tender. Taking hold of her hands he raised first one and then the other to his lips, the brief touch on her skin sending a warm thrill shooting through her. "Do you know how much I love you, Mrs. Ingleby?" he asked gently.

"Mrs. Ingleby!" she repeated almost reverently, her hands trembling in his. "I like the sound of that."

"So do I," he agreed in a deep voice, "so much so that should you ever discover you have mistaken your heart it is much too late. I am never going to let you go!"

"My heart decided on you a long time ago," she told him unsteadily, "and I *never* want you to let me go."

He kissed her hands, his eyes never leaving hers. "I have scarcely been able to take my eyes off you all day," he told her, his voice deepening, "not that that is anything unusual," he assured her, clasping her fingers a little tighter. "As I watched you walk down the aisle this morning, the sight of you took my breath away, in fact," he told her, "it was all I could do to stop myself from taking you in my arms there and then."

"Mamma," she replied a little breathlessly, "did not quite approve of my appearance."

"Mammas," he told her lovingly, releasing her hands and gently taking her in his arms, "are honour bound to disapprove, but speaking as the man who loves you," his voice a caress, "I most *definitely* approved."

"She did, however," Sophy told him huskily, laying the palms of her hands against his chest, "like my necklace, indeed, she approved of your excellent taste."

"Most kind of Mamma," he acknowledged, his voice deepening, lowering his head.

"Yes," she managed, "and you know what I think of..."

"I do," he confirmed against her lips, "but since you told me at a moment when it was impossible for me to respond in the way I would have liked, you must allow me to do so now."

Sophy was perfectly happy to allow it and, sliding her arms around his neck, welcomed his lips on hers. It may not have been a passionate kiss, but nevertheless his warm and deliberate caressing of her lips had the immediate effect of relegating her mamma to the back of her mind.

"Do you know how I have *ached* for this moment?" he asked a little hoarsely, easing himself a little away from her. "Just the two of us – alone."

"Because I love you so very much," she told him huskily, "yes, I do."

He drew in his breath at this, but deeming no words were necessary he lowered his head and unhurriedly kissed her, delicately persuasive caresses which made her tremble in his arms. His whole body cried out to make love to her but at no time was it his intention to rush her, but the low evocative sound which came from deep within her throat and the feel of her soft pliant body in his arms, irresistibly pressed against him, were enough to break down whatever restraint he had.

She could feel the urgency which emanated from his strong, hard body as he pressed it against her own and the warmth of his hands as they slowly and seductively travelled up and down her back, seeping deliciously through the fine material of her nightdress, stimulating her into meeting his increasingly ardent demands in a way which did nothing to stem either his need or desire, and it was therefore some little time before he released her lips from the confinement of his. "Do you have any idea how I felt all that time?" he asked raggedly, as he reluctantly eased himself a little away from her to look down into her radiant face. "Knowing how much I loved you yet dare not show it? Wanting you so much that it was almost like a physical pain until I thought I was going insane and, worse," he groaned, "being absolutely powerless to help you!"

The look on her face and in her eyes told him that she too had ached and yearned for the same thing, tantalisingly and frustratingly just out of reach, and if he needed further confirmation of this he only had to feel her trembling body in his arms, impatiently awaiting what she had desperately longed for, for a very long time. Whenever Sophy, in moments of wretchedness and despair, had allowed herself to imagine what it would be like to have Marcus make love to her, she realised now that not all her imaginings had prepared her for the wonderful reality of it. She liked the feel of his hands and lips on her body, so much so that she never wanted him to stop, but when his fingers slowly, and very deliberately, began to tantalise her skin as they moved from the small of her back up the length of her spine until entwining themselves in her thick long hair, she thought she would die from the sheer joy of it, her head instinctively tilting back as his lips paved a seductive trail along the soft white column of her neck and throat with delicate feather-light caresses until he reached her mouth.

"*Never* stop loving me, Sophy!" he cried hoarsely, urgently kissing her. "I couldn't bear it if you did! I couldn't live without you; I wouldn't want to!"

She looked up into his eyes, as darkened with desire as her own, her smile hovering somewhere between empathy and provocative enticement. "I couldn't stop loving you if I tried," she told him huskily against his lips.

"*I love you, Sophy!*" he groaned, looking down at the vital woman he had always known her to be, her eyes reflecting all the love she had for him and, in that moment, any remnants of self-control deserted him. Pulling her urgently to him he kissed her with such intense hunger that she shuddered, putting up no resistance when he began to unfasten the mother-of-pearl buttons on the bodice of her nightdress with fingers that were far from steady, provocatively sliding it off her shoulders until it slid silently to the floor. Something very like a cry of pain ripped from his throat as he looked at the beautiful and passionate woman whose love and need was as urgent as his own before setting in motion a devastatingly seductive assault which she welcomed eagerly, until eventually he could contain himself no longer, picking her effortlessly up in his arms and carrying her over to the bed, laying her gently down.

For two people, finally at liberty to express their love, the fulfilment of all their needs and desires was a glorious abandonment of restraint of any kind. Sophy gave herself to him as completely as he gave himself to her and the experience of sharing their love was an unknown and wonderful experience, so much so that she knew nothing would ever quite equal this moment. Here was not a husband simply doing his duty but a man making love to her; a man who loved and needed her just as much as she loved and needed him and knew a moment of intense pain at the thought of how close she had come to never knowing or sharing this depth of intimacy with him.

The whole night lay before them, as did the rest of their lives, but as she basked under the pleasurable demands of his love there was no room for thoughts, just the wonderful joy and sweetness of being with the man who was taking her into a world she had never entered before and from which neither of them were eager to leave.